LAST STAND

Keyoke surveyed his defenses, his plumed head held high despite the arrows arcing overhead. The Minwanabi seemed frantic to engage the Acoma. Why? Why should two men so skilled in war spend men by the hundreds? To capture the silk would be no mortal blow to the Acoma and certainly not worth the lives that would be sacrificed before the sun reached midheaven. Time must be a factor, but . . .

A sudden shout arose from behind Minwanabi lines. They suddenly withdrew.

An object was launched from the retreating enemy into the air from a point beyond the canyon's rim. Dark against the daylight sky, it came flying into the gully, a bundle of soaked rags and knots. The Strike Leader lifted the bundle and unwrapped it.

"It's Wiallo's head," he murmured softly. "Your orders, Force Commander?"

Keyoke's bitterness came near to showing as he said, "Only to stand ready and kill as many Minwanabi as possible. And to die like men of the Acoma."

"[*Servant of the Empire*] combines fantasy and intrigue with an intricate and exotic world. . . . Richly detailed and compellingly written, this sequel to *Daughter of the Empire* is highly recommended."

—*LIBRARY JOURNAL*

SERVANT
OF THE
EMPIRE

by

RAYMOND E. FEIST

and

JANNY WURTS

Bantam Books

NEW YORK TORONTO LONDON SYDNEY AUCKLAND

*This edition contains the complete text
of the original hardcover edition.*
NOT ONE WORD HAS BEEN OMITTED.

SERVANT OF THE EMPIRE
*A Bantam Spectra Book / published by arrangement with
Doubleday*

PUBLISHING HISTORY
*Doubleday edition published October 1990
Bantam edition / December 1991*

*SPECTRA and the portrayal of a boxed "s" are trademarks of
Bantam Books, a division of Random House, Inc.*

ISBN 0-553-29245-5

Published simultaneously in the United States and Canada

*Bantam Books are published by Bantam Books, a division of Random House, Inc.
Its trademark, consisting of the words "Bantam Books" and the portrayal of a rooster,
is Registered in U.S. Patent and Trademark Office and in other countries. Marca
Registrada. Bantam Books. New York, New York.*

PRINTED IN THE UNITED STATES OF AMERICA

OPM   19   18   17   16   15   14   13   12

DEDICATED TO THE MEMORY OF
RON FAUST,
ALWAYS A FRIEND

1. SLAVE

The breeze died.

Dust swirled in little eddies, settling grit over the palisade that surrounded the slave market. Despite the wayward currents, the air was hot and thick, reeking of confined and unwashed humanity mingled with the smell of river sewage and rotting garbage from the dump behind the market.

Sheltered behind the curtains of her brightly lacquered litter, Lady Mara wafted air across her face with a scented fan. If the stench troubled her, she showed no sign. The Ruling Lady of the Acoma motioned for her escort to stop. Soldiers in green enameled armor came to a halt, and the sweating bearers set the litter down.

An officer in a Strike Leader's plumed helm gave his hand to Mara and she emerged from her litter. The color in her cheeks was high; Lujan could not tell if she was flushed from the heat or still angered from the argument prior to leaving her estate. Jican, the estate hadonra, had spent most of the morning vigorously objecting to her plan to purchase what he insisted would be worthless slaves. The debate had ended only when she ordered him to silence.

Mara addressed her First Strike Leader. "Lujan, attend me, and have the others wait here." Her acerbity caused Lujan to forgo the banter that, on occasion, strained the limits of acceptable protocol; besides, his first task was to protect her—and the slave markets were far too public for his liking —so his attention turned quickly from wit to security. As he watched for any sign of trouble, he reasoned that when Mara busied herself in her newest plan she would forget Jican's dissension. Until then she would not appreciate hearing objections she had already dismissed in her own mind.

Lujan understood that everything his mistress undertook was to further her position in the Game of the Council, the political striving that was the heart of Tsurani politics. Her invariable goal was the survival and strengthening of House Acoma. Rivals and friends alike had learned that a once untried young girl had matured a gifted player of the deadly game. Mara had eluded the trap set by her father's old enemy, Jingu of the Minwanabi, and had succeeded with her own plot—forcing Jingu to take his own life in disgrace.

Yet if Mara's triumphs were the current topic of discussion among the Empire's many nobles, she herself had barely paused to enjoy the satisfaction of her ascendancy. Her father's and brother's deaths had taken her family to the brink of extinction. Now Mara concentrated on anticipating future trouble as she maneuvered to ensure her survival. What was done was behind, and to dwell on it was to risk being taken unawares.

While the man who had ordered the death of her father and brother was finally himself dead, her attention remained focused on the blood feud between House Acoma and House Minwanabi. Mara remembered the unvarnished look of hatred on the face of Desio of the Minwanabi as she and the other guests passed his father's death ceremony. While not as clever as his sire, Desio would be no less a danger; grief and hatred now turned his motives personal: Mara had destroyed his father at the height of his power, while he hosted the Warlord's birthday celebration, in his own home. Then she had savored that victory in the presence of the most influential and powerful nobles in the Empire as she hosted the Warlord's relocated celebration upon her own estates.

No sooner had the Warlord and his guests departed Acoma lands than Mara had embarked on a new plan to strengthen her house. She had closeted herself with Jican, to discuss the need for new slaves to clear additional meadowlands from the scrub forests north of the estate house. Pastures, pens, and sheds must be completed well before calving season in spring, so the grass would be well grown for the young needra and their mothers to graze.

As Acoma second-in-command, Lujan had learned that

Acoma power did not rest upon their soldiers' loyalty and bravery, nor upon the far-held trading concessions and investments, but upon the prosaic and dull six-legged needra. They formed the foundation upon which all its wealth rested. For Acoma power to grow, Mara's first task was to increase her breeding herd.

Lujan's attention returned to his mistress as Mara lifted her robe clear of the dust. Pale green in color, the otherwise plain cloth was meticulously embroidered at the hem and sleeves with the outline of the shatra bird, the crest of House Acoma. The Lady wore sandals with raised pegged soles, to keep her slippers clear of the filth that littered the common roadways. Her footfalls raised booming, hollow sounds as she mounted the wooden stair to the galleries that ran the length of the palisade. A faded canvas awning roofed the structure, shading Tsurani lords and their factors from the merciless sunlight. They could rest well removed from the dust and dirt, and refreshed by whatever breeze blew in off the river as they viewed the slaves available for sale.

To Lujan, the gallery with its deep shade and rows of wooden benches was less a refuge than a place of concealing darkness. He lightly touched his mistress on the shoulder as she reached the first landing. She turned, and flashed a bothered look of inquiry.

"Lady," said Lujan tactfully, "if an enemy is waiting, best we show them my sword before your beautiful face."

Mara's mouth turned upward at the corners, almost but not quite managing a smile. "Flatterer," she accused. "Of course you are right." Her formality with Lujan became gentled by humor. "Though among Jican's protests was the belief I would come to harm from the barbarian slaves, not another Ruling Lord."

She referred to the inexpensive Midkemian prisoners of war. Mara lacked the funds to buy enough common slaves to clear her pastures. So, seeing no other alternative, she chose to buy barbarians. They were reputed to be intractable, rebellious, and utterly lacking in humility toward their masters. Lujan regarded his Lady, who was barely as high as his shoulder, but who possessed a nature that could burn the man—Lord or slave or servant—who challenged her indomitable will. He recognized the purposeful set of her dark eyes.

"Still, in you the barbarians will have met their match, I wager."

"If not, they will all suffer under the whip," Mara said with resolve. "Not only would we forfeit the use of the lands we need cleared before spring, we would lose the price of the slaves. I will have done Desio's work for him." Her rare admission of doubt was allowed to pass without comment.

Lujan preceded his mistress into the gallery, silently checking his weapons. The Minwanabi might be licking their wounds, but Mara had additional enemies now, lords jealous of her sudden rise, men who knew that the Acoma name rested upon the shoulders of this slender woman and her infant heir. She was not yet twenty-one, their advisers would whisper. Against Jingu of the Minwanabi she had been cunning, but mostly lucky; in the fullness of time her youth and inexperience would cause her to misstep. Then would rival houses arise like a pack of jaguna, ready to tear at the wealth and the power of her house and bury the Acoma natami—the stone inscribed with the family crest that embodied its soul and its honor—face down in the dirt, forever away from sunlight.

Her robe neatly held above her ankles, Mara followed Lujan around the first landing. They passed the entrance to the lower tier of galleries, which by unwritten but rigid custom was reserved for merchants or house factors, and climbed to the next level, used only by the nobility.

But with Midkemians up for auction, the crowds were absent. Mara saw only a few bored-looking merchants who seemed more interested in the common gossip of the city than in buying. The upper tier of galleries would probably stand empty. Most Tsurani nobles were far more concerned by the war on the world beyond the rift, or in curbing the Warlord Almecho's ever growing power in the council, than with purchasing intractable slaves. The earliest lots of Midkemian captives had sold for premium prices, as curiosities. But the novelty lost attraction with numbers. Now grown Midkemian males brought the lowest prices of all; only women with rare red-gold hair or unusual beauty still commanded a thousand centuries. But since the Tsurani most often captured warriors, females from the barbarian world were seldom available.

A breeze off the river tugged at the plumes on Lujan's

helm. It fluttered the feathered ends of Mara's perfumed fan and set her beaded earrings swinging. Over the palisade drifted the voices of the barge teams as they poled their craft up and down the river Gagajin. Nearer at hand, from the dusty pens inside the high plank walls came the shouts of the slave merchants, and the occasional snap of a needra hide switch as they hustled their charges through their paces for interested customers in the galleries. The pen holding the Midkemians held about two dozen men. No buyers offered inquiry, for only one overseer stood indifferent watch. With him was a factor apparently in charge of issuing clothing, and a tally keeper with a much chipped slate. Mara glanced curiously at the slaves. All were very tall, larger by a head than the tallest Tsurani. One in particular towered over the chubby factor, and his red-gold hair blazed in the noonday sun of Kelewan as he attempted to communicate in an unfamiliar language. Mara had no chance to study the barbarian further, as Lujan stopped sharply in her path. His hand touched her wrist in warning.

"Someone's here," he whispered, and covered his check in stride by bending as if a stone had lodged in his sandal. His hand settled unobtrusively on his sword, and over his muscled shoulder Mara glimpsed a figure seated in the shadow to the rear of the gallery. He might be a spy, or worse: an assassin. With Midkemians scheduled for sale, a bold Lord might chance on the fact that the upper level would be deserted. But for a rival house to know that Mara had chosen to go personally to the slave market bespoke the presence of an informant very highly placed in Acoma ranks. The Lady paused, her stomach turned cold by the thought that if she was struck down here, her year-old son, Ayaki, would be the last obstacle to the obliteration of the Acoma name.

Then the figure in the shadows moved, and sunlight through a tear in the awning revealed a face that was handsome and young, and showing a smile of surprised pleasure.

Mara lightly patted Lujan's wrist, gentling his grip on the sword. "It's all right," she said softly. "I know this noble."

Lujan straightened, expressionless, as the young man arose from his bench. The man moved with a swordsman's balance. His clothing was well made, from sandals of blue-dyed leather to a tunic of embroidered silk. He wore his hair in a warrior's cut, and his only ornament was a pendant of polished obsidian hanging around his neck.

"Hokanu," Mara said, and at the name her bodyguard relaxed. Lujan had not been present during the political bloodbath at the Minwanabi estate, but from talk in the barracks he knew that Hokanu and his father, Lord Kamatsu of the Shinzawai, had been almost alone in supporting the Acoma. This, at a time when most Lords accepted that Mara's death was a foregone conclusion.

Lujan stood deferentially aside and, from beneath the brim of his helm, regarded the noble who approached. Mara had received many petitions for marriage since the death of her husband, but none of the suitors were as handsome or as well disposed as the second son of Kamatsu of the Shinzawai. Lujan maintained correct bearing to the finest detail, but like any in the Acoma household, he had a personal interest in Hokanu. And so had Mara, if the flush in her cheeks gave any indication.

After the subtle flattery of recent suitors, Hokanu's honest yearning for Mara's approval was refreshing. "Lady, what a perfect surprise! I had no expectation of finding so lovely a flower in this most unpleasant of surroundings." He paused, bowed neatly, and smiled. "Although of late we have all seen this delicate blossom show thorns. Your victory over Jingu of the Minwanabi is still the talk of Silmani," he said, naming the city closest to his father's estates.

Mara returned his bow with sincerity. "I did not see any Shinzawai colors among the retainers waiting on the street. Otherwise I should have brought a servant with jomach ice and cold herb tea. Or perhaps you do not wish your interest in these slaves to be noticed?" She let that question hang a moment, then brightly asked, "Is your father well?"

Hokanu nodded politely and seated Mara on a bench. His grip was strong but pleasant; nothing like the rough grasp she had known from her husband of two years. Mara met the Shinzawai son's eyes and saw there a quiet intelligence, overlaid by amusement at the apparent innocence of her question.

"You are very perceptive." He laughed in sudden delight. "Yes, I am interested in Midkemians, and at my most healthy father's request, I am trying not to advertise the fact." His expression turned more serious. "I would like to be

frank with you, Mara, even as my father was with Lord Sezu
—our fathers served together in their youth, and trusted one
another."

Though intrigued by the young man's charm, Mara repressed her desire to be open lest she reveal too much.
Hokanu she trusted; but her family name was too recently
snatched from oblivion for her to reveal her intentions.
Shinzawai servants might have loose tongues, and young
men away from home sometimes celebrated their first freedom and responsibility with drink. Hokanu seemed as canny
as his father, but she did not know him well enough to be
certain.

"I fear the Acoma interest in the barbarians is purely a
financial one." Mara waved her fan in resignation. "The cho-
ja hive we gained three years ago left our needra short of
pasture. Slaves who clear forest in the wet season fall ill, my
hadonra says. If we are to have enough grazing to support
our herds at calving, we must allow for losses." She gave
Hokanu a rueful look. "Though I expected no competition at
this auction. I am glad to see you, but nettled by the thought
of bidding against so dear a friend."

Hokanu regarded his hands for a moment, his brow untroubled, and a smile bending the corners of his mouth. "If I
relieve my Lady of her dilemma, she will owe the Shinzawai
her favor. Say, entertaining a poor second son at dinner
soon?"

Mara unexpectedly laughed. "You're a devil for flattery,
Hokanu. Very well; you know that I need no bribes to allow
you to visit my estates. Your company is . . . always welcome."

Hokanu stared in mock suffering at Lujan. "She says that
very prettily for one who refused me the last time I was in
Sulan-Qu."

"That's not fair," Mara protested, then blushed as she
realized how quickly she had spoken in her own defense.
With better decorum she added, "Your request came at an
awkward moment, Master Hokanu." And her face darkened
as she recalled a Minwanabi spy, and a pretty, importunate
boy who had suffered as a result of the intrigue and ambition
that underlay every aspect of life in the Empire of Tsuranuanni.

Hokanu noted the strain that shadowed her face. His

heart went out to this young woman, who had been so serious as a child, and who had against the greatest odds found the courage and intelligence to secure her house from ruin. "I will cede to you the Midkemians," he said firmly, "for whatever price you can bargain with the factor."

"But I wish not to inconvenience you," Mara protested. Her fan trembled between clenched fingers. She was tense; Hokanu must not be permitted to notice, and to distract him she whiffed air through the feathers as if she were bothered by the heat. "The Shinzawai have shown the Acoma much kindness, and in honor, it is time that we proved ourselves worthy. Let me be the one to cede the bidding."

Hokanu regarded the Lady, who was daintily small, and far more attractive than she herself understood. She had a smile that made her radiant, except that at present the face beneath its thyza-powder makeup was almost wary with tension. Her concern went much deeper than simple forms of honor, the young man sensed at once.

The insight gave him pause: She had been snatched away from taking vows of service to the goddess Lashima to assume her role as Ruling Lady. In all likelihood she had known little or nothing of men before her wedding night. And Buntokapi of the Anasati, an ill-mannered, coarse braggart at the best of times, had been the son of an Acoma enemy before he had become her husband and Ruling Lord. He had been rough with her, Hokanu understood with sudden certainty, which was why this Ruling Lady and mother could also act as unsure as a girl years younger. Admiration followed; this seemingly delicate girl had owned valor out of all proportion to her size and experience. No one outside her inner household could ever guess what she might have endured in Buntokapi's rude grasp. One close to Mara might say much if Hokanu could get him to share drink in a wine shop. But a glance at Lujan's alert pose convinced Lord Kamatsu's son that the Strike Leader was a poor choice. The warrior measured Hokanu, having perceived his interest; and where his mistress was concerned, his loyalty would be absolute. Hokanu knew Mara was a shrewd judge of character— she had proven as much by staying alive as long as she had.

Attempting to lighten her mood and not give offense, Hokanu said, "Lady, I spoke out of sincere disappointment at not being able to see you on my last visit." He concealed any diffidence behind a disarming smile. "No favors do the Acoma owe the Shinzawai. We deal here in simple practicality. Most Midkemian slaves go to the block at the City of the Plains and Jamar, and I am bound for Jamar. Should I make you wait for the next shipment of prisoners to journey upriver, while I drive two score men in a coffle through the heat, house them while I conduct business, then herd them back upriver again? I think not. Your needra pastures are a more immediate need, I judge. Please accept my not bidding against you as nothing more than a tiny courtesy from me."

Mara stopped her fan in midair with barely hidden relief. "Tiny courtesy? Your kindness is unmatched, Hokanu. When your business in Jamar is concluded, I would be most pleased if you would accept my invitation to rest as a guest of the Acoma on your way back to your father's estates."

"Then the matter of the slaves is settled." Hokanu took her hand. "I will accept your hospitality with pleasure." He bowed, sealing their agreement. As he straightened he saw two brown eyes regarding him intently. The Lady of the Acoma had always attracted him, from the moment he had first seen her. When he returned from Jamar, he might have the opportunity to know her better, to explore possibilities, to see if his interest was reciprocated. But now, intuitively, he sensed that his nearness confused her. The public slave market was no place to unravel the reason why, and rather than discomfort her to the point where her pleasure at seeing him changed to regret, he rose from his seat. "Well, then. The sooner I'm off to Jamar, the sooner I'll return this way. I look forward to seeing you again, Lady."

Mara fluttered her fan before her face. Unexpectedly self-conscious, she felt both regret and relief that Hokanu was departing. She nodded with the appearance of poise. "I, too, look forward to that time. Fare well upon your road."

"Fare you well, too, Lady Mara."

The younger of the two Shinzawai sons threaded his way through the benches and left the upper gallery. As he stepped into the sunlight on the stair, his profile showed the straight nose, high forehead, and firm chin that had captured the attention of many a noble's daughter in his home province of Szetac. Even to Lujan's overcritical eye, the man was as well favored as he was socially well placed.

The sound of raised voices drifted up from the slave com-

pound. Mara's attentions turned from the retreating figure of
Hokanu. She pressed close to the gallery rail to view the
cause of the commotion. Since archers could not be concealed among bands of naked slaves, Lujan did not urge her
to stay back within the shadows, but he did continue to observe nearby rooftops.

Mara was surprised to discover that the unseemly shouting came from the factor overseeing the barbarians. Short,
plump, and swathed in costly yellow silk, he stood shaking
his fist under the chin of an outworlder. Facing him stood the
red-haired Midkemian Mara had glimpsed before, his naked
body gleaming in the afternoon light. He seemed to be desperately smothering laughter as he endured the factor's ti-
rade. Mara was forced to admit the tableau was comic; the
factor was short, even for a Tsurani, and the barbarians towered over him. In a vain attempt to look threatening, their
overlord was forced to stand upon tiptoes.

Mara studied the outworlder. Although at any moment he
might be savaged by a whip, he stood with arms crossed, a
study in self-confidence. He was a full head taller than any of
his betters, the overseer and the two assistants who rushed to
the factor's aid. The outworlder looked down on their agitation like a boy noble bored by his jesters. Mara felt a sudden
twist within her as she studied the man's body, made whip-
cord-lean by meager rations and hard work. As she forced
herself to calmness, she wondered if Hokanu's presence had
affected her more deeply than she had imagined. The men
she needed to be most concerned with at *this* moment were
down in the pen, and her interest in them was solely financial.

Mara ended her frank appraisal of the man's appearance
and focused on his interaction with the Tsurani overseer and
his assistants. The factor's rant reached a crescendo. Then he
ran out of breath. He waved his fist one last time at the
height of the barbarian's collarbone. And much to Mara's
amazement, the slave showed no sign of submissiveness.
Rather than prostrating himself with his face pressed into the
earth at the factor's feet, silently awaiting his punishment, he
stroked his bearded chin and, in a resonant voice, began
speaking in broken Tsurani, his gestures those of a confidant
instead of obedient property.

"By the gods, will you look at him!" exclaimed Lujan in

astonishment. "He acts as if slaves were born with the right to argue. If they're all as brazen as this fellow, it's no wonder a slave master must beat their skins off to get a half day's work from them."

"Hush." Mara waved her hand toward Lujan. "I wish to hear this." She strained to understand the barbarian's mangled Tsurani.

Suddenly the outworlder stopped speaking, his head cocked to one side, as if he had made his point. The factor looked overheated. He motioned to the assistant with the tally slate and said in an exasperated tone, "Line up! All of you! Now!"

The slaves unhurriedly strung themselves out in a row. From her overhead view from the gallery, Mara noticed that the barbarians shuffled to their places in such a way as to conceal the activities of two fellows, who were crouched before the log palisade on the side that fronted onto the river.

"What do you suppose they are doing?" she asked Lujan.

The warrior shrugged Tsurani style, the barest movement of the shoulders. "Mischief of some sort. I've seen needra show more brains than that factor."

Below, the overseer and the assistant with the slate began laboriously to count the slaves. The two by the palisade joined the line late, and by dint of a staged trip and some scuffling as the off-balance man crashed into the row, the tally keeper lost track of his count. He started over, looking down to chalk a mark for each slave as he passed, while the factor cursed and sweated at the delay.

Each time the tally keeper consulted his slate, the unruly barbarians shifted position. The man with the whip lashed a few backs in attempt to establish order. One slave shouted something in his native tongue that sounded suspiciously like an obscenity as he jumped away from the punishment, and others laughed. The lash fell to silence the ones nearest the overseer, which caused the line of standing slaves to break and shuffle and re-form behind the man's back. The tally keeper looked up in despair. Once again, the numbers were hopelessly confused.

The factor shouted in a shameful show of impatience, "We'll all be dead and ashes by the time you finish with that!" He clapped his hands at someone on the sidelines, and a moment later, a servant scuttled into the compound with a basket of rough-woven trousers and shirts. These he began to dispense among the slaves.

At this point the red-haired barbarian began to scream insults at the overseer. His Tsurani might be broken and heavily mispronounced, but at some point along his line of march since his capture some nameless beggar child had taught him thoroughly and well. The overseer's mouth opened in incredulity as he considered the biological implications of what the outworlder had just said about his mother. Then he reddened and swung his lash, which the barbarian adroitly avoided. A chase developed between the large Midkemian and the smaller, fatter Tsurani.

Lujan laughed. "It's a shame the barbarian needs to be broken; this is a comedy worthy of any traveling troupe of performers I've ever seen. He certainly seems to be enjoying himself." Movement caught Lujan's eye in the far corner of the pen. "Ah!" he exclaimed. "And to clear purpose, it would seem."

Mara, too, had noticed that one of the slaves had resumed his crouch by the palisade. A moment later he appeared to be stuffing something through. "Lashima's wisdom," she said, startled into a smile of amazement. "They are pilfering the shirts!"

The gallery afforded a view of the operation. The red-headed giant raced around the compound. Despite his height, he moved with the grace of a sarcat—the quick and silent six-legged hunter of the grasslands—at first avoiding every attempt of the overseer to catch him. Then, strangely, he began to plod like a pregnant needra cow. The overseer came close, and as the barbarian dodged the near miss of the lash, he shuffled, slid, dragged his heels and toes, and kicked up an excessive amount of dust. He also crashed often into those of his comrades who had received their allotment of trousers and shirt. These suddenly clumsy men fell and rolled, and under cover of dust and movement, cloth miraculously disappeared. Some was bundled and passed to other slaves; occasionally a shirt would unfurl and land, to be picked up by another man. In this manner the clothing passed at last to the man by the palisade. At opportune moments he stuffed the fabric through a gap and caught the shell counters that served as coin within the Empire that someone slipped through from without. These the Midkemian wiped on his hairy chest. Then he placed them in his mouth and swallowed them.

"There must be beggar boys on the other side." Lujan shook his head. "Or perhaps some bargeman's child. Though why a slave should think he has use for coin is a mystery."

"They certainly show great ingenuity . . . and nerve," Mara observed, and Lujan regarded her keenly. That she had mistakenly conceded honorable attributes to men who by the inflexible laws of society were accorded less stature than the lowest scabby beggars in the gutters made the Strike Leader pause. Desperation had taught Mara to reappraise the traditions of her people with sometimes ingenious results. Yet although Lujan himself had sworn to her service through just such an unorthodox twist, even he could not guess what she might see in a lot of barbarian slaves. Trying to fathom her fascination, the warrior regarded the ongoing conflict down below.

The overseer had called in reinforcements. Several brawny guards equipped with curved hooks of roughened needra hide raced into the compound and ran at the unruly redhead; slaves who tried to hamper them were elbowed aside or kicked with sharp-toed sandals. One barbarian fell with a bloodied shin. Seeing that, the others quickly cleared the soldiers' path. The redheaded ringleader also slowed his pace. He allowed himself to be cornered rather than suffer injury from brutal handling. The warriors took him in hand with their hooks and dragged him before the red-faced and dusty factor, whose robe was now sadly in need of a wash. They pitched their huge captive on his knees and held him, while the overseer yelled for cuffs and straps of hardened needra leather to restrain his unmanageable wildness.

Still the barbarian was not cowed. As if unaware that his life could be taken at a gesture of his overseer's hand, he flung back his tangled hair and regarded his captors with wide blue eyes. At some point in the scuffle he had acquired a slash across one cheekbone. Blood ran down his face and soaked into the fiery brush of his beard. He could not be past his twenties at a guess, and even harsh handling had not tamed his flamboyance. He said something. Mara and Lujan saw the factor's face go stiff, and one of the guards repressed an un-Tsurani-like burst of laughter behind one lacquered gauntlet. The overseer with the whip proved more in control.

He answered with the lash, then kicked the barbarian forward onto his face.

Mara did not flinch at the violence. Disobedient slaves were beaten on her estate for far less cause than this barbarian's outrageous behavior. Still, the fact that the redhead's actions were inconceivable to the mores of society did not shock her beyond thought. She had acquainted herself with the customs of the cho-ja, and come to respect their ways and wisdom, alien though they might be. As she watched the slaves in the compound, it occurred to her that these men were as human as she, but their world was far different from Kelewan. Being strangers, perhaps they did not comprehend the scope of their lot: for on Kelewan a man left slavery only through the portals of death. He was honorless, soulless, insignificant as an insect, to be raised to comfort or ground down in misery with as little thought as a man might regard a red-bee who gathered his honey.

A Tsurani warrior would die by his own hand rather than allow himself to be taken alive by an enemy—captives were usually wounded, unconscious, or cowards. These Midkemians presumably had the same options, and in living on past honor, they had chosen their lot.

The redhead seemed anything but resigned. He rolled to escape the whip and crashed into the factor's ankles. The fat man yelped and staggered, saved from a fall by the tally keeper, who hurriedly dropped his slate and grabbed a double handhold of creased yellow silk. The chalkboard fell flat in the dust, and the barbarian, with enviable subterfuge, rolled over it. The tally marks were obliterated by a smear of sweat and dirt; and Mara, in the gallery, saw with a queer thrill that the hamper was empty. Only a third of the men in the yard were clothed; some lacked breeches and others had no shirts. Although the redhead had gained himself a beating, perhaps even death by hanging, he had won a small victory over his captives.

The men with the hooks closed in. The heat and the exertion had stripped them of patience, and this time their blows were aimed to cripple.

On an impulse, Mara of the Acoma leaped to her feet. "Cease!" she called over the railing. The command in her voice compelled the warriors' obedience. She was a Ruling Lady, and they no more than servants. Conditioned to follow orders, they lowered their hooks and halted their rush on the Midkemian. The factor straightened his robes in surprise, while, on the dusty, torn earth, the barbarian slave rolled uncomfortably onto one elbow and looked up.

That his rescuer was a small, black-haired woman seemed to take him aback. Still he brazenly continued to stare, until the tally keeper slapped his face to make him avert his gaze.

Mara's brows knitted in anger. "I said cease! Any more of this, and I will demand that you be obliged to pay for damaging goods while a bidder stands waiting to make an offer."

The factor snapped straight in stupefication, his spoiled yellow silk forgotten. He brushed sweaty hair from his temples, as if by mending his appearance his lapse in decorum might be forgotten. Seeing the Lady of the Acoma in the buyer's gallery, he bowed very low, almost to his knees. After the redhead's bad-tempered display, he knew he would be lucky to sell this lot of Midkemians for the price commanded by a pet fish. That this Lady had witnessed and yet still wished to purchase, was a marvel no sane man would question.

Aware he was in no position to bargain, Mara swished her fan with a studied show of indifference. "I might give thirty centuries for these barbarians," she said slowly. "If the big one bleeds too much, I might not."

At this, even Lujan raised his brows. He, too, questioned his Lady's wisdom in purchasing unruly slaves, but it was not the place of a warrior to advise. He held his silence while, in the compound, the factor turned on the tally keeper and sent the man scurrying off for cloths and water. The man returned and was immediately assigned the humiliating task of bathing the redhead's cuts.

But the barbarian ringleader would endure no solicitude. He reached with one huge fist and, despite the restraint of cuffs and strap, moved fast enough to catch the tally keeper's wrist. What he said could not be overheard from the gallery, but the servant abandoned both rag and basin, as if his fingers were burned.

The factor glossed over this disobedience with a smile of nervous improvisation. He had no wish to try Mara's patience by ordering reprisal against the slave. He tried to behave as if everything had gone according to plan as one of the barbarian's fellows stepped forward and briskly began cleansing the whip wounds of his companion.

"Lady, the purchase papers can be drawn up at once, in the private comfort of my office. I'll send for iced fruit for your thirst while you wait to sign. If you would be so kind as to join me in my office . . ."

"That won't be necessary," Mara said crisply. "Send your scribe to me outside, for I wish that these slaves be removed to my estates at once. The instant I have a bill of sale, my warriors will take them into custody." She made a last study of the compound and added, "That is, I will sign for my purchase after these slaves have been provided with proper clothing."

"But—" spluttered the factor in dismay. The tally keeper looked sour. Although the hamper brought out from the storerooms had originally held enough trousers and shirts to clothe three incoming coffles from Jamar, many of these men still stood naked or half-clothed. There should be a proper inquiry over that, and no doubt a round of beatings, but the Lady's impatience ended the matter. She wanted to sign and buy at once. With a furious gesture, the factor urged the tally keeper to overlook the lapse and be done. At thirty centuries, these slaves would bring little profit, but worse was the risk that they would linger unsold, swelling the holding pens and eating thyza that might better be used to fatten more amenable slaves—each worth five to ten centuries alone.

Aware of which shortfall he would rather report to his investors, the factor regained his poise. "Send my runner for a scribe to draw up the Lady's document." He snapped something under his breath as his underling began to protest, surely an urge to make haste lest the Lady come to her senses and change her mind.

The assistant rushed off. The Lady in the gallery paid his departure no heed; her own gaze turned toward the red-headed barbarian acquired on impulse and intuition. He in his turn stared back, and something about the intentness of his blue eyes caused her to blush as Hokanu of the Shinzawai had not.

Mara suddenly turned away and without a word to her Strike Leader hurried down the steps from the gallery to the street level. The Strike Leader needed but a step to overtake her and resume his position. He wondered if the speed of her departure resulted from her impatience to return to her home or from another discomfort.

Putting aside speculation, Lujan bent to assist Mara into her litter. "Jican's going to be thrown into a dither." Mara studied her officer's face and found none of his usual amusement. In place of mocking humor she saw only concern—and perhaps something more.

Then the factor's scribe appeared with documents to finalize the sale. Mara signed, impatient to be away.

A noise of alien chatter and grumbling, and the slaves were herded out the gate from the holding area. Lujan gave the barest motion of his head, and Mara's company of guards busied themselves with readying two dozen Midkemians for the journey back to the Acoma estates. The task was made difficult by the slaves' poor comprehension of the language and an unbelievable tendency to argue. No slave of Tsurani birth would ever think of demanding sandals before being required to march. Stymied by seemingly irrational defiance, the soldiers first threatened and finally resorted to force. Their tempers grew shorter by the minute. Soldiers were not overseers, and beating slaves was beneath their station. To be seen manhandling chattel in a public street shamed them and reflected no honor upon the mistress now ready to depart.

Mara's too-straight back as she sat motionless on her cushions showed her discomfort at this coarse display. She gestured for her bearers to shoulder the litter poles. The pace she commanded from them at least assured that passage through the streets of Sulan-Qu would be brief.

Mara motioned to Lujan and, after the briefest conference, determined that she and her party should drive the Midkemian slaves by the least conspicuous route. This involved crossing the poorer quarters by the river, over streets rutted with refuse and puddles of sewage and wash water. Now the warriors drew swords and shoved laggard slaves on their way with the flats of their blades. Footpads and street thieves were little threat to a company of their vigilance and experience, but Mara wished for haste for other reasons.

Her enemies always took interest in her movements, no matter how insignificant, and gossip would arise about her visit to the slave pen. Even now the factor and his handlers were probably heading for the local wine shop, and if just one trader or merchant overheard their speculation upon Mara's motives in buying outworld slaves, rumors would instantly begin to spread. And once her presence in the city was widely known, enemy agents would be racing to overtake her and track her movements. Since the Midkemians were intended for the clearing of new needra meadows, Mara wished that fact kept secret as long as possible. No matter how trivial, any information gained by her foes weakened the Acoma. And Mara's supreme concern, since the day she became Ruling Lady, was to preserve the house of her ancestors.

The litter bearers turned into the street that flanked the riverfront. Here the byway narrowed to an alley between ramshackle buildings, providing scant room on either side for the litter. Atop the walls, galleries with rough hide curtains loomed above the streets, their roof beams crowding together, swallowing sunlight. Successive generations of landlords had added additional floors, each new story overhanging the previous one, so that to look upward was to view a narrow slice of the green Kelewanese sky, brilliant against the oppressive dimness. Mara's soldiers strained to see in the sudden gloom, always watchful for threats to their mistress; this warren provided ample opportunity for ambush.

The river breeze could not penetrate this tight-woven maze of tenements. The air hung motionless and humid, fetid with garbage, waste, and the pungency of decaying timbers. Many foundations were eaten away with dry rot, causing walls to crack and roof beams to sag. Despite the repellent surroundings, the streets teemed with humanity. The inhabitants hurried clear of Mara's retinue, commoners ducking into doorless hovels at the sight of an officer's plume. Warriors of great Lords would instantly beat any wretch slow to clear their path. Only throngs of shouting and filthy urchins tempted such misfortune, pointing at the Lady's rich litter and darting clear of the soldiers who jabbed spear butts to move them away.

The Midkemians had ceased their chattering, much to Lujan's relief. At present his warriors had enough to occupy them without that added irritation. No matter how often the barbarians were ordered to silence, as befitted slaves, they tended to disobey. Now, as the Acoma retinue passed between the overcrowded tenements, the spicy, smoke-scented air that issued from the dens of the drug-flower sellers became prevalent. The eaters of the kamota blossom resin lived in dreams and hallucinations, and madness came upon them in fits. The warriors carried their spears in readiness, prepared for unexpected attack, and Mara sat behind closed curtains, her scented fan pressed close to her nostrils.

The litter slowed before a corner, its occupant jostled as the bearers shifted grip and jockeyed their load past the posts of a sagging doorway. One of the poles caught upon the dirty curtain that hung across the entrance, pulling it askew. Within huddled several families, crowded one upon another. Their clothes were filthy and their skins wretched with sores. A pot of noisome thyza was being shared out among them, while another, similar pot collected the day's soil in one corner. The stench was choking, and on a tattered blanket a mother suckled a limp infant, three more toddlers lying across her knees and ankles. They all showed signs of vermin, ill health, and starvation. Inculcated since birth to know that poverty or wealth was bestowed as the gods willed—in reward for deeds in past lives—Mara gave their wretchedness no consideration.

The bearers cleared the litter from the doorway. As they regrouped, Mara caught a glimpse of the new slaves who followed behind. The tall redhead muttered something to another slave, a balding, powerfully built man who listened with the respect of one deferring to a leader. Outrage, or maybe shock, showed in both men's expressions, though what might inspire such depths of emotion within a public place, before individuals almost as honorless as the slaves themselves, seemed a mystery to the Lady.

The poor quarter of Sulan-Qu was not large; still, passage through the jammed streets was painfully tedious. Finally the tenements fell behind as the road crooked with the bend in the river Gagajin. Here the gloom lessened, but only slightly. In place of the mildewed tenements were warehouses, craft sheds, and factories. Dye shops and tanneries, butchers' stalls and slaughterhouses crowded the way, and the blended stinks of offal, dye vats, and steam from the tallow renderer's left a reeking miasma in the air. Smoke from the resin maker's fires coiled in clouds from the chimneys, and at the riverside, docked to weathered pilings, lay commerce barges and other floating house-shacks. Vendors vied for any cranny that remained, each crowded, tiny stall serving its wares to clusters of wives and off-duty workers.

Now Lujan's warriors were forced to shove the crowds aside, shouting, "Acoma! Acoma!" to let the commoners know a great Lady was passing. Other warriors closed tightly against the sides of Mara's litter, placing their armored bodies between their mistress and possible danger. The slaves they kept herded together, and the press became so tight that no man could look down to check his footing. The soldiers wore hardened leather sandals, but the slaves, including the bearers, had no choice but to tread on bits of broken crockery and rivulets of sewage and other refuse.

Mara lay back against her finely embroidered cushions, her fan pressed hard to her face. She closed her eyes in longing for the open meadows of her estate, perfumed with summer grass and sweet flowers. In time the factory quarter changed, became less odorous and crowded, more inclined toward industries of the luxury trade. Here weavers, tailors, basket makers, cordwainers, silk spinners, and potters toiled. An occasional jeweler's stall—guarded by armed mercenaries —or a perfumer's, frequented in this less fashionable quarter by painted women of the Reed Life, was nestled between shops offering less luxurious merchandise.

The sun had climbed to midday. Drowsy behind her curtains, Mara fanned herself slowly, thankful that, at last, the bustle of Sulan-Qu fell behind. As her retinue continued down roads shaded by evergreens, she was lying back, attempting to sleep, when one of the bearers developed a limp. At each step she was jostled uncomfortably on her cushions, and rather than cause a man needless pain, she ordered a halt to look into the matter.

Lujan detailed a soldier to inspect the bearers. One had cut his foot in the poor quarter. Tsurani, and aware of his place, he had striven to continue his duty to the verge of fainting from pain.

Mara was still nearly an hour from her estate house, and, maddeningly, the Midkemians were once again speaking among themselves in the nasal braying that passed for their native language. Irked by their jabbering as much as by the delay, she motioned to Lujan. "Send that redheaded barbarian over to replace my lame bearer." Slave he might be, but he acted like a ringleader, and since the stinks of the poor quarter had left Mara with a headache, she was willing to consider almost any expedient to make the barbarians less quarrelsome.

The warriors immediately brought the chosen slave. The bald one called out in protest and had to be cuffed aside. Knocked to his knees, he continued to shout, until the redhead bade him be silent. Then, blue eyes fixed in curiosity on the elegant Lady in the litter, he came forward to shoulder the vacant left front pole.

"No," snapped Lujan at once. He waved for the slave to the rear to come forward and assigned the redhead to stand behind. This way a warrior with an unsheathed sword could march at the barbarian's back, insurance against trouble or threat to their mistress.

"Home," she ordered her retinue, and her bearers crouched to shoulder their burden, the redheaded barbarian among them.

The first steps forward were unmitigated chaos. The Midkemian was over a head taller than the other bearers, and as he straightened with his load, and strode ahead, the litter canted forward. Mara found herself starting to slide. The silk trappings and cushions offered no resistance to her motion. Lujan's fast reflexes spared her an unceremonious spill onto the ground, and a slap of his hand warned the barbarian to hold his pole level. This the huge man could only by hunching his back and shoulders, which placed his curly head just inches from his mistress's curtains.

"This won't do at all," Mara snapped.

"A fine triumph for Desio of the Minwanabi, if you came to hurt through a slave's clumsiness," Lujan said, then he added a hopeful smile. "Maybe we could dress these Midkemians as house slaves and give them to the Minwanabi as a gift? At least they might break much of value before Desio's First Adviser orders them hung."

But Mara was in no mood for jokes. She straightened her robe and removed mussed pins from her hair. All the while the barbarian's eyes watched her with a directness the Lady found disturbing. At length he cocked his head to one side and, with a disarming grin, addressed her in broken Tsurani as he stumbled along.

Lujan drowned him out with a shout of outrage. "Dog! Slave! On your miserable knees!" He snapped his head at his warriors. Instantly one rushed to take the litter pole, while others seized the redhead and threw him forcefully down. Strong arms pummeled his shoulders, and still he tried to speak, until a warrior's studded sandal pressed his insolent face into the dust.

"How dare you address the Lady of the Acoma, slave!" shouted Lujan.

"What is he trying to say?" asked Mara, suddenly more curious than affronted.

Lujan looked around in surprise. "Can it matter? He's a barbarian, and that brings you no honor, mistress. Still, his suggestion was not without merit."

Mara paused, her hand full of tortoiseshell pins. Sunlight glinted on their jeweled heads, and on the shell ornaments sewn to her collar. "Tell me."

Lujan raked his wrist across his sweat-streaked brow. "The wretch suggested that if you would call over three of his fellows, and dismiss your other slaves, they might carry your litter more easily, since they are closer to the same height."

Mara lay back, her pins and fallen hair momentarily forgotten. She frowned in thought. "He said that," she mused, then looked at the man, who lay face down in the dust with a soldier's foot holding him immobile. "Let him up."

"Lady?" Lujan said softly. Only his questioning tone hinted how close he dared go in direct protest of her given order.

"Let the barbarian up," said Mara shortly. "I believe his suggestion is sensible. Or do you wish to march through the afternoon, delayed by a lame bearer?"

Lujan returned a Tsurani shrug, as if to say that his mistress was right. In truth, she could be as stubborn as the barbarian slaves, and rather than try her further, the Acoma Strike Leader called off the warrior who held the redhead down. He gave rapid orders. The remaining bearers and the one warrior lowered Mara's litter to the ground, and three of the taller Midkemians were selected to take their places. The redheaded one joined them, his handsome face left bloody where a stone in the roadway had opened the gash on his cheek. He took his place no more humbly than before, though he must have been bruised by rough handling. The retinue started forward once again, with Mara little more comfortable. The Midkemians might have meant well, but they were inexperienced at carrying a litter. They did not time their strides, which made for a jolting ride. Mara lay back, fighting queasiness. She closed her eyes in resignation. The slaves purchased in Sulan-Qu were proving far too much of a distraction. She made note to herself to make mention to Jican; the Midkemians should perhaps be assigned to duties close to the estate house, where warriors were always within call. The more experienced overseers could keep watch until the slaves had been taught proper behavior and could be trusted to act as fate had intended.

Irritated that something as trivial as buying new slaves had evoked so much discomfort and confusion, Mara pondered the problems sent against her by her enemies. Eyes closed against the onslaught of a burgeoning headache, she thought to herself, What would I be plotting if I were Desio of the Minwanabi?

2. PLANNING

The air was still.

Desio of the Minwanabi sat at the desk in his late father's study contemplating the tallies before him. Although it was midday, a lamp burned near his elbow. The study was a shadowy furnace, all screens and battle shutters tightly closed, denying those inside the afternoon breezes off the lake. Desio seemed immune to the discomfort. A single jade-fly buzzed around his head, apparently determined to land upon the young Lord's brow. Desio's hand moved absently, as if to brush away the troublesome insect, and for an instant the sweating slave who fanned him broke rhythm, uncertain whether the Lord of the Minwanabi gestured for him to withdraw.

An elderly figure in shadow motioned for the slave to remain. Incomo, First Adviser of House Minwanabi, waited patiently for his master to finish the reports. Desio's brow knitted. He dragged the oil lamp closer and sought to concentrate upon the information listed on the papers before him, but the characters seemed to swim through the humid afternoon air. At last he rocked back on his cushions with an angry sigh of frustration. "Enough!"

Incomo regarded his young master with a blandness that hid concern. "My Lord?"

Desio, never athletic, pushed the lamp aside and rose ponderously to his feet. His massive stomach strained at the sash of the lounging robe he wore in his own quarters. Perspiration streamed off his face, and with a pudgy hand he swept damp locks out of his eyes.

Incomo knew that the cause of Desio's agitation was more than the unusual humidity, the legacy of an unseasonable tropical storm to the south. The Lord of the Minwanabi had ordered the screens latched closed ostensibly for privacy. The old man knew the reason behind the seemingly irrational order: fear. Even in his own home, Desio was afraid. No lord of any house, let alone one of the Five Great Houses, could admit to such weakness, so the First Adviser dared say nothing on the matter.

Desio stalked heavily around the room, his rage slowly building, his torturous breath and bunched fists sure sign that within minutes he would strike out at whichever member of his household happened to be nearest. The young Lord had evidenced a nature of petty cruelty while his father ruled, but that vicious streak had bloomed in full since the death of Jingu. With his mother having retired to a convent of Lashima, Desio showed no restraints on his impulses. The fan slave paced after his master, attempting to discharge his tasks without getting in the way.

Hoping to avoid the incapacitation of another house slave, the First Adviser said, "My Lord, perhaps a cool drink would restore your patience. These matters of trade are urgent."

Desio continued pacing as if he did not hear. His appearance revealed his recent personal neglect and indulgence, florid cheeks and nose, puffy dark circles beneath his red-rimmed eyes, grimy hair hanging lankily around his shoulders, and greasy dirt under his fingernails. Incomo reflected that, since his father's ritual suicide, the young Lord had generally acted like an itchy needra bull in a mud wallow with a dozen cows, an odd way to show his grief, but not unheard of: those confronted by death for the first time often embrace life-affirming behavior. So, for days, Desio had remained drunk in his private quarters with his girls and ignored the affairs of House Minwanabi.

On the second morning some of the girls reappeared, bruised and battered from Desio's passionate rages. Other girls replaced them in a seemingly inexhaustible succession, until the Lord of the Minwanabi had finally thrown off his fit of grief. He had emerged looking ten years older than at the moment he had silently watched his father fall upon the family sword.

Now Desio made a pretense of running the far-flung hold-ings he had inherited, but his drinking began at midday and continued into the night. Although Lord of one of the Five Great Families of the Empire, Desio seemed unable to ac-knowledge the enormous responsibility that went with his power. Tormented by personal demons, he tried to hide from them in soft arms or wash them away with a sea of wine. Had Incomo dared, he would have sent his master a healer, a priest, and a child's teacher who would issue a stiff lecture on the responsibilities that accompanied the ruler's mantle. But one look in Desio's eyes—and the madness hinted there—warned the First Adviser any such efforts would be futile. Desio's spirit boiled with a rage only the Red God might answer.

Incomo tried one last time to turn Desio's attention back to business. "My Lord, if I may point out, we are losing days while our ships lie empty in their berths in Jamar. If they are to sail to—"

"Enough!" Desio's fist crashed against a partition, tearing the delicate painted silk and splintering the frame. He kicked the wreckage to the floor, then whirled and collided with his fan slave. Enraged beyond reason, the Lord of the Minwa-nabi struck the man as if he were furniture. The slave crashed to his knees, a broken nose and lacerated lip spraying blood across his face, his chest, and the smashed partition. In fear for his very life, the slave managed to keep the large fan from striking his master, despite being half-blind from pain and tears. Desio remained oblivious to the slave's heroic defer-ence. He rounded to confront his adviser. "I cannot concen-trate on anything, so long as *she* is out there!"

Incomo required no explanation to know to whom his master referred. Experience taught him there was nothing to do but sit back and endure another outburst. "My Lord," he said anxiously, "no good will be gained in yearning for ven-geance should all your wealth dwindle through neglect. If you will not attend to these decisions, at least permit your hadonra to take matters in hand."

The plea made no impression on Desio. Staring into the distance, his voice a harsh whisper, as if to speak the hated name were to give it substance, he whispered, "Mara of the Acoma must die!"

Glad now for the dark room which hid his own fears,

Incomo agreed. "Of course, my Lord. But this is not the time."

"When!" he shouted, his bellow hurting Incomo's ears. Desio kicked at a pillow, then lowered his voice to a more reasonable tone. "When? She contrived to escape my father's trap; and more: she forced him to dishonor his own pledge for the safety of a guest, compelling him to kill himself in shame." Desio's agitation simmered higher as he recounted Mara's offenses against his house. "This . . . girl has not merely defeated us, she has humbled—no, *humiliated* us!" He stamped hard on the pillow and regarded his adviser with narrowed eyes.

The fan slave shrank from the expression, so like that of Jingu of the Minwanabi when roused to rage. Bleeding from nose and mouth, but still trying valiantly to cool his sweating master, he raised and lowered his fan in barely unbroken rhythm while Desio's voice turned conspiratorial, a harsh whisper. "The Warlord looks upon her with amusement and affection, even favor—perhaps he beds the bitch—while our faces are pushed into needra slime. We eat needra droppings each day she draws breath!" Desio's scowl deepened. He stared at the tightly closed screens, and as if seeing them stirred a memory, a glint of sanity returned to his eyes for the first time since Jingu's death. Incomo restrained a sigh of open relief.

"And more again," Desio finished with the slow care a man might use in the presence of a coiled pusk adder. "She is now a real threat to *my* safety!"

Incomo nodded to himself. He knew that the root of Desio's behavior was fear. Jingu's son lived each day in terror that Mara would continue the Acoma blood feud with the Minwanabi. Now Ruling Lord, Desio would be the next target of Mara's plotting, his own life and honor the next to fall.

Although the stifling heat shortened his patience, Incomo attempted to console his master, for this admission, no matter how private between a Lord and his adviser, was the first step in overcoming that fear, and perhaps in conquering Lady Mara, as well. "Lord, the girl will make a mistake. You must bide your time; wait for that moment. . . ."

The jade-fly returned to pester Desio; the slave moved his fan to intercept its flight, but Desio waved the feathers away.

He glared through the gloom at Incomo. "No, I cannot wait. The Acoma cow already has the upper hand and she continues to grow stronger. My father's position was more advantageous than my own; he stood but one step away from the Gold Throne of the Warlord! Now he is ashes, and I can count loyal allies on one hand. And all our pain and humiliation can be placed at the feet of . . . *that woman!*"

This was sorrowfully true. Incomo understood his master's reluctance to speak his enemy's name. Barely more than a child when her father and brother died—with few soldiers and no allies—within three years Mara had secured more prestige for the Acoma than they had known in their long, honorable history. Incomo tried in vain to think of something soothing to say, but his young Lord's complaints were all justified. Mara *was* to be feared, and now her position of power had increased to the point where she not only could protect herself, but could directly challenge the Minwanabi.

Softly the First Adviser said, "Recall Tasaio to your side."

Desio blinked, momentarily looking stupid as his father never had. Then comprehension dawned. He glanced about the room and noticed the fan slave still at his post, despite the blood trickling from his broken nose and torn lip. In a moment of unexpected consideration, Desio dismissed the unfortunate wretch. Now alone with his adviser, he said, "Why should I call my cousin back from the war upon the barbarian world? You know he covets my position. Until I marry and sire children, he is next in succession. And he is *too* close to the Warlord for my taste. My father was wise to keep him busy with affairs upon a distant world."

"Your father was also wise enough to have your cousin arrange Lord Sezu and Lanokota's deaths in the first place." Hands tucked in his sleeves, Incomo stalked forward a step. "Why not let Tasaio deal with the girl? The father, the son, now the daughter."

Desio considered. Tasaio had waited until the Warlord had been absent from the campaign upon the barbarian world to order Lord Sezu and his son into an impossible military situation. He had ensured their deaths without exposing the Minwanabi to any public culpability. It had been a brilliant stroke, and Desio's father had ceded some desirable lands in Honshoni Province to Tasaio as reward. Tapping his cheek with a pudgy finger, Desio said, "I am uncertain. Tasaio might prove dangerous to me, perhaps as dangerous as . . . that girl."

Incomo shook his head in disagreement. "Your cousin will defend Minwanabi honor. As Ruling Lord, you are not a target for Tasaio's ambition, as you were when Lord Jingu was alive. It is one thing to seek a rival's demise, quite another to attempt to overthrow one's own lawful Lord." Incomo pondered a moment, then added, "Despite his ambitions, it is unthinkable Tasaio would break his oath to you. He would no more move against you than he would have against your father, *Lord Desio.*" He stressed the last to drive home the point he wished to make.

Desio stood, ignoring the fly, which at last perched upon his collar. His eyes fixed on a point in space, and he sighed aloud. "Yes, of course. You are correct. I must recall Tasaio and have him swear fealty. Then he must defend me with his life, or forfeit Minwanabi honor forever."

Incomo waited, aware his master had not finished. Sometimes clumsy with words, Desio still possessed a cunning mind, though he lacked his father's instincts or his cousin's brilliance. He crossed to the windows. "I shall include all other loyal retainers and allies in my summons," he declared at last. "Yes, we must have a formal gathering." He faced his adviser with finality. "No one shall think I have hesitated in calling my cousin to serve at home. No, we shall have all our vassals and allies here."

Decisively the fat man clapped his hands. Two servants in orange livery slid aside painted doors and entered to do his bidding. "Open these damned screens," commanded Desio. "Do it quickly. I am hot." As if a great burden had been lifted from his soul, he added, "Let in fresh air, for the gods' mercy."

The servants busied themselves with latches and bars, and presently light flooded the study and cool air flowed inside. The fly on the young Lord's collar took wing toward freedom, and the lake beyond. The waters sparkled silver in sunlight, dotted with fishing boats that plied nets from dawn to dusk. Desio seemed to shed his self-indulgence as he strode across the room to stand before his First Adviser. His eyes came alight with newfound confidence as the paralyzing fear brought on by his father's death fled before his excited planning. "I will make my vows upon my family's natami in the Holy Glade of Minwanabi Ancestors, with all my kin in attendance.

"We shall show that the Minwanabi have not fallen. . . ." Then, with unexpected dry humor, he added, "Or at least not very far." He shouted for his hadonra and began relaying orders. "I want the very finest entertainment available. This celebration will outshine that disaster my father arranged to honor the Warlord. Have every family member attend, including those who fight upon the barbarian world. . . ."

"This shall be done, my Lord." Incomo sent a runner scurrying with instructions for officers, senior advisers, servants, and slaves. Within moments two scribes were furiously copying Desio's commands, while, close by, the family chop bearer hovered with hot wax.

Desio regarded this bustle with a cold smile on his lips. He droned on a few minutes more, his orders and grandiose plans making him feel better than wine. Then suddenly he stopped. To all in the room he announced, "And send word to the Grand Temple of Turakamu. I will build a prayer gate, so that each traveler who passes through will invoke the Red God's indulgence, that he will look favorably upon Minwanabi vengeance. To the god I vow: blood will flow freely until I have the Acoma bitch's head!"

Incomo bowed to conceal his sudden concern. To pledge so to Turakamu might bring fortune during a conflict, but one did not vow lightly to the Death God; disaster could befall if vows went unfulfilled. The patience of the gods in such a matter was a fickle proposition. Incomo gathered his robe about him, finding the air off the lake suddenly chilling. At least, he hoped it was the breeze and not a premonition of doom.

Sunlight streamed through the tree branches within the largest of the Acoma gardens, painting patches of light upon the ground. Overhead, leaves rustled, while the fountain in the center of the courtyard sang its never-ending melody of falling water. Despite the pleasant surroundings, all those called to council shared their mistress's concerns.

Mara sat within her circle of senior advisers, her thoughts

troubled. Clad in her thinnest lounging robe, adorned by a single green jewel on a cho-ja–carved jade chain, she seemed almost abstracted, the picture of the Lady in repose. And yet her brown eyes held a glint that these, her closest advisers, all recognized as puzzlement.

One by one the Lady studied the officers and advisers that were House Acoma's core. The hadonra, Jican, a short, nervous man with a shrewd mind for commerce, sat diffidently as always. Under his detailed management, Acoma wealth had multiplied, but he preferred progress in small, secure steps, avoiding the dramatic gambles that appealed to Mara. Today Jican fidgeted less than usual, which the Lady of the Acoma attributed to the news that the cho-ja silk makers had begun their spinning. By the winter season their first bolts of finished cloth would be ready. Acoma riches, then, were on the increase. To Jican, this was of vital concern. But Mara knew wealth alone did not secure a great house.

Her First Adviser, Nacoya, had repeated this to no end. If anything, Mara's recent victory over the Minwanabi made the wizened old woman more nervous than ever. "I agree with Jican, Lady. This expansion could prove dangerous." She fixed Mara with a steady gaze. "A house can rise too fast in the Game of the Council. The lasting victories are ever the subtle ones, for they do not call for preemptive action by rivals unnerved by sudden successes. The Minwanabi will be moving, we know, so let us not bring uninvited appraisal from other houses, too."

Mara dismissed the remark. "I have only the Minwanabi to fear. We are at odds with no one else at present, and I wish things to remain that way. We must all prepare for the strike we know will come. It's just a question of when and in what form." Mara's voice held an uncertain note as she added, "I expected a swift reprisal after Jingu's death, even if only a token raid." And yet, for a month, no changes had been observed in the Minwanabi household.

Desio's appetite for drink and slave girls had increased, Mara's spies reported; and Jican's quick eyes had noticed the drop in Minwanabi trade goods sold within the Empire's marketplaces. This decrease in wares had driven prices up, and other houses had prospered as a result: hardly the desire of the power-hungry Minwanabi, particularly after that family had suffered such a loss in prestige.

Neither were there any overt preparations for war. The Minwanabi barracks maintained practice as usual, and no recall orders had gone out to the troops at war on the barbarian world.

Force Commander Keyoke had not taken the spies' reports to heart. Never complacent where Mara's safety was concerned, he labored among his troops morning until nightfall, reviewing the condition of armor and weapons, and overseeing battle drills. Lujan, his First Strike Leader, spent hours at his side. He—like all Acoma soldiers—was lean and battle-ready, his eyes quick to fix upon movement, and his hand always near his sword.

"I don't like the way things look," Keyoke said, his words sharp over the fall of water in the fountain. "The Minwanabi estate might appear to be in chaos, but this could be a ruse to cover preparations for a strike against us. Desio may be grieving for his father, but I grew up with Irrilandi, his Force Commander, and I will tell you there is no laxity in any Minwanabi barracks. Warriors can march in a moment." His capable hands tightened on the helmet in his lap, until the officer's plumes at the crest quivered with his tension. Ever expressionless, Keyoke shrugged. "I know our forces should be preparing to counter this threat you speak of, but the spies give us no clue where we should look for the next thrust. We cannot keep ourselves at battle readiness indefinitely, mistress."

Lujan nodded. "There has been no movement in the wilds among the grey warriors and condemned men. No large force of bandits is reported, which should mean it's safe to assume that Minwanabi is not staging for a covert attack, as they did against Lord Buntokapi."

"Seems not to be," Keyoke amended. "Lord Buntokapi," he said, naming Mara's late husband, "was given ample warning." His eyes showed a fleeting bitterness. "For Lord Sezu, warning came too late. That was *Tasaio's* plotting, and a more clever relli has never been birthed by the Minwanabi," he observed, referring to the deadly Kelewan water serpent. "The moment I hear Tasaio has been recalled, I will begin sleeping in my armor."

Mara nodded to Nacoya, who seemed to have something to add. The old woman's pins were askew, as always, but her gruff manner seemed more thoughtful than sharp. "Your Spy

Master's agents will pay very careful attention to important matters within the Minwanabi household." A shrewd expression crossed the adviser's face. "But he is a man, Lady, and will concentrate on numbers of soldiers, stockpiling of stores for battle, the comings and goings of leaders, messages to allies. I would suggest that you put your agent under orders to watch for the moment when Desio tires of his slave girls. A man with a purpose does not dally in his bed. This I remember well. The moment Desio ceases drinking wine and fondling women, then we *know* he plots murder against your house."

Mara made a faintly exasperated gesture. The slightest hint of a smile curved her lips, making her radiantly pretty. Though she was unaware of the fact, Lujan was not; he watched his mistress with devoted admiration and added a playful comment. "My Lady, First Adviser"—here he nodded to the wizened Nacoya—"I will bid the warriors who sweat through their drills at noon to await the exhaustion of Desio's member. When the Minwanabi flag droops, we will all line up for the charge."

Mara blushed and threw the First Strike Leader a dark look. "Lujan, your insight is apt, even if your example is not." Since her wedding night, Mara had little comfort with such talk.

Lujan bowed. "My Lady, if I have given offense . . ."

She waved away the apology—she could never stay angry with Lujan—then turned her head as her runner rushed up and bowed at her elbow.

"Speak, Tamu," she said gently, for the young boy was new to his post and still uncertain of himself.

Tamu pressed his forehead to the floor, still intimidated by being in a noble's presence. "Lady, your Spy Master awaits in your study. He says he has brought reports from Hokani Province, particularly from estates to the north."

"At last," said Mara in relief. She recognized in the runner's choice of language what her Spy Master, Arakasi, had striven to impart. Only one estate in Hokani mattered. He would have word of the countermove her people had been awaiting through four strained weeks. To her advisers she said, "I will speak with Arakasi at once, and meet with you all later in the afternoon."

Breezes played through the ulo leaves, and the fountain

still sang its splashing song, as the Acoma officers bowed to acknowledge their dismissal. Keyoke and Lujan were first to rise. Jican gathered his tally slates and asked his Lady's permission to look in on the cho-ja silk makers. Mara granted his request, but waved him off before he could reiterate any of his constant concerns.

Nacoya was last to rise. Arthritis had slowed her movements of late, and Mara was jolted by the unpleasant recognition that age was taking its toll on the indomitable old woman. Nacoya's promotion to First Adviser had been well earned, and despite her belief that she had risen higher than she deserved, Mara's former nurse had worn her mantle of office with grace and shrewd intelligence. Thirty years serving the wives and daughters of Ruling Lords had gained her a unique insight into the Game of the Council.

Mara watched Nacoya's stiff bow with trepidation. She could not imagine Acoma prosperity without the old woman's acerbic guidance or her strong, affectionate nature, which had supported Mara through worse troubles than she had ever imagined she might survive. Only the gods knew how long Nacoya might live, but, with a chill, Mara sensed that her First Adviser's days were limited. The Lady of the Acoma was in no way prepared for the loss. Save for her son, the old woman was all Mara counted family in the world. If she lost Nacoya unexpectedly, there was no clear choice among her servants for the role of First Adviser.

Mara pushed such gloomy thoughts away. Best not to think of future sorrows when the Minwanabi were busy plotting vengeance, she justified to herself.

Mara bade her runner slave rise and inform Arakasi that she would be joining him in the study. Then she clapped for a servant and sent to the kitchen for food. For unless Arakasi changed his manner, he had come straight to his mistress from the road and had not eaten since the night before.

Mara's study was dim and cool, even during early afternoon. Furnished with a low black table and fine green silk cushions, it had hand-painted screens opening onto a walkway lined with flowering akasi plants. When open, the outer doors provided a view of the Acoma estates, needra meadows rolling away to the wetlands where the shatra birds flew each sunset. But today the screens were only partially open, and the view was blocked by filmy silk drapes that admitted air while keeping out prying eyes. Mara entered a room that appeared at first glance to be empty. Experience had taught her not to be deceived; still, she could not entirely control her slight start.

A voice spoke without warning from the dimmest corner. "I closed the drapes, Lady, since the work crew is trimming the akasi." A shadowy figure stepped forward, graceful as a predator stalking prey. "Although your overseer is honest, and Midkemians are unlikely to be spies, still, I take precautions out of habit."

The man knelt before his mistress. "More than once such practices have saved my life. I bring you greetings, Lady."

Mara gave him her hand as a sign he should make himself comfortable. "You are doubly welcomed home, Arakasi." She studied this fascinating man. His dark hair was wet, but not from a bath. Arakasi had paused only to rinse off travel dust and slip on a fresh tunic. His hatred of the Minwanabi equaled any harbored by those born on Acoma lands, and his desire to see the most powerful of the five Families ground down into oblivion was dearer to him than life.

"I hear no sounds of shears," Mara pointed out. She permitted her Spy Master to rise. "Your return is a relief, Arakasi."

The Spy Master straightened and settled back onto his heels. Mara had a quick mind, and, with her, discussions tended to thread through several topics simultaneously. He smiled with genuine pleasure, for in her service his reports bore rich fruit. Without waiting for her to be seated, he answered her earlier query. "You hear no sounds of shears, Lady, because the overseer sent away the workers. The slaves on the first shift complained of sunburn, and rather than sweat over the whip, the overseer chose to shuffle the work roster."

"Midkemians," Mara said shortly, as she settled onto her cushions. With Arakasi she felt familiar, and since the day waxed hot, she loosened her sash and allowed the breeze through the drapes to cool her through her opened robe. "They are recalcitrant as breeding needra. Jican advised against my buying them, and I fear he may have been right."

Arakasi considered this with a birdlike cock of his head. "Jican thinks like a hadonra, not a ruler."

"Meaning he does not see the whole picture," Mara said,

and the light in her eyes intensified with the challenge of matching wits with her Spy Master. "You find the Midkemians interesting," she surmised.

"Passingly so." Arakasi turned at a slight step in the corridor, and seeing that the disturbance was nothing more than a servant approaching from the kitchen, he again faced his mistress. "Their customs are not like ours, Lady. If there are slaves in their culture, my guess is they are very different creatures from ours. But I digress from my purpose." His eyes grew suddenly sharp. "Desio of the Minwanabi at last begins to show his hand as Ruling Lord."

The servant arrived at the doorway with platters of fruit and cold jigabird. Arakasi fell silent as Mara motioned for the tray to be placed on the table. "You must be hungry." She invited her Spy Master to take his ease upon the cushions. The servant departed silently, and for the moment all was quiet outside. Neither Mara nor her Spy Master reached for the dishes. The Lady of the Acoma spoke first. "Tell me of Desio."

Arakasi became very still. His dark eyes showed no emotion at all, but his hands, so seldom betraying his mood, went tense. "The young Lord is not the player of the Great Game that his father was," he opened. "This if anything makes him more dangerous. With Jingu, my agents always knew where and when to listen. This is not so with the son. An experienced opponent is somewhat predictable. A novice may prove . . . innovative." He smiled slightly and nodded in Mara's direction, acknowledging that her own successes bore out his observations. "He's no creative thinker, but what Desio can't gain by wit, he may yet bungle into having." The Spy Master poured himself a cup of jomach juice and took a tentative sip. He would find no poisons in this house, but the subject of the Minwanabi, as always, made him prickle with uneasiness and caution. Seeking a lighter tone, lest he needlessly alarm his young mistress, Arakasi added, "Desio has a lot of soldiers to bungle with."

Mara considered her Spy Master's mood, perhaps brought on by his own need for self-control, for to give his hatred free rein he would seek the destruction of his enemies without regard for the safety of any and all things near to him.

"But Desio himself is weak, no matter how strong those who serve him." Arakasi abandoned his juice cup on the table. "He has inherited all his father's passions, but not Jingu's restraints. If not for Force Commander Irrilandi's vigilance, his enemies might have torn through his defenses and fed off his wealth like a pack of jagunas over a dead harulth," he said, referring to Kelewan's doglike carrion eater and most feared predator: a giant, six-legged terror, all speed and teeth. Arakasi steepled his hands and looked keenly at Mara. "But Force Commander Irrilandi kept his patrols in first-class order. Many exploratory raids were mounted within days of Jingu's death, and Minwanabi left only a few survivors licking their wounds."

"The Xacatecas were among those enemies," Mara prompted.

Arakasi returned a nod. "They bear the Minwanabi no affection, and my agent in Lord Chipino's household indicates that the Xacatecas First Adviser raised the possibility of alliance with the Acoma. Others in his council are still opposed; they say you have shown the best you have, and wait for you to fall. But Chipino of the Xacatecas listens without making final judgment."

Mara raised her eyebrows, surprised. The Xacatecas were one of the Five Families. Her victory over Jingu had indeed raised regard for her name, if Chipino's advisers would debate a possible alliance that would be a virtual declaration of war on the Minwanabi. Even the Shinzawai had skirted the question of open ties, content for the moment to keep a friendly but neutral position.

"But the Xacatecas can wait," said Arakasi. "Desio will not formulate policy on his own, but come to depend on advisers and relations. Power and leadership will be spread over several men, making a clear-cut picture very difficult for my agents to gather. This will make our predictions unreliable where broad policy is concerned, and certainty impossible when it comes to assessing the Minwanabi's immediate plans."

Mara watched an insect advance across the fruit dish, sampling each variety. So would Desio surround himself with ambitious and power-hungry individuals, and though their desires might differ, all could be depended upon to wish the Acoma downfall. Perhaps ominously, the insect settled on one slice of jomach, where several of its fellows joined it. "We are fortunate that Tasaio is away in the wars upon Midkemia," the Lady mused.

Arakasi leaned forward. "Fortunate no longer, mistress. The man who arranged the murder of your father and brother is returning through the rift on this very day. Desio has called a great gathering of relations and supporters for the week following next. He will take oaths of fealty, and more. He has paid in metal for the erection of a prayer gate to the Red God."

Now Mara went very still. "Tasaio is dangerous."

"Ambitious as well," added Arakasi. "Desio might be ruled by his passions, but his cousin's only interests are war and power. With Desio firmly upon the Minwanabi throne, Tasaio will advance his own cause for command over Imperial troops and will serve Desio faithfully—albeit with an occasional silent wish for Desio to choke on a jigabird bone, I wager. Tasaio may try a military solution to his uncle's fall from power. A smashing victory over House Acoma, with some damage to other great houses as well, and Desio will stand next to the Warlord in power in the council."

Mara considered this. Jingu's death had caused the Minwanabi to lose honor, allies, and political strength, but their garrisons and capability for warcraft were still undiminished. Acoma forces were well on their way to recovery since the destruction that had accompanied the fall of her father and brother. But too much relied on the cho-ja guards. At present the insectoids would act only on Acoma lands, a deadly and reliable defensive army, but useless for offensive strategy. In war or conflict beyond the estate borders, the Acoma could not match the military might presently commanded by Desio.

"We must know what they plan," she said tensely. "Can your agents penetrate this Minwanabi gathering and report what Desio's advisers whisper in his ear?"

Arakasi returned a bitter smile. "Lady, do not overestimate any spy's abilities. Remember that the man who reports was very close to Jingu. That servant still commands the same post, but as the son begins to exercise his powers, we have no guarantee he will remain there. Of course, I have begun to groom a replacement should things go amiss, but remember that the agent we place must be tailored to Desio's tastes. He will not be able to rise in the young Lord's confidence for a few years at best."

Mara anticipated Arakasi's next thought. "And Tasaio is the greater danger."

The Spy Master returned a slight bow. "Lady, be sure that I will do all that is possible to compile an accurate report of what transpires at Desio's gathering. Should the young Lord remain as stupid as I think he is, Tasaio will be but one voice among many. If he shows an unexpected flash of intelligence and assigns the campaign against us to Tasaio, we are doubly endangered." He set aside a barely nibbled piece of bread. "Worrying about what may occur has limited benefit. Have your factors and servants listen in the market for gossip and news. Knowledge is power, remember that always. On this will the Acoma come to triumph."

Smoothly Arakasi arose, and Mara waved him permission to withdraw. As he slipped unobtrusively from her presence, she noticed with a chill that this was the first time she had ever known him to leave food when he was hungry. The room seemed suddenly too silent, oppressive with her own doubt. The image of Tasaio returning reawakened the desperate sense of helplessness she had known when she had learned of the deaths of her family. Unwilling to dwell upon the blackness of the past, Mara clapped for her servants.

"Bring me my son," she commanded. Though she knew Ayaki would be soundly asleep, she had a sudden yearning for his noise, his mischief, and the warm weight of his small, muscular body in her arms.

3. *CHANGES*

The child turned over.

Ayaki sprawled upon the cushions, asleep. Boisterous for a short time, he had finally succumbed to exhaustion. Mara stroked his black hair away from his forehead, filled with love for her son.

Although the boy had his father's stocky build, he had inherited quickness from her family. In his second year, he showed remarkable coordination, a fast tongue that drove the servants to distraction, and continually bruised knees. His smile had won the hearts of even the most hardened warriors who served on the Acoma estates.

"You will be a fine fighter, and a greater player of the game," Mara mused softly. But now the boy's toughness and quick wit had one opponent he could not overcome, his need for an afternoon nap. Though he was the light of Mara's life, these brief interludes were welcome, for when awake Ayaki required three nurses to keep him occupied.

Mara tucked her son's robe about him and straightened his outflung limbs. She settled back upon her cushions in thought. Many recently planted seeds must bear fruit before Ayaki came of age. When that day dawned, her father's old enemies the Anasati would end the alliance begun for the sake of the boy. What goodwill Mara had secured through giving birth to the first grandson of Lord Tecuma of the Anasati would end, and the debt incurred by Buntokapi's premature death would be extracted. Then must the Acoma be unassailably strong, to weather the change in rule as Mara turned over control of her house to an inexperienced son.

The Minwanabi menace must be fully eliminated before another powerful enemy challenged a young Lord.

Mara considered the years ahead, while afternoon sunlight striped the drapes and slaves returned to trim the akasi. The gardening around the walkways occurred often enough that she had become indifferent to the clack of shears. Except for today, that normal household sound was repeatedly interrupted by sharp commands from the overseer and the frequent slap of the short leather quirt he carried. Normally the lash was ceremonial, a symbolic badge of rank carried on the belt—Tsurani slaves seldom required beating. But the slaves from Midkemia were indifferent to their overseer's displeasure. Their respect for their betters was nonexistent, and whippings shamed them not at all.

Tsurani slaves found the Midkemians as enigmatic as Mara did. Raised in the knowledge that their humble devotion to work was their only hope of earning a higher place upon the Wheel that bound the departed to rebirth and life, they worked tirelessly. To be beaten for laziness, or to disobey their lawful masters in any way, was to earn the permanent disfavor of the gods, for below slave was only animal. And once returned from the Wheel of Life in a lower form they would find salvation from the countless rebirths in pain and deprivation impossible.

Disturbed from contemplation by a heated argument, Mara realized with annoyance that the barbarians still had not learned proper manners. The only change in them since the slave auction seemed to be the increased number of lash welts on their backs and a marked improvement in the command of their masters' language.

"The gods' will? That's *hogwash!*" boomed one in heavily accented Tsurani. For a brief moment, Mara wondered what "hogwash" meant. Then the barbarian voice resumed. "I call it plain stupidity. You want work from these men, you'll take my suggestion, and thank me for it."

The overseer had no ready reply for slaves who talked back at him. Such things did not arise in Tsurani culture, and he had no means of coping except to slap the offender with his quirt and swear in an embarrassing display of temper.

This had no effect. Disrupted utterly from her thoughts, Mara heard sounds of a scuffle, and then words of unmistakable rage.

"Strike me again with that, little man, and I'll drop you head first into that pile of six-legger's dung on the other side of that fence."

"Put me down, slave!" screeched the overseer. He sounded genuinely frightened, and since the situation had plainly gotten out of hand, Mara arose to intervene. Whatever "hogwash" might be, it wasn't something that indicated proper deference to authority.

She crossed the study, whipped the drapes back, and found herself looking up across an impressively muscled expanse of shoulder and arm. The redheaded Midkemian who had been at the root of the commotion at the auction had a fist twined in the overseer's robe, lifting him into the air, his feet kicking above the ground. When he saw his mistress, the overseer's eyes rolled back in his head, and his lips moved in prayer to Kelesha, goddess of mercy.

The barbarian simply looked down at the diminutive lady in the doorway, his expression bland but his eyes as blue and hard as the sword metal that abounded on the Midkemian side of the rift.

Mara felt her own anger rise at that openly rebellious stare. She curbed her temper and spoke evenly. "If you value life, slave, let him go now!"

The redhead recognized authority in her dark eyes. Still, he was insolent. He considered her command an instant; then a wicked grin spread across his face and he opened his fist. The overseer dropped without warning, buckled at the knees, and landed on his seat in the middle of Mara's favorite flower bed.

The grin sparked Mara's anger. "You lack any hint of humility, slave, and that is a dangerous thing!"

The redhead stopped smiling, but his eyes remained upon his mistress with an interest that now had more to do with her thin robe than any respect for her words.

Mara was not too angry to notice. Suddenly made to feel undressed by the barbarian's frank appraisal, she felt her temper mount. She might have ordered the redhead's immediate death as an example to the others, except that Arakasi's earlier expression of interest in the barbarians made her pause. None of the Midkemians behaved in an appropriate way, and unless she could learn the reason why, the only expedient that could end the problem was to slaughter her purchases out of hand. Still, an object lesson was required. Turning to a nearby pair of guards, she said, "Take this slave out of sight and beat him. Do not let him die, but make him wish to. *If* he resists, then kill him."

Instantly two swords appeared, and, with clear intent to brook no resistance, the guards led the outworlder away. As he moved down the path, the imminent prospect of a beating seemed to have no effect on his self-important posture. The barbarian's lack of fear at his coming ordeal served only to irritate Mara more, for it was the one thing about the man that was Tsurani-like and admirable. Then Mara caught herself: about the man? What could she be thinking of? He was only a slave.

Jican chose that moment to make an appearance. His polite knock on the doorframe broke through Mara's angry contemplation.

She whirled and snapped across the room, "What!"

The sight of her hadonra jumping back in fright made her feel foolish. She motioned for her overseer to remove himself from the flower bed, then retired to her cushions, where Ayaki still lay asleep.

Jican stepped into the room from the hallway. "Mistress?" he inquired meekly.

With a wave at her hadonra, Mara said, "I am about to learn why Elzeki here must argue with slaves."

The overseer stepped through the outer door, flushing visibly at his mistress's disapproval. Elzeki was little better than a slave himself, an untrained servant given the office of managing workers about the estate. And authority given to him could be taken away. He prostrated himself upon the waxed wood floor and protested hotly in his own defense. "Mistress, these barbarians have no sense of order. They are without *wal.*" He used the ancient Tsurani word meaning "center of being"—the soul that defined one's place in the universe. "They complain, they malinger, they argue, they make jokes. . . ." Frustrated to the point of tears, he finished in an angry rush. "The redheaded one is the worst. He acts as if he were a noble."

Mara's eyes widened. "A noble?"

Elzeki straightened from his obeisance and glanced in appeal at the hadonra. Jican still winced at the poor choice of words. With no support forthcoming from the hadonra,

Elzeki prostrated himself again, his forehead pressed to the floor. "Please, mistress! I meant no disrespect!"

Mara waved away the apology. "No. That is understood. What did you mean?"

Peeking up, he saw that his mistress's anger had changed to interest. "The other barbarians defer to him, my Lady. Maybe this redhead was an officer too cowardly to die. He might have lied. These barbarians mix truth and untruth without distinction, I sometimes think. Their ways are strange. They confuse me."

Mara frowned, thinking that if the redhead were cowardly, or frightened of pain, he would not have shown such nerveless composure at the prospect of a beating by her guards.

"What were you and he arguing about?" Jican demanded.

Elzeki, the overseer, seemed to shrivel, as if to review the events leading up to his shameful embarrassment were to relive them. "Many things, honorable hadonra. The barbarian speaks with such a savage accent, he is difficult to understand." Through the screen beyond the drapes came the sound of a distant thud, followed by a pained grunt. Mara's orders for punishment were plainly being carried out by the guards. Since his own hide might be whipped over the barbarians' disobedience, the overseer began visibly to sweat.

Mara motioned for the screen door to be closed, lest she be further disturbed. As a house servant rushed to do her bidding, she saw that the remaining barbarians were gathered on the walkway, their shears idle in their hands, regarding their mistress with open hostility and resentment. Stifling outrage at such blatant disrespect, Mara snapped at the overseer. "Then tell us just one thing that red-haired barbarian dared to feel important enough to argue about."

Elzeki shifted his weight. "The redhead asked to move one of the men inside."

Jican glanced at his mistress, who nodded permission for him to cross-question. "What reason did he give?"

"Some nonsense about our sun being hotter than the sun on their own world, and this other man being stricken by the heat."

Mara said, "What else?"

Elzeki glanced at his feet, like a boy caught sneaking sweets from the kitchen. "He also complained that *some* of the slaves needed more water than we were giving them, because of the heat."

Mara said, "And?"

"He gave excuses for laziness. Rather than work hard, he objected that a few of the men who were set to tend the flowers knew nothing of plants upon their own world, let alone ours, and that to punish them for working slowly was foolish."

Jican sat back, astonished. "These sound like excellent suggestions to me, my Lady."

Mara expelled a long-suffering sigh. "It seems that I acted too hastily," she said ruefully. "Elzeki, go and put a stop to the beating. Tell my guards to have the redheaded slave cleaned up and brought to me here in my study."

As the overseer hurried obsequiously away, Mara regarded her hadonra. "Jican, it would seem that I ordered punishment for the wrong man."

"Elzeki has never had much perception," Jican agreed. Silently he wondered why that admission seemed to cause his Lady distress.

"We'll have to remove him from office," Mara summed up. "Slaves are much too valuable to be mismanaged by fools." She appealed at last to her hadonra. "I'll have you break the news to Elzeki, and then trust you to appoint his replacement."

"Your will, my Lady." Jican bowed low and departed. As he passed through the screen to the corridor, Mara stroked Ayaki's cheek. She then called for her maid to remove him to his sleeping mat in the nursery. If she was to deal with this redheaded barbarian personally, she wanted no other distractions. That thought made her smile, as the maid lifted her stocky son and he murmured angry protest in his sleep. Ayaki awake was as much of a disaster as the redhead, and with a shake of her head, Mara sat back to await the arrival of the guards with the barbarian offender who had single-handedly managed to ruin her contemplation.

The guards stepped in soon after, the Midkemian between them, his hair and loincloth drenched. Mara's request that he be cleaned up had been interpreted in the most uncomplicated way possible: the guards had simply dropped him into a convenient needra trough. The beating and subsequent soaking had dampened his spirit only slightly. The amusement in his eyes had changed to anger barely held in check. His defiance disturbed Mara. Lujan had often crossed the line of good manners with his playful banter, but never had a socially inferior man dared to look at her in such an openly condemnatory fashion. Suddenly sorry she had not called for a more modest house robe, Mara nevertheless refused to summon her maid, lest she grant significance to the stare of a barbarian slave. Rather than feel embarrassment before the outworlder, she matched his gaze with her own.

The guards were uncertain what to do with the wretch they had half dragged into their Lady's presence. Still gripping the huge man tightly, they offered ineffectual bows. The more senior of the warriors broke the silence with ill-concealed diffidence. "Lady, what is your wish? A barbarian in your presence would perhaps be more seemly on his knees."

Mara noticed the guards as if for the first time, and the water pooling on her waxed floor. There was blood mixed in the puddles.

"Let him stand, if he wishes." She clapped for her servants, and sent the first one to answer off at a run to fetch towels.

The house slave reappeared with a pile of scented bath towels. He entered the study, bowed, and only belatedly realized that his Lady's request had been made in behalf of the scruffy barbarian who stood pinioned in the hands of the guards.

"Well," snapped Mara, at her servant's hesitation, "dry the brute off before he ruins the floor."

"Your will, Mistress," the slave murmured from a position of prostration. He arose and began to daub the reddened skin between the barbarian's shoulder blades, this being the highest place he could reach.

Mara assessed the huge slave in a relatively calm moment, then came to a decision. "Leave us," she commanded her guards. They released the barbarian, bowed, and let themselves out through the screen to the corridor.

The barbarian rubbed his wrists where the guards' grip had restricted circulation. The slave attempting to dry him seemed an irritation, and after a glance at Mara, the outworlder reached out, took a clean towel from the pile, and finished the task himself. His hair stood up in spikes when he finished, and the slave looked in dismay at the pile of blood-soiled, damp towels heaped about the barbarian's feet.

"Give those to my washing maids," Mara said. She motioned for the redhead to select a cushion and be seated.

Mara studied the barbarian's face; the gaze he returned was as penetrating as her own. Suddenly she felt out of her depth. Something about this man disturbed her. The reason struck her: she still considered him a man! Slaves were *livestock*, not people. Why did this one cause her to feel . . . uncertain? Her practice in the role of Ruling Lady allowed her to assume the mask of command. She felt challenged to discover why this barbarian made her forget his station. She forced her voice to calm. "I was hasty, perhaps." As the house slave scooped up the towels and hastened away, she added, "It would appear, upon examination of the matter, that I ordered you beaten unfairly."

Taken aback, but covering it well, the redhead selected a cushion and gingerly sat down. The scar left on his cheek by the overseer at the slave market did not detract from his appearance; rather, the flaw gave heightened contrast to his handsome features, and his heavy beard was a novelty not seen in Tsurani freemen, who shaved as a matter of tradition.

"Slave," commanded Mara, "I wish to know more of the land you come from."

"I have a name," said the redhead in his deep-throated voice, which now was bristling with antagonism. "I am Kevin, from the City of Zūn."

Mara replied with irritation, "You might have been counted human once, upon your world, but now you are a slave. A slave has no honor, nor does he have a spirit in the eyes of the gods. This you must have known, Kevin of Zūn." She spoke the name with sarcasm. "You chose your lot, chose to forfeit honor. If not, you should have died before an enemy took you captive." She paused as another thought occurred to her. "Or were you vassal to another more powerful house, whose Lord refused you permission to take your own life?"

Kevin raised his brows, momentarily baffled by confusion. "What? I'm not sure what you mean."

Mara repeated herself in terms a child would understand. "Did your house swear vassalage to another?"

Kevin straightened his back, winced, and raked a hand through his damp beard. "Zūn swore allegiance to the High King in Rillanon, of course."

The Lady nodded as if all were explained. "Then you were forbidden permission by this King to fall upon your sword. Yes?"

Thoroughly mystified, Kevin shook his head. "Fall on my sword? *Why?* I might be a third son of a minor nob—er, family, but I don't need my King's permission to sanction what seems an act of total idiocy."

Now Mara blinked in surprise. "Have your people no honor? If the choice was yours, why allow yourself to be taken captive into slavery?"

Careful of his welts, which were swelling uncomfortably, Kevin regarded the diminutive woman who through misfortune had come to be his mistress. Forcing a smile, he said, "Trust me, lady, I had no option, otherwise I wouldn't be enjoying your . . . *hospitality* now. Had I a choice, I'd be at home with my family."

Mara shook her head slightly. This was not the answer she sought. "We may be having difficulty because of your barbaric use of the Tsurani tongue. Let me ask a different way: when you were taken captive, were you not spared a moment by fate in which you could have taken your own life rather than face capture?"

Kevin paused, as if weighing the question. "I suppose so, but why would I think about killing myself?"

Without thought, Mara blurted, "For honor!"

Kevin laughed bitterly. "What good is honor to a dead man?"

Mara blinked, as if struck by harsh lights in a dark room. "Honor is . . . everything," Mara said, not believing anyone could ask that question. "It is what makes living endurable. It gives purpose to . . . everything. What else is there to live for?"

Kevin threw up his hands in exasperation. "Why, to enjoy life! To know the company of friends, to serve men you admire. In this case, to escape and go home again, what else?"

"Escape!" Thoroughly shocked, and unable to conceal the fact, Mara needed a moment to regroup. These people were not Tsurani, she reminded herself; the codes of behavior that bound slaves to service on her world were not shared by the folk beyond the rift. The Lady of the Acoma went on to wonder whether others of her culture might have discovered how different the Midkemians were from themselves. Hokanu of the Shinzawai sprang to mind. Mara made a mental note to pry loose information on Lord Kamatsu's interest in the barbarians during the son's forthcoming visit. Next she considered whether this Kevin of Zūn might hold strange knowledge or ideas that might prove helpful against her enemies.

"You must tell me more of the lands beyond the rift," she demanded abruptly.

Pained by more than cuts and bruises, Kevin sighed. "You are a woman of many contradictions," he said with some care. "You order me beaten, dipped in a livestock trough, and then dried with what must be your finest towels. Now you want speeches without so much as a drink to wet my throat first."

"Your comforts, or lack of them, are beyond your right to question," said Mara acidly. "You happen to be bleeding on a cushion that cost much more than your worth on the open market, so be careful how you speak of my consideration."

Kevin raised his brows in reproof. He intended to say more, but at that moment someone outside chose to scratch on the screen to the Lady's private study.

Since no Tsurani would signal his mistress for attention with anything but a polite knock, Mara did not immediately respond. Whoever waited without seemed entirely unfazed by this fact. The wooden frame slid on its oiled track, and the bald-headed slave who had abetted the clothing scam at the slave auctions poked his face inside. "Kevin?" he said quietly, oblivious to the fact that he trespassed upon nobility without spoken leave or invitation. "You all right, old son?"

Mara gaped, as the redhead returned a reassuring grin. The bald-headed man smiled at Mara, then withdrew without further ado. Mara sat speechless for a long moment. In all the memory of her ancestors, she had never known a slave with the effrontery to admit himself to his ruling master's chambers without any summons, to hold a personal conversation with another slave, then withdraw without leave, making only the most perfunctory attempt at acknowledging his rightful mistress. Mara curbed her first impulse to call for punishment, now being totally convinced of the need to understand more of these barbarians.

She sent her runner to find another overseer to manage the barbarians and set them to cutting akasi, as they should have been doing all along. Then Mara returned her attention to Kevin.

"Tell me how servants treat their mistresses in the lands where you were born," she demanded.

The barbarian returned a provocative smile. His eyes wandered boldly over Mara's body, which was covered only by an almost transparent silk robe. "To begin with," he said brightly, "any lady who wore what you do in front of her servants would be begging to get herself . . ." He struggled for a word, then said, "In my language it's not a polite term. I don't know how you folks feel about it, but given you're showing me all you've got without a thought, you obviously don't consider such things."

"What are you talking about?" Mara snapped, at the edge of her patience.

"Why . . ." He touched himself upon his dirty loincloth, then made an upward gesture with his extended forefinger. "What men and women do, to make babies." He pointed in the general direction of her groin.

Mara's eyes widened. She might be having difficulty thinking of this barbarian as a slave, but obviously he had no difficulty thinking of her as a woman. Softly, in tones that could only be called dangerous, she said, "To suggest such a thing, even indirectly, could mean a slow and painful death, slave! The most shameful execution is hanging, but if we wish the condemned to suffer, we hang them by the feet. Some men have been known to last two days that way. With a pile of hot coals just below your head, it can be a most unpleasant way to die."

Aware of Mara's anger, Kevin hastily amended, "Of course, Zūn has a much cooler climate than you are accustomed to." His phrases became broken as he searched for unfamiliar words, or substituted ones in his own tongue where his knowledge was incomplete. "We have winters, and *snow,* and cold rains during other seasons. The ladies from my lands must wear heavy skirts and animal skins for warmth. Tends to make the uncovered female body something . . . something we don't see a lot."

Mara's eyes flashed as she listened to the slave. *"Snow?"* She sounded the barbarian word awkwardly. "Cold rains?" Then what he meant registered and she said, "Animal skins? Do you mean furs? Leather with the hair not scraped off?" as her anger lessened.

"Something like that," Kevin said.

"How strange." Mara considered this like a child presented with wonders. "Such clothing must be uncomfortably heavy, not to mention being difficult for slaves to wash."

Kevin laughed. "You don't wash furs if you don't want them ruined. You beat the dust from them and set them in the sun to air." Since her features again clouded over at his amusement over her ignorance, he quickly added, "We have no slaves at Zūn." As he said this, his mood turned darker and more subdued. His shoulders stung yet from his beating, and despite the padding of the cushion, he ached even from sitting. "The Keshians keep slaves, but Kingdom law severely limits such practices."

Which explained much of the unmanageability of the Midkemians, Mara concluded. "Who does your menial work, then?"

"Freemen, Lady. We have servants, serfs, and franklins who owe allegiance to their Lords. Townsmen, merchants, guildsmen as well."

Unsatisfied with such a brief explanation, Mara plied Kevin for details. She sat motionless as he described the structure of Kingdom governance in depth. Long shadows striped the screens by the time her interest flagged. Kevin's voice by then sounded worn and hoarse. Thirsty herself, Mara sent for cool fruit drinks. When she had been served, she motioned for Kevin's comforts to be looked after.

Mara asked then about metalworking, an art her people knew little of, since such substances were rare in Kelewan. That Midkemian peasants owned iron, brass, and copper seemed inconceivable to her. Kevin's assertion that occasionally they possessed silver and gold was beyond credibility. Her astonishment at such wonders made her forget the differences between them. Kevin responded by smiling more. His easy manner awakened a hunger she had never allowed herself to explore. Mara found her eyes wandering over the lines of his body, or following the gestures of his strong, fine hands as he sought to explain things for which he lacked words. He spoke of smiths who fashioned iron and shaped the hard, crescent shoes that were nailed to the hooves of the beasts their warriors rode. Quite naturally the discussion turned into a lively talk over tactics, and the mutual discovery that the Midkemians found the cho-ja as terrifying an adversary as the Tsurani found mounted horsemen.

"You have much to teach," Mara said at last, a flush of pleasure showing through her fine complexion. That moment Nacoya knocked upon the door, to remind her of her afternoon meeting with her councilors.

Mara straightened, startled to realize that most of the day had fled. She regarded the deepening shadows, the plates of fruit rinds and the emptied pitchers and glasses strewn on the table between herself and the slave. Sorry that the discussion between them must end, she waved for her personal servant. "You will take this barbarian and see to his comforts. Let him bathe and apply unguents to his wounds. Then find him a robe, and have him await me in my personal quarters, for I wish to speak further with him when my business is concluded."

The slave bowed, then motioned for Kevin to follow. The barbarian unfolded his long legs and arose stiffly to his feet. He winced, then saw that the Lady still watched him. He returned a wry smile and, with no humbleness whatsoever, blew a kiss in her direction before he started after the servant.

Nacoya watched his parting gesture with narrowed eyes, a frown on her leathery face. Her mistress exhibited more amazement than outrage at such familiarity. Suddenly Mara hid a smile behind her hand, seemingly unable to contain herself. Nacoya's displeasure deepened into suspicion. "My Lady, have a care. A wise ruler does not reveal her heart to a slave."

"That man?" Mara stiffened, surprised into a blush. "He is a barbarian. I am fascinated by his alien people, nothing more." Then she sighed. "His blown kiss was a gesture Lano used to make when we were little," she explained, referring to the dead brother she used to idolize as a child. "Remember?"

Nacoya had raised Mara from infancy and the memory of Lanokota's gesture did not worry the old nurse. What troubled Nacoya was the reaction she saw in her mistress.

Mara straightened her robe carefully over her thighs. "Nacoya, you know I have no wish for a man." She stopped smoothing her silken hem, and her hands tightened into fists. "I know some ladies keep handsome men as litter bearers, so that more . . . personal needs can be satisfied at whim, but I am . . . uninterested in such diversion." Even to herself, Mara sounded unconvincing.

Irritated by the urge to discuss what should have needed no denial, Mara closed the topic with an imperious gesture. "Now, send for servants to remove these plates and cups. I will see my advisers, and Arakasi will relate his report on Lord Desio of the Minwanabi."

Nacoya bowed, but as a house servant arrived and began clearing the table for the meeting, the old First Adviser watched closely. A wistful smile came and went on Mara's lips. Shrewdly intuitive, Nacoya knew Mara did not contemplate the coming meeting, but, rather, the bronzed and red-haired barbarian who had whiled away an entire afternoon with talk. The sparkle in Mara's eyes, and the half-excited, half-frightened clenching of hands betrayed the Lady. Fears of pain and humiliation—memories of a brutal and insensitive husband—warred with new desire. Nacoya might be old, but she remembered younger passions; twenty years ago she might have given serious thought to having the slave brought to her own sleeping room. Aware of Kevin's attractions, and foreseeing trouble, the former nurse sighed silently. Mara had proved herself a clever player of the Game of the Council; but she had yet to understand the most basic things about relations between a man and a woman. Already under siege, she lacked instinct to know an attack from that quarter was even possible.

Fighting tears of concern, the former nurse composed herself for the forthcoming meeting. If Mara was to have her world turned over by an unexpected passion, she had chosen the worst possible time to have it happen.

4. VOWS

Horns sounded.

A thunder of drums joined in as the assembled crowd knelt, bowed, then sat back upon their heels in the ancient Tsurani position of attention. Arranged according to rank, but clothed in no other finery than white robes tied with an orange-and-black sash, they awaited the arrival of the new Lord of the Minwanabi.

The Minwanabi great hall was unique in all the Empire; some ancient Lord had employed a genius for an architect, an artist of unsurpassed brilliance. No visitor to the house of Desio's ancestors could fail to be awed by the engineering, which couched a supreme comfort within what amounted to a fortress.

The hillside chosen for the estate house had been hollowed out, the upper third pierced with arches that were left open to the sky, admitting light and air. Screens designed to protect against inclement weather were presently drawn back, and the entire hall lay awash in noonday sunlight. The lower portion of the hall was cut into the mountain. Its central chamber measured a full three hundred paces from the single entrance across a richly patterned floor to the dais. There, upon a throne of carved agate, Desio would receive fealty offered by the retainers and vassals summoned to do him homage.

Minwanabi guards in ceremonial armor stood at attention, their black lacquered helms and officers' orange plumes a smart double line in the gallery overlooking the main floor.

The musicians by the entry completed their fanfare, then lowered their horns and drums. Silence fell.

A piercing note cut the air. A door slid open to one side, and a priest of Turakamu, the Red God of death, spun on light feet into the hall. The bone whistle between his lips was a relic preserved from the ancient days. A feathered cape fell to elbow length, and his nude body was painted red upon black, so he looked like a blood-drenched skeleton as he danced in praise of his divine master. He wore his hair slicked to his scalp with heavy grease, the ends plaited into two braids tied with cords from which dangled bleached infant skulls.

The priest circled three times around the dais, joined by four acolytes, each in red robe and skull mask. Their appearance caused a stir through the assembly. Many in the hall made surreptitious gestures to ward off ill luck, for to encounter the Death God's minions was unpleasant at the best of times. The whistles shrilled, and the skulls clacked in time to the head priest's step. His dance grew faster, and the acolytes initiated a series of gyrations and leaps that described the throes of human suffering, the Death God's ultimate power, and the punishment meted out to mortals who displeased him.

Now a muttering disturbed the hall as Desio's guests asked in whispers why Red Priests should be chosen to invoke a blood ritual at this gathering. Normally the priests of Chochocan, the Good God, or in rare cases the priests of Juran the Just would be asked to bless a new Lord's reign, but a Death Priest was a rare and unsettling presence.

The dancers spun to a standstill and the whistles ceased. The chief priest advanced on soundless feet and mounted the dais. He removed a scarlet dagger from a pocket inside his cape and, with a high, keening yell, severed his left braid. This he hung upon the corresponding arm of the new Lord's throne. Then he touched his forehead to the chairback, and cut his right braid. The tiny skull at the end clicked ominously against agate carvings. When this talisman had been affixed to the right arm of the great chair, none present were left in doubt. The Red God's priests did not cut their hair except in expectation of great sacrifice to their divine master. Desio of the Minwanabi was pledging his house to violent undertakings.

Uneasy quiet reigned as Desio's honor guard made their entrance. The customary twelve warriors were led by Force Commander Irrilandi and First Adviser Incomo. Last came the new Lord, resplendent in a plumed overrobe of orange trimmed in black, his dark hair tied back.

Incomo reached the dais, turned, and sank to his knees at his master's right hand. He watched critically as his Lord completed the steps to his seat of power. Desio was holding up well, despite the heat and the unaccustomed weight of the armor beneath his finery. As a boy, Jingu's heir had lacked any skill at warcraft. His efforts in the practice yard had earned only silent scorn from his instructors. When old enough for active service, he had marched with a few patrols in safe areas, but when the officers in command had politely complained about his ineptness, the boy had gratefully become a permanent fixture in his father's court. Desio inherited the worst attributes of his sire and grandsire, Incomo judged. It would be a miracle for the Minwanabi to prosper under his rule, even should the Acoma pose no threat.

Studying the assembled crowd, Incomo's attention was caught by a striking figure in the first row of guests. Tasaio wore Minwanabi armor like a warrior born. He was perhaps the most able family member in three generations. Bored with the ceremony, Incomo considered what it would be like to serve under a clever-minded ruler such as Tasaio. Then the First Adviser banished such fanciful thoughts. In a moment he would swear to obey Desio in all things.

The new Lord managed to seat himself upon his great chair without mishap, for which Incomo was thankful. Clumsiness at this time would be inauspicious, an omen that the gods' disfavor had fallen upon the Minwanabi. Anxious sweat dampened the First Adviser's brow as he endured the time-honored formalities before Desio arose to speak. The young Lord of the Minwanabi began in a voice surprisingly strong in the silent hall.

"I welcome you," Desio intoned, "my family, my allies, and friends. Those who served my father are doubly welcome, for your loyalty to him in the past and to myself in the future."

Incomo drew a relieved breath, his immediate worries assuaged. His young charge went pompously on to thank the attending priests; then he waved his florid hands as his words became more passionate. Convinced of his own importance, Desio called attention to his more prominent guests. Incomo was trying to look attentive, but his mind became increasingly preoccupied: What move would the Lady of the Acoma make next?

How had a girl turned Jingu's plans for her murder to her own ends? As many times as Incomo reviewed the events of that cursed day, he could not determine what had reversed things to bring about such a tragic pass.

One thing he knew: the Minwanabi had relied too heavily upon a hired courtesan as agent. She had a reputation as thoroughly professional, yet at the last she had failed to carry out her duty. The result had cost the beautiful woman her life. Incomo vowed never again to depend upon one not sworn to Minwanabi service. And what of the part played by the Strike Leader Shimizu, one who was oath-bound to service? His assault upon Mara's bodyguard had gone as planned, but the following night a simple "accident" that should have ended the Acoma line turned into a debacle.

Desio announced another honored guest come to see him take his office. Incomo glanced in that Lord's direction, attempting not to look bored. His thoughts returned again to that terrible day.

Incomo repressed a shiver as he remembered the horror upon Lord Jingu's face as the Warlord's magician companion had employed magic to prove the misfortunate treachery of courtesan and Strike leader against Mara. Shamed before the eyes of guests, Jingu had been forced to make amends on behalf of his house in the only appropriate way. In all history no Minwanabi Lord had ever been required to preserve family honor by suicide. Incomo still awoke in a cold sweat each night as he dreamed of the moment Jingu had seized bravery and thrown himself upon his family sword.

Incomo remembered little after that; the march back to the estate house, his Lord upon the funeral bier, with his armor polished and shining, and his hands crossed upon his sword, were vague images. Instead the First Adviser was tormented by the moment of death: his Lord sprawled upon the ground, life's blood and entrails spilling out of his stomach, his vacant eyes filming over like those of a fish dying upon the docks. The priest of Turakamu had quickly bound Jingu's hands with the ritual red cord and hidden his face with a scarlet cloth. But the memory remained, indelibly. The reign of a great and powerful master had ended with terrifying swiftness.

A movement reawakened Incomo to the present. He nodded in greeting to another ruler come to pay homage to Desio. Then the Minwanabi First Adviser took a deep breath and collected himself. He had managed the household through Desio's days of dissipation with what seemed unassailable calm. But behind his emotionless, correct bearing, Incomo battled with terror. For the first time in a long life of playing the Game of the Council, he knew paralyzing fear of another ruler.

His only defense against this dread was an anger fueled by the image of Mara and her retinue crossing the lake. Dozens of other lords had departed with her, their colored craft flocked together like waterfowl in mating plumage. Among that flotilla had been the massive white-and-gold barge of the Warlord. Almecho had moved his celebration from Jingu's estate to the lands of the Acoma, as telling a sign of the Minwanabi fall from grace as any single thing could be.

That moment a shadow crossed Incomo's face, ending his interval of reflection. A lean, graceful warrior mounted the dais to kneel at the feet of the new Lord. Tasaio, son of Jingu's late brother, bowed low and presented himself to his rightful master. Tasaio's auburn hair was clipped short in a warrior's style. His profile was slightly aquiline, and his bearing was impeccably correct; hands, scarred lightly from past battles, possessed the beauty of strength honed to an edge of perfection. He was the image of a humble warrior, sworn to serve his master, but nothing could hide the burning intensity in his eyes. He smiled up at his cousin and gave his pledge. "My Lord, this I swear, upon the spirits of our common ancestors, even to the beginning of time, and upon the natami wherein resides the Minwanabi spirit: to you I pledge honor in all things. My life and my death are yours."

Desio brightened as the most able rival to his place as ruler bowed to tradition. Incomo put away his futile wish that the cousins' roles had been reversed; had it been Desio bending knee before Tasaio, then would the Acoma have trembled. Instead, irrevocably, the cleverer, stronger man bound his fate to the weaker. Incomo found his hands clenched to fists, his nails gouging into his palms.

Something still nagged at him from the night when Minwanabi fortunes had soured. As Tasaio arose and marched from the dais, the First Adviser considered a new thought. Mara had managed to discover the plot to end her life—but no, Incomo corrected himself, of course she expected the attack—yet somehow she had sensed the moment and the manner of the strike. Luck could not explain such fortune. Coincidence on that scale was unlikely to the point of impossibility. The Mad God of Chance would have had to have been whispering in the Lady's ear for her to have simply guessed what Jingu and his courtesan agent had planned.

The last Minwanabi allies were filing by, completing their assurances of friendship to Desio. The First Adviser regarded each expressionless face and concluded that their protestations were about as useful as weapons made from spun sugar. At the first sign the Minwanabi were vulnerable, each Lord here would be seeking new alliances. Even Bruli of the Kehotara had refused to renew the vow of complete vassalage his father had embraced with Jingu, leaving doubts as to his reliability. Desio had barely hidden his distaste as Bruli mouthed a promise of friendship, then departed.

Incomo smiled mechanically at each passing noble as he reviewed his own concerns. He replayed the events of the past again and again, until logic at the last yielded answer. His conclusion was shocking, unthinkable: the Acoma *must* have a spy within the Minwanabi household! Jingu's plot had been carefully laid, inescapable without privy information. Incomo found his pulse racing as he considered the ramifications.

The Game of the Council knew no respite. Always there were attempts to infiltrate the rival houses. Incomo himself had several well-placed agents and had personally thwarted attempts to penetrate the Minwanabi household. But somewhere, all too obviously, he had missed one. The Acoma spy might be a servant, a family factor, a warrior wearing an officer's plume, even a slave. Now enmeshed in thought to trace the culprit, Incomo viewed the ceremony with impatience. Protocol demanded he remain at his post until the formalities closed.

The last Lord made his appearance. Desio dragged through an interminable speech of thanks. Incomo almost fidgeted with restlessness. Then the priests of Turakamu resumed their cursed whistle blowing and another ritual dance. At last the recessional began, Desio's honor guard marching in measured steps out the portals from the great hall. Posted at Desio's shoulder, but a half pace behind, Incomo reviewed each senior member of the household.

His quick mind narrowed down the possibilities, eliminating blood relations and those in service since early childhood. But even after these were put aside, the possibilities for enemy agents were still vast. So many servants had been acquired over the last three years that Incomo faced a daunting search. To dismiss these new staff members in large numbers would be a clear admission of weakness. To use torture to discover which one might be the turncoat would only alert the spy. He, or she, might then slip between their fingers. No, far better to move with caution.

The procession continued through the tunneled hallway. Outside, the late afternoon sun dipped behind the trees. Long shadows fell over the column as honor guard and guests marched in measured step to the place appointed for the next part of the ceremony. Benches had been laid in a circle in a natural amphitheater formed by a fold in the hills. The guests found seats in silence, and looked down upon the expanse of cleared ground in the center. Four large holes had been dug there, a pair flanking the main road. A company of soldiers and workers awaited in neat array beside a huge, newly erected wooden frame bedecked with pulleys and ropes.

Incomo took his place on one of the central benches and strove to focus on the proceedings. Unlike Desio's assumption of office, this was no mere formality. To build a prayer gate was to invoke the presence of a god and beg favor; to erect a monument to Turakamu, the Red God, was to risk destruction should the act be looked upon with disfavor.

The priest of Turakamu and his acolytes began dancing around the four painted beams that awaited placement in the waiting holes. They spun with mad energy, accompanied by eerie yells and blasts on the sacred bone whistle. The head priest's naked flanks heaved with exertion, and sweat traced clean patches in his red and black ceremonial paint. The bouncing of his flaccid genitals amused Incomo. The First Adviser scolded himself for his impiety. Rather than laugh and earn the Red God's displeasure, he averted his eyes slightly, out of respect for the holy performance.

Two groups of workers waited nearby in silence. Among them, out of place and oddly ill at ease, stood servants and their families. A girl of about seven cried and clung to her mother's hand. Incomo wondered if the spectacle of the priest frightened her. The next moment, the head priest ended one of his spins in a motionless crouch before the little girl's father. The acolytes screeched in unison. They sprang forward, caught the man by the shoulders in a ritual grip, and led him to the nearest of the holes. The bone whistle shrilled in the afternoon heat. The chosen man closed his eyes and silently jumped down into the hole, which was deep, and wide.

Then the act was repeated with the other man, whose wife hid her face in a most unseemly way. When the second hole was occupied, the priest gave a tortured shriek. Then he intoned, "O Turakamu, who judge all men at the last, welcome to your service these two worthy spirits. They shall stand eternally vigilant over this, your monument. Look upon their families with charity, and when their children pass at length through your hall, judge them kindly and return them to life with your blessing."

Incomo heard the opening ritual with a rising unease. Human sacrifice was rare in the Empire, and while no longer common, it was still a practice in the Red God's temple. Obviously, these two workers had volunteered to become gate sacrifices, in exchange for the hope their children might return to their next life born to higher station: warriors, or perhaps even lords. Incomo considered that a thin bargain at best. If a man was pious enough, should the gods not grant him favor, as temple aphorism stated?

Yet only a fool would speak against an offering to the Red God. Incomo watched in stony stillness as the volunteers were tucked into their holes, knees under chin and hands crossed in semblance of eternal prayer. The priests screeched a paean to their divine master, then signaled work crews to hoist the massive timbers that would support the arch of the gate. Ropes creaked under the strain as the workers hoisted the first upright high; they chanted and swung the beam, and a scythe of shadow crossed the pit as the end was jockeyed into position. Now the crowd of Minwanabi supporters was frozen, awaiting the moment of sacrifice. A foreman with a squint judged the position correct; he signaled to the head priest, who touched his bone whistle to his lips and blasted the quavering note that would summon the god.

As the call faded, and a hush claimed the gathering, two lesser priests raised a sacred ax of shining obsidian and slashed the ropes. The carved pole released, thudded downward into the waiting hole, and crushed the first servant like a bug. A spatter of blood sprayed up from the earth, and the sobbing child tore from her mother's hold and threw herself against the post that had slain her father. "Bring him back! Bring him back!" she cried repeatedly as Minwanabi soldiers dragged her away.

Incomo knew the Red Priest counted this an inauspicious start. In an attempt to appease his god, the priest revised the ritual from first-level sacrifice to second. He clicked his bone rattle with his fingernails, and his acolytes donned ceremonial masks. The second victim was dragged from his hole, confusion plain in his eyes. He had expected his end to be the same as his predecessor's, but apparently this was not to be.

The first masked acolyte stepped forward with a bowl and obsidian knife. He said no word, but at a gesture from the head priest, the men gripped the farmer spread-eagled over the bowl. The acolyte raised his knife, chanting, and called for the god's favor. He laid the blade first on one side of the pinioned man's temple, and then the other, consecrating the sacrifice. The unfortunate farmer trembled under the touch of the stone knife; he flinched as its keen edge cut a symbol into his forehead, and strove to endure without outcry as a slash from the priest opened his right wrist.

Blood pattered into the dust like obscene rain. Acolytes became spattered as they rushed to catch the drops in the bowl; and like a litany of the damned, the whistle of the priest shrilled again. The second upright was hoisted. The obsidian knife darted again and drank from another vein. Now the farmer whimpered. He felt his life draining away, but the end could not come quickly enough to deaden his fear. He stumbled against the priests as they lifted him and lowered him head downward into the pit. The beam swung overhead. The whistle wailed, entreating the god to grant his favor. The head priest signaled, hastening the ceremony, since, for the gift to be acceptable, the waiting sacrifice must not lose consciousness and die before time. Yet haste canceled precision. As the ropes were slashed, one acolyte hesitated, and the massive timber turned slightly as it fell. Its bole crashed against one lip of the hole; dirt and rock cascaded downward, bringing an involuntary yelp of terror from the victim. Then the full weight of the trunk sheered down the sidewall. The timber crushed the legs and hips of the farmer but did not kill him outright. He screamed uncontrollably in pain, and the ceremony became shambles.

In vain Desio shouted for workers to right the tilted trunk. Pale in his rings and finery, he threw himself face down on the bloodied earth and begged the Red God's forbearance. The head priest advanced, his whistle silenced. Before all the waiting company, he rattled his beads and bones and solemnly announced his divine master's displeasure. Over the wail of the maimed sacrifice he demanded to hear what the Lord of the Minwanabi would pledge to regain the Red God's favor.

Behind the tableau of Lord and priest, slaves strained at ropes, and the gate timber was slowly dragged upright. The farmer's screams changed pitch but did not stop. Workers rushed forward with baskets of earth and upended them into the pit, and gradually the cries became muffled; no one dared end the farmer's agony. His life had been consecrated to the god, and to interfere would bring curse.

Sweating, his face smeared with dust and gore, Desio sat up. "All-powerful Turakamu," he intoned, "I pledge you the lives of my enemies, from the highest of noble blood to the life of the lowliest relations. This I promise if you will stay your wrath and allow Minwanabi victory!" To the priest he said, "If the all-powerful sees fit to grant my humble appeal, I promise a second grand prayer gate. Its posts shall be consecrated with the lives of the Acoma Lady and her firstborn son and heir. The path beneath shall be paved with the crushed stone of the Acoma natami, and polished by the feet of your devoted worshippers. This I will give to the glory of the Red God if mercy is shown for the transgressions that have happened this day."

Desio fell silent. The priest stood over him for a moment, unmoving. Then he assented with a sharp jerk of his head. "Swear your promise," he boomed out, and extended his bone whistle for Desio to seal his pledge to the god.

Desio reached out, convinced that once his hand clasped the bone, he was committed irrevocably. He hesitated, and a hiss from the priest warned he was close to bringing the Red God's wrath. Feverishly he grasped the relic. "I, Desio, Lord of the Minwanabi, swear."

"Upon the blood of your house!" commanded the priest. Onlookers could not help but gasp, for the priest made clear the Red God's price for failure. Desio embraced the same destruction for his entire house—from himself down to his most distant relative—the same ruin he promised the Acoma should he fail. Even should both sides come to desire truce in the future, no quarter was now possible. Within the near future one of two ancient and honorable houses would cease to exist.

"Turakamu hears your offering," the priest cried. As Desio released the relic, the priest spun and gestured to the incomplete gate, which arose like blackened pillars against the sky of sunset. "Let this gate stand incomplete, from this day forth. Its posts shall be carved into columns with the promise of the Minwanabi inscribed on each side. Neither shall this monument be changed or taken down until the Acoma are ashes pledged to the glory of Turakamu!" Then he looked at Desio. "Or the Minwanabi are dust!"

Desio dragged himself to his feet. He seemed shaken, overwhelmed by a poor beginning to the grandiose oath he had sworn. Incomo's lips thinned with anger. If there was an Acoma spy in the Minwanabi household, he had more to worry about than rumors as aftermath from this day's affairs. The First Adviser studied the expressions of the family members as they departed; most showed strain, a few looked frightened, and here and there a noble swaggered with his chin jutted aggressively. Many would seek to advance themselves in the family hierarchy if Desio proved a weak ruler, but no one seemed particularly satisfied by the terrible turn of the day's events. Abandoning the attempt to divine the spy by naked will, Incomo sought his master.

Tasaio stood at the side of his Lord, supporting Desio's elbow. Although the Lord was the one wearing armor, there was no mistaking which was the warrior. Tasaio's carriage held the unthinking and deadly grace of the sarcat. Incomo hurried closer. Words reached his ears, blown on the rising winds of an incoming storm.

"My Lord, you must not look back upon the mishaps of

today as ill-omened. You have sworn our family to a power-ful oath. Now let us see what we can do about fulfilling it."

"Yes," Desio agreed woodenly. "But where to begin? Mara has cho-ja warriors guarding her estate house; outright assault is folly without the Warlord's favor. Besides, even should we be victorious, we would be weakened, and a dozen other houses would rush to seek advantage over us."

"Ah, but, cousin, I have ideas." Tasaio sensed an approaching step, looked around, and identified Incomo. His quick, flashing smile seemed calculated to the First Adviser, despite its apparent spontaneity. "Honored First Adviser, I urge that we convene a meeting. If our Lord can fulfill his oath to the Red God, much glory may be gained for our house."

Incomo searched the words for irony—to fail a promise to the Death God would bring the Minwanabi to final ruin—and saw that Tasaio was sincere. Then he examined the usually stern face for any hint of deceit, but found none. "You have a plan?"

Tasaio's smile widened. "Many plans. But first I understand we have to flush out an Acoma spy."

While Desio's soiled face showed muddled astonishment, Incomo struggled to conceal suspicion. "How could you know about that, honored cousin?"

"But we have no Acoma spies in our midst!" Desio broke in, suddenly and righteously outraged.

Tasaio laid a calming hand on the young Lord's arm, his words directed mostly toward Incomo. "But we must. How else could that stripling bitch know our last Lord intended to kill her?"

Incomo inclined his head as if acknowledging a victory. That Tasaio had also surmised the cause of Mara's survival at the Warlord's celebration showed the depth of his thinking. "Honored cousin, for the good of us all, I think we should listen to your plans." With a withered scowl, he reached out and helped the tall warrior shepherd his Lord back to the shelter of the estate house.

Ancient parquet floors creaked as servants hustled about, adjusting screens and drapes against rising breezes from the south. An approaching storm scudded clouds over the lake's silvered face, offering early but unmistakable presage of the wet season. The smell of rain mingled with the indoor scents of furniture oils and dust that ingrained the small study, a private chamber used by Jingu and his predecessors to formulate their deepest plots. The painted window screens were small, to discourage observers from the outside, yet the air was never stifling.

Damp made Incomo's bones ache. Concealing an urge to frown, he folded himself neatly onto the cushions opposite the Lord's seat, an elaborate nest of pillows atop a two-inch-high dais. Some long-past Minwanabi ancestor had decided that a Lord should at all times be raised above his retainers, and most rooms in the older portions of the estate house bore the token of his belief.

Incomo had been reared to the inconvenience of multilevel floors and of flagstones on certain walkways that were a half-step higher than those adjacent; but a new servant was always conspicuous by the number of times that he tripped. Sourly, his thoughts preoccupied by spies, Incomo considered which factors and servants had been clumsiest while serving his late-departed Lord; none came immediately to mind, which added to the First Adviser's discomforts. In frustration, he awaited his master.

The servants had departed by the time Desio could be unlaced and divested of his ceremonial armor and be wrapped in an orange silk robe sewn with black symbols connoting prosperity. He did not dally longer with bathing, as his father had been wont to do; smelling faintly of nervous sweat, he entered with his cousin in attendance and levered his bulk onto the precious gilt-edged cushions that his predecessor had worn thin before him. Desio was agitated. Incomo decided he looked as if he was coming down with a cold, pale as reed paper about the face, except for his nose, which was pink. Beside him, his cousin looked tanned and lean and dangerous.

While Desio squirmed his way into a comfortable position, Tasaio settled and rested his elbows on his knees. Beside Desio's fidgeting, Tasaio owned the taut stillness of a predator while it tests the air.

Tasaio had lost nothing by serving in the barbarian wars for the past four years, Incomo concluded. Although the war had not advanced as well as the Warlord had promised, the time away from the Game of the Council had only sharpened the young man's wits. He had risen to the position of First Subcommander to the Warlord, Almecho, and had gained great advantages for the Minwanabi—until Jingu's death had humbled them.

"My esteemed cousin and my First Adviser," Desio opened, struggling to mask his inexperience and at least act the part of Ruling Lord, "we are gathered here to discuss the possibility of an Acoma spy in our midst."

"No possibility, but a certainty," Incomo snapped. What the household needed was action, swiftly and decisively carried out. "And we must not assume there is only one."

Desio opened his mouth in outrage, both against his First Adviser's impertinence and also to rebut the idea that the Acoma could have infiltrated Minwanabi ranks more than once.

Tasaio's lips tightened in barely withheld contempt; but no disparagement showed through his tone as he smoothly and gently interjected. "Your father was a great player of the game, Desio. If not through underhanded treachery, how else could a girl child have come to best him?"

"How could a girl child, as you call her, have managed to place such a masterful network of spies?" Desio spluttered. "Damn her to Turakamu's pleasures—and may he take her to his bed of pain for ten thousand years—she was in Lashima's convent until the day she came into her inheritance! And her father had no such penchant for implanting agents. He was too straightforward in his thinking to have much use for spies."

"Well then, cousin, those are things we must find out." Tasaio made a gesture, symbolic of the sword's thrust. "You speak as if the girl leads a charmed life. She does not. I arranged to have the outworld barbarians kill her father and brother on our behalf—rather neatly if I may say so. Sezu and Lanokota bled and died as other men do, clutching their opened guts and squirming in the mud." Passion lent fire to Tasaio's words. "If the Acoma claim the Mad God's luck, it certainly didn't serve Mara's father and brother very well!"

Desio almost smiled, before he recalled that his father had ended the same way, in agony on his own sword. Petulantly he poked at the pillows that crumpled under his weight. "If there are spies, then, how shall we flush them out?"

Incomo drew breath to answer, then deferred to a glance from Tasaio. "If my Lord permits, I would offer a suggestion."

Desio waved his assent. Interested enough to forget his various aches, Incomo leaned forward to hear the young warrior's advice.

Instinctively, Tasaio made use of the wind that rattled the screens. Timing the gusts to mask his voice against the chance he might be overheard, he said, "A spy is of little use if his information is not employed. So we turn that fact to our advantage.

"I recommend that you formulate some activities that would be detrimental to Acoma interests. Order your Force Commander to mount a raid against a caravan or outlying holding. Next day you let slip to your grain factor that you intend to undercut the Acoma thyza prices in the markets in the City of the Plains." Tasaio paused, lending the appearance that he sat at ease, sharing confidences. And yet Incomo noted with approval that he did not entirely relax; the glitter in his eyes betrayed that he watched, always, for trouble. "If Mara defends her caravans, we know we have a spy in the barracks. If she withholds her thyza crop from market, we establish that we have an Acoma disguised as a clerk. After that, it becomes a matter of digging out the informer."

"Very clever, Tasaio," Incomo said. "I had thought of a similar tactic, but there remains one telling flaw. We cannot afford to sell our thyza at a loss; and won't we reveal our machinations to the Acoma when no attack befalls the caravan?"

"We would if we failed to attack." Tasaio's eyelids hooded slightly. "But we will attack, and be defeated."

Angered, Desio punched his pillows. "Defeated? And lose more position in the council?"

Tasaio raised his hand, thumb and forefinger poised a scant inch apart. "Only a little defeat, cousin. Enough to provide proof that we are compromised. I have plans for that spy, when we find him . . . with your permission, of course, my Lord."

The moment was smoothly handled, Incomo observed with hidden admiration. Without coming to grips with Desio directly, Tasaio had let slip the assumption that the young

Lord would receive his due credit; the other side of the issue being that permission, of course, would be granted.

Desio swallowed the bait, but missed the larger implications. "When we catch this traitor, I will see him tortured in the name of the Red God until his flesh is twitching pulp!" His plump fist pummeled cushions for emphasis, and his nose deepened from pink to purple.

But as if he handled irate nobility on a daily basis, Tasaio showed no alarm. "That would be gratifying, cousin," he agreed. "Yet, to kill that spy, however horribly, would offer the Acoma a victory."

"What!" Desio stopped thumping and shot erect. "Cousin, you make my head ache. What could the Minwanabi gain but insult by keeping a miserable spy alive?"

Tasaio settled back on one elbow and casually plucked a fruit from a bowl on a side table. As though its ripe skin were flesh, he stroked his nail down the curve in what seemed almost a caress. "We need this spy's contacts, honored Lord. It serves our cause to ensure that our Acoma enemies learn only what we wish them to know." The warrior's hands gripped the fruit and gave a vicious twist. The jomach split in half, with barely a splash of red juice. "Let the spy set up our next trap."

Incomo considered, then smiled. Desio looked from his cousin to his First Adviser, and managed not to fumble the catch as his cousin tossed him one piece of the fruit. He bit into the morsel, and then began to laugh, for the first time restored to the arrogant certainty of his family's greatness. "Good," he said, chewing with relish. "I like your plan, cousin. We shall dispatch a company of men on some useless raid and let the Acoma bitch think she has routed us."

Tasaio tapped the remaining bit of fruit with his forefinger. "But where? Where shall we attack?"

Incomo pondered, then offered, "My Lord, I suggest that the raid should be close to her home."

"Why?" Desio wiped juice off his chin with his embroidered cuff. "She will be guarding her estate rigorously, as usual."

"Not the estate, itself, Lord, for the Lady needs no spy's report to maintain vigilance against attack from your army. But she will not expect a raid against a caravan bound for the river port at Sulan-Qu. If we attack between the Acoma lands and the city, and she is prepared for our raid, we can pinpoint the flow of information and find the agent among your household."

Tasaio inclined his head in an unconscious gesture of command. "First Adviser, your counsel is excellent. My Lord, if you will permit, I will oversee preparations for such a raid. A routine trade shipment would warrant little protection, unless the Acoma bitch knows she deals with blood enemies." He smiled, and white teeth gleamed against skin tanned dark on the Warlord's campaign. "We should know when such a caravan is due, simply by contacting shipping brokers in Sulan-Qu. A few discreet questions, and maybe a bribe or two to hide our inquiries, and we should know within the hour when Mara's next caravan is expected."

Desio met Tasaio's offer with a lordly air of industry. "Cousin, your advice is brilliant." He clapped his hands, bringing the errand runner in from his position outside the door. "Fetch my scribe," he commanded.

As the slave departed, Tasaio's composure became that of a man sorely tried. "Cousin," he assayed, "you must not write down the orders that we have discussed this hour!"

"Hah!" Desio released a second snicker, then a full-throated laugh. He leaned from his dais and fetched his cousin a resounding blow in the shoulder. "Hah!" he snorted again. "You must not mock my intelligence, Tasaio. Of course I know better than to include even servants and slaves in our plot! No, I simply thought to pen a notice to the Warlord, begging his forbearance for your absence from his campaign upon the barbarian world. He will acquiesce, as the Minwanabi are still his most valued ally. And, cousin, you have just shown me how much more you are needed here."

Incomo watched Tasaio's reaction to his Lord's praise. He had not missed the battle-trained reflex that had seen the friendly blow coming, nor had he failed to note the calculated and split-second decision that allowed the stroke to connect. Tasaio had grown skilled at politics as well as at killing.

With cold curiosity, the Minwanabi First Adviser wondered how long his master would be amenable to the counsel of one so obviously gifted with the qualities Desio lacked, but who could not be spared in restoring the Minwanabi to their

former greatness. Desio would know that his cousin's cleverness showed him up for a fool; eventually he would become
jealous, would wish more than the puppet title of Lord. Incomo noticed that his headache was back in force. He could
only hope that Desio would wait to turn upon his cousin
until after the Acoma bitch and her heir were pulp under the
post of the Red God's grand prayer gate. Best not to underestimate how long that feat might take. Such vanity on a lesser
scale had cost Jingu of the Minwanabi his life; and through
that misfortune, Mara had received enough recognition to
gain powerful allies.

Apparently Tasaio's mind turned to similar concerns, for
after the message to the Warlord was penned, and while
Desio occupied himself with ordering servants to bring him
refreshments, the warrior cousin turned to Incomo with a
seemingly casual question. "Does anyone know whether
Mara has had a chance to make overtures to the Xacatecas?
When I received my recall orders from the barbarian world,
a friend among his officers mentioned that their Lord considered approaching her."

Here Tasaio revealed his cunning. No friendship might
exist between officers who were enemies; by this, Incomo
understood that the information had been gained by intrigue.
With a grunt that passed for laughter, Incomo shared out his
own latest gleanings.

"The Lord of the Xacatecas is a man worthy of . . . if
not fear, then deep respect. His position in the High Council,
though, is not advantageous at the moment." With a flash of
perfect teeth, he added, "Our most noble Warlord was somewhat put out with the Xacatecas' reluctance to expand his
interests in the conquest of the barbarian world. Some political byplay resulted, and when the dust settled, Lord Xacatecas wound up with military responsibility for our tiny
province across the sea. Chipino of the Xacatecas languishes
in Dustari at the moment, commanding the garrison that
holds the only noteworthy pass through the mountains to
Tsubar. The desert raiders are active, at last report, so I
expect he has his hands full—let us hope too full to concern
himself with advances toward the Acoma."

Finished with his servants, and left with nothing to do but
anticipate his elaborate midafternoon feast, Desio picked up
on the conversation. He waved one pudgy hand to restore

proper attention to himself and said, "I advised my father on that plan, Tasaio."

The First Adviser refrained from pointing out that all Desio had done was sit in the room while Incomo and Jingu had discussed means to get Xacatecas occupied.

"Well then," said Tasaio, "if Xacatecas is busy guarding our frontiers across the sea, we can focus our attention upon Lady Mara."

Desio nodded and leaned back upon his imposing pile of cushions. With his eyes half-closed, and an obvious enjoyment of his newfound authority, he said, "I think your plan a wise one, cousin. See to it."

Tasaio bowed to his Lord as if his dismissal had not been that of a thankless underling; all pride and spare movement, he left the private study. Incomo buried his regret at the young warrior's departure. Resigned to the life the gods gave, he forced himself to attend the less glorious realities of Tsurani life; no matter what plots of blood and murder might drive the Game of the Council, other mundane matters remained to be considered. "My Lord, if you're agreeable, there are some grain transactions your hadonra needs to discuss with you."

More interested in thoughts of his lunch, Desio seemed less than anxious to deal with the prosaic side of family business. But as if his cousin's icy competence had awakened him to responsibility, he realized that he must. He nodded and waited without complaint as Incomo sent for Murgali, the hadonra.

5. ENTANGLEMENT

Breezes rustled the leaves.

The perfume of akasi flowers and trimmed greens filled Mara's personal quarters. Only one lamp was lit against the coming night, and that had but a small flame. The flicker painted a changing picture, as, each moment, details emerged from shadow: a gemstone's glint, highlights on polished jade fittings, fine embroidery or enamel work. Just as the eye beheld the splendid aspect, the gloom returned. Although surrounded by beauty, the Lady of the Acoma was oblivious to the richness of her furnishings; her mind was elsewhere.

Mara reclined amid a nest of cushions, while a maid worked out the tangles in her unbound hair with a scented shell comb. The Lady of the Acoma wore a green silk robe, shatra birds worked in wheat-colored thread around the collar and shoulders. The low lighting touched her olive skin to soft gold, an effect a more self-aware woman would have noticed. But Mara had finished her girlhood as a novice of Lashima, and as Ruling Lady she had no time for feminine vanity. Whatever beauty a man might find in gazing upon her was simply another weapon in her arsenal.

With a directness any Tsurani nobleman would have found disconcerting, she questioned the barbarian who sat before her on his homeworld's customs and cultures. Kevin seemed utterly unaffected by the lack of social protocol, plunging directly to the heart of matters. By this, Mara judged his people blunt to the point of rudeness. She watched as he struggled to describe concepts alien to her language;

haltingly groping to express himself, he spoke about his land and people. He was a quick study, and his vocabulary improved daily. Right now he attempted to amuse her by telling a joke that had been "making the rounds" in Zūn, whatever that meant.

Kevin wore no robe. The servants had tried in vain to outfit him, but nothing on hand had been large enough. In the end they had settled for a loincloth, and had substituted fineness for the garment's brevity. Kevin wore russet silk with midnight-blue borders, tied at the waist by a knotwork sash and obsidian beads. Mara failed to notice the effort. She had weighed Nacoya's advice the night before and realized something troubling: this slave in some way recalled her dead brother, Lanokota. Irritation at this discovery had given rise to resentment. While the slave's outrageous behavior had seemed amusing the day before, now she wanted only information.

Wearied after a day of meetings, Mara remained alert enough to measure the man she had ordered into her presence. Properly groomed, he looked much younger, perhaps only five years her senior. Yet where early struggles with great enemies had given her a serious manner, this barbarian had a brow unlined by responsibility. He was tightly wound but self-contained rather than overwrought. He laughed easily, with a sly sense of the ridiculous that alternately fascinated and annoyed Mara.

She kept the topics innocuous, a discourse upon festival traditions and music, jewelry making and cooking, then metalworking and curing furs, undertakings rare on Kelewan. More than once she felt the barbarian's eyes on her, when he thought she was not paying heed. He waited for her to reveal the purpose behind her interests; the fact he cared at all was curious. A slave could gain nothing by matching wits with an owner—no bargaining between the two stations was possible. Yet this barbarian was obviously trying to divine Mara's intent.

Mara reoriented her thinking: This outworld slave had repeatedly shown that his view of Tsurani institutions was alien to the point of incomprehensibility. Yet that very different perspective would allow her to see her own culture through new eyes—a valuable tool if she could but grasp how to use it.

She needed to assess this man—slave, she corrected herself—as if he were her most dangerous opponent in the Game of the Council. She was committed to these dialogues regarding his people so she might shift the chaff from the grain and discover useful intelligence. As it was, she hardly knew when Kevin was being truthful and when he was lying. For five minutes he had adamantly insisted that a dragon had once troubled his village, town, or whatever the place called Zūn might be. Exasperated, Mara had ceased to dispute him, though every child knew that dragons were mythical creatures, with no basis in reality.

Seeing him tire, she motioned for a fruit drink to be served, and he swallowed greedily. When he sighed, indicating his satisfaction, she changed the subject to board games and, against her usual wont, listened without making observations of her own.

"Have you ever seen a horse?" the slave asked unexpectedly in the pause as servants stepped in to brighten the lamps. "Of all things from home, horses are among those I miss most."

Beyond the screen, full darkness had fallen, and the copper-gold face of Kelewan's moon rose over the needra meadows. Kevin drew a deep breath. His fingers twisted in the cushion fringes, and a wistful gleam touched his eyes. "Ah, Lady, I had a mare that I raised from a filly. Her coat was the color of fire, and her mane as black as your own." Caught up in reminiscence, the barbarian sat forward. "She was fleet, both in the sprint and the long ride, fine-spirited, and a perfect witch on the field. She had a kick that could fell an armed warrior. She stopped swords at my back more times than a brother." He glanced up suddenly and ceased speaking.

Where before Mara had listened with relaxed interest, she now sat stiffly on her cushions. To Tsurani warriors, horses were not animals of admiration and beauty but creatures that inspired terror. Under the alien sun this slave knew as his own, Mara's father and brother had died, their life's blood soaked into foreign soil, trampled under horses ridden by Kevin's countrymen. Perhaps this same Kevin of Zūn had been the warrior who wielded the spear that struck her loved ones down. From some deep place, unguarded because of the day's fatigue, Mara felt a grief she hadn't experienced for years. And with that painful memory came old fears.

"You will speak no more of horses," she said in such a changed tone that the maid ceased her ministrations a moment, then cautiously resumed combing the long, lustrous hair.

Kevin stopped picking at the fringes, expecting to see some sign of distress, but the Lady showed no emotion. Her face remained blank in the lamplight, her eyes cold and dark.

He almost dismissed his impression as fancy. But an intuition prompted him to study her closely. With a look that was not the least mocking, he said, "Something I said frightened you."

Again Mara stiffened. Her eyes flashed. The Acoma fear nothing, she thought, and almost said so. Honor need not be defended before a slave! Shamed that she had nearly forgotten herself, she jerked her head in dismissal to the maid.

To Tsurani eyes, the gesture offered warning like a shout. The servant knelt and touched her face to the floor, then left the room with close to indecorous haste. The barbarian remained oblivious. He repeated his question, softly, as though she were a child who had not understood.

Alone in the lamplight, and arrogant in her annoyance, the Lady's dark eyes bored into Kevin with a fury that sought to sear him.

He misread her temper for contempt. His own raw-nerved anger kindled in response and he surged to his feet. "Lady, I have enjoyed our chat. It has allowed me to practice your language and spared me hard labor under a brutal sun. But from the moment I came into your presence yesterday, you seem to have forgotten that our two nations are at war. I might have been taken captive, but I am still your enemy. I will speak no more of my world, lest I unwittingly lend you advantage. May I have your permission to withdraw?"

Although the barbarian towered over her, Mara showed no change in composure. "You may *not* go." How dare he act as a guest and request his hostess's leave. Checking her anger, she spoke in measured tones. "You are not a 'captive.' You are my *property*."

Kevin studied Mara's face. "No." A grin lit his features, rendered wicked and humorless by the anger that lay behind. "Your captive. Nothing more. *Never* anything more."

"Sit down!" Mara commanded.

"What if I don't? What if I do this instead?" He moved with battle-honed speed. Mara saw him come at her like a blur in the lamplight. She might have shouted for warriors to defend her, but astonishment that a slave might raise his hand to her made her hesitate. The chance was lost. Hands hard with sword callus closed over her neck, crushing jade ornaments into delicate skin. Kevin's palms were broad, and icy cold with sweat. Too late Mara recognized that his banter had been a façade to cover desperation.

Mara gritted her teeth against pain, twisted, and tried for a kick at his groin. His eyes flashed. He shook her like a rag doll, and did the same again as her nails raked his wrist. The breath grated through the back of her throat. He held her just tightly enough to prevent outcry, but not quite cruelly enough to stop her breath. His eyes bent close to hers, blue and hard and glittering with malice.

"I see you are frightened at last," he observed. She could not speak, must be growing dizzy; her eyes were very wide and dark, and filling with tears from pain. And yet she did not tremble. Her hair hung warm over his hands, scented with spices; the breast that pressed his forearm through her silk robe made fury difficult to maintain. "You call me honorless slave, and barbarian," Kevin continued in a hoarse whisper. "And yet I am neither. If you were a man, you would now be dead, and I would die knowing I had removed a powerful Lord from my enemies' ranks. But where I come from, it is shameful for a man to harm a woman. So I will let you go. You can call your guards—maybe have me beaten or killed. But we have a saying in Zūn: 'You can kill me, but you can't eat me.' Remember this, when you watch me die as I hang from a tree. No matter what you do to my body, my soul and heart are free. Remember that I *allowed* you to kill me. I permitted you to live because *my* honor required it. From this moment forward, your every breath is a slave's gift." He gave her a last shake and released her. "My gift."

Humiliated to her very core that a slave should have dared lay hands on her and threaten her with the most shameful death, Mara drew breath to call her warriors. With a gesture, she could subject this redheaded barbarian to any of a dozen torments. He was a slave, he had no soul and no honor; and yet he slowly, and with dignity, sat back upon the floor before her cushions, his eyes mocking as he waited for her to name his fate. Revulsion not felt since she lay helpless beneath her brute of a husband made her shake. Every fiber of her being cried that this barbarian be made to suffer for the insult he had forced her to endure.

But what he had said gave her pause. His manner challenged her: call your guards, his tenseness seemed to say. Let them see the fingermarks on your flesh. Mara gritted her teeth against a shriek of pure rage. Her soldiers would *know* that this barbarian had held her at his mercy, and chose to let her go. Whether she ordered him scourged or executed, the victory would be his; he might have snapped her neck as easily as that of a snared songbird, and instead he had maintained honor as he understood it. And he would die with that honor intact, as if he had been killed in battle by an enemy's blade.

Mara grappled with a concept so alien it raised her skin to chill bumps. To vanquish this man through the use of superior rank would only diminish her, and to be shamed by a slave's action was unthinkable. She had trapped herself, and he knew it. His insolent posture as he sat waiting for her to act revealed that he had guessed to a fine point how her thinking would follow, and then staked his life on his hunch. That was admirable playing for a barbarian. Mara took stock of the result. Shaken again into chills, but Tsurani enough to hide them, she fought for composure. More hoarsely than she intended to sound, she said, "You have won this round, slave. By bargaining the only thing you have to risk, your own existence and whatever faint hope you have for elevation on the Wheel in the next life, you have put me in the position of either destroying you or enduring this shame." Her expression changed from barely controlled rage to calculation. "There is a lesson in this. I'll not forfeit such instruction for the pleasure in seeing your death—no matter how enjoyable that choice appears at the moment." She called a servant. "Return this slave to quarters. Instruct the guards that he is not to be allowed out with the workers." Looking at Kevin, she added, "Have him returned here after the evening meal tomorrow."

Kevin mocked her with a courtier's bow, not the obeisance due from a slave. His erect posture and confident stride as he moved down the hallway forced her to admire him. As the door to her study closed, Mara returned to her cushions, battling chaos within. Shaken by unexpected emotions, she willed her eyes closed and ordered herself to breathe deeply, inhaling through her nose and exhaling through her mouth. She called up an image of her personal contemplation circle, a ritual first practiced during her service at the temple. She focused on the mandala's design and banished all recollection of the powerful barbarian as he held her at his mercy. Fear and anger drained away, along with other strangely exciting feelings. When at last Mara felt her body relax, she opened her eyes once more.

Refreshed, as always from such exercise, she considered the evening's events. Something might be gained from this odd man when all had been assimilated. Then another angry flash visited her. Man! This slave! Again she employed the exercise to calm the mind, but a strange and unsettled feeling lingered in the pit of her stomach. Clearly the balance of the night would hold nothing akin to tranquillity. Why did she find it so difficult to find her inner peace? Except for damaged pride she was unharmed. Early in life she had discovered that pride was a means of trapping enemies. Perhaps, she considered, even I have pride I have not named.

Then, unexpectedly, she giggled. *You can kill me, but you can't eat me,* the barbarian had said. Such an odd expression, but one that revealed much. Caught by rising laughter, Mara thought, I'll eat you, Kevin of Zūn. I'll take your free soul and heart and tie them to me more than your body was ever bound. Then the laughter became a choked sob, and tears trailed down her cheeks. Outrage and humiliation overwhelmed her until she shook in spasms. With that pain came other emotions, equally disturbing, and Mara crossed her arms to hold herself tightly, as if she could force her body to stillness. Control returned with difficulty, as she employed her mental exercises yet again.

When at last she regained her composure, she let out a long breath. Never had she needed to employ that exercise three times. With a muttered "Damn that man!" she called servants to ready her bath. She rose, and added, "And damn his wrongheaded pride!" As she heard the bustle of servants racing to do her bidding, she amended her comment: "Damn all wrongheaded pride."

• • •

Mara studied the outworlder, again in the red light of sunset. Heat invaded her study, despite the open screens to the garden, admitting the faint evening breezes, yet Kevin was more relaxed than previously. His fingers still toyed with the fringes of the cushion, a habit no Tsurani would permit. Mara counted it an unconscious act, signifying nothing. Obviously the implications of being allowed to live had finally registered on the outworlder. He studied Mara as intently as she studied him.

This strange, handsome—in an alien way—slave had forced her to examine long-held beliefs and set certain "truths" aside. For the balance of the previous night and most of the day Mara had sorted out impressions, emotions, and thoughts. Twice she had been so irritated by this necessity she had been tempted to send soldiers to have the man beaten or even killed, but she recognized that the impulse stemmed from her personal frustration and resolved not to blame the messenger for the message. And the lesson was clear: things are not as they appear to be.

For some peculiar reason she wished to play this man in an intimate version of the Great Game. The challenge had been made the moment he had forced her to submit to his rules. Very well, she thought, as she regarded him, you have made the rules, but you will still lose. She didn't understand why it was important to vanquish this slave, but her intent to do so matched her desire to see the Minwanabi ground into the dust. Kevin must come to be her subject in every way, giving her the same unquestioning obedience as every other member of her household.

Kevin had been in her presence for nearly ten minutes, silently waiting as she finished reading reports. Reaching for her opening gambit, she said, "Would you care for something to drink? The interrogation may prove long." He weighed her words well enough to know she did not offer conciliation, then shook his head. After another silence, she asked, "On your world is it possible for a slave to go free?"

Kevin's mouth crooked in irony. His fingers flicked, and fringes scattered in a snap of pent-up frustration. "Not in the Kingdom, for only criminals with life punishment are sold as slaves. But in Kesh and Queg, a slave who pleases his master may earn freedom as a reward. Or he may escape and make his way across the borders. It happens."

Mara watched his hands. Flick, flick, one finger after another lashed the fringes; his emotions could be read like a scroll. Distracted by his openness, the Lady struggled to pursue her line of thought, to explore her improbable supposition one step further.

"And once across the borders, such a runaway might accumulate wealth and live in honor among other men?"

"Yes." Kevin thumped his palms on his knees and leaned back at his ease on one elbow, ready to add more, but Mara cut him off.

"Then you believe that if you were to find a way back across the rift to your own world, you would be able to regain your position, your honor, and your title?"

"Lady," said Kevin with a patronizing smile, "not only would I reclaim my former position, I would have won distinction, for contriving escape from my enemies, to once again take the field to oppose them, and to give hope to future captives that they might also find freedom. It is the duty of a captured . . . soldier to escape, in my nation."

Mara's brows rose. Again she was forced to reexamine her concepts of honor, loyalty, and where one's best interests lay. The barbarian's words made sense, in an oddly disquieting way. These people were not intractable, or stupid, but acting within a strange culture's tenets; she grappled with the concept stubbornly. If, within Kevin's society, his defiance was seen as heroic, his behavior made a perverted sort of sense. Leading by example was a familiar Tsurani ideal. But to endure humiliation . . . degradation . . . so that one could someday return and again contest with the enemy . . . Her head swam from ideas that, until now, she had held to be profoundly conflicting.

She took a moment to sip at cool fruit juices. Dangerously fascinated, like a child shown forbidden rites in a back temple chamber, Mara considered facts sharp-edged as swords: in Midkemia, honorable men did not harm women, and honor did not die with captivity. Slaves could become other than slaves. What, then, did the gods decree for men who lost their souls while still alive? What station could negate honor in a worse way than slavery? Within the framework of this man's culture, honor was gained by upholding their odd codes, and rank was seen as a situation rather than a life. Kevin behaved like a free man because he didn't think of himself as a slave but, rather, as a captive. Mara rearranged her robes, hiding the turmoil brought on by a "logic" that bordered heresy on Kelewan.

These barbarians were more dangerous than even Arakasi had imagined, for they assumed things as foregone conclusions that could turn Tsurani society on its head. Mara earnestly believed it would be safer for her people if she had her barbarians all executed. But sooner or later someone would exploit these perilous ideas, and it would be foolish to let the opportunity fall to an enemy. Mara tossed off her disquiet in a raw attempt at humor. "From what you have said about women being sacrosanct, then your Lords' wives must make the decisions. True?"

Kevin had followed her every move as she smoothed her silks. Drawn to the visible cleft between Mara's breasts, he tore his eyes away regretfully and laughed. "In part, they do, my Lady. But never openly, and not according to law. Most of their influence is practiced in the bedchamber." He sighed, as if remembering something dear to him, and his sight lingered over the exposed bosom above her robe and the long length of leg that extended below the hem.

Mara's eyebrows rose. Aware enough of nuance to blush, she reflexively drew her legs under her and closed the top of her scanty robe. For an awkward moment she found herself looking at anything else in the room but the nearly nude slave. Enough! she scolded herself. In a culture where nakedness was commonplace, why was she suddenly discomforted?

Irked at her mistake, she stared directly into Kevin's eyes. Whatever this man might think, he was still her property; she could order him to his death or her bed with equal disregard for consequences, for he was but a thing. Then she caught herself and questioned why her mind turned to the bedchamber. Struck by her unexpected angry reaction at such foolishness, she took a deep breath and turned the discussion away from things remotely personal. Soon she was lost in an indepth exploration of Lords and Ladies and their responsibilities in the lands beyond the rift. As on the night before, one subject led to another series of questions and answers, with Mara providing Kevin with the words he needed to flesh out his descriptions of his nation, the Kingdom of the Isles.

A quick man, he needed scant tutelage. Mara was impressed by his ability to discourse on many topics. The room dimmed as the lamp burned low; Mara was too distracted to call in a servant to trim the wick. The moon rose beyond the open screen, casting a copper-gold glow across the floor and throwing all else into shadow. The flame burned lower still. Mara lay back on her cushions, tense and not ready for sleep. Beneath her fascination with Kevin's world, anger still smoldered. The memory of his physical touch—the first man's upon her skin since her husband's death—occasionally threatened to disrupt her concentration. It took all her will at such instants to stay focused upon whatever topic the barbarian was addressing.

Kevin finished describing the powers of a noble called a baron, and paused to take a drink. Lamplight gleamed upon his skin. Above the rim of his cup his eyes followed her body's contours through the thin silk robe.

Unreasoning distaste stirred through Mara, and her cheeks flushed. Picking up her fan, she kept her face expressionless as she cooled herself. Bitterly she understood that new information could only temporarily divert her from her inner turmoil.

The intelligence brought in by Arakasi had unsettled rather than reassured, and the fact her enemies offered no immediate threat to counter left her uncertain which flank to guard. Her resources were thin, too few men guarding too broad a front, while she tried to arrive at a useful strategy. She found herself fretting endlessly over what she could most afford to lose, this warehouse or that remote farm. The daring victory she had won over Jingu had not blinded her to reality. The Acoma were still vulnerable. She might have gained prestige, but the number of soldiers in her garrisons had not changed. When enemies chose to move against her in force, a wrong guess would be dangerous, even fatal.

Kevin's culture offered strange concepts, like a salve against fear's constant ache. It occurred to Mara that she must keep the barbarian close at hand, both to dominate him and to pick at that confused treasure-house of ideas he carried with him.

Now better acquainted with the slaves' attitudes, she deemed it safest if their ringleader was kept away from them. Without Kevin, the slave master reported, the barbarians were less prone to grumbling and indolence. And if Kevin was at her side through most of her daily activities, his close-hand observation of high Tsurani culture might better enable him to apply his wits to her problems—a potentially priceless perspective. To that end, Mara decided she must allow him to know something of the stakes at risk. She must acquaint him with her enemy, and let him discover what he stood to lose if Desio of the Minwanabi should triumph over the Acoma.

The next time that Kevin interjected a personal question, Mara lowered her lashes to give the impression of a girl about to exchange a confidence. Then, hoping she acted rightly within the framework of his alien culture, she looked up brightly. "You shouldn't expect me to answer that."

Some of the vulnerability that leaked through was genuine, and the result struck Kevin like a blow. She was not remote, or icy, but a young woman who struggled to manage a sprawling financial empire and command of a thousand warriors. Mara responded to his bewildered silence with an air of mischievous deviltry. "You shall act as my body slave," she announced. "Then you must go everywhere that I do, and you might observe the answer to your question yourself."

Kevin stilled into watchfulness. He had caught the calculation behind her ruse, she saw, and was not amused by it. That he would be separated from his men bothered him, and also the fact that he could not read her motive. Absently his fingers worried at the fringes again. This time the strands parted to threads under his hands. Mara watched through lowered eyelids: he was growing rebellious again. Rather than risk having him move on her person a second time, she clapped for a manservant. The pattern she used also alerted the guards beyond her door, and they opened the screen, then faced into her chamber.

"Take the slave to quarters," she instructed her bowing servant. "In the morning I want him measured for house robes. After the fitting, he will be assigned duties as body servant."

Kevin bristled as the servant took his elbow. The guards' vigilance had not escaped him, and with a last, rancorous glance at Mara, he allowed himself to be led away. The servant was shorter than him by a head, and he, in pique, extended his stride until the little man had to stumble into a run to keep up.

In the doorway, Lujan shoved his helm back on his forehead. "Lady, is that wise? You can hardly keep that barbarian civilized without holding him with a leash. Whatever your ploy, even one so lacking in wit as myself can see that he's aware of your game."

Mara lifted her chin. "You too?" Amusement showed through her strained poise. "Nacoya already lectured me yesterday about learning evils from demons. Arakasi said the barbarians think as crooked as streams twisting through swamps, and Keyoke, who usually has sense, won't say anything, which means he disapproves."

"You left out Jican," Lujan said playfully.

Mara smiled and with the greatest of tact released a sigh. "The long-suffering Jican has stooped to bets with the kitchen staff that my pack of Midkemians will slaughter one another within the next season. Never mind that the trees for the needra fields won't get felled, and we'll be eating calves like jigabirds to keep down the cost of grain."

"Or we'll be beggared," Lujan added in tones an octave higher than usual, in a wicked imitation of the hadonra's fretful diffidence.

He was rewarded by a gasp of laughter from his mistress. "You are an evil man, Lujan. And if you weren't so adept at keeping me amused I'd have long ago packed you off to the swamps, to guard insect-infested hovels. Leave me, and rest well."

"Sleep, my Lady." Gently he slid the screen closed enough for privacy, but left enough of a gap that armed help could reach her on an instant's notice. Mara sighed as she saw that Lujan assumed the role of guard before her door, rather than retiring for the night. She wondered how long the Acoma could suffer an honorably plumed Strike Leader standing duty like a common warrior outside her chambers.

Desio, if he knew, would be gloating.

Ayaki grabbed a fistful of red hair. "Ow!" yelled Kevin in mock pain. He reached up to the boy who straddled his shoulders and tickled his silk-clad ribs. The young Acoma heir responded with an energetic howl of laughter that caused half the soldiers in Mara's escort to suppress a flinch.

The litter curtains whipped aside, and Mara called through the gap. "Will both of you children quiet down?"

Kevin grinned at her and gave Ayaki's toe one last tweak. The youngster screeched and burst into giggles. "We're having fun," the barbarian responded. "Just because Desio wants you dead is no reason to spoil a perfectly fine day."

Mara made an effort to lighten her frown. That both Ayaki and Kevin had made their first visit to the cho-ja hive with her retinue was reason enough for boisterous spirits. But what one was too young and the other too inexperienced to understand was that a messenger sent to recall her from the hive meant an event of unsettling importance. If the news had been good, inevitably it followed that it could have waited for her return to the estate house.

Mara sighed as she settled back against her cushions. Sunlight washed across her lap, and humid air made her sweat. It had rained during the night, for the wet season was beginning. The ground where her soldiers marched was thinly filmed with mud, and the shadier hollows in the road sparkled with puddles like jewels. The added moisture caused even the commonest weeds to flower, and the air was oppressive with perfumes. Mara felt a headache coming on. The past month had worn her nerves, as she waited for the Minwanabi under Desio to establish some predictable pattern. So far the only concrete thing Arakasi's spy network had turned up was that Desio had informed the Warlord that his cousin Tasaio was needed at home.

That by itself was ominous. Tasaio's cleverness had nearly brought the Acoma to ruin in the first place, and recovery was too recent to withstand another major setback.

As the litter rounded the last curve on the approach to the estate house, Mara felt apprehension that this summons from her Force Commander resulted from a move instigated by Tasaio. The man was too good, too subtle, and too ambitious to stay a minor player in her enemies' ranks. Had she been Desio, she would put the entire conflict with the Acoma into Tasaio's hands.

"What did you see that made you wonder?" Kevin inquired of Ayaki. The two of them had been instant friends since the morning the boy had tried to instruct the huge barbarian in the correct manner of lacing Tsurani sandals, even though he really didn't know himself. The barbarian's winning over the boy had given him some added protection against Mara's anger at his having put hands upon her. As she came to know Kevin, she found herself developing something resembling affection for him, despite his outrageous behavior and a total lack of civility.

"Funny smell!" shouted Ayaki, for whom enthusiasm was measured in decibels.

"You can't see a smell," Kevin protested. "Though I admit the cho-ja's hole reeked like a spice grinder's shed."

"Why?" Ayaki thumped his chubby fist on Kevin's crown for emphasis. "Why?"

Kevin caught the boy's ankles and flipped him off his shoulders in a somersault. "I suppose because they're insects —bugs."

Ayaki, upside down and turning red with pleasure, said, "Bugs don't talk. They bite. Nurse swats them." He paused, dangling his hands downward and rolling eyes. "She swats me, too."

"Because you talk too much," Kevin suggested. "And the cho-ja are intelligent and strong. If you tried to swat one, it would squish you."

Ayaki howled denial, claiming he'd swat any cho-ja before they could squish him, then howled again as the barbarian slave tossed him and restored him upright into the arms of his disapproving nurse. The retinue had reached the estate house. The bearers squatted to lower Mara's litter, and the soldiers who accompanied her on even the most innocuous errands stood smartly at attention. Lujan appeared on station to help the Lady to her feet, while Jican offered a deep bow by the doorway. "Arakasi awaits with Keyoke in your study, my Lady."

Mara nodded abstractedly, mostly because Ayaki's retreating noise still foiled conversation. She tipped her head at the bearer who carried new silk samples and said, "Follow." Then she paused, considering. After a moment she glanced to Kevin. "You too."

The barbarian bit back an impulse to ask what the topic of conversation would be. Since his assignment to the Lady's personal retinue, he had met most of Mara's advisers, but the Spy Master was an unknown. Always when he delivered his reports, Mara had sent her body servant off on some task that would occupy him elsewhere. Curious what could have made her change her mind, Kevin had acquired enough sense of Acoma politics to presume the reason would be significant, even threatening. The more he observed, the more he understood that behind the Lady's poised assurance lay fears that would have crumbled a lesser spirit. And despite his anger at being treated as little more than a talking pet, he had grudgingly come to admire her steely toughness. Regardless of age or sex, Mara was a remarkable woman, an opponent to be feared and a leader to be obeyed.

Kevin stepped into the dim hallway, following the Lady. Unobtrusively Lujan accompanied, a proper full step ahead of the slave. The Strike Leader would stand guard at the study door throughout the meeting, not only to protect his mistress, but to ascertain no servant lingered in the corridor to eavesdrop. Even though Arakasi had exhaustively scrutinized every domestic who worked in the estate house, he still urged Mara to take precautions. Seemingly loyal servants had been known to sink to dishonor and succumb to bribes, and a ruler who was slack in security habits invited betrayal. Warriors sworn to service and ranking advisers could be trusted, but those who picked fruit in the orchards and tended flowers in the garden could serve any master.

The screens were drawn in the study, making the air more damp and close. The Force Commander's plumed helm showed as a shadow in the dimness; Keyoke sat with the patience of a weathered carving on the cushions before the shut screen. His scabbarded weapon rested across his knees, sure sign that he had spent the interval while he waited for his mistress inspecting the blade for flaws that only his eyes could discern—if not cared for, Tsurani blades of cured hide could delaminate, leaving a warrior disarmed.

Mara nodded curt greeting, shed her outer robe, and loosened her sash. Kevin tried not to stare as she tugged the thin silk of her lounging robe from her sticky skin. Despite his care, his groin swelled in response to the sight of her bare breasts. In surreptitious embarrassment he hitched at the inadequate hem of his slave livery to hide the result. As often as he reminded himself that concepts of modesty differed here from those of his native Midkemia, he could not become accustomed to the casual near nudity adopted by the Kelewanese women as a consequence of the climate. So involved was he in trying to curb the involuntary response of his body that he barely noted Mara's words as she waved away her maidservant and sat.

"What do you have to report?"

Keyoke inclined his head. "There has been a raid, a very minor one, launched by the Minwanabi against a thyza caravan."

Mara pushed back a loosened strand of hair, quiet a moment before she said, "Then the attack came as Arakasi's agent predicted?"

Again Keyoke inclined his head. "Even the numbers of the soldiers were accurate. Mistress, I don't like the smell of the event. It appears to have no strategic relevance at all."

"And how you hate loose ends," Mara concluded for him. "I presume the Minwanabi soldiers were routed?"

"Killed, to a man," Keyoke amended. His dry tone reflected little satisfaction at the victory. "One company less to harry our borders, if Desio chooses war. But it's the ineptness of the attack that troubles me. The warriors died like men sworn to honorable suicide, not those bent on taking an objective."

Mara bit her lip, her expression darkening. "What do you think?" she said into the shadows.

Something moved there in response, and Kevin started slightly. He looked more closely and made out the slender form seated motionless, with folded hands. The fellow's uncanny stillness had caused Kevin to overlook him until now. His voice was dry as a whisper, yet somehow conveyed the emphasis of a loud expostulation. "Lady, I can offer you little insight. As yet I have no agent who is privy to Desio's private councils. He discusses his intentions only with his First Adviser, Incomo, and his cousin Tasaio. The First Adviser is, of course, not given to gossip or drink, and Tasaio confides in no one, even the warrior who was his childhood mentor. Given the circumstances, we do well to know that the agents we have are reporting accurately."

"Then what is your surmise?"

Silent a long moment, Arakasi replied, "Tasaio is in command, I would wager. He has a mind as devious and keen as any I've encountered. He served Lord Jingu well in the obliteration of the Tuscai." All, save Kevin, knew the fallen house was the one Arakasi served before coming to Mara's service. "Tasaio is a very sharp sword in his master's hands. But working under his own direction . . . it is hard to judge what he would do. I think Tasaio probes. His warriors could have been ordered to die so that he might test something about House Acoma. I judge it a gambit."

"For what?"

"If we knew, mistress, we would be planning countermeasures, instead of pondering possibilities."

Mara paused through a tense moment. "Arakasi, is it possible we have a spy in our own ranks?"

Kevin watched in curiosity as the Acoma Spy Master subsided once more into stillness. Close scrutiny revealed that the man had a knack for arranging himself in a fashion that caused him to blend with his surroundings. "Lady, since the day I swore oath on your natami, I have instigated diligent checks. I know of no traitor in our midst."

The Lady made a frustrated gesture. "But why attack a thyza caravan between the estate and Sulan-Qu, unless somebody guesses what plans we have afoot? Arakasi, our next grain shipment is to conceal our new silk samples. If that was information the Minwanabi sought to discover, our troubles might be grave indeed. Our cho-ja silk *must* take the merchants at the auctions by surprise. Revenue and standing will be lost if our secret is discovered beforehand."

Arakasi inclined his head, conveying both agreement and assurance. "The raid by Desio's soldiers might have been coincidence, but I concur with you. We dare not presume so. Most likely he probes to discover why we arm our caravans so heavily."

"Why not give them a red herring?" offered Kevin.

"Herring?" snapped Keyoke with impatience. By this time, Mara's Force Commander had grown resigned to the barbarian's out-of-turn remarks; he could not be made to think like a slave, and the Lady at some point, and for reasons of her own, had decided not to enforce protocol. But Arakasi and the Midkemian had never encountered each other previously, and the impertinence came as a surprise.

The Spy Master's eyes glinted in the shadows as he looked at the tall man who stood behind Mara's shoulder. Never one to entangle his intellect with preconceptions, he discarded both the man's rank and his insolence as irrelevant, and fastened what proved to be an almost frighteningly intense interest upon the concept behind Kevin's suggestion. "You use a word for a species of fish, but imply something very different."

"A ruse of sorts." Kevin accompanied his explanation with his usual expansive gestures. "If something is to be hidden in a thyza shipment, confuse the enemy by burying wrapped and sealed packages in every wagon that carries goods. Then the enemy must either spread his resources thin and intercept all outgoing caravans, and thereby make plain his intentions, or else abandon the attempt."

Arakasi blinked very fast, like a hawk. His thoughts moved faster still. "And the silk samples would be in none of these shipments," he concluded, "but concealed somewhere else, perhaps even in plain sight, where silks might ordinarily be in evidence."

Kevin's eyes lit up. "Precisely. Perhaps you could sew them as the lining of robes, or maybe even as a separate shipment of scarves."

"The concept is sound," Mara said, and Arakasi nodded tacit agreement. "We could even have servants wear underrobes of the fine silk beneath their usual traveling robes."

That moment, someone outside knocked insistently at the screen. Arakasi faded into his corner as if by reflex, and Mara called an inquiry.

The screen whipped back to admit the disheveled Acoma First Adviser in a red-faced state of agitation. Keyoke settled back on his cushions and loosened his tense hand from his sword hilt as Nacoya descended upon her mistress, scolding even as she made her obligatory bow.

"My Lady, just look at your clothes!" The former nurse turned her eyes heavenward in despair.

Surprised, Mara glanced at her lounging robe, draped open in the heat, and showing dust about the collar from her earlier visit to the cho-ja hive.

"And your hair!" Nacoya ranted on, now shaking a wizened finger in reproach. "A mess! All tangles, when it should be shiny-clean and scented. We're going to need a dozen maids, at least." Then, as if noticing Keyoke's and Arakasi's presence at the same time, she clucked in renewed affront. "Out!" she cried. "Your mistress must be made presentable very quickly."

"Nacoya!" Mara snapped. "What gives you cause to descend upon my private council and order my officers about like house staff? And why is the matter of my personal appearance suddenly so urgent?"

Nacoya stiffened like a stung jigabird. "By Lashima most holy, Lady, how could you forget? How could you?"

"Forget?" Mara shoved back a fallen strand of hair in honest confusion. "Forget what?"

Nacoya huffed, speechless at last. Arakasi intervened very gently and answered for her. "The little grandmother most likely refers to Hokanu of the Shinzawai, whose retinue I passed on the road from Sulan-Qu."

The Acoma First Adviser now recovered poise with acerbity. "That young gentleman's letter of inquiry has sat on your desk for a week, my Lady. You answered him with an acceptance, and now you offer him insult by not being ready to greet him upon his arrival."

Mara used a word not at all in keeping with her station. This brought another squawk from Nacoya and an outright grin from Kevin, whose command of Tsurani obscenities had been learned from a particularly colorful slave driver and remained his most comprehensive vocabulary.

Nacoya vented her frustration by clapping sharply for Mara's bath attendants. Through the resulting pandemonium as slave girls descended with basins and towels, and armloads of fine jeweled clothing, Mara dismissed her Force Commander. While three sets of hands removed her clothing, she fought one wrist free and gestured at the bundled silk samples brought from the cho-ja hive. "Arakasi, decide what to do with these. Jican will tell you when they're due to arrive at Jamar. Contrive some subterfuge to get them there unnoticed."

The Spy Master returned an unobtrusive bow and departed with the bundle. Kevin remained. Forgotten in his place behind his mistress's cushions, he spent the next minute being tantalized by the sight of Mara standing in her tub while her servants poured hot water over her lithe body. Then she sat slowly, gracefully. While she rested in the tub, her woman servants soaping her down and washing her hair, Kevin repeatedly caught glimpses of nude flesh. Motionless in the corner, he inwardly cursed the inadequate coverage of his brief Tsurani garment, as the sight of his pretty young mistress caused his manhood to rise up again in appreciation. Like an embarrassed kitchen boy, he stood with both hands folded before his groin and tried to focus on unpleasant thoughts to bring his unruly body back under control.

When the Lady of the Acoma emerged at speed from the attentions of her maids and bath servants, Kevin followed in his accustomed place, mostly because no one in authority had bothered to tell him otherwise. Jeweled, primped, and clad in a fine overrobe sewn with seed pearls and emeralds, Mara was far too agitated to note the barbarian slave who had been a part of her retinue for almost a month now. She swept through the hallways with a frown pinching the skin between her eyebrows. Kevin, grown familiar enough to guess at her moods, determined that this Hokanu of the Shinzawai came for something outside the usual social visit. In many ways, Mara preferred involved financial discussions with her hadonra to meeting the social obligations that fell to her as ruler of a time-honored Tsurani house.

At Nacoya's furiously whispered reminder, Mara slowed her step before the entry to the enclosed courtyard, which at this hour was the coolest place in which to make a guest comfortable. The First Adviser patted her charge's wrist and delivered last-minute instructions. "Be charming with this man, daughter of my heart, but do not underestimate his perception. He is no importunate boy like poor Bruli, to be swayed by the follies of romance, and you have certainly offended him by keeping him waiting."

Mara nodded distractedly and shed the protective Nacoya. With Kevin still on her heels, she stepped out into the dappled shade of the courtyard.

Cushions had been laid by the fountain, and a tray with refreshments close by. Both appeared untouched. At Mara's entrance, a slim, well-muscled man paused between steps in what must by now have been the last of a dozen restless tours along the garden pathways. He wore blue silk sewn with topaz and rubies, robes obviously tailored for the son of a powerful family. Now more practiced at reading Tsurani inscrutability, Kevin did not look at the handsome but expressionless face for enlightenment; instead he checked the hands, which were well formed and strongly sword-calloused. He noted the slight spring in the stride as the young man turned to greet the Lady, and also noted the tenseness in carriage that conclusively betrayed annoyance.

Still, the voice emerged pleasantly tempered. "Lady Mara, I am pleased. Are you well?"

Mara swept him a bow, her jewels flashing in stray flecks of sunlight through the leaves. "Hokanu of the Shinzawai, I am well enough to know better. You are irked at my tardiness, and for that I plead no excuses." She stood upright, the top of her forehead barely level with his chin. To meet his dark eyes, she had to tilt her head up in a manner that, entirely without artifice, made her stunning. "What can the Acoma do but ask your forgiveness?" Mara paused with a disarmingly sheepish smile. "Quite simply, I forgot what time it was."

For a second, Hokanu looked outraged. Then, obviously at a loss before the Lady's appeal, and taken by the fact she had not lied to him, his teeth flashed in a burst of honest laughter. "Mara, you confound me! Were you a warrior, I should be trading sword blows with you. As it is, I can only note that you owe me a debt. I'll claim your company as my compensation."

Mara stepped forward and allowed him a briefly formal embrace. "Maybe I should have met you at the door in the crumpled robe I wore to council," she suggested wickedly.

Hokanu continued to grip her hand in a manner Kevin interpreted as possessive. The young man's ability to conceal his eagerness behind a façade of astonishing grace annoyed the Midkemian slave, although he could not have said why. When the nobleman responded to the Lady's quip with another laugh, saying, "Do that next time," Kevin found himself scowling.

Normally Mara was quick-witted and assertive when dealing with her male staff and those few state visitors Kevin had observed during his tenure as her body servant. With Hokanu, her wit became less acerbic, and the spirit he had grudgingly come to admire became obscured by inexplicable diffidence. Mara seemed guarded against showing pleasure as she allowed the young warrior to settle her down on the cushions; plainly she found the young man's company enjoyable. With submissive courtesy she called Kevin to serve food and drink. Hokanu accepted a dish of spirit-soaked fruits and a goblet of sā wine. His dark eyes flicked with interest over the Midkemian. Kevin momentarily felt inspected inside and out, like merchandise; then the nobleman turned teasingly to Mara.

"I see that you have tamed this sarcat of a barbarian most admirably. He appears to have learned his place somewhat better than others of his kind."

Mara hid amusement behind the rim of her chocha cup as she took a small swallow. "So it might seem," she said quietly. "Did you find the slaves your father required in the ngaggi swamps?"

Hokanu's eyes flickered as he inclined his head. "The matter has been resolved satisfactorily." Then, as though aware that Mara had been as reticent with him as he with her concerning their mutual but unspoken interest in Midkemians, he returned the subject to Kevin's physical attributes, as though the redheaded Midkemian were not present and listening.

"He looks as strong as a needra bull and should do very well at clearing the land for your pastures."

Ill accustomed to being discussed like an animal, Kevin opened his mouth and observed that he would rather take wagers over arm wrestling. Before he could be so bold as to challenge the elegant Shinzawai warrior to a match, Mara's face paled. With dramatically fast timing, she forestalled his next line. "Slave! You are no longer needed here. Send Misa to attend us. Then go to the front courtyard and help Jican see to the needs of Hokanu's caravan."

Kevin's lip curled daringly into a half-smile as he made his slave's bow, still slightly less than custom dictated, to Mara's everlasting irritation. Then, with a glance at Hokanu that came just shy of spiteful, he spun on his heel and departed. The only flaw in his performance was the fact that the short Tsurani robe looked ridiculous on him, a detail Hokanu did not overlook.

The comment half-heard as Kevin stepped through the screen into the corridor was close to indecent, considering the presence of the Lady. With a vicious twist of anger, Kevin wished he could pick a fight, then, with equally surprising candor, he realized he felt jealous. "Damn him, and damn her, too," he muttered to himself. To even think of an infatuation with Mara was sure invitation to get himself strung by the neck from the nearest ulo tree, probably head down over a slow fire. If he was to gain anything from this woman, it would not be through dalliance. Somehow, against all expectations and traditions, he would contrive a way to be free again.

The outer courtyard was dusty, as if last night's rains had been a dream dispelled by sunlight. Needra and wagons jammed the latticed enclosure; drovers' shouts and the snorts of gelded bulls overlaid the confusion as slaves ran to and fro with fodder, thyza bowls, and water basins. Kevin strode into the midst of the bustle still preoccupied with his pique, and almost stepped on Jican.

The little hadonra yelped in affront and leaped back to avoid being knocked down. He peered upward, took in the muscled expanse of Kevin's chest that the scant robe failed to cover, and frowned with a fierceness that his mistress had never seen. "What are you doing idle?" he snapped.

Kevin disarmingly raised his eyebrows. "I was taking a walk."

Jican's expression turned thunderous. "Not anymore. Fetch a basin and bring water to the slaves in the caravan. Move smartly, and don't offend any of the Shinzawai retinue, or by the gods, I'll see you strung up and kicking."

Kevin regarded the diminutive hadonra, who always in his Lady's presence seemed shy as a mouse. Although shorter by more than a head, Jican held his ground. He snatched a basin from a passing slave and jabbed the rim into Kevin's middle. "Get to work."

The larger man grunted an expelled breath of air, then leaped back as a flood of cold water drenched his groin. "Damn," he muttered as he caught the wooden implement before it fell and insulted his manhood more permanently. When he straightened, Jican had moved on. Having lost his chance to slip through the press unobserved, Kevin located the water boy and obediently filled his basin. He carried its slopping contents across the dusty pandemonium and offered drink to two rangy, sunburned slaves who perched at their ease on the tailboard of a goods wagon.

"Hey, you're Kingdom," said the taller, who was blond and bore two peeling scabs on his face. "Who are you? When were you captured?"

The three slaves exchanged names as Kevin offered his

basin to the slighter, dark-haired one whose right hand was bound in a bandage, and whose expression was strangely cold about the eyes. This man proved to be a squire from Crydee and was not known to him, but the other, who called himself Laurie, seemed familiar.

"Could we have met before?" Kevin asked as he took back the basin from Squire Pug. The blond man shrugged with an instinctively theatrical friendliness. "Who knows? I roamed the Kingdom as a minstrel and sang in the court at Zūn more than once." Laurie's eyes narrowed. "Say, you're Baron—"

"Quiet," cautioned Kevin. He glanced quickly to either side, ensuring no soldiers could hear. "One word of my rank and I'm a corpse. They kill officers, remember?"

Conscious of how thin and weatherbeaten his fellow countrymen looked, Kevin asked after their lot following capture.

The dark, enigmatic man, named Pug, gave him a hard look. "You're a quick enough study. I'm a squire, and if they had figured out that meant minor nobility, I'd have been killed the first day. As it is, they've forgotten my rank. I told them I was a servant to the Duke, and they took that to mean a menial." He glanced around at the hurrying Acoma slaves, who moved with single-minded purpose to do the hadonra's bidding. "You're new to this slave business, Kevin. You would do well to remember these Tsurani can kill you with no pangs of conscience, for here they hold the belief that a slave possesses no honor. Kevin of Zūn, tread most carefully, for your lot could be changed on a whim."

"Damn," said Kevin softly. "Then they don't give you concubines for good conduct?"

Laurie's eyes widened a moment, then his broad laugh attracted the attention of one of the Shinzawai warriors. His plumed head turned in their direction, and instantly the expressions of the two Midkemians on the wagon went blank. When the soldier turned away, Laurie let out a quiet sigh. "They've not spoiled your sense of humor, it seems."

Kevin said, "If you can't laugh, you're as good as dead."

Laurie wiped his face with a rag dipped in the basin Kevin held and said, "As I tell my short friend here, many times over."

Pug regarded Laurie with a mixture of affection and aggravation. "This from a fool who almost got himself killed saving my life." He sighed. "If that young Shinzawai noble hadn't been in the swamps . . ." He left the thought unfinished. Then his tone turned somber. "All the men captured with me in the first year of the war are dead, Kevin. Learn to adapt. These Tsurani have this concept of wal, this perfect place inside where no one can touch you." He put his finger on Kevin's chest. "In there. Learn to live in there, and you'll learn to live out here."

The redhead nodded, then, aware that Jican watched his back, took his basin back for a refill. With a regretful nod to Laurie and Pug, he proceeded to the next wagon in line. If he could, he'd slip out of the slave quarters in the evening and spend some time with these two. Trading some information might not prove useful, but it might ease the pain of homesickness a bit.

But as the evening wore on, he was given more work, until, exhausted, he was led back into the great house and commanded to sleep in the room set aside for him. A guard outside his door made any attempt to visit his former countrymen useless. But in the night he could hear faint voices, speaking words barely understood, yet familiar with accents well known.

Sighing in frustration, he knew his own companions were visiting with the two Islemen from the Shinzawai caravan. He would get his gossip secondhand when he next had a chance to speak with Patrick or one of the other men. Yet the lack of firsthand contact caused the most bitter pangs of homesickness he had felt since capture. "Damn that bitch," he whispered into his hard pillow. "Damn her."

6. *DIVERSIONS*

The wet season ended.

Lengthening days brought back the dry dust, and strong sunlight faded the plains grass surrounding the Minwanabi estate house; within weeks the hills would begin to lose their lushness, until by midsummer all would be golden and brown. During the hotter weather, Lord Desio preferred to remain within the shaded comfort of his estate house, but admiration for his cousin often lured him outdoors.

Tasaio might be serving his family as a senior adviser, but the day never dawned that he failed to maintain his battle skills. Today, while the morning mists burned off the lake, he stationed himself on a hillside with his bow and sheaves of arrows, and straw figures set at varying distances for targets. Within a half hour they bristled with shafts fletched in Tasaio's personal tricolors: Minwanabi black and orange, cut with a band of red for Turakamu.

Desio joined him as his battle servant retrieved arrows between rounds. Aware of the young Lord's approach for some time, Tasaio turned at precisely the correct moment and bowed. "Good morning, my Lord cousin."

Desio halted, panting from his climb up the hill. He inclined his head, wiped sweat from his pink brow, and regarded his taller cousin, who wore light hide armor studded with precious iron garnered as a war prize from the barbarian world. Tasaio wore no helm, and the breeze stirred his short auburn hair. The bow in his hand was a recurve, lacquered shiny black and tasseled at each horn with orange silk. Politely Tasaio offered the weapon. "Would you care to try a round?"

As yet too breathless for speech, Desio waved to decline. Tasaio nodded and turned as the servant approached, a bin of recovered arrows in each hand. He bowed before his master. While he remained on his knees, Tasaio removed the shafts by their nocks and pressed them one by one, point first, into the sandy soil. "What brings you out this fine morning, cousin?"

Desio watched the arrows pierce the earth, in perfect lines like warriors arrayed for a charge. "I could not sleep."

"No?" Tasaio emptied the first bin and started on the second. A jade-fly landed on the battle servant's nose. He twitched no muscle and did not blink as the insect crawled across his cheek and began to suck at the fluids of his eye. To reward his perfect composure, Tasaio at length gave the man leave to brush the insect away. The man gratefully did so, having learned under the lash to ease himself only when given permission.

Tasaio smoothed a parted cock feather and waited for his cousin to continue.

"I could not sleep because months have passed, and still we have not uncovered the Acoma spies."

Tasaio set arrow to bowstring and released in one fluid motion. The shaft arced out through the bright morning and thumped into the painted heart of a distant straw figure. "We know there are three of them," the warrior said evenly. "And the field has narrowed. We have disclosed information leaks from our barracks, from our grain factor, and also from someone who has duties in the kitchens or among the house staff."

"When will we know the names of these traitors?"

Drawing his bow, Tasaio seemed totally focused, but an instant after the arrow left his string he said, "We shall learn more this morning, when we hear the fate of our raiding party. The survivors should have returned by now." Nocking another arrow to his bow, he continued, "Besides, discovering the spy is but the first step in preparation for our much larger plan."

"So when does your grand campaign take effect?" Desio burst out in frustration. "I want the Acoma ruined!"

Two more arrows flew and sliced into targets. "Patience,

cousin." Tasaio notched a third shaft and sent it through the neck of the straw figure farthest from his position. "You wish the Acoma ruined beyond recovery, and the wise man plans carefully. The best traps are subtly woven, and unsuspected until they close."

Desio sighed heavily. His body servant rushed to set a cushion under him as he settled his bulk upon the grass. "I wish I had your patience, Tasaio." Envy showed through his petulance.

"But I am not a patient man, cousin." The arrows flew at regular intervals, and a straw figure toppled, riddled like a seamstress's pincushion with feathered shafts. "I chafe at delay as much as, perhaps more than, you, my Lord—I hate waiting." He studied his distant targets as if evaluating his performance. "But I hate the flaw of impatience within myself even more. A warrior must strive toward perfection, knowing full well that it will forever be unobtainable."

Desio pulled his robe away from sticky flesh and fanned himself. "I have no patience, I admit, and I was not gifted with coordination enough for the field, as you were."

Tasaio waved his servant off to fetch arrows, though the line by his feet was not depleted. Then he set his bow across his shoulder and looked at his more corpulent cousin. "You could learn to be, Desio." There was no mockery in his tone.

The Lord of the Minwanabi smiled back. "You have finalized your plan to destroy Mara."

Tasaio remained still a moment. Then he threw back his head and sounded a Minwanabi battle cry. When he finished his ululation, he looked back to his cousin, a sparkle of excitement in his eyes. "Yes, Lord, I have a plan. But first we must speak with Incomo and discover if the runners he dispatched have returned with word of the ambush."

"I will go back and call him," Desio grunted as he pushed to his feet. "Join us in my chambers in an hour's time."

Tasaio acknowledged that his Lord paid him deference by complying with his request for a meeting. Then his eyes narrowed. He spun, slipped his bow, and set another war arrow to his string.

The servant on the field retrieving arrows saw the move and dropped to earth just a heartbeat before the shot hissed past the place his body had just vacated. He remained prone as more shafts whined by, peppering the dummy by his elbow. Wisps of straw drifted down and made his face itch, yet he did not move to brush them away until he saw that his master had depleted his arrows.

"You play with your men as a sarcat plays with his prey before the kill," Desio observed, having lingered to watch the display.

Tasaio raised one cool eyebrow. "I train them to treasure their lives," he amended. "On the battlefield, they must fend for themselves against our enemies. If a servant cannot keep himself alive, and be where I need him, he is of no use, yes?"

Desio conceded the point with an admiring chuckle.

Tasaio said, "I am done, I think. No need to wait an hour, my Lord. I will accompany you back now." Desio clapped his cousin on the shoulder, and together they started down the hill.

The Minwanabi First Adviser met them in the private study, his grey hair damp from his bath, and his back erect as a sword blade. He was an early riser, inspecting the estates with the hadonra in the morning hours. Afternoons he spent over paper work, but years of watching sunrises had given him the weatherbeaten appearance of an old field general. He watched with a commander's perception as he made his bow before the cousins.

Lord Desio was sweating, though he had already consumed three mugs of rare, iced drinks. Runners continually drove themselves to exhaustion to provide him with the luxury; as the summer progressed, and the snowline receded up the northern peaks, the young Lord's craving for cold dishes could no longer be satisfied. Then he would turn to drink to dull the heat, but unlike his father Jingu, he did not slacken his intake after sundown. With an inward frustrated sigh, Incomo regarded Tasaio, who still wore his armor and archer's glove, but who showed no fatigue from his hours of practice in the hills. His only concession to comfort was the slightly loosened lacing at his throat; at all times, even just after rising, Tasaio seemed but a half second away from being ready to answer the call of battle.

"Tasaio has finally devised his plan to defeat the Acoma," Desio opened as his First Adviser took his place on the cushions beneath the ceremonial dais.

"That is well, my Lord," answered Incomo. "We have just received word of our ambush on the Acoma thyza wagons."

"How did it go?" Desio rocked forward in his eagerness.

"Badly, my Lord." Incomo's expression remained wooden. "We were defeated, as we expected, but the cost was much higher than anticipated."

"How costly?" Tasaio's voice seemed detached.

Incomo shifted dark eyes to the cousin. Slowly he said, "Every man we sent was killed. Fifty raiders in all."

Desio sat back, disgust upon his face. "Fifty! Damn that woman. Is every move she chooses ordained to win her victory?"

Tasaio tapped his chin with a finger. "It may seem so now, cousin. But victory belongs to the last battle. In the end, we shall see where Mara is vulnerable." He inclined his head to Incomo and asked, "How did our enemy achieve so total a success?"

"Simple," answered the First Adviser. "They had three times the guards on the wagons that we would expect."

Tasaio considered this, his fingers motionless on his knees. "We expected them to know we were coming. That they responded with so much force tells us two things: first, they did not want us to capture that wagon, at any price, and second . . ." His eyes widened in sudden speculation. "That damned cho-ja hive must be breeding warriors like jade-flies!"

Desio seemed confused. "What does this have to do with uncovering Acoma spies?"

Incomo smoothed his robes with the fussiness of a bird ruffling feathers. Unbreakably patient, he qualified. "Our offensive was aimed at tracing information leaks. Mara's too competent Spy Master has just confirmed the guilt of one, or all three, of our household suspects. Timing is all, my Lord Desio. Had we planned our attack on commerce more consequential than the grain trade, we would certainly have drawn notice to our purpose."

Tasaio broke his silence. "There could well be something else at play here: a garrison as undermanned as Mara's should not have responded so forcefully to so minor a threat. This overreaction is meaningful." Tasaio paused, his brow furrowed. "Suppose our action has in some way disrupted a plan the Acoma have under way. Suppose we just blundered into their next move against our interest? They were desperate for us not to capture that wagon, willing to pay a price far above the worth of the grain or the minor loss in honor of abandoning a small caravan."

"Now, there is a point to pursue," Incomo broke in. "Our factor in Sulan-Qu reports that since our raid the Acoma have doubled the guards on all their trade caravans. Rumors circulate that secret goods lie hidden under every bushel of grain. By the flurry of covert activity, we could conclude that one real treasure exists, a treasure our enemies have determined at all costs to keep secret." Incomo's excitement dissolved in a frustrated sigh. "How I wish we had an informant in Mara's inner household! Something important is under way, something we nearly discovered accidentally in our raid near Sulan-Qu. Why else should a minor sortie provoke such elaborate countermeasures?"

Desio reached for his ice glass and swirled the last, fast-melting chips in the dregs. "She's sent messengers to Dustari, too. No doubt to invite Chipino of the Xacatecas to parley on his return from the borders. If he accepts, the Acoma will almost certainly gain an alliance."

Only Tasaio remained unmoved before the evidence of setbacks. Gently he said, "Let that bide, cousin. I have a long-range plan for Mara that might take two years to bring to fruition."

"Two years!" Desio slammed his mug on a side table. "If that cho-ja hive is breeding warriors, each spring Mara's estates become that much more unassailable."

Tasaio waved this aside. "Let Mara grow strong at home. For we will not deal with her on her own ground. Gone are the days we could dream of overwhelming her estate by main force." His voice turned reflective. "We would win, of course, but be so depleted we would not survive the certain onslaught from other enemies. Were I Chipino of the Xacatecas or Andero of the Keda, I would welcome an open confrontation between the Acoma and the Minwanabi."

Desio became sulky when anyone else tried to tell him what to do. Incomo watched as his master sucked his last ice cube between his teeth. Finally the Lord of the Minwanabi said, "I may come to regret my rashness in vowing Minwanabi blood should we fail to crush the Acoma. I had hoped to spur our people to end the matter quickly. But the Red God gave us no time limit"—he glanced heavenward and made a luck sign, just in case he was wrong—"so we might do well to proceed cautiously. We cannot spare fifty seasoned warriors for each grain wagon Mara sends out." With a nod, Desio said, "Cousin, let's hear your plan."

Tasaio responded obliquely. "Do smugglers still operate between the Empire and the desert lands in Tsubar?" he asked the First Adviser.

Incomo shrugged. "Almost certainly. The nomads still covet luxuries, especially jades and silk. And they have to import swords from somewhere, since resin-producing trees do not flourish in the desert."

Tasaio nodded almost imperceptibly. "Then I suggest we send an envoy to the ruins at Banganok, to offer the nomads weapons and jades and rich bribes to step up their raids on the borders."

"Xacatecas' forces would stay preoccupied." Desio jumped ahead. "His return to the mainland would be delayed, along with any possible alliance with Mara."

"That is the least advantage, my Lord." Tasaio slipped the fingers out of his archer's glove. He flexed his hands as though warming up his grip for the sword, and outlined the steps of the bold plot.

The Minwanabi would cultivate relations with the desert raiders, beginning with bribes to keep the Xacatecas forces pinned down in defense. Over a period of two years, the bribes would be escalated, forming the pretense of alliance. Minwanabi soldiers would add to the raiders' ranks, disguised as tribesman allies. At a moment judged most propitious, a grand offensive would be mounted on the Empire's borders. In emergency meeting, the High Council would order the Lady of the Acoma to go to the aid of the Lord of the Xacatecas.

At mention of this, Incomo brightened. "Mara must lead her relief troops in person or spoil her overtures toward alliance. And if she sends less than her full support in the field, she proves lack of sincerity in her promises."

"She would be drawn far from her estates, along with most of her cho-ja," Desio cut in. "We could mount raids."

Tasaio silenced him with a slightly raised eyebrow. "Better than that, cousin. Much better." He went on, ticking off points on his fingers in the manner of a tactician. Mara had no military training, and her only officer with command experience in the field was Keyoke. If her call to arms in Dustari could be timed as a surprise, she would be handed a crisis. She must strip her outer holdings, hire mercenary guards to flesh out those garrisons of least strategic importance, and then leave the heart of her estates under the care of an officer only recently promoted. Or she must assign Keyoke to protect her family natami, and expose herself to risk. Tasaio elaborated. "Isolated in Dustari, far from help from her clan or allies, there would be no miracles for Mara. She would be alone on a field of our choosing, and forced to rely on the guidance of an inexperienced officer." Tasaio paused, licked his lips, and smiled. "At best, Mara's lack of preparation will do our work for us. She may be killed, or captured by desert raiders, or, at the least, blunder in the assignment and earn the Xacatecas' wrath, while losing the heart of her army."

"Interesting," said Incomo. "But the weak link is evident. The assignment left to Keyoke will almost certainly not be bungled."

Tasaio slapped his empty glove against his palm, and his smile widened. "That is why Keyoke must be removed. A raid that will deliver him to Turakamu must be carefully planned. Let us say the Lady will receive summons from the High Council on the day of her Force Commander's death." Tasaio folded his hands, the model of a Tsurani warrior in repose. "With Keyoke dead, Mara must leave Acoma welfare in the hands of lesser servants, a Strike Leader named Lujan, most likely, a flutterbug of a hadonra, and an old nurse who calls herself First Adviser. Among these may be one we can subvert."

"Brilliant!" muttered Desio.

Tasaio summed up. "As I read the situation, without experienced officers, Mara could never gain from assignment to Dustari. Whichever Strike Leader she promotes to oversee the attempt at relieving Xacatecas will quickly learn the difference between commanding a strike force and planning a battle."

"Brilliant," Desio said, loudly and with shining enthusiasm.

Incomo considered more practical ramifications. "Lord Desio would need to call favors from a great number of allies in the council—even become indebted—to contrive for Mara to be assigned to a post in Dustari. Getting Xacatecas there was quite costly, and keeping him on the frontier another two years will be difficult. The nobles who supported us will demand even more concessions to be bought a second time, particularly since the setback of Jingu's death. We are not as strong or as influential as we once were, I regret to remind you, and the debt incurred will be great."

"What price the death of Mara of the Acoma?" Tasaio said softly. "Desio swore blood oath to the Red God. The alternative is for us to slaughter every woman and child wearing Minwanabi black and orange, then march to Turakamu's temple and fall upon our swords."

Incomo nodded and turned shrewd eyes on his Lord.

Hot as Desio was to see Mara compromised, he still recognized the gravity of his decision. He did not commit himself or the resources of his house thoughtlessly, but pondered with knitted brows. "I think my cousin advises me well," he said at last. "But can we be sure of the desert men?"

Tasaio looked out the window, as if something in the distance shaped his answer. "It's immaterial. For among those 'allies' attacking will be a field commander ready to take the necessary steps to ensure Mara's failure. I will supervise the battle personally."

The suggestion filled Desio with delight. "Wonderful, cousin. Your reputation credits you too little. You are more crafty than I had been told." He nodded enthusiastically. "Let preparation for these plans begin. We shall put aside haste in favor of completeness."

Tasaio nodded. "I have much to arrange, my Lord. Our plan must proceed with perfection, or we risk enmity from two great houses rising in power. The army we gather two years hence must be smuggled in small numbers by boat to Ilama, then westward along the coast trail to Banganok. No one must suspect the movement of troops. And when Xacatecas is hard-pressed, we must be ready to kill Keyoke the first moment he's vulnerable." He blinked, as if recalling his focus to Desio. "Yes, I have much to see to. I ask my Lord's permission to depart."

Desio waved him on his way. Though matters of protocol were furthest from his mind, Tasaio arose and made his bow, correct to the last. Incomo watched and wondered again if undue ambition lay behind such perfect poise. As the Minwanabi cousin departed from the study, he leaned close to his Lord and murmured a soft-spoken question.

Desio stiffened in surprise. "Tasaio? Turn traitor to his Lord?" he exclaimed, entirely too loudly. "Never." His conviction rang with blind faith. "All my life, cousin Tasaio has been an example to us all. Until the moment of my ascension to the rank of Lord, he would have happily slit my throat to gain the mantle of the Minwanabi, but the moment I took my father's place, Tasaio became mine to command. He is the soul of honor, and a devil for cleverness. Of all the men in my service, that one will bring me the Acoma natami."

Satisfied with his own judgment on the matter, Desio ended his clandestine council. He clapped for servants, and asked for pretty serving girls to bathe with him in the cool waters of the lake.

Incomo bowed, content that while Desio fathered bastard children, Tasaio would need his help to begin plotting the vast design to destroy Mara. If the Minwanabi First Adviser felt any resentment at Tasaio's usurpation of his role, he hid it even from himself; he was loyal to his master. As long as Tasaio served Minwanabi interests, Incomo had no jealousy within his breast. Besides, the wry thought intruded, Lords of great houses quite commonly came to youthful deaths; until Desio married and fathered an heir, Tasaio remained next in line for the ruler's mantle. Should Desio perish untimely, it would never do to have one unexpectedly inheriting the title be displeased with the resident First Adviser.

Incomo motioned for a servant to attend his desires. "Send word to Tasaio that I am at his disposal in any fashion for which he deems me worthy and that I will happily lend my feeble efforts to his great work."

As the servant hurried off, Incomo considered ordering a cool tub and a pretty woman to wash his sweaty, tired body. Shrugging off the wistful image, he arose from his cushions. Too much work remained undone. Besides, if he read young Tasaio correctly, he would be sent for within the hour.

Mara moved between nodding rows of kekali blossoms, a basket on her arm. She pointed to a bloom and said, "That one," and the servant who trailed her obligingly cut the stem with a sharp knife. Another held up a lantern so the first might clearly see in the shadows of early evening. The servant lifted the indigo flower, inspected it briefly to see that the petals were unharmed, then bowed and handed the blossom to the Lady. She pressed it to her nose to enjoy the fragrance before she added it to others already piled in her basket.

The hadonra, Jican, trailed her as she turned down a bend in the path. "The ravine between your southernmost needra meadows has been flooded, my Lady."

Mara pointed out another flower she wished cut, and a smile curved her lips. "Good. The bridge across our new river will be completed before market season, I trust?"

Now Jican chuckled. "Planking is being added to the framework even as we speak. Jidu of the Tuscalora sweats as he writes daily, begging permission to transport his chocha-la crops down the ravine by boat. However, as I politely pointed out on your behalf, my Lady, the right-of-way you granted when you purchased the land permitted only wagons."

"Very good." Mara accepted the indicated blossom from her servant, and carelessly stabbed her finger on a thorn. The pain she accepted with Tsurani impassivity, but the blood was another matter. Kelewanese superstition held that chance-spilled blood might whet the Red God's appetite, making the deity greedy for additional death. Jican hastily offered his handkerchief, and Mara bound up her stinging finger before any droplets could fall to the soil.

Her plan to beggar Lord Jidu of the Tuscalora and force him to become her vassal had been delayed by a season because of the attentions received by her house following the death of Jingu of the Minwanabi. Now, as events resumed their proper course, she found her planned victory over her neighbor to the south had partially lost its savor. Hokanu's visit had offered a welcome interlude, but his stay had been brief, owing to his need to return home.

Nacoya blamed her restlessness on the lack of male company. Mara smiled at the thought and shifted her basket of flowers. The First Adviser insisted that no young woman's life could be complete without a healthy male diversion now and again. But Mara viewed romance with skepticism. As greatly as she enjoyed Hokanu's company, the thought of taking another husband to her bed made her hands turn clammy with apprehension. To her, marriage and sex were simply a woman's bargaining chips in the Game of the Council. Love and pleasure had no place in such decisions.

"Where's Kevin?" said Jican unexpectedly, making his Lady start.

Mara settled on a stone bench and motioned for her hadonra to join her. "He's being fitted for new clothes."

Jican's eyes brightened. He loved to gossip, but was seldom so bold as to trouble his Lady outright on matters outside of estate finance.

Mara indulged him. "Kevin went out with the hunters yesterday, and when he complained that his legs and backside had suffered from thorns, I allowed him to be measured for Midkemian dress. He's off to show the leather workers and tailors what to do, as they know little about his nation's odd fashions. I told him the colors must not be other than a slave's grey and white, but maybe he'll behave with more dignity once his knees are covered with—what did he call it? —ah yes, hose."

"More like he'll complain he's too hot," the little hadonra returned. Then, as Mara dismissed the other servants, he added, "I have news of your silk samples, Lady."

Instantly he had Mara's entire attention. "They were safely stowed aboard your message barge yesterday. The factors in Jamar will have them before the close of the week, in time for inspection before the price auctions."

Mara sighed with relief. She had worried endlessly that the Minwanabi might discover her move into the silk market beforetime and give warning to their silk-producing allies in the north. Most Acoma revenues came from needra raising and weapon craft; but now she needed to strengthen her army and outfit the ever rising numbers of cho-ja warriors bred by the new Queen. Hides and armor would be needed at home, cutting back on her marketable goods. The silk trade Mara hoped to create must balance out the loss. If the timing were spoiled, the northern silk merchants would undercut her prices and offer early deliveries to starve out her fledgling enterprise. Years of established trade had given them influence over the dyers' and weavers' guilds. Paying costly bribes to ensure guild secrecy and goodwill was an unavoidable necessity until Acoma craftsmen could be schooled to mastery of these specialized new skills. But if Acoma silks arrived on the market at just the right moment, not only would Mara gain income, she would upset the revenues of the Minwanabi allies.

"You have done well in this, Jican."

The hadonra blushed. "Success would not have been possible without Arakasi's planning."

Mara stared out over the gardens, into the gathering gloom of twilight. "Let us not speak of success until the price auctions are dominated by demand for Acoma goods!"

Jican returned a deep bow. "Let us hope the day comes without mishap." He made a sign for the Good God's favor and quietly retired from her presence.

Mara lingered, alone except for a few servants. She set down her basket and surveyed the gardens that surrounded the estate house's east wing. This had been her mother's favorite place, or so Lord Sezu had told the daughter whose birth had caused that Lady's premature death. From this seat the Lady Oskiro had watched her Lord select his hunting dogs as the young ones were brought out for his inspection. But the kennels runs were empty now, by Mara's command; the baying of the hounds had reminded the new Ruling Lady too painfully of the past. And her husband had cared more for battle practice and wrestling with the soldiers than coursing after game with fleet dogs. Or perhaps he had not lived long enough to appreciate the sport.

Mara sighed and shook off her regrets. She excused her servants and stared over the distant meadows as the shatra birds flew at sundown. Normally their flight calmed and reassured her, but today she felt only melancholy. That no attack upon the Acoma seemed imminent did not reduce the threat. The most brilliant moves within the Game of the Council were those that came without warning. The tranquil passage of days only made her skin creep, as if assassins lurked in hiding at her back. Knowing that Tasaio stayed on as Desio's adviser promised subtle and devious trouble. Arakasi was worried also. Mara knew by his stillness as he stood to deliver his reports. He had survived the fall of one Lord and lived to serve another; a matter that could trouble him would not be anything slight.

Mara lifted a kekali blossom from the basket at her feet. The petals were soft and fragile, susceptible to the slightest chill, and fast to wilt in extreme heat. The bushes themselves were hardy, and armed with thorns for defense; but the flowers were short-lived and vulnerable. This evening, surrounded by the perishable beauty of the kekali, Mara missed the baying of the hounds at their dinner. More, she missed the strong presence of her father as he sat in the garden, enjoying the cool of the oncoming night, sipping on a bitter ale while his son and daughter prattled on about childish things. Gold light faded from the western sky, and the shatra flocks settled to rest after their sky dance. A barefooted slave lit the last lanterns along the path; the instant he finished his task he hurried away for his meal of thyza mush. In the kitchens and common dining hall, estate workers gathered for the evening meal. Still Mara lingered.

Dusk deepened. Stars appeared, and the western hills became a silhouette against the last trace of afterglow. The silence peculiar to the hour descended, the birdsong of daytime now stilled, while night-singing insects in their myriad thousands had yet to waken and trill. Since this garden was farthest removed from the soldiers' barracks and servants' quarters, it was silent; Mara enjoyed a rare moment of peace.

She found herself thinking of Hokanu. His visit a few months earlier had been disappointingly brief—a lingering dinner; then at first light, after breakfast and what seemed a short chat, he took his leave and departed. Some development in the game had compelled his return to the Shinzawai estates sooner than Mara would have liked. Left with a sense that Hokanu felt he should have bypassed the house and returned straight upriver to his father's estates, Mara felt flattered he had compromised his sense of duty a little and stolen a visit with her.

But she had said nothing to him, sheltering her feelings behind tradition's accepted behavior. His wit might make her smile, and his intelligence inspire her, yet she shied from contemplating any final outcome of this handsome noble's attentions.

Attractive as she found Hokanu, the thought of returning to any man's bed made her shudder. Even now she had nightmares of her late husband's rages and the bruises he had inflicted in his passions. No, she decided, she had no desire to encourage the company of a man.

And yet, when Hokanu's small caravan had drawn out of

sight, Mara had been astonished at how swiftly the time had fled. The young man's company had pleased her. She had not had a comfortable moment while he had been there, but she missed his lively companionship.

Footsteps approached on the gravel path. Mara turned in time to see a tall, long-strided figure invade her temporary sanctuary.

"There you are," called a voice. Even without the heavy accent, the disrespectful address and the boisterous tone identified her visitor as Midkemian. And as often as Mara was astonished by such directness, she was also attracted to it.

"I've been looking for you since sundown," Kevin added, treading a winding path between kekali bushes to reach the bench where she sat. "I asked Nacoya, and the old witch just grunted and shrugged. The servants looked nervous when I spoke to them, and finally I had to track down Lujan at the change of the guard."

"He must have known you were following him," said Mara, unwilling to believe her best soldier would be so lax in his duties.

"Of course." Kevin rounded a last island of flower bed and paused before her. "We were discussing the fine points of swordplay. Your methods differ from ours. Ours are better, naturally," he added. Irritated that his intentional baiting always worked, Mara raised her head. She found him grinning in anticipation of her rejoinder, and realized he played with her. She refused to be teased and studied his new attire.

The lantern light caught Kevin in profile, burnished his wavy hair copper, and touched the long, flowing sleeves of the white shirt just collected from the seamstresses. Over this he wore a jerkin belted tightly around his waist, and hose that clung to a muscled length of leg. The neutral grey color flattered him, for it set off his hair and beard and the deep tan of his face, and somehow made his blue eyes more intense. Mara glanced down, to find the effect spoiled at the ankle by the same worn sandals he had been given on the day of his arrival. Aware of the Lady's gaze on his feet, Kevin laughed. "The boots aren't finished yet."

He looked very exotic, handsome in a barbaric way. Fascinated by the sight of him, Mara forgot to reprimand his lack of form. However, this time, Kevin kept courtesy. He made his bow Midkemian style, from the waist.

"Is that how you show respect for your Kingdom ladies?" Mara asked somewhat acidly, mostly because she could not take her eyes off his wide, strangely clothed shoulders.

Kevin gave back a wicked smile. "Not quite. Have I your permission?"

Mara inclined her head, then started as he reached and took her hand. "We greet our ladies like this." He confidently touched her fingers to his lips. The caress was very soft, barely a brush of flesh against flesh. Mara shivered slightly and stiffened to pull away.

But Kevin was not finished taking liberty. The feel of proper clothing and the mildness of the night lent him a spirit of recklessness. He firmed his grip, not so much that his mistress could not break away, but enough that she must struggle or follow his lead. "Sometimes we take the ladies dancing," he invited, and he drew her to her feet, grasped her lightly around the waist, and spun her in a circle through the lantern light.

Mara laughed in surprise, not feeling in the least threatened. Glad to be distracted from the morass of difficult memories, the Lady of the Acoma abandoned herself to this single moment of fun. And between Kevin's breathless laughter and the heady perfume of the flowers, she discovered that the touch of him was pleasing. His strength did not intimidate but warmed her. Small as a doll in his arms, she tried to keep pace with him; yet she did not know the steps of his wild dance. Her feet got in his way, and he stumbled. She felt his muscles tense in response. He had reflexes swift as a cat's. But the backstep he initiated to save his balance met disastrously with the basket she had abandoned on the path.

The wicker container overturned, showering the gravel with kekali. Kevin tripped sideways, dragging Mara with him. The plunge happened too suddenly to allow the Lady to cry out. Caught in Kevin's embrace, she felt him turn his shoulder to cushion her fall. She landed sprawled across his chest, slightly breathless, and still entangled in his arms. His hands moved, slid down her back, and paused at her waist.

"Are you all right?" he said in a voice that was unfamiliarly deep.

Overwhelmed by a rush of strange sensations, Mara did not answer at once. Kevin shifted under her. He freed one hand and picked up a kekali blossom from the ground. He pinched the stem in his teeth and, by touch, stripped off the thorns. Lantern light softened the planes of his face as he finished and carefully wound the flower in a strand of Mara's hair. "At home we call flowers that look much like these by another name."

Mara shut her eyes against a strange rush, something like dizziness, yet not. His fingers brushed her neck as he finished with the flower, then withdrew, leaving her aching. Huskily she asked, "What name?"

"Roses." Kevin felt the slight quiver that coursed through her flesh. The hand on her back moved, drew her closer. Softly he added, "though we've none this wonderful shade of blue." His touch was tentative, and gentle in a manner that did not frighten. Aware through her confusion that he offered comfort, Mara did not tear herself away. For a moment he went still, as if he awaited some form of reaction.

Mara returned none. Her body felt strangely languid. When she made no move, Kevin held her more firmly. He shifted again, until her hip lay cradled in the hollow of his flank, and her hair loosened from its pins and cascaded in a rush across the opened laces of his shirt. The hand on her back slid down and under her arm, and traced the neckline of her robe. The touch raised fire in her, a warmth that seemed to melt her from within.

"Lady?" he said softly. His other hand brushed the hair back from her face. She saw that his eyes were very wide, the pupils dark in the lantern light, and the irises narrow bands of silver. "Do you want this? A man on my world gives roses to a Lady when he loves her."

"I care very little for love," Mara answered, her voice oddly rough to her own ear. Now her body tensed against his. "My husband taught me more than I ever wished to know." Kevin sighed, changed his position, and lifted her.

Overwhelmed by his strength, she felt a giddy sense of familiarity, reminiscent of a time when a tiny girl was held gently by her warrior father's powerful hands. Yet Mara sensed no danger, for despite the power of those hands, their touch was only loving. Mara felt a chilly rush of air as she and Kevin separated, when he gently sat her upon the bench.

Her robe had pulled askew. He did not stare at her exposed breasts but sought something within her own gaze. Her eyes followed his as he carefully stepped back, awaiting her command.

Mara settled against the stone seat and recovered the semblance of poise. Yet the control she had schooled to be second nature came with difficulty. Inside, she remained in turmoil; despite the memory of her former husband's brutality, despite the ingrained fears, her body ached to be touched again by such tender strength. Kevin made no move toward her, and this only made her flesh cry out all the more. Battling to impose logic over confusion, Mara said nothing, which left Kevin the task of smoothing over the awkwardness of the moment.

"My Lady," he said, and bowed again from the waist. For some reason the movement gave her the shivers. He turned his back, bent, and methodically began to gather the blossoms strewn across the path. "A man might also give a woman a rose if he admired and respected her. Keep the flower in your hair; it truly does become you."

Mara reached up and touched the blossom which rested, still, twined in the lock above her ear. She became absorbed by the play of muscles under his loose-fitting white shirt. The sensation in her middle mounted to an ache. She shivered again as Kevin stretched and recovered the tipped basket. Lantern light caught his hair and his sinewy wrists as he laid the recovered flowers inside. A few remained, crushed by his body during the fall, and as he arose to return the basket to her, he grimaced and said, "Curse the thorns."

Instantly Mara felt contrition. Moved by an unfamiliar instinct, she reached out and touched the back of his hand. "Did you receive a wound?"

Kevin looked at her wryly. "No, Lady. I'd hardly call a few pricks in the back on your behalf a wound."

"Let me see," demanded Mara, pressed by a recklessness that made her giddy.

The barbarian regarded her, his moment of surprise well hidden. Then his wryness expanded into a smile. "As my Lady wishes." He loosened the laces of his cuffs, shed the shirt in an enviably smooth movement, and straddled the bench by her side.

Presented with a view of his back, Mara hesitated. Plain

in the light she could see scratch marks, studded with imbedded kekali thorns. Shaky now, and frightened, still she fumbled until she found the handkerchief lent by Jican. Tentatively she dabbed at a cut. Kevin held motionless. The feel of his skin was silken smooth, not at all what she expected. The handkerchief fabric caught on a brier. Gently Mara drew it out. She ran her fingers down and down, found more thorns, and drew them, until finally none were left. Her hands did not want to leave him. She traced the side of his flank, felt the hard muscle there, and then flinched back with a gasp as memory of Buntokapi made her start.

Kevin swung his knee over the bench and spun to face her. "Lady? Is something wrong?"

The concern in his voice suddenly broke her heart. She fought against tears, and lost.

"Lady," whispered Kevin. "What makes you cry?" He gathered her to him, held her shaking against the hollow of his shoulder. Mara tensed, at any moment expecting his hands to turn brutal, to twist at her clothes and seek out her most tender parts. But nothing happened. Kevin simply held her, unmoving, and in time her fear unlocked. Mara realized that he was not going to be rough, but would only offer her comfort. "What troubles you?" he asked again.

Mara stirred, then surrendered to his warmth and leaned against him. "Memories," she said softly.

Now Kevin's hands did harden. He caught her firmly, lifted her, and resettled her in his lap.

Mara caught herself just short of a scream. Shame burned her cheeks, that she had so nearly disgraced her heritage. She choked a breath to call Lujan, but Kevin's hold loosened. He stroked her hair, gentle once more, and relief made her cry all over again.

"Your memories must be painful," Kevin murmured in her ear. "I've never seen a beautiful woman so frightened at a man's attentions. It's as if someone beat you when another man would have kissed you with tenderness."

"Bunto," said Mara, her voice lowered to a near whisper. Her coldness was unexpected, and prompted by a resentment she had never before given rein, except in confidence with Nacoya. "He liked his women bruised. His concubine, Teani, loved such abuses." She paused, then added, "I don't think I ever could. Perhaps that makes me a coward. I don't care. I'm just glad I no longer have a husband to share my bed."

Now Kevin was silent, shocked to an outrage that made him cup her chin until she faced him. "In my land, a husband who strikes his wife is nothing but a common criminal."

Mara managed a weak smile. "How different our cultures can be. Here a woman has no power over her fate, unless she is Ruling Lady. A man may dominate his wife as he would a slave, and in the eyes of other men, his manhood is increased by her submissiveness."

Now Kevin's anger could be heard in his voice. "Then your lords are no better than barbarians. Men should treat women with respect and kindness."

Excitement coursed through Mara. Time and again Nacoya had told her that all men did not behave like Buntokapi; yet the fact that they owned the god-given right to be brutal had caused her to distrust even Hokanu, whose outward manner seemed mild. Where she had not dared to give herself to a suitor of her own culture, with Kevin she felt oddly safe.

"Then your people treat their wives and lovers like flowers, cherishing them without causing pain?"

Kevin nodded, his fingers stroking her shoulders as lightly as the wings of small birds.

"Show me," Mara whispered. The touch of him made her tingle, and she felt, through his breeches, the pressure of his own aroused manhood.

The barbarian's brows rose mischievously. "Here?"

The ache inside Mara mounted, became unbearable. "Here," she repeated softly. "Here, now, I command you." When he looked as though he might protest, she added, "No one will disturb us. I am Ruling Lady of the Acoma."

Even now she tautened, as if at any moment she expected to be manhandled. Kevin sensed her tension. "Lady," he said softly, "right now you rule more than the Acoma," and he bent his head and kissed her lips.

His touch was soft as a whisper. Reassured, she yielded almost immediately. Then, as his lightness teased her to desire, she leaned into him, demanding more. But his hands stayed soft. He stroked her breast through the fabric of her robe, maddening her with his gentleness. Her nipple turned hard and hot. She wanted his fingers on her bare skin, more desperately than she had ever wished for anything.

He did not comply. Not all at once. Barbarian that he was, he acted as if her very robe were precious. He slipped the silk slowly from her shoulders. Mara moaned and shivered. She tugged at his shirt, wanting the feel of him, but her hands tangled in his unfamiliar dress, and as her fingers encountered his skin, she hesitated, wanting to return the feeling he gave her, but uncertain what she should do.

Kevin caught her wrists, still handling her as if her flesh were fragile. His care made her desire mount further, tormented her to an ecstasy she had never dreamed existed. She could not have named the moment he slid her robe off and touched his lips to her breast. By then her world had dissolved into dizziness, and she moaned for his touch against her loins.

Midkemian clothing was more complicated than Tsurani dress. He had to shift her to remove his breeches. Somehow they ended up in the grass, lit by the golden sliver of Kelewan's moon, and also by a soft wash of lantern light. Abandoned to pleasure amid the scent of blooming kekali, swept away by the passion of a redheaded barbarian, Mara discovered what it was to be a woman.

Later, flushed with the elation of newfound release, Mara returned to her chamber. Nacoya awaited her there with news of a business transaction in Sulan-Qu, and a tray of light supper. One look at her mistress's face, and she forgot the contents of the scroll. "Thank Lashima," she said, correctly interpreting the cause of Mara's euphoria. "You've discovered the joy of your womanhood at last."

Mara laughed, a little breathless. She pirouetted like a girl and sat on the cushions. Kevin followed her, his hair still tousled and his face more guardedly sober. Nacoya regarded him closely for a moment. Then, her lips pursed in mild disapproval, she turned upon her mistress.

"My Lady, you must excuse your slave."

Mara looked up, her first flush of surprise changing to annoyance. "First Adviser, I shall do as I please with my slave."

Nacoya bowed deeply in respect for her mistress's prerogative. Then she went on as though Kevin were not present. "Daughter of my heart, you now have learned the wonder of sex. This is good. And you are not the first great Lady who has used a slave. It is not only useful, it is even wise, for no slave can use you. However, Desio of the Minwanabi will be waiting to take advantage of every weakness, however small. You must not make mistakes and let the pleasures of the flesh grow into infatuation. This Midkemian should be sent away to keep your thinking clear, and you should take one or two different men to your bed soon, to learn they are merely . . . useful."

Mara stood motionless, with her back turned. "I find this discussion inopportune. Leave me at once, Nacoya."

The First Adviser of the Acoma returned a deeper bow. "Your will, Lady." Stiffly she arose, and with a last lingering glare at Kevin she left the room. As the indignant tap of her sandals faded down the hall, Mara motioned to her slave.

"Join me," she invited. Then she shed her loosened robe and dropped naked upon the cushions of the mat that served as her bed. "Show me again how the men in your land love their women."

Kevin returned his familiar wry grin. Then he raised his eyes toward heaven in a show of mock appeal. "Pray to your gods to give me the strength," he murmured. Then he slipped off his shirt and his drawers, and joined her.

Later, when the lamps burned low, Mara lay awake in the clasp of Kevin's arms and reflected upon the joy she had found in the midst of so many worries. She reached out and smoothed back her lover's tousled hair. She regarded the punctures traced across his shoulder by the sharpened thorns of the kekali; the wounds were slight, already scabbed over. Only then did Mara appreciate the bittersweet nature of the love that had overtaken her at last.

Kevin was, and always would be, a slave. There were certain unarguable absolutes in her culture, and that fact was one.

Caught up in a moment of melancholy, and frowning at the waning moon through the screen, Mara wondered whether the bad luck that had brought down her brother and father might not stalk her yet. Desperately she prayed to Lashima that the blood from Kevin's scratches had not seeped through his shirt and touched the ground. Lord Desio of the Minwanabi had sworn the vengeance of his house into the hands of Turakamu. And with or without invitation, the Death God walked where he would. If he chose to favor the Minwanabi, the Acoma would be swept away without trace from the land and the memory of man.

7. *TARGET*

Mara stirred.

Her hand brushed warm flesh, and she started awake. In the predawn gloom, she saw Kevin as a figure of greys and blacks. He was not asleep but propped on one elbow looking at her. "You're very beautiful," he said.

Mara smiled drowsily and snuggled into the crook of his elbow. She felt tired but content. Through the months since Kevin had come to her bed, she had discovered new aspects to herself, a sensual side, a tender side, kept hidden away until now. The pleasures she shared with the barbarian made the brutalities of her marriage seem a distant and unpleasant dream.

Playfully she ran her fingers through the hair on Kevin's chest. She had come to value their morning chat after lovemaking as much as council with her advisers. In ways not fully realized, she was learning from him. His nature was far more guarded than she had guessed upon first impression; she now understood that his direct and open manner stemmed from a cultural surface trait that masked an inner privacy. Kevin remained intentionally vague about his previous life and family, and though she asked often, he avoided talk of the future, as if he concealed his plans in that regard, as well. Different as he was from a born Tsurani, Mara judged his character to be complex and deep. She found it astonishing that such a man could be a common soldier, and wondered if others with like potential lay undiscovered among her warriors.

Kevin said something, disturbing her contemplation.

Mara smiled indulgently. "What did you say?"

Caught up by a thought, he mused, "What strange contrasts your world has."

Brought to alertness by his uncharacteristic intonation, Mara focused her attention. "What troubles you?"

"Are my thoughts so transparent?" Kevin shrugged in partial embarrassment. He remained silent for a moment, then added, "I was thinking of the poor quarter in Sulan-Qu."

"But why?" Mara frowned. She attempted to reassure him. "You will never be permitted to starve."

"Starve?" Surprise made Kevin pause. He drew a fast breath, then stared at her, as if he might fathom her woman's mind by studying her intently. At last, moved to some inner conclusion, he admitted, "Never in my life have I seen people suffering in such numbers."

"But you must have poor folk in the Kingdom of the Isles," Mara returned without inflection. "How else do your gods show their displeasure at man's behavior than by returning him to his next life in low estate?"

Kevin stiffened. "What do the gods have to do with starving children, disease, and cruelty? And what of the righteousness of good works and charity? Have you no alms in this land, or are all Tsurani nobles born cruel?"

Mara shoved herself upright, spilling cushions across the waxed floor. "You are a strange man," she observed in a voice that hid a note of panic. As often as she had bent tradition, she had never questioned the gods' omnipotence. To dare that heresy was to invite utter destruction. Mara realized that other nobles might be less firm in their adherence to their ancestors' faith, but she herself was devout; had fate not destined her for the ruler's mantle, she would have dedicated herself to a life of contemplative service to the goddess Lashima. The ultimate truth was that the gods decreed the order of the Empire. To question this was to undermine the very concept of honor that was the foundation of Tsurani society. It was this divine mandate that imparted order to the Empire and made sense of everything, from the certainty of ultimate reward for honorable service, and the right of nobles to rule, to constraints in the Game of the Council so that wholesale carnage never resulted.

With one careless remark, the barbarian had challenged the very fabric of Tsurani beliefs.

Mara clung to her poise, inwardly battered by a host of alarming implications. The pleasures Kevin brought her could never compensate for the dangerous new bent of his thoughts. He must not be allowed to speak such blasphemous idiocy, especially not within Ayaki's hearing; the boy had grown to dote upon Kevin, and the future Lord of the Acoma's resolve as he led his house to greatness must never be shaken by uncertainties. To conquer the might of other families because the gods looked favorably upon such efforts was one thing; to vainly think accolades came solely through wit and skill and some random factor of luck was . . . was morally destructive and unthinkable. Cornered, with only one option, the Lady of the Acoma chose her course.

"Leave me," she said sharply. She arose at once from her bed and brusquely clapped for servants. Although the sun had not yet risen, and the screens were still closed for the night, two maids and a manservant answered her summons.

"Dress me at once," the Lady commanded. One maid rushed to select a robe, while the other took up brush and comb to attend to her mistress's tangles. The manservant tidied the scattered cushions and adjusted the screens. The fact that Kevin got in his way seemed not to faze him. Wizened and old, and ingrained in the habit of his duties, he went about straightening up the chamber as though he were deaf.

Mara slipped her arms into the rose-colored silken robe the maid held up for her. She turned and saw Kevin standing naked, his breeches and shirt across his arm, and a dumbfounded look on his face. The Lady's expression remained stern, her dark eyes fathomless and hard. "Jican tells me that the work clearing the forest for my needra fields goes slowly. This is mostly owing to your countrymen, who complain and malinger over their appointed share of work." The maid with the comb lifted the hair from Mara's nape and began expertly piling it into an elaborately knotted headdress. Mara continued in a level tone, despite the fact that her head was tugged this way and that as the maid separated each long lock for arrangement. "I wish you to take charge," Mara announced. "Spring will be upon us all too swiftly, and the needra herds will increase. You shall have power over my overseers and the authority to change any detail you see fit. In return, your countrymen will cease their laziness. They will cut timber and clear the new fields before the first calf is thrown. You may coddle their needs so long as the work gets done. Fail to complete this task, and I shall have one man chosen at random and hung for each day my new pastures remain unfinished past the Spring Welcoming Festival."

Kevin appeared puzzled, but he nodded. "Shall I return tonight, or—" he began.

"You will need to stay with the workers in the meadow camp."

"When shall I return—"

Coldly Mara interrupted. "When I choose to send for you. Now go."

Kevin bowed, his face revealing bafflement and anger. Still carrying his clothing, he departed the room. The soldier on duty by the door showed no change in expression as the barbarian stepped into the corridor. The Midkemian looked at the impassive soldier as if he had said something, then let loose a burst of ironic laughter. "Damned if I can figure her out, either," he confided in tight frustration. The soldier's eyes fixed upon Kevin, but the features remained unchanged.

Despite being surrounded by servants, Mara overheard Kevin's comment. She heard the pain that he did not bother to conceal, and closed her eyes against inexplicably threatening tears. Tsurani decorum kept her from showing emotion, though her inner self might cry out with the desire to call Kevin back. As a lover she wished to ease his pain, but as Lady of the Acoma she must not be ruled by the heart. Mara kept her anguish behind a mask, while her servants worked unobtrusively on her person.

Afraid to move, afraid even to sigh lest her control break into an uncontrollable bout of weeping, Mara called in a small voice for a meal. As much as she longed for release, tears would be shameful for the Lady of the Acoma. To be shaken by a barbarian slave's words, to feel desolate over his absence, was not appropriate for the Lady of a great house. Mara swallowed her pain, which was doubled by knowing she had wounded Kevin in saving herself. She found no relief in restraint, nor did the silent disciplinary chants learned in Lashima's temple help ease the ache. When her breakfast tray arrived, she picked at the food without appetite and stared into empty space. Her servants remained dutiful and silent. Bound to traditions as rigid as her own, they waited for her next command without judgment upon her behavior.

Mara at last signaled, and servants removed the breakfast tray with the food barely touched. Determined to master her inner turmoil, Mara called her advisers to conference. They met in her study, Keyoke alert as always, his Force Commander's plumes the only decoration on his well-scarred, common armor. He had been up before dawn to oversee a patrol on the borders, and his sandals were still dew-drenched and dirty. Nacoya, who usually dragged in the mornings, perked up sharply as she completed her bow and noticed Kevin's absence. She breathed a perceptible sigh of relief: at long last her mistress had come to her senses and sent the tall barbarian away.

Angered by the old woman's worldly-wise satisfaction, Mara repressed a desire to slap Nacoya's wizened cheek. Then, shamed by her inappropriate resentment, she looked for her hadonra's arrival. At the point when she was ready to send her runner slave to find him, Jican arrived. Puffing, he bowed very low and apologized profusely for his tardiness. As Mara belatedly recalled that his delay had been caused by her summarily rearranging the work roster, she cut Jican's apologies short.

"I want a list of every asset we have that you feel might be vulnerable to exploitation by enemies," Mara instructed. "There must be other transactions aside from our silk interests that Desio could damage, either by undercutting prices, or through buying off the guilds who rate the quality of our goods. There are markets he might strangle, trade routes he could disrupt, agents that could be bribed, and buyers who could be threatened. Boats could be sunk, wagons overturned, warehouses burned; none of this must be allowed to occur."

"That does not seem to be Desio's style," a dry voice said from the doorway that opened onto the outer pathways. Arakasi stepped in through the partially opened screen, a shadow against the misty grey of dawn.

Mara barely managed to repress her surprise; Keyoke and the guards in the hallway all lowered their hands from their weapons. The Spy Master bowed and chose a place among the advisers, and the furrow over his brows indicated he had more to say. Mara indicated her permission, and the Spy Master sat at the table, his long fingers folded in his lap.

He continued as if his presence had been expected all along. "Except that the young Lord of the Minwanabi has not held power for long enough to evolve much style." As if he were still formulating his conclusion, the Spy Master stroked the merchant's plaited scalp lock he had cultivated for his latest guise on the road. "One thing is clear, though: Desio is spending huge sums of money upon something. The markets from here to Ambolina are choked with Minwanabi goods, and from the scant information from our clerk in Desio's employ, I would presume the unaccounted moneys are being invested in gifts, bribes, or favors."

Agitated at this news, Mara chewed her lip. "Bribes for what?" she mused softly. "There must be some means of finding out."

Keyoke's deep voice interrupted. "This morning, my soldiers caught a strange herder lurking in the needra fields that border the Tuscalora estates. They took him for questioning, but he died on his dagger rather than name his true master."

Arakasi's eyes slitted speculatively as Nacoya said, "He was probably one of Lord Jidu's spies, sent to check the guard on the bridge across the gorge." The First Adviser pursed her lips, as if thought of the Acoma's southern neighbor brought a bad taste to her mouth. "The Tuscalora chocha-la harvest is nearly ready for market, and by now even Jidu's thick-witted hadonra must guess that his wagons will not be using Mara's bridge to reach the road without paying toll for their passage."

The Spy Master leaned sharply forward. "I would not count on the possibility that herder was Jidu's."

Mara nodded. "Neither do I take your hunches lightly, Arakasi." To Keyoke she added, "We must send a patrol to guard Lord Jidu's borders—unobtrusively, of course. His warriors are good, but they may not realize how much my enemies might gain if their masters' crops burned."

Keyoke nodded, the hands at rest upon his sword unmoving as he contemplated this touchy assignment. Lord Jidu of the Tuscalora might be lax in his spending habits, but his soldiers were fine warriors.

Jican diffidently offered advice on this point. "Lord Jidu

hires on migrant workers from Nesheska to help with the harvest, when his crop is abundant. This has been a bountiful year. Perhaps some of our warriors could disguise themselves as chocha-la pickers and infiltrate the workers in the fields. The overseers would not know every strange face, and since our men would be drawing no pay, their presence might pass unnoticed for many days."

Keyoke expanded this proposition. "Better, and for our warriors' honor, we could stage battle maneuvers in the meadows beside Lord Jidu's estates. Our own workers can infiltrate the groups of Tuscalora pickers, and if trouble arises, they could slip away and alert our troops."

Mara nodded decisively. "Let this be done." She dismissed her advisers, assuring Jican she would study the finance papers brought for her review after the midday meal.

Then, atypically vague and aimless, Mara retired to the garden, seeking solace. But the paths between the flowering kekali bushes seemed lonely and empty in the morning light. The growing heat of day oppressed her. As the Lady wandered among the fragrant akasi blooms, her thoughts returned to her nights in Kevin's arms. Her feelings at the time had seemed so profoundly right, and now his absence made her ache, as if a piece of her being were missing. She contrived a thousand excuses to send for him—only for a moment, to answer a question, to play with Ayaki, to clarify some obscure rule in the game his people called knucklebones. . . .

Mara's eyes sheened over with tears, and she misstepped, stumbling over a raised stone in the path. Her musing dissolved into anger; she needed no reason, she was Mara, Ruling Lady of the Acoma! She could order her slaves where she would without explanation to anyone. Then, wakened to her own folly before she gave in to impulse, she firmed her inward resolve. Her house had stood at the brink of ruin since the death of her father and brother. She must do nothing to risk the gods' displeasure. If she failed, if she lost sight of the ways of her ancestors over an affair of the heart, every Acoma retainer from the least servant in her scullery to her beloved senior advisers would suffer. Their years of loyal service and the honor of her family name must never be sacrificed for the sake of dalliance with a slave. Nacoya had been right. Kevin was a danger to her, best put aside without regret.

Damn the barbarian, she reflected with irritation. Couldn't he learn his place quickly, and become a Tsurani slave? Couldn't he cease his poisonous, perilous thinking? Sadness pushed through her confusion and mixed with annoyance at herself. I am Ruling Lady, she scolded inwardly. I should know what to do. Miserably, Mara admitted, "But I don't."

The servant by the garden gate who awaited his mistress's command called out, "My Lady?"

Mara bit back a needlessly harsh reply. "Send for my son and his nurse. I would play with him for a while."

The man returned a proper bow and hurried to do her bidding. Immediately Mara's mood brightened. Nothing brought a smile to her lips more reliably than the boisterous laughter of her son as he chased after insects, or raced till he was breathless through the garden.

Desio hammered his pudgy fist into the tabletop, causing a candle to topple, and a dozen jade ornaments to scatter and roll upon the carpet. A nervous servant hurried to gather the fallen items, and First Adviser Incomo stepped aside to avoid being struck by the rolling pedestal that had supported a goddess figurine.

"My Lord," he implored cautiously, "you must have patience."

"But Mara is about to gain a vassal!" Desio howled. "That lazy idiot Jidu of the Tuscalora doesn't even see what's coming!"

The servant arose, a half-dozen precious carvings clutched to his chest. Desio chose that moment to bang the table again. The servant cringed, and with shaking hands began to restore the ornaments to their former resting place. Incomo regarded his Lord's flushed face and sighed with restrained impatience. He was weary from days spent indoors, each one filled with long and profitless hours in attendance upon a Lord whose mind held no subtlety. Yet until cousin Tasaio returned, Incomo could do little except endure Desio's ranting.

"If only we could arrange a raid to burn those chocha-la

bushes," the Lord of the Minwanabi complained. "Then Jidu would see his ruin staring him in the face, and we could rescue him with a loan that would compel his loyalty to us. Where did that fatheaded needra bull find the foresight to disguise informants among his workers? Now we dare not intervene without damaging our credibility in the council."

Incomo did not trouble to voice the obvious: that with their current outlays in bribes to get Mara assigned to duty in Dustari, the Minwanabi finances could hardly be extended any thinner; and Lord Jidu was a poor prospect for a loan at any time, with his reputation for drinking, gambling, prostitutes, and bad debts. Not to mention that Mara would most certainly counter a Minwanabi loan by ruining Jidu, ensuring no funds could be recovered. Even if she remained ignorant of an enemy's transaction, the problem would simply recur next year. Incomo knew better than to waste his breath with explanations. He prepared to endure another hour of complaints, when a voice interceded from the doorway.

"The informants among the workers were not Lord Jidu's, but spies set in place by Keyoke," Tasaio said as he entered. "They are the reason two hundred Acoma warriors stage maneuvers on the borders of Jidu's estates."

"Keyoke!" Desio echoed. His face turned deeper purple. "The Acoma Force Commander?"

Tasaio's smile thinned at this statement of the obvious. "Seeing the Tuscalora chocha-la safely through the harvest is in the Acoma's best interest," he reminded.

"Mara's security is too tight," Desio grumbled, but with a shade less heat. While the relieved servant finished with the ornaments and scuttled into the background, the portly young Lord sought his cushions. "We could not send an assassin to poison this Force Commander with any assurance of success—we've already lost a man trying to infiltrate the Acoma herders. And from what we've discovered about that gods-lucky Strike Leader, Lujan, we might not benefit so greatly from Keyoke's death. The upstart might be recently promoted, but he could prove just as able a defender of Acoma honor. I say he needs to be killed, as well, but he guards the Lady's own chambers!" Desio's anger reasserted itself. "And if I could get an assassin that damn close, I would order him to murder Mara instead!"

"True," Tasaio agreed. Before Desio's disgruntlement

could mushroom further, the warrior threw off the mantle that draped his armored shoulders. He tossed the garment to a hovering servant and bowed before his cousin with flawless deference. Then he sat. "My Lord, there has been a new development."

Incomo lost his sour expression, admiring the tact that transformed the Lord's ill-tempered restlessness into attentive eagerness.

Tasaio smiled, revealing straight white teeth. "I have ascertained the identity of Mara's three spies."

Desio was silent a moment. The anger fled his visage, quickly replaced by astonishment. "Wonderful," he said softly. Then, with more pleasure than Incomo had heard since the death of Desio's father, the young Lord repeated himself. "Wonderful!" He clapped his hands together. "This calls for a celebration, cousin." While a servant hastened off to fetch refreshments, and a carafe of a rare vintage sä wine, the Lord sank back on his cushions, eyes narrowed with rapturous speculation. "How do you plan to punish these traitors, cousin?"

Tasaio's expression never changed. "We shall use them as our pawns, send falsified reports to the Acoma, and arrange Keyoke's demise."

"Ah!" Desio echoed his cousin's smile as his thoughts leaped ahead. The plan conceived in words the season before at last seemed a reality to him: to kill the Acoma Force Commander, and force Mara to personally command troops in the field, where Tasaio could seek her out and kill her. He clenched a fist, his pleasure almost sexual in intensity. "I look forward to seeing the Acoma bitch's head on the floor before me. We shall feed the spies our false information this afternoon."

Incomo muffled a grunt of annoyance behind his hand, but if Tasaio shared his impatience with Desio's short-sightedness, he showed no sign. "My cousin," the warrior said evenly, "to send the reports today would be gratifying, I admit. But we must bide our time until precisely the right moment to utilize our knowledge. To use Mara's agents now would certainly reveal our infiltration and waste our advantage. These men are not simple servants but men who, in their own way, are fierce in their loyalty to the Acoma. Like warriors, they have made peace with the gods and are ready

to die at any moment. Should Mara learn that we have uncovered them, she will simply cut them loose. They would
welcome death at her order, rather than betray her trust.
They might try to flee to the safety of her estates, or they
might fall upon their swords. If their courage fails, we might
have the small satisfaction of executing them, but for Minwanabi advantage, we gain nothing."

Incomo added his agreement. "Given the fact Mara has
three agents here, her Spy Master will certainly work to install replacements. We could then be reduced to another
lengthy search to smoke out the new culprits."

Tasaio urged his cousin, "Make no overt move until the
fall. By then I can smuggle enough of our warriors into Dustari to have a fair chance against the army Xacatecas and
Acoma will send against the nomads. All through the summer, Mara must wonder what our crucial move will be. She
will lie awake at night and sweat in the darkness, and send
out informants, and learn nothing. Are we trying to strangle
her grain markets? she will ask. Will we insinuate ourselves
between her and potential allies in the council? Might we raid
outlying warehouses when her finances are vulnerable? Let
her conceive of a thousand possibilities and agonize over
each and every one."

Tasaio sat forward, his amber eyes afire. "Then, after harvest, when she has exhausted herself with worry and taxed
her useless spies to their limits, we strike." Fast as a sword
stroke, the Minwanabi cousin clapped his hands. "Keyoke
dies, along with a company of Mara's best soldiers—perhaps
her First Strike Leader, Lujan, falls as well. The Acoma
household is left without military cohesion, and whatever
surviving officer the lady promotes to wear plumes must assume a post for which he is unpracticed. Troops that have
served under the same commander for thirty years cannot
help but become disrupted." As he looked directly at Desio,
Tasaio's manner embodied confidence. "Now, cousin, suppose we further the Acoma's disarray? Suppose that the summons to Dustari arrives from the High Council before
Keyoke's ashes have a chance to grow cold?"

Desio's eyes lit. Though the plan was as familiar to him as
a prayer, the repetition swept away his doubts; his anger
dissolved, and as Incomo observed his master, he saw the
wisdom of Tasaio's manipulation. When Desio doubted, he

became unstable, a danger to his house, as he acted on impulse. The oath sworn to the Red God at the young Lord's investiture might have brought such a disaster. But like a master tactician, Tasaio would turn the blunder into victory. Not for the first time, Incomo wondered why the gods had not switched the fathers of the two cousins, that the truly brilliant man might wear the Lord's mantle instead of the one who at best was merely competent.

Desio heaved his bulk straight on his cushions and released a deep-chested chuckle. The sound gained force, until the young Lord rocked with laughter. "My cousin, you are brilliant," he gasped between paroxysms, "brilliant."

Tasaio inclined his head. "All for your honor, my Lord, and for the triumph of the Minwanabi."

Summer came, and the Acoma silk samples disrupted all of the southern trading districts' markets. The factors for the northern guilds were taken entirely by surprise. No longer could they market their lesser-quality goods for premium prices in the south. The auctions were an Acoma triumph, and the talk of every clan gathering the breadth of the Tsurani Empire. Supplied with enough orders to busy the cho-ja for five years, Jican had to restrain himself to keep from dancing in his mistress's presence. At one stroke, the Acoma's monetary position had gone from critically overdrawn to abundant. From a well-to-do house without much liquidity, the Acoma had become among the wealthiest in the central Empire, with enough cash reserves to narrow any threat posed by enemies.

Mara smiled at her hadonra's elation. This victory upon the silk market had been a long time in the planning, but she was given no time to appreciate her hard-won fortune. Just one hour after word arrived from the auctions, another messenger delivered fresh news. Her southern neighbor Jidu of the Tuscalora presented himself, asking audience, presumably to beg for Acoma vassalage to save his house from irremediable debt.

This touched off a flurry of activity. The Acoma senior advisers all gathered with Mara to meet Lord Jidu in the great hall. An honor guard in ceremonial armor stood arrayed behind her dais. With Nacoya on her right hand, and

Keyoke and Lujan on her left, the Lady observed the proper forms as the fat Lord—splendid in pale blue robes and clouds of expensive perfumes—presented his appeal. Once Mara's Tsurani soul would have reveled in the sight of an antagonist brought to his knees before her, particularly since Jidu had tried to bully her as if she were an importunate girl after her husband's death. Though she and her honor guard had suffered an attack at this neighbor's command, and she had come close to being killed, the humbling of a man twice her age had lost all sense of triumph. Perhaps Mara had matured in the past year; certainly the exposure to Kevin's alien concepts had changed her.

Where once she would have seen only glory gained for the Acoma, now she could not escape noticing the hatred in Lord Jidu's pouched eyes as he paid her obeisance. She could not block her ears to his overtones of anger, nor entirely absolve herself from his self-made burden of shame. With stiff shoulders, and eyes that sparkled with frustration too private for expression, Lord Jidu admitted his dependence upon Acoma good grace.

Almost, Mara found herself wishing she could turn this event to another ending: allow Jidu to redeem his honor through Acoma generosity, and gain his gratitude and willing alliance. As Jidu ground out his last sentence, she was haunted by Kevin's accusation on the last morning she had seen him: *"Are all Tsurani nobles born cruel?"*

And yet leniency where Lord Jidu was concerned was a dangerous indulgence. In the machinations of the Great Game, mercy could be dispensed only by the unassailably strong; in the small or the weak, it was considered cowardly. The ruler of the Tuscalora might be lax in matters of finance, but he had strong warriors and a gift for strategy on the field. Given his penchant for gross overspending, his loyalty could all too easily be bought by an enemy, and Mara dared not leave such a threat unattended on her southern border. As her vassal, Jidu could make no alliances without Acoma sanction. The honor of his house would be entrusted to Mara's hands, and those of Mara's heirs, for the span of Lord Jidu's living days. Her sovereignty would become such that he could not fall upon his sword without her leave to die.

"You drive hard and dangerous bargains, Lady Mara," the Lord of the Tuscalora warned. Should the Tuscalora effectively be reduced to a pawn for Acoma ambitions, his clan and fellow members of the Yellow Serpent Party would be less willing to treat with her because of Acoma domination over one of their own.

"The Great Game is a dangerous undertaking," Mara replied. Her words were not empty platitude; Arakasi kept her informed of politics afield. If clan or party action brewed up against her family, she would hear well in advance of the fact. Her heart might be divided concerning Jidu, but her options stayed unequivocally clear. "I choose to take your oath, Lord Jidu."

The ruler of the Tuscalora bowed his head. Pearl ornaments chinked on his clothing as he knelt in submission, to recite the formal words. Mara signaled, and Lujan stepped from the ranks, the rare metal sword of her ancestors in his hands. As the Acoma Strike Leader poised the shining blade over Jidu's bent neck, the Lord swore his oath of vassalage, his voice hard and deep with pent-up hatred, and his fists clenched helplessly in rage. He ended the last phrase and arose. "Mistress." He pronounced the word as if he tasted poison. "I ask your leave to withdraw."

On impulse, Mara withheld her consent. While Lord Jidu flushed red, and her honor guard went from ready to tensely nervous, she weighed her need for control against her wish to ease this man's humiliation. "A moment, Jidu," she said finally. As he looked up, suspicious, Mara strove to impart understanding. "The Acoma need allies, not slaves. Give up your resentment over my victory, and willingly join with me, and both of our families will benefit." She sat back upon her seat, speaking as if to a trusted friend. "Lord Jidu, my enemies would not treat you so gently. The Lord of the Minwanabi demands Tan-jin-qu of his vassals." The word she used was ancient, describing an absolute vassalage that granted the overlord powers of life and death over the members of a subservient household. Under Tan-jin-qu, not only would Jidu become Mara's vassal, he would be her virtual slave. "Bruli of the Kehotara refused to continue that abject service to the Minwanabi when he inherited his office, and as a result, Desio withholds many of the protections the Kehotara have known for years. Bruli suffers because he wishes the appearance of independence. I do not shame you by demanding the lives of all your subjects, Jidu."

The stout Lord conceded this point with a curt nod, but his anger and humiliation did not lessen. His was not an enviable position, to be at the mercy of a woman he had once tried to kill. Yet something in Mara's sincerity caused him to listen.

"I will establish policies that benefit both our houses," Mara decreed, "but the daily affairs of your estates remain yours to oversee. Profits from your chocha-la harvest shall stay in the Tuscalora coffers. Your house will pay no tribute to the Acoma. I shall ask nothing from you save your honor to serve ours." Then, given insight on how she might mollify this enemy, Mara added, "My belief in Tuscalora honor is such that I shall entrust the protection of our southern borders to your troops. All Acoma guards and patrols will be withdrawn from the boundary of our two lands."

Keyoke's expression did not change at this development, but he scratched his chin with his thumb, in a long-standing secret code of warning.

Mara reassured her Force Commander with a suggestion of a smile. Then her attention returned to Lord Jidu. "I see you do not trust that friendship might exist between us. I will show my good intentions. To celebrate our alliance, we shall mount a new prayer gate at the entrance to your estate, in glory to Chochocan. This will be followed by a gift of one hundred thousand centuries to clear your past debts, that the profits from this year's harvest may be used for the good of your estate."

Nacoya's eyes widened at the amount, fully a fifth of the funds being forwarded from the silk auction. While Mara could afford to be generous, this honor gift cut considerably into Acoma reserves. Jican was certain to become apoplectic when his mistress ordered the sum transferred to the wastrel Lord of the Tuscalora.

Jidu searched Mara's face. But study as he might, he saw nothing to indicate that she toyed with him. Her words were spoken sincerely. Considerably subdued, he said, "My Lady of the Acoma is generous."

"The Lady of the Acoma strives to be fair," Mara corrected. "A weak ally is a drain, not a benefit. Go, and know that should you have need, the Acoma will answer your call, as we expect you to honor ours," and she gracefully allowed him leave to withdraw.

No longer angered, but profoundly puzzled by his sudden shift in fortune, Jidu of the Tuscalora left the hall.

As the last of his blue-armored guardsmen marched out, Mara abandoned her formal posture. She rubbed tired eyes and inwardly cursed her weariness. Months had passed since she sent Kevin off to oversee the crew clearing forests. She still slept poorly at nights.

"My beautiful Lady, let me compliment you on your deft handling of a particularly vicious dog," said Lujan with a respectful bow. "Lord Jidu is now well collared, and he may only whine and snap at your command, but he dare not bite."

Mara focused her attention with an effort. "At least we won't need soldiers guarding that cursed needra bridge day and night after this."

Keyoke burst into sudden laughter, to the astonishment of both Lujan and Mara, for the old soldier rarely showed pleasure.

"What?" said Mara.

"Your stated intention to strip our southern border had me concerned, my Lady." The Force Commander shrugged. "Until I understood that without needing to patrol the Tuscalora side of our boundary, we have freed several companies to reinforce more critical defenses. And with no further worries from the north, Lord Jidu can mount more vigilant defenses on other fronts. We have effectively gained another thousand warriors to guard one larger estate."

Nacoya joined in. "And with your generous gift, daughter, Jidu can afford to ensure his men are properly armed and armored, and that cousins can be called to serve to expand his army."

Mara smiled at the approval. "Which will be my first . . . ah, 'request' of my new vassal. His warriors are good, but they lack the numbers for our needs. When Jidu recovers from wounded pride, I shall 'ask' that his Force Commander consult with Keyoke on a the best ways to protect our common interests."

Keyoke returned a guarded nod. "Your father would look upon your farsightedness proudly, Lady Mara." He bowed in respect. "I must return to duty."

Mara granted him permission to leave. Beside her, Lujan inclined his plumed head. "Your warriors will all drink to your health, pretty Lady." A playful frown creased his forehead. "Though we might do well to assign a patrol to ensure that Lord Jidu does not tumble headfirst from his litter and bash in his skull on the way home."

"Why would he do that?" Mara demanded.

Lujan shrugged. "Drink can spoil the best man's balance, Lady. Jidu smelled like he had been guzzling since dawn."

Mara's brows rose in surprise. "You could smell through all that perfume?"

The Strike Leader returned an irreverent gesture around the scabbard of the ancestral sword. "You didn't have to lean over the Lord's bared neck with a blade."

Mara rewarded him with a laugh, but her moment of levity did not last. She waved dismissal to her honor guard, then retired to her study with Nacoya. Since her wedding to Buntokapi, she was disinclined to linger in the great hall, and with the redheaded Midkemian slave sent away, she found no relief in solitude. Day after day, she immersed herself in accounts with Jican, or reviewed clan politics with Nacoya, or played with Ayaki, whose current passion was the wooden soldiers carved for him by her officers. Yet even when Mara sat on the nursery's waxed wooded floor and arranged troops for her son—who played at being Lord of the Acoma, and who regularly routed whole armies of Minwanabi enemies— she could not escape the realities. Desio and Tasaio might die a hundred deaths on the nursery floor, to Ayaki's bloodthirsty and childish delight, but all too likely, the boy who played at vanquishing his enemies would himself become sacrificed to the Red God, victim of the intrigue that shadowed his house.

When Mara was not fretting about enemies, she sought diversion from heartache. Nacoya had assured her that time would ease her desires. But the days passed, and the dust of the dry season rose in clouds as this year's needra culls were driven to market. Mara still woke in the night, miserable with longing for the man who had taught her that love could be gentle. She missed his presence, his blundering ways, his odd thoughts, and most of all his intuitive grasp of those moments when she most wanted sympathy, but was too much the proud Ruling Lady to show her need.

His willingness to give strength and his kindness were as rain to a heart parched by troubles. Damn that man, she thought to herself. He had her trapped more helplessly than any enemy ever would. And perhaps, for that reason, Nacoya was right. He was more dangerous to her house than the most vicious of her foes, for somehow he had insinuated himself within her most personal defenses.

A week passed, then another. Mara called on the cho-ja Queen and was invited to tour the caverns where the silk makers industriously worked to meet the auction contracts. A worker escorted Mara through the hive to the level where dyers and weavers labored to transform the gossamer fibers into finished cloth. The tunnels were dim and cool after the sunlight outside. Always when Mara visited the hives, she felt as though she entered another world. Cho-ja workers rushed past her, speedily completing errands. They moved too swiftly for the eye to follow through tunnels lit by globes that shed pale light. Despite the gloom, the insectoid creatures never blundered into one another. Mara never felt more than a soft brush as the rapidly moving creatures negotiated the narrowest passages. The chamber where the silk was spun was wide and low. Here Mara raised a hand to make sure the jade pins that held her hair would not scrape the ceiling.

The escort cho-ja paused and waved a forelimb. "The workers hatched for spinning are specialized," it pointed out.

When Mara's eyes adjusted to the near darkness, she saw a crowd of shiny, chitinous bodies hunched over drifts of raw silk fibers. They had comblike appendages just behind their foreclaws, and what looked like an extra fixture behind the one that approximated the function of the human thumb. While they crouched on their hind limbs, the forelimbs carded fibers that seemed almost too delicate to handle without breaking. Then the midlimbs took over and, in a whirl of motion, spun the fibers into thread. The strand created by each cho-ja spinner led out of the chamber through a slot in the far wall. Beyond this partition, dyers labored over steaming cauldrons, setting color into the threads in one continuous process. The fibers left the dye pots and passed through yet another partition, where small winged drone females fanned the air vigorously to dry them. Then the passage opened out into a wide, bright chamber, with domed roof and skylights that reminded Mara of Lashima's temple in Kentosani. Here the weavers caught up the colored strands and performed magic, threading the fine silk weft through the warp into the finest cloths in the Empire.

The sight held Mara in thrall. Here, where Tsurani protocol held little importance, she acted like a girl, pestering the escort worker with questions. She fingered the finished cloth and admired the colors and patterns. Then, before she was aware of herself, she paused before a bolt of cloth woven of cobalt and turquoise with fine patterns of rust and ocher threaded through it. Unconsciously, she imagined how this fabric might set off Kevin's red hair; her smile died. No matter what the diversion, it never lasted. Always her thoughts returned to the barbarian slave, however much she might long to sink her attention into something else. Suddenly the rows of bright silks seemed to lose their luster.

"I wish to go back, now, and take my leave of your Queen," Mara requested.

The cho-ja escort bowed its acquiescence. Its thought processes differed from a human's, and it did not think her change of mind was either unmannerly or abrupt.

How much simpler life must be for a cho-ja worker, Mara thought. They concerned themselves entirely with the present, immersed in the immediacy of the moment and guided by the will of their Queen, whose interest was the needs of the hive. These glossy black creatures lived out their days untroubled by the thousand nagging needs that human flesh was heir to. Envying them their peace of mind, Mara wended her way back through the press toward the Queen's chamber. Today, unlike every other day, her curiosity was quiescent. She did not long to beg the silk makers' secret from the cho-ja Queen, nor did she make her usual request to visit the nurseries, where newly hatched cho-ja young blundered on awkward legs to complete their first steps.

Her escort guided her to the junction of two major passages, and was about to turn downward to the deepest level where the Queen's chamber lay when a warrior in a plumed helm raised a forelimb and intercepted them. Confronted by the razor-sharp edge of chitin that the cho-ja could wield like a second sword, Mara stopped at once; though the edge was turned away at an angle that indicated friendliness, she did not know why she was being stopped. Cho-ja did not think like individuals, but reacted according to the mind of their hive, and the consciousness that directed that collective purpose was the Queen's. Cho-ja reactions were frighteningly fast, and their moods could change as suddenly.

"Lady of the Acoma," intoned the warrior cho-ja. He squatted down into the same bow he would give to a Queen, and as his plumed helm bobbed, Mara recognized Lax'l, Force Commander of the hive.

Reassured that his intentions were not hostile, she relaxed and returned the nod due a commander of Lax'l's rank. "What does your Queen require of me?"

Lax'l stood erect and assumed a statuelike stillness that seemed unreal amid the bustle of workers that continually passed around him and the Lady with her escort. "My Queen requires nothing of you, but wishes your best health. She sent me to report that a messenger has arrived from your estate house asking with some urgency for your presence. He waits on the surface."

Mara sighed in frustration. Her morning should have been free of commitments; she had scheduled no meetings until afternoon, when she was due to review figures from the needra sales with Jican. Something must have come up, though it was summer's end, and the game usually underwent a lull as most Lords involved themselves with finances prior to the annual harvest. "I must return to find out what has happened," the Lady of the Acoma said regretfully to Lax'l. "Please convey my apology to your Queen."

The cho-ja Force Commander inclined his head. "My Queen returns her regards, and says further that she hopes the news that awaits you holds no word of misfortune." He flicked a forelimb to the escort worker, and Mara found herself turned around and bustled toward the upper tunnels almost before she had a chance to think.

As she stepped outside, the sudden reentry into sunlight dazzled her. Mara squinted against the glare while her eyes adjusted. She made out the presence of two officers' plumes among the slaves who awaited with her litter. One was Xaltchi, a junior officer recently promoted by Keyoke for his valor in defense of a caravan. The other, with a longer, more sumptuous plume, could only be Lujan. Surprised that he should be bearing the message, and not a lesser servant or her runner slave, Mara frowned. Whatever news awaited her would not be a matter for ears that could not be trusted. She dismissed her cho-ja escort with absentminded politeness, and hurried toward her Strike Leader, who had seen her emerge from the hive and who strode briskly to meet her.

"My Lady." Lujan completed a hasty if proper bow, then took her arm and guided her through the traffic of cho-ja workers streaming to and from the hive. The instant they reached open ground, but well before they came within earshot of the slaves within the litter, Lujan said, "Lady, you have a visitor. Jiro of the Anasati is currently in Sulan-Qu, awaiting your word. His father, Tecuma, has sent him to discuss a matter too sensitive to entrust to a common messenger."

Mara's frown deepened. "Go back and send a runner to town," she instructed her Strike Leader. "I will see Jiro at once."

Lujan saw her to her litter, helped her inside, and bowed. Then he was off at a run down the lane that led back to the estate house. The bearers shouldered the Lady's litter and Xaltchi mustered the small company of soldiers who marched as her escort. More slowly, the cortege followed in Lujan's footsteps.

"Pick up the pace," Mara commanded through the curtains. She fought to keep the concern from her voice. Before her marriage to Buntokapi of the Anasati, that ancient house had been second behind only the Minwanabi among Acoma enemies. Since she had engineered her husband's death, the family had more cause than ever to hate her. Only the common interest in Ayaki, son of Bunto and grandson of Lord Tecuma, kept the two houses from open conflict. The thread that held that alliance together was slender indeed. For very little excuse, Tecuma might wish her out of the way, so that he could install himself as regent of the Acoma until Ayaki came of age to assume the title of Lord.

A matter too sensitive for even a bonded messenger was unlikely to be good news. A familiar tightness clutched Mara's middle. She had never underestimated her enemies' ability to plot, but lately a lack of any overt threat had caused her to come dangerously close to complacence. Mentally she readied herself for a difficult interview; she would need five hundred warriors armored and at the ready, and an honor guard of twelve within the hall where she received Jiro. Any less would offer him insult.

Mara settled her head against the cushions, sweating in her thin silks. Maddeningly, endlessly, between planning that her life might depend on, she thought of a barbarian slave, who at this moment stood in hot sunlight directing men cutting timber into fencing, six rails to a span, and shoulder-high to a tall warrior. The needra fields were nearly finished, too late for this season's calves, but well in time to fatten the weanlings for the late-fall markets. Mara blotted her brow in fussy annoyance. She had enough on her mind without adding the question of what she was going to do with Kevin when the new pastures were finished. Perhaps she would sell the man . . . But her mind dwelt on this idea only a moment before she resolved that some other task must be found to keep him away.

Mara took her place beside the entrance to the estate house, while Jiro's litter and escort approached the Acoma borders. The First Adviser stood at her side, looking uncomfortable beneath sumptuous fine robes and jewels. Although Nacoya enjoyed the authority inherited with her promotion, in some things she outspokenly preferred the duties of a nurse. State dress was one of them. Had Mara been less nervous, she might have smiled at the thought of the elderly servant resenting the fussing and attentions of maids that Mara had been forced to endure life long, at Nacoya's tireless instigation. The only surcease the Acoma daughter had known had been during her novitiate in the temple of Lashima. Those days, with their tranquil simplicity and hours of scholarly study, seemed far behind her now.

Mara glanced about her to be sure all was in readiness. Amid the clutter of footmen, soldiers, and servants, she noted one person missing. "Where's Jican?" she whispered to Nacoya.

The First Adviser inclined her head, forced to raise a hand to rescue a loosened hairpin. She reset the errant finery with an impatience that had much to do with being awakened from a nap for the purpose of greeting a personage still regarded with venom. Nacoya's dislike of Buntokapi extended to all his relations, and though Mara knew she could rely on the ancient woman to maintain perfect protocol, the household was likely to suffer several days of grouchy aftermath.

"Your hadonra is in the kitchens, making sure the cooks slice only first-quality fruit for the refreshment trays," the former nurse answered tersely.

Mara raised an eyebrow. "He's more of an old lady than you are. As if the cook needs to be told how to prepare a meal. He would do no less than his best for the sake of Acoma honor."

Nacoya whispered, "I told Jican to supervise. The cooks might wish to slip an Anasati guest something less than appetizing—their view of honor is different than yours, daughter." Buntokapi had not made himself popular in the kitchen, either. Still, Mara kept to herself the thought that even the Acoma chief cook would not shame her house for something as petty as slipping sour fruit to Jiro—no matter how much he would have enjoyed doing so.

Mara glanced at Nacoya. Silently she considered how easily she had come to regard her house servants as part of the furnishings. That they had actively resented Bunto's brutality as much as she had never occurred to her; she remembered how rough he had been on them. Her servants and scullions had perhaps suffered worse than she during Buntokapi's tenure as Lord, and belatedly, Mara remembered to sympathize. Had she been one of those kitchen girls—or her brother, father, or lover—who had been dragged into service in Bunto's bed, she, too, might have been tempted to feed his brother leavings from the garbage set aside for the jigabirds. Mara repressed a smile at the thought. "I must pay more attention to the feelings of my staff, Nacoya, lest I perpetuate Bunto's thoughtlessness."

Nacoya only nodded. Time for talk was past, as the painted red-and-yellow litter and rows of marching warriors filed into the dooryard. Mara fingered the emerald and jade bracelet on her wrist and strove to maintain decorum as the Anasati honor guard snapped to a halt and Jiro's bearers set down his litter before her doorway.

At the last possible moment, Jican hurried through the door to take his place beside Nacoya and Tasido, who as senior Acoma Strike Leader commanded the Lady's honor guard. Wishing Keyoke or Lujan were present in his stead,

Mara observed the Anasati soldiers through narrowed eyes. They were not relaxed but spaced in a formation that allowed free access to draw weapons. She had expected no less, yet to be confronted by such readiness for hostility with an elderly officer in charge was not a comfortable circumstance. Old Tasido had arthritis and cataracts; in better times, he would have seen honorable retirement by now. But the Acoma forces had taken too many casualties on the barbarian world when Lord Sezu was betrayed to his death for even one officer to be spared. In another year, or perhaps two, the old man would be given a hut near the river where he could live his remaining days in peace. But today not one sword could be dispensed with.

Mara had not seen Jiro since her wedding day nearly four years past. Curious as well as cautious, she watched the young man step from his litter. He was well dressed, but not in the gaudy style preferred by his father. His robe was black silk, sparingly trimmed with red tassels. His belt was tastefully adorned with shell and lacquer bosses, and his hair was cut plainly as a warrior's. He stood taller than his brother Buntokapi had; his build was leaner and he held himself with considerably more grace. The face resembled his mother's, with high cheekbones and a haughty mouth. His square jaw kept him from looking overbred, but his hands were fine as a woman's. He was a handsome man, save for a certain cruelty betrayed around his lips and eyes.

Jiro bowed with sarcastic perfection.

"Welcome to the house of the Acoma," Mara greeted without inflection. She returned his bow, but kept the courtesy brief, in pointed reference to the fact that the Anasati son had brought an armed retinue into her courtyard out of all proportion for a social visit. As was her right as senior in rank, she waited for her guest to begin the formal enquiries. After a pause through which Jiro kept still in the expectation that Mara might blunder and ask after his health, he finally said, "Are you well, Lady?"

Mara gave a curt nod. "I am well, thank you. Are you well, Jiro?"

The young man smiled, but his eyes stayed serpent-cold. "I am well, as is the father who sent me." He rested a languid hand on the dagger sheathed at his belt. "I can see that you are well also, Mara, and if anything, grown more beautiful in motherhood. It is a pity for one so lovely to be widowed so young. Such a waste."

If his tone was impeccably polite, his words bordered upon insult. This was no visit of reconciliation. Aware that his attitude approached that of an overlord visiting a vassal, Mara swept up her robes and led the way through the entry, leaving him to follow like a servant. Let him play his parlor games too long, and she might be maneuvered into putting up with him for more than the afternoon. Since Tecuma would be expecting the boy to bring back whatever information on the Acoma he might be able to pry loose, Mara had no intention of letting Jiro gain excuse to stay the night.

Servants had laid trays of light refreshments in the great hall. Mara seated herself on the dais. She appointed Nacoya the place on her right, and granted Jican the permission to retire that he longed for. Then she waved for Jiro to make himself comfortable on the cushions across from her; the place she accorded him was that of an equal. Given this voluntary courtesy, he could not protest the fact that Tasido and his subofficers would be standing at his back. To place her honor guard on the dais was done only when hostile parties met for parley. This not overtly being the case, Jiro's bodyguard must remain by the door. Mara's most trusted house servant plied her noble guest with a bowl to wash his hands, and a towel. He politely inquired what Jiro would prefer to drink, his timing perfectly arranged to keep the guest occupied with trivia. The Lady of the Acoma spoke before Jiro could seize the chance to regroup. "Since a man would not require so many soldiers on a visit to console his brother's widow, I presume your father has some message for me?"

Jiro stiffened. He recovered his bearing with admirable control and looked up; Mara had struck hard and to the heart. She had turned the memory of the brother who had died to further Acoma standing in the game back upon him, and also implied that Jiro wished to "console" his brother's widow in a manner more intimate than Tsurani custom found acceptable—and further, that he was nothing more than his father's errand boy. It was the verbal equivalent of a slap to the face. The look the Anasati son turned upon her was icy and possessed a fathomless hatred.

Mara hid a shiver. By Nacoya's white-lipped stillness, she

was aware that she had made a mistake; she had also underestimated Jiro's enmity. This boy despised her with a passion beyond his years. In his cold silence, Mara realized he would lurk like the poisonous relli of the swamps, biding his time until he saw his opening. He would not move against her until his trap was perfected and he was absolutely certain of his victory.

"I will not repeat the rumors concerning my Lady's preference in lovers since the loss of her noble husband," Jiro said with a diction so clear that, while not overloud, could be understood by even the door servants. To emphasize how demeaning the matter was, he raised his drink and sipped with a steady hand. "And, yes, I did leave off an important trade transaction in Sulan-Qu to stop here, by my father's suggestion. He has heard of secret meetings between certain council members that he believes might indicate plots that pose danger to his grandson, Ayaki. As regent to the Acoma heir, you are being sent a warning."

"Your words are vague," Nacoya pointed out with the acerbity of an elder who has lived long enough to see many a youth succumb to folly. Using a tone well practiced from her days as a servant in the nursery, she added, "Since neither the Anasati nor the Acoma stand to gain if Ayaki fails to inherit his Lordship, I suggest you be more specific."

Jiro inclined his head with the barest suggestion of malice. "My father is not privy to these plots, First Adviser, dearest Lady. His allies have not spoken directly to him, which he believes might be due to heavy bribes. But he has eyes and ears in strategic places that see and hear for him, and he wished you to know that factions who are partial to the Minwanabi have met more than once in secret. The Omechan were heard to compliment Lord Desio's restraint in the face of Acoma affront, and while they are powerful, their dependence upon Minwanabi goodwill in the Alliance for War makes them chary of losing supporters at this time. More than the Omechan applaud Desio's cold-blooded planning, and that approval works against your heir's interests. In short, you have few allies voicing support in the High Council."

Mara waved for a servant to carry away the refreshment tray, which Jiro had not touched. Although she regretted provoking Jican's disappointment that the finest fruits in the kitchens should be spurned, she was too tense to indulge herself. She did not like the way Jiro's eyes darted about, taking in every detail of the Acoma hall, servants, and guardsmen. His interest held the hunger of an officer in an enemy camp who gathered information in preparation for an assault. Never as straightforward as his elder brother, Halesco, Jiro thought in subtleties that were rooted in ambition. Mara strove to sort out how much of what he spoke was truth, and how much was exaggeration designed to scare her. "What you say is not exactly unknown to me, Jiro, at least in general. Surely your father need not have sent you from your important transaction to tell me these things," she ventured, testing. "A bonded messenger might have sufficed."

Jiro returned a detached poise. "This is a family matter," he replied. "My father wished you to understand that the plot within the council is deeply disguised, and clever. He would not compromise his sources by trusting a hired runner. The sending of a bonded guildsman would remain on public record, and watching enemies would know. Desio has paid to have every guildbook in Sulan-Qu open for his inspection. A message from Anasati sources would be too obvious." Jiro inclined his head with the barest suggestion of irony. "But none would question an uncle who stops to visit a fatherless nephew."

"Not even one who interrupts an important transaction to pay social calls on a three-year-old?" Nacoya interceded politely.

Jiro did not even blush, which required commendable control. "We are none of us in a position to trade accusations, as the First Adviser to my brother's widow should remember. Besides, what harm if Desio thinks we share secrets? He can only imagine what they may be." His look at Mara was a disturbing mix of covetousness and hatred.

Mara regarded Jiro with a searching stare until he could not but feel uncomfortable. His family had treated Buntokapi as an awkward afterthought; it had been their own neglect of his education that had permitted her an opening to exploit. Although the fact that she had taken advantage of a man's frustrated desires and clumsiness did not make her proud, Mara had reviewed the situation through eyes tempered by regret; she knew she did bear all the guilt by herself.

Tired of Jiro's intensity, and more stung than she dared to

admit at his implied slander of Kevin, Mara prompted an end to the visit. "I thank you for the news of Desio's compromising the commercial guilds—that is valuable to know. And of the Omechan willingness to pander to the Minwanabi. You have done your duty by your father, none could say different. I would not delay you from completing your important transactions in Sulan-Qu."

Jiro returned the driest smile, and anticipated her closing line. "Unless I should wish to stay for a meal, which your servants would take elaborate and lengthy pains to prepare?" He inclined his head in the negative. "Your company has no compare. But I am forced by circumstances to decline. I shall be on my way."

"Without so much as setting eyes on the fatherless nephew you came to visit," Nacoya interjected. More pointedly dry than usual, she turned shrewd eyes on her mistress. "Your guest sets great store by your security, my Lady, that he feels confident no rumors of this will reach the wrong ears."

Now Jiro did change color, but his pallor was more due to annoyance than embarrassment. He rose and bowed shortly to Mara. "I see that the regent for the Acoma heir learns much by keeping the company of sour old women."

"They keep impertinent young men in their places far more readily than their younger, prettier sisters." Mara rose also. "Return my regards to your father, Jiro."

The fact that the young noble bore no title before his name plainly vexed him no end. Given this insight into what might have motivated his bitterness, Mara saw her guest to the door. He climbed into his litter without once looking back at her, and snapped his curtains closed the instant she completed the obligatory words wishing a departing guest safe journey. As the bearers bore up their haughty burden, and the Anasati soldiers formed into columns and began their departure down the lane, Nacoya sighed with relief. "Thank the gods you did not marry that one, daughter of my heart. He is much too clever for his own good."

"He bears me no friendship, that much is certain." Mara turned back into the cooler shadow of the house, her brows tightened into a frown.

Nacoya regarded her mistress keenly. "What did you expect, after you chose his younger brother over him? From the first instant you and Tecuma agreed to your handfast with Buntokapi, that boy began to hate. He considered himself the better candidate for your title, and he will carry that grudge to his dying day. More, he hates doubly because at the root he desires you. He would take you still, should you but allow him your bed." Then the old woman sighed. "Yet after, he would still kill you, daughter, for I think this one has been permanently twisted by envy."

Mara captured a strayed wisp of hair, then lowered her hand, the rare metal bracelet on her wrist jangling. "Lashima's folly, but men's pride is easily bruised!" Her eyes betrayed pain that had nothing to do with Jiro's anger over her past rejection of him.

Nacoya shook a finger at her. "You're thinking of that no-good barbarian again."

Mara ignored the accusation. "Kevin has nothing to do with this. Why should Jiro come all this way, and take such elaborate lengths to provoke me, all on the excuse of some not so very well documented clandestine meetings within the council?"

Now Nacoya looked shocked. "My Lady, you would do well to heed Lord Tecuma's warning—his spies may not be as widespread as yours, but they are no less gifted. Never mind that Jiro's passions clouded the delivery. You stand in very grave danger."

Mara dismissed her First Adviser's concern with irritation. "Nacoya, surely I have enough of real import on my mind without burdening myself with trivia. If there was plotting afoot in the council, surely Arakasi's network would keep me informed of the fact."

Sunlight fell through a half-opened screen, catching the First Adviser's face, like some wizened caricature of a cameo. "Lady," she said gravely, "you rely far more on Arakasi's spies than you should. They are only men. They cannot see into Desio's mind, and they cannot hear every whisper that is exchanged in dark corners behind closed doors. They can be in only so many places at one time. And as mortal men, they may be corrupted or misled."

"Nacoya, you worry beyond duty's call. You have my permission to retire and pursue some recreation." While Nacoya completed a stiff-backed bow, Mara pulled at her heavy robes. She wanted a bath and a change, and maybe some players to make her laugh. Her morning with the cho-ja seemed very far away. Jiro's icily schooled antagonism bothered her far more than Tecuma's concerns with the council; and she missed Kevin, unbearably. Starved for his friendly company in a way that made her ache, she impulsively sent her runner to fetch a scribe. When the man she had summoned made his bow, burdened down with chalks and slates, she cut his courtesy short with a gesture. "Go out to the new needra fields and observe the workers. Make a transcription of everything that happens there, with particular regard for the redheaded man who is slave master. I wish to know all that he does and says, so that I may evaluate the efficiency of his work team."

The scribe bowed low over his satchel. It was not his place to question his mistress's will; but he left with a puzzled look, for the Lady concerned herself with a detail that was normally her hadonra's responsibility. In the days he had served since apprenticeship, the scribe had never received so unusual a request.

8. *RECONCILIATION*

Tasaio smiled.

Startled by his unusual expression, the Lord of the Minwanabi watched suspiciously as his cousin crossed the grand hall upon his return from his trip downriver. Then, recalling that Sulan-Qu was the city nearest the Acoma estates, Desio recovered his wits. "What has passed?" he inquired as his cousin paused and bowed before the dais, not the large one with its throne, but a cushioned level off to one side reserved for less formal occasions where Desio was not forced to loom over his councilors.

To one side, Force Commander Irrilandi waited without resentment to listen to the man who had supplanted him in everything but title. Tasaio was both nobly born and a brilliant field commander; as the Warlord's second-in-command in the campaign on the barbarian world, he was surrogate for Desio as Clan Warchief. By Tsurani tradition, service to such greatness could bring only honor to the Minwanabi.

"My Lord," said Tasaio, rising in full and flawless courtesy before his cousin, "it has begun."

Desio tensed with anticipation. Inspired by his cousin's example, he had undertaken to practice the martial traditions. As he sat in his finery on a brocaded mat, his waistline sagged less, and his florid face had lost its puppyish appearance. Diligent work on his swordsmanship had improved his skills to the point where his sparring partners need not offer a blatant opening to allow their Lord the victory. Desio no longer cut a comic figure when he wore armor for ceremonies; the older servants whispered among themselves that the boy carried himself at least as well as his father, Jingu, had in his youth and perhaps was even more manly.

Physical prowess was not the least of Desio's gains. In Tasaio's absence, he had successfully pressed his claim as Warchief of Clan Shonshoni, the first public step toward recovering the prestige surrendered upon his father's death. More assured than ever before, Desio drew himself up to full height. Afternoon sun from the skylight slashed down upon his shoulders, raising sparkles from his precious metal ornaments. "Tell me the details!"

Tasaio handed his helm to a waiting servant. He ruffled sweat-slicked hair from his temples, then began unbuckling his gauntlets while he spoke. "We have again received word from Mara's clansmen." Two servants rushed forward; one poured water from a ewer into the bowl held by the other. Without break, Tasaio rinsed hands and face, then allowed himself to be dried by a third servant. "They would consider the utter obliteration of Mara's house a difficult proposition, but they are also disinclined to incur our wrath should they discover it an accomplished fact."

The servant folded the soiled linen and departed, while from the shadowed alcove beside Desio's cushions Incomo thrust forth a withered hand. "My Lord, it is as Bruli of the Kehotara claimed."

With novel lack of petulance, Desio allowed his First Adviser to continue. "Clan Hadama is politically factioned. They squabble among themselves enough that they never keep common war council. They will seek no quarrel with Clan Shonshoni, yet we must be cautious. We must not grant them incentive to unite. In the heat of crisis, I suggest they would put aside differences and come to Mara's aid should she call upon clan honor with any justification. We must ensure we give them no such cause lest we face an entire clan. We would be forced to marshal Clan Shonshoni in turn."

"Any conflict of that magnitude would bring intervention from the Assembly of Magicians," Tasaio pointed out. "Which would be disastrous." He flicked a fingernail that harbored an invisible fleck of dirt. "So we act with circumspection, and after Mara and her son are dead, Clan Hadama will cluck their collective tongues, mouth regrets, and go about their usual business, yes?"

Desio held up his hand for silence and considered.

Incomo withheld his urge to press counsel, pleased by his Lord's newfound maturity. Tasaio's influence had proved a gift of the gods, for the young Lord seemed on his way to becoming the confident, decisive leader not seen in the Minwanabi great hall since his grandfather's reign.

Now sensitive to nuance, the Lord surmised, "So you have determined the moment to spring the first part of our trap?"

Tasaio smiled again, broadly and slowly as a sarcat's yawn. "Less time than I had anticipated. But not as swiftly as we would like. Word must be passed through the Acoma spies that we are moving to attack their cursed silk shipments."

Desio nodded. "Logical choice. We were punished enough by the chaos caused by their surprise entry into the silk auction. Mara's advisers will readily believe that we raid to regain some lost wealth and damage her ill-gotten profits."

Tasaio fingered the marks left by his gauntlet straps, yet if this was a sign of eagerness, the rest of his demeanor stayed cool. "On your word, should we let it be known that 'bandits' will raid the caravan heading down the river road to Jamar?"

Once, Desio would have nodded in transparent eagerness. Now he frowned in concentration. "Foot troops will not be enough. Be sure to send the impression that we hold boats in readiness as well. Should Mara's hadonra reroute the caravan by barge, have her understand that river 'pirates' will fall upon them."

"But of course, my Lord!" Tasaio no longer needed to act as if the suggestion were novel. "Such tactics will force Keyoke to send a strongly guarded decoy caravan by the main highway, while he personally escorts a small, fast-moving band of wagons across Tuscalora lands."

"Where will you take him?" Desio asked, intense concentration on his face.

Tasaio signaled the runner slave, who in turn summoned the aide who waited outside the main hall. The warrior entered, bearing a heavy roll of parchment. He made proper obeisance before his Lord, then threw his burden to the floor, where two servants rushed to unroll it.

Tasaio drew his sword. In a short, neat movement, he indicated the meandering blue line that represented the river Gagajin. "Once through Sulan-Qu, Mara will send her wagons southward on the Great River Road, or else she will put them aboard barges and take the water route. She will draw much attention upon this false caravan, so she will not risk her real wares to follow through the woodlands to the east of her holdings. It is too close to the false cargo." His sword scratched across the river that offered the main avenue of trade through the heart of the Empire; east and west, major roads were inked in red lines. "Here," said Tasaio, stabbing his sword at a minor line twining south from the Acoma border. "Keyoke is certain to cross south through Tuscalora lands and pass through the foothills of the Kyamaka Mountains. He will make for the delta north of the Great Swamp, and continue directly for Jamar, gateway to the southern markets."

Leaning forward over the chart, Desio anticipated him. "You'll attack in the foothills?"

Tasaio tapped his weapon at a serpentine bend in the road. "At this narrow pass. Once into it, Keyoke's forces can be bottled up at both ends, and with the Red God's blessing, no Acoma warrior will survive."

Desio tapped his full lips with a finger, silent. "But Mara might keep her Force Commander with her. Suppose her Strike Leader, Lujan, is sent in Keyoke's place?"

Tasaio shrugged. "Mara has shown cleverness in trade, but in battle she must delegate command. Her options besides Keyoke and Lujan are a half-blind old Strike Leader soon to retire and two others newly promoted. She'll do the only intelligent thing: send her proven officers with her two caravans, and trust her cho-ja allies' raw power to protect her home estates."

Yet Desio was not satisfied. "Can we arrange an accident for Lujan, also?"

Tasaio considered this with abstracted interest. "Difficult. Mara's soldiers will be expecting trouble, and even a gifted assassin would be unlikely to get near their commander."

"Unless . . ." Desio arose from his mat and squatted on the stair above the map. After a studied moment, he said, "What if we arrange to have our young Strike Leader come rushing down to aid his commander?"

Tasaio's eyes widened. "You'll need to be clearer, my Lord."

Pleased to have surprised his cousin even slightly, Desio

set his chin on clenched knuckles. "We 'expose' one Acoma spy, torture him enough to convince him we're serious, and while doing so, brag about our trap—we'll even tell him where it will occur. Then, at the moment Keyoke cannot be recalled, we'll let him escape."

Tasaio's face was expressionless. "And he'll run home to the Acoma." Deliberate in his movements as always, he returned his sword to its scabbard. The click as the laminated blade slid home resounded through the near-empty hall.

"About here," Desio went on, shifting position to touch the river road line with his toe, "just to the south of Sulan-Qu, our released spy will encounter Lujan and his caravan. By then the Acoma Strike Leader will be jumping at every sound, expecting our overdue ambush. When he hears that Keyoke is the real target, he'll turn his army and race downriver to try a rescue." Smugly Desio concluded, "By the time relief arrives, Keyoke will be dead and our men in position to ambush Lujan's force."

Tasaio's lips thinned in serious doubt. "I think the plan a bit overbold, my Lord. Removing Keyoke with his little troop should pose no problem, but Lujan will be commanding as many as three companies of a hundred, hundred and twenty men each, hot for a battle."

Desio brushed such concerns away. "At the worst, Lujan will prove too difficult a foe and we'll withdraw, leaving Keyoke dead and the Acoma's most likely new Force Commander shamed by his failure to effect a rescue.

"Better," Desio finished, a finger upraised for emphasis, "with a little luck, we could remove at one stroke the only other able field commander the Acoma bitch has. That's worth the risk."

"My Lord—" Tasaio began.

"Do it!" Desio shouted, overriding his cousin's caution. Then, with all his lordly authority, he calmly repeated his command. "Do it, cousin."

Tasaio bowed his head, turned, and left. While the aide who had carried the map hurried belatedly to catch up, Desio motioned to Incomo. "I shall be drilling with my personal guard for the next hour. Afterward I shall bathe. Instruct the hadonra to have serving girls ready. Then I shall dine."

Uncaring that he had demeaned his First Adviser with

instructions more suitably put to a body servant, the Lord of the Minwanabi arose. Slaves hastened to set crumpled cushions to rights and to clear away trays that held discarded fruit rinds. Force Commander Irrilandi, in his orange-plumed helm, trailed his master unobtrusively from the hall. Incomo watched with narrowed eyes. As the doors boomed closed, and only slaves and servants remained, he bent his leathery neck and regarded the map still spread on the floor by the dais, creased now where the Lord had trodden across it. Incomo descended the stair. Posed like a shore bird with one foot in Lash Province and the other poised over the border to Hokani, he shook his head sharply. "If Lujan is a fool, our Lord is a genius," he mused to himself. "But if Lujan is a genius . . ." He pored over the map and muttered, "Now if our headstrong young Lord would listen, I would—"

"I see several problems," a crisp voice interjected.

Startled by Tasaio's silent return, Incomo jerked his chin upward. "You might explain."

Tasaio pointed. "I came for the map."

Incomo removed himself from the parchment as if walking on eggs. Tasaio was dangerously annoyed, and if he chose to elucidate, he would do so best without badgering.

Tasaio motioned, and his aide knelt down to roll the chart. The First Adviser waited, still with patience.

"What could go wrong?" said Tasaio in candor. He took the rolled map from his officer and slung it casually under his arm. "My cousin's boldness does him honor as head of the clan. However, he depends far too much on events proceeding as Minwanabi desires would have them. From experience I suggest it is wiser to prepare for the worst."

"Then you expect the double raid to go wrong," Incomo prodded, skillfully implying a defeat that Tasaio would face death rather than to allow.

Tasaio lifted tawny, black-lashed eyes and returned a merciless stare. "I will not be able to stay and lead this raid to ensure that things will go right. Nevertheless, it is often said that battles are won and lost before the first arrow is shot. The Acoma will certainly emerge with losses. I will spend my last hours before I depart for Dustari preparing for every imaginable contingency, and our Force Commander will receive instructions as detailed as I can make them. Irrilandi was Keyoke's boyhood friend and knows his temper. He should be able to anticipate which action Keyoke will take in response to our efforts. If I give Irrilandi detailed instructions for each option, he will emerge victorious."

Incomo bristled at the doubt implied in Irrilandi's skills; still, the criticism was fair relative to the man who had been the Warlord's Subcommander, the First Adviser conceded as Tasaio and his aide marched smartly from the hall. Desio's cousin was probably the most skilled field officer in the Empire, having earned a reputation for valor and cunning in the rise of the Minwanabi under Jingu, then refining his natural talents through four years commanding the Alliance for War on the barbarian world.

Incomo sighed, his only sign of regret that after one last night of planning, this gifted young noble would depart by river to begin his journey across the Sea of Blood to the ruins at Banganok. There Tasaio would join the men already in camp with the desert raiders, to effect the second stage of the plot to be set in motion by the silk raid. The campaign against the Xacatecas in Dustari must be stepped up, else the demand for an Acoma relief force could never be bribed through the council. Assigned the more demeaning worries of bath water and pretty serving girls, the Minwanabi First Adviser skirted a sweeper as bent as time, and shuffled his way out of the vast hall.

Mara paced. She spun in a tight circle, repressed an impulse to kick a pillow, and said, "Call him back. At once!"

The scribe, whose slates lay in a disorderly stack by the desk in the Lady's study, bowed low and touched his forehead to the floor. "Your will, Mistress." He scrambled erect and hurried from the room, too intimidated by Mara's anger to resent the fact that she had ordered him off to the farthest reaches of the estate as though he possessed a runner slave's fitness.

As the servant's footsteps dwindled down the passage, Nacoya clucked in reproof. "Daughter, the troubles you shoulder are difficult, but that should not let you take liberties. You have worked yourself into a deplorable state."

Mara whirled, white with fury. "Old woman, your nattering is most unwelcome."

Nacoya raised a furrowed brow. "Worry has made you

unreasonable." Her gaze fastened unerringly upon Kevin's name, repeatedly scribed on the slates strewn around the floor. Narrowing her eyes as if trying to peer into her foster-daughter's heart, the former nurse said, "Or love has."

Now Mara did kick the cushion. It sailed through the screen and through close-woven branches of akasi; flower petals exploded in profusion, and a cloud of pollen showered the floor. "Old woman, you try me beyond tolerance! Love has nothing to do with this. I'm angry because I allowed myself to send him away out of fear, and cowardice of any sort is unacceptable."

Nacoya fastened at once on the key phrase. "Fear . . . a barbarian slave?"

"I feared his blasphemous opinions on the working of Fate's Wheel, and the effect that attitude might have upon my son. And I'm put out with myself for feeling this. Kevin is my property, is he not? I may have him sold or killed at my whim, yes?" Mara sighed in frustration. "For these last months I've had his behavior watched, and he has conducted himself well. The fields are at long last clear, and not one of his countrymen has been hung to speed things along. And the entire time he has shown the proper respect toward his superiors."

Nacoya's sternness softened. She considered her mistress's fevered eyes and the flush on her cheeks, then regrettably concluded that little more could be done. The girl had come to love the barbarian. Though Mara didn't understand that fact yet, neither tact nor reason could turn back time. Against any sane judgment, Kevin would be back by nightfall.

Nacoya shut her eyes in long-suffering patience. The timing could hardly be worse, with news of a coming Minwanabi offensive just delivered from Arakasi's able hands. But one could not fault a young woman for turning to comfort in a crisis. Nacoya could only pray that Mara would tire of the slave quickly, or at least learn that nothing more than sexual release could come from such a relationship. The Lady must see reason, and give attention to more appropriate suitors. Once married to a man of rank, firm on her seat as Ruling Lady with a fit consort at her side, Mara could sleep with anyone she chose—her husband must accept this was a right of her office, as mistresses would be for a Ruling Lord. But finding a consort, that was the problem.

Since the shaming of poor Bruli of the Kehotara a year before, most young noblemen shied clear of the Ruling Lady of the Acoma; Tsurani street gossip consistently took the breath away with its detailed accounts of what occurred in supposedly private bedchambers. While only a handful of servants had witnessed Bruli's embarrassment, within days every street vendor in the Central Provinces had repeated the tale.

Perhaps some potential suitors had learned of that incident and decided the strong-willed Lady was more trouble than her wealth and title were worth, or perhaps lingering suspicions regarding Lord Buntokapi's dishonor and death kept others away. Certainly a majority of potential suitors were simply waiting to see if Mara survived much longer.

Even someone as overt in his interest as Hokanu of the Shinzawai could not be expected to wait while Mara indulged in her follies. Each night that Mara dallied with Kevin was an hour she was unavailable to entertain noble sons. Nacoya threw up crabbed hands and made a disgusted sound through her nose. "My Lady, if you must call him back, at least ask the herb woman to mix you a potion of barrenness. Bed sport is all to the good, but not if you have the misfortune to conceive accidentally."

"Out!" Mara flushed red, then paled, then blushed again. "I am calling my slave back for reprimand, not to indulge his rampant lust!"

Nacoya bowed and beat a retreat as quickly as her ancient bones allowed. In the hall she sighed. Reprimand for what? For being efficient and showing respect to his betters? For extracting more work from his barbarian countrymen than anyone else had been able to do? With a look of unbreakable patience, Nacoya walked to the servants' building and called upon the herb woman herself, to ensure that an elixir of teriko weed would be left in the Lady's room by nightfall. With the Minwanabi hot for Acoma blood, all the family needed for folly was a Ruling Lady burdened with a pregnancy.

•   •   •

The afternoon was well spent by the time the exhausted scribe returned from the farthest meadows accompanied by Kevin the barbarian. Having forgotten she had sent other than a runner slave on the errand, Mara's temper had not improved with the delay, nor at the realization her judgment had been clouded by emotion. Hungry, but too nettled to eat, she waited in her study, while a poet whose verse she had not listened to for the better part of two hours read from a seat on the bare wooden floor. Mara waved him silent each time she heard footsteps in the corridor. The poet resumed with feigned patience each time the tread turned out to be that of a passing servant. If not for the great Lady's patronage, he would be on the streets in Sulan-Qu, trying to eke out a living composing verse for passersby. When the expected party arrived at last, he graciously bowed at his dismissal; Mara was generous in her ways, and if he felt slighted by her inattention through the afternoon, she would make up the discourtesy to him later.

Cued by striding footfalls, accompanied by the quick patter of feet as a much shorter servant attempted to keep up with the long-legged barbarian, Mara bade the pair enter before either had a chance to knock. The nearly incapacitated scribe pushed the screen open, his face bright red as he gasped, "Lady . . . Kevin."

Too preoccupied to be contrite, Mara dismissed him to rest and leave her alone with her slave. When the screen clicked shut, she regarded Kevin, framed in the space before the doorway. For a long moment neither spoke, then Mara made a curt gesture for the barbarian to step closer.

Kevin complied, deeply suntanned and freckled over the nose, his blue eyes in startling contrast to his darkened skin. His hair had bleached red-gold, and the untrimmed ends fell curling to his shoulders. He wore no shirt. Hours spent digging with his work crews had left him calloused and heavily muscled across the back and arms. The intensity of the summer's heat had taken its due: his precious Midkemian-style trousers had been hacked short at the thigh, and his knees showed old scars and new scratches from the briers. Absorbed with taking in details, and unprepared for the leap of her heart as she saw him again after so long, Mara did not anticipate his anger.

Kevin bowed with insulting brevity. He locked gaze with

her and gestured in his un-Tsurani fashion. "What do you want of me, Lady?" He fairly spat out the title.

Mara stiffened on her cushions and the color left her face. "How dare you speak so to me?" she whispered, barely able to talk.

"And why should I not?" Kevin shot back. "You push me about like a chess . . . shāh pawn! Here! There! Now here again, because it suits you, but never one word of why, and never one second of warning! I've done as you've bid—not for love of you, but to save the lives of my countrymen."

Startled into the defensive, Mara broke poise and found herself near apology, as she attempted to justify her acts. "But I gave you promotion to slave master and allowed you charge of your Midkemian companions." She gestured at the slates. "You used your authority to see them comfortable. I see they have been eating jigabird and needra steak and fresh fruits and vegetables along with their thyza mush."

Kevin threw up his hands. "If you work your men at heavy labor, you've got to feed them, or they weaken and take ill. That's common sense. And those fields are a lousy place to be, filled with stinging flies and insects, and all manner of six-legged pests. Any kind of cut gets infected in this climate. You think my men have been enjoying banquets— you try sleeping on the ground out there, where the dust chokes your nostrils, and what passes for slugs and snails on this godsforsaken world invading your blankets after dark. And when you do rid your kit of guests, you lie awake unable to catch a breath of air."

Mara's eyes darkened. "You will all sleep wherever I bid, and keep your complaints to yourselves."

Kevin tossed back his untrimmed bangs, the better to glower at her. "Your damned trees got cleared, and the fences are nearly complete—give me another week. That's something, considering our Tsurani counterparts wilt and take siesta every time the sun crosses the zenith."

"That does not give you leave to take liberties," Mara snapped. She caught her voice rising, and controlled herself with an effort.

"Liberties, is it?" Kevin sat down without permission. Even then she had to look up to him, and that gave him perverse satisfaction.

Mara reached out, picked up one of the slates scattered at

her feet, and read: "The barbarian's words to the overseer as follows: 'Do that again and I'll rip off your . . . balls, you lying son of a ditch monkey.' " Mara paused, sighed, and added, "Whatever a 'ditch monkey' is, my overseer took it as an insult."

"It was intended that way," Kevin interrupted.

Mara's frown darkened. "The overseer is a free man, you are a slave, and it is not permissible for slaves to insult free workers."

"Your overseer is a cheat," Kevin accused. "He steals you blind, and when I found that the new issue of clothing for my men went to the markets to line the man's pockets, while they continued to wear rags, I—"

"Threatened to stuff his ripped-off manhood between his teeth," Mara interjected. She touched the slate. "It's all here."

Kevin said something rude in Midkemian. "Lady, you had no business spying on me."

Mara's brows rose. "About my overseer you happened to be right. He has been punished for his thefts, but as to spying, these are my estates, and what happens is certainly my affair. It is not spying to oversee one's estate operations." She paused, about to say more, then changed course. "This interview did not begin as I had planned."

"You expected me to come back to you with kisses after sending me off like that? After months of breaking my back laboring to get fences built, under a threat of death for men whose only crime was to suffer from heat and malnourishment?" Kevin said another word in Midkemian, this one short and to the point. "Lady, I might be forced to serve as your slave, but that doesn't make me a mindless puppet."

Mara bridled again, controlled herself, then threw up her hands in a manner more Kevin's than her own. "I had intended to compliment you on your work team's efficiency. Your methods might be unorthodox, even rough by our standards, but you got results."

Kevin regarded her keenly, his mouth a compressed line. "Lady, I can't believe, after being silent so long, you called me all the way back here to give me a pat on the head."

Now Mara felt confused. Why had she called him back? Had she forgotten how much of a distraction he could be, with his outspoken barbarities and headstrong manners? She felt his anger toward her, and his bleak and frustrated resentment. Having smoothed over the intensity of him in her memories, she tried to distance his presence, and the appalling havoc he was playing with her heart and mind.

"No, I did not call you back here for compliments. You are here because"—she glanced around, apparently seeking something, while she calmed herself, then reached out and selected another slate, the one that had touched off her fury in the first place—"of fence rails."

Kevin rolled his eyes, his hands clamped hard enough to bring white marks out on his forearms. "If I'm going to build a fence, I'm not going to do it with rotten posts that will fall down in the wet season, sure's the're flies in the fields. I can see me sitting here being lectured for shoddy 'barbarian' workmanship. Not to mention the fact that next year I'll be stuck with repairing the miserable job."

"What you'll be doing next year is not your concern." Mara fanned herself with the slate. However she tried, she could not seem to control this conversation. "But taking the merchant who sells us the posts and tying him upside down over the river by the feet is an outrage."

Kevin unlocked his hands, folded his arms across his chest, and looked smug. "Oh? I thought it was perfect justice. If the post held, the merchant stayed dry. If the wood was unsound, he got a dunking. Made him think twice, when we pulled him out of the water, about selling us inferior lumber."

"You shamed my name!" Mara broke in. "The man you dunked happened to come from a guild house, and an honorable family, even if they are not noble. Jican had to pay significant compensation to redress the injury done to the man's dignity."

Now Kevin sprang to his feet with the sudden wild grace that always startled Mara. He paced the floor. "That's what I don't understand about you Tsurani," he shouted, shaking an accusatory finger in the air. "You're obviously cultured, educated, and the factors you have in your service aren't stupid. But this confounded honor code you have, it makes me crazy. You cut off your toes to spite your feet with it, keep lying, lazy, or just plain incompetents in positions of authority because they happen to be born to an honorable house while better men are wasted in jobs of low demand and reward." He spun in a tight stride and faced Mara. "No wonder your father and brother got killed! If your people thought in straight logic, instead of in tangles of duty and tradition, your loved ones might still be alive."

Mara went white. Kevin didn't notice, but went on shouting, "And my people from the Kingdom might not be in such straits were your generals to play a straight war. But no, they advance here, savage a town without mercy, then retreat for no apparent reason and go off and ravage someplace else. Then they camp for months and do nothing."

Mara fought to hold her ebbing composure. "Are you saying my people are fools?" Vivid in her mind were the memories of the family killed through Minwanabi treachery. The thought that fate might have provided means to bring them home alive, if Tsurani honor had been somehow ignored, was cause for unanticipated anguish. Though the loss by now was years past, the grief still lingered.

Kevin drew breath to answer, but Mara interrupted. "Say no more." Her voice broke over the words, and tears welled in her eyes. Daughter of a proud heritage, she tried to rein them in, but did not succeed. She averted her face to hide this shame, but not quite quickly enough.

Kevin saw the sparkle in her eyes, and his anger abruptly drained away. He knelt down and reached an awkward hand toward her shoulder. "Lady," he said, his tone gone gritty with honesty. "I never intended to hurt you. Mostly I was mad because I thought I pleased you, before you sent me away." He took a deep breath and shrugged. "I am only a man, and like most, I don't like to find out I'm wrong."

"You weren't wrong." Mara spoke softly, without turning her head. "But you frightened me. Many of your ideas are constructive, but others are an affront to the gods—to what I believe in. I would not see the Acoma be ground down into the dust because I listened to your outworld 'logic' to the exclusion of wisdom, and spurned divine law."

Her shoulders spasmed with a sob, and Kevin's heart went out to her. Had he stopped to think, he would have hesitated, but analyzing emotions was not his habit. He gathered her small, tense form into his arms. "Mara," he spoke softly, into her hair. "Sometimes powerful, greedy men interpret the laws of heaven to suit themselves. I've learned a bit of your gods from your countrymen. Your Lashima is much like our Kilian, and Kilian is a kind and loving goddess. Do you think Lashima in her generosity would shrivel the hands on your wrists if you took pity and gave coins to the poor?"

Mara shivered in his grip. "I don't know. Please say no more. Keyoke and Lujan lead our warriors to counter a Minwanabi offensive, and at such a time the Acoma must not tempt the gods' anger."

His hands gentled her, pulled her around to face him. His calluses felt rough, and his person and his hair smelled of sun-warmed sweat and meadow grass. Yet the feel of his skin upon hers made her heart race. Finding a calm in his presence that until now had eluded her, Mara wrinkled her nose. "You need a bath."

"Do I?" Kevin drew her closer and lingeringly kissed her lips. "I missed you, though I'm foolish to admit it."

Mara's body burned in response and she leaned into him, feeling his strength. The pressure of his hands on her flesh made her throw caution, and Nacoya's advice, to the winds. "I missed you also. Maybe we both need a bath."

Kevin's face split into a grin. "Here? Now?"

Mara clapped her hands, and servants rushed in, ready to answer whatever request she might choose. Impishly, the Lady of the Acoma looked up at the tall barbarian who held her. "Call my attendants and have them draw bath water." As an afterthought, she added, "And erase these slates. They contain information that could start a rebellion, and I don't want my other slaves to learn impertinence, as this one has." As the servants hurried about their assigned tasks, she reached up and touched the scratch of stubble that grew on Kevin's cheeks and chin. "I don't know what it is that I see in you, dangerous man."

Unaccustomed to sharing intimacies in a room filled with bustling activity, Kevin flushed beneath his tan. One by one he pulled out the pins that bound up Mara's hair. When the rich locks fell free, he reached into the midnight mass and used it to screen both of their faces from public view. "You're quite the Ruling Lady," he murmured into the scented gloom, and their next kiss swept away reason. Letting his hands slide playfully along the curve of her neck, he felt her shiver in delight and anticipation. Whispering in her ear, he said, "And, sorry sod that I am, I have missed you . . . Lady."

Mara moved far enough away to see if his expression was mocking, but instead she read something in his eyes that caused a weakness to flow through her. Leaning against his hard body, the sunburn on his chest hot against her cheek, she answered back, "And I have missed you, my barbarian. Gods, how I've missed you."

9. AMBUSH

Keyoke motioned a halt.

Behind him, the first heavily laden silk wagons creaked to a standstill, the stamp of the needra teams scattering ocher dust on the breeze. Keyoke blinked grit from his eyes. The weight of his much-used battle armor made his knees ache and his back cramp; getting too old for campaign in the field, he thought.

Yet the warrior within him prevailed. Neither age nor fatigue reflected in Keyoke's stance as he turned keen eyes toward the crest of the hill and scanned the roadway ahead. To the men who stood in neat ranks behind their officers, Keyoke was as he had always been: a craggy, sun-beaten figure that seemed carved from indestructible rock.

Ahead, the trail wound like a looped cord through promontories of cracked granite; dirt lay rutted where the rainy season had gouged away soil loosened by needra hooves and caravan wheels. But the rise ahead of the pass was not empty, as it should have been. Against a sky fogged with dust, Keyoke perceived movement, and a sparkle of sunlit green armor. A trailbreaker had lingered in wait for the caravan, sure sign that something was amiss.

Keyoke motioned to his newly promoted Strike Leader, a short man with a scar that marred an eyebrow, named Dakhati. "Pass the word to be ready."

The order was superfluous. Warriors stood poised in their lines, hands rested lightly on sword hilts. They had marched at the ready since leaving friendly borders. Not one had been lulled by the uneventful passage of days or the fatigue of levering wagon wheels mired in the ruts of ill-kept mountain roads. These lands were rife with bandits, and laid out by the gods for ambush.

Mara's finest soldiers had been selected to escort the precious silk to Jamar, for while attack was expected upon the decoy wagons, they were defended by a large force. Should Keyoke's small band encounter battle, each warrior would be required to fight like two. And no one doubted that the scout who waited in the roadway meant trouble. The trailbreakers had been men who had once foraged in these very hills as grey warriors. They knew these valleys and would not be jumping at shadows.

Keyoke motioned broadly, and the scout up ahead disappeared. Moments later, he arrived at the head of the caravan, striding out of the roadside brush with the silence of sun-moved shadow. He paused before his Force Commander and gave a stiff nod of respect to Keyoke and Dakhati.

"Report, Wiallo," Keyoke said. His body might feel its burden of years and service, but his memory was yet sharp; he made a point of knowing every soldier's name.

The scout passed a last, uneasy glance over the slope, then spoke. "I've hunted here often, sir. Before evening, mulaks and kojir birds should be flying about the lake beyond that ridge." He indicated the sun-dappled shade of the forest. "And sanaro, li, and other songbirds should never be quiet at this hour." He glanced meaningfully toward Keyoke. "I do not like the silence and the sound of the wind."

Keyoke knuckled back his helmet, letting a gust of breeze evaporate the perspiration under his hair. Then, slow and deliberate, his seamed fingers tightened the chin strap. Veteran Acoma warriors knew their Force Commander prepared for a fight. "Other birds roost in those trees, do you think?"

Wiallo grinned. "Large birds, Force Commander. Ones who wear dogs' tails instead of feathers."

Dakhati licked his teeth, uneasy. "Minwanabi, or bandits?"

Wiallo's smile died. "Grey warriors would give this company a wide berth."

Keyoke snapped his chin strap tab through the keeper under his jawbone. "Minwanabi, then. Where would they be likely to hit us?"

Wiallo frowned. "A clever commander would see us over this next small rise." He pointed at the ridge that rose like a knife cut against late-day haze. "About halfway up the slope on the far side of the next valley, the road rises sharply again and snakes through a chain of steep gullies."

Keyoke nodded. "The enemy would keep to higher ground, while we, under bowfire, would be forced to whip the needra uphill over rocks to escape." His clear eyes met those of Wiallo. "That's where I would strike, with a follow-up company to plug the valley from the rear, and cut off our chance of retreat." He glanced around. "They are most likely infiltrating behind us right now."

Behind the rows of nervous soldiers, a needra bawled. Traces creaked, and a carter cursed, and a patter of running footsteps approached.

"Make way! A scout returns!" somebody called from the rear.

Neat ranks parted, and a warrior stumbled through, white-faced and gasping for breath.

Dakhati stepped forward and caught the runner as he rocked unsteadily to a stop. "Force Commander!"

Keyoke turned with a calm he did not feel. "Speak clearly."

"Soldiers upon the road behind us." The man dragged in a painful breath. "Perhaps a hundred, a hundred fifty, and Corjazun says he recognized their officer. Minwanabi."

Keyoke's first reaction was a softly spoken "Damn." Then he touched the heaving shoulder of the runner and added, "Well done. Is this army traveling covertly?"

The runner scrubbed his palm over his salt-wet brow. "They march openly. We estimated the troop size by the cloud of dust they raised."

Keyoke's eyes narrowed. Briskly he concluded, "That's no raiding band; that's company strength, a hundred men at least, to drive us into the trap."

Dakhati ventured an opinion. "If we have an ambush waiting for us, and an army closing from behind—"

"They knew we were coming," finished Keyoke. The implications were chilling, but academic, unless someone survived to warn Lady Mara she had an intelligence leak within her household. "I hate to abandon the silk wagons, but if we don't, we're all sacrifices to the Red God and the silk's lost anyway." The Force Commander prepared to deliver grim orders.

A touch from Wiallo stopped him.

"Force Commander," offered the onetime grey warrior. "There might be another way."

"Tell me quickly," Keyoke demanded.

"There's a foot trail hidden by boulders near the base of this rise. It leads to a narrow canyon that bandits used as a camp. The wagons cannot pass, but the silk could be hidden, and the position at least offers hope. There is only one entrance, and that can be defended with very small numbers of men."

Keyoke's gaze shifted to the horizon, as if searching for sign of the army that approached to destroy them. "How long could we last there? Long enough to get word to Lady Mara? Or to recall Lujan?"

Wiallo was silent. He said, on a frank note, "A message, perhaps, to our mistress. Long enough to hold until relief arrives from home? The Minwanabi could force their way through if they were willing to endure a terrible slaughter."

Dakhati slapped his thigh in a startling display of anger. "What honor to abandon that which we are pledged to defend?"

Curtly Keyoke said, "The wagons are lost in any event. We cannot defend them and sally against a hundred men in the open." More important, Mara must not go uninformed of Minwanabi's access to her secrets. No, better to make a stand, and send a messenger while the Minwanabi are kept occupied at the canyon.

Lashima's wisdom guide us all, Keyoke prayed inwardly. Then he raised his voice and said, "There are better ways to defend a trust than to fight to the death before letting the enemy seize the prize." He added a swift string of orders.

The soldiers made a display of relaxing. They removed their helms and shared refreshment from the bucket and dipper carried around by the water boy. They gathered in knots, and told jokes, and laughed as though nothing under the sky could be wrong, while behind them servants worked swiftly to unlash the covers from the wagons, and bundle the precious silk bales inside. Wiallo showed them where the rocks dipped into crevices. A third of the silk was quickly hidden out of sight and covered with brush, but room remained for no more. The servants redistributed what remained in the wagons, and spread the covers to hide the gaps. Then Keyoke shouted, and the soldiers formed up, and the caravan creaked forward once again. The company wound downward from the crest into a valley mantled and deep with late afternoon shadows.

The caravan reached the base of the hill, and the needra bawled as the drovers reined them in once again. Through the rising pall of their own dust, Keyoke squinted behind and saw a sky gone light with the gold of coming sunset; but the heights they had recently left were now marred with a cloud of dull gray. A moment later, a scout confirmed his foreboding over that patch of dirty sky.

"It's dust kicked up by marching soldiers. The Minwanabi tire of waiting," the runner reported breathlessly. "Perhaps they think we camp here."

Keyoke pursed creased lips. He waved for Dakhati's attention and called, "We'll need to hurry." Then, feeling every mile his feet had traveled, the Force Commander watched his Strike Leader give orders. In an unusual moment of reflection, he wished for Papewaio's intuitive presence. But Pape was dead, murdered by a Minwanabi assassin while defending Mara. Keyoke hoped he would accomplish as much. For he had no illusions: he knew that every warrior here would likely meet the Red God on the end of a Minwanabi weapon.

Masked from observation by the trees, the silk was unloaded, the needra unhitched. Then, with poles cut from the forest, the Acoma soldiers levered the wagons onto their sides, forming a barrier behind which twenty archers took cover. These men volunteered to stay behind and fight to the death, buying time for the rest of the company to make their way to Wiallo's canyon. That such a haven might not exist, or that the ex–grey warrior could have mistaken its location, posed a possible disaster no one spoke of.

Sunlight left the valley early but held the heights in bright aspect like fingers dipped in gilt. The dust raised by the Minwanabi army deepened the gloom down below.

Keyoke ordered, "Let every man carry as much of the silk as he may." Wiallo returned a puzzled glance. Keyoke said, "Those bolts can be better used to stop arrows, or build a bulwark against a charge. Now have the servants lead the needra, and guide us quickly to this canyon."

Soldiers with silk bales piled on their shoulders marched between drovers and servants who whipped the balky needra over a ragged barrier of boulders. Darkness fell fast, and the footing was poor. The gutted remains of the caravan moved over treacherous terrain, pushing past branches that whipped and caught at armor, and over gullies that grabbed at the ankles. Several times men fell, though not one uttered an oath. In silence they arose and gathered up their dropped bundles, and pressed forward into brush-dense forest.

By moonrise the company reached a narrow defile in the trail. Here forest vines clutched at the trees as if they sought to strangle, and from their choking outgrowth thrust an upstanding promontory of rock on either side.

"The canyon lies just ahead, perhaps three bowshots from that formation," Wiallo said.

Keyoke peered through the gloom and made out a boulder that bulked like an overhang above the path. He raised his hand, and the column behind came to a halt.

A bird called and fell silent; no way to determine whether the creature wore feathers or armor. Keyoke touched two of the nearest warriors and waved them forward. "Stand guard here. The moment you see any sign of pursuit, one of you send me word."

The chosen men shed their bundles and assumed their posts without protest. Keyoke saluted their bravery and wished he had time to say more. But words could not lighten necessity: when the Minwanabi marched on their position, one man would race with the warning, and the other would die to provide his colleague enough of a lead to get through. Mara would be proud, the Force Commander thought sadly.

The company and its servants scrambled along the trail. They moved in the half-dark like men driven by demons. At a narrow V in the rocks, where each man needed to scramble on hands and knees and have his bundled goods passed through, and the needra had to be forced against their nature to jump downward, Keyoke waved Wiallo to his side. Above the bawling of frightened animals, he asked, "What chance you could make your way cross-country from here to our Lady?"

Wiallo shrugged in impassive Tsurani modesty. "I know this area as well as any man, Force Commander. But, in the dark, with Minwanabi soldiers coming from all sides? A shadow would need the gods' favor to pass unseen."

The squealing bawl of a needra momentarily defeated thought. Keyoke glanced to one side and pointed to a slight overhang. "Then climb up there and hide. When the Minwanabi dogs march past, judge your moment and double back to the main road. Make your way swiftly to the estate. Tell Lady Mara where the goods have been hidden. When it is clear the Minwanabi are close to breaking through, I shall burn the silk we carry. With luck, our enemies will assume we have destroyed all to deny them spoils. Most important, tell our mistress that we have been betrayed; we may have a spy in our house. Now go."

Honored at being chosen for the important assignment, Wiallo nodded smartly and began to climb. At the top of the boulder, he removed his helm and crouched to avoid being seen by the enemies soon to pass below. Starting downward, Wiallo called, "May the gods preserve you, Force Commander; send many Minwanabi dogs to the halls of Turakamu tonight!"

Keyoke returned a quick nod. "And may Chochocan guide your steps."

The next man in line gathered up Wiallo's abandoned bolt of silk and stoically resumed his march. Silent, grim, and too preoccupied to dwell on his aches, Keyoke bent his knees and crawled over ground turned jagged with gravel. With the reek of needra droppings sharp in his nose, he wormed under the stone outcrop and pressed forward to lead his struggling company.

The night deepened, and the moonlight flashed and vanished behind a rim of black rock. Insects chittered in a forest where night birds did not sing, and the wind whispered secrets in the leaves. Men moved like ghosts through the mist-shrouded defile, their feet sliding to find purchase upon wet roots and moss-covered rocks. The clack of lacquered armor echoed down the ravine, cut by the whine of the hide whips the drovers used to prod the needra. Of the soldiers and servants hurrying through the night, none reached the small canyon without bloodied arms and knees, and the needra stood shivering and lamed, their coats rankly matted with sweat.

Under starlight, Keyoke issued brisk orders as he surveyed the canyon where they would make their stand. Men shed their loads of silk and began to throw up a barricade of boulders, logs, and earth dug in haste from the stream bed, between the water-smoothed walls of rock that formed at the canyon's entrance. Servants slew needra and piled the still-kicking carcasses into breastworks to provide cover from the archers that would surely be deployed above them on the canyon's rim. The night air grew thick with the reek of fresh blood and the heavier odor of excrement.

Keyoke ordered the servants to butcher one of the carcasses, and build a small fire to cook and dry the meat. Soldiers could not fight without sustenance. Finally, soldiers stacked the bolts of precious silks like a palisade in a hollow to the rear of the canyon. Piled before the rise of the cliff wall, the beautiful, iridescent rolls of cloth would serve as a niche to fall back to, in the extremity of a final stand.

Then, hoarse from calling orders, Keyoke knelt before a pool of water fed by a small waterfall that splashed through an unscalable cleft in the rim. He unstrapped his helm, rinsed his parched face, then did up the buckle with hands that betrayed him by shaking. He was not afraid, he had led charges in too many battles to fear any death by the blade. No, it was age, and weariness, and sorrow for his Lady that set his fingers trembling at their task. Keyoke checked his sword, and then his knives in their sheaths, and lastly looked up to find the water boy with his dipper awaiting a turn at the brook. The boy was also shaking, though his shoulders were held straight as any man's.

Proud of even the smallest member of his company, Keyoke said, "We have enough water here to last as long as we need. See that the soldiers drink deeply."

The boy managed an unsteady smile. "Yes, Force Commander." He splashed his pail into the pool, as ready to die for his mistress as the most hardened soldier.

Keyoke arose and turned his gaze over the bustling activity, the servants huddled over the smothered campfires, the warriors on guard at the barricades; there was no laxity in discipline. These soldiers resisted the novice's tendency to look toward the light; they needed no reminder to know their survival depended upon unspoiled night vision. Keyoke sighed imperceptibly, knowing nothing was left to be done but to make rounds and give encouragement to men who knew their lives were measured now in hours.

Keyoke swallowed needra steak whose juices held no savor. To the cook who took his empty plate he said, "Be my spokesman to the servants; should the Minwanabi break past our front barricade, and our last soldiers lie dying, use the shields to scoop up the burning brands and hurl them into the silk. Then throw yourselves at the Minwanabi, that they must kill you with swords and grant you honorable deaths."

The cook bowed his head in abject gratitude. "You honor us, Force Commander."

Keyoke returned a smile. "You will honor your Lady and your house by carrying out your orders. In this you must be like warriors."

The old man, whose name Keyoke couldn't recall, said, "We shall not fail Lady Mara's trust, Force Commander."

Keyoke had given orders that one man in every three should move in turn to the rear of the narrow canyon and eat a quick meal. The second company had finished eating, and now the third took their places near the campfire. Strike Leader Dakhati held back as Keyoke left the cook fire. In barely suppressed uneasiness, the younger officer fingered the unblooded crest of his officer's plume. "What are your tactics, Force Commander?"

Keyoke glanced one last time around the gully that already smelled like carrion, now rendered grey, black, and flickering orange by the blaze of shielded fires. Since nothing more could be done, he answered with clipped deliberation. "We wait. Then we fight."

With a wariness learned during his years as a bandit leader, First Strike Leader Lujan scanned the perimeter. The moonlight shone down much too brightly, and the flatlands along the river road were open, not at all to his liking for a pitched fight. But level ground gave him the advantage of seeing an enemy's approach, and he had at his command every soldier that could be spared from Mara's estate. It would take a major assault by at least three full companies of warriors to break through the circled wagons. And the Minwanabi would need to send no fewer than five hundred men to be certain of victory. Nonetheless, Lujan suffered an uneasy stomach and an urge to pace. Again he reviewed his defenses, studying the archers atop the wagons, and found nothing amiss as cooks cleaned up after the evening meal. His foreboding did not lessen, but only increased, for battle was long overdue.

The Minwanabi should have struck by now. At first light tomorrow his caravan would roll toward the gates of Sulan-Qu. The report from Arakasi's spy said a major attack was a certainty. And to Lujan's practiced military mind, the most likely site for ambush had been a forested bend in the road passed uneventfully the previous afternoon. That left a night attack, for it was inconceivable the Minwanabi would try to seize the caravan inside the city.

Again Lujan surveyed the road. His instincts screamed that something was wrong. For lack of anything better to do save sleep, he walked the perimeter, and as he had done only minutes before, he spoke a quiet word with guards who were growing edgy from his repeated surveillance. His worry was hampering the vigilance of the sentries, Lujan knew.

The Strike Leader passed through the narrow corridor between the backs of his guards and the rows of leather-lashed wagons shielding the central fires, the needra pickets, and the men who slept in shifts. The wagons were laden with thyza bags under their linen coverings; for appearance sake, two bolts of silk showed beneath one bulging, mistied corner. The cloth glistened by moonlight, smooth as water and opulently perfect in quality.

Lujan fingered his sword. He repeatedly reviewed what he knew and couldn't escape the same conclusion: the delayed attack made no sense. After sunrise, the enemy would be forced to wait until the caravan left the gates on the south road to Jamar. Ambush then would be complicated by the possibility that the cargo might be loaded onto barges and sent downriver by water. Could the Minwanabi have mounted two forces, one on shore and one on boats to attack upon the river? They had enough warriors, gods knew. But battle on the swift-flowing Gagajin would pose difficulties—

"Strike Leader!" hissed a nearby sentry.

Lujan's sword left its sheath, seemingly by its own volition. The Acoma Strike Leader forced a calm he did not feel into his words as he urged the man to speak.

"Look there. Someone comes."

Lujan cursed his nerves, which had caused him to face the fires but a moment before to inspect his sleeping men; now he waited impatiently for his night vision to return. Shortly he made out a lone figure down the road from their position.

"He staggers like he's drunk," observed the sentry. The approaching man stumbled unsteadily on his feet. His stride was awkward, as if could not use the heel of his right foot, and the arm at his side swung slack like something gutted.

As he closed the last few yards, and came into the light, Lujan saw that he wore a bloodstained loincloth and clutched a rag of a shirt over his shoulders. His deadened eyes did not register the presence of soldiers or camped caravan. Lujan said, "He's not drunk—he's half-dead."

Lujan motioned a nearby warrior to accompany him as he stepped away from the perimeter. Together, officer and soldier caught the man by his shoulder and upper arm, and the half-held shirt fell away to reveal a chain of bruises, overlaid with scabs and dusty clots of dried blood. Looking in horror at a face that showed no expression, Lujan forced his breath past his teeth. This man had been beaten to madness.

"Who did this?" demanded the Strike Leader.

The man blinked, worked his lips and seemed to emerge from a daze. "Water," he whispered hoarsely, as if he had been screaming, full-throated, and for a long time. Lujan called a servant to fetch a waterskin, then gently eased the injured man to the ground. Something inside the man seemed to break as he drank. His abused legs quivered in the dust, and suddenly he was fainting. The soldier's strong hands propped him upright, and the servant splashed water on his wrists and face. Dust and blood rinsed away to reveal more bruises, and a sickening smell of burned flesh.

"Gods," said the soldier. "Who did this?"

Ignoring his abused state, the man attempted to rise. "Must go," he muttered, though it was clear he could not continue.

Lujan ordered two warriors to lift the man up and carry him through the wagons to a fire. Settled on a blanket, and exposed at last to the light, the extent of what he had suffered was revealed. No portion of his body had been spared from torment. The tale was told in ugly lesions, ragged at the edges where caustic solutions had been applied; the hand wrapped in the shirt tatters was a mass of blackened burns and without fingernails; and the skin over sensitive nerve centers was congested and purple with bruising. Whoever had tortured this man had been an artist of pain, for while the man yet survived, several times during the process he must have begged for passage to the halls of Turakamu.

Lujan spoke softly in sympathy. "Who are you?"

The man's eyes struggled to focus. "I must warn her," he insisted in a voice made feverish by pain.

"Warn?" asked Lujan.

"I must warn my Lady. . . ."

Lujan knelt and bent closer to the man, whose voice grew faint. "Who is your Lady?"

The man thrashed feebly against the soldier's grasp, then seemed to weaken, "Lady Mara."

Lujan glanced at the soldiers who stood upon either side. "Do you know this man?" he questioned quickly.

A warrior from the old Acoma garrison indicated he had never seen the wounded man, and he knew every servant by sight.

Lujan motioned the others to stand away and leaned down. Near the man's ear he whispered, "Akasis bloom . . ."

The man struggled upright and fixed a bright, fevered gaze on Lujan's face. ". . . in my Lady's dooryard," he muttered back. "The sharpest thorns . . ."

Lujan finished, ". . . protect sweet blossoms."

"Gods, gods, you're Acoma," said the man in relief. For an instant it looked as if he might shame himself, and cry.

Lujan rested his knuckles on his knees. His eyes never straying from the tortured man's face as he called for the healer to dress and bind the wounds. "You are one of my Lady's agents," he concluded softly.

The man managed a nearly imperceptible nod, "Until a few days ago. I . . ." He paused, winced, and seemed to maintain lucidity with an effort. "I am Kanil. I served in the Minwanabi household. I carried food to Desio's table and stood by to meet his demands. Much of . . ." His voice faded.

Gently as possible Lujan said, "Slowly. Tell us slowly. We have all night to listen."

The injured servant jerked his chin violently in the negative, then sank back into a faint.

"Give him air, and tell the healer to bring a restorative to rouse him," Lujan snapped. A warrior hurried off to comply, while the men who had been steadying the man gently eased a blanket under his head. Moments later the healer arrived, unlimbering his bundled box of medicines and bandages. He quickly prepared and pressed a strong-smelling medicine to the unconscious man's nose. He roused with a groan and thrashed his arms.

Lujan caught his tortured gaze. "Tell me. You were discovered."

"Somehow." The man blinked, as if trapped by unpleasant memories. "The First Adviser, Incomo, found out I was an Acoma agent."

Lujan said nothing. Besides the Spy Master, only four people in the Acoma household, Mara, Nacoya, Keyoke, and himself, knew the passwords, changed at irregular intervals, that would identify an Acoma agent. The possibility could not be dismissed that this man might be a Minwanabi imposter. Only Arakasi would know for certain. If torture could force the password from the real agent, any number of enemy warriors might agree to this abuse to ruin the Acoma.

Kanil clawed weakly at Lujan's wrist. "I don't know how they found me out. They called for me and then took me to this room." He swallowed hard. "They tortured me. . . . I lost consciousness and when I awoke I was alone. The door was unguarded. I don't know why. Perhaps they thought I was dead. Many Minwanabi soldiers were rushing to board boats and cross the lake. I crept out of the room in which I was a prisoner and stowed away on a supply boat. I passed out, and when I was again conscious, the flotilla was docked at Sulan-Qu. There were only two guards at the far end of the docks, so I slipped off into the city."

"Strike Leader Lujan," the healer interjected, "if you question this man too long, his survival may be threatened."

At the mention of Lujan's name, Kanil stirred in sudden and shattering agitation. "Oh, gods!" he whispered hoarsely. "This is the false caravan."

Lujan's only betrayal of shock was a tightening of his

hand on his sword hilt. Taut, dangerous, and wary, he ignored the healer's plea and leaned close to the man. Too softly he said, "For what reason would the Spy Master inform you of this deception?"

The man lay uncaring of his peril. Whispering, he said, "Arakasi didn't. The Minwanabi know! They laughed and boasted of what they knew of Lady Mara's plan while they tortured me."

Chilled by this answer, Lujan pressed, "Do they know about the real silk shipment?"

Kanil returned a nod. "They do. They sent three hundred men to plunder it."

Lujan stood. Curbing an impulse to fling his plumed helm to the ground, he cried, "Damn the fickleness of the gods!"

Then, aware of curious eyes that turned in his direction, he waved healer and soldiers away, leaving him alone with the tortured man. Night wind stirred the fire. Kneeling, Lujan seized Kanil by the back of the neck and hauled his battered face near to his own so they might speak without being overheard. "Upon your soul and life, do you know where?"

Tremors coursed through Kanil's body. But his eyes were steady as he said, "The attack will happen on the road through the Kyamaka Mountains, beyond the Tuscalora border, in a place where wagons must climb up out of a depression toward a western ridge. That is all I know."

Lujan stared unseeing into features ravaged by enemies. He thought with a clarity that came on him in moments of crisis, and reviewed every dell and hideout and cranny he remembered in the mountains where he had once led his band of grey warriors. There were many an army might use for an ambush. Yet only one place that was suitable for concealment of three full companies matched the description. As if dreaming, Lujan said, "How long ago did the Minwanabi dogs pass Sulan-Qu?"

Kanil's head sagged sideways. "A day, perhaps two. I cannot say. I fainted in a hovel in the city, and the gods only know how long I lay unconscious—an hour or perhaps a full day." He closed his eyes, too spent to add more; and the strength of purpose that had sustained him drained away with the deliverance of his message. Lujan lowered his hands and settled the limp head on blood-marked blankets. He made no protest as the healer hurried forward and began to tend the man.

Lujan completed his inner calculations. Knotted inside with concealed rage, he shouted loudly enough to wake the most sluggish of the sleeping servants. "Break camp!"

To the worried presence of his subcommander he added, "Assign a patrol and wagon to take this man to Lady Mara in the morning, and then detail half a company to see the rest of the wagons safely to our warehouses in Sulan-Qu at dawn."

The officer saluted. "Yes, Strike Leader."

"The rest of us march now," Lujan finished. He wasted no breath with elaboration; every second counted. For if the Minwanabi attacked Keyoke in the pass, there was only one place to make a stand. The bandits' canyon would be known to the scouts; but in the heat of ambush and battle, had any of them found the chance to mention its presence? Curse of Turakamu, Lujan thought. The silk could be lost already, and Keyoke might at this moment be a corpse staring sightless at stars. Only a fool would hold to hope, and only an even greater fool would risk another two companies . . . yet Lujan could not conceive of any alternative but action.

For Lujan loved Mara with a devotion deeper than life: she had returned him to honor from the meaningless existence of a grey warrior. And the Force Commander Lujan had come to admire with the affection a son reserves for a father had become ensnared in a Minwanabi trap. Keyoke had embraced the tattered soldiers from Lujan's band as if they had been born to Acoma green, and he had supported Lujan's promotion to First Strike Leader with a fair judgment few men maintained in old age. Keyoke was more than a commanding officer; he was a teacher with a rare talent for sharing, and for listening.

Looking southward with eyes flat as pebbles, Lujan raised his voice to his company. "We march! And if we must steal every boat and barge in Sulan-Qu to make passage southward, we shall! By dawn I want to be on the river, and before another day passes, I want to be hunting dogs in the foothills of the Kyamakas!"

•   •   •

The forest was silent. Night birds did not cry, and the high, steep rim of the canyon cut off even the whisper of wind. Except for a brief hour when the moon had crossed the narrow slice of sky overhead, the darkness was unrelenting.

Keyoke refused all pleas to unbank the fires, though the air was chill at this altitude and the lightly clothed servants shivered. Soldiers sought to snatch sleep in full armor on damp ground, while others stood at their posts, carefully listening.

Only unwelcome sounds reached their ears: the scrape of disturbed stones and the muffled grunts of effort as climbers tested canyon walls in the dark. The enemy had arrived, but the wait, most cruelly, did not end.

Keyoke remained by the barricade, his face impassive as old wood. Committed to battle in a place he had never seen in daylight, the Acoma Force Commander prayed that Wiallo's assessment had been accurate: that the cliffs above were too steep to descend. As it was, Keyoke could do little but detail sentries to follow the rattling falls of pebbles set off by men prowling the heights. Once his soldiers were gratified by a muffled cry and the thud of a fallen body. The corpse that lay sprawled in the canyon was raggedly dressed, but too well fed and kempt for a bandit; his weapons were first-quality and stamped with the maker's mark of an armorer well known in Szetac Province. No further proof was needed. That craftsman's trade supplied the Minwanabi, as his forebears had for several generations.

Keyoke squinted at stars and found them paling. Dawn was approaching, and soon the enemy would have light enough to try arrows. Keyoke knew that if the Minwanabi Force Commander, Irrilandi, opposed him, he would have archers in crannies in the rock against any counterattack—one of Irrilandi's more predictable tendencies was always to be ready for a counteroffensive. Come daylight, his archers could fire blindly down into the ravine. Most bowshafts might fall harmlessly, but some might strike chance targets. A secondary but nonetheless pressing worry was the shortage of healers' herbs and unguents. The wagons had carried little by way of supplies, and no healers traveled with the soldiers.

The assault came as the Kelewanese sky brightened to jade green in the east. The first wave of Minwanabi soldiers struck the rough barricade with a battle scream that shattered the stillness. They could charge only four abreast through the rock passage, and their attempt to climb the breastwork brought them swift death on Acoma swords and spears. Yet the enemy came on, climbing over dead and dying comrades in bloodthirsty waves. At least a dozen Minwanabi soldiers lay fallen before the first Acoma warrior took a wound; almost before his sword faltered, a fresh man shouldered forward to take his place. Minwanabi archers fired ineffectively over their comrades' heads.

For nearly an hour the enemy hammered at the barricade. By ones and threes they died, until the corpses lay close to a hundred deep. Acoma casualties numbered fewer than a dozen injured and only one dead. Keyoke detailed servants to give what care they could to the injured. Although movement within the canyon was hampered by the insistent fall of enemy arrows, no man who took wounds for Acoma honor was permitted to lie without care.

Keyoke raised his voice to Dakhati. "Bring up fresh soldiers to the barricade."

Dakhati dashed to relay the order. Within minutes the relief company undertook the defense of the barricade, and the Acoma Strike Leader brought word back. "The enemy are making little progress, Force Commander. They've tried having men crawl on their bellies to pull away some of the dead, and to undermine our breastworks. If they try sappers, we're in trouble."

Keyoke shook his head. "Sappers are useless here. The soil is sandy, yes, but the water lies too close to the surface and there is not enough room for engineers to dig." The Force Commander pushed his helm back to fan cool air on his scalp. The chill of mountain night had fled, and the breezeless canyon warmed under even the earliest sunlight. "Our flimsy breastworks are the greater problem. If they charge the line, and send men behind the assault to pull at the breastwork . . . Put spearmen on their knees behind the first line, and see if they can discourage any such activity."

Dakhati hastened to effect this deterrent.

Keyoke surveyed the rest of his defenses, his plumed head held high despite the arrows arcing overhead. Most shafts bounced off the sheer walls of the canyon, but a few sped downward. One struck a handspan from Keyoke, but he barely noticed. As if the quivering shaft by his foot had no existence, he motioned for servants to carry water to his fighting men. Then he surveyed his command yet again.

The Minwanabi seemed frantic to engage the Acoma. Why? Keyoke considered. If the canyon was defensible, it was also a trap. The Minwanabi would pay dearly to enter, but the Acoma would die attempting to leave. An attacker not pressed to haste would be better to sit and wait, holding the canyon until starvation forced the defenders to desperation, then let Acoma bodies be the ones piling up at the base of the barricade as hunger drove them to escape. Keyoke reviewed what he knew of his opponent: Irrilandi was in no way stupid—he'd been competent enough to remain the Minwanabi Force Commander for nearly two decades—and in this foray he was almost certain to be operating under battle orders from Tasaio. Why should two men so skilled in war spend men by the hundreds? To capture the silk would be no mortal blow to the Acoma and certainly not worth the lives that would be sacrificed before the sun reached mid-heaven. Time must be a factor, but why?

Disturbed, Keyoke turned away from unanswerable questions and selected soldiers for the next rotation. Before each warrior took his turn behind the barricade, Keyoke inspected weapons and armor, and briefly placed a hand upon each lacquered shoulder guard. He spoke quiet words of encouragement, then sent the relief forward. There they waited, until a weary Acoma warrior would step back and his replacement move forward, the change taking only a moment.

Keyoke assessed the blood-spattered soldiers who removed their helmets and washed sweat-soaked hair and faces in the creek. He decided to step up the rotation. The Minwanabi were still able to send only four men at a time against the barricade, and the spearmen had held off any further attempts to destroy the fortification of tangled branches and rocks. Better to keep the men as fresh as possible, Keyoke judged.

A sudden shout arose from behind Minwanabi lines. Uncertain what this might signify, Keyoke signaled every man in the canyon to stand ready. Strike Leader Dakhati hastened to his Force Commander's side, sword pointed at the barricade. But no foray came against the defenders. Rather than choke the defile with more soldiers, the Minwanabi unexpectedly withdrew.

Dakhati expelled a pent breath. "Perhaps they tired of seeing their men die for naught."

Keyoke shrugged, noncommittal. Retreat was not Irrilandi's style, and certainly not Tasaio's. "Perhaps," he conceded. "But our enemies were willing enough to waste lives until this moment."

On the verge of speaking, Dakhati fell abruptly still as an object was launched into the air from a point beyond the canyon's rim. Dark against the daylight sky, it came flying into the gully, a bundle of soaked rags and knots. It struck the hard dirt and rolled, servants scattering from its path in case it contained a nest of stinging insects—an old siege trick —or something equally unpleasant. Keyoke signaled and Dakhati moved to investigate. The Strike Leader lifted the bundle and unwrapped it. When he pulled away the last turn of cloth, his lips tightened and his face blanched grey beneath his tan.

As Dakhati glanced up, Keyoke nodded almost imperceptibly. His Strike Leader covered the bundle in response. "It's Wiallo's head," he murmured softly.

"I thought so." Keyoke's voice betrayed no hint that he shared the same hopeless, helpless rage. Mara, he thought, you and Ayaki are in grave danger and I can do nothing to help.

Equally mindful of the threat to the Acoma household, Dakhati added more. "They included a bit of rope, so we might know they hung him before they cut his head off."

Keyoke repressed a flinch at the mention of an honorless end. "Wiallo told them he was a deserter, no doubt. He may have been hung, but he died with courage. I'll attest to that before the Red God himself."

Dakhati nodded grimly. "Your orders, Force Commander?"

Keyoke did not answer immediately. He was pained beyond measure by the fate of his messenger to Mara; the canyon was sealed, irrevocably. Now no one could win free to warn her of the spy unnoticed in her house. His bitterness came near to showing as he said, "Only to stand ready and kill as many Minwanabi as possible. And to die like men of the Acoma."

Dakhati saluted and returned to the barricade.

• • •

The assaults continued through the day, halting only to allow the Minwanabi to regroup and send fresh soldiers into the van. They no longer made pretense of being outlaws, Keyoke observed with old hatred. The ranks that assaulted the breastwork now wore orange-and-black armor. Dedicated to their mission, the enemy warriors threw themselves against the Acoma defenders; they died and died, until the flow of their lifeblood soaked the soil and mixed into sucking mud. The Minwanabi were not the only casualties. Acoma soldiers fell also, more slowly, but with a finality that wore away at their numbers.

Keyoke tallied eleven dead and another seven wounded beyond the ability to serve. He estimated this had cost the Minwanabi ten times that number dead or critically injured. More than a company of slain enemies would rise to sing of his valor when Keyoke's soul stood in judgment before the Red God, but he despaired to be sent in defeat, that his mistress might never discover that her security network had been breached until too late. For while Lujan was a quick enough study that Keyoke counted him a fit successor as Force Commander, he was untested in large battles, and his training was unfinished.

Keyoke forced himself away from agonizing over this. There was no profit in it. He approached the senior servant. "How fare our stores?"

The man bowed. "If our soldiers take minimum rations, we have ample food for several days."

Keyoke considered a moment. "Double the rations, instead. I doubt we'll survive for several days. The Minwanabi seem determined to waste lives as a drunkard spends centis in a tavern."

Shouting arose from the canyon mouth, and Keyoke spun around, his sword out of its scabbard with the speed of reflex. Minwanabi soldiers had contrived to gain a position on a ledge behind their own lines, and archers were shooting at the hondo of the Acoma defenders, forcing them down while the attackers at the barricades threw shields across the bodies of fallen comrades to enable them to leap over the top into the canyon.

The first Minwanabi soldier attempted the jump only to

land upon a ready Acoma spear, but the soldier who made the kill took an arrow for his trouble. Keyoke whirled and shouted to Dakhati, who stood by with a reserve company. "Prepare to sortie!"

Dakhati called his men into ranks.

To the men at the barricade, Keyoke shouted, "Withdraw!"

The defenders fell back in tight order, and a pair of Minwanabi soldiers sprang into the clear space behind the barricade, only to crumple as Acoma archers cut them down. The grating sound of rocks and heavy branches pushed across stone resounded through the canyon as the Minwanabi attempted to force through the barricade. Keyoke issued a command and a pair of husky servants hauled on ropes tied to the end of the heavy log that was the mainstay of the defenses. The tree trunk drew aside, and the barricade gave way. Branches and rock shoring burst inward, and off-balance Minwanabi soldiers fell forward onto their faces.

Keyoke showed his teeth in satisfaction, just as Dakhati called for the charge, hurling his company at a run into the astonished and ragged line of attackers. The fresh Acoma reserve pushed the vanguard back, while archers on the Acoma flanks fired upon their Minwanabi counterparts. The air was alive with arrows, thick enough to shadow the sunlight that now beat unmercifully from above; with the enemy unable to fan out past the rocks, their concentrated numbers made them easy targets. Within moments the orange-and-black arrows ceased.

The vigorous assault by the Acoma drove the Minwanabi up the defile, and Keyoke called the next wave of soldiers forward. They rushed to the breached barricade, pulled the dead from the branches and rocks, and threw Minwanabi as well as Acoma corpses into the canyon. Servants stood ready to strip the fallen of armor and arms, saving anything that might be turned to Acoma use. Swords that were not too badly damaged, shields and daggers, an occasional hip bag of food—all were quickly added to the Acoma stores. Other servants scrambled around the area, inspecting arrows in a search for those that hadn't been broken against the stone walls of the canyon. Acoma archers fired black-and-orange-marked arrows as often as green ones.

The bodies were left naked where they lay while soldiers

and servants rushed to restore the barricade. Keyoke mourned inwardly for Dakhati's reserves, still fighting on the other side; he prayed their deaths would be hard-won and their pain honorably brief. The sacrifice would lend their fellows the time to restore the broken barricade and inflict more disproportionate damage on the Minwanabi.

Fifty or more Minwanabi casualties lay in the clearing. Keyoke revised his estimate to nearly three hundred enemies dead or critically injured. The sky showed the day half-done and their position no worse—perhaps even stronger—than at first light.

And yet no man knew how many companies the Minwanabi had sent against them.

Keyoke repositioned himself to gain a view over the barricade. If any in Dakhati's small band were alive to effect a retreat, they would shortly be attempting to return. Keyoke knew his own soldiers were well drilled in the plan, but more than once he had seen battle stress confuse orders. The Acoma Force Commander stayed at hand to restrain any hotheads from attacking their brother soldiers.

They waited under the blistering sun in an airless defile that now stank of sweat, excrement, and death. Sounds of battle echoed off sheer walls of damp rock. Minutes dragged by, and flies swarmed. Keyoke and the other seasoned warriors watched anxiously for the first green Acoma helm to appear on the trail beyond the barricade.

In time, Keyoke accepted what he had expected all along: Dakhati and his company had continued their charge past all chance of retreat. They had no intention of returning. The Strike Leader who led them understood as well as Keyoke that eventually the Minwanabi must prevail. Beyond hearing orders, Dakhati's little band was simply intent on killing as long and as many as possible before death overtook their company.

Keyoke raised his eyes to heaven and silently wished them a great killing. Putting aside feelings of loss for his own brave warriors, or concerns for what this defeat would mean for Lady Mara, Keyoke bid three more servants and the small, nimble water boy to attempt to slip away over the barricade. If Dakhati had driven the enemy far enough up the defile to enable the four to escape into cover in the wood, word might yet reach the estates.

But such hopes were dashed in an instant as a wave of Minwanabi soldiers still bloodied from dispatching Dakhati's men took the lives of the four even before they could turn and run. If there was panic, there were no screams; and the water boy died on his feet, facing the enemy with a kitchen knife clutched in his hand.

Turakamu receive such valor kindly, Keyoke prayed, as quietly he accepted his coming death as inevitable. He fingered his battered sword hilt, familiar to him as a brother. What a price his foe would pay!

Sundown came. Gloom fell into colorless twilight, smothered under a descending mantle of mist. Exhausted soldiers trudged from their shifts at the barricade, and stiffly Keyoke limped over to assess their condition. His forces had dwindled. Of the hundred soldiers and fifty servants who had left the Acoma estates, fewer than forty soldiers and twenty servants remained on their feet to serve. Most of the rest were dead, though about a dozen wounded soldiers and a like number of servants were ministered to in a makeshift camp around the pool. The incessant random arrows of the Minwanabi still caused enough damage to keep men on edge. No one could lie down, lest he offer a better target for a descending shaft. A few men attempted to rest under a pair of shields, but the experience encouraged cramping rather than rest. Most warriors simply sat with knees drawn up under chin, shoulders hunched, and heads bowed, as tight against the walls of the canyon as possible.

Night came, and the fighting wore on by the flickering flames of enemy brands. The mist in the defile glowed with their light, like some twisting fog-tendriled spirit. The Acoma warriors considered that light, and sharpened their weapons, and if their voices expressed courage through quips, their thoughts were bleak. The fighting would probably not last until the morning, and certainly not to midday. They knew this as well as the Force Commander who tirelessly made his rounds to bolster their spirits.

Hours passed, and men died, and the stars stayed hidden by the mist. Keyoke was crossing the clearing to inspect two men who appeared injured by thrown rocks when something struck him in the right leg like a needra calf's kick. He staggered and all but dropped to his knees as pain exploded in his right thigh. Two soldiers ran to assist him as he began to collapse from the arrow that protruded from his upper leg. They carried him a short way and gently placed him so he could sit with his back against a relatively sheltered part of the canyon wall.

Fighting off a threatening blackness that circled his vision, Keyoke said, "Gods, that hurts." He forced himself to look at the shaft that was buried in his thigh. It had struck downward—one of the random shots into the canyon—and he could feel the head scrape the bone. "Push it through and cut off the feathers," he ordered. "Then pull it out."

The two soldiers exchanged glances, and he had to repeat his order, shouting through clenched teeth that they should pull the accursed shaft free.

The soldiers' eyes met again, over the dusty plumes of Keyoke's helm. Neither wished to speak the truth: that to pull the arrow free would likely tear an artery and cause death in a spurting flow of blood.

Keyoke cursed, very clearly. He pulled one gnarled arm from the supporting hold of one warrior and, with a surprisingly steady hand, reached out, grasped the arrow, and snapped the wood. "Push it through!" he demanded.

The shaft that still held the head remained embedded in flesh. The hole bled sullenly, swelling rapidly to purple.

"That will fester," one warrior said gently. "It should be cut out, and the wound allowed to drain."

"I haven't time," Keyoke said, his voice not as steady as his hand. The agony that cut through him had little to do with pain, which he had known before and endured, as now, when necessary. "If the arrow is not removed and the gods-damned head keeps rubbing against my leg bone, I will likely lose consciousness. Most certainly I will not be able to walk and continue commanding our troops."

The soldiers said nothing, but their unspoken reproach was noticed.

Keyoke relied in his anger. "Do you think any one of us will be alive for long enough for me to die of a wound gone bad? Tie off this leg and *push the damn thing through!*" They reluctantly obeyed. Pain caused Keyoke's vision to swim, and for a few minutes he lost his sense of time and place. After a few moments of darkness, his wits returned and he found the soldiers binding the wound; the agony in his leg fell off to a dull ache.

Keyoke ordered the warriors to help him to his feet and he stood unsteadily a few moments. He refused to cut a cane from the brush, but stumped about with half-steps, his thigh throbbing angrily and each bump and jostle of motion a torment. But no man in Acoma green would dispute his authority; he was still in command of his army.

He promoted a particularly bright young soldier, Sezalmel, to acting Strike Leader, only to watch the man die less than an hour later. Reacting in inspired frenzy, Sezalmel had repulsed the largest Minwanabi offensive since sundown, the second near breaching of the barricade. His sortie drove the attackers back, but only in exchange for heavy losses. The Acoma were tiring, while the Minwanabi warriors seemed inexhaustible. Keyoke took no time to promote anyone else. There was no need, with Acoma numbers fallen below that of a small strike force. A second commander would be superfluous.

Keyoke shuffled wearily over to the servants and instructed a distribution of rations. Given the fatalities, there was now enough food for every man to eat as he wished. If the soldiers could not have enjoyed a hot meal, at least they would be restored by a full stomach. Keyoke took a cake and piece of jerked needra. He had no appetite, but he forced himself to chew. The painful throbbing in his right leg and the burning ache of swollen tissue were incessant. In the end, when no one was looking, he spat the tasteless morsels on the ground. He drank when the waterskin was passed, and controlled the heave of his stomach. His throat still seemed dry from the cakes, and he wondered if he was beginning to get feverish. Then, as always, his thoughts returned to his command.

Keyoke estimated that more than three hundred fifty Minwanabi had fallen before the barricade throughout the day. The night's numbers would be fewer, lessening as his soldiers tired. At least fifty enemies had perished after the hour of sundown. His soldiers were killing Mara's foes at a rate of five to one. Losses were increasing, however, and very soon would become critical as his own forces were cut down until, inevitably, the Minwanabi would win past the barricade and rush through to slay the survivors. Keyoke concluded his review with pride. The Acoma forces had surpassed expectations, and the end might be prolonged until dawn.

Sitting back against the icy damp of the rock wall, Keyoke removed his helm. He scraped back soaked grey hair and reflected that he had never known such fatigue in his life.

The exhaustion brought on a regret: that he should be guilty of an old man's vanity. He berated himself for not spending more time training Lujan and the other Strike Leaders. He should have insisted all the officers dine with him in the servants' hall, instead of in the barracks with their own companies, while he took his meal with Lady Mara, or Nacoya, or Jican. Every chance missed to educate those young soldiers came back to haunt him.

Too late, now, to wish a younger man here in his post. A hot flash of pain from his wound reawakened anger. Cursing himself for a fool, he put aside his sorrow. He refused, at the last, to be a man caught up in black contemplations. A battle continued to be fought, and morbid reflections required effort better spent on the field.

Keyoke propped his wounded leg out before him and was racked by a stab of agony. He made no sound, but only sweated under the weight of his armor. By the gleam thrown off by banked coals, the flesh around the puncture looked red —a deception of light, or inflammation, he had no means to tell—and it throbbed unmercifully. No matter, he thought. A wound was but a way to measure growth for a warrior. Life was pain and pain was life. His circling thoughts drifted as his body attempted to fight off the aches of battle, injury, exhaustion, and age.

He must have dozed, for the next he knew, a soldier was shaking his shoulder, exhorting him to wake. Keyoke blinked gummed eyelids and fought to clear senses that normally came instantly alert. Without thought he attempted to rise, but pain seared the length of his leg and caused him an audible gasp for air. The soldier offered a steadying hand and tried to keep pity from his eyes. "Force Commander, we hear armed men approaching in the hills above the canyon!"

Keyoke squinted at the narrow crack of sky above the cliff walls. There were no stars, nor any lessening of darkness to indicate the hour. He had no way to estimate how much time had passed. "How long until dawn?" he asked.

The soldier frowned. "Perhaps two hours, Force Commander."

"Bank the fire," Keyoke snapped. Sure that the enemy had by now encircled the mountains and flanked his position, he hobbled over to the men who readied themselves for the next assault. A frown marred his forehead. "If Irrilandi has sent troops to crush us from the hills, why attack in the darkness?" he said softly, unaware, through his fever and his pain, that he did his musing aloud.

Then a crack resounded across the clearing. The barricade exploded backward under a wave of orange-and-black-armored bodies, and Acoma defenders were hurled in all directions. A heavy log burst through with a grind of stones and a tearing of stinking needra flesh. The canyon had been breached by a ram, run up the short defile under cover of darkness, and wielded with devastating effect.

Minwanabi soldiers rushed screaming into the canyon while the Acoma sprang to engage them. Keyoke called to the servants to take cover behind the bulwark of silks. Soldiers fell thrashing in death throes or groaning in mortal pain. The fighting spread into the breached canyon. Bodies draped twitching and crushed between the stones and large branches of the shifted barricade; others writhed, impaled. Some few fumbled to lift swords while they lay with broken legs and backs.

Keyoke absorbed this without pause to register the horror, for Minwanabi soldiers poured through the gap. The defile might only admit one or two men at a time, but it was open, and the Acoma were in retreat.

Keyoke drew his sword. His helm was off, abandoned on the ground where he had slept. He rejected the idea of searching for it, not trusting his balky leg enough to attempt unnecessary steps. Only the will of the gods might determine whether he should die proudly as Acoma Force Commander or as just another nameless old soldier. With Mara left threatened, in the end, he judged, it mattered little.

"Burn the silk," he called to a servant, who hovered awaiting orders by his elbow. The man bowed swiftly and left, and in the soft, untrustworthy light of blossoming torches, as loyal hands threw flaming brands upon piled silk,

Keyoke hurried forward in a stumbling half-hop. Through a spinning haze of fever he was aware of the screams of dying soldiers and the clash of arms punctuated by the crackle of silk and dry wood exploding at his back in a leaping wash of fire. A Minwanabi soldier spun backwards, stumbling from the blow of an Acoma warrior. Keyoke dispatched him with a reflexive slash, and a grim smile stretched his lips across his teeth. His leg might be ruined, but by Turakamu, his sword arm still functioned. He would see the Minwanabi as his escorts into the halls of the Red God.

The battle raged across the narrow draw, hemmed between rock walls and a blazing barrier of silk. Men struggled in a dance with death, their swords shining red in the night. Fighting, stumbling ahead, Keyoke squinted against the glare and tried to sort friend from foe. The warriors of both sides looked like nothing so much as a scene from some demented battle hell as the fire burned in brilliant fury.

Beset by another Minwanabi, Keyoke ducked a sword thrust and countered with a single chop to the throat. The warrior fell, gurgling, and precious seconds were lost because Keyoke could not raise his injured leg high enough to step over the man's death throes. The Acoma Force Commander's knee trembled as he limped around, and pain jabbed him from ankle to thigh each time the limb bore weight. The agony knotted his belly, and he swallowed to keep from voiding his stomach. Dizziness teased at his balance, and his vision swam.

Keyoke hobbled headlong into his last fight, where two Minwanabi soldiers hammered at the shield of an Acoma. Hide and wood parted with a crack, and a blade struck home. The Acoma warrior went down, and his dying eyes met those of his officer.

"Force Commander," he called clearly, before an attacker trampled over his face.

Then a figure in orange and black was shouting and pointing his sword, and warriors turned and converged. The clash of arms swelled on all sides. Believing the sound to be amplified by his fever, Keyoke focused only on the recognition reflected on enemy features.

"The Acoma Force Commander!" someone called clearly, and Keyoke was beset by enemies. His sword spilled their blood, but his feet were not nimble. His guard was hampered by his lameness, and in the press of cut and thrust he was aware of other soldiers rushing him from behind. He could do nothing to prevent himself being surrounded. Driven to his knees and crippled, he wrestled through spinning vision to ward off the blows hammered down on him. The Minwanabi soldier before him suddenly stiffened. His expression of astonished disbelief was swallowed by darkness as he fell. Keyoke caught sight of a meat cleaver protruding from Minwanabi armor, and a frightened servant backing away. Keyoke cut sideways with his sword, and at least one more enemy died before he could avenge his fallen comrade. The servant perished anyway, cut from chest to crotch by another soldier, and then the same bloody sword was pointed and slashing at Keyoke. More men pressed in from the sides. He fought them, with a skill honed by forty years on the field.

Sweat ran down Keyoke's temples. He blinked salty drops from his eyes and slashed through a white haze of pain. Dimly he noticed an Acoma servant crouched near him, and hands attempting to prop him upright. Then the servant's eyes went round and he lurched forward. His back lay opened to show the white ribs, and his weight drove Keyoke to the ground.

Blinded by dust and agony, Keyoke struggled to rise. His ears rang and his hands would not grip. Numbed fingers could not find his sword, and he was conscious of wetness flooding down his flank beneath his armor. He gasped, but there seemed to be no air to fill his lungs. Above him he made out the shape of a Minwanabi soldier, pulling back his blade from the thrust that had dispatched the valiant servant.

Keyoke groped in the dirt, found his sword, and struggled against the twitching weight of the corpse to raise his guard. The soldier pulled the servant aside, then aimed a killing stroke at the beaten old Force Commander at his feet. Keyoke raised his arm to parry and drew upon his last shred of strength to commend his wal to Turakamu. Then sword met sword, and the laminated hide screeched with the impact. The blow deflected, but barely. The Minwanabi stroke missed the heart and glanced down to pierce through armor and gambeson and, finally, through the flesh of Keyoke's belly.

The soldier jerked back his blade. Flesh tore and bled, and Keyoke heard a distant, hoarse cry, as torment forced his own lips to betray his weakness before an enemy. At the ending of life, Keyoke invoked his soldier's will to greet death with head up and eyes open. Through the pounding of blood in his own ears, the Force Commander heard a distant voice crying, "Acoma!" He felt only pride for that one brave soldier.

Blurred shapes swam in and out of focus. Time seemed unnaturally slowed. Through the darkness, a hand caught the Minwanabi soldier's arm, yanking back the descending sword. Keyoke frowned and faintly wondered whether this was the god's reward for lifetime service: for his valor in Acoma defense, he would not feel the death blow. "Tura-kamu," he muttered, believing himself bound for the Red God's halls; then the earth overturned, and he knew nothing as the sword slipped from his hand.

10. *MASTERPLOT*

Sounds intruded.

Through an encompassing dark, Keyoke heard voices. They echoed dreamlike through his mind, amid a growing awareness of pain. He listened for the singing of warriors, the Minwanabi dead who would attest to his valor as he entered the halls of Turakamu.

But there came no singing, only spoken words in a voice that sounded like Lujan's.

No, thought Keyoke. No. Through a stirring rush of anguish that mushroomed into despair, he listened more carefully. There had to be singing.

". . . not regained consciousness since the battle," Lujan's voice continued, ". . . been delirious with fever . . . serious wounds in his belly and side . . ."

Another voice interjected, Nacoya's surely. "Gods. Mara must not see him like this. It will surely break her heart."

And then a bustle amid the darkness, and someone that sounded like his mistress crying out in an anguish too sharp to rein back. "Keyoke!"

There was to be no singing, then, the old warrior understood in cold sorrow. Accolades would not herald a warrior who died in defeat. The Acoma must have been vanquished for Mara, Lujan, and Nacoya to be present here, in the halls of Turakamu. The Minwanabi army must have gone on from the canyon to attack the estate, and the cho-ja defenders must have fled or been overwhelmed. The end must have come with the enemy in triumph, and the Acoma crushed.

"Mistress," murmured Keyoke in his delirium. "Lady."

"Listen! He speaks!" someone exclaimed.

"Keyoke?" Mara's voice said again. Cool hands brushed his brow, the fingers lightly trembling.

Then light shone, blindingly bright through half-opened eyelids, and consciousness flooded back, along with full awareness of the pain.

"Keyoke," Mara said again. Her hands settled on either side of his temples, gently and insistently framing his face. "We are all well. Ayaki is well. Lujan speaks of a battle bravely fought in a canyon. The Minwanabi brought five hundred men to attack, and we hear your small company battled to the death defending the silk."

The Force Commander struggled through a haze of fever and managed to focus his eyes. His mistress bent over him, her dark hair still loose from her sleeping mat, and her pretty brow furrowed with concern. He was not in the halls of the Red God but in the courtyard before the doors of the Acoma estate house. The grounds were peaceful. Shapes stirred in the surrounding mists as warriors of Lujan's company dispersed to their barracks. A servant with a cloth hovered nearby, ready to wipe his sweating face. Keyoke drew a difficult breath. Through the fiery pain of his injuries he gathered his wits and spoke. "Lady Mara. There is danger. Lord Desio has breached your security."

Mara stroked his cheek. "I know, Keyoke. The spy who was tortured escaped and brought us word. That's how Lujan knew to rush his company to the mountains to your aid."

Keyoke thought back to the sounds of fighting that had broken out at the last, in the hills behind the canyon. Lujan, then, had flanked Lord Desio's army and put it to rout up the ravine.

"How many are alive?" Keyoke asked, his voice barely a croak.

Lujan said, "Six men, Force Commander, counting yourself. All seriously wounded."

Keyoke swallowed hard. Of the hundred warriors and fifty servants, only five beside himself survived the Minwanabi trap.

"Don't mind that the silk has been lost," Mara added. "The cho-ja shall eventually make more."

Keyoke fumbled a hand free of the blankets that lapped

over his chest. He grasped Mara's wrist. "The silk is not lost," he gasped clearly. "Not all of it."

This brought an exclamation from Lujan and a whispering stir among the servants. Only then did Keyoke notice the presence of Jican, hovering, bright-eyed, to one side.

He forced out the necessary phrases and told where the bolts were left concealed in the rocks leading into the pass.

Mara smiled. The expression lent her face the delicate, glowing beauty that had once been her mother's, Keyoke recalled. He also noticed the tears that glittered brightly at the corners of her eyes, which she bravely blinked to keep back. "No mistress could have asked so much. You have served honorably, and superbly well. Now rest. Your wounds are very grave."

Keyoke did not ask how grave; the pain told all he needed to know. He loosed his breath in a sigh. "I can die now," he added in a whisper.

The mistress did not protest but arose and imperiously called out orders for her Force Commander to be given her finest chamber. "Light candles for him, and call poets, and musicians to sing him tribute. For all must know that he has fought as a hero, and given his life for the Acoma."

Ruling Lady she might be, Keyoke thought, but her voice shook. From him, who knew her as a daughter, she could not hide her grief. "Do not weep for me, Lady," he whispered. "I am content."

There was noise and a jostle of motion, and consciousness wavered. "Do not weep for me, Lady," Keyoke repeated. If she heard, he could not tell, for the darkness lapped over him once more.

Later he was aware of scented candles, and soft music, and a stillness that enveloped him like peace, except for the pain, which seemed endless. Forcing his tired eyes open, he saw that he lay on a mat in a beautifully appointed chamber, one painted with scenes of warriors displaying the virtues of arms and valor. Between the reedy notes of two vielles playing in counterpoint, he heard a poet reciting the deeds and the victories he had accomplished, which extended back into Lord Sezu's time. Keyoke let his eyes fall closed again. He had not lied to his Lady. He was content. To die of great wounds for her honor was a just and fitting destiny for a warrior grown old in her service.

But a disturbance outside in the corridor rang over the notes of the instruments, and the poet faltered in his lines.

"Damn it, are you just going to let him lie there until he dies?" cried a strident, nasal voice.

The barbarian, Keyoke identified, as always challenging custom.

Lujan's voice interjected, unaccustomedly distressed. "He has served honorably! What more can any of us do?"

"Get a healer to fight for his life," Kevin almost shouted. "Or do you wait for your gods to save him?"

"That's impertinence!" snapped Lujan, and there followed the sound of a hand striking flesh.

"Stop it! Both of you!" Mara broke in, and the voices merged together in a spill of sound that rose and fell like waves.

Keyoke lay still and wished the arguing would end. The poet had reached the stanzas that referred to the raid he had once staged with Papewaio against Tecuma of the Anasati, and he wanted to listen for inaccuracies. No doubt the bard would not mention the celebration that had followed, nor the jars of sā wine he and Pape and the master had shared to celebrate the victory. They had all paid with a hangover, Keyoke recalled, and he had hurt afterward nearly as much as he did now.

But the poet did not resume his verses. Instead, Keyoke heard Mara's voïce carrying from the hallway. "Kevin, it would be no kindness at all to save the life of a warrior who is missing a leg. Or didn't you know that Lujan's field healer had it cut off, since Keyoke took an arrow wound that festered?"

Keyoke swallowed hard. The agony that racked his body masked his awareness of the missing limb. He kept his eyes closed.

"So what!" Kevin said in exasperation. "Keyoke's value lies in his expertise, and even *your* gods-besotted healer knows a man's brains are not in his feet!"

Silence followed, then Keyoke heard the screen swept back and someone step through.

Keyoke opened one eye and looked in the direction of the disturbance. Entering the room was the tall barbarian. His hair blazed like fire in the candlelight, and his height threw dark shadows on the wall. He shoved determinedly through the musicians, then shot a glance of disgust at the poet. "Get out," he said imperiously. "I want to talk with the old man and see what he thinks about dying."

Keyoke looked up into the face of the barbarian slave, his eyes dark with fury. He forced his voice to be as firm as his condition permitted. "You are impertinent," he echoed Lujan. "And you intrude upon matters of honor. Were I armed, I would kill you where you stand."

Kevin shrugged and sat down at the old warrior's side. "If you had the strength to kill me, old man, I wouldn't be here." He crossed his arms, leaned his elbows upon his knees, and regarded Keyoke who was very much a general of armies, even propped like a figurehead amid a sea of cushions. His flesh might be drawn with illness, but his face was still that of a commander. "Anyway, you are not armed," Kevin observed with his shattering, outworld bluntness. "And you'll need a crutch to rise from that bed. So maybe your problems can't be answered with a blade anymore, Force Commander Keyoke."

The pain dragged at his belly as the old man drew breath to reply. He could feel the weakness sucking at him, the darkness in the wings that waited to draw him in, but he gathered himself and managed to speak with the tone that had stopped many a young warrior from cockiness. "I have served."

The words were delivered with unassailable dignity. Kevin shut his eyes for a moment and inwardly seemed to flinch. "Mara still needs you."

He did not look at Keyoke. Apparently his rudeness had limits; but his hands tightened white against his forearms, and Lujan, in the doorway, turned away his face.

"Mara still needs you," Kevin grated out, as if he struggled for other words that eluded him. "She is left with no great general for her armies, no master tactician to take your place."

No sound and no movement issued from the man in the cushions. Kevin frowned and, with obvious discomfort, tried again. "You need no legs to train your successor, nor to advise in matters of war."

"I need no legs to know that you have overstepped yourself," Keyoke interrupted. The effort taxed him. He sagged back against his pillows. "Who are you, barbarian, to judge me in my service to this house?"

Kevin flushed darkly and rose to his feet. Embarrassed, in his transparent way, but also unknowably stung, he clenched his fists and added, "I did not come to hound you, but to make you think." Then, as if angry, the huge redhead stalked from the bedside. At the doorway he half turned, but still would not meet Keyoke's eyes. "You love her too," he said accusingly. "To die without a fight is to deprive her of her finest commander. I say you seek an easy way out; your service is not discharged, old man. If you die now, you desert your post."

He was gone before Keyoke could summon the strength for rejoinder. The candles seemed suddenly too bright, and the pain intense. Quietly the musicians resumed their play. Keyoke listened, but his heart found no ease. The poet's verses lost their luster and became just empty words, recounting events long done and mostly forgotten as he lapsed into sleep.

Mara waited outside in the hallway. No attendants were with her, and she stood so still that Kevin almost missed her in the shadows. Only quick reflexes stopped him as, wiping moisture from his eyes, he saw her barely in time to prevent crashing into her.

"You will answer to me for this," she said, and although her poise was perfect, and her tone even, Kevin knew her well enough to read the anger in her stance. Her hands twisted in the fabric of her sleeves as she went on. "Keyoke has led our soldiers into battle for more years than I've been alive. He has faced enemies in situations the rest of us would have nightmares just contemplating. He left a war, and his own Lord to die, though the orders broke his heart, to keep the Acoma name alive by coming to take me from Lashima's temple. If we have a natami in the glade to hold our honor sacred, Keyoke is worthy of the credit. How dare you, a slave and a barbarian, imply that he has not done enough!"

"Well," said Kevin, "I admit that I have a big mouth, and also that I don't know when to keep it shut." He smiled in that sudden, spontaneous way that never failed to disarm her.

Mara sighed. "Why must you continually interfere with things you do not understand? If Keyoke wishes a warrior's death, it is his right, and our honor, to grant him his passage in comfort."

Kevin's smile vanished. "If I have any quarrel with your culture, Lady, it is that you count life much too lightly. Keyoke is a brilliant tactician. His mind is his genius, not his sword arm, which a younger man can beat anyway. Yet all of you stand back, and send poets and musicians! And wait for him to die his warrior's death, and waste the years of experience that your army so sorely needs to—"

"And you suggest?" Mara interrupted. Her lips were white.

Kevin shivered under the intensity of her gaze, but continued. "I would appoint Keyoke to the position of an adviser, make up a new office if necessary, and then call in the most skilled of your healers. The wound in his abdomen might kill him still, but I believe that human nature between your culture and mine cannot differ so widely that a man, even a dying one, wants to let go of life feeling useless."

"You presume to a great deal of knowledge for a commoner," Mara observed acidly.

Kevin stiffened and all at once fell into one of his strange, inexplicable silences. He locked eyes with her, still unwilling to end the discussion; and so wrapped up was she in trying to read why he should suddenly become secretive, Mara did not notice the runner slave at her elbow until the second time he addressed her.

"Mistress." The boy bowed diffidently. "My Lady, Nacoya bids you come at once to the great hall. An imperial messenger awaits your attendance."

The flush of anger drained out of Mara's cheeks. "Find Lujan and send him to me at once," she instructed the runner. As though she had forgotten Kevin's existence and the fact she had been deadlocked in an argument only seconds before, she spun on her heel and departed down the corridor in almost unseemly haste.

Kevin, predictably, followed after. "What's going on?"

She didn't answer, and the runner slave had dashed beyond earshot. Undeterred, Kevin lengthened stride until he overtook his diminutive mistress. He tried another tack. "What's an imperial messenger?"

"Bad news," Mara returned shortly. "At least, this close upon the heels of a Minwanabi attack, a message from the Emperor, the Warlord, or the High Council speaks of a great move in the game."

Mara skirted the bows of a cluster of house slaves bent over buckets and brushes, scrubbing the lacquered wood floor. She crossed the atrium that led toward the great doubled doors to the hall, and Kevin followed. His Lady's poise had seemed brittle since the return of Lujan's companies. The purpose of the Minwanabi raid, she insisted, had not been simply to ruin her silk in the marketplace. Being unable to follow every twist of Tsurani politics, which to his Kingdom mind still seemed convolutedly illogical, Kevin was determined to stay at Mara's side. What threatened her threatened him, and his feelings toward her were protective.

The great hall held the damp in the mornings, and the old stone floor transmitted chill even through the soles of leather sandals. Crossing the echoing expanse of empty space, shuttered into gloom by closed screens, Kevin saw Nacoya awaiting on the dais and heard Lujan's step enter from the passage behind. But the barbarian's attention stayed riveted ahead where, even in the dimness, the sparkle of gold stood out, an unexpected and unnerving sight in a land where metals were a rarity.

The messenger sat on a fine, threadworked cushion, and even his posture was imposing. He was a young man, powerfully muscled, and beautiful to look upon in a simple kilt of white cloth. Cross-gartered sandals hugged his dusty legs, and his skin sparkled with perspiration. Binding shoulder-length black hair from his brow was his badge of rank, a cloth of alternating bands of gold and white that sparkled and flashed through the shadows. The thread of the weave was metallic, true gold, the symbol of the Emperor of Tsuranuanni, whose bonded word he carried.

Upon Mara's entrance, he rose from his seat and presented himself with a bow. The gesture denoted arrogance, for although he was a servant and she a noble Lady, his master's word was the law of the land, to which all great houses must submit. The head badge made this man sacrosanct within the Empire. He could safely run through a battlefield, between warring houses, and no soldier would dare impede his passage, upon pain of the Emperor's wrath. The messenger knelt with beautifully studied poise and presented a gilt-edged scroll, tied also with ribbons of gold, and sealed with the imprint of Ichindar.

Mara accepted the weighty missive, her hands looking fragile against the parchment. She broke the seal, unrolled the scroll, and began to read, while Lujan took his place on the side once occupied by Keyoke, and Nacoya visibly restrained herself from craning her neck to make out words over her mistress's shoulder.

The document was not lengthy. Kevin, who was tallest, could see that the sentences were brief. Yet Mara paused a lengthy interval before she raised her face and spoke.

"Thank you. You may go," she said to the messenger. "My servants will see you refreshed and housed, if you wish to rest while my scribes take dictation and prepare my return message."

The imperial messenger bowed and departed, the tap of his nail-studded sandals loud in the closed hall. The moment he passed beyond the doorway, Mara sank down upon the nearest empty cushion.

"Tasaio's hand is at last revealed," she said, and her voice sounded hollow and small.

Nacoya took the scroll and read its lines with a steadily deepening scowl. "The devil!" she exclaimed when she finished.

"Pretty Lady," Lujan interjected, "what are the Emperor's wishes?"

It was Nacoya who answered, her aged voice like acid. "Orders, from the High Council. We must, with all haste, send our army to lend support to Lord Xacatecas in his war against the nomad raiders in Dustari. Lady Mara has been commanded to appear in person, with a levy of four companies of troops, to be ready to depart within two months."

Lujan's eyebrows jerked up and froze. "Three companies would be too many," he said, and his hand tapped furiously on his sword hilt. "We're going to have to buy favors of the cho-ja." His gaze shifted significantly to Kevin. "And you're right, damn your barbarian ideas. Keyoke cannot be granted the luxury of dying, or else the estate will be left stripped of its last experienced officer."

"That's surely what Desio intends. We must thwart him." Mara turned her head. Her eyes were black sparks, and her cheeks were flushed in shock as she voiced her orders. "Lujan, you are now promoted to the post of Force Commander. Take Kevin and go to Keyoke. Tell him I wish to appoint him as First Adviser for War, but will do so only with his permission." Her voice went distant with memory or maybe tears withheld as she added, "He will think other warriors will ridicule him for carrying a crutch, but I will see his name honored. Remind him that Pape once found pride in wearing the black rag of the condemned."

Lujan bowed, a suggestion of sorrow in his own stance. "I doubt Keyoke would leave us in such perilous straits, my Lady. But the gods might overrule his will. The wound in his abdomen is not the sort that a man is likely to recover from."

Mara bit her lip. As if the words pained her, she said, "Then, with his permission, I will send runner slaves and messengers throughout the Empire, to seek a healing priest of Hantukama."

"The offering such a priest will demand for a healing will be great," Nacoya pointed out. "You may have to build a large shrine."

Mara came close to losing her temper. "Then speak to Jican about rescuing the remnants of our silk from the mountains and getting it to market at Jamar! For we need our Keyoke alive, or all will be lost. We cannot afford to slight the Lord of the Xacatecas." Even for Kevin's sake, this statement needed no elaboration. The promise of Lord Xacatecas' alliance had held many enemies at bay; should the Acoma give a family that powerful any cause whatsoever for enmity, they would beg a swift ruin, engaged as they were in their blood feud with the Minwanabi. "The estate here must not be left in jeopardy," Mara finished.

"Dustari is a trap," Nacoya said, voicing a point all except Kevin was aware of. "Tasaio will be there, and no move you or your four companies can make will not be anticipated in advance. You and the men you take with you will go the way of Lord Sezu, betrayed to your deaths on foreign soil."

"All the more reason why Keyoke must hold these lands secure for Ayaki," Mara finished. And the last high color fled her face.

•   •   •

The Imperial messenger departed with Mara's written acquiescence to the High Council's demands. After that, her household factors and advisers hurried off to initiate a frenzied list of preparations. Lujan detailed officers to make an inventory, then he and Kevin departed for Keyoke's bedside, neither with enthusiasm.

Jican arrived as they departed, summoned from the needra fields by the runner slave.

"I need a full accounting of Acoma assets," Mara demanded before the little man had entirely risen from his bow. "How many centis we have in cash, and how many more we might borrow. I need to know how many weapons our master armorers can turn out in two months, and how many more we might purchase."

Jican's brows went up. "Lady, did you not already decide to send our new arms to the markets? We will need the sale to balance our deficit in the silk."

Mara frowned and restrained a sharp impulse to snap. "Jican, that was yesterday. Today we must outfit four companies to relieve Lord Xacatecas in Dustari."

The hadonra was adept at figures. "You'll be bargaining for more warriors from the cho-ja, then," he surmised. His straight brows tightened into a frown. "We'll have to sell off some prime stock from your needra herds."

"Do it," Mara said at once. "I'll be with Ayaki. When you have the accounting complete, bring your slates to the nursery."

"Your will, Lady," said Jican unhappily. Wars were the perpetual ruin of good finance, and that Mara must indulge in one through the plotting of dangerous enemies made him frightened. So had great houses fallen in the past; and the disaster of Sezu's betrayal and death had happened too recently for any servant on the estate not to feel the threat of annihilation. Word did not take long to spread among the servants, and in a household that was bustling with activity, the talk was ominously hushed.

Mara spent an hour with her son that seemed all too terribly brief. He would soon be five, and had a temper that occasionally burned to rages that defeated the skills of his nurses. Now, lying on his stomach with his ankles crossed in the air, playing at soldiers, he pushed his plumed officers to and fro and cried commands in a treble child's voice. Mara watched him with a wrenching in her heart and tried to memorize the small face, shadowed by a fall of dark bangs. She clasped cold hands and wondered if she would live to see her child grow to manhood. That he very well might not was a possibility she forced out of her thoughts. She, who had come into power too young, burned with the wish that her son might have the chance to grow, and learn, and have years to be guided into preparedness for the ruling Lordship that awaited him. She must live and return from the desert, and make sure that this became so.

Until Jican arrived with his figures, she prayed long and desperately to Chochocan. At her feet, Ayaki obliterated company upon company of Minwanabi enemies, while his mother racked her mind for solutions to impossible equations.

Jican arrived and presented his slates, their columns impeccably neat despite the haste in Mara's command. The hadonra looked hollow-eyed and worn as he bowed. "Lady. I have done as you commanded. Here are three calculations on your liquid financial assets. One depends upon the remaining silk arriving safely to market. The other two include what you might spend comfortably, and what you might call on, with variable lists of consequences. If you go by the last slate, be warned. Your herds will take another four years to build back to their present levels of productivity."

Mara flipped through the slates, then unhesitatingly selected the final one. She glanced down at Ayaki, who watched her with liquid dark eyes. "The needra are replaceable," she pointed out, and briskly sent her servants to fetch retinue and litter. "I'll be visiting the cho-ja Queen for the rest of the afternoon."

"Can I come?" Ayaki shouted, springing up and scattering toy warriors in a bounding rush toward his mother.

She reached out and ruffled his hair with the hand not clutching the slate. "No, son. Not this time."

The boy scowled, but did not talk back. At last his nurse was succeeding in teaching him the manners his dead father had never acquired. "Kevin will take you for a wagon ride," she consoled, then remembered: Lujan and her barbarian had not reported back from Keyoke's chamber. "If he has time for you," she amended to the son who tugged at her elbow. She cupped his tiny face gently in her hand. "And if you

allow the bath maid to wash the fruit juice off your chin."
She gave his face a playful shake.

Ayaki's scowl deepened. He rubbed his soiled mouth,
made a sound through his lips, and said, "Yes, Mother. But
when I am Ruling Lord, I shall keep my chin sticky if I
please."

Mara gave an exasperated glance toward heaven, then disentangled her sleeve from her son. It smelled of jomach and
cho-ja–made candy. "Boy, if you do not worry first about the
lessons of growing up, there will be no estate for you to
manage."

A servant appeared at the doorway. "Lady? Your litter
awaits."

Mara bent and kissed Ayaki, and came away with the
taste of the candy. The mishap did not irritate her. All too
soon she would be breathing and tasting the dust of the
southern deserts, and home would be an ocean's width away.

Although many times a haven in times of trouble, the cho-ja
hive with its cool dimness for once brought no comfort. Mara
knotted sweating fingers under the sleeves of her overrobe.
An unfamiliar officer accompanied her where once Keyoke
would have walked, half a pace to her rear, exchanging greetings and courtesies with the hive's Force Commander, Lax'l.
The warrior, Murnachi, had never fought with a company of
cho-ja. Although he was honored to be asked to accompany
his mistress on this important mission to the Queen, his stiffness denoted his discomfort and desire to be returned to the
open air as soon as possible.

Mara made her way through the tunnels leading to the
Queen's chamber, by now a familiar route. But this was no
social visit, and instead of her customary small gift, the servant who followed her escort carried a slate that listed all of
the Acoma cash assets.

She had not attempted to bargain with a cho-ja Queen
since her negotiation for the hive that had settled permanently on her estates. Now that she had need, she had no clue
to how she would be received, particularly on the heels of the
news that two thirds of the new silk shipment had been lost
to Minwanabi attack. The sweat on Mara's hands went from

cold to hot. No past experience in her memory foretold how the Queen would react.

The corridor widened into the antechamber before the throne room; too late now to turn back, Mara reflected, as the cho-ja worker who escorted her small party rushed ahead to announce her presence. Mara continued on, into the warm vastness of the Queen's cavern, lit day and night under the blue-violet light cast by cho-ja globes suspended from brackets set in the massive vaults of stone ceiling. Like an island surrounded by polished floor, a pile of cushions awaited her, with a low table bearing cups and a steaming pot of chocha. Yet Mara did not step forward to sit and take refreshment and exchange gossip, as was usual. Instead she performed the bow one ruler of equal rank might make before another to the enormous presence of the cho-ja Queen, who reared up in massive height, attended by a scurry of workers. Her midsection was surrounded by screens, behind which the breeders and rirari labored continually over the eggs that ensured the continuity of the hive.

Well accustomed to such activity by now, Mara felt no need to stare. She straightened from her bow, alerted by the cant of the Queen's head that the cho-ja ruler was aware something grave was afoot. Mara composed herself. "Ruling Lady of the hive, I regret to inform you that trouble has been visited upon the Acoma by its enemy, House Minwanabi." Here Mara paused, awaiting out of courtesy for some sign from the Queen to continue.

Except for the bustle of the breeding attendants, which never ceased, there came no move within the chamber. Ranks of warriors and workers might march past in the corridor beyond the antechamber, but those who squatted on their forelimbs in the Queen's presence remained as still as statues.

Given not the slightest wave of a forelimb in reassurance, Mara faced the hive's Queen. The next sentence required all of her courage to speak.

"Great Queen, the Emperor's High Council requires a levy of four companies of warriors from the Acoma to defend the Empire's borders in Dustari. If the estate here is not to be left stripped of its protection, I can muster only three human companies to be sent across the ocean. It is my hope, therefore, that you will consider a bargain, to breed an additional company of warriors to fulfill the High Council's command."

The Queen remained still. Breath held, Mara waited, fighting to keep her own poise. Out of the corner of her eye she noted her Strike Leader's tension, and his cho-ja counterpart motionlessly squatting.

At last the Queen twitched a forelimb. "Who will be outfitting this company, Mara of the Acoma?"

The Lady expelled a long-pent breath and tried not to shiver with the relief that her request had not been regarded as impertinence. "My treasury would bear the cost, noble Queen, if it please you to grant my request."

The Queen tilted her massive head, her mandibles working gently to and fro. "I will grant your request for sufficient remuneration," she said, and the discussion broke down into what, to Mara's ear, seemed remarkably like a haggling match between merchants.

The Queen's demands were steep. But Jican had instilled in her a fine appreciation for the value of things, and Mara was a quick study. She seemed to sense which demands were nonnegotiable and which were outright exorbitant and expected to be rejected. In the end, she settled for an amalgamation of coin and goods that equaled a worth about a third higher than what she would have paid to hire mercenaries; which was probably fair, since the cho-ja company would answer only to her, would not be infiltrated with spies or suborned by enemies, and would not flee the field at first sign of possible defeat.

Her needra herds would be depleted for perhaps the next three seasons by what she would be forced to sell to meet the Queen's price. When the negotiation concluded, Mara dabbed moisture from her brow with a small embroidered cloth and released an almost imperceptible sigh.

The cho-ja Queen noticed all. "Lady of the Acoma," she boomed in her friendlier tone, "it would seem to my eyes that you are nervous, or if not that, then recovering from some discomfort. Has our hospitality failed to meet your needs?"

Mara recovered with a start. "No, Lady Queen. The hospitality of the hive is never at fault." She paused, took a chance, and answered honestly, "I confess that I was not sure of protocol when I came to buy this boon of warriors."

"Boon?" The Queen reared back in what might have been

surprise. "You are my friend, it is true, and were you to come asking favors, I would consider them, of course. The fact that you visit here often and take pleasure in our company and affairs is a welcome diversion, never doubt. But when it comes to bargaining for workers, warriors, or services, such things are commodities for trade."

Mara raised her brows. "Then your kind do not require an army for protection."

The cho-ja Queen considered this. "We interact within the Empire, and so are a part of its politics, its Great Game of the Council. But thousands of years past, before the coming of men? We bred warriors then to establish new hives, to protect us from predators like the harulth, and to hunt game. Now, if there are conflicts, they are between the houses of men who have purchased alliances. The cho-ja of themselves do not battle, except for the causes of men."

This was a revelation. Mara tried not to reveal her rising sense of excitement as she folded her damp square of linen. She had studied the alien cho-ja culture, but still had much to learn. If the cho-ja warriors were not loyal to the Lords of men, but simply mercenaries, the fact opened interesting possibilities. . . . But, sadly, the summons to defend the borders of Dustari allowed no leisure to pursue the matter further.

So thinking, Mara politely exchanged banalities with the cho-ja Queen, then courteously took her leave. So much remained to be done, and departure must occur in two months!

Kevin and Jican waited upon her return to the estate house. Mara stepped from her litter into wilting, late-afternoon sunshine, and turned over the slates to the hadonra. He glanced at them surreptitiously as he bowed, and went away clicking his teeth. Mara took that to mean that she had bargained well, but that Acoma finances were stressed. She pushed back a sticky lock of hair, put aside her wish for a bath, and looked up at an unaccustomedly silent Kevin.

"What is it, tall one? The matter must be serious, or you would not have forgotten to kiss me."

"I never forget to kiss you," Kevin countered and remedied the matter forthwith. But his lips did not linger on hers, and his thoughts were clearly not of passion. "Keyoke asks to see you, Lady."

"I thought so." Mara removed her overrobe and passed it to a waiting servant. Slipping her arms into the fresh garment held out for her by a slave, she forcibly smoothed away a frown. "Where is Lujan?"

Kevin fell into step beside her as she moved ahead through the doorway. "He's at the barracks, overseeing a drill, upon Keyoke's suggestion."

Mara absorbed this, thinking; the old man would accept her promotion to the position of Adviser of War; else he would have appointed Lujan to break the news of his refusal, rather than send him off to hard duty. Keyoke adhered to obligations to the very letter of tradition. He would not send personal news in the mouth of a slave, and though Kevin was given privilege as a family member, or consort, Keyoke would never treat him above his station. Considerate of the old one's sense of etiquette, Mara sent Kevin away. She went alone down the corridors of the estate house and entered the candlelit chamber where the old man lay sweating in blankets.

He had been waiting for her, his eyes brilliant with fever. "My Lady," he murmured the instant she appeared in the doorway. She had to hasten to stop him from attempting to rise and bow.

"Don't. Grandfather of my heart, you are hurt, and I am not one to stand upon ceremony. You honor me with your wounds, and your loyalty is beyond question." She knelt on a cushion by his side and broke protocol by taking his hand, holding it fiercely. "I have told Nacoya how I love her many times. I have never said so to you."

The ghost of a smile tugged at Keyoke's lips. He was pleased, but too much the Tsurani commander to show more than the glimmer of emotion. "Lady," he said gruffly, "Tasaio holds your death in his hands, in Dustari."

So Lujan had told him; Mara swallowed against a clenching tide of tears. Most likely that had been what it took to make the old man agree to live.

Even ill, Keyoke read her. "No, Lady. I needed no coercion to serve the Acoma. I am honored to become Adviser for War, never doubt." He paused, seeking words. "I prepared to die as a warrior because that was the only destiny I ever saw for a Force Commander grown too old for the field."

Mara would not settle for this. "And the leg?"

Keyoke did smile, very fleetingly. "Papewaio is my teacher. If he could bear the black rag, I shall bear my crutch." An instant later he added, "Kevin suggested that the armorer make one that holds a concealed sword."

"You like that idea," Mara observed. She allowed herself to smile also. "Grandfather of my heart, I shall make your crutch your staff of office and see the armorers about a blade myself."

She regarded his sweating face, too grey and gaunt, and against all his wishes showing tiredness. "You will train Lujan, and between us we will find a way to rout Tasaio's desert men."

Keyoke's eyes flicked open wider, nailing her with their intensity. "Daughter of my heart, there is no strategy that will help you on treeless sand, except sheer numbers. That my wisdom cannot arrange."

He sank back after that, exhausted beyond bone and sinew. His will was not enough, Mara saw; he was sincere in his gratitude for his new office, but the body was too battered. The Red God might not let him keep the life that had burned itself recklessly until news of the foray could be delivered.

"Leave Dustari to Lujan and me," Mara murmured. "Ayaki is your last responsibility, and the natami in the sacred grove. Should all else fail, and the Minwanabi overrun our borders, you and one picked company can see the boy safe. Take refuge in the hive with the cho-ja Queen, and ensure the Acoma name survives."

Keyoke lay with his eyes closed. He did not speak, but the hand within Mara's returned a light squeeze. She smoothed the fingers against the coverlet and noticed the fast, thready pulse that raced through the veins on his wrist. He was dying. The fact could not be denied.

"Rest well, grandfather of my heart," Mara whispered. In a forced show of calm she arose and stepped to the doorway. "Get my runner slave, and every available messenger," she murmured to the servant outside. "I also want guild runners hired in Sulan-Qu."

She spoke quickly, unaware of the rotund man in the

smock who hurried down the corridor and stopped, quizzically, at her side. He carried a bulging bag of elixirs, and his person smelled fustily of herbs. "You will send for a priest of Hantukama?" he asked, in a voice that was schooled to be mild.

Mara spun, noticed the presence of her personal healer, and returned a quick nod. "It is necessary, don't you think?"

The healer sighed in sympathy. "Lady Mara, I doubt that your Adviser for War will remain conscious past the dawn, or breathe for two more days after that."

"He will live," Mara returned fiercely. "I will find him a priest, and pay for a prayer gate to have the magic of the god invoked for healing."

The healer rubbed arched brows and looked weary. "Lady, the priests are not so easily moved. They are loyal to no one but their god, and they consider common villagers the equal of even the Emperor. If you do find a priest of Hantukama, and they are rare, no prayer gate will lure him to forsake the sick already in his care for the sake of one dying warrior."

Mara regarded the man with his sacks of useless remedies and his unwelcome truths. Her eyes lacked even a spark of compassion. "We shall see, master healer. We shall see."

Before that look the healer quailed, and ducked hastily into the sickroom. Mara's voice pursued him, low and determined as a spear thrust. "Keep him alive and comfortable. That is all that need concern you."

She resumed her instructions to the servant, and to the runner slave recently arrived.

Bent at Keyoke's side, counting the pulse in one dry, heated wrist, the healer turned his eyes heavenward and prayed to Chochocan and Hantukama for a miracle. Keyoke was weakening, and not a remedy in his satchel could stay the spirit from Turakamu's call. The healer went on to examine the whites of Keyoke's eyes, and then to check his bandages; of the two, his gods and his mistress, this moment he feared the wrath of the Lady the more.

Preparation for the war in Dustari overturned the quiet routine of the Acoma estate. In the crafts compound, the constant hiss of the sharpener's wheel sang in rhythm with the calls of slaves and apprentices directing the unloading of supplies, and the thick, pitchy odor of the resin pots overlaid the akasi blossoms' sweeter tang. The smell lingered in the air, invading even Mara's quarters, where, at dawn, she stood by the screen looking out.

"Come back to bed," Kevin murmured, his eyes admiring her slender, nude silhouette. "If you're determined to worry, you'll do a better job of it if you're relaxed and rested."

Mara did not answer but continued to stare through the mists and the moving shadows of the herd boys hurrying out to tend the needra in the meadows. She did not see the slaves, though, or the soft beauty of the lands she had inherited from her forefathers. She saw only a thousand Minwanabi soldiers crossing her borders bent on conquest.

Keyoke must stay alive to manage while she was away, Mara thought. As if her lover had not spoken, she began a ritual prayer pattern invoking Lashima's protection upon the life of her Adviser for War, who lay in a coma on his cushions, with the Red God poised for final conquest.

Kevin sighed and uncurled like a hunting cat from the pillows his Lady had vacated. Plainly this was not to be a morning for talk and lovemaking. They had done enough of that last night, anyway, the Midkemian reflected, running his fingers through his hair. Mara had come to him tense, almost to the point of anger, and their interaction had held little tenderness. Though usually content to be stroked into passion, Mara had hurled herself upon him as if frenzied with lust. Her hands came as close as they ever had to scratching, though violence of any sort in the bedchamber abhorred her. And when she found her release in a convulsive burst of emotion, she had sobbed stormily into his shoulder and soaked her hair with her tears.

Not being Tsurani, Kevin had not been repulsed by her break in composure. Sensitive that his woman needed comfort, he had simply held her and stroked her until she fell into exhausted sleep.

Now, watching her stand, sword-straight and slim as a girl in the frame of the opened screen, he saw that she had recovered her resilience; she was very strong. But upon her shoulders rested the well-being of all who made their livelihood on her far-flung holdings, from respected factors and advisers to the lowliest of her kitchen scullions. Fear for her young son haunted her, waking and sleeping, and Kevin wondered how long she could last before she broke under the strain.

He arose, tossed a robe over his shoulders—even after three years, he could never quite feel comfortable with the Tsurani disregard for modesty—and joined Mara by the screen. He slipped an arm over her shoulders, surprised to find her rigid and shivering.

"Mara," he said gently, and opened his robe and wrapped one side of it around her, bundling her against his warmth.

"I'm worried about Keyoke," she admitted, snuggling against him. "You've been a great comfort." She rested her head against his forearm and tickled a playful hand down his groin.

Kevin considered sweeping her up and carrying her back to the bed; but once again her thoughts carried her away from him, and after a moment she pulled clear of his embrace and clapped her hands sharply.

Servants invaded the chamber, clearing away sleeping mat and cushions, and hustling to assemble Mara's wardrobe. Kevin retired to a screened-off corner to dress. When he emerged, he was surprised to see a breakfast tray laid with fruit, chocha, and bread, but untouched; and although a staff of three remained standing by to serve, Mara was no longer in the room.

"Where is the Lady?" Kevin inquired.

The house servant in charge regarded him with no sense of humility; no matter how fine the embroidery on Kevin's Midkemian-style shirt, he was still a slave, inferior in station, and not worthy of courtesy from a free man. "The Lady has gone to the front entrance." He fell silent, and a small battle of wills ensued. At last, seeing that Kevin would neither demean himself further by speaking, nor go about his business, but would stand staring down from his immense height with unblinking blue eyes, the servant sniffed. "A messenger has arrived."

"Thanks," Kevin muttered with dry irony, wishing as always that the Tsurani caste system were less rigid, and that someone in the whole bowing and scraping lot had thought to inform him of the arrival. Even Mara, but she had worries enough. He pulled on his sandals in hopping leaps through the door and hurried down the corridor to join her.

The messenger proved to be one of Arakasi's, dust-covered and travel-worn. A boy in his teens, he had plainly run through the night, and from a distance much farther than Sulan-Qu.

"We are committed to three shrines," he was saying as Kevin drew close. "One must be stone. And we must also build a prayer gate on your estate, to the Gods of Fortunate Aspect."

This meant Chochocan, Lashima, Hantukama, and half a dozen others Kevin could not separate, their names and their qualities being strange to one of foreign origins. In Kelewan there was even a god who governed the concept of honor.

"The facing must be of corcara," the messenger ended, in pointed reference to the prayer gate.

The promised structure would become a costly undertaking, Kevin realized, as he sorted through his growing Tsurani vocabulary and identified corcara to be a shell resembling abalone.

But matters of finance and debt left Mara surprisingly unconcerned. "When will the healer priest arrive?"

The messenger bowed. "Noon today, Lady. Arakasi's man arranged for hired bearers and paid the premium for haste."

Mara closed her eyes, her face delicately pale in the thinning mists of dawn. "Pray to the Gods of Fortunate Aspect that we have that long." Then she seemed to notice the messenger's weariness as if for the first time. "Rest and refresh yourself," she said quickly. "You have done well, and your master's pledge to Hantukama shall be met. I will speak to Jican at once, and by the time the priest arrives we will have artists at work on drawings for the shrines and prayer gate."

She would need to sell some outlying holdings to pay her account to the healer priest, but that was of decreased concern, with the Dustari campaign in the offing. Some of the outlying properties must be sacrificed, anyway, and their garrisons brought home to deter any threat to the estate. But although Mara usually attended to such important matters personally, this time she delegated responsibility to Jican. She heard and granted a list of requests from Lujan concerning immediate outfitting needs for her soldiers. Then, without a thought for the breakfast she had forgotten, she continued onward to the chamber where Keyoke lay, surrounded by candles and eased by servants, but unconscious beyond recall, and breathing so shallowly that it seemed impossible he was alive. Kevin waited respectfully in the doorway while Mara crossed the lit expanse of the floor and fell to her knees on the cushion by Keyoke's side.

"Honored one, stay with us," she murmured. "Help will be coming by noon today. Arakasi has found a priest of Hantukama, who travels even now to aid the Acoma."

Keyoke lay utterly still. Not even his eyelids flickered, and his skin remained white as nut paste.

Inescapably, he was a man at death's door. Kevin had observed enough battle wounds and their aftereffects to recognize the facts. In pity, he left the doorway and crouched down behind his mistress. His hands locked solidly around her waist, and he said, "Dear one, he cannot hear you."

Mara shook her head stubbornly, and her unbound hair filled his nostrils with its scent. "We believe differently. The Wheel of Life is many-sided, so say our priests. Keyoke's fleshly ears may not hear, but his spirit, resting within his wal, never sleeps. His spirit will know I have spoken, and will take strength from Hantukama to hold Turakamu at bay."

"I hope your faith bears fruit," Kevin murmured. But he looked at Keyoke's wasted flesh, and the hands upon which past sword scars showed like a white intaglio design, and he felt his own hope falter. His hands tightened upon the Lady to share comfort, and also sadness, and a fear he lacked the courage to face. Should he lose her, he thought—and banished the idea at once. An uneasy discovery followed, that should he be offered the chance for free return to his homeworld, he might not wish to leave her side.

"Live, Keyoke," he said. "You are needed." And whether or not the wal of the warrior could hear him, the tall Midkemian spoke the words equally for himself.

The healing priest of Hantukama arrived just past the hour of noon, with such marked lack of ceremony that his presence came as a surprise.

Mara had not left Keyoke's chamber. She had answered the questions of her advisers there, and turned away the servants who offered food. When noon came, she arose and began to pace, her brows drawn into a frown. Occasionally she would turn a concerned glance at the too still figure amid the cushions. Kevin, sitting quietly to one side, observed his Lady's agitation, but knew better than to speak or offer sympathy. She might appear to be wholly absorbed in her worry, but the distance in her eyes warned otherwise. Her thoughts were very far from this sickroom, enmeshed in rituals of prayer and meditation learned in Lashima's temple. There was rhythm to her movements, a dancelike adherence to forms that bespoke purpose rather than an aimless burning of energy. She finished one such pattern, blinked like a dreamer roused from sleep, and found a plainly robed figure standing before her.

Dust-streaked, slender to the point of fragility, he wore robes that were almost as coarse as a slave's. His hands were dark from the sun, and his face like a wrinkled, dried fruit. He did not bow, but looked upon the Lady of the Acoma with dark eyes that burned with a tireless energy.

Mara started slightly. Then she made a holy sign with one hand. "You serve Hantukama as healer?"

The man did bow, then, but not to her. "The god walks in my presence." His brow furrowed. "I did not interrupt your do-chan-lu?" he inquired, referring to the exercise of walking meditation.

Mara waved the apology aside. "I welcome your presence, holy one, and would gladly suffer interruption, had there been one." With no apparent strain, and not even a glance at the comatose form of Keyoke, she went on to offer the little priest refreshment, and food, if he required.

He looked at her, considered, and then smiled, a startling expression that radiated a warmth of compassion. "The Lady is gracious, and I thank her, but my need is not so great."

"Hantukama bless you, holy one," Mara said, and relief showed plainly in her voice as she indicated the sick warrior upon the mat. "There is one here in grave need of healing."

The priest nodded once and moved beyond her. The back of his head was shaved in a semicircle that began just behind his ears and ended at the nape, where the hair had been allowed to grow long in a lustrous tail of intricate braid. "I will need basins, water, and a brazier," he said, not looking around. "My assistant will bring in my herbs."

Mara clapped for a servant, while the priest bent and, with neat economy of movement, removed his dirty sandals.

At his request, a servant washed his hands and feet, but he refused the use of a towel. Instead, he laid his damp fingers upon Keyoke's forehead and stood for an interval, not moving. His breathing slowed to match that of the injured warrior's. For a long minute nothing happened. Then he ran his fingers lightly down Keyoke's jaw and neck, and on, over the coverlet and bandages that clothed the warrior's sinewy body. Over the site of each injury the priest paused, profoundly still, then at last moved on. When he reached the warrior's one foot, he stopped, slapped the sole gently with his palms, and said a word that seemed to ring with echoes.

He turned at last to Mara, and now his face looked grey and worn and weary. "The warrior is at the gates of the halls of Turakamu and holds back his entrance only by great force of will," he said sadly. "He is nearly beyond recall. Why do you wish him to live?"

Mara stepped backward into the unyielding wood of the doorframe, and wished that Kevin's arms were there to support her now. But she had sent the barbarian off, out of fear that his outworld beliefs might unwittingly offend the priest. She looked at the ragged little man, whose hands were heavy with calluses, and whose eyes saw far too much. She weighed his question carefully, aware that much depended upon her answer. She sorted through her memories of Keyoke, from the strong hand that lifted her when she fell and scraped her knees as a child, to the sword that had never faltered in defense of her father in the face of his enemies; how greatly the Acoma name depended upon Keyoke's expertise. The reasons she should want him back were myriad, too many to say in one breath. She considered her former Force Commander, for himself, his loyalty and his honor a shining inspiration to all of the soldiers he had led. She opened her mouth to say that he belonged at the head of her army, but something Kevin had once observed jostled the words from her mind. *Your people and mine are not so different on the inside; just your counting your Kelewanese honor ahead of caring, which to a Midkemian is wrong way about.*

Swayed by this markedly foreign concept, Mara blurted something very different from what she initially intended. "We wish Keyoke among us because we love him."

The priest's critical expression broke into a surprised but heartwarming smile. "Lady, you have answered well and wisely. Love by itself is the healer, not honor, not need, not duty. For love alone will my god Hantukama answer summons, and lend your warrior the strength to live."

Mara felt weak in the knees. In an overwhelming rush of relief she heard the priest excuse her from the room, that he have solitude to invoke his sacred rituals.

Alone except for his assistant, a boy with shorn hair and a loincloth not so very different from a slave's, the priest of Hantukama set up his brazier. All the while that he worked, his voice intoned a chant that rose and fell, like poetry, like music, but not; the guards beyond the closed screen felt the hair prickle at their napes, and they sweated, aware of powers beyond their understanding being summoned beyond the wall.

The priest opened a voluminous satchel and set forth small bundles of herbs, each one painstakingly blessed, and tied with threads spun in a ritual known only to the handful of his brethren who wandered the Empire in Hantukama's service. Each little bundle had a packet attached, labeled with holy symbols and sealed with scented wax. Not even the assistant knew what ingredients made up the fine powders inside. Out of respect, the boy had never dared to ask.

The priest sorted through his sacred remedies, lifting them, weighing them, sensing to the depths the virtues imbued within each. He discarded the ones made for coughs, and others ensorcelled to encourage fruitful childbirth. He laid others, for blood loss, and infections, and fevers, and proper digestion, in a neat array to one side. To these he added still more, for reinstatement of the spirit, and restoration of circulation, and the knitting of injured bone and sinew. He deliberated a moment, touched Keyoke's hand, and added another, for strength. Over the leg, he clicked his tongue. He could not restore tissue that had been severed and discarded. Had the cut limb been saved in turpentine, he might have managed; but maybe not. The belly wound offered difficulty enough.

"Old warrior," murmured the priest between invocations, "let us hope that you love yourself enough to transmute the shame of bearing a crutch into the pride of wearing a badge of honor."

His wizened hands rearranged the remedies into patterns, and blessed them, again and again; at one point Keyoke's body lay ringed with little bundles of herbs. At another, he wore them in rows down the nerve centers of his torso and abdomen. Then the boy assistant lit the brazier, and one by one, with the appropriate song of praise to Hantukama, the bundles were lit and consumed. The packets of powder were dusted in the air above Keyoke, with murmured exhortations to breathe deep, breathe in the strength of the earth and the regenerative powers of the god.

The last of the herbs went up in smoke, and the chamber swirled with incense. The priest gathered his inner energies into a tight knot and became a channel for the glory of his god. He bent over Keyoke and touched the chilly hands that lay unmoving on the coverlet. "Old warrior," he intoned, "in the name of Hantukama, I ask that you give up your sword arm. Your hands are not yours but my god's, to work for peace and harmony. Give up your striving, and walk in love, and find your strength returned in full measure."

The priest paused, then, waiting as quietly as a fish in the depths of a noon-heated pool. "Find your strength," he murmured, and his voice held a coaxing tone, as though he spoke to a tiny child.

At last, reluctantly, a warming began beneath his fingers. The sensation grew to a glow that brightened softly yellow.

The priest nodded and set his hands over Keyoke's face. "Old warrior," he intoned, "in the grace of Hantukama, I ask that you give up your senses, vision, hearing, taste, smell, and touch. Your senses are not yours but my god's, for experiencing the glory that is life. Give up your speech, and walk in joy, and find your senses enhanced and fully vital."

The glow happened more slowly this time. The priest fought sagging shoulders, while he moved on and laid dry hands over Keyoke's heart. "Old warrior, by the will of Hantukama, I ask that you give up your desires. Your spirit is not yours but my god's, for reflecting the perfection that is wholeness. Give up your wants, and live in compassion, and find your being filled in full measure."

The priest waited, huddled into himself like old stone. The assistant watched with folded hands and wide eyes. And when the glow came, it crackled and blazed like new fire and bathed the sick man from head to foot in curtains of impenetrable brilliance.

The priest withdrew his hands, cupped as though they held something inestimably precious. "Keyoke," he said gently.

The warrior opened his eyes, stiffened sharply, and cried out at the blinding light that stabbed into his eyes and filled his spirit with awe.

"Keyoke," repeated the priest. His voice was tired but kindly. "Fear not. You walk in the warmth of my god, Hantukama the healer. Your Lady has petitioned for your health. If my god grants you life and restored health, how will you serve her?"

Keyoke's eyes stared straight ahead, into the blazing net of healer's spells. "I serve her, always, as a father does a daughter, for my heart knows her as the child I never had. Sezu I served for honor; his children I served out of love."

The priest's weariness fled. "Live, Keyoke, and heal by the grace of my god." He opened his hands, and the light flashed intolerably, blindingly bright; then it faded, leaving only the dying embers in the brazier, and the played-out smoke of burnt herbs.

On the mat, Keyoke lay quiet, his eyes closed, and his hands as still as before. But a faint flush of rose showed beneath his skin, and his breathing was long and deep, that of a man in sleep.

The priest sat carefully on the cushion Mara had used earlier for kneeling. "Fetch the Lady of the Acoma," he told his young assistant. "Tell her, with joy, that her warrior is an extraordinary man. Tell her that he will survive."

The boy started up and ran to do the bidding of his master. By the time he returned with the Lady, the priest had packed up his brazier. The ashes and the coals were mysteriously disposed of, and the little man who had brought them the miracle was curled up in sleep upon the floor.

"The healing was a difficult one," the boy assistant confided. Then, as Mara's servants attended to the needs of his master and brought dishes of food for the boy, Mara went to the pallet and quietly regarded Keyoke.

"He will sleep for several days, probably," the boy explained. "But his wounds will slowly close. Do not expect him to be on his feet too quickly."

Mara smiled wryly. She could see the changes that indicated a return to vitality, and her heart sang inside with gratitude for the gift of the priest and his god. "We're going to require a warrior of extraordinary strength and courage to tell this old campaigner that he must keep to his bed. For as I know Keyoke, he's going to wake up asking for his sword."

The days passed in a rushed flurry of activity. Factors arrived and departed at Jican's direction, settling the sales of needra stock, and incoming shipments of supplies. The sheds that once housed breeding bulls were now half-filled with chests of new armor and swords. Acoma leatherworkers stitched tents for barracks in the desert, and the potters fashioned clay hurricane lamps, pierced in patterns, to cradle oiled rags for torches. Dustari was a barren land, and devoid of trees; the woodworkers fired their ovens to make charcoal.

The bustle was not confined to the craftsmen's compounds. The practice yard lay under a continual cloud of dust as Lujan drilled his soldiers and green, newly promoted officers. He staged maneuvers in the fields, swamps, and woodlands and came back with chosen soldiers, to walk barefoot, their muddy war sandals in hand, through the main house to the chamber where Keyoke lay recovering. The Adviser for War reviewed their performance, criticized their weaknesses, and praised their strengths. He spent the hours in between poring over maps of the estate and working out strategies of defense; from his mat he held classes for officer training. For no one doubted that Tasaio of the Minwanabi had contrived the Dustari campaign for no other reason than to leave the Acoma vulnerable.

Mara herself was everywhere, overseeing all aspects of the endeavor that prepared her army for departure. On the morning that Nacoya finally contrived to overtake her, with Kevin absent and no servants or advisers at hand, the Lady was seated in her garden by the fountain under the ulo tree. She often used the place for informal meditation, but lately her free time had gone exclusively to her son. Nacoya peeked surreptitiously at her Lady's quiet pose, and the frown that faintly marked the skin between her brows; she measured the hands, which were still, and judged the moment propitious for talk.

Nacoya entered the garden and bowed before her mistress.

Mara bade her rise and sit on the cushions with her. She regarded her First Adviser with eyes that had circles under them and said, "I wrote the letter to Hokanu yesterday."

The old woman nodded slowly. "That is well, but not my reason for seeking you."

Mara's frown deepened at the tone of her adviser's voice. "What is it, mother of my heart?"

Nacoya loosed a deep sigh and plunged. "Lady, I would suggest that you be thinking of choosing my successor. Do not think I dislike my duties, or that I feel the honor of my post as a burden. I serve my Lady gladly in all ways. But I am growing old, and it is in my heart to point out that you have no younger servants in training to assume the mantle of adviser when I am gone. Jican is middle-aged, but he lacks canniness in politics. Keyoke has the perception to take on the role of First Adviser, but he and I are of an age, and there will not always be a priest of Hantukama to defer the Red God's due."

A breeze sighed through the ulo leaves, and water splashed in the fountain. Mara's fingers stirred against the loosened folds of her robe and gathered the fabric about her. "I hear you, old mother. Your words are wise, and well considered. I have thought upon the issue of your replacement." She paused and softly shook her head. "You know, Nacoya, that too many of our best people died with my father."

Nacoya nodded. She gestured to the fountain. "Life continually renews itself, daughter of my heart. You must find new minds, and train them."

That was a risky venture, as both of them knew. To take on new servants and raise them to high levels of responsibility invited the chance for an enemy to infiltrate a new spy. Arakasi's network was good, but not infallible. Yet the necessity could not be denied. Mara needed trusted people around her, or she would be too encumbered by everyday decisions to maintain her status in the Great Game.

"I will put effort into finding a new cadre of advisers, but after the campaign in Dustari is completed," she concluded at last. "If I return home, and the natami remains in the sacred glade, then we will search for new talent. But the risk is too great to be taken beforehand. Ayaki must be surrounded only by servants who were born here, and whose loyalty remains beyond question."

Nacoya arose and bowed. "My Lady's permission to leave?"

Mara smiled slightly at the stoop-shouldered figure of her adviser. "Permission given. Take a nap, old mother. You look as if you could use it."

"I just got up!" Nacoya snapped. "Take a nap yourself, and without that needra stud of a barbarian for a change. When he's there you get no sleep, and you'll be needing thyza powder to cover the wrinkles that come before you're thirty."

"Sex does not make wrinkles!" Mara laughed. "That's an old nurse's tale. Don't you have duties? The day's messages to sort through?"

"I do have that," Nacoya conceded. "You're getting more inquiries from suitors."

"Opportunists," Mara said, suddenly annoyed. "They think to marry me as consort and inherit if I fall in Dustari; or else they are agents of Desio, thinking to open my gates to his army. Why else petition the Lady of a house that's entering into peril?"

"Yes, Lady," Nacoya said quickly, and the smugness behind her meek tone betrayed her satisfaction. Mara might be young, and foolish in the bedchamber; but when it came to politics, she had an excellent grasp indeed. What remained to be seen was whether she was gifted with the mind of a general of armies. Dustari and the desert men were going to offer a swift and perilous education.

11. *DESERT*

The journey began.

Mara pulled free of Ayaki's embrace, trying with all of her will not to cry. She climbed into her litter and looked one last time on the faces of her advisers, whom she might never see on this side of the Wheel of Life: Nacoya, frowning harder than usual, probably to conceal her grief; Jican, who had a harder time hiding his emotion, since his hands were empty of slates; Arakasi, shadow-still, silent and against his nature looking grim. And Keyoke, dependably expressionless, standing erect on the leg he had left, the crutches leaned unobtrusively against the doorjamb. He wore his sword, but seemed a stranger without armor and warrior's plumed helm.

"Guard Ayaki and the natami, and may the Gods of Fortunate Aspect look favorably upon our endeavors," Mara said; somehow she managed to finish in the proper firm tone. Her advisers and the house servants arrayed behind them looked on with pride as she waved to Force Commander Lujan to signal her army to march. The tramp of many feet lifted a dust plume over the road, as it had not since Sezu's time. That army had departed, and only forty had survived to return. An older generation of servants wondered if the past would repeat itself, while the newer generation sensed their fear. They watched three companies in green and a shiny black company of cho-ja march out bravely under the shatra bird banner. The sun burned down through the morning mists and flashed off polished lacquer armor. It caught on the streamered points of spears, and on the feathered crests of Strike Leaders, Patrol Leaders, and officers' aides.

At Sulan-Qu the Acoma host boarded barges. Naked slaves poled them downriver through the press of commercial traffic, and grain barges, guild boats, and raftsmen pulled aside to let them pass. Southward they floated, through Hokani Province, past the lands of the Anasati, where warriors in red and yellow offered them salute from the shore. Although Lord Tecuma was a reluctant ally, Mara did not stop. He would make no overtures toward social friendship unless Mara returned from Dustari with her family honor intact.

For Kevin, the river offered endless fascination. He spent even the hottest hours by the rail, talking to the barge master and the slaves who manned the poles with equal interest. He studied the water craft, so different from those of his homeworld, and within days became expert at distinguishing guild colors from house crests, hired craft from those privately owned.

Mara's army drew steadily toward the south, past flotillas of barges bearing market goods, some lashed together into permanent stalls that were patronized by the nobles who used the river as transport between Jamar and Sulan-Qu. Fast messenger boats raced between slower craft, furiously paddled by sweating slaves. Once they passed an imperial barge, bright with gilt and hung with banners, its white and gold coloring a dazzling change from the many-colored craft of the nobles. Mara traveled in her barge of state, which was green and adorned with a shatra bird figurehead. She sat beneath a feathered shade, fanned by her slaves, and comfortably surrounded with perfumed flowers to mask the less pleasant stinks of sewage and river mud. Kevin saw other Lords traveling in style, attended by musicians, poets, and performers. One even had a troupe of traveling players performing upon a stage for his pleasure. Overflowing baskets of fruit lay before him, and fat lapdogs lounged all over his pillows, like so many beribboned sausages. Unlike the pets and hunting dogs of Midkemia, the dogs of Kelewan were short-haired and sleek, as a consequence of the climate.

They passed thyza barges, and traveling farm workers, and what looked like the Kelewanese equivalent of traveling gypsy musicians. "Khardengo," Mara identified, when Kevin mentioned the comparison, giving a brief description of gypsies. "It is written in the old chronicles that they were a family that preferred wandering to taking land. They lived in barges and wagons, it is true, much like your gypsies of Midkemia. But unlike your barbarians, the Khardengo have honor. They do not steal for their living."

Kevin laughed. "The gypsies have their own culture. By their mores, they do not steal, only"—he paused, unable to find the right word, and settled for his own language—"borrow."

"Borrow?" Mara squinted· up at him where he lounged chewing sekka rinds dipped in vinegar. "What is that?"

Kevin used other words to explain, and saw her raise her eyebrows in astonishment. Strange, he thought, that the Tsurani concept of honor allowed goods to be exchanged as purchases, gifts, and spoils; but no equivalent to the neighborly concept of lending a thing between friends existed at all. He prepared himself for another afternoon of talk, as Mara explored the concept exhaustively.

The river flowed into the great delta above the city of Jamar. There they held to the west side of the river, which took them into a deep channel leading to the harbor. To the east the great delta fanned out, alive with rafts scurrying across the water, as fishermen netted the soft-shelled denizens of the shallows, or sought to capture game birds.

Kevin openly stared as they entered the river traffic at Jamar, the major seaport and trade center for Szetac and Hokani provinces. Larger than Sulan-Qu, the city was grander and more sprawling. The wharves were built as wide as an avenue, and elevated enough to loom over high tides when storms struck from the south. The length was as crowded as any thoroughfare, bustling with stevedores unloading the blue-water ships that made port from all parts of the Empire. The ships rode high, as the tide was almost full, and Kevin could see the rich tapestry of alien sights along the warf as the Acoma barges passed.

Bales of dyestuffs lay piled next to lashed stacks of rare woods, alongside chests whose chops were ribboned and complex. Mercenaries stood guard over such shipments, indicating their value.

The Acoma barges passed by a low-riding series of ferry barges, loaded to near sinking by stout crates. They leaked exotic smells, of spices used to cure hides, perfumes, and the rich aroma of ground chocha-la.

The Acoma craft passed by landings piled high with rugs, prayer mats and yarns, leather and lacquer, spirits and resin. Each valuble shipment was shepherded by slate-bearing factors, hadonras, and caravan masters. Under hot sunlight, two-wheeled vehicles pulled by slaves transported the goods from shipboard to docks, and from docks into wagons on dry land.

Kevin watched with interest those Tsurani he had never had a chance to glimpse before. Sly-eyed sailors drank jugs of liquor in the shadows of the alleys, or paired off with the painted ladies of the Reed Life who displayed their fleshly wares from gallery boudoirs hung with perfumed silks. Street urchins begged coins and cart vendors hawked wares in a variety of singsong calls. Bead sellers vied for shorefront space where incoming ships landed tenders, to be the first to sell trinkets for sweethearts to sailors coming ashore.

Kevin felt a chill as they rounded the bulk of a large ship and the slave market came into view. Though it was ignored by the others on Mara's barge, Kevin recognized the compound at once from its high picket fence, and the naked men standing in coffles with overseers snapping their goads. The female slaves were kept from the sun under canopies, and if they were no more clothed, the pretty ones were clean so they might attract masters who would buy them for pleasure.

Reminded by the sight that he was still Mara's property, Kevin's interest in Jamar's strange sights flagged at last. He felt no regret when the ship hired to carry the Acoma army across the sea came into sight. Nets were lowered for the cho-ja to scramble up, and then the Acoma soldiers. Mara's litter was lifted, while she calmly sat inside, by the hoist used to load cargo. Then supplies were hurried aboard.

The captain that Lujan had engaged to provide their overseas passage was efficient and determined to make the peak tide that was but minutes away. He called the dock crews to cast off, even as his sailors were lashing down boxes of Acoma supplies.

The vessel drew away from the wharf, dragged into deeper, less crowded waters by a longboat with a dozen oarsmen. Slaves rowed in time to a drum pounded by a fat man in a loincloth, who called off rhymes to synchronize the dip, pull, and lift of the heavy looms. The blades rose from the water in a flash of bright colors. Slaves had painted them in bright patterns, to ward off ill luck at sea.

Coalteca was the name of the vessel Lujan had hired. She carried three masts, and a massive, carven tiller that took seven slaves to man. The ship drew off from the land, and the smaller craft used by fishermen and shore traders thinned out. The towboat cast off lines, and the pilot on board waved the disengaged signal to *Coalteca*'s captain, who barked commands to raise sail. Deckhands scurried aloft and loosed lines, and yards of fiber sails cascaded down and bellied into the wind. Standing in kaleidoscopic patterns of reflected light, Kevin saw that the canvas, like the slaves' oars, was painted with symbols and patterns. The result lent the air of a circus tent, a mad riot of colors that held no harmony, except to Tsurani eyes. Kevin squinted, rubbed his temples, and decided that if he was a god of ill fortune, he would avert his gaze from such a ship if only to keep from getting headaches. As he leaned on the rail and hoped he would escape the seasickness he had suffered on board a Kingdom ship, he stared at the waves and wondered if *Coalteca*'s keel was painted in patterns to ward off attack by sea serpents.

After sundown, in a comfortable cabin lit with the fireless blue-violet globes made by the cho-ja, he asked Mara. This required learning a new word, as the concept of sea monsters had never before been discussed.

"Ah," Mara cried in discovery, after a quarter hour of gestures, and finally crude chalk drawings on a slate. "I understand what you want to say. You ask about the egu, large creatures, similar to relli, that live in the deeps beneath the waves. Yes, the Sea of Blood is filled with them. Each ship carries lances tipped with oiled rags. You called them 'harpoons' earlier, but they are not the same as darts to kill fish. An egu lance is always lit when fired. Sailors say only flame or a Great One's spells will repel attacks by egu."

Kevin rubbed his temples again. Dinner did not find him with any appetite, and he decided to retire to sleep.

"My great barbarian gets seasick," Mara teased, the healthy flush of her own cheeks a sure indication that the malady was no problem for her. She shot her lover a flashing glance and said, "I know an infallible cure for bellyaches." She then shed her robe without ceremony and tumbled into the alcove where he knelt, trying to sort cushions from blankets.

His robe soon joined hers, abandoned in a heap on the floor. Further thoughts of egu did not trouble his sleep after that, for he had no energy left to think.

Coalteca completed her crossing inside a week, untroubled by egu and tossed by surprisingly few squalls.

"It is summer," Lujan said in answer to Kevin's inquiry. "The winds are steady, and rainfall slight." He raised a sunburned arm and indicated the shoreline of Dustari, rising purple off *Coalteca*'s painted prow. "Look, you can see our destination, the city of Ilama."

The port in Dustari differed greatly from what Kevin had observed of Jamar, built on granite hills, and backed by jagged mountains. The wood-and-paper-screen construction favored throughout the mainland Empire was here augmented by stone. Immense, multitiered towers arose, their pyramid structures serving as watch stations for a massive crenellated wall. Other towers with light beacons marked the string of scattered islets that extended seaward arms to the west. The headlands bulked darkly rocky, between expanses of reddish black sand of volcanic origin. The contours of the hills were steep-sided, and lush with trees that had unfamiliar shapes. The smells on the breeze were also strange, and peppered with a pungence of spice.

"The grinders of condiments have sheds at the harborside," Lujan said, when Kevin commented. "Ilama does great trade in spices that grow only in the mountains to the south."

The folk were also famous for their weaving, and prayer mats woven in Dustari were reputed to carry good fortune in their threads. Fey blood ran strong in the folk from that shore; many children born here grew up to take service with the Assembly of Magicians.

Kevin longed for the chance to explore the town, and watched the street traffic avidly as *Coalteca* dropped anchor in the bay. Two-wheeled carts moved along the docks, hauled by a beast he had never seen before, a six-legged creature much slighter than a needra. Weaving flocks of scarlet-and-white shore birds screamed and dove above the masts, chasing one another for the chance to snatch scraps tossed overboard by the cooks. Dirty urchins shouted, their voices echoing across the harbor, as they likewise sought handouts. Suddenly their cries stilled and they wheeled and fled into waterfront alleys. Kevin's interest sharpened.

Onto the wharf marched soldiers armored in yellow and purple. Bearers carried a lacquered litter hung with banners bearing the symbol of a catlike animal entwined with a snake. Servants hurried aside to clear the way for the company, and the dock crews bowed low in deference.

"The Lord of the Xacatecas comes personally to meet us," Mara commented in some surprise. Poised by Kevin's shoulder, and dressed in rich robes of green, she wore makeup that artfully managed to play down her youth.

"You didn't expect him?" Kevin asked, turning to assess the reason for her nerves.

"I did not." Mara considered, frowning. "That he has left his war camp to attend the arrival of the Acoma honors us." She waved to one of her maids and said quickly, "Unseal my black-lacquered carry chest. I'm going to need a finer over-robe."

Kevin's eyes widened in surprise. "The jewels you wear now are already blinding."

Mara fingered the seed pearls and emeralds stitched in rows and whorls at lapel and cuffs. "For a Lord who rules one of the Five Families, and the Warchief of Clan Xacala, I shall wear metal. To appear in less than my finest apparel might be taken as insult, and this man is one my people must never risk offending."

Sailors began to lower *Coalteca*'s tender, and under Lujan's direction Mara's honor guard assembled on the deck, their armor polished, and their spearheads adorned with streamers. The Lady hastened off to change her robe. Kevin, dressed in Midkemian-styled trousers and shirt, took his place among her cortege like a grey-and-white dove in the midst of a festival.

Shortly after, Mara reappeared, clothed in an emerald silk overrobe tastefully sewn with copper sequins. Kevin preferred it to the pearls, and said so; the reddish glint of the copper set off the deep brown of her eyes. But the compliment brought no smile from her.

Lujan saw his Lady settled on board the canopied tender

that would bear her party ashore. The new Force Commander's light brand of humor also seemed absent, which Kevin interpreted as a cue to be restrained. Changed from the brash captive freshly taken from the battlefield, the Midkemian had finally learned the wisdom of keeping quiet when the time warranted. That Lord Xacatecas was immensely powerful was apparent by the depth of Mara's bow, made the moment she stepped onto the stone wharf, to the personage in yellow armor and dazzling gold wristbands who sat like a king enthroned upon his litter.

The Lord of the Xacatecas inclined his head, arose, and returned a polite bow. He was an older man, who did not appear dissipated. His flesh was sunburned and hard, and his hazel eyes shrewd amid their wrinkles. His dress was fine, yet not frivolous, and his mouth was bracketed by deep folds that hinted at irony as he smiled.

"Lady Mara, are you well?"

His voice was gruff, but well modulated. And Mara, looking up at him, smiled also. "You honor me too much, my Lord," she said in quick deference, by which Kevin knew the man had higher rank, but had not insisted she speak first. Lord greeted Lady in friendliness, with a public display of favor. "I am well," Mara continued, her poise belying her strain. "And greatly flattered to see you here. You are well, Lord Chipino?"

"Well indeed," the man replied, with sudden, acid sarcasm. He tossed back steel-colored hair and laughed; Kevin could not see why, but decided the Lord was responding to some subtle nuance of Mara's as he offered his arm and led her forward. "Lord Desio, may he and his cousins die choking, shall be made to regret this day."

Mara murmured something in reply that caused the Lord of the Xacatecas to laugh again, and to eye her with fresh appreciation. He completed a gracious motion, and the Lady was handed into the Lord's own litter, a thoughtful courtesy, since his personal appearance had not been expected, and time had not allowed the Acoma servants to unpack her palanquin. The company of warriors moved off in squares of purple and yellow offset like a checkerboard with squares of green.

"If I were younger," boomed the Lord in his gravelly

voice, "I would be minded to give young Hokanu some competition."

Well, Kevin decided—with a small pang of jealousy—at least the Lord of the Xacatecas seemed charmed by the Lady who desired his alliance.

"For which your beautiful Lady wife would wish me poisoned," Mara demurred smoothly. "Is Isashani well?"

"Well, thank you, and grateful for my absence, which keeps her from becoming pregnant again. Turn here," Lord Chipino instructed his bearers. The company wheeled smartly across a narrow intersection and entered the canopied shade of an open-fronted hostel.

A refreshment bar extended the length of the back wall, and the sides were open framework. Soups, pastries, and assorted blends of local herb brew, called tesh, as well as the usual chocha were sold here. Benches and tables emptied as patrons of lesser rank scurried to make room for their betters, and a flurry of servants in smocks descended to clean up leavings and lay out clean cups and plates. Chipino saw Mara to a seat, took the Lord's place at the head of the table, and set his elbows on the sanded planks, chin rested on his steepled fingertips. He regarded the girl who had routed Lord Jingu of the Minwanabi in his own home, and whose quickness at the game was earning her notoriety. Around him, Lujan's warriors and Xacatecas's were arrayed in defensive formation, leaving Kevin standing with the bearers just beyond earshot of the conversation. He could tell by Mara's bearing that the social chat ended, and that discussion of serious matters began almost immediately. Servants brought food, which was laid aside barely touched, to make room for parchment maps, and a series of slates brought in by a servant in yellow-and-purple livery.

Presently Mara waved for Kevin to come and stand at her shoulder. "I want you to hear this," she said, and by her tone the Midkemian understood that she intended to ask his opinion later, when they had time in private for talk.

The afternoon passed in discussion of the previous year's succession of skirmishes, which had resulted in Mara's summons from the High Council.

"There is only one thing to be concluded," Xacatecas wrapped up. "The raiders from Tsubar are growing vastly more numerous, and aggressive beyond their normal nature. What I would ask you is, why?"

Mara regarded the older man steadily, thinking. "We shall find out, Lord Chipino." She spun her empty tesh cup with her fingers and said obliquely, "Rest assured, my estates are vigorously fortified."

The Lord of the Xacatecas smiled to show even teeth. "Then, daughter of Sezu, we understand each other well. The enemy shall gain nothing of advantage." He reached out, and lifted his goblet of Jamar crystal in hands that bore no rings. "To the victory," he said softly.

Mara met his eyes and nodded, and for some unknown reason Kevin felt chilled.

The *Coalteca* had been unloaded by the time the Lord and Lady emerged from their table of refreshment. Mara's palanquin awaited beside Lord Chipino's, and servants had commandeered a herd of pack beasts. These were lightweight, six-legged, and to Kevin's eyes, resembled a cross between a camel and a llama, except for the ears, which were scaled and whorled like a lizard's. Mara's wardrobe chests and the tents, braziers, charcoal sacks, oil barrels, and stores and supplies for her army had all been strapped to strange, U-shaped racks that rode the creatures' backs like saddles. The train was a very long one, noisy with the bleat of animals and the calls of swarthy-faced tenders who wore loose scarves at their throats. Drovers in baggy garments striped in garish colors prodded their charges into a straggling order of march; the human and cho-ja companies formed up more quickly, and ascent into the mountains began.

Kevin followed with the rest of Mara's house servants. Distracted by a giggling child who rolled in the gutter by the roadside, he was startled by a splash of warm fluid.

He spun, discovered a white gobbet of saliva dripping from his shirt sleeve, and grimaced. "Damn it to hell," he said in Midkemian.

Lujan smiled broadly in commiseration. "Don't stand too close to the querdidra," he called in caution. "They spit."

Kevin flicked his hand, and shed a foaming mess on the pavement. It reeked unpleasantly, like rotted onions.

"Evidently they don't like your smell," the Force Commander finished, laughing.

Kevin eyed the offending pack beast, which was looking at him through violet, long-lashed eyes and curling its monkeylike lips. "Feeling's mutual," he groused. And he wished it a painful attack of constipation, and thorns in all six of its padded feet. Dustari was going to be peachy, he groused to himself, when the querdidra that carried the supplies seemed to outnumber the soldiers.

The mountains changed drastically as they approached the passes. Forested slopes fell away, scoured by winds and driven sand to bare rock. The smells of sun-heated stone replaced those of greenery and soil, and the land became a vista of bleakness. The high country dropped sharply off into a broken series of buttes awash in vast oceans of sand. The sun burned in a sky pale green with drifts of airborne dust, and cooked the lands beneath to a shimmering curtain of heat waves. The rock itself seemed to smoulder, rough-grained, and textured red, black, and ocher. The fires of its forming seemed very recent, and renewed each day with the sharp blaze of sunrise.

In contrast, the nights were chill, with dry gusts cutting through clothing like ice. It became no surprise that the drovers and native guides wore their neckerchiefs over their faces to protect them from wind-driven grit. Centuries of such weather had chiseled the rocks into odd formations resembling towers or stacks of crockery, or sometimes demonlike pillars that seemed to prop up the Kelewanese sky. Kevin and Mara both stared at such shapes in fascination, early on—but not after the first raid by desert men, which happened on the steep trail leading to the top of a pass.

Aware first of an earcurdling yell, and a disturbance in the line of pack beasts up ahead, Mara whipped aside the curtains of her palanquin. "What's amiss?"

Lujan motioned for her to stay back, and then drew his sword. Mara peered around him and through the ranks of her honor guard saw small, broad-shouldered figures in dun-colored robes leaping in a screeching charge from a cleft between the rocks. They grabbed the bridles of several querdidra and dragged them, bleating, off the road. Sure-footed even on loose stone, the creatures bucked and shied as warriors in Xacatecas colors jumped downslope in pursuit.

Lujan shouted to his First Strike Leader and signaled broadly with his sword. Acoma warriors broke from the caravan line lower down, on a switchback curve below their position. Their sally was joined, then overtaken by a fast-moving strike force of cho-ja. Less sure than the insects, the humans fanned out in a wide ring to cut off the desert men, while the cho-ja under their Strike Leader slipped past them and cut in an arc across the path of the raiders' descent.

"Defer to Lord Chipino's officers," Lujan commanded the Acoma. Then, as the Lord of the Xacatecas called something to Mara from his litter, the Lady touched her officer's sleeve.

"The Lord would have no live prisoners," she instructed. Lujan relayed the order.

Kevin watched, wide-eyed, as the cho-ja overtook the raiders. Seeing the shining black insectoids race upslope to take them, with their helmets sitting square on faces that were nothing close to human, and upraised forelimbs lifted like razors to kill, the diminutive mountain men skidded to a stop. They drove the querdidra forward with slaps and curses, trying to disrupt the cho-ja ranks. But Lax'l's warriors were fast, almost black blurs in the sunlight as they swerved around the fear-maddened beasts. And uncannily, they made no sound, beyond the click of hooked feet on broken rock. The cho-ja flowed past the disturbance and came on, while the desert men spun and tried frantically to run.

The slaughter was swift. Kevin, who had never seen cho-ja in war, felt gooseflesh rise beneath his sleeves. He had seen men die, but never disemboweled *from behind,* with a single stroke of those black, chitin-bladed forelimbs. The cho-ja were deadly swift, and they slew with a machinelike thoroughness.

"Your cho-ja make short work of the nomads," Lord Chipino observed, his grim tone revealing he derived no enjoyment from the deaths. "Perhaps they will think twice about harassing our supply trains into Ilama henceforth."

Mara lifted a fan from her cushions and tapped it open, thoughtfully. She cooled herself, more from nerves than heat. Though blood sports did not appeal to her, she did not show squeamishness at the sight of battle and death. "Why attack so heavily guarded a caravan? By Lashima, can't they see we have your honor guard as well as three companies of warriors?"

Downslope, the Acoma Strike Leader's men were ineffectively trying to round up the frightened querdidra. Lord Chipino dispatched some of his own drovers to help, since their knowledge of the beasts' handling was a necessity if the caravan was to be moving again before sundown. "Who can say what motivates the barbarians," he concluded, regarding Mara across the space between palanquin and litter. "If I did not know better, I would say we were fighting fanatics of the Red God."

But the Dustari nomads did not believe in Turakamu, or so said the texts at Lashima's temple where Mara had studied during her youth. The increase in border unrest made no sense, and the descriptions of engagements Lord Chipino had offered in the hostel over maps added up to nothing but a profligate waste of lives.

Mara flicked her fan closed. More than ever, she feared for Ayaki, left at home on her estates. She had expected to cross the ocean to provide support and swift solution for the troublesome attacks on the border. Longing for a quick return home, she sensed that the problem was worse than she'd initially thought. She might not be back for the fall planting, and that turned her heart icy with foreboding. Yet she did not speak aloud of her worries. When the caravan regrouped and started forward, she asked to be shown the mountain landmarks. Kevin walked beside her litter, listening to Chipino's best scout name the peaks, the valleys, and the rock tables that sometimes spanned the trail in wind-carved archways of stone.

They need not have been in a hurry to orient themselves to this new, strange land. Time weighed heavily during the months between engagements, and after the novelty of the early weeks the stark, barren valleys sawed at the spirit and the vast desert horizons scoured the soul to insignificance. As often as he could, Kevin retired to Mara's command tent, which, though constructed of layers of sewn needra hide, oiled to keep it pliable against the weather, was nonetheless opulent inside.

"Who passes?" called the guard at the door flap.

Kevin lowered the cloth he held pressed against his face and sucked in a dust-laden breath. "It is I."

The armored guard waved him past with his spear butt. Kevin stooped, ducked through an inner door of fringes that filtered out most of the dirt, and blinked at the abrupt change in lighting. The main chamber of the command tent was lit by torches of oiled rags, supported in crockery sconces on poles jabbed upright into the earth. Hanging from the roof peaks were cho-ja globes, an eerie blue-violet that mixed uneasily with the warmer glow of flame light. The colors of woven rugs, cushions, and hangings sparkled strangely, spiked by starred shadows that formed a mosaic of geometric patterns of their own, as though the belongings and their assorted shadow shapes formed some alien game board upon which people were the players.

Try as he might, Kevin had never been able to liken the Game of the Council to chess; the Tsurani system of honor was far too convoluted a custom for a foreigner to break down into moves. The desert men's strategies, on the other hand, were less opaque. He had studied them exhaustively through the seasons that had passed since their arrival. The nomads sent raiders against the fortified passes, mostly at night, and always in stealth. They sought to wear away at the armies of Xacatecas and Acoma, here through attrition, and there through the nerve-sawing, actionless boredom. Day after day dawned with no battle, beyond the wasp stings of raiding at night. The forays were just frequent enough, and just well enough engineered, to keep the armies on the hair-trigger edge of vigilance.

The Xacatecas forces had been stretched thin to keep all the minor trails through the mountains adequately guarded. With the support of the Acoma companies, Lord Chipino had hoped the raiders would acknowledge superior numbers and abandon incursions across the borders. Yet the desert men had done no such thing; rather, they stepped up the frequency of their strikes, goading like insects flying at needra bulls.

As the months dragged by with no change, Kevin had been hesitant to venture his full opinion, that the attacks held purpose behind them. He'd had the experience on the field to justify his hunches; but Tsurani killed Midkemian officers taken captive, and in preservation of his life he had never dared admit his birth was noble to anyone this side of the rift save a handful of Midkemian slaves. Shedding his headcloth and sandals and leaving them for servants to beat clean, he now walked across beautifully woven carpets to where his Lady sat on cushions, a sand table depicting the mountains and the desert border of the Empire spread before her and Lujan.

"There you are," Mara said, looking up. A river of raven hair spilled loose over one shoulder; she caught it back with a hand like fine porcelain and smiled her welcome. "We were discussing a change in strategy," and she nodded to indicate Lujan.

Interested, Kevin quickened his step. He knelt on the cushions opposite the sand table and studied the small clusters of green and yellow markers that represented Acoma and Xacatecas companies. The positions were clustered like chains of beads along river courses, passes, and rocky, steep-sided valleys through which the winds keened after dark. Unless a sentry happened to catch the movement of the enemy silhouetted against stars or sky, he would not hear footsteps; only a chance rattle of gravel, which often as not was set off by wind, and an attack that happened in a flurried, surprise ambush. The knives of the desert men were not metal, but they cut throats readily enough.

"We want to eradicate their supply caches," Mara said. "Burn them out. Your opinion is of interest, since you have as much knowledge of the terrain here as any of us."

Kevin licked his lips, a chill chasing his skin under the sleeves of his shirt and the broad-banded desert robe he wore like a cloak overtop. He looked at the sand map and wondered silently whether this was precisely what the enemy hoped to do: lure their warriors out of the defensible passes and harry them into ambush in the open. "I suggest again, Lady, that we not sally forth against these desert men. They hold all the advantage in their own country. I say, as I have before, that we let them come to us, and die on our spears with little cost to your companies."

"There is no honor in hanging back from attack," Lujan pointed out. "The longer the Lady is absent from her estates, the greater the danger to Ayaki. To wait through another turn of seasons wins her no gain in the Game of the Council, nor any stature in the eyes of the gods. It is not the fate of warriors to wait idly by while desert men treat their presence like that of querdidra herders, staging small raids at their pleasure."

"Then you have no use for my opinion," said Kevin, biting back exasperation. "I believe there is strategy in the movements of these nomads. You insist there is not—"

"They are barbarians!" Mara cut in. "They raid across our borders because the land is rich and green. Why should tribes of desert men suddenly organize against a nation armed and prepared against them? What could they hope to gain, except obliteration?"

Kevin heard her anger, and took no offense, aware as he was that the time away from home had stretched out into almost a year, and the separation from her son was wearing at her. Each month the traders' ships made port at Ilama, and Jican's messenger reached her, but no word arrived of an attack by the Minwanabi. She had left her best troops to guard the estate; here, with the ones that remained, she had expected to lend support to Xacatecas, and then be free to depart. But the attack at home had not happened, or at least, if it had, word had not reached them; and on this side of the Sea of Blood, the campaign was unexplainably drawn out and showed no signs of resolution.

"We must find the nomads' supply caches and burn them out," she insisted emphatically. "Or else grow old in this wretched waste, and never see satisfaction against Minwanabi." Her pronouncement ended discussion.

The scouts went out. They made a five-day sweep of the lowlands that extended into a month of seeking. The nomads could not be tracked across sands continuously shifted by the winds, nor over swept slabs of rock. The Tsurani were forced to search for the smoke of cooking fires in a land that had no trees but imported oil or charcoal for heat and light. The warriors had to lie for days in hiding, scanning the barren horizons for signs of enemy encampments. They marched across smoldering hardpan, and found nothing: just old fire rings filled with ash and burned bones, and sometimes the imprint where a hide tent had stood, or broken bits of discarded crockery. The nomads' caches of supplies remained elusively hidden.

After three unfruitful months, Xacatecas and Acoma soldiers began taking captives. These unfortunates were dragged back to Chipino's tents for questioning. The desert raiders were small, of wiry stature, and often bearded. They smelled of querdidra and sour wine, and they wore leather studded with bosses of the pack beasts' horn and bone. Over this primitive light armor they threw loose-fitting robes in beige colors, tied with beaded sashes that held talismans denoting their prowess and tribe. Very tough, with skins weathered by the climate, few could be induced to talk. The ones that had looser tongues were not highly placed in their clan hierarchies; the caches they disclosed in the following four months were of little consequence; just a few skins of wine and some grains stored in earthen jars. Not enough to be worth losing warriors over, Lord Chipino said to Mara in a frustrated talk after a day spent in blazing sunlight, digging one such cache from the sandy floor of an arroyo.

The Acoma command tent was still under the gloom of twilight. The calls of the sentries as the watch changed mingled with smells of roasting meat that drifted in through the flaps, opened to the cooling evening breeze; charcoal smoke arose in blue puffs against darkening hills, and inside, the smoldering of oiled rags threw cherry-colored light through the decorative pierced patterns in the light sconces.

Mara clapped hands for a servant to bring the Lord of the Xacatecas some tesh, sweetened as he preferred it. She said, "Then you think we waste our time by searching the foothills?"

"I do." Lord Chipino emphasized his frustration with a jerk of his chin. "The supplies of the nomads must be held in the deep desert, beyond our scouts' line of sight, and where no trails exist to leave tracks. I believe we must attempt an incursion with perhaps two companies of warriors."

The servant arrived with the tesh, lending Mara a moment for thought. She had also come to feel that some similar tactic was necessary, and Lujan supported her. The only dissenter was Kevin, who tirelessly insisted that the nomads might be planning for just such contingency. She gave a small shake of her head. Why should barbarians taunt her people to invade? What possible need might motivate them?

"None of this makes sense," Chipino said, tugging the straps at his neck to loosen his dust-caked armor. He scratched the leathery skin of his throat, almost frowning, then wet his gullet with the tesh. Its sweetness rinsed the taste of the desert grit from his mouth and also eased his temper. "Isashani wrote me to say that Hokanu of the Shinzawai came visiting in Ontoset."

Mara raised her eyebrows. "Is your wife by chance trying to matchmake?"

Xacatecas laughed. "Perpetually. But in this case with Hokanu's enthusiastic interest, so it would seem. The younger Shinzawai misses you. He asked after you, more than once."

"And Isashani kept score?" Mara prompted. At Chipino's resigned nod, she added, "What brought Hokanu to Ontoset? That's a bit far afield for him, I should think."

"That's just what Isashani pointed out," Chipino added. "The interfering woman suggests that the young man came to trade for spices that can as easily be purchased in Jamar."

Which implied he had gone specifically to speak with Lady Isashani to hear direct news of Dustari. Mara was unsure how to react to this, not certain that Hokanu's overt interest in news of her might not simply mask his father's latest ploy in the Great Game.

The thought was interrupted by the return of that day's officer of the watch, with the dispatches brought in by the scouts. He bowed in deference. Mara gave him permission to speak before her guest, saving herself the trouble of sending word across to the Xacatecas camp later.

"No findings to report, my Lady," the armored man recited, his plumed helm crooked in one dirty elbow. "One man was injured in a rockslide, and two more were killed in an ambush. The wounded are being tended in the camp by the south mesa. The other five bands of scouts found nothing."

Which added up to a loss that had no purpose, Mara concluded in silence. Needled by the progression of useless days, useless deaths, and no sign of change beyond attrition, she found her patience at an end. The nomads were just toying with them—about this Kevin was correct—but to sit and wait without action was unacceptable. Mara excused her tired officer from duty, then met the dark, sardonic eyes of the Lord of the Xacatecas. "The Acoma offer one company, to march out in a foray beyond the foothills. My First Strike

Leader, Migachti, will command, and a half patrol of cho-ja will go along to act as message bearers between here and the main camp."

Lord Chipino of the Xacatecas inclined his head. He set his tesh cup on the low table, between the stone-weighted corners of the map scrolls, and the slates, and the ground-down ends of chalk, and reached for his sun-bleached helm. "To the honor of our houses, and the ruin of enemies," he intoned. "I will send a company also, and a gift, to recompense for your cho-ja, whose abilities I cannot match from my own ranks. The hive on our lands had no warriors to spare, with the unrest of House Zirentari on the northern borders of our home estate."

Mara did not venture the fact that she had bargained with her own Queen to breed extras; one did not divulge the unnecessary even to friends, for in the Great Game today's allies could be tomorrow's bitterest enemy. She arose out of politeness and bowed to her social superior, though between herself and the Lord the forms were not always observed in private. "I waive the need for the gift."

Lord Chipino studied her, squinting slightly in the spangled light thrown off by the pierced designs of the sconces. "You are wrong," he said gently, as he might perhaps have corrected a daughter. "A woman in the beauty of her youth should never be permitted to languish in a desert without gifts."

Mara flushed. She found no words to cover her intense moment of self-consciousness, so Lord Chipino smoothed over the embarrassment for her. "Hokanu made Isashani promise to see that your charms were not forgotten in this desolate, barbarian land."

The Lady of the Acoma laughed, freely, which was a change after two years that felt, in isolation, like captivity. "You and Hokanu are both flatterers!"

Chipino turned his head, then shoved his helm over rumpled grey hair and left the chin strap hanging. "Well, it's true there are no women here to exorcise that failing of mine. I'd flatter the querdidra mares, if I could." He shrugged. "But they spit. Do you spit? No? I didn't think so." Then the true compliment came, underhandedly, so she would not brush it off in a change of subject. "Hokanu is a man of shrewd sense, and fine taste, else Isashani would have shown him and his questions out her door, you can be certain."

The gift, when it came, was a copper bracelet, wrought in the form of a shatra bird on the wing, and set with a solitaire emerald. It was beautiful, made specially for her, and at a cost beyond the worth of a mere half patrol of cho-ja, even were such warriors to die in the course of their duty. Mara laid the jewelry back in the velvet-lined box it had been delivered in. "Why would he do this?" she asked what she thought was an empty tent.

Kevin spoke up from behind her shoulder, making her start. "Chipino admires you, for yourself. He wants you to know that."

Mara's frown deepened. "Lord Xacatecas? Why should he admire me? He is of the Five Families, preeminent in the Empire. What does he hope to gain from a house under siege by the Minwanabi?"

Kevin shook his head in a flash of impatience and sat on the cushions beside her. He reached up, lifted her masses of loose hair, and gently began to knead the tense muscles in her shoulders. Mara leaned into the caress with a sigh and surrendered knots of tension she had not noticed were there. "Why should he?" she persisted in reference to the Lord of the Xacatecas.

Kevin's hands rested warmly on either side of her chin. "Because he likes you. Not because he has designs on you— though I'll wager he might indulge in a little discreet dalliance if he thought you were of a mind. But he has no overt designs on you, or your house, or what gain he might make in the Great Game. Lady, not all of life is bloody politics. Too often you seem to forget that. When I consider your gift, and Lord Xacatecas' motives, I see nothing but a man the age of your father who is pleased with you, and who wishes to give you something that you yourself seldom do: a pat on the back, because you are competent, and caring, and well loved."

"Well loved?" A wicked smile curved Mara's lips, which Kevin echoed. His hands moved and gently slipped the clothing from her shoulders. Together they sank back into the cushions in the soft warmth of the flamelight, and their passions kindled in swift and wordless rapport.

• • •

The patrols marched out the next morning, to a blast of horns blown by the cooks from Lord Chipino's compound. So long had the Xacatecas troops been stationed here that they had taken on the nomads' custom, used to inform the gods and the enemy that the day began in triumph. An army marched at sunrise, and the fanfare was intended to make its enemies tremble.

In the months that followed, nothing happened quickly. Mara took to waiting on the heights in the lookout nook manned by the scouts. The windswept table of rock had no shade, so she exchanged her woven straw headdress for a boy's helmet, wrapped with a gauze-thin silk scarf. As the days passed, she grew as adept as her warriors at spotting the trailing puffs of dust that signaled the return of a cho-ja messenger. At such times she would send a runner slave to inform Lord Chipino, then scramble down the rocky trail at speed to meet the incoming warriors. Her legs grew as firm as any boy's from such climbing where litter and slaves could not bear her. Lujan was a wise enough commander to observe that the Lady's presence had the effect of inspiring his men to diligence. Unlike many Tsurani nobles, this lady gained thorough understanding of the conditions under which her sentries and patrols addressed their duties. She did not demand that they keep impossible hours under the noon sun, nor did she complain when the heat waves off the distant sands obscured the visibility and caused conflicting reports. Although she vastly preferred finance to warfare, she made it her business to study the fine points of strategy and supply. She had as good a grasp of their predicament as any of her officers, but her innovative perceptions could not affect what seemed to lack purpose or pattern.

The reports sent back by the companies assigned to patrol in the desert did little to relieve the border deadlock. One small cache was discovered, and destroyed, along with the nest of nomads that protected it. Two more months passed in fruitless search, and then another, spent chasing down false leads. The cho-ja brought word of an oasis gone dry, and the remains of a stock burrow that had been uprooted in apparent haste. The patrol who gave chase to see if they could overtake the nomads who had deserted the site exhausted themselves in a fruitless march. Of those who remained to investigate, two soldiers were injured when the ground gave way over a pit trap. Infection claimed the life of one; the other was sent back by litter. He would never walk again, and requested honorable suicide by the blade. Mara granted permission, and barely managed not to curse Chochocan for the waste of a fine man.

Another season passed without event. The Lady of the Acoma grew sharp-tempered with brooding.

"We should send out more soldiers," she snapped to Kevin, while combing her hair with sweet oils, since water for baths was wasteful and one had to remove the dust somehow.

The Midkemian paused, then pointedly went back to restringing a broken lace on his sandal. This discussion had taken place repeatedly, and each time he had insisted that a march from the mountains in strength was what the enemy desired of them. The words had been said. But the one fact that would have lent his advice credence remained an unvoiced secret. Month after sun-blazing month, Kevin bit back any comment that might reveal his prior military experience. To admit he had been an officer in command on the field in Midkemia was to ask for a sentence of death.

Yet even ignorant of his past, Mara did not discount his opinion entirely; though she was the more impetuous of the two family rulers charged with border patrol in Dustari, it was Lord Chipino who brought up the need for aggressive tactics at the last.

He came into her tent just past twilight, bringing the smell of charcoal fire and roast chal nuts that he had been sharing over coals with his Strike Leader. "I've had word from the desert companies," he opened without bothering with social ceremony. "They captured a nomad trader, and I think we have a lead. At least, we know where large caravans from the other side of the desert have been leaving off grain parcels."

Mara snapped her fingers for servants to set out warm tesh. "My cho-ja say the same, but add that the sand smells of footsteps." By now all had learned to trust the fact that the insects could scent traces of the oils the nomads used to cure their sandal leather. "The caravans are no falsehood sent to lead us astray."

She gestured to her sand table, which through nearly two

weary years had come to dominate the front chamber of her command tent. Over the course of the campaign, the mountains had been leveled and re-formed to one side, allowing space for the broad, undulating valleys of desert dunes that lay beyond the border. The topography was done by a wizened old man with a squint, paid exorbitant rates to be absent from his large family and trade in Ilama. But on that table, laid out in pins with beaded heads, Mara knew the location of every one of her soldiers. "Let us compare what we know," she invited Lord Chipino in what had lately become an evening ritual.

But, in a departure from routine, she and the lord began a parley that lasted deep into the night. Their voices rose and fell with planning, over the moan of the wind across the tent ridges, and around the sigh of the drafts that rippled the hangings and fanned the embers in the light sconces scarlet. Lord and Lady reached an accord without argument: come the morning, they would each call up another company. Leaving two companies of mixed troops to keep the border, they would journey with the rest into the desert and join the army there. A faster patrol would hasten ahead, with orders to pursue the newest leads and locate the nomads' main supply caches.

"When we arrive with the two new companies," Lord Chipino concluded, "we will have an army of a thousand with which to formulate our attack."

He rose, his multiple shadows thrown by the cho-ja lights swooping across flame-patterned carpets. "Better we attack in force than sit like poets in the heights. To wait out the year is to give those barbarian nomads more honor than they justly deserve."

That night, Kevin lay sleepless in the dark. He listened to Mara's breathing and the endless moan of the winds, and the creaking of the lines that lashed the tent. To leave the mountains with an army would be a mistake; he knew it. But a slave in the Empire was accorded no honor, and his voice would not be heard. But where the Lady of the Acoma went, so he would go also. He loved her too well to stay behind.

The huge center pole crashed down, and what seemed acres of canvas billowed slowly down to the ground. Kevin dashed, tripping, over a mound of rolled throw rugs and all but knocked over Mara.

"You're taking the command tent?" he asked, using his own clumsiness as an excuse to capture her in an embrace.

Mara raised her eyebrows in reproof. "But of course." She sounded as if carting chests of tapestries, carpets, sconces, and braziers into a hostile and barren desert were a foregone conclusion. "The Acoma are not barbarians. We do not sleep on the ground like peasants, unless we are traveling in disguise." She waved at the swarms of servants who labored to dismantle her dwelling. "Lord Chipino's tent is far larger. By the size of our pavilions, the nomads will know they reckon with great families."

Kevin pulled a face. "And seeing the size of your respective tents, they will run like jigabirds from trouble?"

Mara's brows rose a notch higher. "They are not civilized."

"Meaning if they were, they'd run like jigabirds," Kevin qualified.

"You have a habit of repeating the obvious." Mara pushed impatiently at his hands, which were stroking her intimately through her thin robes. "Not now, busy man. When I insisted that you stay at my shoulder, I did not mean bed sport in plain view of gods and sky."

Kevin backed off, smiling. "The querdidra drivers have rounded up their herds." He glanced at the growing piles of chests, carpets, and cushions. "Are you certain you have enough pack saddles for all this stuff?"

Mara looked exasperated. "One more comment, and I'll have you carrying a share like a bearer slave. Very likely you belong with them anyway, as punishment for incurable insolence."

Kevin bowed with mock deference and hurried off to help bridle the insufferable and fractious-tempered six-leggers. "By damn, we'll be lucky be have this army marching before sundown," he muttered as he passed out of earshot.

In fact, it took until noon. The army under Lord Chipino and Lady Mara moved off to a fanfare of horn calls and the snap of querdidra drivers' goads. The litters of the Lord and the Lady moved in the center of the column, surrounded by the protection of their soldiers. With cho-ja patrols leading and following, and an advance guard of scouts, the columns wound their way downward from the heights and into the dense heat of the flatlands, looking more like a merchant's caravan than an army.

The pace set was brisk, despite the unrelenting heat. Once the mountains fell behind, the warriors marched over the loose, ever-shifting sands, their progress marked by a rising trail of dust that was visible for miles in all directions. Any nomad child with eyes would know that a large force was moving against them, and sound carried far on the winds. Secrecy was impossible in any event, with the dunes devoid of plant life or shelter of any kind.

Barren tables of rock thrust up through the sands, wind-carved into fantastic shapes, and sliced by deep-chasmed arroyos that sometimes held springs in their shadowed, almost cavelike depths. Any of these might hide a camp of enemies. The tribes would be watching the armies of the Acoma and the Xacatecas, trying to determine whether to stay where they were and stage ambush, or to slip away under cover of blown dust and nightfall, to avoid getting bottled up inside and slaughtered.

The land was unsuitable for pitched battle of any sort, Kevin decided. Superior numbers were the only assurance of victory, and no one could guess how many desert clans were allied for the campaign against the Empire. They could be holed up in the rocks on all sides, or they might melt away, invisible, while the army marched itself to exhaustion in search of them. Gouging loose sand from beneath the straps of his sandals, and feeling the blisters starting underneath, Kevin swore. If you were a desert man armed with long knives and poisoned arrows, your tactics in provoking a large war force made sense only if you had a trap out there, carefully set, and awaiting the army to spring it. The whole thing reeked of long-range planning.

Yet Mara stayed reluctant to see reason. "The desert tribes cannot be bought," she said, under the stars, when at last they made camp. It was too hot and still yet to retire into the command tent, and slave and Lady sat companionably on a carpet, snacking on dry wine and querdidra cheese. "There are too many tribes, and too many split loyalties. Wealth has no meaning to a chief if he cannot carry it with his tents."

Kevin conceded this point in silence. He had observed enough of the desert men taken captive to appreciate the point. They might be diminutive, but they were as fiercely proud as the dwarves on his homeworld, and argumentative as a sand snake: they tended to bite first and worry about survival after. They were children of a harsh country, where death walked behind every man. Most would jump through fire rather than betray their tribes; and their chieftains, as near as Kevin could see, fought and killed one another as readily as they raided the Tsurani border.

"We should sleep soon," Mara said, interrupting her barbarian's brooding. "We shall have to be up well before the dawn to allow the servants enough time to dismantle my quarters."

Kevin shook grit from his tunic and cursed as it contaminated the last few swallows of his wine. "We might sleep right here," he suggested.

"Barbarian!" The Lady laughed. "If there were an emergency, how would my Force Commander find me?"

"If an assassin chanced to come for you, that could be an advantage." Kevin arose and extended a hand to lift her.

"Show me the assassin who could get through Lujan's patrols," Mara retorted, slipping comfortably into his arms.

Which was true enough, Kevin reflected, but not in the least reassuring. If the nomads had intended to send assassins, they would have done so without baiting a whole army.

The next week's march led them into a country of rocky tablelands and dunes crowned with broken clutches of boulder. The army was hemmed in by poor footing, forced to straggle through deep sand in a twisting succession of narrow valleys. The place had a canyonlike feel not at all to Kevin's liking, and even Lujan voiced doubts. But messengers from the advance troops rushed in with excited word that there was a cache, a large one, as well as a sizable force of desert men encamped on the hardpan on the other side of the hills.

Mara and Lord Xacatecas held parley and decided to press on.

"The cho-ja do not get mired in this sand," Mara explained to Kevin when the latter questioned the decision. "They are fast and fierce, and the heat does not slow them. One company of cho-ja is worth two of humans in this desert, and what can the barbarians do as counteroffensive against that?"

There was no ready answer. The army marched on until night fell over the land and the copper-gold moon of Kelewan rose and bathed the dunes in metallic light.

Mara retired to the comfort of her command tent and the soothing voice of a musician, while Kevin paced the camp perimeter and wrestled with conflicts of his own. He loved the Lady; she was in his blood, and nothing could change that. But did he love her enough that he should risk his own life? The Midkemian walked, listening to the talk of the warriors and the banter that passed between them. The language might be different, but soldiers on the eve of a conflict were no different here from those in the Kingdom of the Isles. Honor notwithstanding, the warriors of Mara's army diced and joked and upbraided one another; but they did not mention death, and they avoided talk of loved ones left home on the estate.

Dawn broke in a haze of fine dust thrown up by restless breezes. The servants by now had the knack of collapsing the great tents; the querdidra had stopped spitting and grown resigned to their added burdens. Or else they were too thirsty and too wise to waste fluid, Kevin thought, as he worked grit from between his teeth and sipped sour water from a flask. Too soon, the army was gathered into ranks and marching through the defile that wound down between mesas to the hardpan.

The nomads were massed there, waiting, a motley spread of perhaps eight hundred drably clothed warriors, clustered around tribal banners woven in bright colors and embellished with the cured tails of kurek, an animal resembling a fox. Kevin looked on them and felt the skin on his arms crawl with gooseflesh. While the warriors of the Acoma and the Xacatecas formed ranks and readied weapons, he retied the laces on his light, Midkemian-style brigandine and hung close by Mara's litter. There Lujan, Lord Xacatecas, Mox'l, the cho-ja Force Commander, and Envedi, who commanded the Xacatecas army, held conference. They would attack the ragtag force of tribesmen; their honor required it, as performance of their duty as guardians of the Empire's southern border. Kevin wished Tsurani custom allowed a slave to bear weapons; for that this army prepared for disaster he had not the smallest doubt.

"I will lead my two companies into the valley and attack in a frontal charge," Lord Xacatecas rumbled in his bass voice. "If the barbarians break and flee before us, your cho-ja company can flank and engage from the rear, and cut them off. If the desert men do not run, then Xacatecas will send a great offering to Turakamu."

Mara inclined her head. "As you wish," she intoned formally. Although Lujan would have preferred to send in a mixed company of Acoma and Xacatecas warriors, Lord Chipino had social seniority. His were the more experienced officers, and Mara had made it clear that she desired alliance, not rivalry, between her house and that of Xacatecas. To contend over war honors and protocol would not be to Acoma advantage.

The sun climbed toward noon, and the shadows shrank beneath the rocks. The army of Lord Xacatecas formed up into battle array and aligned itself for the charge. Mara set observers upon the crests of the escarpments on either side and arranged messenger runners to carry dispatches. The air was still, the silence complete; Kevin stood sweating at Mara's shoulder, almost wishing for the scrape of chitinous shell that the cho-ja made while whetting their bladelike forelimbs to a razor sharpness for killing. His teeth were on edge anyway, and the sound would have justified the discomfort. Then the horns sounded, and the Xacatecas Force Commander signaled the charge. In a wave, the warriors in yellow and purple broke into a run toward the valley.

Kevin shivered before a horrible, gut-wringing premonition that disaster was about to overtake them.

"Lady," he said hoarsely, "Lady, listen to me. There is something I desperately need to tell you."

Wholly engaged with watching the army that descended at a run toward the hardpan, and the screaming, ragged ranks of desert men who surged yipping to meet it, Mara barely glanced in Kevin's direction. "Let it wait," she snapped. "I'll hear you after the battle."

12. *SNARES*

The army charged.

From a niche in a cleft of rock behind the desert men's lines, Tasaio licked his teeth. "Good, good," he murmured gently. "At last we have the Lord of the Xacatecas precisely where we want him."

The Strike Leader at Tasaio's shoulder restrained an urge to scratch an itch beneath his armor. "Do you wish our offensive to begin now, sir?"

Tasaio's cat-yellow eyes blinked once. "Fool," he said, with no change of tone, but the Strike Leader squirmed back. "We do not attack now, but when Lord Xacatecas has fully engaged his troops and is absorbed with the slaughter of tribesmen."

The Strike Leader swallowed. "Sir, that is not what you told their chiefs in last night's council."

Tasaio lounged back, his hair like dark copper against his cheek, a fine stubble showing just in front of his ear where his helm strap had worn the growth short. "Of course not," he said in the same velvet tone. "The tribes would hardly have committed their people to a battle to the death, the slinking cowards."

The Strike Leader of the Minwanabi tightened his lips and said nothing. Tasaio laughed brightly. "You think I have acted dishonorably?"

"Uh, of course not, sir," the Strike Leader stuttered hastily. He had heard that laugh before and learned to fear what action might follow.

"Of course not!" snapped Tasaio in disgusted imitation of

his junior officer. "The desert men are barbarians, without honor, and a promise to their chiefs is as wind. Turakamu will avenge no people who question his divine truth. The desert men are soulless bugs, and even a land such as this will be cleaner without them."

"As you say, sir," the Strike Leader said obsequiously.

His fawning disgusted Tasaio. He turned aside and watched the oncoming ranks of the Xacatecas crash into the lightly armed desert men. Weapons clattered against weapons, and screams arose as the first of the fallen watered the dry sands with their blood.

"Wait," Tasaio soothed his near-to-fidgeting Strike Leader. "We shall attack in due time." He leaned against the shoulder of stone, totally at ease, as if the sounds of death and battle were music to his ears.

The Minwanabi Strike Leader maintained his own calm by strength of will. If he was disturbed by the sight of their desert men allies being cut down and slaughtered as a sacrifice, he said no word. Stiffly correct, and obedient to his master, he observed without flinching as the desert men were driven back, and back again, leaving their numbers in thrashing, bleeding heaps upon the sand. The soldiers of Lord Xacatecas were thorough, efficient, and in no mind for showing mercy. They had been prisoned for years in a backlands post with a cruel climate and had suffered the insect stings of a thousand covert raids. Their swords reaped lives in bloody slaughter until the surviving desert men broke and fled.

Tiny as a doll on the distant field, the Lord of the Xacatecas raised his blade and his Force Commander called the companies to form ranks and pursue. For the honor of the Empire, and in hopes that the border unrest might be ended, his warriors regrouped and surged forward.

Tasaio's eyes narrowed slightly, measuring distances. As if the Xacatecas forces crossed a line invisibly drawn in his mind, he said to his sweating subofficer in an inflection that did not change from the beginning, "Now, Chaktiri. Now signal the start of our offensive."

On the rise overlooking the hardpan, Lujan nodded to himself. "They're routed. Look." And he waved a hand as the ranks of the desert men broke apart into fleeing knots. "Xacatecas will regroup and pursue now, without needing help from the cho-ja."

Mara looked up from her seat on the litter, which rested on the ground at the top of a knoll. She pushed aside the gauzy fabric that served as a veil to keep the blown dust off her face. "You sound disappointed."

Lujan shrugged. "What newly appointed Force Commander would be pleased to sit idly by with a battle going on?" He gave a wry smile. "My Lady's honor is mine. I accept the wisdom of her choice."

Mara smiled also. "Nicely spoken. Also a forgivable lie. I promise you all the action you wish when we get out of this desert, and if there is an Acoma natami to return to."

As if her words were an omen, a horn call split the air. Far down in the valley, on either side of the hardpan where Xacatecas' two companies were pursuing tribal warriors, a dark tide flanked the dunes. Lujan spun, his humor fading and his hand half-clenched to his sword hilt.

Mara turned also, her veils whipped aside by the motion. She saw tribal banners, and rank upon rank of figures in odd bits of armor and desert garb, advancing to hit Lord Xacatecas' troops in the flank from two sides; when the forces met, they would seal off retreat into the hills, where Mara's support companies waited. Swiftly, with eyes sharpened by Keyoke's training, the Lady counted phalanxes. She estimated quickly and found Lord Chipino's force was outnumbered two to one. Worse—her heart slammed in recognition —these were not desert men. To a man, the advancing army stood full height; there was not a diminutive figure of a tribesman among them, which meant but one thing: they were not of this land, but impostors, enemies from within the Empire in this war to see an end to her house, despite their barbaric aspect.

"Minwanabi!" she cried sharply. "So *this* is what Desio planned!" She raised widened eyes to her Force Commander and tried not to show the knife thrust of fear that pierced her. "Lujan, rally our men. We must hit this new army from the rear, or Xacatecas will be slaughtered in the field."

Lujan began a hasty bow, his lungs already filling with air to raise his shout of command.

"Wait!" Kevin's cry cut between, with an intensity that demanded hearing.

Mara turned white. "Kevin!" she snapped in a near whisper. "You presume too much if you think to interfere between sworn allies. There is honor at stake here." She jerked her head at Lujan. "Continue, Force Commander."

Kevin shot up from his crouch, very fast for a man of his size. He reached out, caught Lujan's arm, and then froze as the Force Commander's blade cleared its scabbard, snapped down, and stopped, in perfect control, against the bones of his wrist. A fine line of scarlet opened where the skin split under the edge.

"Stop!" Mara said. Her voice shook, as it never had in the memory of any man present. In the valley, the shouts of the armies reached a crescendo, and the rattle of shields and swords clashing together added to the din as the Xacatecas forces wheeled to take the shock of the enemy reinforcements. Mara flicked dark eyes from her Force Commander to her slave, and even her lips were white. "You might lose your head for this transgression." Her expression showed that with house honor resting on her aiding Xacatecas, even her feelings for Kevin were of no consequence.

Kevin started to loosen his grip, then reversed the motion. He looked at his Lady, grim with an expression she had never seen. His eyes were too wide, his mouth tight, and his breathing shallow and fast. "I have reason."

Lujan stood like a statue, his blade a whisper of a touch against skin that bled a trickle of scarlet.

"Speak, then," Mara said tersely. "Quickly, for Xacatecas soldiers are dying while we delay." She did not add that if this was another of his barbarian whims, he would hang for it. No matter what her love for him, the name of her ancestors must never be disgraced.

Kevin swallowed. "Lady, if your warriors charge in Xacatecas' defense, they will all die in a trap."

Her eyes did not change, but stayed flat without feeling.

"Lady, I know!" Almost, Kevin found himself shouting. He controlled himself. "I have seen these tactics before, on my world. There was a small company of our people in a glade before a walled city. They routed the local conquerors and were advancing, only to be attacked from the rear. The force that rushed to support was set upon by ambush, and they were, all of them, cut to pieces."

Mara's manner did not thaw. Still, she jerked her chin at Lujan, who withdrew his blade in silence.

Kevin loosened his fingers. They were shaking. "Lady, on my life, withhold your charge."

Her eyes yet bored into him. "You were a common soldier. How do you presume to advise?"

Kevin closed his eyes, shrugged in his brazen, offhand manner, and seemed to come to an inward decision. Apparently careless, and hiding his inner desperation, he spoke what should have been his death warrant. "I was an officer on my homeworld of Midkemia. I commanded my father's garrison when taken captive in the field."

He waited. Mara said nothing. He realized that, against custom, she was granting him further leave to speak. He went on. "You have said that Tasaio of the Minwanabi was Subcommander of the Warlord's troops beyond the rift. I have fought against him, and I earnestly believe that the battle plan before us on the hardpan has his stamp and signature."

Mara moved her hand, indicating he should be silent. Kevin stopped talking. He searched her face for some clue upon which to gauge the reception of his remarks.

"You realize," she said presently, "that if you are wrong, I must have you hung. More, you will have brought ruin to us all, even to my young son at home."

Kevin expelled an explosive breath. "I am not wrong, Mara." And he stared levelly back.

Mara seemed to stir, as if from a spell. "We are better off dying in defense of Lord Chipino than surviving in cowardice by hanging back."

Lujan nodded grimly at her shoulder.

Exasperated, Kevin rubbed the shallow cut on his wrist. "There might be a way to save your bacon."

"Bacon?" Mara said in puzzlement. "What has this to do with animal fat?"

"I meant turn the tables on the Minwanabi," Kevin snapped. The clamor of battle on the hardpan was drawing closer, with the Xacatecas taking losses, and the desert men survivors fleeing in small puffs of dust over the farther dunes. "If I am right, Tasaio will have another war host concealed in these hills. He will expect us to charge onto the hardpan—his reserve troops wait in hiding to hit us from the rear. Then the companies engaging Xacatecas would split themselves into two forces." He held his hands to illustrate. "One company would simply hold Xacatecas in place, while the other counterattacked your force. Your companies would find themselves surrounded and annihilated, with Xacatecas' troops cleaned up afterward."

"And you propose?" Lujan prompted urgently.

Kevin raised his eyebrows. "I say we send a small company down to aid Lord Chipino. We send the rest of our troops back down the valley we marched in through. Then we send a fast-moving company with the cho-ja, to surround the hills where Tasaio's troops are in hiding, and harry them out into the open, over the hills, and into the company in the valley. Our attacking companies will have the advantage of height. With decent timing, our archers can pick a third of them off before they hit our center lines in force. We'll have a battle in the valley, but one we stand a chance of winning, with all our enemy surrounded. We could drive them into Xacatecas' waiting spears."

Lujan spun his blade, expertly flicking off the fine traces of blood that marred the edge. His voice held disgust as he answered Kevin's bold plan. "Your ideas are no better than a dream. Only cho-ja could move fast enough to effect the maneuver you describe, and one company of them will not be enough to surround this stand of hills."

"We'll have to try," Mara cut in, "or else be caught in this Minwanabi snare and break our trust with the Lord of the Xacatecas."

"No," Kevin corrected. He glanced across the incline to where the cho-ja waited, still as statues in their ranks. He wondered briefly whether the creatures had a prickly sense of dignity, then gave that up as moot. Mara and all of her following were going to be cut down where they stood if Minwanabi had the chance to complete his offensive as planned —not to mention the fact that he, Kevin of Zūn, would be hung in disgrace if he proved wrong. With a fatalistic sigh that approached a laugh, the Midkemian sucked in new breath and related his intentions to Mara and her Force Commander.

• • •

Tasaio repressed a shameful desire to slam his fist agaist the rocks. "Damn her, why does the whore not order her troops to charge? Her father and brother were not cowards. *Why does she hesitate?*"

On the hardpan, cooked under the merciless noon sun, the Xacatecas forces retreated into a tight-knit, defensive shield ring. Pinned in place and surrounded by enemy warriors, they could do nothing but close ranks and suffer losses until Mara sent in relief companies to save them. The purple-and-yellow banner with its sigil poked stubbornly from the the the press of defenders, now and then obscured by blown dust kicked up by the battle. Tasaio squinted across the hardpan, littered with the limp, blood-soaked dead of the tribes and the yellow-and-purple armor of fallen Tsurani. He stared until his eyes burned at the low stand of hills beyond, seeking to sort out the movement that ran like the seething of water on the boil through the Acoma troops still stationed there.

"Why does she hold back?" Tasaio snapped impatiently. "Her ally stands in peril of his life, and all her family honor is in jeopardy."

On the hardpan, pinned down by enemies, Lord Chipino was likely wondering the same thing. A horn call arose from the company beleaguered on the plain, signaling urgently for aid. In answer, a small, dense square broke away from the rise of the hills and advanced upon the battle that swirled the lowland dust.

"A half company, looks to be," offered the Minwanabi Strike Leader, trying to be helpful.

"I see that." Tasaio stroked his weapon hilt, repressed a peevish impulse to pace, and instead gathered up the plain, unplumed helm he had acquired for his campaign in the desert. "I need a better vantage point." He snapped the buckles and jerked the strap adjustments tight. "And find me runners! We're going to have to send messages to the companies in hiding behind the ridges, to inform them the battle is not proceeding at all as we had planned."

"Yes, sir, as you command." The Strike Leader hastened off, clumsy before Tasaio's angry grace. Yet the irritation of his senior held nothing of discouragement. Battles did not always go as intended; the brilliant man, the master tactician, was the one who could turn setbacks to advantage.

• • •

Lujan placed a hand in trepidation on the slick, horny carapace of the cho-ja. He resisted the impulse to ask the insectoid Strike Leader again if he minded the idea of carrying a human rider. The creature and its fellows had agreed to Kevin's outlandish request, and to question again would be to cast doubt on cho-ja dignity. "Mox'l, you will tell me if I discomfort you," the Acoma Force Leader offered by way of compromise.

Mox'l turned his rounded, black-armored head, his eyes lost in shadow beneath his plumed helm. "I have strength sufficient for the purpose," he intoned. "Perhaps I should crouch lower for you to mount?"

Lujan cringed inwardly. "No," he said quickly. "That's not necessary." He decided that he would rather split his britches than allow the cho-ja officer to act in the least bit subservient. He wondered, as he searched for a nearby rock to use for a mounting block, whether if their roles were reversed, the human warriors in his company would take as kindly to the dictates of necessity. Perhaps Kevin was right, that the Tsurani concept of honor was self-limiting. Then, as Lujan scrabbled ungracefully to find purchase on the smooth, chitinous shell of his mount, he banished such impious thoughts. It was ill to contemplate blasphemy with battle in the offing. If the Acoma had earned the wrath of the gods, he would find out soon enough.

Feeling a trepidation that for honor must never be revealed, Lujan gripped the cho-ja behind its neck segment and swung his leg over its rounded, faintly ridged middle. He sprang, and hauled himself astride. The creature's triple sets of legs depressed and recovered to compensate for his weight; and around him, the company of human warriors paired off with an equal number of cho-ja followed his bold lead and mounted. If they found their seats slippery or uncomfortable, they withheld complaint.

"How do you feel, Mox'l?" Lujan asked.

The cho-ja's voice sounded strange coming from a point to the front of and below him. The creatures habitually walked upright when in the presence of humans, using all six of their legs only to run at need. "You are considerate to ask this of me, Force Commander. I am not in distress. Instead I would ask that you have a care for the safety of your lower hind leg-limb, that my bladed lower fore hand-limb not give you injury when we run."

Lujan looked down, and saw that, indeed, his ankles and shins would be at risk of getting diced when the cho-ja extended to full stride.

"I presume to suggest," Mox'l continued politely. "Fix your knee behind the lateral knob on my carapace. The protrusion might offer you support."

"You presume in kindness, and I thank you," Lujan replied, in the somewhat stilted politeness that marked the etiquette of the hive-born. He slid his leg farther underneath himself, and found that the bodily feature Mox'l mentioned did indeed serve as a wedge to steady his seat. Then, at a loss, he searched the top of the insectoid shell for somewhere to grip with his hands.

His efforts met with Mox'l's tinny laugh. The creature tilted its head and managed to twist its face around to look at him in a manner no human could repeat. "Force Commander, my parts are not soft, like yours. Your hands may grasp my throat joint with safety. My windpipe is protected quite sufficiently by my exoskeleton and will not be disturbed by your strength."

Still gingerly, Lujan did as he was bid. The moment his fingers found their place, Mox'l faced forward. "We are ready, Force Commander. It is time now for haste."

The cho-ja scuttled ahead with the startling shift into motion that characterized his race. All but thrown from his perch, Lujan clutched and precariously maintained balance. Around him, with near-mechanical precision and never a single vocal order, the cho-ja company formed ranks. Then, perhaps newly appreciative of his rider's fragile balance, Mox'l poised and held his company, awaiting Lujan's order.

The Acoma Force Leader raised his arm to signal his half of the mounted strike force to move out. Then a voice called out from the sidelines.

"Don't pinch so hard with your calves, or you're certain to land on your butt!"

Lujan turned his head and found his Lady's barbarian slave grinning from ear to ear on the sidelines. The Force Commander considered a retort, but decided that ignoring the taunt would be more dignified. Kevin was a master of crudities, but lost when it came to subtle insult. Then, belatedly, Lujan recalled that in Midkemia the barbarians were said to ride upon great beasts into battle; the advice, perhaps, was quite valid and genuinely offered as well. "Worry instead about the safety of my Lady," the Acoma Force Commander called back. Then he waved to the ranks surrounding him, and the cho-ja surged forward into a run.

Their long, many-jointed legs adjusted to the uneven terrain with inhuman agility. Heat did not trouble them. Their gait had a slight surge to it, back and forth, but almost no sway. A rider did not feel the jolt of each leg striking ground. Lujan reveled in the sensation of speed beyond his imagination; he felt the wind whip his officer's plumes and trappings, and the snap of loose hair against his cheek. His heart surged with the thrill of the unknown, and before he realized the lapse in manners, he found himself grinning like a boy. His levity vanished soon after, as Mox'l reached the edge of the tableland and rushed headlong down a rocky gully toward the lowlands backing the hills.

Lujan bit back trepidation. The pace of the cho-ja was dizzying, too fast for human reactions to encompass.

The Acoma soldiers clung in fear of life and limb. The ground rushed by very fast. Mox'l and his warriors leaped over washes and boulder-strewn scree. Now and again one clawed foot appendage would scatter a fall of loose stones. Human riders squeezed their eyes shut and thought ahead, anticipating battle with the enemy. Facing death by the sword seemed less risky than this headlong dash on cho-ja backs. By the grace of the gods, the Acoma Force Commander could do nothing but cling and hope that his company of humans would survive the ride without breaking their necks.

The land leveled out into sand flats. If Mox'l tired from his burden, he showed none of the signs a human might. His chitinous body did not sweat, and his armored flanks did not labor with fast breathing. Lujan unglued watering eyes and glanced to either side. His fellow warriors were all still in place, though not a few looked white-faced and stiff. He called encouragement to his subofficers, then faced forward, into the whip of the air, to mark their progress.

The cho-ja had borne the warriors better than three leagues in a fraction of the time a human company could march. They made even better time in the flatlands, their quick, clawed feet raising minimal puffs of dust. In the distance, Lujan caught sight of a lone runner. Confident now, even exhilarated, he leaned down and pointed past Mox'l's many-faceted eye.

The cho-ja Force Commander nodded without breaking stride. "A messenger of the enemy flees before us," he elaborated, his eyesight being keener than a human's. "We must overtake him, else risk the success of our mission."

Lujan opened his mouth to agree, then checked in a moment of inspiration. "No," he decided. "Let the man race in terror and reach his commanders unharmed. We will follow on his heels, and let his fear sap the heart from our enemies."

"Humans know humans best," Mox'l recited from hive proverb. "We shall proceed as you think best, for the honor of your Lady and our Queen."

The ride ended at the base of the hills, before a chain of grottos that notched the slopes opposite the valley where the allied armies of Acoma and Xacatecas had marched the day before. Lujan saw the runner scurry like a gazen into shadow, and then there rose a flurry of movement as warriors too tall for desert men emerged from hiding, in a rush to buckle their helms. They were not fully in armor, having expected to climb over the hills and then march upon Mara's troops through the knolls overlooking the hardpan. Now, caught unprepared, they formed ranks in disarray, shouting for haste and cursing their loosened sword belts.

Lujan and his mounted strike force raced in until they were scarcely beyond bowshot range. Then the cho-ja stopped sharply. Human warriors dismounted from their insectoid companions, and the companies flowed into battle lines and charged. The maneuver could not have gone off more smoothly had they practiced: apprehension kept the Acoma men from recklessness. They did not know how many of the enemy they might be facing. Mindful of their fellows, even the most hot-blooded of the warriors held their places as they ran screaming battle calls into the ranks of their enemy.

They struck, and the conflict was closed. Outnumbered, perhaps, but outraged at the trap that had been set to dishonor their Lady, the Acoma fought as though inspired. They had done the impossible, crossed leagues of hostile desert on cho-ja back; their muscles were fresh, and their bodies charged with the adrenaline of daring the unthinkable. Danger from the unknown was replaced by the familiar rhythm of thrust, parry, and lunge, as Mara's green-armored warriors engaged the enemy with a will.

Void of such emotions, but bred expressly for killing, the cho-ja cut a swath into the ranks of Minwanabi in disguise. Razor-edged, chitinous forelimbs clove through shields and wristbones like butcher's blades, while clawed hind and middle limbs stabbed out, dispatching the fallen wounded who strove to thrust swords through softer segmented abdomens.

Lujan ducked an enemy spear, sliced an enemy wrist, then followed through with a killing stroke to the neck. He stepped over the corpse, unmindful of fountaining blood, and engaged the next man in line. On both sides he saw his companions advance with him. The Minwanabi were shade-blind and blinking, brought out into sunlight, into the thick of battle, in a totally unanticipated attack. The Acoma fared well in these first minutes of engagement. It remained to be seen whether they could stay the distance and maintain the advantage when the surprise wore off and the enemy rallied to the task at hand. Thrusting, parrying, battering his way forward with almost maniacal inspiration, Lujan spared small thought for worry. He had once been a grey warrior and would not willingly be inflicted with such a fate once again. Death was preferable to the loss of his Lady's honor. He was too busy fighting and staying alive to wonder more than fleetingly whether the other company of cho-ja and Acoma under the command of his First Strike Leader had met with as resounding a success on the far side of the hills across the valley. And if the patrols sent on the march down yesterday's back trail were not in place, Mara was left as defenseless as a sacrifice, alone on the hillside with her honor guard of twelve.

On the hardpan, the sun beat down with the merciless might of full noon. The token Acoma force sent down to Xacatecas' aid had not significantly altered the odds, except to draw some of the overwhelming numbers of attackers away from

Lord Chipino's shield ring. The Acoma forces soon became as beleaguered as their allies, but with one difference: they had a purpose to their defense. Huddled together in a wedge, they appeared to be fighting as desperate a defense as the Xacatecas; except that, step by gradual step, they seemed to be winning their way closer to their allies.

Not one to miss nuance, Tasaio noticed. His frown darkened. That his enemy should take more losses than strictly necessary just to gain an insignificant bit of ground discomforted him. He might call Mara coward for sending so small a relief force, but he was too cold-bloodedly wise to discount that another purpose beyond fear might motivate her actions. His suspicion was confirmed a moment later when an archer within Mara's shield wall fired off a signal arrow in a high arc.

Tasaio cursed more fervently when the shaft reached its height, tipped into downward flight, and landed, unrecoverable, in the midst of Xacatecas' troops.

"Suppose she has gotten a message through," worried the interfering Strike Leader.

"No doubt," Tasaio snarled. His plot had gone wrong, he was sure of it. There was dust rising beyond the ridge at the edge of the hardpan, which warned of another battle well in progress. His hidden troops had certainly been discovered, which explained much, and none to the good.

"Quickly, we must call off half of the troops that pin down Lord Chipino," Tasaio concluded. "Our best chance now is to charge upon Mara's command position and hope she has engaged the bulk of her soldiers elsewhere. If she has done so, we stand good odds of overrunning her honor guard and killing her. If we act swiftly, Lord Chipino and that ridiculous little company she sent to distract us will have no opportunity to win free."

The Strike Leader raced off to sound the appropriate horn calls, and Tasaio, slit-eyed, arose from his position and checked his sword belt. With a stiff nod to his battle servant, who accompanied him always, he stalked off to join his warriors. Nothing would go amiss this time, he swore by Turakamu the Red. Against whatever outside contingency might arise, and even should his life become forfeit, Lord Desio's cousin would personally lead the foray against the notch where Mara had taken refuge.

"You won't come out, little bitch. Then I will send killers in after you." So saying, Tasaio drew his sword and took his place at the head of the warriors called into position by his Strike Leaders.

The scout bowed to Tasaio. "It is as you suspected, sir. Mara has sent all of her companies around the ridges to attack our forces in hiding. She keeps with her one officer, as honor guard, to stand by her litter."

"Then we have her." Infused by a glow of confidence and satisfaction, Tasaio dismissed half of the warriors he had called from the battle of the hardpan. "Return to support our fellows against the Acoma and Lord Xacatecas. One patrol should be more than enough to ensure the Acoma bitch dies."

He waved, and the company started forward. Tasaio marched them up the slope toward the saddle between two knolls, where Mara and her honor guard held position. He made no effort at concealment; indeed, it would only be a satisfaction to him if his quarry trembled in fear at his approach. If the Lady broke in terror before his threat, he would bring home to his cousin and Lord the gratifying story of Mara's shame. Very much he would enjoy seeing her cringe before him at the end.

The warriors crested the rise. Tasaio had time to notice that the curtains of Mara's litter were drawn closed, her form but a shadowy presence through layers of gauzy silk. Eyes narrowed against sun glare, Tasaio also saw that the honor guard who stood vigil was exceptionally tall, and red-haired. His greaves were too short for his long shanks. The helm pressed over his unkempt locks was not snapped in the heat. As he sighted the advancing ranks of the Minwanabi, he widened eyes of a rare deep blue.

Then, to Tasaio's ultimate surprise, the redheaded guardsman, who should have been the first pick of Mara's warriors, gave a gasp of alarm. He plucked at the gauze curtains and whined, "Lady, the enemy comes!"

Enjoying the moment hugely, Tasaio signaled the charge. Around him, his warriors leaned into full stride for the attack.

With a strange expression on his face, the Acoma guard

braced his spear. Then, as if he rethought the matter, and as his attackers came within arrow range, he dropped his weapon with a noisy clatter, spun on his heel, and ran.

Tasaio loosed a startled laugh. "Take the bitch!" he called and waved his following onward.

The strike patrol raced for the kill, sandals scattering stones as they pressed eagerly into the draw. Tasaio, in the lead, loosed an ululating cry that was half battle yell and partly a paean to the Red God. He dashed to the green-lacquered litter, slashed the silken curtains aside, and thrust his sword deep into the silk-clad figure inside.

A cloudy puff of jigabird feathers burst outward from the pillow his blade impaled. Caught between fury and reflex, Tasaio struck again. Silk split, and a second gutted cushion disgorged its contents into the air.

Tasaio inhaled a lungful of down and cursed aloud. Enraged and forgetful of decorum, he slashed a third time in an explosion of sheer temper. The litter contained only pillows, wrapped up in a lady's fine robe. The honor guard, the red-head, had too obviously been a slave set up as decoy, and this litter a gambit and a trap.

Tasaio's mind reasoned quickly, even though he was irate. This minute, hidden in the surrounding rocks, Mara was certainly enjoying a rich laugh at Minwanabi expense.

Tasaio scanned the nearby knolls, to glean some clue where to send his shamed patrol of warriors, who were now as mortified and hot for blood as he was. To follow after the fleeing slave was too obvious; Mara surely would be more clever—

That moment, the arrows began to fall.

The man next to Tasaio caught one just above his cheek guard. He fell, clawing at his face. Tasaio saw other warriors stagger out of their ranks, and he himself took a glancing blow to his armor that scored deeply through hide layers before rebounding and leaving him unharmed. His instinctive reaction as a commander was to call orders and prevent a sloppy retreat. His warriors were seasoned. They responded as the trained elite they were and withdrew in orderly fashion into the cover of rocks and outcrops. At once Tasaio began to trace the flights of the arrows, and to formulate a counter-attack to obliterate the Acoma archers.

But a clattering of loose rocks sounded on the ridge he

had only recently climbed. Distracted by the disturbance, Tasaio spun, and saw the plumed helm of an Acoma officer flash past a gap in the rock. Green-armored shapes followed, accompanied by the unmistakable hiss of blades being drawn. Voices added to the din, ordering ranks to close in preparation for a charge.

"They seek to cut us off," the Minwanabi Patrol Leader said quickly.

"Impossible!" Tasaio snapped. There was no way Mara could have moved warriors so swiftly to flank Tasaio and attack from the rear.

More canny to the ways of his superior than the Strike Leader, the Patrol Leader said nothing but waited for his senior to issue commands.

"Cho-ja," Tasaio said abruptly. "She must have kept some of them in reserve." They could move swiftly enough in this uncertain terrain—and yet the voices and the noise from beyond the ridge sounded distinctly human. Tasaio hesitated only a moment more. He could not afford a mistake; if Mara had lured him here, surely she had means to cut him off and annihilate both him and his men. And that would spell disaster for his Minwanabi master.

His face would be known, if not to her, then to Lord Xacatecas. He had cut too forward a figure in the War Party not to be recognized. To have the body of so highly placed a cousin in House Minwanabi would be solid evidence of treason. For although this incident had happened outside the borders of the Empire, to treat with the desert men was to support the enemies of the Emperor. Although Tasaio personally would have been willing, if not eager, to trade his life for the chance to send Mara to Turakamu, he dared not do so in a fashion that left the honor of his ancestors compromised. No, Mara had him trapped. He had but one alternative, however distasteful the necessity.

"Fall back," Tasaio called curtly. "Move in good order, but quickly. We must give the enemy no victory."

The warriors obeyed without question, abandoning the safety of cover. They ran in neat zigzags and suffered renewed assault by Acoma archers as they withdrew toward the hardpan. Their faces showed no expression, in true warrior fashion. So did Tasaio reveal no emotion, but every step that he took in retreat burned. *Never* had he been forced to flee from the field of battle. The ignominy cut into him like physical pain. He had reviled Mara, until now, as an enemy of his house and people. This moment, that hatred assumed a personal score. For this current shame, brought about by an error in tactics and his own overeagerness and bloodlust, the Acoma Lady must in the future be made to pay. He would hunt her, and all of her issue, until his last breath was drawn. Arrows clattered around him in concert with the suppressed grunts of warriors who fell and died. Tasaio swore as he ran he would arrange her downfall coldly, each plot made and executed in icy surety, until this insult was avenged.

One of the fallen was his personal battle servant. Aware the man no longer ran behind his shoulder, Tasaio cursed yet again. He would have to train another, and that was wasteful, since many candidates usually died before he found one with reflexes quick enough to suit him. Here was another personal score to be settled, another reason Mara must be made to bleed and suffer. Absorbed in his hatred, Tasaio raced across the hardpan without once looking back. And so he did not know, until he reached the safety of the half company he had rashly and prematurely dismissed, that he and his strike force had been routed by a handful of cho-ja and soldiers, who had duped him into the belief he was surrounded. In fact they had carried nothing better than some spare helms mounted on poles, and loose bits of armor dragged on cords through the sand to create plentiful noise and much dust.

The Strike Leader laboriously pointed this out, and though his face was woebegone, and not in the least bit mocking, Tasaio whirled on him in a fury.

"Silence that man," he called to his Patrol Leader. "Cut his throat, and take his plumes. You are this moment promoted to his position."

The Patrol Leader bowed to his superior. No hint of distress showed on his face as he drew his sword to carry out his superior's orders.

Tasaio glared at the ridge where Mara and her honor guard must lie hidden, mightily enjoying his defeat. The fact that he had Xacatecas surrounded and all but at his mercy did not ease his disgrace. Tasaio did not turn a hair as his Strike Leader was cut down behind him. As if the man did not gurgle out his last breaths on the sand, the cousin of

Desio turned his resources to salvaging what he could of the afternoon, by ordering renewed assault upon Lord Chipino and the isolated half company of Acoma the Lady had sent out as sacrifice. If he could not get at Mara, at least he could ensure that her honor perished with her ally.

And yet, as the sun passed its zenith and descended through the layered dust toward the horizon, Lord Chipino's warriors held without breaking. Many of them lay dead, but the survivors did not lose heart. Tasaio's mood worsened when an exhausted runner brought word that the warriors behind the west ridge had been attacked and decimated by Acoma. The east ridge perhaps held its own; no messenger arrived to say for sure. Tasaio sent scouts to check, but none returned.

"Damn the Lady's cho-ja," the messenger ended. "Without them, her victory would not have been possible."

"Explain what you mean," Tasaio demanded irritably. But a short time later he saw with his own eyes, as a company of Acoma warriors rushed from the valley, between knolls, to come to Xacatecas' defense. They arrived with impossible speed, mounted on the backs of their cho-ja allies. When they reached the fringes of battle, they dismounted, assembled ranks, and charged with a vengeance upon his troops.

Tasaio's warriors had been fighting all day in the relentless sun of the hardpan. They had sweated out their freshness and had no edge to bring to bear against this new and unexpected threat. In contrast, the soldiers of Lord Xacatecas took new heart from their rescuers and pressed back with freshened hope. The Minwanabi could not hold them, and once again Tasaio found himself calling the order for retreat.

He spoke between clenched teeth, pale to the point of nausea with mortification. His plot in Dustari was in ruins, an unmitigated failure; and all because he had been outmaneuvered on the field, a thing that had never happened on Kelewan, nor in the Warlord's campaign against the Midkemians.

The taste of defeat was new and all too potently bitter. Tasaio oversaw the withdrawal of his army, what remained of it; his stomach churned with the realization that he had destroyed his chances to retaliate. He could not remain in the desert to mount a second assault. The desert men he had sent forth as bait would not forgive his betrayal. The tribes would now be set against him, their chiefs perhaps angry enough to swear blood debt. Though Tasaio looked with scorn upon tribal custom and was not in the least afraid of any retaliation the desert men could call down upon his house, he could not discount their retaliations. All the way to Banganok and the ships that would return him to the mainland, he must endure petty raids as the desert men sought to settle blood score against his company.

That night, sitting tentless and tired in camp between a fold of dunes to the east, Tasaio brooded in solitude. He would take no sā wine to blunt the aches left from battle. He shut out the voices of his soldiers, raised in bitter complaint, as they wrapped their wounds and sharpened the chips from their swords. Above all, he would not look to the west, where the afterglow of sunset was displaced by the glimmer of Acoma and Xacatecas victory fires. Soon enough, he promised, those fires would be as ashes. Soon enough would Mara come to regret this brief victory, for next time he matched wits against her, Acoma defeat would be utter and final.

In the command tent of the Lord of the Xacatecas, surrounded by the soft light of lamps and by hushed conversation between a healer and a favored wounded soldier, Mara made the bow that was proper from a Ruling Lady to a social superior. Although hers had been the triumph in the day's rout, she had chosen not to press the acknowledgment of her laurels. She did not wait haughtily in her own tent and insist that the Lord of the indebted house come to her; wisely, subtly, she did not force her new-won position upon a Lord who could potentially cause the Acoma more harm than help were his pride unduly ruffled. Neither did she attempt to ingratiate herself, but passed off her presence as a social visit of little consequence.

"My Lord Chipino," she opened, smiling slightly as she arose, "you expressed an interest in my honor guard, and specifically the soldier who betrayed such remarkable cowardice, that Desio's much praised cousin, Tasaio, was set off his guard."

Lord Chipino waved away the servant who applied a hot compress to the sore muscles of his back and neck. Glistening with massage oils, and smelling of sweet ointments, he gestured to a waiting slave boy, who slipped a light robe over his body. "Yes." Chipino fixed bland eyes on a tall figure in the shadows behind Mara, and said, "Come forward."

Kevin stepped forth, dressed in his Midkemian trousers and a loose-sleeved shirt, gathered at the waist with a Tsurani belt of overlapping shell disks. His blue eyes were laughing as he stopped, hands on hips, to suffer Lord Chipino's scrutiny.

The Lord of the Xacatecas' eyes widened at the sight of the barbarian slave, whom he had observed often enough in Mara's tent. And yet, having been told by the Acoma Force Commander that the day's tactics had been Kevin's, and that all of them lived and breathed as a result of barbarian logic, he looked more carefully at the man from beyond the rift. Politely he cleared his throat. Since his culture had no protocol for addressing a slave who had been heroic, he settled with inclining his head. "Fetch the lad a cushion," he told his slave boy.

One was plucked from the master's own sleeping alcove. Nonplussed, the Lord bade the barbarian sit. Then, satisfied in his paternal way that the fellow was comfortable, Lord Chipino opened what he held to be a most sensitive topic. "You are a slave, and so you were able to run from the enemy in cowardice, since your Lady ordered you to do so, yes?"

To Chipino's startlement, Kevin laughed. "Being a slave has nothing to do with it," he said, in his booming Kingdom voice. "Just to see the look of surprise on Commander Tasaio's face was satisfaction enough."

Lord Chipino frowned, then covered his puzzlement by sipping at the tesh that waited on the tray by his elbow. "Yet you were an officer in the army in your own land, or so your mistress tells me. Did you not feel shamed to show cowardice?"

Kevin's eyebrows slanted up. "Shamed? Either we tricked the enemy, or we died. I hold shame to be a pittance beside the permanent state of being dead."

"His people esteem life far more than we do," Mara interjected. "They do not acknowledge the Wheel of Life, nor do they comprehend divine truth. They do not understand that they will return in their next incarnation based upon the honor they acquire in this present state."

Here Kevin snorted. "You people have tradition, but no sense of evolving style. You don't appreciate jokes as do the folk in the Kingdom of the Isles."

"Ah," Lord Chipino broke in, the puzzlement on his leathery features relenting as if all was explained. "You fled from Tasaio and experienced no shame because you perceive the action as a jest."

Kevin buried an amused irritation behind tolerance. "You could simplify the issue that way, perhaps, yes." He tilted his head to one side, raked back red bangs, and added, "The worst thing about the assignment was that I could barely keep from laughing outright. Good thing the straps of Lujan's spare armor were too tight, or I might have exploded in spite of my best efforts."

Chipino stroked his chin. "A joke," he concluded, though underneath he was obviously mystified afresh. "You Midkemians are wondrously strange in your thinking." He shifted his glance to Mara and smoothly ascertained that his servants had anticipated her needs and brought chocha as she liked it. A man who lived by subtleties, he had trained his staff to observe his guests, learn their needs, and respond in their duties of hospitality without spoken orders from him. The practice had rewards. It was amazing how soft an opponent could become when he was personally catered to with as little fuss as though he sat in his own hall. Mara was not here as an enemy, but Lord Chipino recognized his debt to her and was anxious to negotiate a favorable settlement. He chose his moment, broaching the subject after Mara was settled with refreshment, but quickly enough that she had little space for deep thinking.

"Lady Mara, your soldiers and the brilliance of your war tactics today spared House Xacatecas from yet more tragic losses. We are in your debt for the occasion, and are prepared to offer fair and honorable reward."

The Lady was young; she was gifted, but she still had much hardening to undergo before she became practiced in the Great Game. She proved so now, for she blushed. "My Lord, the Acoma soldiers achieved only what was proper between allies. Little reward is required, beyond a formal swearing of alliance with witnesses upon our return to the mainland."

She paused, dropped her eyes, and seemed more than ever

the young girl. A slight frown creased her forehead, as she thought upon the matter and realized that she must ask something more of House Xacatecas, lest she leave a social superior with an implied debt of obligation. To leave such business unfinished was an unwise move that could strain further amicable relations. "Lord Chipino," she added formally, as if the matter were an embarrassment to her, "for the actions of the Acoma in behalf of your house, I ask one boon: that, at a time of my choosing, you grant me your vote in the Imperial Council to be cast as I wish. Will this be acceptable?"

Lord Chipino inclined his head, well pleased. The request was a pittance, and the girl was cautious beyond her years, to keep her asking modest. He murmured a command, and his runner hurried to fetch his scribe, to set the matter officially under seal. To Mara's most appropriate response he added one thing more. "Let a suit of fine armor be made for the barbarian slave, in Acoma colors, that he may serve his Lady in comfort the next time she requires to bait her traps with an honor guardsman." Kevin smiled in appreciation of the dry Tsurani humor: he would never be permitted to wear this armor, but he would have it as a trophy of sorts. Then, the matter disposed of in lasting satisfaction of the debt, Chipino clapped for servants to bring food. "You shall dine here," he said, and he waved to indicate the barbarian slave was to be included. "Together we shall drink fine spirits, to celebrate the defeat of our enemies."

Mara woke to the touch of a hand shaking her shoulder briskly. She rolled over. Dark hair caught in her lashes, and she sighed, still deep in sleep.

"Lady, you must wake up," Kevin said in her ear.

The bedding seemed much too warm and comfortable. Reluctantly Mara stirred. Though weary still from the battle the previous day, and no little bit discomforted by the sā wine consumed with Lord Chipino to celebrate the victory, she forced her heavy eyes to open. "What is it?"

Dawn greyed the sky beyond the tent flap, left open to catch the night breezes. In the sandy dunes of the low country, the temperature did not fall after sundown, as happened in the mountains. Mara blinked and rolled closer to Kevin's warmth. "It's too early," she protested, and began provocatively to tickle him.

"Lady," the tall barbarian scolded gently. "Lujan is waiting with a message."

"What?" Now fully wakened, Mara sat up. Loose hair spilled like ribbons over her shoulders as she clapped sharply for a servant to bring a robe. Across the command tent, seen as a shadow against the lamplit antechamber, Lujan stalked the breadth of the carpet in long strides, his officer's helm crooked in his elbow. Quickly the Lady of the Acoma shoved her hands into waiting sleeves. She rose, leaving Kevin fumbling for his trousers, and hurried through the fringed partition between the rooms.

"What's amiss?" she said in response to Lujan's agitation.

The Acoma Force Commander completed a swift bow. "Lady. Come quickly. I think the best thing would be for you to see for yourself."

Made tolerant by curiosity, Mara followed her officer, pausing only to slip on the sandals brought to her by a servant as she stepped into the thin light of dawn.

Her eyes adjusted to the gloom, and she halted very quickly, colliding with Kevin, who hurried less gracefully after her. Involved with fastening his buttons, and still barefoot, he had not seen her stop.

Yet his clumsiness raised no imprecations. Mara was utterly absorbed by the sight of seven motley figures who descended the dunes just beyond the perimeter of her camp. They were short, almost dwarf-like in stature. Their robes were fringed with beads of glass, horn, and jade, and their hair was braided. The ends were tasseled in colors, though the rest of their clothing was drab. And around the wrist of each, in varied and elaborate patterns, were blue tattoos like bracelets.

"They look like tribal chiefs," Mara said in wonderment.

"So I thought," Lujan replied. "And yet they come alone, and unarmed."

"Fetch Lord Chipino," Mara ordered.

Her Force Commander inclined his head in his usual wry fashion. "I have already taken that liberty."

Then, acting purely on instinct, Mara added, "Ask our sentries to disarm. Now. At once."

Lujan directed a suspicious glance at the approaching figures, then shrugged. "Let us pray the gods are with us. After Tasaio's performance yesterday, the clan chiefs will have small cause to love us."

"That's just what I am hoping," Mara said quickly.

She stood, a frown on her face, while Lujan carried out her wishes. All around the camp, Acoma soldiers removed their sword belts and laid their weapons flat upon the sand.

"You think these chiefs come as peace emissaries?" said a voice, Chipino's, still gruff from sleep. The Lord of the Xacatecas stepped up to Mara's side, his robe sash half-tied in his haste.

"That's what I am counting on," Mara murmured.

"And if they are not?" Chipino prompted. He sounded dryly interested rather than worried.

And Mara smiled back. "You guess right, my Lord, I am not without reservations. Lujan was told only to ask the sentries to disarm. The reserve troops, no doubt, are even at this moment being mustered into armor behind the cover of the command tent."

Lujan stepped back into view from that very quarter, looking faintly sheepish. "Someone has to keep a weather eye open for trouble," he said cheerfully.

Then his levity faded, and he, too, looked southward, to where the seven small visitors paused by the still rows of sentries. The one in the lead, who wore the most beads, performed a flourishing salute.

"Let them pass," called Lord Chipino. "We are willing to parley."

The sentries obediently parted, and without speech the desert men came through. They walked on short, bandy legs across the camp, looking neither to the right nor to the left. Unerringly they proceeded until they reached the Lord and the Lady before the tent. They stopped, arrayed in a semicircle, and stared without speaking like sand-carved wooden icons, their beads swinging gently in the breeze.

"Send for an interpreter," Lord Chipino said softly to one of Mara's servants. Then, taking the Lady's hand, he led her forward two measured paces. Together Lord and Lady inclined their heads. In the sign language of the desert tribes, they held forth opened hands, signifying suspension of hostilities.

At once the lead chieftain repeated his salute, which involved a series of gestures that framed his nose, mouth, and ears. He bowed, Empire style, his beads jouncing briskly on their fringes. Then, quite at odds with his precise movements, he broke into excited speech.

The interpreter, a rotund little fellow hired out of Ilama, had to hustle to arrive in time to catch the gist, for the desert man's onrushing babble abruptly ceased.

"What did he say?" Mara demanded, losing her poise to impatience.

The interpreter raised sandy eyebrows in a look of unfeigned surprise. He seemed to try the words out on his tongue once, to ascertain their validity before he answered. "These are the Chiefs of the Seven Tribes of Dustari's northern desert, called the Winds of Sand, in their dialect. They are here to swear enmity and blood debt against the man whom you know as Tasaio of the Minwanabi. Further, since the lands of Minwanabi are across the great sea, and warriors from the Winds of Sand may not travel within the Empire, these, the Chiefs of the Seven Tribes of the Winds of Sand, are here to ask an alliance between your tribes and theirs."

Mara and Lord Chipino locked eyes in satisfaction. Then Mara inclined her head, granting the Lord of the Xacatecas his right to speak for them both. Lord Chipino gave answer, looking directly into the hot, dark eyes of the desert chief, and not waiting for the interpreter to keep up. "Tell the Chiefs of the Winds of Sand," he intoned, "that our tribes would welcome such alliance. Further, our tribes of Acoma and Xacatecas will promise to send to the Chiefs of the Winds of Sand Tasaio's sword, as evidence that blood debt has been met and paid in full." It was assumed the desert men would know enough of imperial custom to know the only way a warrior's sword could be acquired would be to take it from dead fingers. "But if the Acoma and Xacatecas so swear to this alliance, they must have assurance upon clan honor that the tribes of the Winds of Sand will sign treaty with the Empire in Dustari. Raids upon the borderlands must stop, so that the Acoma and Xacatecas may be free to pursue the tribe of Minwanabi and claim blood price. So that the tribes of the Winds of Sand need no reason to raid, we shall establish an outpost that will be a free trading town for the tribes." He smiled at Mara. "It will be jointly administered by the Acoma." Turning back to the chieftains, he said,

"Any traders seeking to cheat or rob our new allies will have to deal with the Xacatecas and the Acoma."

The interpreter hastily caught up, and silence fell. The faces of the desert men stayed inscrutable for an interval. Then the leader stamped his foot and spat upon the sand. He ejected one curt syllable, spun on his heel, and departed, the others falling in after him.

The interpreter, looking astounded, turned to Mara and Chipino. "He said yes."

Lord Xacatecas laughed in disbelief. "Just like that?"

The interpreter returned a gesture betraying that he had desert blood somewhere in his ancestry. "The Lord of the Seven Chiefs of the Winds of Sand spat water."

When nobody's puzzlement cleared, he made a small sigh of impatience. "That is life oath, for a chief and all of his tribe. He, and his heirs, and all of his clansmen and relations would die by ritual starvation were any of the Winds of Sand to break trust. My Lord, my Lady, you have just concluded a treaty with the desert men more binding than any ever sealed in all the long history of the Empire."

This took a second or two to sink in. When it did, Lord Chipino grinned delightedly. "A worthy exchange for Tasaio's sword, I should think. Certainly that part of the bargain will not be a bother to carry out."

Then Kevin whooped and caught Mara into a hug, and spun her around. "You can go home," he said delightedly. "Home to your estate and Ayaki."

Lujan stood bemused, scratching his chin, and Chipino, with characteristic dry irony, summed up. "Our houses will receive recognition and honor from the Emperor himself for this. And Lord Desio will chew rocks when he finds out." Then, as if his own thoughts turned toward home, he muttered, "Isashani will be furious to know how much weight I have lost. Shall we retire to my command tent and share breakfast?"

13. *REALIGNMENT*

The guard signaled.

Desio of the Minwanabi strode into the vast conference chamber, his nailed sandals striking the flagstone with a surprisingly loud snap. Incomo watched his master approach the dais, his broad hands stripping off his battle gloves, which he flung to the body servant who scurried to keep up. While still not the crafty schemer his father had been or as brilliant a strategist as his cousin, Desio now threw himself into the tasks he had avoided at the start of his rule.

Before his First Adviser could speak, the Lord shouted, "Is it true?"

Incomo clutched the latest report tighter to his chest and nodded.

"Damn!" Still heated from his hour of exercise with his honor guard, the Lord of the Minwanabi vented his rage, hurling his helm with total disregard for rich furnishings and glass ornaments. The servant dove, but missed the catch; the helmet bounced across polished flooring, fortunately missing anything of value, skipping twice before it hammered against the far wall with enough force to mar its shiny finish.

The servant distastefully picked a path through a scattering of lacquer chips to effect a retrieval. Miserable as a whipped dog, he crept back to his Lord's side, holding the battered helm.

But Desio was too intent on upbraiding his First Adviser to curse the servant for damage to his armor. "You hold a report less than an hour from the boat and every servant and soldier knows the news before I do." Desio stuck out a sweaty hand, impatiently raking damp hair from his eyes with the other.

Incomo surrendered the parchment, struck that the pudgy fingers he recalled in the boy were hardened to heavy calluses. The fat, self-indulgent youth who had sought to lose himself in drink and women had changed to a self-assured ruler. Desio was far from the ideal Tsurani warrior; but he now looked the part of a soldier rather than a caricature of one.

Desio scanned the opening lines with narrowed eyes, flipped through pages still gritty with desert dust, then, disgusted with the contents, tossed aside the stack. "Tasaio is nothing if not thorough in admitting his failure." His lips white with anger, the Lord sank heavily into the cushions he preferred for conducting court. A sigh escaped him. "And our defeat."

Incomo surveyed his master's flushed features and warily hoped he would not be asked for advice. After years of stalemate, Mara's triumph in relieving Lord Xacatecas in Dustari came as a bitter surprise. Until today's report, every communiqué from Tasaio had indicated the plan was proceeding as designed. For close to a season, Minwanabi Lord and First Adviser had waited in keen anticipation for word of the final victory over the Acoma. But when the jaws of Tasaio's trap snapped shut, Mara had eluded capture once again. Worse, her brilliant counteroffensive, using tactics never seen within Tsuranuanni, had established the first treaty with the Tsubar desert men who had preyed upon the borders for generations.

Desio pounded a fist into his pillows. "Breath of Turakamu, how could Tasaio have bungled his job?" Waving at the report on the floor, he said, "Our own factor in Jamar reports that the combined armies of Xacatecas and Acoma were greeted there with fanfares! He even suggests Mara may receive a citation from the Emperor! She has gained her alliance. Instead of two solitary, weakened enemies, we now face powerful families on the verge of joining to oppose us!"

Wincing at Desio's ranting, Incomo tried gently to ease matters. "While the treaty is a noteworthy accomplishment, master, Chipino of the Xacatecas is not a man to enter into binding commitments—at least, not without strong motives and sureties. Mara accomplished no more than her duty to the Empire when she rescued his army in the desert. Her victory may have impressed the Lord enough to rethink his position once more, but—"

"If it didn't impress him, he's a fool!" Desio raked angry fingers across some nameless itch on his neck, then dropped his hand in befuddlement. "How does the woman do it? Luck must sleep in her bed."

Incomo stepped to the table and dressed the scattered pages into a meticulous pile. "We shall know soon how she . . ." He was about to say "defeated us," but thought better of that, and said, ". . . again managed to avoid ruin." Frustrated by a report that still seemed offensively untidy, with bent corners and musty ribbons, as if the writing had been done under adverse circumstances, the First Adviser indulged in a sigh of irritation. "We will need time to dig out the truth of the matter."

Desio snapped out of his black musing. "Mara is coming."

"But of course." Incomo laced dry hands at his belt. "She would hasten to her estate after so long an absence from her son—"

Desio interrupted. "No. She'll be coming here."

Eyebrows raised, Incomo said, "What makes you say this, Lord?"

"Because it's what *I* would do!" Desio heaved his bulk off his cushions, and the servant with his load of sweaty armor ducked clear as his master stamped across the dais. "Strike while strongest. Allied to Xacatecas, and safe from attack from the Anasati, Mara is free to savage us. Even if Chipino is tentative in his support, the bitch has won public favor. She need do nothing more than invoke a Call to Clan!"

Desio glared at Incomo as if expecting agreement, but the First Adviser held up a placating hand. "In all this, there is some good emerging, my Lord." With a faint smile, he offered another parchment.

The Lord's expression grew thunderous as he saw the proffered scroll bore the personal crest of Bruli of the Kehotara. Desio refused to look at the document. "Bruli has been whining for our patronage for years now, but he lost my father's goodwill, and mine, when he refused to swear as vassal upon his father's death—he wants the benefits of Minwanabi protection without being under our rule." Frustrated further by suspicions that Mara might somehow be behind House Kehotara's truculence, Desio flopped back on his cushions. "Another request for alliance should be refused." Then Desio sighed. "But right now we can use all the friends we can manage. What does the weakfish say?"

Dryly Incomo said, "I suggest my Lord read the message."

The parchment changed hands. Stillness fell, marred by the creak of armor as the slave who bore the Lord's gloves and helm shifted his burden from one tired arm to the other. Desio laboriously scanned the closing lines, and his eyes widened with pleasure. "Is Bruli's observation reliable?"

Incomo tapped his cheek with a finger. "Who can ever be certain? I read into this situation as you might, my Lord, that sundry factions in Mara's clan fear her sudden rise. Should she gain much more honor and wealth, she'll certainly come to dominate Clan Hadama. No other house is more powerful now, if the truth were known; only divided loyalties prevent Mara from dictating clan policy. That, however, could change. These worthy lords who have presumed to contact Bruli of the Kehotara are careful to let us know they do not see their own fortunes necessarily tied to those of House Acoma."

Desio sat forward, elbows rested on his knees. He pondered, realized he was thirsty, and waved for his slave to carry his armor off and fetch refreshments. "We can thank the gods for small favors. Still, better Clan Hadama's families remain neutral than join their ranks against us."

Incomo said, "I think my Lord has missed the other implication."

Matured by his power, and less intolerant of correction, Desio returned a penetrating gaze. Plainly his First Adviser had best be concise if he wished to escape his Lord's ire. "What implication?"

"Our agents have progressed in their work to infiltrate Mara's spy network." Fired by acerbic enthusiasm, Incomo spread his bony palms. "We have isolated still another Acoma agent; nearly all their contacts have been traced, their couriers identified. Occasional plants of useful information have kept those lines open. At need, we can manipulate these Acoma dogs to our advantage."

A strange look passed over Desio's face, and a head shake

prevented his adviser from disturbing thoughts not yet formed as he stretched to grip a notion that tantalized his mind. When his servant returned with the refreshment tray, the Lord had lost his appetite. "I must think on something. Have my bath prepared. I stink like a needra pen."

Incomo bowed. "Which girls does my master wish to attend his comforts?"

Desio silenced his adviser with a raised palm. "No. I need to think. Just the bath attendant. No women. No musicians. A large mug of spiced juice will do nicely. I must have quiet for contemplation."

Intrigued by this sudden turn toward asceticism, Incomo stepped from the dais to carry out instructions. At the door, he stopped on an afterthought. "Any new orders for Tasaio, my Lord?"

Fury smoldered under Desio's hooded eyes. "Yes, my *brilliant* strategist. After four years of squandering our resources on his masterful plan in Tsubar, he must be tired. Let us see that he's given a post that will not tax his depleted energies. We still command that fortress at Outpost Isles; send him there. Let him protect our westernmost holdings from the seabirds and fish."

Incomo lowered his round shoulders into a bow, then left his master to his brooding and continued down a stone corridor that cut into the hill upon which the estate house rested. The cool passage was lit at long intervals with torches. Sheltered from view by thick shadow, the Minwanabi First Adviser let his frustration show. His pace turned brisk, and his robe of office flapped around thin ankles. A pity that Desio's wits had not developed to match his resolve. For if Tasaio's failure was dramatic, no plot in the game could ever be guaranteed. If there had been fault with the plan, it was simply that no provision had been made to allow for failure.

Down a shallow flight of steps, and through a worn postern, Incomo arrived at the wing that jutted out of the hill toward the lake shore. While not as closely situated to the great hall as lesser quarters, the Lord of the Minwanabi's chambers had an unobstructed view of the lake at sunset that made the walk worthwhile. Incomo clapped for servants and ordered his Lord's private bath chamber made ready.

As the servants hurried off to assign slaves to heat the water, Incomo crossed back through the mazelike house to his own less sumptuous quarters. There, surrounded by screens painted with patterns of killwings and clouds, he cursed at his master's orders to Tasaio. His bitterness must never be shown in public, that fate would send away the truly gifted son of the house and leave Minwanabi fortunes in the hands of . . . Incomo slammed his fists on a chest in a display more like his master than himself—the thoughts he entertained were unthinkable for a loyal servant, even in strictest privacy. Desio must somehow contrive to lead the Minwanabi out of this dilemma.

Incomo sank onto a cushion and clapped for his personal servant. "Fetch my writing desk and move it over to my contemplation mat," he commanded, rubbing his temples. "Then open the screen to admit the evening breeze, and depart."

Alone once more, and confronted by his pens and his desk, the First Adviser thumbed a blank sheet of parchment and pondered how to compose his missive to Tasaio. While the man was ostensibly transferred to command of another Minwanabi garrison, Desio had effectively ordered banishment. The fortress in the Outpost Isles had only been established to protect Minwanabi shipping from piracy; and those waters had been cleared of such brigands for over a century and a half. The fort still stood due to the hidebound Tsurani reluctance to surrender any ground once taken. The Minwanabi manned that desolate, fogbound chunk of rock simply to prevent anyone else from supplanting them. Now one of the most gifted military minds in the Empire was being sent to the hinterlands to grow moss.

Disgusted by what he perceived as a waste, Incomo reminded himself that as the price of a grand failure went, life on that rock was light punishment. Had Lord Jingu remained alive to wear the Lord's mantle, Tasaio would have answered for such disgrace with his head preserved in a jar of vinegar and red-bee honey. Setting brush and ink to parchment, the First Adviser sighed that so painful an order should be relegated to written correspondence. Tasaio surely deserved better. A slight word of personal regret would be appropriate; seasoned with the reverses of politics, Incomo knew better than to burn any bridge at his back. Fortune in the Great Game could turn all too quickly, and a man never knew where he might owe his loyalty in the future.

• • •

As the litter rounded the last bend in the road, Mara leaned out of the curtains with childish eagerness. The Tsurani bearers shouldered their off-balanced burden in stoic silence; they could sense their mistress's excitement.

"Nothing has changed," Mara said breathlessly. "The trees and the grass look so green." The wet season lushness of the landscape was a balm to the eye after years of barren desert. Over the final knoll, past the fences of the outermost needra fields, the well-kept estate spread across the land. Dead branches and brush shoots had been pruned back, and the grass under the hedges stood neatly clipped. Mara could see the advance scout waving from the top of the next rise. For an instant she worried: Could some clever enemy have set an ambush to turn her homecoming to disaster? Had she, in her excitement, pushed her warriors and her scouts ahead too rapidly to ascertain the safety of the road? Then logic absolved her fear; she rode at the van of a triumphant army —more than one foe must join ranks in force to threaten her at her own borders.

A scout reported to the head of the column.

Mara pushed impatiently at the gauze hanging that separated her from the officers who marched beside her. "What news, Lujan?"

Her Force Commander flashed a smile, his teeth vividly white in his desert-tanned face. "Mistress, a reception!"

Mara smiled. Only now could she admit to anyone, most of all herself, just how desperately she had longed for home. The fanfares that had greeted her and Lord Xacatecas in Ilama and Jamar had been flattering, but even celebrations that heaped her with honors had proven taxing. Close to three years had passed since the orders to send her garrison in defense of the borders; too long a time in the life of a young son for a mother to be absent. Nights in Kevin's arms and the rigors of battle by day were only a distraction from her ache to see Ayaki.

The returning army crested the hill, the tramp of three thousand feet in the damp soil of the road a dull thunder in the morning quiet. Mara breathed in the scents of rich foliage and akasi, then went wide-eyed with wonder.

At the junction of the imperial way and the road to the

Acoma estate rose the ornate, towering arch of a magnificent prayer gate. New paint and enameled roof tiles sparkled in sunlight and in the gate's deep shadow a hundred Acoma soldiers stood in ceremonial armor. Before their rows of shining shields were other well-loved figures—Keyoke, correct as his warriors but wearing the embroidered badge of an adviser; Jican dwarfed by the hadonra's staff of office; Nacoya, her bothered expression buried in smiles—and a pace ahead of her, a boy.

Mara's breath caught. She fought a rush of tears, determined not to succumb to unseemly display. But the moment she had longed for, that at times had seemed elusive as a dream, overwhelmed her resolve. Kevin acted the role of body servant to perfection, lifting aside the hanging and offering his free hand to Mara. His steadiness allowed her to recover decorum as she stepped onto her native soil at last.

She had to wait, as befitted her rank, for the party by the gate to approach her. The delay was torture, and her eyes drank in details. Keyoke had mastered his crutch. He moved with barely a hitch in stride despite his missing leg, and Mara exulted in her pride for him. Nacoya had not aged so smoothly, but had acquired a slight limp. Mara smothered an impulse to rush and offer an arm; the First Adviser would never forgive such a breach of manners over something as trivial as an aching hip. Lastly, in tingling apprehension, Mara dared a look at the boy who strode resolutely toward her, head held high, back straight, and chin outward. He was so tall and rangy!

Mara's throat tightened as she took in his child's armor, the miniature sword at his side, the helm he lifted from ink black hair with the bearing of a perfect little Acoma warrior. Her child had grown nearly twice the size she remembered on her departure.

With rehearsed dignity, Ayaki completed the bow of son to mother. He spoke out, his child's treble carrying solemnly over the ranks of still warriors. "I bid welcome to the Lady of the Acoma. We are a hundred times blessed by the good gods for her safe return to our home."

Mara's resistance crumbled. She knelt before her son, and suddenly the boy's arms were around her neck, hugging fiercely enough to crumple her fine silks. "I missed you, Mommy." The boy's voice quavered into her hair.

Moisture trembled in Mara's eyes as she answered, though somehow she kept her voice firm. "I have missed you, my little soldier. More than you can ever know."

Standing with pursed lips to one side, Nacoya allowed mother and son a moment of public indiscretion before pointedly clearing her throat. "The entire House of Acoma waits to welcome our mistress. So gladdened were our hearts at news of your triumph that this prayer gate was erected to honor your victory. We trust it pleases you, Lady."

Mara raised her face from Ayaki and examined the brilliant panels of the prayer gate, each one carved and painted with the icons of the felicitous gods. Chochocan, the Good God, seemed to smile directly upon her, while Hantukama, the Bringer of Blessed Health, spread his hands in benediction toward her army. Juran the Just beamed down from the crest of the crossbar, as if in blessing of those about to pass through. Lashima the Wise seemed to gaze with affection at one who almost had been committed to her service. The artisans had done superlative work, and the figures seemed charged with divine wisdom; but the allure of the images quickly palled. Mara took in the familiar faces of servants and soldiers, advisers and friends, then glanced back to Kevin, who returned his barbaric wide smile. Lost in a daze of happiness, she answered her waiting First Adviser. "Yes, Nacoya, I am pleased." She gave the son at her side another squeeze and added, "Let us return to the house of my ancestors."

Despite the fatigue from a long journey home, Mara's spirits soared as the night fell. The grounds of her family estate were decked out in grand celebration, colored lanterns hanging from the trees in all the gardens, and bright bunting festooning the rails of the central entrance. Candles flickered in courtyards, porticos, and halls. Strings of tiny bells, strung from every doorway and screen, chimed sweet melodies in thanks for the gods' blessings with each person's passage. Hired musicians from Sulan-Qu added their melodies to those played by performers under Acoma patronage, and song rang gaily across the grounds. Everyone, free workers, guests, and advisers, danced to celebrate Acoma triumph. Maids and serving girls laughed as they waited upon victorious soldiers, who regaled them with tales of the campaign against the desert men. In time honored Tsurani fashion, the warriors were modest about their own achievements, but lavished accolades upon one another; to a man they praised the daring tactics that had reversed a bitter defeat into a brilliant victory. What their Lady had done in the Game of the Council she had accomplished on the battlefield: make innovation her ally.

From his place at the mistress's shoulder, Kevin smiled indulgently at her beaming expression. Ayaki perched like a miniature soldier at his mother's right hand, determined to stay the course until the festivities ended, but battling drooping eyelids. He had been appointed "defender of the house" in the army's absence, and though the real military orders came from Keyoke, the boy revealed a single-minded devotion that astonished his elders. Unfailingly he had turned out to oversee every change of patrol. Ayaki was much like his father in that regard; no matter what else might be recalled of Lord Buntokapi, none spoke ill of his sense of duty or bravery. But the excitement bested the boy, finally. His chin slowly lowered until he dozed against his mother's side.

Presuming to speak without being addressed, Kevin whispered, "Should I carry the boy to bed?"

Mara stroked her son's soft cheek and shook her head. "Let him stay." Then, as if her own happiness made her sensitive to the needs of others, she said discreetly, "Go say your greetings to your countrymen. You need not return until later."

Kevin smothered a smile as he stepped through sumptuous piles of cushions and made his bow. The long journey from Dustari had permitted little privacy for Mara to consort with her body slave. Unlike the huge command tent on the field, with its many rooms, and the comings and goings of servants a matter beneath notice, the trader's galley which had borne them back across the Sea of Blood and up the river Gagajin had been too cramped to allow intimacy. As much as Kevin longed to visit his fellows, he ached for the moment he could return to Mara's side.

He might have won his mistress's lasting love, but Tsurani culture would never change; Kevin slipped from his Lady's hall with the briskness of a man dispatched on an errand. Once outside the main house, he crossed the lighted grounds at a jog. His favor as Mara's lover would avail him nothing should Jican find him "lazing about" with work to be done.

Kevin kept to the shadows, an easier task as he drew away from the kitchens and barracks; fewer lights burned in the servants' compound, and the slaves' quarters beyond were almost dark.

The music of the victory festivities seemed distant, too faint to make out a melody. Kevin stumbled over ruts in the packed earth until his eyes adjusted to the night. Left only a coppery half moon for guidance, he passed the outermost buildings and entered the cluster of board-walled shacks beyond. There were no trappings of gaiety here. Kevin felt his chest tighten as he noticed: the slave quarters might wear fresh whitewash for the celebration, but they were still only bare little huts. Seated on the ground before the doorways, clusters of ragged, dirty men shared the contents of several ceramic kettles. They ate their portion of the banquet given in Mara's honor with their hands, wolfing down each bit as if it might be their last meal.

One man noticed Kevin's approach and whispered, and instantly conversation broke off. All eyes turned from the food pots. Someone commented in Midkemian that a body as tall as Kevin's could never be a Tsurani overseer.

Then another voice shouted through a hut's open doorway, "I'll be damned! They haven't hung you yet?" A laugh followed, and a bulky figure in a patched grey robe rushed outside to meet him.

Kevin returned the laugh and hugged the broad-shouldered man, playfully rubbing his bald head. "Patrick! They haven't hung you either, I see."

Patrick gave a wide grin. "Not hardly, old son. I'm the only one who can keep this murderous crew in line." Lowering his voice to a whisper, he added, "Or at least that's what we convinced the runts."

Stiffly Kevin broke off the embrace. For three years he had lived with only "runts" and the derogatory term shocked the recognition that his view of the Tsurani had changed. Now, confronted by the gaunt faces of his countrymen, he could not escape the fact that his perspective was unique. Familiar features had changed, become suntanned and hard despite the smiles that welcomed the discovery that their liege lord's son still survived. Kevin surveyed the ragged gathering, his joy dampened further as he took stock of who was absent. "Brandon and William of LaMut, where are they?" As if more men might be hidden within the dim doorways, Kevin cast about. "Marcus, Stephen, and Henry. The two Tims? Brian, Donell, and Jon: where are they, Patrick?"

"Things changed when you left, old son." Patrick expostulated with a tired sigh. "This Jican's a fiend for cutting expenses, so the favors you arranged from her Ladyship vanished. We're treated the same as any other slaves now."

"But where are the rest of us?" Kevin demanded in concern.

A mutter ran through the men, while thin-lipped, Patrick answered. "Brian's stomach turned sour and he died in a week. The runts let him lie there and wouldn't call any doctors for a slave. Donell was killed by a needra bull, during breeding last spring. Marcus died from the fever the wet season after you left. Some sort of snake—called a 'relli' by the runts—bit Tim Masonsson, and the guards killed him without batting an eye. They claimed they spared him a slow death."

"That, at least, was a kindness," Kevin cut in. "Relli poison kills very slowly and painfully, and nobody knows of a remedy."

Unconvinced, Patrick put his arm around his countryman's shoulder; he smelled of dirt, and needra, and unwashed sweat, but Kevin noticed little beyond his whispered words. "Some of these runts understand bits of the King's tongue, we suspect. Jon was sent elsewhere to work with wood; somehow they discovered he was a carpenter. We've not seem him for a year. Samuel of Toren lost his temper and struck a runt, and him they hung within minutes." Glancing nervously across the compound, Patrick dared one last line. "But Tim Blodget and the others have escaped."

Kevin forgot himself. He jerked back, eyes wide, and exclaimed, "Escaped!"

Patrick caught Kevin by the wrist and pulled him strongly away from the huts, past the perimeter hedge and over to the bank of a small brook. Jumpy, tense, and looking often over his shoulder, he continued in a low murmur. "There are camps of bandits in the foothills to the west. The runts call them grey warriors. We overheard some soldiers speaking of them after the army left. William of LaMut escaped and then snuck back to tell us it was true. Brandon, Tim Blodget, and Stephen went with him and we've gotten a few messages back and forth."

The streamlet chuckled quietly over its bed of stones; the music could not be heard at all here, only the scraping of night insects. Kevin sat down, his hands gripped tightly to his forearms. "Escape," he muttered.

Patrick chose a worn rock, sat also, and absently pulled a grass stalk. "Security's tighter now. That Keyoke's no fool. Once the overseers figured out the boys had cut and run, he changed the patrols and doubled the guards who escort us to work." Patrick sucked his grass stem, found it bitter, and spat. "Leaving would be tougher, now the runts have puzzled out what took place. Before, they never imagined a slave might want to escape." He chuckled in bitter irony. "Odd lot. Lived here five years and I've still got no clue how they think."

Kevin shrugged. "I understand them better now."

A snap to his words, Patrick said, "Well, you should. You're the educated one, Kevin, being a noble and all. I'd have taken the other boys into the hills by now, but I thought it wiser to leave that to you. We need your leadership. Because one chance is very likely all we're going to get, and—"

"Wait!" Kevin kicked a clod with a splash into the stream. "Escape to where?"

"Why, to the mountains." Patrick peered closely at his companion, but the gloom hid details of expression. "These grey warriors want nothing to do with us, but they will trade a bit. They're not about to hunt us down. So, I figured we'd wait for our moment, then bolt and make our own camp in the high country."

"And do what?" Exasperated, Kevin shook his head. Though Patrick had been born a commoner, they had been friends, hunting companions, and later soldiers together; while a loyal man and a staunch fighter, Patrick had little imagination. On campaign in Dustari, Kevin had been quartered among Mara's soldiers often enough to learn that some had once been grey warriors. Their existence, as they told it, had been a misery of poverty and starvation.

"Kevin, damn it, we'd be free!" Patrick insisted, as if that settled things.

"Free to do what?" Kevin pried loose another bit of dirt.

He tossed it hard into the water, and the splash startled nearby insects to silence. "Ambush patrols of Acoma soldiers? Cho-ja? To fight our way back to wherever the hell we came through that magical hole from our own world? Or, far more likely, we can die of fever or starvation."

Patrick answered in anger. "We're nothing here, Kevin! If we kill ourselves working, do we get thanks? A better meal? A day of rest? No, we get the same treatment as the animals. Damn it, man, today was the first we've not had to labor from dawn to sunset since you left. At least in the mountains we can lead our own lives."

Kevin shrugged in resignation. "I don't know. You're a gifted enough hunter in the Grey Towers," he said in reference to the mountains near Zūn. "But up there?" He sliced a hand at the dark. "So you snare some six-legged creature, do you even know if you can eat it? Half the damned things are poisonous. Not like the game at home."

"We can learn!" snapped Patrick. "Would you rather work until you die of old age?" A thought struck him. "Or is there another reason, old son? Maybe you've come to appreciate the runt way of looking at things?"

Surprisingly stung, Kevin stood up and spun away. "No, I . . ." He sighed, shed his hurt, and tried again. "It's different for me, Patrick. Very different."

"You don't work as hard as us, for one thing." The insects scraped loudly and long through a silence. Then Patrick rose also. "I see that much."

Kevin whipped irritably around. "No, I don't think you do." Aware he had reached a sort of watershed, he struggled for words to tell his friend what he had come to know and feel for Mara. His hands twisted in frustration. No matter what he said, Patrick would only see the Lady as his captor. A man of plain tastes and simple intellect could not appreciate her ingenious way of seeing things, or Kevin's own delight when she laughed at his jokes when they were alone. Neither could he explain the magic, the fulfillment of his life as he lost himself in her.

Too tired to communicate the impossible, Kevin threw up his hands. "Look, we'll talk about this again. I . . . can't promise anything in a hurry. But we can always leave, and since Dustari, things are not quite so hidebound as before."

"In what way?" Patrick snorted, unconvinced. "Are the

overseers going to treat us like drinking pals now that you've come back with her Ladyship?"

Kevin shook his head, the gesture mostly lost in the dimness under the trees. "No. But I think I'm making progress. Someday . . ."

"Someday we'll be dead," Patrick said brutally. He gripped Kevin's shoulders and all but shook him. "Don't go daft, man, over a little soft thigh. I know you've always been one to moon after this pretty face or that, thinking a ready sword meant you were in love. But, Kevin, there are no lovely ladies for us to cuddle." In the murk Kevin could see Patrick nod toward the distant estate house. "While you enjoy your silks, we sleep in mud. When you dine with the mistress in the morning, we're three hours in the field already, and when you take supper with her, we're just coming back. You're only spared our lot as long as you can keep your sword sharp, and the woman doesn't get tired of you. She'll choose herself another lover one day, and then you'll come to know how we live."

Kevin wanted to argue, but in gritty honesty, he knew Patrick spoke the truth. Mara might love her tall barbarian, but he must never fool himself: she would order his death without an instant's hesitation if the honor of her house became compromised. Generous, innovative, even softhearted as Mara could be, she was equally capable of ruthlessness.

Kevin placed his hands over his friend's taut wrists. "I'm not saying I'm against the idea of escape. Just I'm not convinced that living as outlaws, eating whatever we can steal and sleeping on the run in the forest, is one whit better than slavery. Give me time. Let me see what I can do about arranging better food and less work." He pulled away, torn by a conflict he had rashly never foreseen. "Don't let the lads do anything stupid. I'll use my influence with the mistress and find another way to recover our freedom."

"Don't linger too long, old son. If you've come to like the runts, that's your affair—I'll never stop loving you like a brother." Patrick spun away from the stream bank, his voice suddenly cold. "But know this. I'd kill you if you try to keep us here. The lads have decided; we'd rather die free than live as slaves. We've figured the Tsurani out enough to know that if your Lady had failed down south, it would have been every man for himself, demons take the hindmost. So we waited for news. If the Lady was dead, we'd be off with no one to tell us to stay. When we heard she had won . . . we agreed to wait for you to come back, you being our officer and most likely to get us out safe." He fixed his countryman with a hard gaze. When Kevin didn't answer, Patrick added, "We won't stay much longer. With you or without you, old son, we'll go."

Kevin sighed. "I understand. I won't try to keep you. Just . . . give me a few days."

"A few days it is."

Wrapped in uncomfortable quiet, the two men picked their way back to the slave huts. Kevin lingered to chat with the men he had known as soldiers in the field, and a few others he had met in the slave pens and coffles enroute to Sulan-Qu. The captive Midkemians had formed a tight-knit friendship since coming to Mara's estate; except he was a man marked apart. That had not been so apparent during the year he had worked on the needra fields; but now, the distance between Mara's bed and a miserable life in the slave huts left an unbridgeable alienation.

Kevin listened to gossip, and commiseration over insect bites, hunger, and sores. He had little to contribute to such talk. The exhilaration of a triumphant homecoming faded, and he did not mention the marvels he had encountered in Dustari. Well before midnight, the slaves began to rise and seek their huts. They would be roused before dawn, celebration notwithstanding, and Tsurani overseers used the whip on any laggards. Kevin made excuses and departed. As he walked alone through the night, past sentries who nodded him greeting, and servants who made way to let him pass, each small privilege galled him. As he passed on into the lantern light, and laughter, and pretty serving maids who teased and called for him to dance, his discomfort sharpened to bitterness. For the first time since his headlong plunge into love, he wondered how soon he would come to curse himself for a fool.

Incomo hurried into his Lord's chamber. Desio sprawled before an open screen, his robe flapped open to allow the lake-shore breeze to cool him. Stacks of reports from his various holdings lay scattered at his feet, but he had taken a break from reading to hear a trio of poets recite ballads from the

Empire's history. Incomo heard enough to identify a stanza from "The Deeds of the Twenty," a tale of ancient heroes revered for extraordinary service. Titled *Servants of the Empire* by some long-past Light of Heaven, they were fondly recalled, although the scholars of present generations insisted they were legends.

Since Tasaio's influence had bent Desio toward the martial tradition, the Lord's tastes had shifted from pursuit of lascivious adventure to the glorified exploits of champions; his choice of activity may have changed, but his resentment of interruptions remained in force. The Minwanabi Lord glanced aside at his First Adviser's abrupt entry and, as if his scowl were a signal, the chorus trailed raggedly into silence. "What is it?"

Incomo bowed. "We have an unexpected visitor." Since the poets were traveling players, and not given patronage by the household, the First Adviser leaned close and whispered, "Jiro of the Anasati awaits at the far dock, asking permission to cross the lake."

Desio blinked in surprise. "Jiro of the Anasati?" At Incomo's near reprimand, he prudently lowered his voice. "What possible reason could bring Tecuma's brat here unannounced?" Then, aware he inconvenienced himself by whispering for the sake of hired entertainers, Desio waved the poets away. A servant would pay them; they had not been gifted enough to retain.

The First Adviser watched the doorway until the chamber was private. "I have little to add. Jiro sends you greeting. He regrets the informality of his call and begs a few moments of your time. The messenger in from the river gate adds that the boy travels with a minimal honor guard, only twelve men."

"Twelve men!" Desio's annoyance evaporated. "I could take him at the docks. With Jiro to ransom, Lord Tecuma would . . ." He broke off at his First Adviser's stillness, then sighed. "No, the old man would not trade a younger son for his only grandson. Jiro isn't quite stupid."

"Certainly so, my master." Incomo backed clear as Desio shoved to his feet, flung open the screen to the side hallway, and shouted, "Send guards to escort our guest to the main house docks." The Lord clapped briskly for servants, and demanded dressers and formal robes, then a large tray of refreshments to be brought to the great hall.

Incomo heard the list of preparations through without comment. Early on, Desio had decided that even trivial entertaining must take place in the grand hall. The vast stone amphitheater with its high-vaulted roof was resplendent enough to unsettle most guests. No other estate house in the Empire could match its construction; imitators had tried, but their efforts had lacked the natural site, ringed by stone-crested hills, and situated on a lakeshore that even in spring was not marshy. Easily the most splendid court this side of the Emperor's palace, Desio believed that confronting anyone there lent the Minwanabi the advantage. Puffed by his own self-importance, he said, "What would lure Jiro here?"

"Honestly, my lord, I suspect nothing and everything." Incomo ticked points on dry fingers. "Perhaps the Lord of the Anasati grows feeble. As heir, Halesko might send his younger brother as emissary to propose something."

Servants knocked and entered, bearing folded silk and ropes of tasseled sashes, slippers, jewels, and pins. They bowed, shed their burdens, and helped their master strip off his crumpled day robe. As the fabric was whisked aside, Incomo was struck that Desio's sleekness now overlay heavy slabs of muscle. The boyhood fat of five years before had nearly vanished, along with the vacuous attitude. Slipping his arms into his knot-worked orange-and-black robe, Desio said, "I don't know. Old Tecuma keeps his household on a short leash, especially his two sons. The last time I met Halesko at the games, he seemed just like his father. But Jiro is an unknown."

The conversation lapsed as body servants applied combs to the master's hair, and hung his pink ears with ornaments. As attention shifted to slippers, and the servants washed and toweled Desio's feet, Incomo stole the moment to draw upon the detailed information that any good adviser kept current, concerning every important figure in the Empire.

"Jiro is something of an enigma. Very bright, so don't let anything he says mislead you into thinking him witless."

Raising his other foot to be washed, Desio frowned; he would never be taken in by so transparent a ploy. Though he hated to be made to feel stupid, the Lord listened carefully as Incomo went on and described Mara's past proposal to take an Anasati son in marriage. All present presumed she sued for Jiro, but the younger brother, Buntokapi, had become her husband instead.

Desio grinned. "Ah, she slighted Jiro and gained an enemy."

Incomo sniffed. "One could safely assume that much."

A slave proffered a jeweled slipper. Desio shoved in his foot, then peered at his reflection in a precious metal mirror. "Now, what sort of man is he?"

"He's quiet," Incomo recited. "Jiro keeps to himself and has few friends. His vices are moderate: a little gambling, but never to excess like his deceased brother, nor does he drink like Halesko. An occasional woman, but never a favorite. He's inclined to say little, but implies a lot."

"Cryptic, but each word has meaning," Desio defined.

Impressed that he need not spell out subtleties, the First Adviser listed the rest. Jiro lacked his elder brother's military experience, but was an avid student of history. He preferred scroll books to poets and ballads, and spent hours with scribes in the libraries.

"Well." Desio pouted at his reflection. "I hate to read, so he would hardly be coming here for scholarly conversation. I shall meet our uninvited guest at the dockside, and if I don't care to hear out the younger son of the Anasati, I can send him packing without wasting any more bother."

"Does my Lord wish an honor guard?"

Desio straightened one of his jewels and laid the mirror in the hands of a servant, who reverently returned it to a velvet slipcase. "How many men did you say Jiro brought?"

"Twelve."

"Then order twenty soldiers to the docks. It's too hot for a crowd, and I feel no need to put on a display."

Noon sunlight beat down on the grey boards of the dock, and flashed reflections off the trappings of the honor guard. Sensitive to the light, Desio squinted across the water toward the approaching Anasati barge. The craft was not imposing enough to indicate a state visit; it was smaller, adorned only with paint, and its primary service was running messages along the river Gagajin; except this journey was not made for dispatches. Between the ranks of Jiro's honor guard, Desio made out the bulk of a heavy slatted cargo crate.

His curiosity became piqued. As the polemen maneuvered the barge to the dockside, Desio had Force Commander Irrilandi call his warriors to attention.

The Anasati craft bumped against the landing. Slaves at bow and stern leaped ashore to secure lines. A strange and unsettling growl issued from the depths of the crate; apparently the container confined a vicious animal. An avid enthusiast of the Imperial Games, which held spectacles of beastfights and warriors, Desio craned his neck until a nudge from Incomo recalled decorum.

Soldiers in Anasati red and yellow were already stepping onto the wharf. In their midst, robed in velvet stitched with river pearls, Jiro greeted his host with a graceful bow. He was slightly older than Desio, decisively more poised, and strictly observant of the forms. Without hesitation, he said, "Are you well, Lord Desio?"

"I am well, Jiro of the Anasati." Eyes narrowed, Desio returned the proper response. "Is your father well?"

"Well, indeed, my Lord." A louder, more savage growl issued from the depths of the cargo crate; Jiro gave the haughty suggestion of a smile. Careful of his timing, he drew breath to continue the tiresome, formal ritual of greeting.

But Desio's patience deserted him. Afire to ask after the beast in the crate, he blurted, "I am happy to say all of my family is well."

Released from protocols, Jiro glanced smugly at Incomo, who radiated intense annoyance, but who at this moment was powerless to intervene. "Thank you," murmured the Anasati son. "My Lord Desio is kind to welcome an unexpected visitor. I apologize for my rudeness, but I chanced to be in your area and I felt it would be useful for us to speak."

Something clawed at the crate slats, and the slaves on the barge shifted nervously. Desio twitched from foot to foot: the moment had come to invite his guest inside for refreshments, or turn him away at once. The irritation of honoring an enemy's son was balanced by fascination.

While Desio dithered, Jiro seized the initiative. "Please, Lord, I had not intended to presume upon your hospitality. I have live creatures on board that dislike the motion of the barge. It is well for me, and best for them, if we may speak here."

Perspiration made Desio's face itch. If Jiro could do without a cool drink, the Lord of the Minwanabi preferred not to. He waved magnanimously to his guest and the entire Anasati honor guard. "Come in and sit where we need not hasten our talk." As his visitor darted a concerned glance at the crate, Desio added, "I'll have servants move your beasts into the shade so they will not suffer."

Jiro hesitated. Indelicately caught between refusing the kindness of a superior, or acknowledging fear of an enemy's hospitality—an implied shame—he fingered his shell and lacquer belt. "My Lord is generous, but the beasts I transport are too vicious to be left in strange hands. I would not risk an injury to any of the servants in your household."

A strange, deep light touched Desio's eyes. "Then bring the beasts along; they sound interesting."

Jiro bowed. To the servant who lingered on the barge, he ordered, "Leash the hounds and bring them. And as you value honor, make sure no hapless Minwanabi servant stands too close and takes harm."

The servant paled at the command, Desio saw. His own palms grew moist in excitement. As Irrilandi formed the Minwanabi honor guard into ranks for the march indoors, he could not resist a look back. On the barge, the white-faced servant donned a heavy pair of gloves. He then gathered two thick-braided leashes and signaled the slaves, who hesitantly dragged the cover off the cage. A strident bark and more growls answered the unveiling and the slaves jumped back in fright. Then the servant raised a bone whistle to his lips. He blasted a single note, and two muzzles poked through the opening, followed by wide-set slanting eyes, and ears trimmed short into points. Two dogs of ferocious aspect braced long forepaws on the cage; the slaves cowered back, and every warrior in the Anasati honor guard surreptitiously touched their weapons.

"Magnificent," Desio breathed, as the servant stepped in and looped the leashes through two jewel-studded collars. The dogs flowed out of their prison with sinuous grace. Massive of shoulder and jaw, and brindled in light tan and black, the creatures sprang over to the dock, then sat as regally as if they owned it.

"My Lord would be wise to stand back," murmured Jiro.

Desio did so, too rapt to notice that an enemy had told him what to do. "Magnificent," he repeated, and he stared at

amber eyes that were passionless in their canine ferocity as
Tasaio's, out on the archery field. Then, annoyed by a re-
minder of the cousin who had failed him, and made aware by
Incomo's quiet hiss that he stood gawking like a farmer,
Desio motioned for his honor guard and adviser to follow,
and strode off toward the entrance to the great hall.

"What sort of hounds are those?" he asked as he crossed
the hall and mounted his cushioned dais, his First Adviser a
half-step behind.

"They are hunters without peer." A gesture from Jiro,
and the servant led the dogs to a safe corner, out of reach of
passing servants and set back from any doors. The animals
sat, too poised for relaxation, their eyes restless and hungry.

By now, Incomo's headshakes had drawn notice. Desio
understood that his eagerness set him at a disadvantage. As
he sat down, he sniffed with intent to diminish. "We have fine
tracking dogs."

Jiro rebutted him quietly. "None like these, my Lord. Perhaps when our conference is over, I could offer a demonstra-
tion?"

Desio brightened. "Indeed, perhaps you should." He
sighed in restrained anticipation, then waved for his guest to
choose a cushion. "Come. Let us be refreshed." Slaves
rushed in with laden trays of food and drink. Keeping his
bearing erect and proper, Desio resisted the urge to turn to
look at the dogs, who were offering low, menacing growls to
everyone that passed. At Desio's gesture, Irrilandi withdrew
the Minwanabi honor guard a discreet distance away; Jiro's
Strike Leader did the same, and across the vast chamber
came more slaves with bowls and towels, to assist both nobles
to wash.

One of the dogs whined. Jiro paid it no mind, but dipped
his fingers in the scented water and held them out to be dried.
"You have an impressive home, my Lord. When I imagine
this hall filled with grand entertainment, I deeply regret that
I missed attending the Warlord's birthday celebration."

Incomo froze, caught in the motion of sitting down at his
master's right hand. He looked urgently at Desio, and by the
hardness of the Lord's expression, knew that he need not
take action; the reference to the event when Lady Mara had
trapped the former Minwanabi Lord into dishonor and ritual
suicide had not escaped his master's notice.

The vast hall was silent. Desio reached out and took a glass of fruit juice from the tray; that he eschewed stronger spirits showed his inner anger. He sipped, pointedly withholding permission to eat from his guest. No fascination with hunting dogs could ease the Anasati's current danger. Desio was a powerful Lord, seated within his own hall; the silence would stretch to eternity before he stooped to ask what this upstart second son might wish.

Jiro let the stillness extend enough to show he was not cowed. With sudden brightness, he said, "Splendid news from Dustari. Now the desert men and their allies are routed, the Empire shall enjoy peace on the southern border for many years to come."

Desio flicked a glance to his First Adviser, who signaled a discreet warning. By his reference to allies, Jiro either guessed the desert men had acted under Minwanabi influence, or else the Anasati had spies as cleverly concealed as Mara's.

A dog whined; its attendant whispered a frantic reprimand.

The Minwanabi Lord said nothing.

"Except for the fabled Acoma luck, this triumph would never have come to pass," Jiro finished, then proved that he also could wait.

In leisurely fashion, Desio drained his glass. He listened to a few whispered words from his adviser, then answered in faultless form. "Any action undertaken in defense of the Empire is to be applauded. Or do you think otherwise?"

Jiro smiled without warmth. "The duty of every ruler is to serve the Empire. Naturally."

Conversation faltered to a halt; Incomo's shrewdness rescued the issue from stalemate. "I wonder how Tecuma views Lady Mara's brilliant victory."

Given the cue he had sought for, Jiro gave the skinny old adviser a polite nod. "We Anasati find ourselves bound to a difficult course, since blood relation to Mara's heir forces adherence to goals that occasionally align with Acoma interests."

"Go on," Incomo encouraged, with a sidewise glower at his master to recall courtesy and offer refreshments. Desio complied with a sulky wave.

Jiro accepted a fruit drink, the same variety the Minwanabi Lord had chosen. He took a sip, shook back burnished brown hair, and stared off into the distance. "That such a condition should endure is unnatural, of course." His manner turned disarmingly offhand. "I share concern for my nephew, well enough, but let me speak forthrightly." He delayed for another drink until Desio once again leaned raptly forward on his cushions. Jiro resumed. "Ayaki's mother has too few friends to warrant such a dangerous course for the Anasati." He allowed a suggestive pause. "So if harm comes to my nephew, I would understand. My father is less given to bending with the whims of fate, but my brother and I see things differently."

Here Incomo had to touch his master's arm to remind the young Lord not to show his interest; but where Mara's name was at issue, tact was lost on Desio. "If fate should remove a nephew from this life—"

Fine crystal clanged and raised echoes as Jiro set down his glass. The dogs whined in unison, as if they sensed tension in the air. "I must correct you," the Anasati son said coldly. "My brother and I honor our father as dutiful and loving sons. As long as Tecuma lives, his wishes are to be obeyed— instantly!" His emphasis word made clear beyond doubt: Jiro was not dissembling. If his father so ordered, he would fight and even die in Mara's defense. "But," Jiro qualified delicately, "should the woman come to misfortune, and the boy survive, my Lord father need not be bound to reprisal."

Desio's eyebrows rose. He looked at his guest, and saw in Jiro an abiding, bitter anger. A thought struck him, and he leaned toward Incomo. "He really hates the bitch, do you see?"

The Minwanabi First Adviser gave a fractional nod. "A personal feud, it would appear. Go softly. I would hazard the boy is here without his father's knowledge."

Trying to sound disinterested, Desio spoke around a mouthful of sweet roll. "Your ideas are intriguing, but not feasible. My house has sworn oath to the Red God, that the Acoma bloodline must perish."

Jiro took a slice of cold meat. He did not eat, but fingered the morsel thoughtfully. "I had heard of your vow of sacrifice. Of course, if Mara were dead, and her natami were broken and buried, the little heir would be a Lord with no resources." He tore his tidbit in two with his nails. "Lacking a house and loyal warriors, Ayaki would have only his father's family to shelter him. Perhaps he would be called to swear loyalty to the name of Anasati."

So this was the ploy that had brought Jiro into the house of an enemy! Desio considered, searching for duplicity in his guest. "The boy would swear?"

Jiro twisted on his cushions and tossed the meat toward the dogs. Obedient to command, they did not arise, but snapped the snack out of the air with a clash of strong jaws. "Ayaki is a boy. He must do as his grandfather and uncles instruct. As Lord of the Acoma, he can release anyone from house loyalty, including himself. Should he bow to the Anasati natami, Acoma blood would cease to exist. The Red God must be satisfied."

"That is a bold presumption," Incomo interjected. He looked askance at his Lord. "Perhaps too bold."

"But enjoyable conjecture, nonetheless." Desio arose from his cushions. "This discussion has its merits. Well, Jiro, should the gods look favorably upon the demise of Mara and her house . . . we will hope for the sake of goodwill that events transpire as you suggest."

"For friendship's sake," agreed Jiro, rising also, and taking his cue to depart. "For it would be poor judgment for any house, no matter how mighty, to think they could bloody themselves upon the Acoma and emerge with strength enough to withstand my father's rage."

Desio's face darkened so swiftly that Incomo almost could not rise fast enough to touch his master's sleeve. In a whisper he said, "The point to remember, my Lord, is that without the backing of Tecuma, the Acoma are just another small house. Consider this also: the Lord of the Anasati is aging, and Jiro has taken risks to let you know that his brother, the heir, may not share the father's sentiment for a nephew born to Mara."

Desio turned toward Jiro, his face composed and smiling. "I will take up your offer to see your dogs hunt now." He stepped down from the dais.

The Anasati son repeated his courtier's bow as Desio passed. "As you wish, Lord Desio. For the display, we will need your practice field, and a dummy dressed in man's clothing."

Desio's interest sharpened. "Your beasts course after humans?"

"You shall see." Jiro snapped his fingers, and the servant with the leashed dogs nervously commanded them to heel as Desio led them back out of the hall. "They are bred from herd dogs in Yankora. But these I call Mankillers."

At the first scent of fresh air, the dogs growled and barked. They strained at their leashes, yellow eyes quick to follow the movement of any passing human. Slaves and servants backed away in fright, and the Minwanabi honor guard marched close on the heels of their master, lest some trickery be in play.

Only Desio and Jiro seemed unfazed by the beasts' ferocity as they reached the wide practice field where Irrilandi customarily drilled his soldiers. Two slaves were sent across a small gully to dismantle an archery target, and stuff the old robe of a slave with wheat straw to make a dummy. Desio watched, eyes glittering, as his guest explained how such dangerous beasts should be handled.

"Do you see the gloves and the whistle?" Jiro pointed to the servant who managed the hounds, tugging now at their restraint, the muscles under their brindled hides quivering in high-strung eagerness.

At Desio's nod, Jiro continued. "The leather has been soaked in bitch urine. These particular hounds have been trained to recognize that odor as belonging to their master. These dogs were trained as a gift, so they answer only to the whistle. Once in the hands of their owner, they will come to know his personal scent as the smell on the gloves wears away, and eventually mind only his voice. The gloves and whistle allow them to be controlled in the meantime."

"An admirable system," Desio observed enviously.

Jiro did not miss the note of longing. He motioned magnanimously to the servant. "Would my host care to course the dogs himself?"

Desio's face lit. "I would be honored, Jiro. And grateful."

One at a time, the Anasati servant relinquished the gloves. Desio shoved large hands inside, and grasped the leashes. The magnificent dogs now eyed him with expectancy, and tugged against his hold. He laughed in a rush of elation. Recklessly he stroked one brindled head.

The dog he fondled flashed him an impatient look, then

resumed watching the men, servants, and soldiers who stood well clear on the practice field. "Very soon, my beauties," Desio soothed. He glanced across the gully, where the servants seemed slow in tying the robe to the dummy. He quivered, just like the hounds.

Incomo noted, and felt consternation. Thus had the past Lord, Jingu, appeared, when he pursued unwholesome pleasures. Jiro also saw, and the barest hint of distaste marred his veneer of courtesy.

Desio fingered the bone whistle. "You," he called to the slaves. "Don't bother with those stupid targets. Run that way!" He gestured across the practice field.

The slaves hesitated, horror on their sun-browned faces. Then, more afraid of the hanging they would receive if they dared to disobey their master's order, they let fall the robe half-stuffed with straw and sprinted into the open.

They ran as if all the demons of hell were behind them.

A hungry smile curled Desio's lips.

With flawless politeness, Jiro finished his instructions. "My Lord, one long blast on the whistle will order the dogs to hunt. Two short whistles will recall them."

Desio savored a moment of soul-deep anticipation. He felt the surge of the dogs against his hand, as they strained and whined to be cut loose. A moment longer he teased them, withholding them from their desire. Then he raised the whistle and slipped the leashes from their collars.

The dogs bounded forward, dark shadows against sunlit grass. "Hunt!" murmured Desio. "Hunt until your hearts burst."

The hounds surged across the ground, reaching full stride within seconds. Their tails streamed on the wind, and their savage baying echoed off the hills. They ate up the distance that separated their fleeing prey in long, elastic strides. The slaves flashed terrified glances over their shoulders, and suddenly the dogs were upon them.

Wind brought back a human scream as the lead hound sprang stiff-legged upon the trailing man's back. He pitched forward, flailing desperately, but jaws closed on the nape of his neck. The cries ceased but only for an instant. The other hound overtook the leader, ripped out a hamstring, and the slave went down with a shriek. A chorus of harrowing wails and snarls rang across the practice field. Desio licked his lips.

He watched the thrashing victim with wide, fascinated eyes, and laughed at his feeble attempt to save himself. The dogs were clever and swift. They darted and circled, tearing exposed flesh, then dodging as swiftly away.

"A man armed with a knife would not easily escape them," Jiro observed. "They were trained to kill carefully."

Desio sighed. "Magnificent, truly magnificent." He savored every moment of the carnage, until the struggles of the slaves subsided, and the hounds closed in for a firm grip. One tore its victim's throat out, and the last cry died away. Into uncomfortable stillness Desio said, "Like the legendary battle hounds in the sagas."

Jiro shrugged. "Perhaps. The war dogs of legend might have been akin to these." As if he were bored by the topic, he bowed to Desio. "Since they please you, keep them as my gift to you, Lord of the Minwanabi. Hunt them, and as they kill at your command, think kindly on our afternoon's discussion."

Flushed with delight, Desio returned the bow. "Your generosity enriches me, Jiro." Softly he added, "More than you will know."

Jiro could not match his host's enjoyment; but the Lord of the Minwanabi barely noticed, absorbed as he was by the hounds' bloodthirsty feasting. "Allow me to provide you and your men with quarters," he murmured. "We will dine and I shall see your every need is met."

"I regret to decline your kindness," Jiro returned, almost quickly. "But I am expected downriver to sup with a trade factor of my father's."

"Another time, then." Desio whistled twice, and the dogs ceased worrying the mangled corpses. The beasts stood alert, scarlet, dripping muzzles trained toward their new master. Desio blew another shrill pair of blasts. As the beasts raced obediently toward him, he thought of Mara, and long white fangs rending her hated flesh. Then he laughed aloud. Unmindful of soiling his robes, he patted each square head before slipping the leashes on the collars. "Wonderful," he observed to the silent ranks of his honor guard, and the stiff-faced presence of his First Adviser. "A worthy gift for one of my lineage." Gripping the slightly larger dog's muzzle, he said, "You I shall call Slayer." Stroking the other dog on its smeared nose, he added, "And you shall henceforward be Slaughter."

The hounds whined and meekly settled at his feet. Desio raised blue eyes to the guest he had all but forgotten. "Your generosity is unparalleled, Jiro. I must see that your visit with us results in a fruitful reward."

The shadows of the hills had lengthened. Regretfully Desio whistled his new pets to heel. His gaze never left them, the entire distance back to the docks, and he sighed with regret when the crate was unloaded, and the dogs securely locked inside for transfer to the Minwanabi kennels. Jiro took his leave and boarded his barge, and his polemen sculled him out across waters deepening with the approach of sunset.

Desio stripped off the stinking gloves, and gestured for Incomo to accompany him to his quarters. "I wish a hot bath."

The First Adviser restrained a curl of his lip. His master reeked of the urine that soaked the gloves, and his sandals had been spattered by the dogs. Drenched in perspiration, and talking excitedly, Desio glowed as if with a lust for sex. Incomo realized he hadn't seen the master so aroused since Jingu had ordered slave girls whipped for his amusement.

"Those dogs are . . . unusual," the First Adviser ventured.

Desio said, "More than that. They are a reflection of myself. Unrelenting, unmerciful, bringing pain and destruction to enemies. They are Minwanabi dogs."

Incomo hid consternation as he followed on his master's heels into the estate house. Desio clapped for his bath attendants, then added, "I know Jiro has his own reasons for tempting me to betray my oath to Turakamu, but whatever they may be, he has gained my favor with Slayer and Slaughter."

Incomo managed a magnanimous tilt of his head. "I am sure my master will be cautious of unreasonable . . . ah . . . requests."

Sensing buried disapproval, Desio scowled. "Leave me. Return to the great hall when dinner is served."

Thin fingers clasped at his belt, Incomo bowed low and departed from a bath chamber that suddenly seemed crowded with steam and scented slave girls. As his slippered feet whispered down the corridors, he ruminated sadly on

Tasaio's loss of favor. No stranger to Minwanabi excesses, Incomo knew by his sour stomach that the day's bloodletting had struck a responsive chord in Desio. The master was acting more the bold Lord with each passing day; but if his future choices followed his taste for the hounds, Incomo felt Minwanabi fortunes would not be better for it. Undeniably Jingu's excesses had brought the house to the brink of disaster. Sighing at the trials forced upon mortals by the whims of gods and capricious masters, Lord Desio's First Adviser retired to his quarters. He stretched on his cushions to nap, but the bloodthirsty baying of hounds marred his rest and his dreams.

14. *CELEBRATION*

T
he boy screamed.

Kevin yelled back as he dodged away between flower beds. Ayaki gave chase, shouting Acoma battle cries in a boyish imitation of bloodlust. At times he became too intense, and Kevin would reverse course, capture the boy in his arms, and tickle him. Then Ayaki would shriek in delight and fill the garden with his laughter.

Mara allowed herself pleasure at the sight of their play. Kevin was often a mystery to her, despite their years of intimacy, but one thing she knew: without doubt the man was devoted to her son. His companionship was good for Ayaki; approaching seven years of age, the boy had a tendency toward brooding, intensified during his mother's lengthy absence. But Ayaki could not lapse into dark moods with the Midkemian near. For as if he sensed the onset of the boy's troubled thoughts, Kevin was instantly diverting him with a fanciful story or riddle, a game or physical contest. Through the months since her return from Tsubar, Ayaki became more the boy Mara remembered. She reflected with wistfulness that Kevin could not have shown more affection had he been the child's father. Putting aside daydreams, she returned her attention to the document with its weighty seals and ribbons.

Motionless in the shade before her, Arakasi awaited his mistress's response. Finally Mara said, "Must we go?"

Arakasi stayed quiet as the leaves in the still air as he

answered. "Imperial peace will be enforced, so no overt threat can be mounted."

"Overt," she said. "That is scant reassurance against Minwanabi plotting. Need I remind you the first attempt upon my life was by an assassin of the Red Hands of the Flower Brotherhood in my own contemplation glade?"

The event had occurred before Arakasi's service, yet he knew the story well. He inclined his head. "Mistress, there is a good chance Desio will behave. Your standing in the council is the highest in memory, higher than your father's, if truth be told. And our remaining agents in the Minwanabi house have sent us word that Jiro of the Anasati visited with Desio not two weeks ago."

Mara raised her eyebrows. "Go on."

Dapples of sunlight slid across Arakasi's face as he sipped at a cup of fruit juice. "Our agents were unable to overhear them directly, but after Jiro departed, Desio raged for an entire day, complaining bitterly that he would not be dictated to in his own house by a rival family. From this we might surmise that Tecuma of the Anasati has sent his son to warn against precipitate actions against his grandson."

Mara glanced at Ayaki, shrieking his enthusiasm as he leaped upon the now prone Kevin. "Perhaps. Though I find it difficult to believe Tecuma would send his second son. Jiro's hatred of me is no secret."

Arakasi shrugged. "Possibly Tecuma sent his son to emphasize his serious intentions."

The flowers' perfume suddenly seemed oppressive. "Emphasize to whom?" Mara said. "Desio or Jiro?"

Arakasi showed a faint smile. "Perhaps both."

Mara shifted on her cushions. "I would like to know for certain before I risk a trip to the Holy City."

Her restlessness signaled decision, intuitively grasped by Arakasi. "Mistress, I think I had best be present when you attend this celebration to honor the Light of Heaven. For reasons that elude my network, the Blue Wheel Party's sudden reversal of loyalty has vaulted the Warlord into an almost unassailable position. Almecho can dictate to the council now, and should Ichindar break tradition—as gossip says he might—and attend the games in person . . ."

Excited that his assessment matched hers, Mara nodded. "The Emperor's appearance would endorse Almecho's acts, effectively undermining the High Council for the span of this Warlord's rule."

In a rapport that only deepened with time's passage, mistress and Spy Master contemplated possible ramifications. Much would occur in Kentosani beside games and celebrations. Those families who seized the initiative would not hang back at home. The Warlord might become dictator for life, but he could not live forever. Sooner or later the Great Game would resume.

Arakasi tensed as the patches of sunlight on his knees fell into sudden shadow. Kevin's approach had gone unnoticed until he stood, holding Ayaki on his shoulders, looming over the mat where Mara held her conference.

"My Lady," the Midkemian said formally, "the heir to your title is hungry."

Gladdened by the distraction, Mara smiled. To Arakasi she said, "Speak with Nacoya and Keyoke and make ready to leave tomorrow. You shall travel to Kentosani with the servants and slaves sent ahead to prepare our city house and our apartment in the Imperial Palace. Confirm all the resident staff's loyalty. We dare not assume all plotting will be directed at the Warlord."

Well satisfied with his assignment, Arakasi rose, made his bow, and departed. When the Lady still lingered in serious thought, Kevin broke her abstracted mood. "Are we going somewhere?"

Mara met his blue eyes with a look too deep to interpret. "The Warlord has announced a major celebration to honor the Emperor. We leave for the Holy City next week."

Her news was met with equanimity, even by the volatile Ayaki. In the months since her return from Dustari, life had settled back to routine; Mara had acceded to Kevin's wish to ease the Midkemians' lot; and with better food and housing, new blankets, and a lighter work schedule, Patrick's impatience had subsided. But the schism remained between Kevin and his fellow countrymen; pretending otherwise would not heal it. While escape was not mentioned, freedom was never far from the other captives' thoughts; they might not press, but they knew that Kevin visited only out of duty. He would never join them as long as he shared Mara's bed.

Ayaki kicked at his mount. Jarred from uncomfortable reflection, Kevin gave a feigned cry of pain. "Someone is hungry. I think I had best hurry the young Lord to the kitchen so he may plunder the larder."

Mara laughed and gave leave. Kevin reached up, grappled Ayaki by the wrists, and swung him down to his feet, then swatted him on the backside. The future Lord of the Acoma shouted another battle cry and charged toward the shade of the estate house. As Kevin raced after with no more sense of decorum, the Lady of the Acoma shook her head. "Nacoya hates it when those two eat in the kitchen," she said to on one.

The birds in the treetops returned to their interrupted song. Mara let her mind wander. Weary of the pressures of leadership, she had lately given thought to reviving Hokanu's interest. The Shinzawai had shored up their weakened stock in the council by rejoining Almecho's Alliance for War, making a Shinzawai-Acoma union yet more desirable. The radicals in the Party for Progress made enough noise about social change in the council for the Blue Wheel Party's errant behavior to pass without comment, but Mara sensed something larger was afoot. At the least, she could use the excuse to probe Hokanu for information.

Bothered that her interest should shift so quickly from romance to politics, Mara sighed.

"My Lady?" Nacoya appeared in the doorway, regarding her mistress with concern. "Is something amiss?"

Mara waved the old woman to the mat Arakasi had vacated. "I grow . . . tired, Nacoya."

Slowly, painful with her years, Nacoya knelt. The rampages of Ayaki and Kevin were forgotten as she took Mara's fingers in her own, grown daily more gnarled with infirmity. "Daughter, what weighs down your heart so?"

Mara pulled away from Nacoya's hold. As one of her ever present servants arrived to remove Arakasi's refreshment tray, she took a dried bread crust and tossed it into the path. Two small birds swooped down to peck after the crumbs. "Just this moment I was considering paying court to the Lord of the Shinzawai, for Hokanu, thinking a consort might ease my burdens. But then I found myself wanting to take the excuse to wrest information on the affairs of the Blue Wheel Party. This saddens me, Nacoya, because Hokanu is too fine a man to be used so."

Acting more as nurse than as First Adviser, Nacoya nodded her understanding. "Your heart has no room for romance, daughter. For good or ill, Kevin holds all your affections."

Mara bit her lip, while the birds stabbed and scrapped for the last bit of bread. For years her household had kept silence before the obvious: that her love for the barbarian slave was more than a woman's need for a man's arms to comfort her against loneliness. Dutiful to a fault, Nacoya had not broached a subject the mistress had forbidden to her—no matter how often she might ignore Mara's wishes about trivial concerns. But since Mara had matured enough to question her own course, the elderly woman spoke plainly. "Daughter, I warned you the first night the barbarian slave came to your bed. That is as it has been. Nothing can change what has occurred. Now you must face your responsibility."

Mara bridled, and the small birds spread nervous wings and flew. "Do I not spend my life protecting what shall be Ayaki's someday?"

Her eyes on the abandoned bread crust, Nacoya said, "Your father would glow with pride to know you have prevailed against his enemies. But your days are not your own. You are the life of House Acoma. No matter how great your desire, daughter, you must rule first and find your happiness second."

Mara nodded, her face an emotionless mask. "I have moments . . ."

Nacoya recaptured Mara's hand. "Moments that none who loves you begrudges, daughter. But the time will come when you must seek a firm alliance, if not with Hokanu of the Shinzawai, then with another noble's son. This new consort must father a child, to seal the alliance between our house and his. As Ruling Lady, you may ask to your bed whoever pleases you, and none may say no, but only after you bear a child to your husband. Before that, there must be no question who the father is. None. For that child must be as a bridge of stone across a deep chasm."

"I know." Mara sighed. "But until that time I shall pretend . . ." She left the thought unfinished.

When Nacoya made no move to leave, Mara forced aside her melancholy. "You have news?"

The former nurse scowled to hide a smile of pride. "The visiting emissary of Lord Keda is at the end of his wits and patience. He will press for a settlement this afternoon. You will need to eat, and see to your appearance, for Jican has used up excuses. The time has come for you to take charge of negotiations."

Mara summoned up an impish grin. "The desperate and vexing matter of grain warehouses. I had not forgotten." She rose, offered a hand to the elder woman to ease her back to her feet, then made her way to her quarters, where maids awaited with an exhaustive array of formal robes.

Two hours later, with the hair at her temples pulled painfully taut by the weight of the pins that secured her headpiece, Mara entered the great hall of the Acoma. Awaiting her, looking hot, stood the dignitary who had spent most of two frustrating days in contention with her hadonra. Equally bothered, and near to bristling with nerves, Jican arose to announce her.

"My Lady of the Acoma," he called to the visitor, who swiveled around and regarded her down a beaked nose with the stuffiness of a clerk. Behind him, but less quick to stifle expressions of irritation, a rumpled-looking contingent of scribes and trade factors shoved to their feet and offered bows.

Mara waited until their senior had performed the obeisance due her station before she advanced to her dais. All eyes marked her progress, and the tap of Keyoke's crutch as he followed on her heels made a counterpoint to the creak of Lujan's armor.

His sulkiness buried under silken tones, for his master's family was one of the Great Five and above Mara's in station, the tall emissary offered his respects. "Are you well, Lady of the Acoma?"

Cautious of her elaborately piled hair, Mara tipped her head. "I am well, First Adviser Hantigo. Is your master, Lord Keda, well?"

The Keda emissary responded stiffly to her courtesy. "I can say he was, when last I saw him."

Mara took care not to smile in the face of the man's veiled bitterness. Distantly related to the Shinzawai, his master was a powerful man, not only above her in family standing, but Warchief of Clan Kanazawai. Lord Keda's was not a house she cared to offend, though at her instruction Jican had spent the last day and a half balking the man's First Adviser.

Settled on her cushions, her robes arranged in layers like flower petals, Mara gestured leave to her advisers and the Keda's emissaries to be seated. She opened promptly, as if her hadonra had not done his best to stall through the days of negotiations. "Nacoya tells me we are close to an understanding."

The Keda First Adviser maintained his impeccable manners, but his tone left no doubt as to his mood. "With due respect to your most esteemed First Adviser, Lady Mara, the matter is far from settled."

Mara raised her eyebrows. "Really? What more is there to discuss?"

The Keda First Adviser smoothed irritation with the skill of a seasoned politician. "We require access to the docks in Silmani, Sulan-Qu, and Jamar, Lady. Apparently your factors have purchased so much of the available warehouse space that you hold, in effect, a monopoly."

Soured by sarcasm, one of the lesser factors broke in, "Given the lack of visible Acoma commerce in these areas, I would hesitate to suggest you had anticipated Keda needs and sought to frustrate them. We remind that the season is short. Time compels us to arrange an accommodation to store our goods upon the river docks. The commerce of House Keda must not suffer a detrimental interruption."

Lest the angry clerk reveal too much, the Keda First Adviser took matters back in hand. "My master has ordered me to make inquiry into your requirements and bargain for purchase of your contracts for warehouse leases in the three cities mentioned. After two days of talk, we are unclear exactly what price you demand."

A movement in the shadows at the far corner of the hall drew Mara's eye; unobtrusive, silent as always, Arakasi entered. He saw at once that his mistress had noticed him, and gave her a clear signal to proceed with the matter at hand. Mara concealed her satisfaction over the Spy Master's efficiency and looked pointedly at the Keda First Adviser. "Hantigo, Acoma plans for those facilities are Acoma business. Suffice it to say that we will be relinquishing advantage in the fall markets next year if we do not retain our current contracts."

"My Lady, if I may presume," the Keda First Adviser said with the faintest hint of acerbity. "Next fall's markets are of little concern to Keda interests. It is this spring that our grain must be upon the river at flood. When our factor at Jamar was ignored by your own, we made efforts to negotiate rights to sublet the warehouses." He cleared his throat and forced himself not to sound patronizing; this was not a capricious girl he confronted but a proven player of the game. "Because it is not common for a Ruling Lady to be concerned with minor matters of trade, we were slow to bring the matter to your attention, but, my Lady, the days that remain now are crucial."

"For the Keda," interjected Mara. Arakasi's intelligence had hinted that Keda spring crops were sitting in granaries upon farms upriver, awaiting word that dockside storage was available. When the spring floods began, the grain needed to be close at hand for transport by boats and barges downriver to the markets at the Holy City, Sulan-Qu, and Jamar. The dry winters of lowland Kelewan were the only season when travel on the Gagajin—the heart line of commerce in the Empire—was restricted. While smaller craft could negotiate the shoals during winter, deep-draft barges laden with cargo could not pass the shallows between Sulan-Qu and Jamar. Only when the spring snow melt from the mountains High Wall swelled the waters could heavy cargo make passage. Mara had tried to tie up the dock space at Kentosani, the Holy City, as well, but had failed, owing to imperial edict—no one could commandeer the warehouses under long contracts, against the possibility of imperial need.

Yet even with this setback, Mara had established a barrier to an opponent's trade, but in such a way that no overt act or threat was ever made. That Lord Keda sent his First Adviser to another house as negotiator proved her impulsive plot had touched a weakness; the dilemma concerning the grain impasse was a matter of critical urgency.

Mara feigned consternation. "Well then, if my advisers have not been clear, let me set the terms." She paused, as though counting on her fingers, then said, "We shall grant you full rights to our warehouses in Silmani, without restriction, from this day to the day after your crops leave for the south. And equal access to warehouses in all your southern market cities, again without restriction, until you have sold the last of this year's crops, but no longer than until the first day of summer."

The First Adviser of the Keda sat motionless, no expression on his face, but his weary manner turned avid as he waited to hear the price.

Almost, Mara regretted to disappoint him. "In exchange, your Lord must grant to me the promise of a vote in the council, to be cast as I require, without reservation or question."

In violation of protocol, the Keda First Adviser blurted, "Impossible!"

Mara returned only silence. On cue, Nacoya said, "First Adviser! You forget yourself!"

Stung to shame, Hantigo flushed and fought to recover poise. "I beg the Lady's forgiveness." Coldly he narrowed his eyes. "Nevertheless, I would be less than faithful to my Lord should I answer this request in any way save no."

Aware that Lujan was smothering an ill-timed smile, and that Arakasi watched her in appreciation from his vantage at the rear of the hall, Mara managed her part to perfection. "That is our price."

The clerks and factors looked miffed, and Hantigo's flush receded to a pallor that left him trembling. "Lady, you ask too much."

"You could hire wagons and drive the grain to the southern markets," whispered a mortified factor. Hantigo glowered and answered through clenched teeth. "Had that been a feasible option, I should never have left the shade of my master's estates. The margin we had for alternatives has been wasted, and even should our wagons depart this hour, the grain would arrive too late to catch the market at peak. We would be forced to take whatever price the brokers offered."

Hantigo faced Mara, his features a bland mask. "Keda honor has no price."

But Arakasi had disclosed that this year the Lord of the Keda was overextended. If pride was paramount to him, he could sell the grain at a loss and wait for another year to recoup. Yet Mara sensed that to force him to such a pass would be dangerous, perhaps even earn his enmity. She smiled, and warmth seemed to radiate from her. "First Adviser Hantigo, you mistake me. I intend no disrespect toward

Andero of the Keda. Allow me to pledge before these witnesses that I shall ask your master to support me only in a matter that holds significance to House Acoma. I will promise further that no vote shall be demanded that can adversely reflect upon the honor of House Keda. No demand of mine would call for military aid to the Acoma, or attack upon a third party, or any other act that would require Keda property or wealth to be placed at risk. I merely seek sureties to block any future attempts to disadvantage me in the High Council. Surely you recall the difficulty the imperial call to muster on the border imposed upon my house?"

Hantigo rubbed dampness from his temples, reluctant to concede her point. Minwanabi's plotting had certainly inconvenienced Acoma fortunes for three years; the house's entry into the silk trade had been nearly ruined by that one action alone. But if the First Adviser sympathized, he could not grant Mara's terms without leave from his master; the transfer of a vote in the High Council was not a concession to be granted by an emissary. Regretfully, Hantigo said, "Even with such assurances, I doubt my master will accept your terms."

That the man had ceased protesting impossibilities was significant. Confident of victory, and knowing Andero of the Keda for a man of steadfast integrity, Mara concluded the interview. "Then you had best fly to your master and apprise him of my offer. We shall await his decision with interest. Tell him that we leave for the celebration at Kentosani within a week. Here, or in the Holy City, let him know I will be at his disposal"—she gave a precise smile—"to hear his reply."

The First Adviser of the Keda rose and bowed, his disappointment masterfully hidden. Attended by his troop of scribes and factors, he departed from the hall with dignity.

Mara dispatched Jican to attend the Keda First Adviser's departure. Then she waited a prudent interval and motioned Arakasi to her side. "Shall we count upon a Keda vote in the council?"

Her Spy Master turned a look as keen as a killwing's through the doorway the emissary had just vacated. "I suspect the Lord may relent, but you will have to provide him with sureties. Lord Keda is firm in his role of Clan Warchief. He'll do nothing to compromise house or Kanazawai interests, and most particularly he would not become embroiled in any conflict with the Minwanabi."

Lujan took a step away, toward the door and his awaiting duties, but observed, "Still, even if they're publicly in the Jade Eye Party, the Keda have many relatives involved with the Blue Wheel Party. If they're as deep into the Game of the Council as that suggests, perhaps giving Desio only one more reason to hate them won't matter very much?"

A faint smile was all that remark earned from Mara. Worn by the aftermath of a trying afternoon, she tugged out an itching hairpin. "We've done all we can without risking insult." She turned the pin over in her hands, watching the light flash and sparkle in the small bead at the end. "I don't enjoy twisting the tail of a Clan Warchief, but I'll need all the support I can garner to thwart Minwanabi in the High Council. Our house cannot afford a repetition of our near disaster in Tsubar."

Mara pulled out another hairpin, then motioned for a servant to remove her headpiece. Dark locks cascaded down her back, making her more comfortable, but hotter. "Where does that leave us now?"

Nacoya furrowed her brow, then snapped fingers for a maid to attend to her mistress's loose hair. "If every promise made to you is kept, you could sway close to one third of the High Council."

Weighing the odds as he had once done on the battlefield, Keyoke added, "I would wager some will dishonor their vow, given adverse circumstances, my Lady."

But the game was never assured; Mara had learned the pitfalls of Tsurani politics at a very tender age. While the fingers of her servant worked her hair into a comfortable braid, she hugged her elbows against her chest and rested her chin on her fists. "But if the Clan Warchief of the Kanazawai were to yield me his vote, others who might be inclined to waver would follow the stronger man's lead."

Unspoken beneath her conjecture was the fear that she had gone too far and goaded House Keda into enmity; if Lord Andero took offense, not even the fact that the Acoma and he both held to the Jade Eye Party would prevent a move in retaliation.

But uncertainties did not make for greatness. As the maid finished off her braid with a velvet tie, Mara asked for a lighter, plainer robe, then regarded her circle of advisers. "We have much to do in preparation for the journey." A glance at the window showed several hours of daylight still remained. "Lujan, please assemble an escort. Ayaki and the natami must be secured against attack during our absence, and a shipment of our silk bales must be sent to those warehouses, so the Keda have no cause to complain that we monopolized the space to disadvantage them. For that I must make arrangements with the cho-ja Queen before nightfall."

Like a patrol crossing an enemy border, the Acoma entered the Holy City. From the lofty warehouses by the riverside to the grand avenues between courtyards, Kentosani was bedecked like a bride before her wedding. Freshly painted walls, garlands of flowers, and colored bunting made each street a joyous vista. Older than Sulan-Qu, and reflecting overlapping centuries of tastes and architecture, the city was the most impressive within the Empire. Multitiered stone buildings crowded against carved and painted balconies; lampposts of cleverly fashioned wood and ceramic rose above boxes of flowers lining the avenues. Everywhere Kevin looked, he was stunned by beauty and stark ugliness in contrast. The scent of temple incense mingled with an underlying miasma of river sewage. Squalid beggars licensed by the Imperial Government sat in rows, open sores and missing limbs displayed to the passing throng—not a few balanced upon crutches while resting naked backs against a mural painted by a master artist. Filthy bands of street urchins shouted and craned necks to catch sight of a great Lady, while Mara's vigilant guard kept them back with shields and spear shafts. Town matrons carrying baskets on yoke poles jeered and pointed at the great barbarian slave who towered over the rest of her retinue, and whose red-gold hair drew admiring eyes.

The knots of merchants avoided by running couriers, processions of priests in their cowled robes and beaded sashes hung with relics, darting house messengers, and city guards in sparkling imperial white lent an atmosphere of bustling prosperity. But Kevin was soldier enough to notice alert eyes peering from men hanging back in shadowed corners; whether they belonged to spies, informants, or rumormongers who sold news for shell coins, the Acoma guards took no chances. Alert scouts checked into every doorway and alley they passed, while Lujan kept his warriors poised to attack at the slightest hint of threat. Imperial peace was a promise of retribution against whoever broke it, not a guarantee for the unwary.

Still, for all the underlying intrigue, the crossing of the trade quarter was spectacular. Only one member of the Acoma retinue was not occasionally drawn by the splendor; forced to ride a litter like a courtier, Keyoke sat impassive as a carved stone icon, no expression on his face.

Mara's cortege passed into the temple plaza, a giant square that served as focal point for twenty vast buildings, raised to praise Tsurani gods and house the priests of their separate orders. Archways inlaid with shell flashed in the sunlight, set off by lacquered tiles, precious marbles, and pillars of malachite and onyx. At the center of the plaza a great bonfire burned, surrounded by incense pots and altars heaped high with bowls of offerings. Kevin walked with difficulty, torn between staring at the splendors of an ancient and alien culture, and watching his feet for paving worn treacherously uneven.

Mara's town house was situated off a quiet residential court, shadowed by the flowering trees that lined the avenue. The front stood enclosed by an opulently tiled wall, above which rose its many-tiered roof, adorned at each gable with carved shatra birds. The wide, semicircular wooden portals at the entry were shaded by an arbor of purple vines that grew on trellises cut from thousands of giant seashells. The effect was designed to impress. Like many older families of the Empire, the Acoma owned quarters convenient to the heart of Kentosani and the halls of the imperial seat. Years might pass between visits, but the stately, centuries-old houses were always maintained against the need to reside in the city for weeks at a time. Each family in the High Council was allotted a tiny apartment within the Imperial Palace, but for comfort and the advantages of private entertaining, most rulers preferred the freedom and spaciousness of their less formal accommodations outside the inner city.

At the outer door to the Acoma town house, Jican awaited, accompanied by a servant in house livery. As Mara's retinue halted before the dooryard, the hadonra bowed. "All is in readiness for your arrival, my Lady." Then he gestured, and on cue the gates swung wide.

Mara's bearers bore their mistress inside, and as Jican and his attendant fell in behind, Kevin realized with surprise that the man in the servant's robe was Arakasi. Under cover of the arbor, shielded by the steps of marching soldiers as the honor guard squeezed through the entry, the Spy Master leaned near to Mara's litter.

Only Kevin walked near enough to note that words were exchanged between them. Then the retinue was fully into the courtyard within the walls, and the gates swung closed and barred. Kevin offered Mara his hand and noticed as he helped her from her cushions that she was forcing herself not to frown.

"What's in play?" he asked. "Did Arakasi bring bad news?"

Mara flashed him a warning glance. "Not here," she murmured, pointedly appearing to inspect the tiny garden that helped damp the street noise from the house. "Everything appears in order, Jican."

Kevin remained puzzled by his mistress's reticence until Arakasi nodded slightly toward the overhanging galleries of the home across the way. Watchers might lurk in the shadows there, and belatedly the Midkemian recalled that spies in this world included particularly sharp-eyed individuals trained to read lips. Mollified, he kept the proper one step behind his mistress as she entered her town house.

The inner hall smelled of waxed wood,, spices, and old hangings; antique furnishings lay everywhere Kevin looked, lovingly polished by generations of servants. The residence in Kentosani was older than the estate home near Sulan-Qu. Most of the screens on the street side were overhung with patterned silk, but the inward wall opened into a central courtyard, green-tinged by the shade of ancient trees. Cramped stairs with balustrades carved with mythical beasts, worn nearly smooth by hands resting upon them, ascended through lofty ceilings. As if the building had once been a walled compound, the ground-level walls were stone, with the upper three stories of wooden frame and cloth walls. Kevin stared in amazement, for the building was like none he had seen on either side of the rift. While tiny compared to the Acoma estate house, Mara's town house was as large as a

Kingdom inn. Massive beams and stonework were cleverly constructed, forming a dwelling that felt open and airy.

Balconies crammed with potted flowers overlooked the inner garden, with its fish pools and fountain, and one gnarled head gardener who brandished his rake at two slaves who scrubbed moss from tiled pathways. To no one in particular, Kevin said, "A man could get used to this."

A jab from behind reminded him of his station. He looked around, and down, into the irascible countenance of Nacoya, who clutched her walking stick at an angle that still meant business. "Your mistress calls for her bath, barbarian."

Belatedly Kevin noticed that the ground floor was suddenly emptier and servants were rushing up the stair. Arakasi did not seem to be among them.

Poked again, and this time in a place that mattered sorely, Kevin said, "All right, little grandmother. I'm going." With an insolent smile, he hurried along.

Mara was already in her chambers, several strange maids busied with her undressing. Two other servants, neither one Arakasi, poured ceramic cauldrons of steaming water into a wooden tub. As Mara stood naked, her servant pinning her hair up, Kevin moved forward and tested the water temperature to ensure her comfort. At his nod, the servants departed.

Mara dismissed the maids, then mounted a small riser and gracefully stepped into her bath. She settled into the soothing warmth, eyes closed as Kevin began applying scented soap to her cheeks. Softly she said, "That feels wonderful."

But the bothered expression did not ease from her face.

"What did Arakasi say?" Kevin asked as he massaged gently and removed the road dust from his beloved's face. He laid his hands upon her shoulders as she bent to rinse off suds, her tension still apparent.

Mara sighed and blew droplets off her nose. "A clan meeting has been called for this afternoon. Someone took care to see that the notice never quite reached me. Sometime tonight an apologetic messenger will give us word upon his return from our estates, I am sure."

Kevin retrieved the soap and resumed his washing. His fingers kneaded the nape of her neck, but she gave no sign of pleasure. Kevin guessed she thought upon that long-past visit from Jiro of the Anasati, when he had warned that factions within the Hadama Clan were alarmed at the Acoma's sudden rise. The victory treaty with Tsubar could only have inflamed existing jealousies. And worse: immediately before their departure for the Holy City, Arakasi's spies had sent news that young Jiro had paid a call upon Lord Desio.

This missed message might be connected to both events. The politics of Kelewan were endless, and deadly dangerous. Unwilling to dwell too long on Tsurani intrigue, Kevin pressed Mara forward and began sluicing her back. "My Lady, mixed messages and clan rivalries will still be there after your bath. Unless you want to confront your kinfolk covered in road dirt?"

He startled an outraged laugh from her. "Beast. I'm certainly no dirtier than you, who walked the entire way in the open."

Playfully Kevin ran a finger over his face and held it out as if inspecting it. "Hmmm. Yes, I do seem to be darker than when we began the journey."

The soft cake of soap he held was unguarded, and Mara gouged out a dollop and seized the moment to deposit it on her lover's nose. "Then you had best wash your own body as well."

Kevin looked around in feigned regret. "I don't see servants at hand to scrub my back, my Lady."

Mara grabbed a sponge and drenched his face with water. "Get in here, you foolish man."

Grinning widely, Kevin dropped the soap, stripped off his robes, and climbed into the tub. He settled in behind Mara and cradled her close, his fingers roaming over her body. Her skin quivered under his attentions. She whispered, "I thought you were going to wash off road dirt."

His hands slipped under the water, still touching. "No one said washing had to be unpleasant."

She turned in the circle of his arms, then stretched up and kissed her barbarian slave. Soon the worries of clan rivalries were forgotten as she lost herself in the pleasures of his love.

Robed in formal colors, Mara waved for her bearers to pause before the Council Hall entrance. Surrounded by her tightly clustered bodyguard, and attended by a withered old serving maid, she endured several last-minute adjustments to her costume while Lujan and an honor company of five warriors waited to precede her into the chamber. Kevin stood behind her open litter. Unable to see past her towering jeweled headpiece to gain a view of the chamber, he settled with staring at the antechamber, its splendor unmatched by anything he had seen in his life. The building that housed the High Council was among the more imposing in Kentosani. The council occupied a complex larger than the entire Acoma estate house, with corridors lofty as caverns, each arch and doorway carved with fantastic creatures that earlier generations intended to repel evil influence. The gargoyles remained long after the names of the spirits had been forgotten, their fearsome countenances ignored by those who enjoyed their protection. The floors and ceilings were elaborately patterned, every inch of wall space painted with historical murals. Many of them showed warriors wearing Xacatecas and Minwanabi colors; sometimes he recognized a contingent in Acoma green. Newly appreciative of the Empire's grand traditions, Kevin felt a stranger to his own culture.

This small city unto itself, with its own entrances and conference chambers independent of the palace proper, was guarded by companies of soldiers levied from all of the houses of the council members. The corridors were lined with armored warriors in a hundred different color combinations. Each company was pledged to preserve the peace, taking no sides should disputes lead to violence; however, every Lord ensured this vow was never put to the test, for Tsurani honor held house loyalty above any abstract concept of fair play.

Kevin lost count of badges and colors long before reaching the anteroom. When he had faced Tsurani in the Riftwar, the armies were homogeneous, with perhaps two or three different houses marching under a combined command. But in this antechamber alone, at least a dozen armor patterns he did not recognize identified the houses that provided security for the meeting of Clan Hadama.

A voice called out beyond the entry, "The Lady of the Acoma!" Then a huge pair of drums boomed. Lujan signaled his men to march in lockstep, and as Mara's bearers moved forward in procession, Kevin caught sight of the drummers.

They stood to either side of the grand entry, clad in what looked like a costume of ancient pelts. The mallets in their hands were carved bone, and their instruments were of painted hide stretched over what close scrutiny revealed to be the inverted shells from gigantic turtles. Kevin made out the tripods underneath, fashioned from a lizardlike creature quilled with spines.

Being a barbarian slave had advantages at times—no one showed surprise that he gawked. If the hallways and corridors had impressed Kevin earlier, the hall of the council itself was overwhelming. Constructed under a circular dome, the hall was surrounded by upper galleries, with polished wooden benches, then descending levels of pillared galleries lined with chairs tantamount to thrones. Each gallery reminded Kevin of the Baron of Yabon's private box on the festival grounds at the city's annual fairs, where the start and finish line for horse races were located. The meanest noble family in the Empire was entitled to a seat the equal of the Baron's in opulence. The most expansive galleries were on the lower levels, nearest the central dais, and many were set back under low canopies painted or embroidered with house symbols—ensuring that those behind and to the sides could not spy upon conferences. Aisles that were really promenades separated them one from the next, so that messengers and retainers might hurry effortlessly about their masters' bidding. The vast size of the room was necessary; Kevin was astonished by the crowd. The lower levels were packed with Lords in full Tsurani panoply. Colors and plumes and jeweled headdresses made a riotous feast for the eyes.

Kevin closed his gaping mouth with an effort. This was only a clan meeting!

Mara had attempted to explain clan relationships to him, and after a long and frustrating discourse Kevin grasped only a fuzzy concept of how all these notables were affiliated. By his understanding, somewhere back in the dim mists of history, these people had ancestors that were cousins. Bound to customs that seemed a knotwork of contradiction, they clung to what was, in Midkemian logic, an outdated concept of relationship, one that might have held significance in an earlier age, but that now seemed mostly ceremonial. Yet when Kevin had voiced this conclusion, Mara had insisted that clan loyalty was no phantom. Given the right motivation, these separate family factions would unite and die in bloody battle defending their elusive code of identity. It was the very urgency of such relationships that had created the Great Game, for once clan honor was invoked, no house could honorably ignore those ties of blood.

Once past the entry platform and the drummers, Kevin could view the entire chamber. The sheer size made him feel dwarfed. On a dais slightly higher than the ring of seats on the central level of the hall, a man in flowing robes and a massive headdress of green and yellow plumes nodded to Mara's bearers to set down her litter. Her honor guard retired, to take up position above and behind the concentric circle of seats cut into the lowest tier of galleries, and a snap of her fingers summoned Kevin to assist her to her feet. With the Lady poised on his arm, the Midkemian guided where she pointed: down a shallow stair, to a green-painted awning and a chair carved with shatra bird symbols, in a gallery large enough for all of Mara's advisers and officers to surround her, should she need them close by. Followed by the ghostly echo of whispered conversation, Kevin kept his eyes down in proper Tsurani submission. He must observe the forms here, distasteful as they were to his beliefs. Fully five thousand people could fill the overhanging galleries, with room for ten thousand more at floor level, if occasion warranted.

As Kevin installed the Lady of the Acoma in her green lacquered chair, he marked that her place was relatively close to the dais. Aware that the time of entry, as well as seating, were cultural indicators of rank, Kevin had already marked the range of fashion and quality of clothing. The lord farthest from the dais was a poor country relative, by all appearance, for his finery was worn and faded.

But the man upon the dais was a peacock in full plumage! As Kevin performed a slave's bow beside his Lady's chair, he risked a peek beneath his lashes.

"My Lord Chekowara," Mara greeted cordially. "Are you well?"

The Lord, whose name Kevin recognized as belonging to the Clan Warchief, nodded back, though how he could do so and not topple under the weight of his jewels and plumes was mystifying; the man seemed something of a fop, yet his face was broad and masculine, and almost as black-skinned as that of a native of Great Kesh, the southern empire in

Midkemia. Muttering as he rose from obeisance, Kevin commented, "If you two are related, it's many generations back."

Mara shot him a glance that was half-irritated, half-amused. From the dais, the Lord of the Chekowara smiled, showing an array of ivory teeth. "I am most well, Lady Mara. We welcome our most august Ruling Lady to our meeting, and presume that you are well also."

Mara returned the ritual assurance, then coolly inclined her head to other surrounding lords. As he assumed a slave's place behind his Lady's chair, Kevin searched faces for signs of displeasure; yet if any notable present was disappointed by Mara's timely arrival, nothing showed but Tsurani impassivity. Nearly seventy families had sent representatives to the gathering, and one or several could have been responsible for Mara's misdirected invitation. Stunned yet again by the scope of Tsuranuanni, Kevin reminded himself that the Hadama were held to be a minor clan in the Empire, no matter how much honor the Acoma had gained. How many powerful houses must a great clan number? By Kevin's rough estimation, this tiny clan meeting, which, with Lords, advisers, servants, and slaves, put the number of people in this building close to five hundred, with an equal number of soldiers waiting in outer halls. When the mighty of the Empire met in council, Kevin could only imagine the place filled to capacity.

Clearly not intimidated, Mara said, "I am most pleased to seek council with our cousins and attend this, the first clan meeting since I assumed the Acoma mantle."

The Lord of the Chekowara's smile broadened. "Much honor and prestige have you brought House Acoma since your father's untimely death, Lady Mara. You bring pride to our hearts."

At this many Lords stamped upon the floor in a show of agreement like applause. Others offered congratulations, shouting, "Yes, it is so! Much honor!" and "Great success!"

Kevin leaned over to remove Mara's outer wrap, a light silk embroidered with her house symbol. "This fellow's a snake oil salesman," he whispered.

Mara's brow furrowed under her formal makeup. She risked a hiss of disapproval. "I don't know what snake oil is, but it has the ring of an insult. Now go and stand with Lujan's guard until I need you."

Kevin folded the wrap over his arm and retreated up the stair. Once in place among the Acoma honor guard, he made a surreptitious study of the proceedings. The Lord of the Chekowara opened by announcing what seemed like social chat, a list of pending marriages, handfastings, and births, and a longer list of eulogies. Few of the deceased had died of age or infirmity; the phrase "fallen honorably in battle" occurred frequently. Kevin was astonished at the clarity of the acoustics in the hall—when the speakers chose not to mask their voices, they carried to the highest galleries. Kevin listened, mystified, as the Lord of the Chekowara's rich voice rose and fell as he mourned the passing of notables in the clan. To Lujan he murmured, "That calley bird on the dais has all the sincerity of a relli."

Silently at ease, the Acoma Force Commander did not twitch a muscle; but deepening laugh lines around his eyes betrayed that he stifled a chuckle.

Resigned that he would get nothing from an Acoma soldier on duty, Kevin moved among the litter bearers. Tsurani slaves were not much of an improvement, but at least they noticed when he spoke, even if they only looked confused. Still, Kevin thought, any reaction was better than the stony manner of the warriors. Kevin idled away the passing minutes, observing the comings and goings of the many servants and retainers of the attending Hadama Lords, when an odd behavior caught his eye. Those who hurried through the vast hall seemed oblivious to the many paintings that adorned the walls save one, a depiction of a fairly nondescript man. Like those around it, it was ancient, but this one had been recently repainted, and for the obvious reason that any who passed by reached out and touched it, often without thought. Kevin nudged the slave next to him. "Why do they do that?"

The slave looked discomforted. "Do what?" he whispered, as if speaking were sure to bring instant destruction.

"Touch that picture of a man." Kevin pointed.

"That's an ancient Lord. He was Servant of the Empire. It's good luck to touch him." The slave withdrew into himself as if that cryptic reference explained everything. Kevin was about to ask for explanation when a warning glance from Lujan silenced him, and turned him back to watching the proceedings.

No serious political discussion ever took place that he

could see. Once the family announcements were finished, slaves thronged in with refreshments, and this Lord or that would arise from his chair and speak with Chekowara or other clansmen. Many flocked around Mara's chair, and all of them seemed civil, if not friendly. Kevin waited for a second call to order, or some sort of announcement of business, but no such thing ever happened. When the afternoon light faded above the domed chamber, Lord Chekowara lifted his staff of office and thumped a ringing blow on the dais. "The meeting of Clan Hadama is concluded," he called out, and one by one, according to rank, the lesser Lords bowed to him in parting.

"Seems like nothing but an absurd party to me," Kevin commented.

A soldier in Mara's honor guard caught his eye, then, in urgent warning to keep silent. Kevin returned his usual insolent grin, and then started: the warrior was Arakasi, clad in full armor and looking every inch the proper warrior. He had perfected military bearing so flawlessly that his presence was overlooked until now. More curious than ever to know why the Spy Master's attendance had been called for, Kevin shifted from foot to foot until Mara waved him over to replace her wrap.

Kevin walked behind Mara's litter as her retinue reentered the twilit streets. Lamplighters had just made their rounds, and the imperial quarter of Kentosani glowed softly gold against the darkened sky. As the honor guard formed up to escort Mara to her town house, Arakasi fell in step beside Kevin. Wise enough not to call the Spy Master by name, the Midkemian simply said, "Was anything of importance achieved in there?"

Arakasi marched with his hand on his sword, deadly and capable in appearance though it was no secret he was not gifted with a blade. "Much."

Exasperated by his brevity, Kevin probed: "Such as?"

The honor guard marched down a wide entrance ramp, with torches blazing in bowls on either side. Below the rise a larger contingent of warriors met them, affording their mistress the added security she would need in the darkening streets. Arakasi said nothing until they had rounded several corners and passed the gates from the imperial precinct.

As they marched into the boulevard beyond, Arakasi murmured, "Lady Mara's clansmen have made plain that she can expect a reasonable degree of support . . . assuming her alliances do not place other houses at risk. If she encounters trouble from her enemies, she'll need to invoke clan honor to gain assistance, and the outcome of such a call for aid could not in any way be assured."

The Midkemian's puzzlement stayed obvious.

"Clan honor," Arakasi repeated, in his manner of piercing perception. "You barbarians." The statement held no condemnation; the Spy Master thoughtfully qualified. "To draw her clansman into war, Lady Mara must convince every Lord, from highest to least, that an affront to her house was an insult not only to the Acoma, but to the Hadama Clan as well."

Kevin inhaled the incense-laden air; they were passing the temple quarter and suffered a momentary interruption as their retinue was forced aside to allow a tribute caravan to pass. The huge, leather-strapped carry cases borne on heavy poles by slaves contained metals, originally brought as plunder from the barbarian world and since dispensed by the Emperor's High Secretary, who portioned out allotments for the temples. Kevin waited until the guarding ranks of white-armored imperial warriors passed on before he said, "So?"

Arakasi tapped his sword. "Calls to Clan are difficult when the families who belong are as politically divided as ours are. For any attacking house is careful to make clear that it is moving against an enemy, not his clansmen. Gifts are often sent as reassurances." After a pause, Arakasi added, "Lord Desio has been lavish."

Kevin grinned in appreciation. "What you're telling me is they're saying, 'Don't invite us unless you're going to win, because the Minwanabi might stop sending us bribes. But if you're sure you can destroy them, then we'll be happy to join in, so we can take our share of the plunder.'"

For the first time since Kevin could remember, the Spy Master smiled outright. Then he loosed a chuckle that swelled into quiet laughter. "I would never have thought to put it that way," Arakasi allowed. "But that's precisely what they told her."

"Damn." Kevin shook his head in amazement. "And I saw nothing going on except a gala."

From the litter, Mara interjected, "Now you understand why I keep him around. His perspective is . . . fresh."

Arakasi resumed his soldier's appearance, but a gleam lingered in his eyes. "I agree, mistress."

"I don't know that I'll ever understand you people," Kevin said. He dodged to avoid a jigabird that had escaped some scullion's cleaver. They had entered the residential quarter now, and the lamps were more widely spaced. "I stood and watched that entire meeting, and the only discussion that got heated enough to seem important sounded like a debate on land reform."

"In council," Arakasi said patiently, "what is not said is far more important: who does not approach a Lord's chair, and who hangs back, and who is seen with whom count for more than words. The fact that Lord Chekowara did not leave his dais to personally congratulate Mara on her border treaty was revealingly significant. The clan will not follow her lead. And all of that shuffling of bodies around Lord Mamogota's chair was proof that two factions within the clan support him, against our Lady. No one would seriously consider that nonsense about giving land to peasant farmers. The Party for Progress is without influence outside the Hunzan Clan, and Lord Tuclamekla of that clan is a close friend of Mamogota's. This was a dead issue before the meeting began."

"So you presume that the intercepted message was arranged by Lord Mamo-whoever?" Kevin surmised.

"We hope so," Arakasi answered. "Mamogota's at least not affiliated with the Alliance for War. He might take Desio's 'gifts,' but he isn't a Minwanabi supporter."

Kevin shook his head in amazement. "You people have minds that twist like knitting. Never mind," he interjected as Arakasi asked after the concept of knitting. "Just take it that I'll be an old codger long before I understand this culture."

The silence between slave and Spy Master lasted until the return to the town house. Kevin entered the lovely inner garden and helped his Lady from her litter. He continued to doubt if he would ever truly know the people whose lives and fates he shared. As Mara retained his hand and smiled up at him, he looked into her dark eyes and found himself utterly lost. Tsurani life might be a puzzle to him, but this woman was a mystery and a wonder.

15. *CHAOS*

The spectacle began.

Banners flew from every tall building along the avenues leading to the arena. Citizens tossed flowers into the street, to assure the gods they held no envy for those of loftier station. For reasons only the God of Trickery might name, city dwellers invested favor in this house or that, cheering more or less vigorously depending upon who passed. Mara's litter and escort were greeted with loud applause. Again dressed as a common servant, and placed behind the litter alongside Kevin in the cortege, Arakasi commented, "It seems the mob favors the Acoma this month, my Lady. The victory in Tsubar has made you a heroine among the commoners."

Noise defeated Mara's attempted reply.

The long, stately boulevard that crossed the imperial precinct was thronged with folk from every walk of Tsurani life. Their clothing ranged from the costliest cloths and jewels worn by high-ranking nobles to the craftsman's unadorned broadcloth and the meanest beggar's rags. The games offered by the Warlord in celebration of the Light of Heaven brought the finest ornaments out of jewel chests—the more daring of the wealthy merchants dressing their daughters for display in the hope of attracting a noble suitor.

Surrounded by the flash of rare metal ornaments as well as lacquer combs, jades, and gemstones, Mara's escort jostled and vied for road space along with dozens of other house guards and their litter-borne Lords and Ladies. Some were carried in palanquins painted in carnival colors or sequined with flecks of iridescent shell; others held whole families, shouldered by as many as twenty slaves. For as far as the eye could see, the festival crowd made a vast, brilliant swirl of a thousand colors; only the slaves stood out, in commonplace robes of dull grey.

Kevin stared like a blind man just given sight. Past a retinue of warriors in red and purple, between the canopy poles of an uncountable crush of litters, he saw a wall hung with ribbons and banners that he took to be the end of the boulevard. But as the Acoma party drew closer, his eyes widened in amazement. The barrier was no wall but a segment of the Grand Imperial Stadium.

The amphitheater was vast, far larger than anything he might have imagined. The litters, soldiers, and commoners on foot poured up a broad flight of steps, then across a concourse to a second flight. At the top lay yet another concourse, and beyond that the entrance to the stadium. As Mara's litter began the ascent, Kevin looked to either side and judged there must be at least another dozen entrances from the palace quarter alone.

Even here the guards had to shove and jostle to clear the way for their Lady's passage. All of Tsurani society had turned out to attend the games in the Emperor's honor, or to line up and gawk at the spectacle presented by their betters. Only great occasions such as this brought them so close to the might of the Empire, and country folk flocked in droves to the city to point, jabber, and stare.

Despite the festive atmosphere, the warriors maintained vigilance. Men of unclear rank and position moved through the crowd. Many wore guild badges; others were messengers, vendors, or rumormongers; a few might be agents, or spies, or thieves; assassins might wear any disguise. Any state festival that intermingled clans and political parties became an extension of the Game of the Council.

Beyond the highest stair arose a stone arch two hundred feet across. Kevin tried to calculate the size of the arena beyond, and failed. The tiers of openair seats must hold a hundred thousand spectators, and no amphitheater in the Kingdom could compare.

At the first terrace, Lujan shouted, "Acoma!"

Individuals of lesser rank hurried clear of Mara's retinue. As the warriors ascended the second flight of steps, Kevin noticed bystanders exclaiming in surprise and pointing. When he realized the stares were for him, his ears reddened. Commoners unaccustomed to his height and barbarian aspect made him an object of gossip and speculation.

At the top of the second terrace, Lujan marched his guard through the crowd and cleared a space beside other noble retinues. The litter bearers lowered their burden, and Kevin assisted Mara from the cushions. The Force Commander, a Strike Leader named Kenji and three guards, and Arakasi fell in at either side of the Lady and her body slave. The balance of the Acoma guard departed with the litter bearers, to wait upon them in the street at the bottom of the stairs.

Lujan led the way into a corridor to the left of the archway. A hundred or more rows of seats rose above the level upon which Mara's party moved, while another fifty rows descended toward the arena floor. To the left, two areas stood cordoned off, one of them dominated by a box adorned in lacquerworked gold and imperial white. The other section was bare of any decoration but was immediately noticeable by contrast. The occupants all wore black robes.

Arakasi noticed Kevin's interest. "Great Ones," he murmured in explanation.

"You mean the magicians?" Kevin looked more carefully, but the men in their dark robes sat silently or engaged in hushed conversation. A few watched the sandy expanse below, awaiting the first contest. "They look entirely ordinary."

"Looks may deceive," Arakasi said. At Lujan's command, he helped the other warriors shoulder through a knot of bystanders.

"Why are all these people hanging about?" Mara wondered. "Usually there are no commoners on this level."

Taking care not to be overheard, Arakasi answered, "They hope to catch a glimpse of the barbarian Great One. The gossipmongers claim he will be in attendance."

"How can there be a barbarian Great One?" Kevin interjected.

Arakasi waved aside a matron with a flower basket who tried to sell Mara a bloom. "Great Ones are outside the law; none may question them. Once a man is taken and trained to wear the black robe, he is of the Assembly of Magicians. What rank he held before is of no consequence. He is only a

Great One, pledged to act in preservation of the Empire, and his word becomes as law."

Kevin stilled further questions as Arakasi shot him a warning glance. They were too close to strangers for chance remarks or improper behavior to be risked.

The arena was not yet one-third full when Mara reached the box set aside for her. Like her seat in the Council Hall, the position indicated her relative rank in the hierarchy of the Empire. By Kevin's estimation, some hundred families were closer to the imperial box, but thousands were farther removed.

Mara sat with Lujan, the young Strike Leader, and the soldiers on either side; Kevin and Arakasi took up positions behind her chair, ready to answer her needs. Kevin studied the surrounding array of house colors and tried to puzzle out the pecking order of Tsurani politics.

Past the magicians' area, and to the right of the Warlord's dais, lay a box dressed out in black and orange, the colors of House Minwanabi. On levels above sat other families of lesser importance, but all clan-related or in vassalage to Lord Desio.

Adjacent came the yellow and purple colors of Xacatecas; the victory treaty with Tsubar had advanced Lord Chipino, and now he was second in power in the High Council. The Lord of the Chekowara took up his position in a box beneath Mara's, on the same level as the Warlord's, but as removed from the white and gold as she was.

A trumpet blast sounded from the arena floor. Wooden doors around the arena boomed open and scores of young men in various colors of armor marched out in formation. As they moved, they sorted themselves out into pairs and saluted the empty imperial box. At a second signal from the games director, who sat in a special niche by the gates, they drew swords and began to fight.

Kevin quickly determined that the matches were to first blood only; the bested man would raise his helm as a sign of submission. The winner would then take on another victorious partner and initiate sparring again.

Lujan answered Kevin's query. "These are young officers of various houses. Most are cousins and younger sons of nobility, eager to show their prowess and gain a sliver of honor." He glanced around the stadium. "This is of little consequence, save for those down there and their families. Still, a man may advance himself in the eyes of his master by winning a contest such as this."

There were no colors on the floor from Minwanabi, Xacatecas, or the other three Great Houses, nor from the Acoma, as houses recently covered in glory needed not bother with trivial displays. Kevin followed the combat with the trained eye of a soldier, but quickly lost interest. He had seen Tsurani warriors much closer and with much more serious intentions than those boys who sparred upon the sand.

Beyond the sunlit sands, lesser relations and servants were drifting into the boxes that would shortly hold the dominant Lords of the Empire. From the small size of their honor guards, none closer than a distant cousin had yet put in an appearance.

The contest among the young nobles ended, and the last-remaining pair departed, the loser with his sword lowered in defeat, and the winner nodding to the scattered cheers of those few interested spectators.

The air off the sand was hot, and the amphitheater's high walls cut off any breeze. Bored with the proceedings, and still finding the social reasons for Mara's attendance incomprehensible, Kevin bent to ask her if she wished for a cool drink. She had ignored him since they had entered public scrutiny, for reasons of appearance, but as she shook her head in curt refusal of his solicitude, Kevin noticed that his lover seemed uneasy. Protocol forbade him to make inquiry after her well-being. When Mara chose to assume Tsurani impassivity, a part of her became unreachable, though in most things he had come to know her moods as well as his own.

As if his unspoken thoughts brought her worry to a head, the Lady of the Acoma beckoned to Arakasi. "I would enjoy a chilled fruit drink."

The Spy Master bowed and departed; Kevin suppressed a reflexive flash of hurt, and only belatedly realized that his mistress would hardly send Arakasi off just to fetch refreshments. On his way to seek a vendor, the Spy Master would doubtless be contacting informants and gauging the activities of enemies. As Mara turned back to face the events below, she paused the briefest moment to catch Kevin's eye. That one glance let him know she was glad of his presence.

Mara inclined her head casually to Lujan. "Have you noticed? Most of the nobles are hanging back this afternoon."

Caught off guard by this unexpected public conversation, the Acoma Force Commander replied without banter. "Yes, my Lady. There seems an unusual quality to this festival."

Kevin peered at their surroundings and determined there was something odd in the crowd rhythm. But he, with his alien viewpoint, had been slow to sense such strangeness.

Distracting peals of laughter drifted up from lower courses of seats as other doors opened and short figures scurried out into the arena. Kevin's eyebrows arose in surprise as a cluster of diminutive insectoids raced back and forth across the sand, waving their forearms in agitation and clicking small mandibles this way and that. From the opposite end of the sand, a group of warriors hurried to meet them, dwarves by all appearances.

Most wore mock body armor and makeup that ranged from the comic to the grotesque. They waved brightly painted wooden swords, formed up for a loose-ranked charge, and sounded war calls in surprisingly deep voices.

The timbre of those cries was all too fresh in Kevin's memory. "They're desert men!"

At Mara's permissive nod, Lujan said, "Many were our captives, I expect."

Wondering that such a fiercely proud race should submit to a demeaning act of comedy, Kevin marveled further that cho-ja, who were allies, should be included in such honorless display.

"Not cho-ja," Lujan corrected. "Those are chu-ji-la— from the forests north of Silmani—smaller, and without intelligence. They are essentially harmless."

The dwarves and the insectoids met in a clash of shields and chitin. Kevin soon reassured himself that the combat was impotent, with blunt wooden swords unable to pierce the armored insectoids, while tiny mandibles and blunt forearms closed and tussled without any injury to the dwarves.

This farcical spectacle drew laughter and jeers from the crowd until a sudden, electrical sense of presence turned all heads away from the field. Kevin's gaze followed everyone else's, like metal after a lodestone, to the entrance nearest the imperial box. There a short man in a black robe made his way to the area set aside for Great Ones.

Lujan said, "Milamber."

Kevin's eyes narrowed to bring his distant countryman into better focus. "He's a Kingdom man?"

Lujan shrugged. "So the rumors say. He wears a slave's beard, which is enough to mark him as barbarian."

Short by Kingdom standards, and quietly unremarkable, the man took his place next to a very stout magician and another, slender Great One. Struck by a sense of déjà vu, Kevin said, "There's something familiar about him."

Mara turned. "Was he a companion from your homeland?"

"I would have to get closer to see . . . my Lady."

But Mara forbade him the liberty, since he would attract too much attention were he to venture off by himself.

Like all in Mara's immediate service, Strike Leader Kenji knew of the relationship between the barbarian and his Lady, but their unaccustomed familiarity left him feeling uncomfortable. "My Lady, your slave should be reminded that no matter what the Great One was before, he is now in service to the Empire."

Kevin found his tone abrasive, just as Mara's had been, and though he knew her pose was necessary in public, it still rankled. "Well, I wouldn't have much to say to a traitor to his own people, anyway."

A swift glance from Mara stilled his tongue before his brashness could demand the punishment that would become necessary should any passing stranger chance to overhear.

Ghost-quiet, and suddenly there, Arakasi bowed and presented a large cool drink to his mistress. Under his breath he said, "The Shinzawai are conspicuous by their absence." He glanced around. Satisfied to find the crowd still absorbed by the mysterious outworld Great One, the Spy Master added, "There's something highly abnormal afoot, my Lady. I urge vigilance."

Outwardly calm, and hiding the movement of her lips behind the rim of her cup, Mara whispered tensely, "Minwanabi?"

Arakasi fractionally shook his head. "I think not. Desio is outside, still in his liter, and half-drunk with sā wine. I would expect him to be sober if he had a plot under way." Looking uncharacteristically harried, the Spy Master made another reflexive check for listeners; the battle between dwarves and insectoids raged on to a crescendo of noise. Using the din as cover, and hiding the nature of his talk behind gestures of submission, Arakasi went on. "But something momentous is stirring, I suspect to do with the Blue Wheel's return to the Alliance for War. Too many things I hear ring false. Too many contradictions go unquestioned. And more members of the Assembly of Magicians are in attendance than a man will be likely to see in a lifetime. If someone seeks to undermine the Warlord . . ."

"Here!" Mara sat up straight. "Impossible."

But the Spy Master confronted her skepticism. "At the height of his triumph, he could be the must vulnerable." After a significant pause, he added, "Nine times since birth, mistress, I have moved upon no more than a feeling, and each time my life was saved. Be ready to depart at a moment's notice, I beg you. Many innocents could become entangled in a trap big enough to overwhelm Almecho. Others may die because enemies reacted swiftly to take advantage of the moment. I point out, the Shinzawai are not the only ones absent."

He need not name the empty chairs. Most of the Blue Wheel Party sent no representatives, many in the Party for Peace had not brought wives or children, and most of the Kanazawai Lords wore armor rather than robes. If such anomalies were taken as pieces of one related issue, a widespread threat might be real. Squads of white-armored warriors were stationed at strategic points and entrances, many more than needed for crowd control should an unfortunate event on the arena floor turn the mob's mood from celebration to riot; more boxes than the imperial one were being watched.

Mara touched Arakasi's wrist in agreement; she would take his caution to heart. The Minwanabi could easily have agents planted nearby, awaiting any excuse to strike. Lujan's eyes began to inventory the location and number of soldiers in the immediate area. Whether events occurred by design or accident made no difference to him, the intrigues of politics could surface just as well in chance opportunity. Should an enemy die of injuries in a brawl, who could cast blame? Such was fate. Such might be the thinking of many of the nobles within striking range should the opportunity only present itself in the heat of a riot.

Arakasi's speculation was suspended as a rush of nobles into boxes signaled the imminent arrival of the imperial party. Nearest to the white-draped dais, a man in ceremonial robes of black and orange entered, a flock of warriors and servants clustered at his heels. His stout bearing carried a sureness of step that hinted at muscle beneath his fat.

"Minwanabi," Arakasi identified with a startling note of venom.

Eager to put a form to the man who was the archfiend in the drama that involved his beloved Mara, Kevin saw only a stout young man flushed by the heat, who looked rather petulant.

Further study was cut short by trumpets and drums that signaled the approach of the imperial party. Conversation hushed throughout the stadium. Handlers raced onto the arena sand and chased off the dwarves and insectoids. Across the cleared field, groundkeepers wearing loincloths hurried out with rakes and drags to smooth the ground in preparation for the coming games.

Trumpets blasted again, much closer, and the first ranks of Imperial Guardsmen marched in. They wore armor of pure white and carried the instruments that sounded the fanfare. These were fashioned from the horns of some immense beast, curling around their shoulders to end in bell-like flares above their heads. Drummers in the next rank came on beating a steady tattoo. The band assumed position in front of the imperial box, and the Warlord's honor guard of two dozen entered after them. Each warrior's accoutrements and helm were lacquered in shiny white, marking them for an elite cadre known as the Imperial Whites.

Sunlight splintered in reflections off gold blazons and trim, which drew a murmur of amazement from the commoners seated highest in the amphitheater. By Tsurani standards, the metal worn by each warrior was costly enough to finance Acoma expenses for an entire year.

The guards took position and the crowds stilled. Into an avid silence a senior herald shouted in a voice that carried to the most distant tier of seats, "Almecho, Warlord!"

The crowd surged to its feet, crying out welcome for the mightiest warrior in the Empire.

Quiet in her place, and sipping at her fruit drink, Mara watched but did not cheer as the Warlord made his entry.

Wide bands of gold adorned the neck and armholes of his breastplate; additional goldwork patterned his helm, which was surmounted by a crimson plume. Behind Almecho trailed two black-robed magicians, named the "Warlord's pets" by the masses. Kevin had heard how, in the years before his capture, one of those distant Great Ones had cast the spell that proved Mara's claim of treachery by the Minwanabi, an action that compelled Desio's predecessor to ritual suicide to expiate the shame to his family.

Then, unexpectedly, the herald announced a second presence. "Ichindar! Ninety-one times Emperor!"

The ovation became a deafening roar. The young Light of Heaven made his entrance. Even Lady Mara threw restraint to the winds. She cheered as loudly as any commoner, her face alight with admiration and awe: this was a man held in near-religious devotion by his nation.

The Light of Heaven made his unprecedented appearance in armor covered entirely in gold. He seemed no more than three years over twenty. His expression could not be interpreted over distance, but his bearing was erect and confident, and red-brown hair flowed from under his high gilt helm, to lie in trimmed curls on his shoulders.

Behind the Emperor filed twenty priests, from each of the major temples. As the Light of Heaven made his way to stand beside the Warlord, the crowd thundered. The cheering seemed inexhaustible.

Through the unnerving din, Kevin shouted to Lujan, "Why is everyone so carried away?"

Since decorum had been totally forsaken, Lujan freely called back, "The Light of Heaven is our spiritual guardian, who through prayer and exemplary living intercedes on our behalf to the gods. He *is* Tsuranuanni!"

Never in living memory had an Emperor blessed his nation by coming among the people. That Ichindar chose to do so now was inspirational, a cause for unrestrained joy. Yet, alone in a crowd of thousands, Arakasi was not cheering. He went through all the motions, but Kevin saw that he scanned the surrounding throng for any hint of danger to his mistress. With Tsurani impassivity abandoned to wild pandemonium, this moment offered the perfect opportunity for an enemy to slip close without notice. Kevin edged closer to Mara's back, prepared to leap to her defense if need be.

The tumultuous ovation rolled on with no sign of waning. At length the Emperor took his seat, and the Warlord raised outstretched arms. His demand took several minutes to be noticed. When the crowd reluctantly quieted, Almecho shouted, "The gods smile upon Tsuranuanni! I bring news of a great victory over the otherworld barbarians! We have crushed their greatest army, and our warriors celebrate! Soon all the lands called the Kingdom will be laid at the Light of Heaven's feet." The Warlord ended with a deferential bow to the Light of Heaven, and the masses roared out in approval.

Kevin stood as if stunned. The pit of his stomach felt like ice. Then, aware through his shock and the howl of the crowd that Arakasi studied him intently, the Midkemian glared back. "Your Warlord means Brucal and Borric's forces were routed, the Armies of the West." Desperate to bridle an anger that could only endanger his life, Kevin qualified. "My own home lies in peril, for now the way lies open for Tsuranuanni to march on Zūn!"

Arakasi looked away first; and Kevin remembered: the Spy Master had lost a master and home to the Minwanabi before he swore service to the Acoma. Then Mara's fingers stole into Kevin's hand and returned a squeeze of understanding. The Midkemian battled a rush of emotion as his conflicts of loyalty, love, and upbringing tore him a thousand different ways. Fate had taken him from his family and forced him away to a distant world. He had chosen life and love as a man may, rather than miserable captivity; but the cost was only now becoming apparent: who was he— Kevin of Zūn or Kevin of the Acoma?

Before the imperial box, the Warlord held up his hands. As the noise subsided, he shouted, "To the glory of Tsuranuanni and as a sign of our devotion to the Light of Heaven, we dedicate these games to his honor!"

The cheering swelled afresh, grating on ears and nerves. Somehow Kevin endured it. Though Lujan and Arakasi might tolerate a breach of manners, any Tsurani warriors who guarded neighboring boxes would cut him down and ask questions later should they suspect him of impudence toward a Lady of Mara's rank.

Numbly Kevin watched the doors open at the arena's far end. Roughly a hundred men shambled onto the sunlit sand. Naked but for loincloths, they were of all ages and states of health; some stood with weapons and shields that were familiar to them, but they were few. Most seemed confused by their circumstances, their grip on their swords uncertain.

"These are not fighters," Kevin observed, a sting to his tone despite his best efforts.

Arakasi quieted him with explanation. "This is a clemency spectacle. All are condemned men. They will fight, and the one who lives at the end will go free."

Trumpets sounded and the slaughter commenced. Before his capture, while soldiering for his father, he had seen many men killed. This was not warfare, not even a savagely matched contest. What took place upon the sands of Kentosani's arena was butchery. The handful of trained men moved like cats through mice trapped in a granary, killing at will. Finally fewer than a dozen men remained standing, and these more fairly matched. Kevin had lost his stomach for watching; he stared blankly at the spectators, but found no relief from his disgust. The Tsurani seemed to enjoy the blood, not the sport. They cheered each painful death and compared the agonies of one disemboweled man with those of another. Wagers were made on how long the wretch who tried to stuff his spilled entrails back into his abdomen would last, and how many screams he would utter before he died. No one seemed interested in the skill of the handful of fighters still living.

Kevin felt his gorge rise and swallowed hard. He controlled his loathing by force until the debacle ended, a man with a sword and knife taking the last of the condemned with a thrust under the shield. From the imperial box the vaunted Tsurani Emperor observed the proceedings impassively, while the Warlord at his side murmured to an adviser as if carnage were a daily event.

Burning now, with a fury fueled by outrage, Kevin looked to see how the Great One who had once been a Kingdom man was handling this atrocity. Even at this distance, Milamber's countenance appeared stony; but to Kevin's dismay, the fat magician by his side had broken off his discussion and appeared to be studying the Acoma box.

Kevin averted his gaze in sudden fear. Could a Great One hear thoughts? He bent without considering to ask Mara, but stopped, recalled to his place by the sight of her. The Lady of the Acoma endured the bloodletting with proper Tsurani restraint, her only sign of discomfort a slight stiffness in her shoulders. The former son of Zūn felt his stomach burn. He knew Mara. Intimate with her throughout five years, he knew she could perceive the difference between the slaughter below and the battle campaign experienced in the desert. Yet she never so much as flinched when the victor swaggered among the fallen bodies, his gory weapon brandished aloft.

Kevin checked surreptitiously to see whether the Great One was still watching; this time, he could see plainly that the bearded one, Milamber, bore an expression of distaste; even his eyes seemed ablaze. Kevin was not the only one to notice Milamber's disgust. Nobles in nearby boxes whispered and glanced toward the magician, and a few looked openly apprehensive.

Arakasi saw the exchange. To Kevin he whispered. "This doesn't bode well. Great Ones may act on a whim, and not even the Light of Heaven dares gainsay their will. If this former countryman of yours shares your distaste for killing, there could be a scene."

In sunlight, on hot sand, the victor finished his strutting. Slaves came and cleared away the corpses, while rakers smoothed over the rumpled, blood-soaked ground. Trumpets sounded the next round of the Imperial Games, while Kevin wished silently for a drink to wet his dry mouth.

A band of men wearing loincloths entered the stadium, taller and fairer than most Tsurani. Kevin instantly recognized countrymen from his homeworld. Their shoulders gleamed with oil and they carried an assortment of ropes, hooks, weighted nets, spears, and long knives. The festival atmosphere did not disorient them, nor did they give the crowds of showy nobles more than a desultory glance. Instead they crouched in awareness that trouble approached, from any of a dozen directions. Kevin had shared such uncertainty, upon patrol and standing the night watch on the edge of the no-man's-land where the enemy might strike at any moment.

But these men had not long to wait for action. A pair of large doors rumbled open at the far end of the arena, and a creature out of nightmare shambled out.

All fangs and lethal claws, it stood the size of an elephant, but moved cat-fast on its six legs. At the sight of it, even Mara lost her composure and exclaimed, "A harulth!"

The Kelewanese predator blinked and snarled at the sudden blaze of sunlight. Scales armored its hide, scattering chilly highlights across its neck as it quested to and fro, sniffing the air. The crowd sat charged with expectation. Then the beast spotted its foe: the tiny men who stood exposed on that cruel vista of sand. The harulth did not paw warning, as a bull or a needra might, but lowered its head in belligerence and instantly sprang to the charge.

It moved with terrible swiftness.

The warriors scattered, not in panic, but in a desperate attempt to confuse. The beast made no sound, but its fury was apparent as it focused upon one unfortunate fellow and gave chase. The end came in a flash of claws and a spinning stop that ground the human underfoot. Unmindful of sand or weapons, the harulth devoured the remains in two bites.

Saddened, revolted, and frozen in sympathy for his countrymen, Kevin could not look away. While the harulth dispatched its meal, the survivors regrouped behind the animal and quickly deployed their nets. Faster than Kevin could imagine possible, the creature spun and charged. The men stood their ground until the last instant, then threw the nets as they scattered. The hooks grappled and caught in thick hide and the creature was entangled.

Kevin watched in admiration and fear as spearmen rushed in to strike. The weapons they had been issued were heavy, but the creature's scales were very tough. It took all of a man's strength just to penetrate, and the wounds were like stings to the monster. Its vitals stayed totally unharmed. The men saw the futility of further attack. Two of them conferred briefly, then ran to the rear, where the creature's huge tail thrashed and flailed up sand. Kevin's breath stopped as, against all rational thought, his countrymen leaped upon the harulth and climbed in an attempt to drive their long knives into the monster's spine. The sheer bravery of the act brought tears to his Midkemian eyes.

Even Lujan was impressed. "These men show courage."

Kevin answered in bitter pride, "My countrymen know how to look death in the eye."

The harulth felt the prick at its back. It heaved and snapped, and nets unraveled, whirled away like torn string. The tail hammered down into sand, and the blow shook one man off. He sailed through the air and crashed, too stunned

to run. The harulth snapped him in half. The remaining man
clung grimly. To jump down was to be trampled; to stay, an
act of sheer folly. The scales made treacherous handholds,
and the harulth was maddened to fury. It spun and snapped
and slashed, missing its mark by scant inches; for the man
had resumed his climb.

The crowds murmured their appreciation. Higher the
man climbed, though tossed on his perch like a monkey on a
storm-shaken branch. He reached the juncture above the
stamping hind legs and drove his blade to the hilt into the
creature's back.

The hindmost pair of legs violently collapsed, all but
throwing the man. He slipped, clawed a hold, and clung as
the harulth shuddered and writhed in rage and pain. It
whipped its neck, trying to bite at its tormentor; but its thick
body lacked the suppleness to bend enough to snatch its tiny
foe.

The man flexed a blood-spattered wrist and jerked his
blade. The weapon cleared bone and hide with difficulty. The
harulth bellowed and slashed, and the drag of useless limbs
gouged up furrows in the sand. The man hung on, inching
torturously forward to the next joint of the spine. Again he
drove his blade between the knobs of vertebrae and successfully severed the spine. The middle segment of legs went
limp.

Quickly the men on the ground raced in to blind and
distract the paralyzed monster until their companion could
jump clear. Once he reached the sand safely, they all gave the
stricken predator a wide berth until its struggles slowed, and
it perished.

The crowd yelled their approval, and Lujan made free
with admiration. As if he momentarily forgot that he addressed a slave, he said, "No harulth has been felled by warriors without five times more losses. Your countrymen do
themselves honor."

Kevin wept unabashedly. Though all of these men were
strangers to him, he felt he knew each one in his heart. He
understood that they took no pleasure or pride from what
they had achieved; what the Tsurani counted pride was to
these men merely survival.

Tears also streamed down the cheeks of Kevin's countrymen. Exhausted, alone, and aware they might never see their

home again, the Midkemians left the arena, while needra teams were rushed in to haul away the harulth's carcass, and rakers and slaves with drags scraped the marks of conflict from the sand.

Abruptly aware that he had drawn Mara's scrutiny, Kevin made an effort to mend his glaring disregard for proper behavior. Though she must show no flicker of sympathy in her pose as Ruling Lady, she handed her empty drink cup to Arakasi and exchanged a surreptitious whisper. "Have we remained long enough to satisfy the needs of our status in the council?"

Arakasi glanced pointedly at Kevin, warning the barbarian not to show reaction to the possibility that the Lady might not care for blood sports. "I wish I could say yes, my Lady, but if you were to leave now, before your enemies move to depart . . ."

Mara returned a slight nod and faced dutifully forward. And the fact that she must endure strictly for the sake of appearances sparked a wild anger in Kevin. Under his breath, in reckless reaction, he hissed, "I will never understand your people and your game—"

The trumpets drowned out his protest. The grounds crew left the arena at a run, as yet another door boomed open. A dozen fighting men in outlandish battle harnesses strutted onto the sand. Each wore leather wristbands set with studs, and headdresses of varicolored plumes. They advanced in total disregard of the audience for whom they were imported to amuse, and halted finally at the arena center, their swords and shields held in relaxed confidence.

Kevin had heard of the proud mountain men who inhabited the far eastern highlands. Alone among the people to defeat the Empire, they had forced a truce between nations some years before the Tsurani invasion of Midkemia.

The trumpets blew again and the herald cried an introduction. "As these soldiers of the Thuril Confederation have violated the treaty between their own nations and the Empire, by making war upon the soldiers of the Emperor, they have been cast out by their own people, who have named them outlaws and bound them over for punishment. They will fight the captives from the world of Midkemia. All will strive until one is left standing."

Trumpets called for the event to begin. As the large doors

at the end of the arena swung ponderously open, Lujan volunteered an observation. "What is the game director thinking of? Thuril will not fight one another if they defeat the Midkemians. They'll die cursing the Emperor first."

"My Lady, be ready to leave quickly," Arakasi broke in. "If the fight is a disappointment, the mob will likely turn ugly. . . ."

Since Tsurani custom seated commoners on the levels above the nobility, in the event of violence the higher classes of the Empire would need to fight their way up through a riot to reach the available exits. Kevin wondered at the much vaunted Tsurani discipline, but as if sensing his thought, Arakasi contradicted.

"These games sometimes awaken a bloodlust in the common folk. There have been riots before, and nobles have died in them."

The seemingly endless contradictions of these people baffled Kevin only briefly, for that moment a dozen Midkemians marched from the opened archway opposite the Warlord's dais. Their original metal armor was far too costly an extravagance to be used for arena entertainment; in place of good chain mail and armored helms and shields, these captives wore garishly painted facsimiles fashioned of Tsurani materials. One shield bore the wolf's head of LaMut, and another, in too bright, splashy colors, the horse blazon of Zūn.

Kevin bit his lip to keep from voicing his anguish. He could not help his countrymen! He would only get himself uselessly killed and leave his beloved Lady an inheritance of shame. But the outrage and the pain he felt would never answer to logic. Smoldering with pent-up emotions, Kevin closed his eyes and lowered his head. These Imperial Games were a barbarity, and he was unwilling to watch good men wasted for the perverse sake of a spectacle.

But instead of the clash of combat, a murmuring arose from the crowd. Kevin risked a look. The warriors of Thuril and Midkemia were not fighting but speaking. Catcalls and whistles drifted down from the highest rim of the stadium as the two combatants faced one another with something less than a bellicose posture. Now one of the Thuril pointed at the crowd. While his words were too distant to hear, his expression reflected contempt.

One of the Midkemians stepped forward and a Thuril

came on guard, but a shout from his companion caused him to retreat a step. The Midkemian removed his leather helm and glared about the arena. Then, unthinkably insolent, he cast both armor and sword upon the sand. His shield followed, the thump of its impact clearly audible in the absolute silence. He spoke something to his companions and folded his arms.

His example was shortly followed by the others in the arena. Swords, helms, and shields tumbled from loosened fingers, until in a moment both Midkemians and Thuril confronted one another, disarmed.

More catcalls came from the commoners, but as yet the higher classes seemed more amused than offended by this odd behavior. Danger did not seem imminent.

Until Arakasi tapped Kevin lightly and quietly on the arm. "Take this," he whispered.

A knife haft slipped into the barbarian's palm. He all but flinched in astonishment before his fingers closed. For a slave to carry arms meant a death sentence, and honorless was the freeman who dared to flaunt this law. That the Spy Master did so indicated a circumstance of deadly peril. To Mara, Arakasi murmured, "Lady, I will fetch your guards and litter and have them brought as close to the arena entrance as the Imperial Guards will permit. Then I will run back to your town house and muster your remaining soldiers. Come away and meet us in the streets, as you can. I have . . . that feeling I spoke of earlier. I fear the worst from this."

Mara gave no visible sign that she had heard, but Lujan set his hand upon his sword hilt, and Kenji and the other two warriors came alert. Arakasi slipped quietly away.

Kevin held the blade against his forearm, eyes glued to the strange tableau, while his peripheral senses took stock of the advisers who conferred with masters and mistresses in the adjacent boxes.

Within the Imperial box, the Warlord surged to his feet. The resounding catcalls and shouts redoubled. Mottled scarlet with rage, he shouted, "Let the fighting begin!"

When the fighters on the sand defiantly held their ground, burly, leather-clad handlers rushed in to end their recalcitrance. They uncoiled needra-hide whips and began lashing the warriors.

The crowd began to shout their impatience. Whistles and

obscenities blended into a note ominously rising, as even the wellborn nobles objected to watching motionless men being whipped. Suddenly one of the Thuril grabbed a handler, jerked the man off balance, and caught the trailing lash. He whipped the leather around his enemy's neck and began strangling the life from him. The other handlers turned upon the renegade and flailed at him viciously. Their blows drove him to his knees, but his determination did not relent. He twisted the leather tighter and tighter, while his victim puffed and turned purple, and finally died.

In the next stunned instant, before any could react, the Thuril soldiers recovered their dropped weapons and surged to the attack. The Midkemians joined them, and handlers died, their whips cut into pieces and spattered red with their blood.

An ugly mutter raced through the upper concourses. Kevin glanced toward the magicians to see if they might intervene, but it seemed they had troubles of their own. The bearded one called Milamber was standing, and though the Black Robes on either side entreated him to return to his seat, the magician would hear no pleas. Rage burned in his eyes, hot enough to be felt across distance, and Kevin knew fear.

He glanced back to Mara, but a slight signal from Lujan indicated they must wait, even yet, to depart. Arakasi must have time to fetch the litter and guard and bring them to the outside stair. To be caught without an escort in the street was far too great a risk.

Suddenly a Black Robe at the Warlord's side rose and swept his hand in an arc. A shudder ran down Kevin's spine and the hair prickled at his nape. Magic! And done with no more effort than a wave of one hand; dumbstruck, the Midkemian saw the rebels on the sand buckle at the knees and fall limp.

The Warlord's shout echoed over their helpless, prostrate forms. "Now go bind them, build a platform, and hang them for all to see."

The crowd went still as a storm front. Lujan murmured, "Be ready!"

Kenji and the warriors shifted forward in their seats. Kevin put a hand upon Mara's shoulder. Poised, and apparently at ease throughout the entire exchange, the Lady was hardly immune to the sense of danger. Through touch, the man who loved her could feel that she trembled. He ached to reassure her, but the tension in the arena continued threateningly to build.

Young officers in the first rank of seats cried out in rage at the Warlord's order. Vociferously they raised objection and demanded the prisoners below be permitted a warrior's death. Many had been Patrol Leaders in the forefront of the war against the Midkemians or the Thuril. Enemies or aliens, the captives on the sand had proven their mettle in battle; to hang them like soulless slaves would bring shame to all the Empire.

Neither were the Great Ones remaining passive. Milamber exchanged what appeared to be heated words with the another Black Robe, who strove unsuccessfully to placate him. At length Milamber shouldered past, still speaking; the stout one rose to hurry after, too late. The Great One who had once been Midkemian was poised midway up the steps that separated the Black Robes from the imperial box.

On the sands of the arena, chaos reigned. Carpenters rushed in dragging tools and lengths of lumber, while warriors in Almecho's white armor escorted handlers to gather up and bind the stunned warriors.

Warned by some nameless instinct, Kevin knew an instant of apprehension. The vast crowd in the amphitheater seemed locked in the grip of the moment, mesmerized by fascination. Catcalls and shouts wavered off into silence, and all eyes watched the dark-robed figure next to the Warlord's box.

Milamber raised his arm. Blue flames slashed the air, scintillating even in full sunlight, and a bolt hurled downward and exploded amid the Warlord's guards. Living men were tossed in all directions, scattered like leaves before wind. Carpenters and craftsmen lost their footing, and the boards and tools brought for scaffolding were whirled away like straw. Nobles in the lower seats were hammered into their chairbacks by the fury of the detonation, and a gust clapped in backlash over the rising tiers of seats. Milamber's hand made a striking motion, and his voice cut through the stunned silence left in the aftermath of the explosion. "No more!"

The fat magician abruptly gave up pursuit. As fast as stout legs could carry him, he rushed into the imperial box, his thin companion right behind him. The two Great Ones conferred briefly with the Light of Heaven, who arose from his chair. The next instant, with no warning, both Great Ones and Emperor vanished.

Too shaken to examine his amazement, Kevin caught Mara's arm. "Right. That tears it." Unceremoniously he raised her from her chair. "If His Majesty sees fit to depart, we're leaving, too."

Lujan raised no objection, but drew his sword and leaped over the back of his bench. At his orders, Strike Leader Kenji and both other warriors formed a rear guard, while the Acoma Force Commander forged ahead to keep up with Kevin and Mara. Down the narrow aisle between boxes, the small party retreated in what approached unmannerly haste. Milamber's actions held most other spectators riveted, and those in the rows above Mara's line of flight called down irritable comments as the passage of the Lady and her escort momentarily interrupted their view.

Tensions built to a fever pitch as the Warlord's voice rang out in unmitigated fury. "Who dares this?"

Milamber shouted answer. "I dare this! This cannot be, will not be!" But the rest of his words went unheeded by Acoma warriors as running footsteps approached their party from behind. By now at the juncture of the aisle and the stair to the upper levels, Kevin spun around. He saw two strange soldiers in maroon armor racing to overtake the Acoma escort.

Mara's rear-guard warriors halted and immediately drew their swords. Left with only Kenji for protection, Kevin shouted warning. "Lujan!"

The Force Commander looked back. He took in the threat and identified the armor at a glance. "Sajaio! They serve the Minwanabi!" Still moving, he signaled to the two warriors who prepared to stand interference: "Keep station at your Lady's back." To Kevin he added, "We could take them. But first we get Mara to safety."

For the commotion in the arena showed no sign of abating. The Warlord screamed at the Magician, "By what right do you do this thing?"

Milamber's reply seemed to scourge the very air with his fury. "By my right to do as I see fit!"

Aware of little else beyond a sense of impending disaster,

Kevin hurried Mara urgently forward. She tackled the stone stair gamely, despite the pegged soles of her sandals, which unreliably caught on the treads and threatened to trip her up. Through whitened lips she gasped, "All we know is in shambles. Chaos is upon us."

Other figures stirred in the cross aisles; the guards of the Sajaio hesitated in their pursuit of the Acoma. They conferred, and one doubled back. The other diligently resumed chase.

Now other retinues crowded the concourse stair, nobles and ladies and warriors withdrawing before the charged air of threat that lapped across the amphitheater like the swelling quiet before cataclysm.

Lujan noted Kevin's shout, that one Sajaio warrior had broken away, presumably with instruction to fetch reinforcements. The Force Commander never missed stride. "Only a fool would start a fight now. Or haven't you been listening?"

Shouts from the imperial box ended with, "My words are as law! Go!"

Mara started in fright and caught her sole on a cracked edge of paving. Kevin snatched her back from a fall, all but scooping her slight weight into his arms to keep her upright. Out of the corner of his eye he saw Milamber directing white-clad Imperial Guards to free the prisoners who still lay in unconscious heaps on the sand.

The Warlord gave way to uncontained outrage. "You break the law! No one may free a slave!"

Milamber's wrath towered and his voice sharpened to steel. "I can! I am outside the law."

Kevin felt a surge of wild hope as he crested the last rise to the concourse. The archway that led through to the street lay barely a dozen strides ahead. "Is that true?" he gasped to Mara. "Can Milamber free a slave?"

Mara returned a stark look of fear. "He can do anything. He is a Great One."

An overwhelming sense of imminent upheaval stirred the beginnings of panic. Spectators started erupting out of their seats and shoving onto the concourses. But their flight began too late.

One of the Warlord's Great Ones arose to challenge Milamber. Aware of mass fear, and the crowd like a rising wave behind him, Kevin pushed Mara toward the exit. Lujan raised his sword to stem the rush, while his warriors shouted, "Acoma!"

But not all in the mob fled the magic. Shouts sounded to the rear, and five warriors in maroon armor raced to engage Kenji and the two soldiers. The Acoma Strike Leader never hesitated. Rather than be attacked in full flight, he spun back with a cry of "Acoma!" and charged the Sajaio attackers.

The warriors rushed with him.

Kevin and Mara raced ahead, with only their Force Commander left in reserve to defend them.

Sajaio and Acoma met between stairs. The clash of their weapons passed unnoticed amid the vast upswelling of sound —the cries of awed spectators and the calls of warriors and guards who sprang to their masters' protection. Other folk cried out in amazement at the interplay between Milamber and the Warlord's pets that developed in the imperial box.

Then above such cries came screams of pain and terror.

Poised on the brink of the stair, Kevin risked a glance back. From the area beside the magicians' box, a sizzling discharge of energy cracked out. Milamber's presence disappeared in a searing dazzle; golden light entangled with blue in a fearful, blinding display. In the unearthly play of shadows and light, the faces of the crowd were etched sharply. Each expression held a reasonless need to flee. People pushed, shoved, jostled, and stumbled in a frenzy to climb the stair. The combat initiated by the Sajaio soldiers was overwhelmed, swept away by the roiling thousands who fled the magicians' wrath.

Kevin gripped Mara tightly. "Run!" Barely ahead of the stampeding masses of spectators, he plunged with her down the stair. In the flickering, incandescent flash of sorcery, the plume on Lujan's helm shone an unearthly green. His repeated cry of "Acoma!" vanished into the angry shouts and terrified cries from behind.

The stair plunged endlessly down. Mara ran and stumbled on her clumsy pegged sandals. Scared beyond propriety by the danger, Kevin bent and caught her in his arms. "Kick your shoes off!"

Mara said something. Words could not be distinguished over the noise.

"I don't care about the emeralds! Kick them off!" Kevin commanded.

Her weight made him awkward on the stair. Despite his best efforts to run, they were falling behind Lujan, and now Kevin felt himself battered by pushing hands and buffeted by fleeing bodies.

Mara shed her sandals. In desperation, Kevin set her down, his hand like a vise on her arm. He towed her relentlessly against the jostle and pull of the mob.

Someone fell to his left. In an instant a thousand remorseless feet stamped over the hapless body. The victim never screamed. The crushing weight of the mob rolled over him, pressing air from his lungs and bruising him into a pulp. A frightened, witless commoner jammed hard against Kevin's linked arm, tearing at his hold upon Mara. By reflex he drew Arakasi's knife.

His Lady's wrist slipped through his grasp; now he held only her fingers. Over the shoulder of the man who still shoved, Kevin glimpsed her expression of sheer terror before he lost sight of her completely.

His hand, joined to hers, all but loosened; he wept as he drove the knife through the back of the person who thrust into them.

The weight fell away, and he jerked in merciless desperation upon the one bit of Mara he still held. She reeled free of a wedge of panicked craftsmen and tumbled into his arms.

"Acoma!" The shout sounded near; Kevin stared out over the heads of the mob and blessed his Midkemian stature. At once he spotted a pair of soldiers in green armor hammering a path through the rush.

"Here!" he screamed. "Here!" He waved his hand, forgetful that he held a bloodied blade. "I have Mara!"

The warriors changed course toward him, their beacon his unmistakable red-gold head.

Suddenly Lujan was with him. "Put that away!" he screamed, pointing to the knife. He fell in before the barbarian and used his bracers like clubs to fend off the worst of the crush.

Kevin hid the knife. He pressed on, burdened with a trembling Mara, who yet bravely struggled to stand. "No!" he shouted in her ear. "You're too small, and barefoot, also. Let me carry you."

The stairs fell away underfoot. Kevin tripped, and recovered, held upright by the shove of the crowd. They had reached the concourse between the outer levels. Vaguely the Midkemian realized that Lujan directed their path with a purpose: by the stadium walls, surrounded by a wedge of beleaguered warriors, Mara's litter showed over running heads, a flutter of green pennons against chaos.

A thunderclap pealed from the heavens. A gust struck down like a blow, as the detonation knocked many of those fleeing to the ground.

Kevin lurched forward, slammed into Lujan, and felt the warrior brace to preserve balance. The effort failed. Both men crumpled to their knees. Ears ringing, Kevin shouldered Mara's weight. He shoved back to his feet, unmindful of scraped knees, and barged headlong toward the litter. The crowd soon recovered, closing in relentless panic, until his elbow and side were jammed painfully into the ridges of Lujan's armor. Kevin held ground grimly, and nearly tripped again as his feet entangled in an obstruction that felt like a rag.

A warm rag: another unfortunate who had been trampled.

A victim who might yet be Mara, if he were to lose her in the chaos. Fighting a sickness in his stomach, Kevin gripped her silk gown until the force left his knuckles bone-white.

That instant, a fountain of energies erupted from the arena and sprayed across sky and clouds. The crowd wailed in consternation, heads turned heavenward to gawk. Driven by morbid fascination, some brash folk tried to stem the flow of mass flight for a better view of the display.

Kevin and Lujan used the respite to reach the wall, where a barrier of warriors in green closed around them, an eddy of calm in the turbulence. As the Midkemian set down his shaking mistress, a voice pealed out over chaos. "That you have lived as you have lived for centuries is no license for this cruelty. All here are now judged, and all are found wanting."

The magician: Milamber. Kevin knew a savage surge of pride, that a man from the Kingdom had dared to place righteous compassion before decadence.

The tone of the mob changed subtly. Driven by curiosity, and also by the beginnings of affront, a few people shouted in amazement. Movement swirled through the masses as more and more bystanders slowed their flight and shoved to reenter the arena.

"They are fools that would linger here," Lujan shouted. "The mistress must be gotten safely home."

Kevin reached out to steady Mara, saw blood on his hand, and belatedly remembered the knife. He made to surrender the weapon, but Lujan sharply shook his head. "I didn't see you take that, and my eyes are blind if you use it in my Lady's protection."

Soldiers fell into a tight cordon, with Mara, Kevin, and a half-dozen hapless bearers clustered in a knot at the center. Out of habit, the slaves moved to their places by the litter poles.

Then the voice of the magician echoed with unnatural force over the stadium. "You who would take pleasure from the death and dishonor of others, see then how well you face destruction!"

Kevin shouted. "To hell with the litter! Just run!"

Still greatly shaken by the commotion, Mara found her voice and shouted, "Yes, we must run!"

At Lujan's order, the cumbersome litter was abandoned. The guards regrouped their formation on the fly, and the dash for safety began afresh.

A wind slapped outward from the arena, raising new screams, and setting the plumes of the officers streaming. Kevin felt his skin raise up into gooseflesh, and he marveled at a sensation nearly forgotten since leaving home: cold. On Kelewan, no natural gust could carry such a touch of ice.

As if in response, Milamber's voice cried, "Tremble and despair, for I am Power!"

A keening wailed upon the air as the Acoma cordon began their rush down the lower stairway. The blustery gust increased as Milamber shouted, "Wind!"

The gale swelled to a howl in response. A stink of death rode the gust and set Kevin and the staunchest warriors choking. They pressed on in their descent, forcing pained lungs to inhale. Mara's face drained of color, but she kept pace with her retinue, down the steep stairs.

Their path was maddeningly crooked. Forced to skirt others who had doubled over with nausea from the foul odor, Lujan called to his soldiers to keep step. Some who succumbed to sickness became trampled, while others were jostled and kicked by the flood of retreating citizens.

A low moan shivered the pavement. Created by nothing

of this world, the sound tormented the ears with subsonics. The warriors increased pace, and Kevin caught Mara's wrist to aid her down the last of the stairs. Ominously, the shadows deepened; the atmosphere darkened, and the sun vanished from view. Clouds gathered above the stadium and swirled in a monstrous vortex.

That Milamber stood at its center Kevin never doubted. He flung off fear with a laugh. "He's going to make one hell of a show!"

Breathlessly jogging at his side, Mara shot him a confused look. Belatedly, Kevin realized he had slipped into the King's speech. He repeated his remark in Tsurani.

She forced a brave smile.

They stumbled to the base of the stairs. Lujan halted as more guardsmen joined ranks, reinforcing the square of protection around their mistress. The outer ranks linked arms, and they resumed course down the avenue as the magician behind them cried, "Rain!"

The resonance of the voice had damped slightly. Kevin sucked air into burning lungs and hoped the change meant their progress had distanced them from the vortex of spells and trauma Milamber called in judgment upon the crowd. The heavens opened, and icy drops slashed the air. The first fall sheeted into a downpour, soaking all in the street to the skin. The last light vanished. Eyes squinting against the storm of elements, Kevin ran. He kept hold of Mara's wrist, though her skin became slippery, and her steps dragged against the cling of sodden formal robes. The rattle of rainfall against cobbles and armor blended with the slap of fleeing feet. The cries of the crowd seemed dimmer, whipped to misery and despair.

"Keep going," Kevin exhorted to Mara.

A few steps more, and he sensed the rain lessening with each stride.

The Acoma retinue reached the street that bordered the arena, and the distant voice of Milamber cried, "Fire!"

A collective peal of terror arose from inside the stadium. Mara looked back in horror, afraid for the unfortunates who were still trapped. Kevin turned to hurry her on and, through the pattering fall of thinning droplets, saw a thing of terrifying, alien beauty. A display of flames played through clouds that even yet splashed icy wetness upon the earth.

Jagged bolts of lighting rent the sky. A burning sting grazed Kevin's cheek as a rain of pure fire began to fall.

Mara screamed. Flame blossomed in the silks that covered her head, and the wet did not stop them igniting. Soldiers slapped at the flames with their gauntlets, and the odor of seared hide and lacquer grew choking on the smoke-filled air. They ran. Falling fires spattered sparks across the pavement, and, in fear for their lives, they ran harder.

Lujan pointed. "There!" A hundred yards away, across a streaming expanse of puddles and flame, sunlight shone down untroubled.

Kevin dragged Mara into a sprint, and still those last hundred yards stretched like miles. And then they were safe in the sunlight. The soldiers slowed to catch their breath at stern orders from Lujan. Winded men made poor fighters, and the streets were a seething mass of frightened people and soldiers battle-ready to defend their Lords. Kevin seized the respite to look back. The madness above the arena had not stopped. Fires splashed down in lurid streaks, and the cries of the dying and the injured mingled into one vast wail.

The streets were packed with suffering, blazing scarecrows that danced and flapped in an agony of burning. Singed survivors raced into safety and collided with craftsmen and slaves who had paused about their business to gape. Many had fallen prostrate out of fear, while others made protective signs against the gods' displeasure; the most simple just stood in mute astonishment.

A faint word carried over the confusion. Kevin couldn't make out the meaning, but at a wave from Lujan he gently urged Mara forward. "Do your feet hurt? We'd better keep moving. I think we're still a little close to the action."

Mara blinked, white-faced with exhaustion. Numbly she said, "The matter of shoes must wait. To the town house."

Lujan sent one soldier ahead to bring more warriors from the garrison to guard the Lady in her walk across town. Skillful in his guidance, the Force Commander kept to quiet streets; he avoided the temple precinct, where worshippers and priests seethed around offering tables, chanting and singing a rush of placating prayers. Runners hastened on unknown errands, and beggars roved districts that were not in their usual province. Wary of attack, the soldiers kept together; Kevin kept a grip on Arakasi's knife. No ambush materialized, but an odd buzzing sensation rippled through the ground underfoot.

The vibration swelled to a deep-throated rumbling, and Kevin knew a flash of fear. "Earthquake!" he shouted. "Into that doorway! Now!"

Lujan and his warriors wheeled smartly. They forced aside a trio of commoners who sheltered under the arch of an alehouse door. Made of solid stone, the portal had once supported two wooden panels, torn down forgotten years before.

The warriors passed Mara between them, sending her reeling into cover under the overhang. Kevin stumbled in behind her, and, pressed on all sides by armored men, he felt the earth fall out from beneath his feet. The warriors staggered and buckled to their knees; others fell prostrate, while the litter bearers whimpered with their arms over their heads. The force of the quake sent people reeling and falling in the street, and screams arose from inside the alehouse as ceiling beams collapsed and plaster and debris rained down. Crockery mugs spilled and clattered; buildings outside shed roof tiles, and cornices, and coping, to crash and shatter on the pavement. Balconies collapsed, and screens tore, and people fell bleeding like tossed litter.

A stone wall nearby collapsed in a grating puff of dust, and the shaking increased. A bucking, surging motion rolled the length of the avenue, and the air rang with the grinding crash of splintering timbers and masonry. Kevin fought the heave of the earth to reach Mara, but a pair of soldiers already lay atop her, shielding her with their bodies.

On and on the madness raged; the very ground writhed like a thing in pain. From across the imperial precinct, in the vicinity of the arena, the noise of wrenched stones rumbled and roared like an avalanche. The sound raged tireless as the sea, cut by tens of thousands of voices shrieking in horror and pain.

Then the earth stilled between one heartbeat and the next. Quiet fell, and sun shone down through a haze of raised dust. The street was left in wreckage, a battleground of rubble and moaning wounded. Mashed between stones, crushed under splintered falls of lumber, lay the silent, bloody dead.

Kevin pulled himself to his feet. His cheek burned with blisters, and his eyes stung from grit. As the soldiers around him also recovered their footing, he helped Mara to rise.

Looking at her soiled face, with cobwebs of charred silk dangling from her tangled headdress, and wet robes plastered to her body, Kevin repressed an urge to kiss her lingeringly on the lips. Instead he dusted a fallen strand of hair from her earlobe and wakened the sparkle of an emerald ornament. He breathed a shaky sigh. "We were lucky. Can you imagine what it must have been like within the arena?"

Mara's eyes were still wide with shock. She was past all attempt to hide her trembling, but her voice held a grim hint of iron as she said, "We can only hope that our Lord of the Minwanabi remained too long at the games."

Then as if the wrecked beauty that surrounded her suddenly wounded her, she gestured curtly to Lujan. "Back to our town house, at once."

Lujan formed up his company and began the long trek back through the devastated avenues of Kentosani.

Arakasi appeared later, his servant's garb dusty and singed. Far from the arena and the site of Milamber's wrath, the Acoma house had taken only mild damage. But now a dozen warriors held the outer door, and more stood guard in the courtyard; the Spy Master advanced with cat-footed caution. Not until he sighted Lujan in the hallway did he finally relax his stance.

"Gods preserve us, you made it," the Force Commander greeted in a hoarse-voiced rush of feeling.

In an instant, Arakasi was directed upstairs, where he bowed before his mistress.

Mara was seated on cushions, freshly bathed, but still pale from the day's excitement. A scraped knee showed beneath her lounging robe, and her eyes were shadowed by an anxiety that lifted at the sight of her Spy Master. "Arakasi! Well met. What news do you bring?"

The Spy Master arose from his bow. "With my Lady's forgiveness," he murmured, and he raised a stained cloth and dabbed at a bleeding cheek.

Mara motioned to a maid, who hurried off for healer's salves and a basin. The Spy Master tried to brush her solicitude away. "The cut is of no consequence. A man sought to take advantage of the confusion and rob me. He is dead."

"Rob a servant?" Mara questioned. The excuse was transparent; more likely her Spy Master had risked grave danger in her behalf, but she abided by his wishes and refrained from embarrassing him with questions.

When Mara's party had arrived at the door to her town house, they had found the Spy Master absent, along with the bulk of her soldiers. Leaving a small garrison with Jican, Arakasi had made his way back toward the arena, but the madness caused by Milamber had disrupted his passage through the streets. The two parties had passed and missed each other in the pandemonium.

The maid arrived back with a basket of remedies. Mara nodded toward Arakasi, who looked irritated but submitted to having his cheek doctored at his mistress's insistence.

While the maid dabbed at the Spy Master's wound, Mara asked, "The rest of our soldiers?"

"Back with me," Arakasi answered, unwarrantably peevish. He flicked a dark look at the maid, then finished his report. "Though one warrior took a blow to his head from falling pottery, if you can believe, and is probably going to die."

Mara watched the filth and old blood that came away on the cloth. "That's more than a scratch. The bone shows." She added the question that burned to be asked. "What of the city?"

Arakasi ducked the maid's hand. In a movement quick as a predator's, he caught up a clean rag and held it pressed to his injury. "My Lady should not bother herself with a servant's aches and pains."

In the softening gloom of twilight, Mara's eyebrows rose. "And servants should not bother to aid their mistresses by risking imperial charges for handing a blade to a slave? No"
—she raised her hand as Arakasi drew breath—"don't answer. Lujan swears he didn't see. There was a knife that turned up bloody in the pantry, but the cooks insist it was used to slaughter jigabirds."

Arakasi loosed a sharp chuckle. "Jigabirds! How apt."

"Very. Now answer my question," Mara demanded.

Still delighted, Arakasi obeyed. "All is in chaos. There are fires everywhere, and many wounded. Kentosani looks as if it has been overrun by an invading army in the quarters around the arena. The Warlord has retired in shame, humiliated by the Great One, Milamber. The spectacle was too public and caused too many innocent deaths. I wager Almecho will end his sorry life within the day."

"The Emperor?" Through her excitement at this momentous news, Mara kept track of the prosaic. She dismissed the maid with orders to fetch a tray of supper.

Arakasi said, "The Light of Heaven is safe. But the Imperial Whites are withdrawn from all parts of the palace save the family suite, where they protect the Emperor and his children. The Council Guards remain on duty, but with no orders from the Warlord to direct them, they will not act. By nightfall, it should be presumed that house loyalty will prevail, and each company will return to its own master. What rules we know are temporarily suspended, with the council weakened and the Warlord shamed." Arakasi shrugged. "There is no law, except as strength demands."

Mara felt chilled in a room that seemed suddenly darker. She clapped for servants to light lamps, then said, "Lujan should hear this. Do you think we could be attacked?"

Arakasi sighed. "Who can know? All is madness out there. Yet if I were to hazard a guess, we are probably safe for the night. If the Lord of the Minwanabi survived the destruction of the games, then he is most likely hiding in his quarters, as we are, taking stock of personal losses and awaiting word that sanity has returned in the streets."

The tray arrived, brought in by a servant with Lujan striding hard on his heels. Mara motioned for her Force Commander to be seated, then had a round of chocha poured. She sat back and sipped the hot, reassuring liquid, while Lujan bullied Arakasi into treating his wound with salve. The warrior's graphic descriptions of suppurating sword cuts were enough to intimidate the bravest, and Arakasi's courage mostly stemmed from stubbornness. Roused to pity by her Spy Master's harried frown, but not enough to let him escape being bandaged by the capable hands of her Force Commander, Mara judged her moment and intervened. "If Almecho takes his own life, there will be a call to council."

Eager for the diversion, Arakasi scooped up a cold meat pie. "A new Warlord."

Lujan tossed the unused bandage back in the basket of remedies. "Any who attend the election will be taking grave risks. There is no clear successor to the title."

Yet that danger, while apparent enough, was not the worst

imaginable. Mara raised steady eyes in the brightening light
of the lamps. "If ever the Acoma presence must be in force in
the council, it's to elect Almecho's successor. Only five Lords
command enough following to strive for the title, and one of
those is Desio of the Minwanabi. His claim must never be
permitted to succeed."

"You have made bargains," Arakasi allowed, "compiled
enough promised votes that you could carry an influence.
But with all normal order overturned, do you dare rely on
who will be present to be counted?"

Now Mara's fatigue showed plainly. "No greater risk
could exist than Desio wearing the white and gold."

Lujan fingered his weapon hilt. "Could that happen?"

"In the normal course of events, no. Now . . . ?" The
Spy Master shrugged. "This morning, would any one of us
have guessed the reign of Almecho could end in disgrace
before sundown?"

The night beyond the window seemed suddenly more than
dark. Menaced by gathering fears, Mara longed for the comfort of Kevin's arms; but he was outside with the warriors,
helping to repair gaps the earthquake had opened in the wall.
Milamber had broken more than stones and heads in his
contest against the Warlord. His deed had undermined all
hierarchy within the Empire, and the dust would be long
days settling.

"It would seem we must be ready for any eventuality,"
Mara announced with firmness. "Arakasi, when you are able,
you will be needed back in the city. Keep abreast of every
rumor. For soon the powers of this Empire will change their
course, and if we do not lay our path carefully, we may be
crushed in the byplay."

There followed a tense, sleepless night, while Lujan's warriors rearranged furnishings and pulled old battle shutters
out of storage. The ancient dwelling in Kentosani had not
taken assault in many centuries, but the old walls were solid.
The warriors fortified the gates and the doorways as best they
could, their work lit by slaves bearing lanterns.

Sounds of strife drifted in from the direction of the inner
city, and running footsteps chased up and down the street.
Whether these were men fleeing thieves, or assassins sent out
to knife enemies, no one within the safety of walls dared open
their gates to know.

Three hours after nightfall, Strike Leader Kenji returned, a sword cut in his shoulder and his armor chipped from hard fighting. He found Lady Mara in the kitchen, deep in consultation with Jican concerning food stores. By the slate in her hand, and the inventory going on, she looked as if she prepared for a siege.

Kenji bowed, and the movement caught Mara's eye. She called for a servant to bring chocha, and settled her Strike Leader on a chopping table, while the battered basket of remedies was once again fetched from the stores.

"The Sajaio were swept away by the mob." Kenji fought back a grimace as he reached to unbuckle his armor.

"Don't," Mara said. "Let me call a slave to help."

But Kenji was too numbly focused on completing his duty to take heed. As the first fastening loosened, he started on another, and torturously resumed his report. "The two men with me were lost. One died fighting; the other perished in the falling fire. The mob drove me far astray, though I fought to return to the town house. Thick crowds jammed the temple precinct, drawn there in fear of their lives. I tried to come by way of the waterfront, but the docks there collapsed in the earthquakes."

A slave appeared at Mara's summons and stooped to help Kenji with his armor. His wound was sullenly bleeding, the silk padding underneath lacquer armor already ringed with stains. "There were riots, Lady." Kenji gasped as the breastplate was lifted from him. Sallow and sweating in his pain, he continued, his words labored. "The poor and the fisherfolk from the dockside started looting moored barges and nearby shops."

Mara glanced anxiously at Jican, who had earlier noticed the scarlet glow of fires and rightly predicted disastrous effects upon trade.

"Some of the warehouses were torn open and gutted. Other folk swarmed away to the imperial precinct to demand food and shelter from the Warlord.

Mara waved Kenji to silence. "You have done well. Rest now, and allow your hurts to be tended."

But the battered Strike Leader insisted on rising to make his bow. As the slave brought warm water to soak the padding away from his half-formed scabs, he sank back and endured the discomfort in a wretched lethargy of exhaustion.

Mara sat down and took the hand of her officer. She remained with him while his shoulder was tended, and listened as sounds of distant strife mingled with the scratch of Jican's chalk. Spread on benches and tables were supplies enough to last for several days. Thirty warriors might be enough to hold the gates against a mob bent on mayhem, but never a foray of armed force.

In the end, toward dawn, when Kenji was bedded down and sleeping, Mara consulted with Lujan, and an officer was chosen to summon reinforcements from the nearest Acoma garrison.

Thuds and screams drifted in through the screens, incongruous against the liquid play of fountains. The sky lay tinged by the glow of raging fires, and the streets were safe for no man. As Lujan let his messenger out the gate, he said in worried parting, "Let us pray to the gods that our enemies are in as much disarray as we are."

"Indeed," Mara murmured. "Let us pray."

16. *REGROUPING*

The trumpet sounded.

After two days behind locked gates, with Acoma soldiers camped in garden and courtyard and even the downstairs hallway, the noise was a welcome intrusion. Mara pushed away a book scroll she had failed to read. Her nerves were like overwound strings, responsive to the slightest movement and sound. She was on her feet ahead of thought, even as the warriors on duty had blades half-drawn from their scabbards.

And then reason caught up with defensive instinct. An attack would not be heralded with a fanfare, nor take place in the light of midday. Trumpets could only signal a long-overdue call to council or other imperial announcement. Grateful the waiting was ended, Mara arose to go downstairs.

Arakasi had dispatched no reports in the interim. Mara had been reliant on hearsay bought by tossing coins over the walls to rumormongers, and what news she managed to glean was far too sparse for the enormity of the events that had transpired. Word had passed like wind through the streets the night before that Almecho had taken his life in shame. Odd talk also circulated that the Assembly had named Milamber outcast and stripped him of his rank. Less reliable sources said the barbarian magician had climinated the Assembly altogether. That version Mara doubted; when she tried to imagine power on a vast enough scale to subdue the tempest that had destroyed the arena, her mind balked at the concept.

Unasked, Kevin had dryly observed that he would not

wish to be the one sent to inform the barbarian magician of his change in status.

Mara picked her way down the grand stair, which was stacked like shelves in an armory with helms and bracers laid aside by resting warriors. Swords lay piled in corners, and the curved scroll of the balustrade became a mustering place for spears. Since the arrival of the relief troops, her original thirty warriors had swelled to a garrison of one hundred, and the guest suites were all jammed with officers.

The horn call had roused more sleepers, and the on-duty patrol of seventy-five was fully armored. Prepared for immediate action, the men formed up at the appearance of their mistress and cleared a path between her and the door. Mara passed through and wondered that Kevin was not among the dicers in the corner.

The dooryard outside was no less jammed with warriors. They formed ranks three deep in the narrow space as she signaled for Lujan to unbar the street gate.

Four Imperial Whites waited on the other side, and a herald in a thigh-length robe of brilliant white. His badges of rank flashed in the sunlight, as did the golden ribbon around his head and his gilt-trimmed rod of office.

"Lady Mara of the Acoma," he intoned.

Mara advanced a step ahead of Lujan and presented herself.

The herald returned a shallow bow. "I bring words from the Light of Heaven. Ichindar, ninety-one times Emperor, bids you retire to your home at your leisure. Go in peace, for his shadow is thrown across the breadth of the land and his arms encircle you. Any who trouble your passage shall be enemies of the Empire. So he has decreed."

The warriors behind Mara maintained an expectant stillness. But to the astonishment of all, the Emperor's herald made no mention of a call to council. Without waiting for response, and speaking no further word, he formed up his escort and marched down the lane to the next house.

Surprised, Mara stood frowning in full sunlight while her officers closed and barred her gates. She had lost weight since the flight from the arena. Worry left her pale, with heavy shadows under her eyes, and now this latest development chilled her with bone-deep foreboding. If the Warlord had died in disgrace, and the Lords of the Empire and their families were being sent home with no call to council, the implication could no longer be debated: the Emperor must have entered the Great Game.

"We need Arakasi," Mara said, coming back to herself with a start. She raised harried eyes to her Force Commander. "If the Emperor's guard keeps the peace, surely we could send out a runner?"

"Pretty Lady, it will be done," said Lujan, in an almost forgotten tone of banter. "Safe streets or not, every man or servant here would run barefoot through mayhem if you asked."

"I would not ask." In a mix of grave amusement, Mara looked down at her own feet, still wrapped in soft cloths from her shoeless flight through the streets. "I've tried the experience. Jican has already received orders: my slaves are all getting new sandals."

Which in its way showed the influence of the Midkemian, though on that point Lujan withheld comment. The mistress was like no other ruler he had met, with her radical ideas, and her unflinching toughness, and her odd moments of compassion. "If you think we could do with more floor space," he said, "half the garrison could be sent to the public baths."

Now Mara did smile. "They don't like being stepped on in their sleep? We are a bit overcrowded," she allowed. In fact, the house smelled like an uncleaned, cheap public hostel. "Do as you see fit, but I want an extra company kept close at hand within the city." As she turned to reenter the town house to arrange her summons to Arakasi, she added a final thought. "The last thing the Acoma are going to do is tuck up tail and run home."

When Lujan bowed, he was grinning.

The runner proved unnecessary. While Mara deliberated over how best to get covert word to one of the agreed-upon places for leaving messages, the Spy Master himself showed up in the guise of a vegetable seller. The first Mara knew of the event was a commotion from the kitchens, and an uncharacteristic bout of temper from Jican.

"Gods, don't slice him with that meat cleaver," Kevin said in a merry baritone. His laughter echoed up the broad staircase, and aware that her irate hadonra would retaliate by having her lover scrape latrines, Mara hurried down to intervene.

She found her Spy Master leaning on the wheel of a handcart filled with a cargo of spoiled vegetables that some thrifty soul had saved to feed livestock. "There aren't any fresh ones in the market," Arakasi was saying reasonably to Jican. When that failed to placate the red-faced little man, he added on a note of hope, "In the poor quarter, these melons would fetch good prices."

In danger of laughing outright after days of trauma and worry, Mara made her presence felt. "Arakasi, I have need of you. Jican, ask Lujan for an escort of soldiers, and go find some edible meat to butcher. If you find none, those melons won't smell so terrible."

Arakasi pushed off from his perch, bowed, and left handcart and contents to the hadonra. "Happy hunting," he murmured as he passed, and earned an intent look from Mara. "You seem in a fine mood this morning," she commented.

"That's because nobody else is," Kevin interrupted. "He does it just to be perverse."

The barbarian fell into step with mistress and Spy Master as she retraced her way through the scullery, then settled for conference on the stone benches laid out in a circle within the courtyard.

Mara liked the place, with its flowering trees and its soft-voiced trio of fountains. But her manner was far from languid as she opened, "Is it certain Almecho is dead?"

Arakasi shed a smock that smelled ripely of fruit mold. "The Warlord performed the rite of expiation before all his retainers and friends, including two Great Ones. His body lies in state in the Imperial Palace."

"You heard there is no call to council?" Mara questioned, and now her concern showed through.

Arakasi's lapse into levity ended. "I had heard. Some Lords are already grumbling, and Desio's voice is the loudest."

Mara closed her eyes and breathed in the sweet scent of flowers. So fast; events were moving all too swiftly. For the sake of her house, she must act, but how? All the known laws had been broken. "Who will rule?"

"The Emperor." All eyes turned to Kevin.

Mara sighed in a burst of impatience. "You do not understand. The Emperor rules as a spiritual leader. While the daily business of Tsuranuanni is conducted by the imperial staff, the High Council governs the nation. All policy begins there, with the Warlord foremost among the great Lords of the land."

Kevin hiked a thumb over his shoulder in the general direction of the palace. "I seem to remember someone saying the Light of Heaven never went out in public, either, but there he was, big as life, sitting at the games. This Emperor has already changed the way of his fathers, as I see things. Ichindar may be more intent on governing than you think."

Arakasi stroked his chin. "If not he, then the Great Ones could be at play here. There were an inordinate number of them present the other day."

"Everyone has guesses," Mara interjected. "What we need are facts. Who survived the debacle at the games, and were there any suspicious accidents in the aftermath?"

"Far more injuries than fatalities," Arakasi said. "I will write you a list before I leave. If a momentous precedent is being set at the palace, there are agents I can approach with questions. For now I advise caution, despite the Emperor's peace. Many streets are still blocked with debris. The priests of the Twenty Orders have opened their temples to house the homeless, but with trade disrupted at the docks, food is scarce. There are hungry, desperate people at large who are every bit as dangerous as assassins. Repair work began at the waterfront this morning, but until the markets reopen, the streets will be perilous to walk."

Mara made a rueful gesture at the wrappings on her feet. "I shouldn't be going out until my litter is replaced, in any event."

Arakasi arose, stretched, and flexed his hands until his knuckles cracked. Mara regarded him narrowly. The cut on his cheek was healing, but the surrounding flesh looked more drawn than she recalled. "How long has it been since you slept?"

"I haven't," said the Spy Master. "There has been too much to do." With the faintest distaste, he picked up the discarded farm smock. "With your leave, my Lady, I will borrow back that handcart and seek your guards and hadonra. The markets may be closed, but I do have ideas on where Jican might buy vegetables." His head vanished briefly behind crumpled, filthy cloth as he tugged the garment over his house robe. Tousled, squint-eyed, and looking every inch the weathered field hand when he emerged, he added, "The price will be very dear."

"Then Jican will owe you no favors. Go carefully," Mara bade him.

Arakasi bowed and stepped under the arch that led into the house, where he instantly became all but invisible; his voice issued softly out of the shadow. "You'll be staying?" Then, after barely a pause, "I thought so."

And suddenly he was gone.

Kevin regarded his Lady in the greenish light falling through the trees. "You won't be persuaded to go home to Ayaki?" He asked also for himself, at the back of his mind a need to speak to Patrick, and share with his countrymen the news that weighed on his heart since the games: Boric and Brucal routed, and the Kingdom open to invasion.

For an instant Mara looked anguished. "I cannot go home. Not with this much change under way. I must be close to the seat of power, no matter in whose charge things fall. I will not have House Acoma crushed as a consequence of other men's decisions. If we are in peril, I will cherish my son beyond the last breath in my body, but I will act."

Her hands rested tense on the stonework. Gently Kevin captured them in his own warm palms. "You are frightened," he observed.

She nodded, which for her was a momentous admission. "Because I can act against a plot by the Minwanabi or any other enemy Lord. But there are two forces in the Empire I must bow before without question, and one or both are at play here."

Kevin needed no prompt to guess she referred to the Emperor and the Magicians. As her gaze darkened and turned inward, the Midkemian knew she worried also for her son.

Three more days passed, filled with the sounds of marching soldiers in the streets, and the grind of carts bearing away wreckage, rubble, and bodies. Mara waited, and took reports from Arakasi, delivered in strange forms and at odd hours of the night. Kevin laconically remarked that the Spy Master had a knack for spoiling their lovemaking, but the truth was that boredom left the couple more time for indulgence. His prediction that the Emperor would undertake the rule of the Empire proved partially correct, but more than one game within politics was under way, and Arakasi diverted all his resources into uncovering whose hand pulled which strings.

As time passed, and the council members scrambled to assemble a profile of the emerging power structure, it became plain that Ichindar's intervention was not a whim. He had planned carefully and kept men ready to step in and conduct the business usually left to the factors and agents of the council Lords. The puzzle came clearer as Arakasi began to unwind which factions provided Ichindar with support. Members of the Blue Wheel Party, nearly all of them absentees from the chaos at the Imperial Games, were at the heart of the plot. Even the old Imperial Party families, who could claim ties of blood, were outsiders in this new order.

Since the declaration of imperial peace, the city began recovery from its wounds. Repairs of the destruction wreaked by the barbarian magician began with the laborious clearing of broken stone and timbers. For days a spire of smoke rose over the vicinity of the arena as the dead were brought there and burned. Stories of Imperial Whites hanging looters or black marketeers who were hoarding put an end to both practices. Moorings were set in the river, and small craft used to ferry goods ashore while new docks were built on old pilings; the shops began slowly to restock. Servants with shoulder yokes and handcarts picked their way around fallen stones to do business.

Ten days after the disaster at the games, Mara received reports from Sulan-Qu. There had been a small influx of refugees there, and some fighting over salvage on the riverbanks, but Acoma interests had not suffered. Nacoya reported that, except for Ayaki's tantrums, all was quiet at the Acoma estate. The worst the First Adviser had contended with was Keyoke, who had to be dissuaded from sending half the standing garrison to Kentosani to extricate his mistress. They had learned she was safe, Nacoya wrote, through Arakasi's agents. Mara set down the inscribed parchment. Tears blurred her eyes as she thought upon the devotion of those who loved her. She missed her son unbearably, and vowed to spend more time with him at the earliest possible opportunity.

Fast footsteps sounded in the hallway. Mara heard her guards snap to attention, and then Arakasi appeared, looking hollow-eyed and grim. In a total breach of protocol, he burst into her private quarters and threw himself face down on the carpet in absolute obeisance.

"Mistress, I beg forgiveness for my rush."

Caught in a moment of weakness, Mara dabbed at her eyes. She knew she ought to feel frightened, but events were changing so quickly, she felt as if they were happening to somebody else.

"Be seated," Mara said. "What is the news?"

Arakasi rose, and his eyes roved the chamber, seeking. "Where is Kevin? He should hear this, as you will certainly want his opinion."

Mara flicked her hand, and her runner departed for the kitchen, where the Midkemian had gone for hot chocha. Already returning up the stairs, the barbarian slave entered almost immediately. "What's the excitement?" he asked as he set down a tray laden with a pot and assorted cups. "A bit of spiced chocha hardly seems cause for getting nearly knocked flat by your runner."

Kevin's back was turned to Mara as he bent to pour the first cup, and he had not noticed Arakasi, who habitually sought the least conspicuous corner.

"First, the barbarians—" the Spy Master began.

Startled into rattling the china, Kevin spun. "You!" He covered his overreaction with a sour smile. "What about the *barbarians?*"

Arakasi cleared his throat. "The outworlders have launched a completely unexpected and massive counteroffensive. Our armies on Midkemia have been overwhelmed and routed back to the valley where we control the rift! We have just suffered the worst defeat of the war!"

Tactful for once, Kevin reined back a laugh of joy. But he could not resist a smug look at Arakasi as he handed his Lady her spiced chocha.

"What else?" Mara asked, sure there must be more because of her Spy Master's precipitous entrance.

"Second," Arakasi ticked off, "the Emperor has agreed to meet with the barbarian King to discuss peace!"

Mara dropped her cup. "What?" Her exclamation cut

across with the smash of china, and steaming chocha splashed in a flood across the floor.

Kevin stood rooted. Mara ignored the drenched tiles, and the fine spray of stains that spread slowly through the hem of her robe. "Peace?"

Arakasi continued, speaking quickly. "My agent in the palace sent word this morning. Before the Warlord's last major offensive, two agents of the Blue Wheel Party slipped through the rift with the outbound troops. They were Kasumi of the Shinzawai and a barbarian slave, and they left the encampment and carried words of peace to the barbarian King."

"That's why your Shinzawai friend wasn't at the games," Kevin said. "He didn't know if he was going to be a hero or an outlaw."

Mara pulled wet cloth from her knees, but called no maids to assist. "Kasumi. That's Hokanu's brother." Her eyes narrowed. "But the Blue Wheel Party would never do something this bold without—"

"Without the Emperor's approval," Arakasi interjected. "That's the gist. Ichindar had to be willing to discuss peace prior to dispatching any envoy."

Mara turned pale as she considered. "So this is why the Light of Heaven was prepared to step in and rule." Slowly she added to Kevin, "Your appraisal of our Emperor may be more accurate than we gave you credit for, my love. Ichindar meddled in the Great Game, and none knew." She shook her head in disbelief. "This goes counter to all tradition."

Kevin pulled a napkin from the tray and knelt to dam the flow of chocha. "You're one to talk. I seem to recall you've bent one or two traditions to the point of twisting them beyond recognition."

Mara protested. "But the Emperor . . ." Her awe made it clear she considered the Light of Heaven to be just short of a god.

"He's a man," said Kevin, the hand with the dripping rag rested on his bent knee. "And he's young. Young men often do unexpected and radical things. But this one's lived a pampered life, for all his boldness. He's surely naïve if he thinks he can skip in and order your power-hungry Tsurani Lords to pack up and go home to grow radishes."

Arakasi said, "Mistress, whatever 'radishes' may be, I fear Kevin is right."

"There's another hand in this," Mara insisted, unsatisfied. She glared at her sodden overrobe, then threw it impatiently off. Fine cloth finished where Kevin's ministrations had left off, but if a few silk cushions had been saved, Mara never noticed. "Had the magician Milamber not caused Almecho's disgrace, how would things have proceeded?"

If the question was rhetorical, the progression was not hard to trace. Even Kevin could follow that the Blue Wheel Party would have once more reversed policy and withdrawn from the Alliance for War. This would have left Almecho with only Minwanabi as a major supporter. With the Acoma and the Xacatecas busy worrying the Minwanabi flank, Desio could not afford to increase support. Almecho and his party would have been deadlocked, after thirteen years of near-absolute rule.

Kevin wrung his rag savagely over the chocha tray and voiced the only viable conclusion. "So your Emperor would have barged into the High Council to announce a peace proposal, and your Warlord would have lacked enough support to confront him. Very neatly done." Kevin finished with a whistle of admiration. "Your Ichindar is a very smart boy."

Arakasi appeared inwardly calculating. "Even had things gone as Kevin surmises, I don't think our Emperor would have risked an open confrontation with the Warlord. Not unless he had some special avenue of appeal."

Kevin's eyes widened. "The magicians!"

Mara nodded. "Almecho has his 'pets,' so Ichindar would need allies to counter them." To Arakasi she said, "Go and speak with your agents. Discover, if you can, who among the Great Ones is a likely candidate to have been involved in this game. See if one has a special relationship to any within the Blue Wheel, especially the Shinzawai. They seem to be at the heart of things."

As her Spy Master bowed and departed, Mara's gaze sharpened as if she viewed some private vista from a place of dizzying height. "Great changes are coming. I feel this like the breeze that brings the butana," she said in reference to the bitter, dry wind that in the old stories raised the spirits of demons and set them free to roam the land. Then, as if thoughts of mythological evils and present-day strife gave her shivers, she ruefully acknowledged her clumsiness. "But one can hardly seize the initiative while swimming in puddles of chocha."

"That depends on what sort of initiative," Kevin countered, and he rescued her from the disaster by sweeping her into his arms.

The upheaval precipitated by Milamber brought in a few small concessions. As trade resumed, and shortfalls opened opportunities, Mara received word from Lord Keda that her terms for the warehouse space had been accepted. The destruction along the dock front in Kentosani had made her offer the only option, and a premium would reward the first grain shipments to reach the market on the flood. Lord Andero conceded her the Keda vote with a minimum of sureties; with no High Council called to session, such a promise held questionable value.

Yet Mara dispatched a messenger with word of her acceptance anyway. Any promise was worth more than no promise at all, and from the information brought by her Spy Master, the ruling Lords who were not busy exploiting trade advantages were displeased with the Emperor's machinations. Peace, they said, was a coward's act, and the gods did not favor weak nations.

The news came thick and heavy after that; Mara spent yet another morning in conference with Arakasi, while Kevin dozed in the shade of a tree in the courtyard. He did not hear until later, when official word came, that the Light of Heaven had departed for the City of the Plains, his intent to cross the rift to Midkemia and negotiate for peace with Lyam, King of the Isles.

Kevin shot bolt upright at the mention of the Midkemian name. "Lyam!"

"King Lyam," Mara repeated. She tapped the parchment delivered to her town house by Imperial messenger. "So it is written here, by the Emperor's own scribe."

"But Lyam is Lord Borric's son," Kevin remembered, a dazed look on his face. "If he's King, that can only mean King Rodric, Prince Erland of Krondor, and Borric himself are all dead."

"What do you know of King Lyam?" Mara asked, choosing a seat by his side.

"I don't know him well," Kevin admitted. "We played together as children one time. I just remember him as a big blond boy who laughed a lot. I met Lord Borric once at a commanders' meeting." He fell silent, wrapped in thoughts of his own land, until curiosity caused him to ask to read the parchment. The Emperor of Tsuranuanni did not believe in traveling without half the nobles in his Empire, it appeared. Kevin's mouth quirked wryly. By imperial command, the Light of Heaven's honor guard consisted of the Warchiefs of the Five Great Clans and the eldest sons of half the other Lords in Tsuranuanni.

"Hostages," the Midkemian said outright. "The Lords will hardly defy edict and make bloody trouble with their heirs in the Emperor's field army."

The arena of politics suddenly paled. Kevin shut his eyes and tried to imagine the brown-haired youth in gilt armor seated across a table with Borric's son Lyam, who was also young . . . and it came home to Kevin, like a slam to the heart, that time had passed. The war had gone on, and people had died in his absence. He did not even know if his father and elder brothers were alive. The thought stung, that for years he had forgotten to care. Seated in a beautiful courtyard, surrounded by alien flowers and a woman from a culture that often seemed incomprehensibly cruel, Kevin, third son of the Baron of Zūn, took a breath and tried to take stock of who he was.

"But why should Ichindar go there?" Mara mused, unmindful of his turmoil. "Such a risk to our Light of Heaven."

Her thoroughly Tsurani viewpoint sparked shock, and Kevin bridled. "Do you think our King would come here? After your warriors have been ravaging his lands for nine years? 'Forget we've burned your villages, Your Majesty. Just step through this gate into our world!' Not bloody likely. Remember, this King has been a field commander with his father's army almost since the start. He knows whom he faces. Trust will be a very thin commodity in the Kingdom of the Isles until your people prove otherwise."

Mara conceded that Kevin was right on all points. "I would guess from your perspective we would be worthy of distrust."

Her equanimity struck a nerve, mostly because he expected a fight. Kevin laughed, a cold and bitter sound. "I love you as the breath of my life, Mara of the Acoma, but there is just one of me. Thousands of my countrymen know the Tsurani only upon the battlefield. What they see are men who have invaded their homeland for bloody conquest. There will be no easy peace in all this."

Framed by an arching trellis of akasi vines, Mara frowned. "Do you infer that Ichindar will be asked to surrender the lands the Warlord has gained?"

Kevin laughed again. "You Tsurani. You believe that everyone thinks as you do. Of course the King will demand you depart. You're invaders. You're alien. You don't belong on the Midkemian side of the rift." Caught by an upwelling tide of irony, Kevin looked into Mara's face. She looked worried, even hurt, but uppermost was her concern for him. That wrenched. She did not share his concept of cruelty, could never grasp what it cost him to beg for the concessions that had given Patrick and his fellow slaves the most basic sustenance. Torn by his improbable love and his inborn sense of justice, Kevin rose precipitately and left.

The trouble with the Kentosani town house was that it had no vast yards to get lost in. Mara found Kevin within a few minutes, crouched on their bed mat, casting small pebbles into the fish pool that separated the outer screen from the wall shared with the building next door. She knelt and circled his waist with an embrace from behind. With her cheek against his back she said, "What do you see in the fish pool, beloved?"

Kevin's reply held flinty honesty. "I see years of pretense. I let myself become lost within your love, and for that I am grateful, but upon hearing of this coming peace . . ."

"You remember the war," she prompted, hoping he would talk.

Mara sensed bitterness behind the fine tremors of rage that coursed through him as he said, "Yes. I remember. I remember my countrymen, my friends, dying trying to defend their homes from armies we knew nothing of, warriors who came for reasons we could not understand. Men who asked for no parley, but who just came and butchered our farmers, took our villages, and occupied our towns.

"I remember fighting your people, Mara. I didn't think of

them as honorable foes. I thought of them as murdering scum. I hated them with every fiber of my being."

She felt him sweat with the memories, but when she did not withdraw, he made an effort to calm himself. "In all this I have come to know you, your people. I . . . can't say I find some of your ways pleasant. But at least I understand something of the Tsurani. You have honor, though it's a different thing from our own sense of justice. We have our honor, too, but I don't think you understand that fully. And we have things in common, as all people do. I love Ayaki as if he were my own.

"But we're people who have both suffered, you at the hands of my countrymen, me at the hands of yours."

Mara soothed him with her touch. "Yet I would change nothing."

Kevin turned within the circle of her arms and looked down at a face shining with tears that were considered an unconditional weakness in her culture. Immediately he felt shamed. "You'd not save your brother and father if you could?"

Mara shook her head. "Now I would not. Most bitter of all is that knowledge, my beloved. For to alter my past griefs, I would never have had Ayaki, or the love I share with you." Behind her eyes were other, darker realizations: she would never have ruled, and so would never have known the intoxicating fascination she found in the power of the Great Game.

Stunned by her soul-baring honesty, Kevin felt his throat constrict. He held Mara close, letting her tears wet his shoulder through his shirt. Half-choked by emotion, he said, "But as much as I love you, Mara of the Acoma . . ."

She let him push her away. Her eyes held his as she searched his face and discovered the harsh truth he could no longer evade. Fear twisted her spirit, and a sorrow not felt since the day fate had forced her to assume the mantle of the Acoma. "Tell me," she snapped. "Tell me all, now."

Kevin looked tortured. "Ah, Lady, I love you beyond doubt . . . I will until death. But I will never embrace this slavery. Not even for you."

Mara could not bear to look at him. In this moment, for the first time, she at last knew the depth of his pain. Gripping him desperately, she said, "If the gods willed it . . . would you leave me?"

Kevin's arms tightened around her shoulders. As if she were his only antidote against pain, he held her; yet he said what could no longer be denied. "If I could be a free man, then I would stay with you forever. But as a slave, I would take any expedient I could to return home."

Mara lost the heart to control her sobbing. "But you can never be free . . . here."

"I know. I know." He brushed damp hair from her cheek and lost his own poise with the touch. His tears fell as freely as hers. The depths had been shared at last, and acknowledged: while they loved each other desperately, there would always be this open wound, as vast as an ocean and as deep as a chasm, and as wide as the rift between worlds.

Events in the Holy City revolved around the coming peace conference. With only days left before the Emperor's departure, the Ruling Lords of the Empire exchanged heated speculation over what terms had been agreed to in advance; yet even Arakasi's network could glean only sparse information on that subject. Mara spent long hours closeted with her scribes, sending messages to allies and tentatively confirming ties. Occasionally she entertained other Lords whose town houses were located nearer to the inner city and whose households had been inconvenienced by damage.

Small frustrations and concessions balanced larger ones. The craftsmen were slow in replacing her lost litter; with every carpenter in Kentosani busy fixing broken rooftrees, lintels, and doorframes, not even an apprentice could be borrowed from the work. Jican bargained to no avail. Imperial decree held a freeze on all private contracts until the dockside warehouses were rebuilt. Mara resigned herself to playing host to those she wished to see, until Lord Chipino of the Xacatecas heard of her straits and sent a replacement litter as a gift.

It was Xacatecas purple and yellow, and well chipped since a succession of Isashani's daughters had used it for shopping excursions. Jican remedied the matter by delving into the cellars after paint, but there were still no craftsmen to be hired. The task in the end fell to Tamu, a runner slave who had outgrown his post and graduated to formal messenger. But for three days after, young Tamu sat idle because his hands and arms were stained green to the elbow.

But at least the litter looked passable. Mara made social calls and compared her findings with Arakasi.

Overtly, the ruling Lords of Tsuranuanni were supportive of the Emperor's intervention; they sent their eldest sons to serve the imperial delegation, and they did not break peace. But beneath compliant manners, each Lord jockeyed for position, and counted enemies, and made compacts. Frustrated in their desire to convene the council, the rulers of all the great houses made covert, alternative plans.

Mara paid particular attention to the movements of the Minwanabi. Tasaio remained in exile in the remote western islands. But Desio had insinuated another cousin, Jeshurado, into the former Warlord's army as Subcommander, which gave Minwanabi an ally in the Emperor's camp. Desio was one of the five Warchiefs who would be in attendance at the conference on Midkemia, along with Andero of the Keda, the Lord of the Xacatecas, and the Lord of the Tonmargu.

But Clan Oaxatucan named no Omechan Warchief, owing to bitter infighting over who should succeed the seat left vacant by Almecho. His eldest nephew, Decanto, was the obvious choice, but another nephew, Axantucar, had shown unexpectedly strong backing from other members of the clan. Since the most vigorous factions were deadlocked, and many held back from supporting either man, Decanto and Axantucar were forced to cede the privilege to a third cousin, Pimaca, to act as Omechan Warchief for the imperial honor guard.

Mara's inquiry into the role taken by the Great Ones had drawn no clear answers. But Arakasi did find a relationship between the Assembly of Magicians and the Blue Wheel Party. As Mara watched the water fall in silver streams from the fountains in her courtyard garden, the Spy Master addressed that point. "It turns out that the Great One Fumita was once the younger brother to Lord Kamatsu of the Shinzawai, and is Hokanu's true father."

Mara showed astonishment. For whenever and wherever arcane talent was discovered, the Assembly took that man for training and broke all ties to family. Children were raised by relatives as if they were their own, their ties to their natural parents "forgotten." "So Hokanu is Kamatsu's adopted son and actually a nephew by blood." Since his mother had sworn service to the temple of Indiri after her husband's departure, Kamatsu and Kasumi were the only family Hokanu had known since the age of ten.

"Do you know if Fumita ever visits his son?" she asked of her Spy Master.

Arakasi shrugged. "Kamatsu's house is well guarded. Who can know?"

Recognizing that the continuance of her house would be better served by cultivating Hokanu's interest, Mara was equally curious to ply him for information on the chance that Fumita's commitment to the Assembly might have a weak point: that he might not have entirely put aside family concerns, and had been influential in bringing the Shinzawai and the Kanazawai Clan aid from the magicians.

But any thought of Hokanu led endlessly back to the thorny hedge of pain concerning Kevin. Mara sighed. In a rare moment of abstraction, she watched the water drops fall and fall, then firmly forced herself to concentrate on more immediate concerns. If she indulged herself in preoccupation with personal troubles, the Acoma would be overwhelmed at the next move of the Great Game.

The Light of Heaven would depart downriver in four days. If he succeeded in his peace with the Kingdom of the Isles, all houses would be equally disadvantaged. But if the Emperor failed, there must be a call for a new Warlord. Otherwise Ichindar, ninety-one times Emperor of Tsuranuanni, would face open revolt in the council. It had been centuries, but regicide had occurred before in the Empire.

A short while later, Mara clapped her hands for her runner. "Tell Jican we shall move our quarters to the apartment in the Imperial Palace this afternoon."

"Your will, Lady." The slave boy bowed and raced off to complete the errand as if happy for the chance to run.

Jican received the order like an antidote to frustration after days of simply assessing damage. Kevin was set to work lifting carry boxes outside to the waiting needra carts. On the stairs and landing, crates of jigabirds rubbed edges with parchment satchels, and the Lady's coffers of shell centis and centuries. At least the number of warriors had thinned down. One half of the company had relocated to a public barracks in the city. Of the others, fifty would serve as escort to see their mistress across town, of which twenty would return to guard the town house grounds.

Removed from the bustle, Mara sat in the courtyard with pen in hand, scribbling notes to Keyoke and Nacoya. To ensure other houses could not pry into her affairs, the Lady entrusted Lujan to carry her missive to the fastest bonded guild messenger. "Add this verbal message to my report," she instructed. "I want the bulk of our army ready to march at a moment's notice, and as near to Kentosani as Keyoke thinks prudent. We must stand prepared for any turn of events."

Dressed in the plain armor he preferred for the field, Lujan accepted the sealed parchments. "We prepare for war, my Lady?"

Mara said, "Always."

Lujan bowed and left without banter. Mara set down her pen and rubbed cramped fingers. She took a deep breath and held it a moment, then let it slowly out, as she had been taught at the temple. Kevin had forced her to see the ways of her people with new eyes; she understood that greed and ambition were masked by tradition, and honor became the justification for endless hatred and blood. The young Emperor might strive to change his people, but the Great Game would not be abolished at a stroke by Imperial edict. No matter what she felt, no matter how tired she became, no matter what regret came her way, Mara knew there would always be the struggle. To be Tsurani was to struggle.

Kevin had thought the great hall was impressive, but the Imperial Palace complex beyond the High Council's meeting place was even more grandiose. Mara's retinue entered portals wide enough to admit three wagons drawn abreast. Behind, doors whose weight required a dozen slaves to shift boomed closed. Sunlight vanished, leaving a dry, wax-scented dimness lit purple-blue by cho-ja globes suspended on ropes from a ceiling over two stories high. The corridor was immense, with worn flagstone floors, and two levels of galleries rising up on either side. Off these were doorways painted in riotous colors; each led to an apartment assigned to a council member's family, with those closest to the outer walls belonging to the lowest in rank.

"Forward," commanded Strike Leader Kenji to the honor guard, his voice a flurry of echoes off a ceiling dim under layers of varnish and dust.

Kevin marched at mid-column, beside his Lady's litter. Except for the Acoma retinue, the hallway was largely empty. Servants in imperial livery moved briskly from this task to that, but otherwise the enormous complex appeared deserted.

"Which is the Acoma apartment?" Kevin inquired of the nearest bearer slave.

The Tsurani returned a look of disgust at Kevin's irrepressible tongue, but out of pride he could not resist giving answer. "We are not on the first hall, but the seventh."

A moment later, Kevin understood the odd reply, when the honor guard turned a corner and he saw a vast intersection ahead, where several other corridors joined in a concourse. "Gods, this place is huge." Then he looked up and saw that this section had four tiers of galleries, accessed by wide stone staircases that zigzagged between landings. Yet for all the grandeur, the building seemed empty.

Then he realized the, that, unlike the area that housed the council hall, these passages had no mixed companies of guards on duty. "It's so quiet."

Mara peeked out of her litter curtains. "Everyone is at the docks, bidding the Emperor and his honor company farewell. This is why we hurried here—a better chance to enter unobserved. I did not want to risk meeting Imperial Guards right now."

They ascended no stairs. The Acoma apartment complex was situated at ground level near a slight bend, and identified by a lacquered green door with a shatra bird seal. The corridor stretched away from the crook for a hundred yards in each direction, with gigantic portals and more intersecting halls at either end. By now Kevin had deduced that the apartments were arrayed in semicircles around the central dome that housed the High Council hall. Set out in blocks, another three hundred or so small complexes turned this section of the palace into a warren of halls and passages.

Two massive apartment complexes stood adjacent to Mara's, and opposite lay the residence of House Washota, its green and blue doors securely closed. Past the bend, the doorways had yet more majestic decorations, from vaulting arches obscured by sixty-foot-high silken hangings, to carpeted stairs and urns overflowing with flowers. These were the apartments of the Five Great Families, with the smaller gallery complexes above reserved for guests and vassals. The allotment of space was by rank, but barracks room did not vary. Every Lord in the Empire could dwell within the Imperial Palace with a maximum retinue of twelve.

Yet Mara had brought fully thirty Acoma warriors into the palace precinct. Though technically she flouted a rule to do so, there were no patrols mustered in the corridors. In unstable times she knew full well that other Lords would do likewise, or bring still more warriors if they could manage it.

At Kenji's discreet tap, the green door opened. Inside, two guards bowed to their mistress and made way for her retinue to enter.

Jican bowed also, as her litter was set down in the small anteroom. "The area is safe, Lady," said the hadonra, and at his shoulder, Lujan gave Mara a slight nod.

Then the rest of the warriors crowded through the outer door, leaving Kevin barely enough space to raise his Lady from her litter. Judged by the standards of the town house, the apartment seemed spartan. The wooden floors held little beyond old woven carpets and cushions, and an occasional ceramic oil lamp. And then Kevin realized: the heavier furniture had been moved to block all the windows and doors. The apartment was three rooms deep, and the inner chambers opened into a small terrace courtyard. But today the Tsurani passion for breezeways and open doors was sacrificed for safety. Several screens had been nailed shut and backed with heavy wooden barricades.

"Expecting an attack?" Kevin asked no one in particular.

"Always," Mara answered. She looked sad as she reviewed the steps her warriors had taken to secure her family quarters. "We may not be the only house to realize that now is the perfect time to enter without attracting notice. Imperial Whites will always be on duty in the Imperial Family's complex, but without council-sanctioned guards, this area is now a no-man's-land. We travel these halls and concourses at our own peril."

While the bearers began the task of piling Mara's carry boxes against an outside screen, Arakasi arrived, his face drenched in perspiration. He wore the loincloth and sandals of a messenger, and his hair was tied back with a ribbon too dirty for anyone to reliably determine its color.

Mara threw off her traveling robe, a look of inquiry on her face. "You look like a merchant's runner."

Arakasi replied, eyes alight with sly humor, "Runners wearing house colors are being waylaid by everybody."

This drew a slight laugh from Mara, who softened at Kevin's blank look and explained. "Merchants' runners often don house colors, because that discourages street urchins from throwing stones at them. But now a messenger in house colors is apt to be seized for information. Since stone bruises are less to be feared than torture, roles have been reversed." She asked Arakasi, "What news?"

"Strange bands of men move through the shadows. They hide their armor under cloaks and carry no badge of house service. Imperial servants give them a wide berth."

"Assassins?" Mara asked, and her eyes held her Spy Master's without shifting as a servant retrieved the robe that trailed from her fingers.

Arakasi shrugged. "They could be that, or some Lord's army being smuggled into the city. They might also be agents of the Emperor sent under cover to see who seeks to break the peace. Someone highly placed let slip some information that has caused a stir of talk."

Mara sank down onto a nearby cushion and motioned permission for the others to retire.

But Arakasi declined. "I won't be staying, except to add that it appears that some of the demands made by the King upon the Emperor are . . . very odd."

This piqued Kevin's interest. "How do you mean?"

"Reparations." In spare tones, the Spy Master qualified. "Lyam demands something on the order of a hundred million centis to compensate his nation for damages."

Mara shot straight on her cushions. "Impossible!"

Kevin calculated and realized that the Midkemian sovereign was being generous. In Kingdom terms, Lyam was asking for something close to three hundred thousand golden sovereigns, which would barely replace the cost of keeping the Armies of the West in the field for nine years. "That's half of what he should ask for."

"The amount is not the issue, but the concept of paying damage," Mara said in acute frustration. "Ichindar cannot do so and keep his honor. It would shame Tsuranuanni before the gods!"

"Which is why the Light of Heaven refused," Arakasi cut in. "Instead, he takes a 'gift' of rare gems to the young King, the value of which should approximate a hundred million centis."

Appreciative of the Emperor's ingenuity, Mara smiled. "Not even the High Council can deny his right to give another monarch a gift."

"There's this other thing." Arakasi's dark eyes flicked meaningfully to Kevin. "Lyam wishes a prisoner exchange."

This drew a strange, emotionally weighted look between the barbarian slave and his mistress. With a strange reluctance to her tone, Mara turned back to Arakasi. "I understand what he asks for, but will Ichindar?"

Arakasi returned the openhanded shrug of the Tsurani. "Who can say? Giving slaves to the King of the Isles is not an issue. Lyam could do as he pleased with them. More to the point, what would the Emperor do with our returning war captives?" A silence developed, for it was true that in Tsuranuanni the honor and freedom of such men could never be restored.

Suddenly tired, Mara studied her feet. The bruises left since her flight from the arena had nearly faded, but emotional wounds between Kevin and herself over issues of slavery and freedom ached still. "You have word on the Minwanabi?"

As if he had prompted the change of subject, Arakasi's mouth thinned. "They ready more than three thousand soldiers for war."

Alarmed, Mara looked up. "They are coming to the Holy City?"

"No." But the Spy Master had only thin reassurance to offer. "They merely ready themselves upon the Minwanabi estates."

Mara's eyes narrowed. "Why?"

But it was Lujan who answered, and bitterly, from the doorway, where he paused after appointing his warriors to guard posts by every window and door. "Desio fears the imperial peace with reason, my Lady. If you abandon conflict with the Minwanabi, you renounce only a commitment to blood feud. Some might judge Acoma honor compromised, but who would fault you for obeying the Light of Heaven? But if the Emperor forces peace among warring houses, Desio forfeits his blood oath to Turakamu. He must destroy us before the Emperor's power becomes too strong to challenge, or offend the Death God."

Kevin took the liberty of asking a servant to bring his Lady a cool drink. He could sense her effort at self-control as she asked, "Would Desio risk attacking the Emperor?"

Arakasi shook his head. "Not openly, but should the High Council find cause to unite against Ichindar's will, Desio would have the largest army within striking distance of the Holy City. That offers a dangerous combination."

Mara chewed her lip. With the Omechan Clan divided between Decanto and Axantucar, the danger was apparent: Desio could become the new Warlord if a large enough faction of the High Council decided to use force to defy imperial edict.

Kevin added an unwelcome observation to this reflection. "Three thousand Minwanabi swords outside the Council Hall could make a persuasive argument even if Desio doesn't have a clear majority."

Wrung by more than fatigue, Mara regarded the drink brought in by the servant as if it contained deadly poison. Then she put off dark thoughts. "The truce meeting beyond the rift won't happen for another three days. Until Ichindar and Lyam fail in negotiations, all is speculation. Now that we are safely within the palace, let us enjoy this quiet time."

Arakasi bowed more deeply than usual and, like a wraith, departed. Mara watched the doorway for long minutes after he left, and returned to life only when Kevin settled beside her and gathered her into his arms. Trembling, afraid to voice the uneasiness she felt inside, Mara finished her thought. "I fear much is carried upon the shoulders of a very young man, and while the gods may favor our Light of Heaven, they also may turn away from him.

Kevin pressed a kiss onto the crown of her head. He held no illusions. Like her, he understood that the best they could hope for was that Arakasi could garner a last-minute warning in the hour before an enemy attack.

• • •

For three days the Empire seemed to hold its breath. Outside the palace, the Holy City struggled back to normality, as workers finished repairs to the last damaged dock and masons borrowed fallen stonework from the arena to fix the gateways to the Imperial Palace. Fishermen left before dawn to draw their nets through the currents of the river Gagajin, and farmers drove the late season's crops in on heavily burdened wagons, or floated them in on barges. Temple incense and flowers prevailed over the smell of the cremated dead, and vendors set up openair stalls within the roofless walls of their shops. Once more their singsong voices called their wares to the attention of passersby.

And yet all these sounds and signs of industry held dreamlike transience, even for the poor and the beggars who stood furthest from the center of power. Rumors respected no class boundaries. And like the wrecked timbers still heaped like bones between the fabric of makeshift walls, disquieting undercurrents dogged the City's normality. Tsuranuanni's Emperor was upon another world, and Iskisu, the God of trickery and Chance, held the balance—not only the peace of two peoples, but the stability of an ancient nation; all hinged upon the meeting of minds between two young rulers from vastly different cultures.

Deprived of the solace of her courtyard and fountains, Mara spent her hours within the small room in the center of the apartment. With soldiers camped in the chambers on either side, and guards at each door and window, she studied notes and messages and maintained cautious contact with other Lords. Arakasi showed up almost hourly, in the guises of bird seller, messenger, and even mendicant priest. He had not slept, but labored tirelessly between brief naps, employing every tool at his disposal to discover even the faintest shred of information that might be of use.

In an adjoining room, Lujan held sword drill with his soldiers, one man at a time. The waiting frayed everyone's nerves, the warriors' most of all, since they could do nothing but stand through endless idle hours on watch. Several more Acoma companies had slipped into the city, and by dint of clever planning and the use of a carpet dealer's cart, more warriors had been smuggled into the imperial precinct. Mara's apartment garrison now numbered fifty-two, and Jican complained. His scullions could not scrub pots without banging into scabbards, and Lujan would have warriors sleeping four deep on the carpets if he continued to muster more troops. But the numbers of warriors were unlikely to swell beyond the current count, for the Acoma as well as other houses. Imperial Guards had noticed the influx of soldiers into the palace and were now inspecting all inbound wagons and servants to limit potential combatants.

Racing footsteps echoed through the outer corridor. The tap of the runner's sandals passed through the walls, a ghostly, whispered counterpoint to the clack and snap of swordplay between Lujan's sparring warriors. Mara heard, from her desk in the middle chamber. She stiffened and looked wildly at Kevin. "Something has happened."

The Midkemian did not ask how she knew, or why this set of hurried steps should be different from those of any of the dozen or so runners that had passed by the apartment within the hour. Bored with being cooped up, and with the endless, dragging hours that passed between Arakasi's reports, Kevin bowed to the warrior he had challenged at dice, and crossed the chamber to sit with his Lady. "What's to do?" he murmured.

Mara regarded the inkwell and parchment on her lap desk. The pen in her hands was dry, and the letter unmarked, except for the name of Hokanu of the Shinzawai in careful characters at the top. "Nothing," she replied. "There is nothing to do, except wait."

She set down her quill and, to keep her hands busy, picked up the Acoma chop. She did not say, and Kevin did not remind her, that Arakasi was late. He had promised to stop by in the morning, and by the white slash of sunlight that glared through the barricaded screens, noon had come and gone.

Long minutes passed, filled with the patter of more runners, and the muffled, excited tones of someone speaking urgently from an apartment several doors down. The thin plaster and lath partitions between domiciles were not impervious to sound. While Mara made a pretense of trying to concentrate on the wording of her message, Kevin touched her shoulder, then slipped away into the kitchen to make hot chocha.

When he returned, the Lady had done little but dip her quill. The ink had set in the nib. Arakasi had not returned. When Kevin set the tray on top of the parchment, Mara did not protest. She accepted the filled cup he handed her, but the drink cooled untasted. By then her nerves were showing, and she started up at the slightest sound. More steps passed by, all running.

"You don't suppose somebody's holding footraces, and making odds to pass the time?" Kevin suggested in an attempt at humor.

Lujan appeared in the doorway, soaked with sweat from his exercises, and still gripping his unsheathed sword. "Footracers don't wear battle sandals with studs," he commented dryly. Then he looked at Mara, who sat as still as a figure in a china shop, with too little color in her face. "My Lady, at your word, I could go out and find a rumormonger."

Mara turned paler. "No," she said sharply. "You are too valuable to risk." Then she frowned, as she weighed whether she should deplete her garrison by two and send a pair of warriors on the errand instead. Arakasi was three hours late, and to hold uselessly to false hope was to invite yet greater risk.

A scratch came at the outer screen. Lujan spun, his sword pointed at the barricade, and every other Acoma guard in the room whipped around ready for attack.

But the scrape was followed by a whisper that caused Mara to cry, "Thank the gods!"

Quickly, cautiously, the warriors let down the wooden tabletop, wedged up by three heavy coffers, and cracked the screen. Arakasi entered, a black silhouette against daylight. For an instant fresh air filled with the sweet scent of flowers swirled through the close apartment. Then Kenji fastened the screen and slotted the wooden pegs that secured it, and coffers and tabletop were replaced with swift dispatch.

In the falling gloom, Arakasi found his way to Mara's cushions in five unerring strides. He threw himself prostrate before her. "Mistress, forgive my delay."

At his tone, a mixture of disbelief and masked anger, Mara's brief joy at his return vanished. "What's amiss?"

"All," said the Spy Master without preamble. "Wild rumors sweep the palace. There has been trouble upon the barbarian world."

Mara relinquished her quill pen before tension caused her to snap it. Somehow her voice remained firm. "The Emperor?"

"He is safe, but little more is known." Arakasi's voice became gritty with rage. "The barbarians acted with dishonor. They sang a song of peace while they plotted murder. At the conference, despite their bond of truce, they attacked suddenly and almost killed the Emperor."

Mara sat speechless in shock, and Kevin cursed in astonishment. "What?"

Arakasi sat back on his heels, his manner bleak. "At the conference, a large company of those you call dwarves and elves massed nearby, and when the Light of Heaven was most vulnerable, they attacked."

Kevin shook his head in denial. "I can't believe this."

Arakasi's eyes narrowed. "It is true. Only through the bravery of his officers and the Warchiefs of the Five Families did the Light of Heaven survive this treachery on your world. Two soldiers carried him back through the rift, unconscious, and there followed a terrible thing. The rift closed and could not be reopened, trapping four thousand Tsurani soldiers upon the Midkemian world."

Mara's confusion sharpened into rapt attention. She drew a quick breath. "Minwanabi?"

"Dead," snapped Arakasi. "He was among the very first to fall. His cousin Jeshurado died at his side."

"The other Warchiefs?"

"Gone. Dead or not, none can say, but the rift exists no more. All of the Warlord's honor guard remain trapped upon the barbarian world."

Mara couldn't comprehend the enormity of this. "Xacatecas?"

The list continued, inexorably. "Gone. Lord Chipino was last seen fighting Kingdom horsemen."

"All of them?" Mara whispered.

"Scarcely a handful returned," Arakasi said, anguished. "The two soldiers who carried the Light of Heaven and a half dozen who served to marshal soldiers waiting on our side of the rift. The Imperial Force Commander was killed. Lord Keda lay bleeding upon the ground. Lord Tonmargu was nowhere to be seen. Pimaca of the Oaxatucan also was unaccounted for. Kasumi of the Shinzawai was the one who forced the Emperor to leave, but he did not himself pass the rift." Arakasi forced himself to take a breath. "The runner who arrived in the city knew nothing more than this, my Lady. I doubt at this time that even those involved could hazard much beyond guesses as to who is gone. The losses are too widespread, and the shock of the event far too sudden. After the Emperor assumes command, we may have a clearer idea of what occurred."

Silent a long minute, Mara leaped to her feet. "Arakasi, you must go out and ascertain an accurate list of losses, and survivors. Quickly."

Her urgency must not be denied. At a stroke the Empire had lost its most powerful older Lords and the heirs to many important houses. The effects would be too widespread to anticipate—houses in mourning, troops lost, and young, untried second sons and daughters thrown headlong into rulership. The aftereffects of such turmoil left only stunned shock. But Mara knew that the ambitious would very quickly transform turmoil to a devastating, bloody grab for power. She understood what it was to have authority and responsibility newly thrust upon one unprepared for them. Knowing who was in that frightening predicament and who was still alive to rule with experience could prove a significant advantage in days to come.

As Arakasi bowed and hurried out, Mara stripped off her lounging robe and called for her maid to bring formal garments. Kevin hurried to help her undress, while she delivered rapid instructions. "Lujan, ready an honor guard. We leave for the Council Hall at once."

Caught with both hands full of pins as the maid began arranging Mara's hair, Kevin said, "Shall I go with you?"

Mara shook her head, then spoiled the maid's efforts by leaning forward and giving him a fast kiss. "There will be no welcome for one of your nation in this council today, Kevin. For your safety, please stay out of sight."

Shamed by his countrymen's broken faith, Kevin did not argue. But a short time later, when thirty Acoma guards marched in lockstep and vanished beyond the far concourse, he wondered how he was going to survive the wait. For the Lady of Acoma did not go to a council but to frightening, unmitigated chaos in which the strongest would move fastest to seize power.

Desio dead did not leave one enemy less on her heels, but rather elevated a more competent foe to primacy. Tasaio now ruled the Minwanabi.

17. *GREY COUNCIL*

The hall filled.

Although there had been no sanctioned call to council, when Mara and her warriors arrived at the great chamber many Lords were there ahead of her. Perhaps a quarter of the seats were occupied, with more arrivals by the minute. The lack of council guards kept no ruler away; each lord had from a dozen to fifty armed men close at hand. No imperial herald announced Mara's name as she entered the wide portals and descended the stair. This unofficial gathering had no pomp or ceremony; house rulers entered in the order that they came, all concerns of rank set aside.

Neither did any particular house act as spokesman. Several Lords conferred near the platform dais that customarily seated the Warlord or, in his absence, an appointed First Speaker of the Council. With Almecho dead, and all of the Clan Warchiefs either killed or lost, no single house held clear-cut supremacy. But sooner or later, some Lord might try to seize power or at least intervene to hinder the advancement of a rival. Those Lords already present stood in tight-knit, whispering groups, divided roughly by faction. They eyed all newcomers with suspicion, and kept their warriors close at hand—no one wished to be the first to draw sword in the council, but everyone was more than prepared to be the second. Mara swiftly scanned the gathering for familiar or friendly house colors. The red and yellow of the Anasati stood out boldly amid a cluster of older nobles who conferred in the aisle between the lower-level seats and the dais. Mara recognized her former father-in-law. She hastened down to meet him, taking Lujan and two warriors for protection.

Seeing Mara approach, Tecuma of the Anasati turned and bowed slightly. He wore armor, but the hair that showed beneath his helm was now more white than iron-grey. His face, always thin, now seemed drawn taut to the bone, and his eyes darkly shadowed.

In acknowledgment of a superior power, Mara returned his bow and said, "Are you well, grandfather of my son?"

Tecuma seemed almost to look through her. He said, "I am well, mother of my grandson." His lips thinned as he cast a glance around the disordered bands of speakers in the hall. "Would that the Empire were as fit."

"The Emperor?" Mara said, hungry for information.

"The Light of Heaven, from all reports, lies at rest in his command tent upon the plain near the rift gate." Tecuma's tone stayed hard. "When Ichindar recovered from his incapacitation, he made known to his officers that he seeks a return to the Kingdom of the Isles to launch another invasion. Yet our desire to punish these barbarians for their treachery may be frustrated. The Great Ones may manipulate a rift, but they do not control all its aspects. Whether this one to Midkemia can be reestablished is doubtful."

Again the Lord of the Anasati regarded the house rulers who gathered in the great hall, in defiance of the Emperor's orders. He softened not at all as he concluded, "Meanwhile, the business of the game continues."

Taking swift stock of other elders present, Mara said, "Who shall speak for the Ionani?"

Secure in his power, and holding a name among the oldest in the Empire, Tecuma said, "Until Clan Ionani retires to elect a new Warchief, I shall be its spokesman." Abruptly he pointed across the room. "There gathers Clan Hadama, my Lady. I suggest you hurry there and make your presence known."

"Lord Tecuma—"

The old man interrupted with his hand. "Mara, I am a grieving man, so forgive my bluntness." His manner grew piercingly forced. "Halesko was one of those trapped upon the alien world—and by all reports he lay dying upon a lance. I have lost a second son this day. I have no time for the woman who took away my first."

Mara felt her throat tighten. She bowed lower in sympathy. "My apologies, Tecuma. I was tactless not to realize."

The Lord of the Anasati shook his head slightly in what might have been a gesture of suppressed disbelief, or pain. "Many of us mourn, Mara. Many brothers, sons, and fathers were trapped upon the alien world. The loss is a blow to our honor and to our hearts. Now, if you would excuse me?" Without waiting for a reply, he turned his back on his former daughter-in-law and resumed the discussion she had interrupted.

Left outside his circle, and given a hostile look from the Yellow Flower Party member cut off when she addressed Tecuma, Mara moved on around the dais to the first set of stairs, where the Hadama Clan chiefs stood in caucus. Several bowed with respect as Mara approached, while others gave her a perfunctory nod. One or two, along with a palsied elder seated in a litter chair, offered the Acoma ruler no sign of greeting at all. Mara took stock and said, "How many losses have we suffered?"

The Lord of the Sutanta, a tall man in dark blue robe with pale blue trim, gave her a perfunctory bow. "Lord Chekowara and his forty warriors are on their way from the City of the Plains. The Lord of the Cozinchach and two vassals remain with the Emperor. Hadama's losses were slight, since smaller clans were not placed in the forefront of the lines at the betrayal. Most of our rulers will be returning to Kentosani within the week."

"Who called this council?" asked Mara.

Lord Sutanta's leathery features stayed carefully blank. "Who called you here?"

Equally noncommittal, Mara said, "I just came."

With a wave of his hand, Lord Sutanta indicated the filling chamber. "No one here would speak against the will of the Light of Heaven." He fixed bird-bright eyes upon Mara. "Also, no one here would see their firstborn son dead of treachery and sit idly at home."

Mara nodded, and inwardly concluded the things that remained unsaid. The defiance of Ichindar's play for power was being politely acknowledged. But in the Great Game, courtesy often masked murder. The High Council of Tsuranuanni intended to make itself heard. There would be no formal meeting this day; too many Lords were absent. No Lord would make a move until it was known which enemies and which allies remained alive to be reckoned with. Today was for taking stock, and tomorrow was for playing, seizing advantage over rivals for the openings that chance had offered. And while this council was unauthorized, this meeting was no less a round of the Great Game, for while a grey warrior could kill as easily as one sworn to house colors, so was this grey council just as deadly as one with imperial sanction.

Mara stole a quiet moment for review. Acoma prospects were not reassuring. The Minwanabi had lost a few opponents and gained a new Lord who could use all their resources, especially military might, to full potential. The odds did not favor Lord Xacatecas. As Warchief of Clan Xacala, Lord Chipino would have stood in the Emperor's front rank; his eldest son, Dezilo, would have represented Xacatecas as third of the Five Great Families. Both were lost, which left Lady Isashani and a brood of offspring, the oldest of which were young and untrained for the Lord's mantle—Mara's strongest ally was now dangerously weakened. All too reliant upon Ayaki's tenuous blood tie with the Anasati for some protection, Mara felt as though a cold breeze blew against her naked back.

Around her, like jagunas sniffing over corpses before deciding which choice bits to fight over, the ruling Lords of Tsuranuanni gathered with members of their clans, then splintered off to speak with allies and factions, usually along party lines.

The Acoma were technically members of a minor political party, the Jade Eye, but the connection had lapsed since Lord Sezu's rule. Mara had little to do with party politics, being far too consumed by the need to preserve her house from obliteration. But with all the Empire now cast into upheaval, no tie was too tenuous to ignore.

Mara threaded her way past Lord Inrodaka, and the Lord of the Ekamchi's fat second son, and a cousin of the Lord of the Kehotara, who conferred together in whispers and cast her cold glances. Finding two other members of the Jade Eye Party beyond them, Mara approached and began a conversation that devolved from lists of sad condolences. The dead and those abandoned beyond the rift seemed to haunt by their absence. Yet life in Tsuranuanni did not retreat from losses. Around the hall, members of the High Council explored byplays behind façades of polite conversation, and all the while they played, once more, the Great Game.

Lightning rent the sky, flashing silver-white on the great house of the Minwanabi. Seated at his lap desk, pen in hand, with fresh ink by his elbow, Incomo reviewed the documents arrayed before him, ignoring the sound of driving rain from outside. He was never a fast thinker, and now his shock and disbelief would not leave him. The events surrounding the Emperor's betrayal still seemed the uneasy aftermath of a nightmare. That Desio was dead was undoubted. Three witnesses reported seeing him go down with arrows in his throat and chest—his cousin Jeshurado already dead at his feet. No friend or retainer had been near enough to rescue the Lord's body from the chaos before the magical rift closed, forever sealing Kelewan from Midkemia.

Incomo pressed dry palms to his temples and inhaled a breath of damp air. Desio of the Minwanabi rested with his ancestors, if indeed a man's spirit could cross the unknowable gulf between worlds. The rites had been said in the Minwanabi sacred glade by a hastily summoned priest, and runners departed with the news. All that remained to be done was await the new Lord's return from the outpost in the western isles.

At that moment the screen at the First Advisor's back slipped open. Warm, damp air swept through the room, ruffling the parchment and spattering a fall of wind-borne drops across the floor. "I left orders not to be disturbed," Incomo snapped.

A dry, incisive voice said, "Then pardon the interruption, First Adviser. But time passes, and there is much to be done."

Incomo started and spun around. He saw a warrior, backlit by a white flash of lightning, step through the doorway. Water streamed off his battle armor and slicked his officer's plume into spikes. Light-footed, lithe, and almost without sound, the man reached the circle of radiance cast by the room's single lamp. He swept off his helm. Shadows circled his honey-colored eyes, and wet hair clung to his neck.

Incomo dropped his quill and bowed from the waist in obeisance. "Tasaio!"

Tasaio looked Incomo in the eyes for a silent moment and then said slowly, "I'll forgive the familiarity this time, First Adviser. Never again."

Incomo shoved his lap desk aside, spilling quill and parchment, and nearly upsetting the inkwell. He unfolded gaunt legs and stiffly touched his forehead to the floor. "My Lord."

The boom of the storm filled silence while Tasaio looked keenly around the room. He did not grant Incomo permission to rise, but studied the painted images of birds, the worn sleeping mat, and lastly, most leisurely of all, the prostrate elder on the carpet. "Yes. Tasaio. Lord of the Minwanabi."

At last given leave to sit upright, Incomo said, "How did you—"

The new master interrupted in a tone that was faintly derisive. "Incomo! Did you think yourself the only one with agents in this house? My cousin commanded my loyalty, but never my respect. Never would I dishonor the Minwanabi name, but in my position only a fool would have left cousin Desio unobserved."

Tasaio smoothed back drenched bangs, then adjusted the set of his sword belt. "Since the moment I set foot on that cursed island, I kept one boat in readiness, manned and provisioned to leave. Day or night, if the call came, the lines need only be cast off. On the instant of my cousin's death, those loyal to me sent word to the Outpost Isles." Tasaio shrugged, scattering droplets in the lamplight. "I took a boat to Nar and commandeered the first ship. When is the High Council to elect a new Warlord?"

Eyes fixed on the runnels of rainwater that threatened his sleeping mat, Incomo reordered his thoughts. "Word came only this morning. The Light of Heaven has called the High Council into session, to meet three days from now."

In almost silken calm, Tasaio said, "You would have let me miss that meeting, Incomo?"

Wet pillows quite abruptly ceased to matter. "My Lord!" Again Incomo pressed his forehead to the floor. "Desio's end was most sudden. Our swiftest messenger departed within the hour, with orders to choose the fastest boat. I humbly submit that I did my best. Do not fault a servant's limits, when my Lord has been clever beyond the expected call of duty."

Tasaio laughed without humor. "I dislike pointless flattery, First Adviser, as well as unconvincing humility. Rise, and remember that."

A loud peal of thunder rattled the house, and echoes boomed across the night-dark lake. With a field commander's ability to adjust his voice to noise, Tasaio said, "Here are your orders, First Adviser. Dismiss Desio's body servants and concubines. I have staff of my own, and they will attend me as I don my robes of mourning. I shall sleep this night in the officers' barracks. Tell my hadonra to clear everything that belonged to Desio from the Lord's quarters. I want the chambers stripped. My carry boxes and personal items will be fully installed by dawn, and the old Lord's robes, bedding, and other personal items will be burned." Tasaio's eyes narrowed. "Tell the kennel master to cut the throats of the man-killer hounds—they will answer to no other master. After first light, assemble every member of this household on the drill field. A new Lord of the Minwanabi rules, and all must understand that inefficiency will not be tolerated."

"As my Lord wishes." Incomo prepared for a sleepless night. He unfolded sore knees and made ready to stand, but his master had not finished.

The Lord of the Minwanabi regarded his First Adviser with flat, unwavering eyes. "You do not need to indulge me as you did my cousin. I will hear your thoughts on all matters, even if my opinion lies contrary. You may suggest as you see fit until the moment I give orders. Then you will silently obey. Tomorrow we shall review the accounts and call together an honor guard. By midday I wish to be in my barge of state, on my way downriver to Kentosani. See that every detail is in order for my journey. For when I reach the Holy City I intend to present my case."

"What case, my Lord?" Incomo inquired in tacit respect.

At last Tasaio smiled, a sword-sharp brightness to his expression. "Why, to assume the seat of Warlord, obviously. Who has a better claim than I?"

Incomo felt the hair stir at his neck. At last, after years of wishful yearning, he would serve a Lord who was clever, competent, and ambitious.

Thunder shook the floor again, and rain slashed against the screens. Straight in the wavering flare of lamplight,

Tasaio finished his thought. "Once I wear the white and gold, we shall obliterate the Acoma."

Incomo bowed again. When he rose, the room was empty, a draft through the darkened doorway the only trace of his master's visit. Silently the First Adviser considered the desire he had never dared utter, but that fate and the gods had freely granted: Tasaio now wore the Minwanabi mantle. Touched by a mood of dry irony, Incomo wondered why the gift left him feeling worn and old.

The storm left runoff that trickled in streams around the luck symbols anchored to the roof peaks of the Imperial Palace, and downspouts dripped into puddles in the courtyards. Inside the building, the sound of falling water became muffled; drafts played like sighs up and down the cavernous corridors, setting streaming the flames of those lamps that servants had bothered to light. Lujan and five armored warriors marched briskly through concourses gloomy with shadows to report back to the Acoma apartment.

Mara met her Force Commander in the middle room, where she conferred with Arakasi. Kevin stood by the wall at her shoulder, his mood of biting sarcasm brought on by inactivity. He had a headache. His teeth were on edge from listening to warriors sharpen weapons, and the reek of the lacquer used to preserve laminated-hide armor made his stomach queasy.

Before the Lady's cushions, Lujan arose from his bow. "Mistress," he said briskly, "we bring word of new movement by Sajaio, Tondora, and Gineisa soldiers into apartments previously unoccupied."

Mara frowned. "Minwanabi dogs. Any word of the kennel master himself?"

"No. Not yet." Lujan unstrapped his helm and scuffed his fingers through damp hair.

Arakasi looked up from the untidy pile of the notes passed on to him that morning by his contacts throughout the palace. He regarded the Acoma Force Commander with hooded eyes. "In three more days, the Emperor will return to the palace."

Propped by one shoulder against the wall, his arms folded

across his chest, Kevin said, "Taking his own sweet time about it, isn't he?"

"There are a great number of rituals and ceremonies along the way," Mara broke in, her irritation barely masked. "One does not travel with twenty priests, a thousand bodyguards, and five thousand soldiers and make speed."

Kevin shrugged. Confinement and stress affected them all. For two days the business in council had been building momentum. Mara spent up to fifteen hours at a stretch closeted in the great hall. At night she returned so exhausted that she barely had inclination to eat. She looked peaked and thin, and despite lavish solicitude from her lover, what little sleep she garnered was troubled. If the nights were unsatisfactory, the days were worse. Inactivity of any sort burned Kevin's nerves, but even boredom had limits. Duty in the scullery drove him to vocal rebellion, and though seldom given to self-indulgence, he lacked the fatalism that enabled the Tsurani warriors to endure in seemingly endless patience.

Mara sighed and took stock of her gains. "So far I have held council with seventeen Lords, and have bound only four to agreements." She shook her head. "A poor record. No one wishes to commit, though many pretend to be willing. Too many factions contend for the Warlord's seat, and to support one candidate openly brings the enmity of all of his rivals."

Arakasi uncrumpled a note that carried a pungent smell of fish. "My agent at the dockside reports the arrival of Dajalo of the Keda."

Mara perked up at this. "Is he in residence at his town house, or the Imperial Palace?"

"Patience, Lady." Arakasi shuffled through his notes, discarded three, then scanned the coded script of another that smelled intriguingly of perfume. "Town house," the Spy Master concluded. "At least for tonight."

Mara clapped hands for the scribe brought in to help with correspondence. "Address this to Lord Dajalo of the Keda. First offer our condolences at the death of his father, along with our certainty that his end was both brave and honorable. Then let Dajalo understand that the Acoma hold a document over Lord Andero's personal chop that binds House Keda to one vote of our choosing. Dajalo, as new ruling Lord, is bound to honor this."

"Mistress," Arakasi broke in. "Isn't this a little . . . abrupt?"

Mara ran her fingers through the masses of her hair, the ends of which were still crimped into curls from being pinned. "Perhaps I have acquired habits from this barbarian I keep around." She paused, as thunder rolled in the distance. "Have no doubt . . . Tasaio of the Minwanabi will be among us quite soon, and then I may need this vote instantly."

A tap at the entry interrupted. A guard appeared in the doorway and bowed. "Mistress, our scouts report armed men moving through the outer hallways of the palace."

Mara glanced at Lujan, who jammed his helm over tangled hair and left still fastening the strap. Lightning flickered silver beyond the outer screens, reduced to slits between barricades now reinforced with raw boards. Kevin resisted a caged animal's need to pace, while Mara and Arakasi made a pretense of reading reports. The scratch of the scribe's quill filled the interval until the Force Commander returned.

His bow was almost cursory as he said, "Our lookouts have spied two bands of soldiers, numbering twenty to thirty each. They pass in the shadows and would seem to be moving toward another section of the palace."

"What house?" Mara asked, half-fearful to hear the reply.

"None, pretty Lady," Lujan's reassurance was dubious. "These wear black armor, without markings or badge."

Mara raised eyes gone wide in the lamplight. "Then it is beginning."

Lujan passed quiet orders to the warriors in the front chamber. The last screen left cracked to let in air was drawn shut and wedged in its frame with wooden pegs. A table was turned on end and levered against the outer door, then braced in place with a massive bar. Now the humidity brought in by the storm became like a stifling blanket. Arakasi seemed unaffected, where he sat in poised stillness poring over his notes.

But Kevin sweated and chafed, his empty hands itching for a blade. The hours wore on toward midnight. Sounds came muffled through the walls. Footfalls splashed through puddles, or pounded down hallways and stairs, sometimes broken by a shout. The rain ceased, and insects in Mara's garden rasped their nightly song.

Since nobody seemed inclined to attend to the commonplace necessities, Kevin finally knelt at Mara's shoulder and pulled away the parchment she had held without reading for an hour. "You must be hungry," he coaxed.

Mara leaned her head against him. "Not really. But I should eat something if I am to be alert in council tomorrow."

Kevin arose, prepared for the inevitable battle of wills that transpired when he invaded the kitchen. Jican considered any slave caught empty-handed to be fair game. Tonight he seemed primed for the fight, since a squad of busy scullions was already scouring kettles and plates. As if the din of crockery were a charm to ward away the distant sounds of conflict, every ladle or cup or soup bowl was getting sanded down and polished. Jican spotted Kevin in the doorway, and his worried face brightened. "The mistress wishes to eat?"

Kevin nodded, and found himself the startled recipient of a tray of warm bread, cheeses, and fruit. Disappointed by his easy victory, he swallowed a carefully prepared retort and returned to his Lady. He set down the supper and sat with her, while she made a concerted effort to take sustenance. In the end, Arakasi finished the food. Kevin urged Mara to bed, while at every window and door the warriors waited like statues, prepared for an attack that never came.

Morning dawned. Mara arose from her cushions and called for her bath and her maids. Makeup erased the shadows of worry from her face, and three layers of formal robes disguised her thinness. At the last minute, just as she was poised to leave, she turned and looked hard at Kevin.

Nettled by the prospect of another tedious day, he regarded her with reproachful blue eyes.

Mostly because she feared an attack on her apartment in her absence, Mara gave in to impulse and relented. "Come with me. Remain close and stay silent unless I tell you otherwise."

Kevin fairly leaped to join her retinue. Lujan called her honor guard to form ranks, and minutes later the Acoma contingent made their entrance into the Council Hall.

Sunlight angled across the dome overhead, spotlighting the yellowed murals above the galleries. The upper seats were already filled, with those lowest still empty. The chaos had subsided enough for Tsurani nobles to be once more attentive to rank, Kevin observed. He followed Mara down the steps, while Lujan took station with two other warriors behind her. The rest of her honor guard remained on the concourse by the door, as if this council were no different from any other.

But as she passed an empty chair on the way to her appointed place, Mara pressed her fingers to her mouth to stifle a cry of shock. "Trouble?" Kevin murmured, his promise of silence forgotten.

Mara returned a barely perceptible nod. Clearly unhappy, she whispered, "The Lord Pataki of the Sida is dead."

Kevin said, "Who?"

"A man who was kind to me once, in defiance of public sentiment. He was also a potential ally. Yesterday he was here, but this morning his seat is vacant."

"How do you know he isn't just lingering over breakfast?" Kevin murmured.

Mara settled into her chair and nodded for her slave to stand behind and to her right. "Only an assassin could have kept Pataki from this chamber." She made an inventory of the nearby galleries. "Three other lords are also absent, from the look of things."

"Friends of yours?" Kevin did his best to keep his voice down.

"No. Enemies of Minwanabi," answered Mara. She snapped her small ornamental fan open and murmured something to Lujan, who arranged his warriors around her seat, then assumed the place nearest the aisle where his sword would be first in her defense.

The lowest gallery was now beginning to fill. Kevin looked around at the great Lords of the Empire, dressed up like peacocks in full plumage. Some sat like royalty in their places, speaking to those who came to petition for favors or alliances. Others stood in clumps, changing position or exchanging confidences like butterflies congregating around flowers. The Game of the Council was less an overt battle for hierarchy than a subtle, endless sequence of encounter, rebuff, and social machination.

"I don't understand," Kevin said after long minutes of study. "No one seems to act as if four of their fellow councilors were murdered."

"Death is part of the game," Mara answered, and as the morning wore on, Kevin came finally to understand. To show undue notice of another's defeat was to imply dishonor, since murder in and of itself meant that someone was responsible. In the absence of proof, the Tsurani perceived only "accidents." A Lord might kill with impunity, and even win the admiration of his rivals for doing so, as long as the forms were observed.

A middle-aged Lord sauntered up to Mara, who rose in greeting and bowed. Social conversation was exchanged, with a word or two concerning trade issues. Kevin was left to his own thoughts. This calm conducting of business during the day, while assassins had roamed the palace the night before, frightened him beyond anything he had known since he was captured.

A rustle of voices swept through the room as a young man strode into the lower gallery. Flanked by six guards in scarlet and grey armor, he assumed one of the more imposing chairs opposite the central dais. Heads turned to watch as he motioned an adviser to his side. After a word in conference, the minister bowed and immediately hurried up the steps to where Mara and the other noble spoke. Aware by a low stir of whispering that something significant had occurred, Kevin watched the exchange.

The adviser made Mara a bow. "My Lady of the Acoma, my Lord wishes you to know that the Keda stand ready to honor any debt incurred in their name."

Mara inclined her head slightly, and the minister departed. This message had a profound effect upon the man whose conversation was interrupted. His entire manner changed, from dominance to sincere subservience. And suddenly several other lesser nobles were making their way down from the galleries, seeking word with the Lady of the Acoma.

Kevin watched in wonder as the subtle currents of Tsurani politics shifted, with Mara becoming more and more a central object of attention. With the leaders of the Five Great Houses lost on the alien world, the more powerful clans were caught up in their own internecine struggle. This left openings for the lesser families within those clans, and for the smaller clans within the council, to negotiate, make promises, and seek out potential support. If the armies of the mighty were to march upon one another in rivalry, the weaker houses needed to stand together, or else insinuate themselves beneath the mantle of more powerful protectors. Treaties and standoffs were arranged, concessions were made freely and under duress, and trade properties changed owners as sureties and gifts. As the day wore on toward noon, Kevin realized that Mara had not yet needed to leave her chair: interested parties came to her, which did not escape the notice of other factions. Inrodaka and Ekamchi glanced often toward the vacant seat of the Lord of the Minwanabi, while members of the Ionani Clan made smiling remarks to a stiff-faced Tecuma of the Anasati.

Just before midday, a company of soldiers in purple and yellow entered and accompanied a slender young man of dark good looks to the chair of the Xacatecas. The heir to Chipino's mantle took his place within the council with all of his father's cool poise. Mara, watching, flipped out her fan and held it pressed for a moment against her forehead. Kevin sensed her distress. He could offer no word of sympathy, but only stand rigid as he, too, noticed with a wrench how much the Xacatecas boy resembled his departed father.

Three Lords waited politely for Mara's attention. She recovered her poise and entertained them with anecdotes until most of the Lords of Clan Xacala had had time to present themselves to the heir of their former Warchief.

A lull came at last. Mara beckoned to Lujan and descended the shallow stair, until she stood before the Lord of the Xacatecas. Up close, Hoppara looked every inch the young raptor, though his hair and eyes were a warmer brown, and his slenderness was his mother Isashani's. But he had Chipino's bearing and presence, even in untried youth. He rose, formally bowed, and said, "Are you well, Mara of the Acoma?"

Mara felt her color rise. By inquiring after her health before she could speak, Hoppara had acknowledged before all present that Mara was his social superior! Since his blood was of the Five Great Families, this gesture was little more than a courtesy, but in some meaningful if subtle way the concession held stunning consequence. Even as Mara drew breath to frame her reply, she could sense the stir in the galleries. Nobles near Lord Xacatecas regarded her with astonished awe, while others looked sourly on from their seats across the dais.

Her answer held true warmth. "I am well, my Lord of the Xacatecas. Your grief is the grief of House Acoma. Your father was a credit to his family and clan, and more. He defended the Empire's borders with courage and honored the Acoma by permitting us to count him an ally. I would consider it a signal privilege if you would number my house among the friends of the Xacatecas."

Hoppara managed a creditable smile, though the effort did not entirely mask his grief. "My Lady, I would count it an honor if you would consent to dine with me this afternoon."

Mara bowed formally, indicating she was at his disposal. The way back to her own chair was suddenly impeded by a wave of flatterers, and until the Xacatecas First Adviser came calling to fetch her to lunch, she had no moment to herself.

The Xacatecas apartments in the Imperial Palace were twice the size of Mara's. The carpets and antiques were sumptuous, black-lacquered furnishings in tasteful contrast to shades of lavender, royal purple, and cream. Li birds in hanging wicker cages filled the room with song and the flutter of brightly colored wings. Mara recognized Isashani's love of comfort and grace, and she settled in relief upon soft, thick cushions. The servants had been trained by Lord Chipino, and one of them had served on the desert campaign. Already familiar with her habits, he held a bowl of water scented with the perfume she preferred. As Mara washed, she thought sadly of the old master, while Kevin found his place on the floor behind her shoulder.

Hoppara shed his heavy outer robe, pushed a hand through tightly curled hair, then seated himself opposite a low table laden with a sumptuous lunch. He sighed, tugged his sleeves back to free strong, suntanned wrists, then offered his hands to be washed by the body slave who waited at his elbow.

When the slave had finished the ablutions, the young Lord turned frank eyes to study the bearded barbarian who stuck to Mara like a shadow.

Kevin stared levelly back until Hoppara raised an eyebrow. "This is your barbarian lover?"

The curiosity did not offend. Hoppara had his father's bluntness and his mother's shrewd judgment of people. He was simply being direct, not mocking her personal choices. Mara returned a slight nod, and Hoppara gave back Isashani's disarming smile. "My father mentioned this man to me. If it is the same one?"

"This is Kevin," Mara said guardedly.

Hoppara nodded in satisfaction. "Yes. The slave who owns a full set of armor in Acoma colors." He sighed, his sorrow barely concealed. "My father told us how this Kevin was more than merely useful in the battle fought in the desert."

Mara smiled slightly, indicating the point was not lost. "He had one or two . . . suggestions."

Li birds sang sweetly through an interval of reflection. "Father was not often free with compliments," Hoppara admitted. He stared at the cutlery as if he saw memories instead of food on the plates. "He credited much of what he saw in the field to brilliantly original ideas. He said no Tsurani would have thought to order his soldiers onto the backs of cho-ja warriors. The tactic impressed him greatly." The young Lord gave his guest another engaging smile. "As he was also impressed with you, my Lady."

Kevin suddenly felt a stir of jealousy as Mara blushed at the compliment. "I thank you, my Lord."

"Is it hot?" Hoppara said suddenly, as if the color on the Lady's face had other cause than his attention. He waved for a servant to open the screen, and sunlight and air spilled into the room. The garden beyond was planted in violet flowers and canopied over with fruit trees. Then, as if Lujan's slight stiffness revealed that a guest might be concerned for her safety in the Xacatecas home, the Lord offered swift reassurance. "This apartment backs up to a barracks that houses the Emperor's honor guard. Eighty Imperial Whites are in residence at all times."

When Lujan stayed unbendingly alert, Hoppara's tone turned genial. "Mother never liked that much. She said she could never wear lounging robes or bathe in her garden without putting the Imperial Family at risk. Assassins could be murdering them all, she insisted, and there the Imperial

Guards would be, peeking over the walls with the wrong spears raised, and not an eye among them on defense."

Mara smiled. Lady Isashani's beauty was legendary—repeated motherhood over the years had done little more than add a mature lushness to her figure—and her forthright, spicy tongue was the outrageous delight of polite Tsurani society. "How is your mother?" Mara inquired.

Hoppara sighed. "Well enough. My father's and older brother's deaths were a blow to her, of course. Did you know," he added, unwilling to lose the thread of his original subject, "that my sire suggested you might marry one of his younger sons one day, should you escape from Desio's attempts to obliterate you?"

Mara's eyes opened wide at that, for gossip said Isashani unequivocally favored Hokanu for her match. "I'm flattered."

"You're not eating," Hoppara observed. He lifted his knife and stabbed a morsel of wine-soaked meat. "Please, refresh yourself. My sisters' lapdogs are all overweight. If the scullions give them more scraps, the poor beasts will end up being mistaken for pillows." Hoppara chewed thoughtfully. He appeared to weigh Mara's expression. Then he arrived at some inward decision, and his manner changed from charming to serious. "My father believed you will become one of the most dangerous women in the history of the Empire. As a man who chose his enemies with great care, he clearly wished to have you as a friend."

Mara could only bow low at the compliment. She sipped at her fruit drink and waited, while the li birds chirped dulcet melodies.

Now convinced beyond doubt that she would not soften to praise, Hoppara tore an end off a loaf of bread. He soaked the crust in a sauce and remarked, "You realize, of course, that many of us are going to die before the new Warlord is invested."

Mara made a spare gesture of assent. The white and gold had too many contenders, and alliances were too much in flux. Even a fool could perceive that rivalries would become bloody.

"I have been ordered to seek you out, and will bluntly make my point." Hoppara motioned to a servant, who bowed and unobtrusively began to remove the birdcages. Into an air of growing silence the young Lord said, "The Xacatecas wish to survive this ordeal without surrendering too much of the prestige my father gained in life. To this end, we look for the situation of greatest advantage. My First Adviser instructed me to offer you informal alliance and to promise whatever aid the Xacatecas can provide as long as—"

Mara stopped him with a raised finger. "A moment, my Lord. Ordered? Instructed? Who directed you?"

The young man's manner turned rueful. "She said you'd ask. My mother, of course."

Kevin laughed, and Mara said, "Your mother?"

Unabashed, Hoppara admitted, "I will not reach my twenty-fifth birthday for three more years, Lady Mara. I am Lord of the Xacatecas, but not . . ."

"Not yet Ruling Lord," she finished.

Hoppara sighed. "Not yet. Mother is Ruling Lady until then—if I can manage to stay alive."

"Then why isn't Lady Isashani here?" Kevin asked.

Hoppara glanced at Mara, who said, "He often forgets his place."

"And he never met Mother, obviously." The young Lord shook off discomfort. "Isashani might seem like a li bird, but she's as tough as any soldier and weighs her options like a silk merchant. She has six sons left, and four daughters. If she lost me, she would mourn, no doubt, but Chaiduni would take my place, and after him Mizu, then Elamku, and so on down the line. After us there are the get of my father's concubines, some eighteen sons, not counting those still in milk teeth, and another batch yet to hit the cradle." Now the boy colored, as he thought of the storms that had rocked the house when Lord Chipino had arrived home from the desert with six new concubines, every one of them pregnant.

"The Xacatecas would be a difficult line to eradicate," Kevin summed up.

Hoppara sighed in appreciation. "Too many babies and cousins with hundreds of offshoots, and every one but a moment away from being recognized as heir to Mother's office, if need be. My mother stays safely upon our estates, deputizing me to come here and conduct the business of the council." He gestured in the direction of the great hall. "Most of our rivals don't realize I am not Ruling Lord yet. And they won't be given cause to pose the question, since I have full authority from my mother to negotiate on behalf of House Xacatecas . . . within limits."

Mara's mind raced along as she examined the implications. "Then we know for a fact what few will guess: you did not come to council to claim the office of Warlord."

"Even had Father lived, he would be no higher than third among those who claim the white and gold," Hoppara said.

"Who stands higher?" Now, at long last, Mara found her appetite.

Hoppara shrugged. "I can only repeat my mother's view. Minwanabi has the most power, but the vote won't give him a clear majority. Should the Oaxatucan cease their internal bickering, an Omechan could succeed their former Warchief. They still wield impressive influence. The Kanazawai are in disgrace because of the failed peace plans, so even the Tonmargu rank higher than the Keda." He shrugged again, then concluded, "Minwanabi is the logical choice. Tasaio is a more than able general. Many will back him who wouldn't have supported Desio."

The meats suddenly lost their savor. Mara abandoned her plate. "We come to the crux of the matter. What are you proposing beyond alliance?"

Hoppara also put down his eating knife. "For all our vaunted power, the Xacatecas are presently disadvantaged. We lost two advisers in the company with my father, and we are short on reliable guidance. I have been instructed to follow your lead, unless your wits should fail you. Otherwise, I am to throw our support to Tasaio."

Kevin said, "You'd support that murderer? After his treasonous manipulations in Tsubar?"

Mara put up a hand, silencing him. "That is logical. Once Minwanabi wore the white and gold, the Xacatecas would be free from the immediate worry of attack from the other four great families."

"We would have time to muster our defenses while Tasaio was occupied destroying the Acoma." Hoppara's tone was matter-of-fact. "However," he hastened to add, "it is only a choice of last resort. While safest for the Xacatecas in the short run, an Empire under the dictates of a Minwanabi Warlord . . ." His voice trailed off in distaste.

Kevin voiced his puzzlement. "Damned if I understand that logic."

Hoppara's eyebrows rose. "I would have thought . . ." To Mara he said, "Have you not explained?"

As if the sunlight through the screen had suddenly lost its warmth, Mara sighed. "Only the roots of our current strife: the death of my father and brother."

A li bird, chirped, muffled, from the adjoining chamber. "Please cover the cages," Hoppara instructed a servant. He looked at his guest. "If I may?" At Mara's nod, he turned, troubled, to Kevin. "The Minwanabi are . . . strange. Inappropriate though it may be to pass judgment upon another noble family whose behavior remains honorable in public, there is something in the Minwanabi nature that makes them . . . more than merely dangerous."

Kevin returned a look of flat confusion. "Any mighty house is dangerous. And to my view, the Game of the Council is just treachery with protocols."

If Hoppara was shocked by the slave's outspokenness, he masked it well. Patiently he sought to elaborate. "You are here more because of Lady Mara's potential to be a threat than her not inconsequential charm." He bowed slightly as he said this. "But the Minwanabi are more than dangerous. . . . They are—"

Mara interrupted, "They are insane."

Hoppara held up his hand. "That is harsh. Understandable, in your case, but still harsh." To Kevin he added, "Let us say they have tastes that are considered unwholesome by many."

Kevin grinned, his eyes very innocent and blue. "You mean they're bent."

Hoppara said, "Bent?" Then he laughed. "I like that. Yes, they are bent."

"The Minwanabi enjoy pain." Mara's gaze fixed on some inward image less pleasant than Isashani's lavender sitting room, "Sometimes their own, always others'. They kill for pleasure, slowly. Past Minwanabi lords are known to have hunted captives like wild animals. They have tortured prisoners and hired poets to compose verse in praise of their victims' agonies. Some have a sickness in them, becoming . . . aroused at the sight and smell of blood."

Hoppara waved for servants to remove the dishes and bring wine. "Some Minwanabi hide it better than others, but they all have this . . . bent appetite for suffering. Sooner or later it emerges. Jingu was obvious in his vices. Several of his concubines were murdered in his bed, and his first wife was strangled while he took her, rumor claims. Desio was held to be less violent, but even the street beggars know he beat his slave girls. Did you never wonder, with all the Minwanabi wealth and power, why noble Lords were not anxious to petition a marriage for their daughters?" He let the question go unanswered. "Tasaio is . . . more guarded. I've served with him in the field and seen him raping captive women like a common soldier. He also makes rounds through the healers' tent, lingering there not to bring comfort to his wounded soldiers but to savor their pain."

His attention returned to the crystal as his servant poured the wine, Hoppara repressed a grimace. "Tasaio is not a man I would wish to see upon the Warlord's throne."

"He is very bent," observed Kevin.

"And very dangerous," Hoppara summed up. He lifted his wine, waited for Mara to taste her own, then drained his goblet freely. "This is why I must either covertly block Tasaio's bid for the white and gold, or openly support him, gaining his favor."

Mara set down her glass, her eyes veiled by lowered lashes as she weighed available options. "So, you ask that I contrive a way for you to support someone else, a candidate who would not stand at odds with your covert alliance with the Acoma, lest the wrath of the Minwanabi be brought down upon House Xacatecas."

Hoppara nodded in obvious relief. "That would be the preferable choice."

Mara rose and waved the young man back as he moved to get to his feet. "Your father was never formal with me in private, and I prefer to keep the custom." As Lujan assembled her honor guard by the outer doorway, she guardedly said, "I will consult with my advisers and keep you apprised, Lord Hoppara. But understand that should I be able to save you and protect your house, you will be required to support me in another matter."

The boy nodded, silent, and motioned his hovering servants not to pour more wine.

Mara bowed slightly and departed toward the door.

Kevin lingered behind, his eyes on the pretty garden courtyard. The wall and the Emperor's barracks were set back a good fifty yards from the screen. Mara's Force Commander had not relaxed one instant throughout the hour's discussion. "One piece of free advice," Kevin said to the Lord of the Xacatecas. "Double your guards, and start turning this apartment into a fortress. Three or four Lords have been murdered in their beds already, and unless Imperial Whites have wings, they won't get over that back wall in any kind of time to help you."

As Kevin hurried to overtake Mara and her warriors at the doorway, the young Lord of the Xacatecas called his Force Commander to attend him. The Acoma party left the apartment, while Hoppara's voice rose in steel-voiced command that could have been an echo of Chipino's. "I don't care if there's nothing to use but purple pillows and birdcages! Just seal these godsforsaken windows and barricade every screen. That barbarian's ideas saved my father's life once in Tsubar, and I have a mind to heed his warning!"

A servant, embarrassed by this outburst, hurried the outer door closed, and Mara smiled at her Midkemian slave. "Hoppara is a very likable young man. I hope he survives to assume his family mantle."

"I hope we all survive," Kevin said sourly as a companionable shove from Lujan jostled him into place. "This jockeying to choose a new Warlord definitely gives me a stomachache."

18. *BLOODY SWORDS*

The council ended.

Long shadows streaked the courtyards between concourses as Mara and her retinue chose an alternate route back to her apartment. Though the meeting itself had gone quietly, the charged air of tension left even the strongest Lords cautious. Tecuma of the Anasati had not objected to Mara's suggestion that they join their honor guards together for their return to their quarters. With Clan Ionani vaulted into unanticipated prominence, whether he wished it or not, the young Lord of the Tonmargu was seen as being in contention for the white and gold, and Tecuma was vital for any support the Ionani wished to give their favorite son. Any who wished to throw the Ionani into disarray could not find a quicker means than killing Tecuma of the Anasati.

Times were uncertain for all. Tecuma gave no nod of farewell as he and his warriors branched off to his red-painted entry. He gave no sign that Mara had been with him at all, lest the wrong eyes see and presume a warmer relation between his house and the Acoma.

Bone-tired, Mara marched on to her apartment. After Xacatecas' airy sitting room, and the enormous, vaulted council hall, the inside of her own quarters seemed stuffy and cramped. Mara settled wearily in the central chamber and was immediately approached by Jican, who offered a note left by Arakasi.

Mara broke the seal and read. An immediate frown

creased her face. "Tell Lujan to keep his armor on," she called, then sent a servant for her pens and writing desk.

Kevin settled resignedly into his accustomed corner. He watched his mistress write two hasty messages. She handed them to her Force Commander for delivery with quick last-minute instructions. "Tell the Lords in question that we have no further details. If they feel unable to protect themselves, have them join us straight away."

"What was that?" Kevin asked over the rattle of men donning armor as Lujan selected an escort from the ranks of off-duty warriors.

Mara passed her soiled nib to a servant and sighed. "One of Arakasi's agents overheard a band of men who were hiding in the imperial gardens. One of them carelessly mentioned names and revealed that they were sent to attack the suites of two Lords who happen to be Inrodaka's enemies. Since any who hinder that faction are potential allies to our cause, I deemed it wise to send warning." She tapped her chin with the note. "I suspect this means that Inrodaka and his gang will support Tasaio."

The single maid in residence entered. At a nod from her mistress, she began to unpin Mara's elaborately high-piled hair and remove her necklaces of carved jade and amber. The Lady endured with closed eyes. "I just wish we had some clear indication of our own danger."

Kevin loosened his Tsurani-style slave robe and, from a pocket that by rights should not have been there, removed what looked like a meat knife. He turned the blade toward the lamp, inspecting the edge for flaws, saying, "We're ready. Should it matter when they come?"

Mara opened her eyes. "Did you steal that from the pantry? It is death for you to have a weapon."

"It is death for a slave to have opinions, and you haven't hung me yet." Kevin looked at her. "If we're attacked tonight, I'm not going to stand by and watch you killed because you think meek behavior is going to gain me a better station in my next life. I'm going to slice some throats." He said the last without humor.

Mara felt too spent to argue. Jican would know the knife was missing; if her hadonra had not seen fit to report the theft, inquiry would be met with shrugs and blank looks unless she were to pose a direct question. The hadonra and her

Midkemian slave had evolved a complex relationship over the years. Between them, most issues were cause for unending bickering, but in the select few areas they agreed upon, it was as if a blood oath held them together.

Near midnight, a knock sounded on the outer door of the Acoma apartment. "Who passes?" called the guard on duty.

"Zanwai!"

Roused from a half-doze where she lay in Kevin's arms, Mara ordered urgently, "Open the door!"

She clapped for her maid to bring an overrobe, then motioned for Kevin to assume a position of more propriety, while her warriors lifted down the heavy bar and slid back the tabletop pressed into service as siege shutter. The portal opened into a dark, lampless corridor and admitted an old man, bleeding from a blow to the head. He was supported by an equally wounded guard, who looked over his shoulder as if expecting pursuit. Lujan hurried the pair into the apartment, then spun to help the guards bolt and bar the door behind. Mara had a sleeping mat pulled out of the room that served as an officers' barracks. Her own servants relieved the injured warrior of his master's weight and made the old Lord comfortable with pillows.

Strike Leader Kenji arrived with a satchel of remedies, and it was he who washed and dressed the old man's head wound, while another of Mara's warriors helped the soldier out of his armor. His cuts also were tended, the deepest ones spread with salve and tightly bound. None were life-threatening. Mara sent her servant to bring wine, then inquired what had befallen.

Still pale from shock and pain, the old man fixed eyes of startling blue upon his hostess. "An inopportune fate, my Lady. I dined late this night with my cousin, Decanto of the Omechan, in celebration of my support for his claim to the white and gold. As I was making ready to depart, his apartment was overwhelmed by soldiers wearing unmarked, black armor. Lord Decanto was the target of their attack. I just happened to be in the way. Decanto was still fighting when we escaped."

The servant arrived with a tray of filled goblets. Mara waited until her guests had been served, the warrior accepting his drink with his one unbandaged hand. Delicately she asked, "Who sent such soldiers?"

The old man tasted his wine, half smiled his appreciation of the vintage, then grimaced as the expression pulled at his cuts. "Any one of six other cousins, I fear. The Omechan are a large clan, and Almecho appointed no clear heir from his Oaxatucan nephews. Decanto was the obvious successor. . . ."

"But someone else disagrees," Mara prompted.

Lord Zanwai pressed the cloth against his scalp and scraped back a damp strand of hair. "Decanto is the first son of Almecho's eldest sister. Axantucar is the older because he was born first, but his mother was a younger sister, so that leaves a mess. Almecho, curse his black soul, thought he was immortal. A wife and six concubines, and not one son or daughter."

Mara considered, sipped her own wine, then said, "You're welcome to stay, my Lord. Or if you prefer your own quarters, I'll offer a guard of my warriors to escort you back."

The old man inclined his head. "My Lady, I am in your debt. If I may, I will stay. It is a killing ground out there. I had an honor guard of five. We eluded no less than six companies of men. . . . I fear four of my warriors lie dead or dying. There were other armored bands afoot, but the gods be thanked, they ignored my last man and me."

Quietly Lujan doubled the guards at the door. Then he leaned on the lintel between the chambers, and out of habit squinted along the edge of his blade. "Did all wear black armor like the ones who attacked you?"

"I did not see," the old man said.

The wounded warrior did better. Revived a bit by the wine, he grated, "No. Some were like that. Others wore Minwanabi orange and black—Lord Tasaio must have arrived in Kentosani tonight. And still others were . . . tong."

Mara almost spat. "Assassins! Here in the Imperial Palace?"

Over the shiningly perfect edge of Lujan's weapon, the eyes of Lady and Force Commander met. The one recalled and the other knew that Mara had once almost died at the hands of a hired tong killer, dispatched to her home by Jingu of the Minwanabi.

The warrior continued bleakly with his tale. "They were

tong, my Lady. Black robes and headcloths, hands dyed in colors, swords across their backs. They swept through on silent feet, glanced at our colors to determine our family, then passed on. We were not their chosen prey this night."

Kevin arose and joined Lujan by the screen track between the rooms. Softly he asked, "What are 'tongs'?"

Lujan ran his thumb over his blade. No unseen flaws met his touch, but a frown marred his complacency nonetheless. "Tongs," he said in a dead, flat tone, "are brotherhoods, families without clan or honor. Each tong hold allegiance to no one and nothing save their 'Obajan,' the Grand Master, and their outlaw code of blood. Politely put, they are criminals who have no respect for tradition." The sword flashed in the lamplight as the Force Commander turned it. "Some of them, like the Hamoi, make of their unclean craft a renegade religion. They believe the souls of their victims are true prayers in praise of Turakamu. To them, murder is holy." Lujan sheathed his sword, and his tone assumed a grudging admiration. "They make terrible enemies. Many of them train since childhood, and they kill most efficiently."

"I know who wants me dead," Mara said, the wineglass forgotten in her hand. "Tasaio has enough strength to threaten me directly. So then, who dares hire tongs into the palace?"

Lord Zanwai tiredly shrugged his shoulders. "These are reckless times. Rivalries run hot enough that a slain man could have had his death bought by any of a dozen factions, and the work of a tong is not traceable."

"Brother could kill brother, and never be accused of disloyalty." Mara set down her goblet and clenched her hands to still their shaking. "Almost, I wish this matter could be settled in open war. The killing at least might be cleaner."

A bitter laugh met her words. "Dead is dead," said Lord Zanwai. "And any contest on a battlefield would see Minwanabi take the prize." He put down his wineglass. "I judge the tong more likely in Tasaio's employ, simply because overt display of Minwanabi arms might frighten potential allies into supporting another claimant to the white and gold—and it is rumored the Minwanabi have had dealings with the tongs in the past." Mara chose not to mention that she had certain knowledge this was correct. "The real question is who sends soldiers without house colors through the palace?"

Sadly, silently, Mara conceded the truth. One could only guess; certain knowledge might never be hers. She called for servants to clear one of the guest rooms of warriors for Lord Zanwai's use. "Rest well," he said as one of her men helped him stiffly to his feet. "May all here live to see the morning."

Throughout the night, the palace echoed with shouts, running feet, and sometimes the crack of swords in distant combat. No one slept, except in snatches. Mara lay long hours in Kevin's arms, but the best she managed was a fitful doze that led to bloody nightmares. Acoma soldiers stood watch in shifts, ready for any attack upon their Lady's quarters.

An hour before sunrise, a bump outside the apartment door caused the warriors on guard to draw weapons. "Who passes?" called Lujan.

The low voice that answered was Arakasi's.

Mara had given up trying to sleep. She waved away the maid who arrived to help her dress, while the door was unbarred and opened and the Spy Master let inside. His hair was matted with dried blood and he cradled one forearm in the crook of his elbow; the flesh above the wrist bore an ugly lump and a purple mass of swelling.

One look, and Lujan said tersely, "We're going to need a bonesetter." He caught the Spy Master strongly beneath the shoulder on his uninjured side, and helped his unsteady feet across the floor and onto the sleeping mat that had served Lord Zanwai the night before.

"No bonesetter," Arakasi grunted as his knees folded and he settled back on the cushions. "It's chaos out there. Unless you sent half a company, a messenger would have a knife in him before he crossed the first concourse." The Spy Master looked meaningfully at Lujan. "Your field medicine will do well enough."

"Find Jican," Mara snapped to her maid. "Tell him to bring spirits."

But Arakasi held up his sound hand, forestalling her. "No spirits. I have much to tell, and a bang on the head has me dizzy enough without making my wits stupid with drink."

Mara said, "What has happened?"

"A battle between unknown warriors in black armor and a dozen assassins of the Hamoi tong." Arakasi fell silent as Lujan examined the cut in his scalp, then unstrapped his bracers and set to cleaning away scabbed blood with rags and water brought in a basin by the maid.

As the injury was bared to light, the Force Commander said softly, "Fetch the lamp."

The maid did so, and Mara waited through a worried interval while Lujan held the flame before Arakasi's eyes and watched for response from the pupils. "You'll do," he said presently. "But the scar might grow back in white hair."

That brought a curse from the Spy Master. The last thing a man in his profession might desire was a distinguishing feature to mark him.

Lujan turned next to the arm. "My Lady," he said gently, "you might do better in the next room, but leave me Kevin and one of the warriors who wins at arm wrestling."

Arakasi murmured a protest, then said clearly, "Just Kevin."

The Spy Master looked paler when Mara was allowed to return. Beneath clipped hair and a fresh dressing, his face was running sweat. Yet he had made no outcry when Lujan had set his arm. Kevin's comment as he returned to his accustomed corner was "Your Spy Master's tough as old sandal leather."

Mara waited patiently while her Force Commander finished with splint and bandages. Once Arakasi was arranged with his arm settled on pillows, she sent a servant to bring wine. "Don't speak until you are ready."

Arakasi looked back in impatience. "I'm ready not to be fussed over." He nodded his thanks as Lujan stood to depart, then turned dark eyes to his Lady, all business. "At least three more Lords were murdered or injured. Several others withdrew from the palace and fled to their town houses or back to their estates. I have a list." He shifted awkwardly and produced a paper from his robe.

The servant arrived with the wine. Despite his insistence on abstinence, Arakasi accepted a glass. He drank while his mistress scanned his hasty notes, and a little color returned to his face.

"The dead are all supporters of Tasaio and Lord Keda," Mara summed up. "You think the killers are being underwritten by either the Ionani or the Omechan faction?"

Arakasi sighed deeply and set down his glass. "Perhaps not. Axantucar of the Oaxatucan also suffered an attack."

Mara heard this without surprise, for he had strong rivals within his own faction. "How did he fare?"

"Well enough." Eyes closed, the Spy Master forced himself to relax. With his head tipped back against the wall, he added, "All the attackers died, which is surprising. They were tong."

But Axantucar was always a competent fighter; he, too, had managed armies on the barbarian world. Mara observed her Spy Master and noted that tension had not quite left him. "You know more."

"I wish that I did not, mistress." Arakasi opened eyes that shone too bleak. "A delegation of Lords went to the imperial barracks and presented the Commander of the Emperor's garrison with a demand. They wished three companies of Imperial Whites to guard the Council Hall. The Commander refused. Since the Light of Heaven has called no official council, the halls were not his responsibility. The duty appointed him was to protect the Imperial Family, and he would send no soldiers away from their post unless his Emperor saw fit to give orders."

Mara tapped her wineglass in a fever of suppressed irritation. "When will the Emperor return?"

"Noon tomorrow, by all reports."

Mara sighed. "Then we have no choice but to endure. Order will be restored when the Emperor steps into the palace."

Kevin raised his eyebrows. "His presence alone will do that?"

Dryly, Arakasi corrected, "The five thousand soldiers he brings with him will do that." He went on to add, "The great Lords have made their case adamantly. Also the Chief Priests of the Twenty Orders adjourned late last night and proclaimed that the betrayal on Midkemia was evidence of divine anger. Tsurani tradition has been broken, they say, and the Light of Heaven strayed from spiritual to mundane concerns. If Ichindar had the support of the temples, he might command still, but at this point he must relent and allow the council to name a new Warlord."

"Then the matter must be settled by noon," observed Mara. The reasons were all too clear. Enough misfortune had occurred since the Emperor set his hand in the game. The High Council Lords had shown they would not be displaced. A new Warlord would greet Ichindar upon his return to the palace.

"Tonight," said Arakasi quietly, "this building will become a battlefield."

Kevin yawned. "Will we get any sleep before then?"

"This morning only," Mara allowed. "We must be at council this afternoon. Today's meetings will largely decide who lives through tonight. And tomorrow, whoever survives will appoint the new Warlord of Tsuranuanni."

As Arakasi gathered himself to rise from his pillows, Mara waved him back. "No," she said firmly. "You will stay and rest for the day."

The Spy Master did little but look at her, yet Mara spoke as if he questioned her aloud. "No," she repeated. "This is a command. Only a fool would assume that the Minwanabi will not make an appearance. You have done enough, and more, and Kevin spoke rightly last night. Whether or not there is a threat against the Acoma, I will not leave this council. We are already as prepared as we can be for an attack. If our efforts are not enough, then Ayaki is protected at home."

Arakasi inclined his white-wrapped head. His fatigue must have been great, for the next time Kevin looked, the nervous intelligence of the man had stilled. Mara's Spy Master lay in a loose-limbed sprawl, soundly and finally asleep.

Disquiet pervaded the great Council Hall. Mara was not the only ruling noble to enter with more than the traditionally permitted honor guard—the aisles between seats and concourses were packed with armored warriors, and the hall looked more like a marshalling yard than a chamber for deliberation. Each Lord kept his soldiers at hand, sitting on the floor at his feet, or lined up along the railings between stairways. Any who needed to travel from place to place were forced to take tortuous routes, often stepping over warriors who could only bow their heads and mutter apologies for the inconvenience.

As Mara picked her way between the retinues of two rival factions, Kevin muttered, "If one idiot draws a sword in here, hundreds would die before anyone had a chance to ask why."

Mara nodded. She said softly, "Look there."

In the lowest gallery, the seat opposite the Warlord's dais at last stood occupied. Warriors in orange and black filled the floor in a wedge formation, and in their midst, clad in battle gear barely more ornamented than an officer's sat Tasaio of the Minwanabi. If Kevin had been disappointed by the late Lord Desio's innocuous appearance, the same could not be said of his cousin's. Tasaio sat his chair with a relaxed and waiting stillness that even from a distance revealed presence. Kevin was reminded of nothing so much as a tiger. Briefly, Tasaio glanced across the chamber. His eyes locked with Kevin's for an instant; yet recognition occurred. The face beneath the fluted rim of the helm stayed impassive, but there was no mistaking the shock of awareness that passed between the two men.

Kevin stared a moment longer, then bent his head toward his Lady. "The tiger knows we're outside his lair."

Mara arrived at her chair, and sat, and by all appearance seemed occupied with arranging her formal overrobe. "Tiger?"

"Like one of your sarcats, only four-legged, twice as big, and a lot more dangerous." Kevin assumed his position behind her chair, crowded into the narrow space by the press of extra warriors who normally would have waited on the upper concourse.

Mara took stock of the hall, which seemed more gloomy and, oddly, more resonant to sound. There were empty chairs, with the gloss of armor and sword scabbards more plentiful than fine silks and jewels among the Lords present. As intrigues became more tangled, the talk turned convoluted; words gained layers of meaning, and looks between Lords were all weighted. Each empty place meant a council member dead or intimidated into withdrawal. The factions that remained were resolute, and some caucuses fairly bristled with unspoken aggression.

A council runner brought Mara a note. She slit the seal,

glanced at the two chops stamped inside, then motioned for the boy to wait while she read. Lord Zanwai entered, along with a dozen warriors. He appeared recovered from his ordeal the night before, and as a blocked aisle forced him to improvise a route, he chose one that brought him close to Mara. He gifted the Acoma Lady with a smile and slight nod as he passed.

She returned his tacit greeting, then penned a response to the note just received and dispatched the runner to another gallery. To Lujan she said, "We've gained two more votes, in thanks for Arakasi's information."

The morning's business wore on. Mara exchanged talk with a dozen lords on seemingly harmless subjects. Although Kevin tried to follow the byplay, he could not discern if the exchanges masked threats or offers of alliance. More and more, he found his eyes drawn to the lower gallery, where Lord after Lord paid court to Tasaio of the Minwanabi. Kevin could not help but notice that the visitors spoke most, while Tasaio largely remained silent. When he did reply, his words were sparse and crisp, as evidenced by the flash of white teeth. The warriors at his sandaled feet moved no muscle all the while, but sat with the inhuman poise of statues.

"His followers fear him," Kevin whispered to Lujan in a stolen moment of confidence.

The Acoma Force Commander returned a barely perceptible nod. "With good reason," he murmured back. "Tasaio is a superb killer, and he keeps his skills sharp by using them."

His gaze on the figure in the orange-and-black chair, Kevin felt a chill skim his flesh. If the Game of the Council was ruthless, there sat the most merciless player of them all.

Mara returned to her quarters for lunch and a consultation with her advisers. Arakasi had tied his arm in a sling and commandeered her writing desk. By the clutter of notes and quills, he had been busy, and remained so as Mara asked her servants to bring up trays of light food. Kevin watched the Spy Master pen three more missives in the interim, the parchments held braced under his splinted forearm, while he wrote in level, left-handed script.

"You're right-handed," the Midkemian accused; he had a

swordsman's eye, and noting which hand a man used was part of an ingrained reflex. "I would have sworn it."

Arakasi did not look up. "Today I cannot be," he said with spare irony.

When Kevin looked to see if the penmanship suffered, he was further awed to find that the handwriting varied like artistry. One of the notes looked as though it had been scribed by a strong male hand; another seemed feminine and delicate, and yet another, as if the author could neither read nor spell with skill, but struggled by with scanty education.

"Do you ever get confused about who you are today?" Kevin asked, for he had yet to find an impersonation that the Spy Master would not try.

Arakasi deemed the question beneath notice and went on with enviable dexterity to fold and seal his letters one-handed. By now Mara had slipped out of her overrobe. She did not ask Arakasi to move, but sat instead on the sleeping mat he had vacated.

"Who is going to deliver those?" she asked tartly.

The Spy Master acknowledged her annoyance by offering a bow made graceless by the encumbrance of the sling. "Kenji volunteered once already," he said gently. "These are the replies to a good morning's work." As Mara's look warmed toward outrage, Arakasi raised his brows in reproof. "You forbade me to go out, and I have not done so."

"So I see," Mara said. "I should have assumed you could feign sleep as well as you shape your disguises."

"The effects of the wine were quite genuine," Arakasi objected, faintly hurt. He looked at the papers scattered around his knees. "You do wish to know what I've learned?"

"Tasaio," Mara cut in. "He's here."

"More than that." Arakasi's air of lightness disappeared. "Most of the struggles so far have been tactical sparring. Tonight that will change. Entire sections of the palace are being set up as staging areas for large numbers of warriors and assassins. Some prior battles were fought simply to gain quarters from which to launch assaults."

Mara looked silently to Lujan, who said, "Mistress, our soldiers are still two days away by forced march. We must rely upon the forces we have here to defend you."

These words left a difficult silence, through which the arrival of the servant with the lunch trays seemed a clattering, alien intrusion. Mara sighed. "Arakasi?"

The Spy Master grasped her meaning by instinct. "Intelligence will not be necessary. Tasaio is preoccupied with gaining support for his own claim to the Warlord's throne. He expects you will throw Acoma support to whichever of his opponents is strongest. Even if he overestimates your courage, and you try to bury your enmity under a show of neutrality, he will still move to obliterate you. Your death would satisfy his family's blood vow to the Red God, and additionally throw your allies into disarray. Your popularity is on the rise. To cut you down would bring notice, perhaps give the Minwanabi enough edge to claim the white and gold over whoever emerges intact from the infighting of the Omechan Clan."

By now, Mara had recovered her wits. "I have a plan. Who else is likely to be attacked tonight?"

Arakasi did not need to consult any notes. "Hoppara of the Xacatecas and Iliando of the Bontura seem high on the list."

"Iliando of the Bontura? But he's one of Lord Tecuma's best friends and an Ionani stalwart." Mara noticed the servant hanging uncertainly by the food trays. She motioned for the man to resume his duties. "Why would an Ionani Lord be singled out as a target?"

"As a warning to the Tonmargu and other Ionani Clan Lords not to oppose Tasaio or the Omechans," Arakasi supplied.

Kevin said, "A polite note would be sufficient, I should think."

Lujan broke in with dry humor. "Killing Lord Iliando is a Tsurani polite note."

Mara gave the interruption short shrift; she asked Arakasi, "Could your contacts get word to the Lords you judge to be highest on Minwanabi's list? I need to ask them for time in council this afternoon."

Arakasi reached for his pen. He dipped the nib, slipped a sheet of fresh parchment under his splint, and said, "You will loan me Kenji and two warriors for the task?" Without looking up between lines, he added, "They need only go to the city and leave the notes with a certain sandal maker in the river stalls. From there the deliveries will be accomplished by other hands."

Mara closed her eyes as though she suffered from a headache. "You can have the use of half my company, if you need them." To Kevin she added, "See what Jican has ready for us to eat. We must be back in council shortly."

While the Midkemian moved off to investigate the trays, Lujan left to review the state of his garrison. "Have the men rest," he instructed his Patrol Leaders. "Tonight we shall fight."

When Kevin returned with a plate and juice, he found Mara still motionless on the mat. Her brows were gathered into a frown, her gaze distantly intense. "Are you all right?"

Mara focused on him as he laid the meal by her knees. "I'm just tired." She looked at the food without interest. "And worried."

Kevin heaved an exaggerated sigh. "Gods, I'm glad to hear you say that."

Mara smiled at his japery. "Why?"

"Because I'm scared senseless." Kevin stuck a two-tine Tsurani fork through a slab of cold jigabird as if he skewered an enemy. "It's good to know you're human under all that hard-boiled Tsurani stoicism. When I set out to do something foolhardy, the last thing I feel is complacent."

From the next room came the rasp of warriors sharpening laminated-hide swords.

"That sound makes me want to commit suicide," Kevin added. He looked at Arakasi, who worked over his notes with economical lack of nerves. "Don't you ever want to throw something?"

The Spy Master looked up, utterly bland. "A knife," he said with ice-cold lack of inflection. "Through Tasaio of the Minwanabi's black heart." He was unarmed, bandaged, a man in tired clothes writing letters in a crowded apartment. But at that moment, through chills, Kevin could not have said which was the more dangerous: Tasaio of the Minwanabi or the man who served Mara as Spy Master.

Warriors stood at the ready. The rooms of the Acoma apartment had become an armed camp, with fourteen additional soldiers in the purple and yellow of the Xacatecas joined to the ranks. Lord Hoppara had seen sense almost immediately when Mara approached him in council. Having too few warriors to fortify his larger quarters, and with Minwanabi already set against him, he saw no point in standing behind an appearance of neutrality that by morning might see him coldly dead. Some of the Xacatecas garrison had fought in Dustari, and Force Commander Lujan was known to them. Warriors sought old companions, or made new, as they waited through the first hours of evening.

Behind furniture barricades in the central room of the apartment, amid a ring of warriors and the last few cushions and sleeping mats, Mara fretted. "They should have been back by now."

Hoppara swirled a finger in his wineglass to stir up the spices and fruit that had been added in accordance with his taste. "Lord Iliando has always been a man to look upon logic with suspicion."

Mara resisted an urge to seek Kevin's comfort as the gloom of twilight deepened, and the first thuds and cries of distant combat echoed through the corridors outside. Against her better wishes, she had granted Arakasi's request to take Kenji and a patrol of five in a final attempt to convince Iliando of the Bontura to see reason. As the muffled clatter of swordplay resounded through the palace, Mara worried that her men had delayed their return until too late.

Then came the signal she longed for, a coded knock at the door. Lujan's men swiftly slid barriers aside and lowered the heavy bar. The portal opened, and Kenji hurried in, a Force Commander in violet and white plumes at his shoulder.

"Thank the gods," Mara murmured, as more warriors entered, the heavyset Lord Iliando of the Bontura in their midst. Last came warriors in Acoma green, and after them, at a flat run, Arakasi. He slipped in just as the door was closing, his helm with its Patrol Leader's badge shadowing a face pale as parchment.

Mara left the inner circle of protection to meet him. "You should not have been running," she accused her Spy Master, aware that his poor color was solely due to pain.

Arakasi bowed. "Mistress, it was necessity." The splinted arm under his officer's cloak was flawlessly hidden; no one would think that the warrior before her was not fully able to defend himself. As Mara began to voice recriminations, the

Spy Master quickly cut in. "Lord Iliando was obdurate until, at the last, we gave him a detailed picture of his own forces, their deployment, and four ways he was vulnerable to attack." He dropped his voice to a whisper. "It was his own weakness that convinced him, not our belief that he is the obvious object lesson for Clan Ionani and Lord Tonmargu."

Arakasi glanced to the doorway, where warriors replaced the bar and barricades, and the Lord of the Bontura and his Force Commander stood in conference with Lujan and Hoppara to formulate a combined defense. "We were none too soon," the Spy Master allowed. His gaze flicked back to Mara. "Lord Bontura's apartment was already under assault when I left, and the chests I shoved under the door will not detain his attackers very long. When they find the rooms empty, they will be coming here." At Mara's slight frown he added. "I escaped out the back, through the gardens."

She dared not ask how he had climbed walls in his condition; only his breathlessness told how hard he had run to overtake Lord Iliando's escort. Now firmly the Ruling Lady, Mara addressed her Spy Master. "Get out of that armor," she commanded. "Find a servant's robe, and hide in the cupboards with the scullions. That's an order," she snapped out as Arakasi drew breath in protest. "When this is over, if I am alive, I will have need of your services more than ever."

The Spy Master bowed. But before he disappeared in the direction of the kitchen he used his Patrol Leader's badge to collar a pair of warriors in Bontura and Acoma colors. "Get your master and mistress back into the fortified room, and convince them to stay there. Attack will be upon us any moment."

Minutes later, the solid ring of axes bit into the outer window frames. Warriors in the rooms on the garden side sprang to the ready, while in the room that faced the corridors a thundering crash hammered at the barricaded front portal. Lujan shouted, "A battering ram!"

Acoma soldiers leaped and threw their weight against the furniture used as shoring, but their efforts availed nothing. The second blow struck. Wood exploded into splinters as furnishings and bar and doors gave way, and the ram burst into the room. The invaders who manned its weight fell forward to allow ranks of swordsmen behind to spring over their backs.

The attackers who poured through the breached door wore black. Dark cloth also veiled their faces. As the leader waved his killers onward, Lujan glimpsed the dyed palm that identified a hired assassin of the Hamoi tong. Then battle closed between his own combined troops and the enemy. Sword met sword with an unnatural, belling clang. As Mara's Force Commander parried and thrust to defend, he realized: some of these tong carried metal swords, a rarity in the Empire. Valued beyond measure, such weapons were never risked in combat, despite their deadly ability to cut through laminated Tsurani armor.

A Bontura warrior went down, pierced through his breastplate. Lujan switched tactics, using his bracer to deflect the stabbing sword point. He called out a warning to his warriors, and two assassins fell before they were six feet into the room. Ordinary blades could not withstand repeated impacts. Metal carved chips from the edges and shattered good resin with cracks. Six Acoma guards went down, and Lujan's men fell back in a race to stop the enemy from gaining the door that connected the outer room to the inner complex. The battle became a two-sided struggle between the doorposts as the remaining Acoma guards, with Bontura and Xacatecas allies, jammed together to defend the rulers who huddled behind a wall of jumbled furniture.

At his Lady's side stood Kevin, his eyes on the outside windows in the farthest, innermost chamber. The frames bounced and shivered, and plaster cracked from the sills, as the ax blows continued from outside. Warriors hammered reinforcements into place: planks ripped at need from screen tracks, shelving, and carry boxes. The shoring would delay the invasion only by minutes, and the frontal attackers were gaining. Within minutes of the first assault, the tong members were joined by an influx of black-armored warriors who carried no house badges or colors.

Kevin weighed the odds and decided. The barricade of furnishings would not withstand assault from three sides. To Mara he said, "Lady, quickly, move over into that corner."

The Lord of the Bontura watched wide-eyed as she arose and changed her position. "You would listen to a barbarian slave?"

Hoppara had better grace. "The man speaks sense, Lord Iliando. If we stay, we'll soon be surrounded." The Lord of the Xacatecas moved to join Mara, then glared long and levelly at Iliando until the fighting edged nearer and the first of the windows gave way. In the instant before more assailants flooded the rear room, the stout older ruler relented.

The two Lords drew blades and positioned themselves before Mara. Kevin stayed close, but a clear step ahead, enough to move should the need arise.

The battle in the outer room intensified; there was no way to guess how many attackers entered through the breached front door. The clack and uncanny clang of metal sword meeting laminate came fast and furious, mingled with horrible cries. Defenders from the inner room rushed in two directions, some to stay the frontal onslaught and others to stave off the influx of assailants who shoved to gain access through the torn window; while at the second window the ax blows suddenly ceased.

Kevin cocked his head. Through the bang and crash of the melee he heard a faint scrape, through the wall at his back. "Gods! Someone's found a way into the sleeping chamber!"

He hesitated, then rushed to the screen that gave access to the hall. One lamp burned, washing the corridor in a wavering interplay of shadow and light. Kevin advanced. His bare feet sensed vibrations through the wooden floor: warriors falling, and the blows of another ax. He hugged the wall by the bedchamber door, waiting, his hand on the meat knife concealed inside his robe.

A man in black armor charged through. Kevin swung around. He drove a knee into the man's groin, then stabbed the meat knife through the hollow of the neck beneath the chin strap. Blood ran hot over his hands as he thrust the shuddering, dying body backward into another man who followed. Both warriors fell with a crash.

There were more, coming in a wave. Kevin cried, "Lujan! Back here!"

Aware that help might never come, the Midkemian crouched, dagger raised to meet the black-armored man who jumped over the fallen pair. Lamplight flickered over a leveled sword, too long for a short blade to thrust past, and thrusting too hard to parry. Kevin backstepped into the room. The black warrior lunged.

Kevin jumped, and all but tumbled over backwards. The

sword grazed the cloth over his stomach. Off balance, sure the next strike would kill him, the Midkemian flailed to stab the wrist above the man's sword guard.

But the knife grazed flesh and bounced off the enemy's bracer. Kevin gasped a curse, tensing to take the killing blow. Then the Lord of the Xacatecas shoved out of the corner and drove his sword into the man's back. The black warrior stiffened. His locked legs skidded across the floorboards and his eyes rolled back as he collapsed.

Another black-clothed assassin charged from the depths of the hall.

"My Lord! Look out!" Kevin cried.

Hoppara spun, his guard up barely in time. The enemy blade did not spit him, but grated edge to edge in a grinding contest of strength. Metal carved the rim of the young Lord's chest armor, gouging a groove in the plate. Hoppara grimaced in pain. He turned his wrist in a disengage, twisted, and returned a ringing blow to the side of his assailant's head. The unarmored tong assassin staggered dizzily back.

From the opened hallway dashed more dark-clad enemies. The Lord of the Bontura threw his stout weight into the fray. And Mara was alone, exposed in the corner. Kevin ducked the swing of swords and crashed into a black-armored elbow. His hand on the meat knife was slick with blood. His grip slipped as he stabbed. The enemy fell writhing between him and his Lady.

Then a pair of axes bit through wooden bracing, and the shutters behind Kevin burst inward. Plaster puffed from the wall as the heavy panels struck and rebounded, to be bashed back again by dyed fists. More tong assassins in black clothing swarmed through. Unencumbered by armor, they leaped to the sill, swords drawn from scabbards in one fluid motion. Kevin grasped the lead man's wrist. The sword descended. He ducked sideways and jerked mightily. The assassin catapulted through the window. Both men overbalanced. In the rolling tumble as they struck the floor, Kevin's short knife held the advantage. He stabbed before the enemy could turn his longer weapon.

Dead man and slave hammered hard into the barrier of furniture. Impact jammed the meat knife into the corpse's sternum. Kevin yanked, with futile result, then abandoned the blade and snatched the sword from dying fingers.

Spinning, on his feet cat-fast, Kevin brought up the sword. Blade struck blade, deflecting a cut coming fast at his neck. A ringing clang met the impact, not the dull thud he expected. Kevin laughed aloud. He held a metal blade. The gods knew how, on this world that had no ores—but this was a weapon he knew.

Kevin lashed out with the strange sword and quickly found its balance. Long as a broadsword, but finely made, the blade handled with murderous ease despite the slightly curved edge.

The first man Kevin engaged stumbled back in confusion before this alien slave who knew his way with a sword. Then the eyes behind the black mask narrowed. The assassin recovered poise and fought back. Slammed by a fast reach and practiced parries, Kevin realized he faced an equal weapon and an opponent of greater skill.

Then a green-clad warrior was at his side, and another sword was harrying the assassin's flank. Shoulder to shoulder, slave and Acoma soldier beat the tong back toward the hall. The man had a sword arm like lightning. Parry after parry, he deflected the strokes that sought his life. The Acoma warrior missed his footing, and staggered a half-step sideways. A weighted cord snapped through the splintered window and circled his unarmored throat. He dropped his sword, fingers clawing his neck as he strangled. As he buckled and crashed to his knees, the tong assassin who had wielded the throwing garrote leaped through.

A second Acoma warrior and another in Bontura colors charged to take him. Alone and beaten backward by his original foe, Kevin skidded helplessly to the side. Luck favored him. The assassin mired a heel in a cushion flung from somewhere; he slipped, and Kevin took him in a thrust under the armpit.

The Midkemian yanked his blade clear. He cast about and saw the Lord of the Bontura backed against the wall by a black warrior. The stout man somehow warded off a stroke that should have killed him—as the next one surely would. Not so fast as the assassin, the Lord was still deadly quick. Kevin rushed the black-armored warrior and struck him full from behind. Metal slid through laminated armor with a slap like a melon being punctured. The enemy died, choking on blood. Kevin leaped clear and came to stand before Mara, sword at the ready. Hoppara had stationed himself by the window; a wad of blood-sodden black lay jammed across the sill: the most recent assassin who tried to enter.

Breathing hard, and running with sweat, Kevin took stock. An insane three-way battle raged in the tiny apartment. Knots of black warriors and robed Hamoi tong thrashed and strained and wrestled to tear down beleaguered defenders. A tong assassin broke free of the fray, spied Mara, and snapped a hand to his belt sash. A knife was going to follow, Kevin knew with a rise of the hair at his nape.

Even as the assassin moved to throw, the Midkemian had a handful of Mara's robe. He let himself collapse, and his weight dragged her down, just as the assassin let fly. The knife thudded into the wall, kicking up grains of burst plaster. Kevin felt a yank at his shirt. He saw the pinned fold of his robe, then felt his left arm slung up at an awkward angle.

Mara lay beneath him, gasping for breath against the press of his weight. The assassin saw his opening. He leaped in, and his raised sword flicked shadow across both victims' faces. Kevin twisted. Cloth tore with a scream as he threw his sword, point first, at the assassin. The blade caught the man in the stomach. He doubled, slammed to his knees, and pitched forward. The sword flew from his hand and skidded to stab into the baseboard. Kevin freed the last shred of his robe, then jerked the still-quivering blade from the wood.

He reached his feet just as another assassin shouldered through the window and bounded into the room. Kevin's stroke decapitated him in midair. The corpse slammed down, spraying blood while the head bounced with a sick, wet thump across the floor.

The head rolled on and slapped into a black-armored warrior who charged through the rear doorway. Kevin spun to meet him. The warrior hesitated only an instant, then leveled his weapon at Kevin. The Midkemian braced for the sword blow, but belatedly realized: the man would not cross blades with a slave. In bull-mad Tsurani outrage, he chose to use his armored bulk to smash an upstart barbarian to a pulp.

Too late, Kevin tried to sidestep. The enemy rammed him, knocking breath from his lungs and driving him backward into the gloom of the hall. His back met heaving bodies. A vicious struggle raged between an invading mass of tong and Lujan's most disciplined defenders. Kevin rolled left as the heavily armored warrior crashed atop him. Half-crushed by his opponent's sword arm, and aware by a repeated jerk beneath his flank that he had managed to fall on the flat of his enemy's blade, Kevin struggled. He could not win free, and his own sword and hand were pinned against the wall. But neither could the other man succeed in grappling his weapon back. The warrior had no choice but let go of the hilt and slam ineffectively at the slave's exposed face. Kevin tried to chop at the man's neck, but his efforts won him only a skinned elbow.

Then Kevin saw his opening. He threw his weight into his assailant and rolled him onto his back. Pulling upward, Kevin dragged his arm across the man's throat; the sword followed, slicing deep. Throat strap, gristle, and cartilage parted. The warrior thrashed and died.

Buffeted by other fighters, Kevin extracted himself from the corpse. He ducked an assassin, raced back into the main room, and tried to locate Mara. Hoppara battled an armored man by the furniture barricade. A Hamoi assassin was besting the fatigued Lord of the Bontura. Kevin slashed the man's black-clothed flank and stepped past. Mara was nowhere to be seen. Leaving Lord Iliando to dispatch the wounded assassin, Kevin raced into the hallway that connected the suite to the garden. Two rooms proved empty. A corpse twitched in the third; another black-armored soldier stared with blank eyes from the bed.

Kevin all but hurled himself through the screen into the last room. There he found Mara backed against a wall, holding a dagger, her robes spattered with fresh blood. His panic found no time for outcry. Two men in black armor were closing in, leaving her no gap to flee. One man showed a nasty cut on his sword arm; already Mara had taught them to treat her with respect.

An animal cry of outrage erupted from Kevin as he surged into the room. The first warrior died before he had time to turn. The second backed a half-step, then stiffened as Mara drove her dagger into the gap between neck and helm.

Kevin spun left, then right, seeking the presence of more opponents. A warm weight crashed into his chest: Mara. She did not weep, but simply clung inside the circle of his arm, trembling with fear and exhaustion. He held her tightly, his sword still angled to fight.

But from the hallway the sounds of struggle had lessened. The crack and clang of sword strokes ended in a scraping thump, and silence descended, ringingly strange after the din of chaos and death. Kevin let out a pent-up breath. He lowered his dripping blade, stroked Mara's hair with fingers that were hardly less sticky, and noticed the sting of cuts and grazes that had passed unnoticed in the action.

After a moment a call came from the outer rooms: "Mistress!"

Mara licked dry lips, swallowed, and forced herself to speak. "Here, Lujan."

The Acoma Force Commander burst into the chamber, snapped to a stop, and said, "Mistress!" His relief was a tangible wave. "Are you injured?"

Belatedly, Mara regarded her smeared and spattered clothing. Her hands, even her cheeks, were covered with blood. She still held the knife in slippery fingers. She dropped it in distaste and absently dragged her knuckles on her soiled robe. "I am all right. Someone fell on me. This is a dead man's blood."

As if aware that she still clung like a child to her slave, she released her hold and straightened. "I'm all right."

Sickened by the thick stink of death, Kevin stepped to the window. The frame was a savaged mass of splinters, and across the small garden he could see a gaping hole in the brick wall. "They came from the next-door apartment," he said dully. "That's why there were so many pouring in from the rear."

Lujan held a sword out for Mara's inspection. "Some of the assassins carried steel."

"Gods!" exclaimed Mara. "That is the blade of a dynasty!" She examined the weapon more carefully and frowned. "But it bears a plain hilt. No clan or house markings." She gestured briskly toward the passage. "Have your men inspect the dead. See if any more such blades are found."

"What's the significance?" Kevin pushed away from the ruined sill and lent his arm to Mara, who still seemed to be shaking. He steered her gently around the fallen and into the corridor beyond.

A step ahead, Lujan answered, "Few true steel swords exist in the Empire. Each house that traces lineage back to the dawn of our history owns one, or is rumored to. Only the master of the house, the Ruling Lord, has access to such a blade. They are priceless, second only to the natami in importance to a house's honor."

Mara agreed. "There is an Acoma family sword that was my father's before me, and that I hold in trust for Ayaki. It is a rare weapon of steel."

They reached the juncture of the corridor and the blood-soaked central room. Already Acoma warriors worked to clear the floor of dead. Five more steel swords lay lined up against one wall, with Kevin's bringing the number to six. "These were found among the dead assassins, Force Commander."

Lujan looked upon the blades in awe. "Where can they have come from?"

"Minwanabi?" asked Kevin.

The Lords of the Xacatecas and the Bontura entered from the front chamber, both as blood-streaked as Mara, but little the worse for the wear. Drawn by the glint of steel in the flickering lamplight, they also examined the weapons.

Kevin drew his blade clean between a fold of his slave robe. "This is new," he said quietly. "It still bears faint marks from the grinder's wheel, and the stamp of the armorer's mallet." He inspected it closely one last time and added, "It bears no maker's mark."

All eyes turned to the slave. Iliando inflated his chest in the beginnings of offense, but Hoppara's curiosity forestalled his response. "Who has the skill to make ancient weapons?"

Kevin shrugged. "Among my people, the art is commonplace. Any one of a dozen good smiths would be able to duplicate this, I think."

Unwilling to be shown up as graceless by a younger Lord, Iliando lifted a blade and stiffly offered comment. "It's sharp, but I think not so finely fashioned as the ones made by our ancestors. These could be copies, made with inferior metals."

"But where would a man get such wealth?" asked Hoppara.

"My world," suggested Kevin.

The Lords exchanged glances, the stouter one taken aback by the slave's forthright manner. Yet no one interrupted as Kevin said, "After a battle, your warriors pick up swords and armor as spoils. Someone gets his hands on enough iron and a good smith, then shows them one of your ancestral blades. . . ." He made a pass with the weapon. "Say he duplicates it. This blade is not so unlike those used by the Hadati mountain people in my homeland. A smith from Yabon could forge its like, and there could easily be such a captive working for one of your Lords."

"Minwanabi," said Mara, her voice almost splitting over the name. "All metals taken across the rift as spoils are property of the Empire, some sent as tribute to the temples, some to the imperial treasury, and the rest to pay the upkeep of the army upon Midkemia. But the collection is overseen by the Warlord and, in his absence, his Subcommander. Tasaio served in that post for five years. That's ample time for a man without scruples to divert contraband resources back to his cousin's estates." Mara's tone grew reflective. "Or to his own estate, for his private use."

Iliando's heavy features showed distaste. "If every assassin carried one, the price of this one attack is incredible."

"For a raid in the Imperial Palace?" Hoppara interjected. "I would wager five times this many swords would be needed." He regarded the red-stained floorboards. "No guarantee of success, and every man expected to die. No, Tasaio is the logical one to have hired the tong."

"Then," said Kevin, kicking the helm of a fallen black warrior with his toe, "who sent this lot?"

Hoppara sank tiredly down on an unstained corner of a bed mat. He regarded his sword, the edge of which was chewed with chips, and the tip long since delaminated. "Whoever it was, their day's work was a blessing. The assassins and these warriors caused each other great confusion. I don't know if we could have withstood the Hamoi tong alone."

Mara crossed the floor and sat next to the young man. Exhaustion made her sigh. "Good men won the day for us, my Lord. You've done your house proud."

Lord Iliando glanced significantly at Kevin, who yet held one of the metal blades. "The gods will find ill in this. A slave—"

But Lujan cracked out an interruption. "I saw nothing."

The heavyset Lord turned toward Mara, incensed at her Force Commander's rudeness. She gave him back his stare with bland eyes. "I saw nothing untoward, my Lord of the Bontura."

Iliando heaved in a great breath, but it was Hoppara who stepped in with diplomacy. "You speak, I believe, of a blade that saved your life?"

The Lord of the Bontura reddened. He cleared his throat, stabbed a glance at Kevin, then shrugged stiffly. "I saw nothing," he allowed grudgingly; for here, in the Acoma apartments, when Acoma guards had died to spare him, to contradict the word of a Lady and her guest was to insult Mara's honor.

Kevin grinned. He held out his bloodied blade to Lujan, who accepted the offering with a flatly impassive face. Quick to ease the tension, Mara said, "My Lords, it would be appropriate if you each took two of the swords, as spoils of war. I plan on awarding worthy soldiers with the others, as a token of esteemed service."

The Lords bowed their heads, for her gift was a magnanimous gesture. Hoppara smiled. "Your generosity is without precedent, Lady Mara."

The Lord of the Bontura nodded; and by the flash of his eyes as he considered the enormous gain in wealth, Mara knew greed had won him. Kevin's transgression would be overlooked.

"Let us clear these floors of honorless garbage," Mara added to Lujan. The surviving warriors went to work. Scabbards were gathered up and swords sheathed, as the dead were examined for any clue that might prove who had ordered the assaults. None was found; tongs earned their pay through anonymity. The black-clothed assassins bore only the blue flower tattoo of the Hamoi tong and the traditionally red-stained hands. The black-armored soldiers were devoid of any common marking at all.

When Lujan was satisfied nothing incriminating would be found, he had men dump the bodies out the back screen into the garden. Then he set squads of warriors to rebarricade the windows and doors with whatever materials were available, and to see to the care of his wounded.

A soldier brought Lady Mara a bowl of scented water and a cloth. "My Lady?"

Mara dabbed at her face and hands, dismayed by the mess that soon discolored the basin. "In the morning, I must have the services of my maid." She looked up at the soldier. "You do well enough, Jendli. But tomorrow I will need more than the mercies of good warriors to make myself presentable for council."

Lord Hoppara laughed at the remark, surprised that a woman of such dainty stature should have the fiber to look beyond the harrowing horror of the past hour. "I begin to see what my father admired in you," he started, and paused as a strange crawling sensation visited everyone in the room.

Kevin whipped around, empty hands groping for the sword he no longer held. A glance at Lujan showed the Force Commander also peering into shadows, seeking the source of this unnamable dread.

Then came a faint hissing sound, like the release of steam from a cook pot. All in the room found their eyes drawn to the floor, where a mote of green light burned into existence. The staunchest of the warriors instinctively cringed back, and those who wore weapons reached for swords.

The glow intensified until it outshown the single lamp. Eyes burned and teared at the brilliance, and a fey energy raised the hair on everyone's arms.

"Magic!" hissed Lord Bontura, the widened whites of his eyes stained sickly green by the dazzle.

The speck brightened and swelled, then smeared to a sinuous form that twisted and undulated in the air. No one was able to move, for the effect of the light was hypnotic.

. The phenomenon coalesced into a horrible, glowing apparition. Scintillating eyes appeared, and a wedge-shaped head, and a deadly, tapered tail writhed against the floor.

Under his breath, Hoppara said, "A relli!"

Kevin knew the poisonous snake of Kelewan, but this surpassed the biggest river viper he had ever seen. Fully two feet in length, the serpent shimmered with a green incandescence that cast an evil glow over every object in the room. The creature slithered forward a few inches, its head slightly raised and its forked tongue flickering from armored jaws to taste the air.

Kevin glanced at Lujan, who gripped his sheathed weapon in taut fingers. Yet even a gifted swordsman could not draw from the scabbard and expect to strike before the serpent.

Still on the mat, barely breathing, Mara whispered, "Don't move, anyone."

As if the sound of her voice keyed response, a low buzz shook the air. The serpent's head snapped toward the Lady of the Acoma. Its eyes brightened and seemed eerily to shine through the body of the soldier who knelt between, the basin by his knees and one hand raised to bathe his mistress's face.

The magical apparition writhed to one side. The slanted head twisted toward Mara and its tail whipped suddenly into a coil. The head rose and arched back.

Lujan nodded to Kevin, who took a slow, soundless step back. Permitted room to swing, the Force Commander snapped his wrist. His blade sang free of its scabbard and descended, edge on, toward the creature's neck.

Yet against an arcane summoning no man could move undetected. The snakelike creature arose until it towered to full height. Then it struck, blindingly fast.

Lujan's sword sliced air, and Mara cried out in shock. The warrior by her side flung his body across hers, and the basin flooded water across the floor; the glowing apparition missed its mark. Fangs like arrows pierced through hide armor with no more resistance than cloth. The wedge-shaped head followed, vanishing into the warrior's body like liquid sucked through a hole, and the sickly illumination poured after.

For an instant, the room crawled with shadow.

Then the warrior screamed. His hands worked and clenched in agony, and his eyes began to glow greenly. The illumination brightened, spilling across his skin in a flood that burned, then blazed, then dazzled. The room held nothing of darkness. Then flesh itself began to pucker and crumple. The whites of the man's eyes swelled and collapsed, and his teeth glittered emerald in gums that smoldered and turned black.

Hoppara and Iliando shrank away in voiceless terror; Mara sat frozen, as if the spell held her rooted. Only Kevin, driven by love, found the will to react. He stepped aside, reached past the shining flesh that now thrashed in mindless torment, and caught Mara's upper arm. With a tortured cry of effort he half lifted, half dragged her beyond reach of the shrieking warrior. Then he flung his own body before hers.

Lujan found his reflexes. His sword spun down in an expert stroke and silenced the harrowing screams. Smoke puffed from the corpse, and the green glow flickered and vanished. Ordinary gloom flooded back, full darkness held off by the flame of one guttering lamp.

Openly shaking, the Lord of the Bontura made a sign against evil. "A magician wishes your death, Lady Mara. That thing sought you out by the sound of your voice!"

Kevin wiped sweating hands on his robe, forgetful that the cloth was already sodden. He shook his head. "I think not."

Lord Bontura looked irritated at the contradiction, but Mara raised herself from the floorboards without offense. "Why?"

The Midkemian looked back at her, his blue eyes level. "If a Black Robe wanted you dead, you would be, and no effort of ours could have spared you. Just one of those lightning globes we saw at the games, tossed in here, would make an end of things. But if someone wanted to scare the hell out of you as a warning, a slow snake would turn the trick nicely."

"Snake?" said Mara. Then comprehension dawned as she pulled her arms around her knees in a huddle. "You mean the relli. Yes, perhaps you are correct."

"There is another possibility," Hoppara offered, blotting sweat from his brow with the back of one wrist. "Lesser Magicians and priests can work magic, and unlike any member of the Assembly, they might be susceptible to bribes."

"Who?" Kevin fought to keep the shiver of reaction from his voice. "Who would have the means?"

Hoppara regarded the corpse left dead by the spell, its lips pulled back in a haunting rictus of pain. "If a man could consign a nation's wealth to the Hamoi tong to buy assassins, might he not also stoop to paying off the priests of a powerful temple, or hire the services of a renegade Lesser Magician?"

"Do you accuse Minwanabi?" said Iliando, his ham hands still clenched in his sleeves.

"Perhaps. Or else the party who sent us the soldiers in black." Hoppara surged to his feet, as if further stillness might burn him. Armored, blood-streaked, and left haggard by stress, he looked the image of Chipino. "We may know tomorrow, if we survive to return to council."

No one spoke.

19. *WARLORD*

Four more attacks came.

Throughout the night the Acoma soldiers and their allies endured assaults by dark warriors without house badges. The Hamoi tong troubled them no more, but the armored soldiers came in waves.

On the last influx the defenders were forced to retreat into the small back bedroom that had no outside door. Jammed in the narrow area, they beat back enemies who sallied from the hall, and others who pressed for entry through the shattered window. Kevin stationed himself before Mara at all times and fought like a man possessed. By the third attack, almost no one remained without injuries. The most tradition-bound Tsurani was too tired to look twice at this redheaded, loud-mouthed barbarian, as he rested with sword and shield in hand after the latest struggle. His blade had stood ground with the best warriors', and let the gods determine the fate of a slave who refused to know his place. While the night wore on, and men died, no hand that could still grip a weapon could be spared.

After the fourth attack, Kevin could barely move. His arms ached with fatigue and his knees shook uncontrollably. When the last black warrior fell under his sword, his legs folded and he hunkered on the floor, while the nervous energy that had sustained him drained away.

Mara brought him a cup of water and he laughed at the reversal of roles. He drank deeply as she moved on to tend to the others able to drink. Kevin surveyed the carnage. The floor, the cushions, the walls, every cranny of the chamber glistened red, and hacked bodies lay sprawled in grotesque positions. The once pleasant room now looked like some nightmare charnel house. Of the thirty Acoma soldiers and two dozen Xacatecas and Bontura who had joined ranks the night before, only ten Acoma, five Xacatecas, and three Bontura warriors stood. The rest lay slain or wounded between heaps of black-clad corpses that no one had energy left to clear. Dully Kevin said, "We must have killed a hundred of them."

"Perhaps more." Called from the pantry cupboard by necessity, Arakasi knelt beside the slave. The sling that supported his arm was splashed red, and the dagger in his left hand seemed glued to his fingers with gore.

Kevin inclined his head. "Doesn't that hurt?"

Arakasi glanced at the splinted arm and nodded. "Of course it hurts." He looked out the door. "Morning is almost here. If they are to come one last time, it will be soon."

Kevin heaved himself to his feet. He would have dropped his sword, could he have done so without cutting his ankles. Bone-tired, and shivering from stress, he crossed unsteadily to where Mara knelt, comforting Hoppara's wounded Force Commander. She looked up at Kevin's approach. She looked painfully thin by the light of the one lamp left burning, her eyes too large in her pale face, and one of her hands was scraped raw across the knuckles. "Are you all right?" Kevin asked.

She nodded absently as she struggled against weariness to rise. "So much . . . waste," she said at last.

Somehow Kevin mustered the will to hold out a hand and pull her to her feet. "Don't let the others hear you, my love. They'll drum you out of the council for un-Tsurani attitudes."

Mara was too beaten to manage even the ghost of a smile.

"You're not safe in here," he added. "We'll get one of the servants to bring Hoppara's officer along."

Mara shook her head. "Too late." She buried her face in the sweaty hollow of her lover's neck.

Kevin looked down and saw that the Xacatecas Force Commander had ceased to breathe. The quiet strength and leadership that had kept men on the march through the burning sands of Tsubar were only a memory now. "Gods, he was a grand soldier."

Kevin guided his Lady back to the small room that had proven the most defensible. There Lujan, two warriors, and Mara's remaining house staff were trying to clear away bodies. Those loyal soldiers who had fallen were carried to another bedroom, waiting a time for honorable cremation, while the black-armored corpses were kicked or rolled through the outer screen into a heap in the garden.

Mara leaned into Kevin. "I don't think I shall ever get the stink of this room out of my nose."

Clumsy with weariness, Kevin stroked her hair. "The reek of a battlefield is not easily forgotten."

A crash from the outer doorway echoed through the apartment. "Lashima, they won't stop," cried Hoppara in a note of desperation. Lord Iliando stood hunched over his sword, wheezing painfully, while Lujan signaled two soldiers to take position close to their lady. Then the Acoma Force Commander shouldered into the corridor, Kevin hard on his heels. There were no longer enough able-bodied defenders for him to hang back beside Mara. As he stepped into the gloom of the hallway, a voice soft as velvet touched his ears.

"Don't worry for her. Just fight as you can, Kevin of Zūn." The barbarian managed a nod over his shoulder at the still presence of Arakasi; then a pair of black soldiers were bursting through the makeshift barricade Xacatecas men had raised in the hall. Kevin charged, while to one side, more enemies shoved at the debris that blocked an adjoining doorway.

A man could not think, but only react by reflex; Kevin lashed out, feeling the jar as his metal blade sliced into the arm of an enemy. Another foe took his place. The pressure of attack did not ease. Slash, backstep, slash again—Kevin moved by ingrained instinct. He was aware of Lujan at his side, and somebody else shouting curses in monotone. Then the warriors at the side door smashed through the rubble, and defenders started dying. Somebody went down under Kevin's feet, and he stumbled, caught from a tumble by the blood-slippery hands of a Bontura warrior. He could only nod swift thanks, for another assailant was upon him. Crazily he wondered where in the Empire anyone had found so many sets of black armor. Or had somebody just lacquered over house colors to loose such an army against them?

The attackers stormed into the first chamber as the defenders flagged. Numbers prevailed. Lujan and his last survivors were driven back, and back. And yet they were not beaten. The Tsurani possessed mulish courage, and they gave no ground freely in retreat.

Kevin felled a black warrior. Behind, an exhausted Lord of the Xacatecas helped the Lord of the Bontura into the second chamber. The heavier man was battling for air, and one leg appeared to be dragging. Kevin felt desperation close around his chest. But the ugly, fearful vision of Mara with a sword through her heart hardened his resolve to keep going. He spun, raised his sword, and attacked with reborn fury. The interval gained the two Lords enough time to make their escape. Another pair of live bodies between Mara and death, thought Kevin with callous practicality. He almost laughed as he recalled Arakasi's words of encouragement. His sword rose and fell, parried and thrust. The fury was gone now; only the pain of exhaustion remained. Then his shoulder slammed against a doorjamb; and his clumsy misjudgment cost. An enemy sword scored his ribs. He hacked it away, metal hammering brittle laminate. The black warrior's sword shattered at the grip. Kevin shoved steel into the man's stark, surprised face, then stumbled over a body and landed on one knee inside the door.

Too slowly, Kevin recovered. A black soldier leaped behind him, turning a backhanded blow upon the barbarian's unarmored back. Pain burned his skin, but a fast parry from Lujan cracked the sword away. Kevin whirled and delivered a heavy-handed thrust to the stomach. The enemy folded.

Beyond stood Arakasi, a sword clutched in his left hand like a boy might threaten with a club. "Are you all right?"

Kevin gasped. "Hurts like hell, but I'll live." Against a pearl-grey light that filtered through gaping screens, he saw black warriors massed for a charge down the corridor. He bit back another crazy laugh. "Did I say live?"

Behind, grunts of effort from Lujan and the bang and hammer of swords sounded warning; once again foes had breached the wall between Mara's quarters and the next-door apartment. Kevin muttered, "Guard this door!" and raced to reach Mara's location. There two Acoma soldiers stood at bay, their mistress behind them, while a half-dozen dark warriors pressed to overwhelm them.

Hoarsely Kevin shouted, "You bastards!" He threw himself against the rearmost. The men he struck carried forward into those ahead. Legs tangled, and sword arms flailed, and the whole mass tumbled to the floor. Kevin slid and rolled on the slick floor, forcing fatigued muscles to respond one more time, and one more time again. He came up sword foremost and staggered a step. Three foes yet survived the sally. Kevin hamstrung the nearest. Another he hacked across the back of the neck, and the blow carried barely enough force to wound. As the two Acoma soldiers rallied to kill the last attackers, Mara cried out, "Kevin! Behind you!"

Kevin spun, peripherally aware that the hamstrung man had a knife. That one he had to leave to fate, because a sword sang down at his head. He jerked right, caught a foot upon the outflung leg of a dead man, and crashed hard into the corpse. The attacker's sword carved a glancing line along his upper left arm. Howling with anger at the pain, Kevin twisted. His blade caught the dark warrior just above the groin. He shook blood out of his eyes. One of the Acoma soldiers jumped to his side, a foot raised in a thrust against the dying man's shield. The enemy crashed back, thrashing, into the narrow hallway, hampering another dark warrior behind him.

Kevin gasped a searing breath. "Gods! There's more of them!" He struggled to stand against a terrible, ringing noise. Trumpets, he realized dully. His back was aflame and his left arm dangled. Wetness dripped off his fingers. Still he staggered upright and dragged after the first Acoma soldier toward the outer door. At his back one last man waited, sword poised in protection before Mara. Kevin managed a lopsided smile of farewell before he stumbled on into the hall. The end was upon them. Lujan, Arakasi, Hoppara, Bontura—all were nowhere to be found, though sounds of struggle issued from the second bedchamber. Without outside help, their numbers were too depleted for them to survive.

As he reached the last doorway, Kevin sighted two soldiers in black armor fleeing out of the hole in the wall toward the garden. Their rush struck him as funny, but tears came instead of laughter. Again a trumpet sounded, louder.

Then the apartment was silent, save for the groan of a wounded warrior and, from somewhere, the labored wheeze of the Lord of the Bontura. Lujan stumbled out of a doorway, his helm gone and blood streaming down his face from a scalp wound. He gave a silly grin at Kevin and rocked to an exhausted halt. "The Emperor! He's here! Those trumpets are the garrison of the palace. The Imperial Whites have returned!"

Kevin collapsed where he stood, and only the wall that banged his shoulder prevented him from hitting the floor. Lujan sank down beside him. A nasty cut on his temple bled freely, and his armor was hacked to scraps. Kevin uncramped his fingers from his sword, groped after a shredded cushion, and used that to stanch the flow of blood. Hoppara stumbled out of the bedchamber door, Lord Iliando leaning on his arm. But Kevin had eyes only for Mara. As weary as the rest, she came to kneel by his side and said, "The Emperor?"

Before Lujan found his voice, a pair of white-clad warriors marched smartly through the door. One of them demanded loudly, "Who claims this place?"

Mara drew herself erect. Her hair in tangles and her robe scarlet, she recovered a Lady's haughty poise. "I, Mara of the Acoma! This is my apartment. The Lords of the Xacatecas and Bontura are my guests."

If the imperial warrior found anything incongruous in her choice of terms, he made no comment. "Lady," he addressed her in formal tones, his brows raised as he glanced around at the carnage. "My Lords. The Light of Heaven commands all house rulers to attend the High Council at noon."

"I shall attend," Mara replied.

Without another word the Imperial Whites wheeled around and departed. Kevin thumped his head back against the wall. Tears of exhaustion ran down his face. "I could sleep for months."

Mara touched his face, almost sorrowfully. "There is no time." To Lujan she said, "Find where Jican is hiding and send him to our town house for clean clothing. He must also bring back maids and servants. This place must be cleansed and I must be ready in full formal attire by noon."

Kevin closed his eyes, savoring one blessed moment of peace. No matter how tired he was, a long, trying day lay before Mara. Where she went, he was bound by his love to go with her.

Pulling himself to his feet, he opened his eyes and motioned to an equally exhausted Acoma warrior. "Come on. Let's start fertilizing the garden."

The pillow cloth pressed to his head, Lujan motioned for the soldier to comply. Kevin had but a step to go to find the first corpse, which he gripped under the arms. As the warrior hefted the feet, and the pair of them stumbled awkwardly to the screen with their burden, Kevin observed, "Too bad it wasn't more of those Hamoi assassins. At least then we wouldn't have to lug armor."

Lujan shook his head slightly, but a faint smile showed his appreciation of Kevin's strange view of life.

After hours of bustling preparation, Mara emerged from an apartment cleared of dead and debris. Her hair was washed and bound back under a jeweled headdress, and formal robes brought from her town house flowed down to slippers unspattered with blood. Her honor guard wore trappings borrowed at need from the house garrison, and Lujan's officer's plumes nodded proudly from his helm, still damp, but at least rinsed clean since the battle. If bracers and flowing cloaks hid scabs and bandages, and if the walk of the warriors was on the stiff side of correct, Mara judged the honor of the Acoma remained unblemished by their appearance as she approached the entrance to the High Council chambers.

Imperial Whites stood guard in the hallways, and a troop of ten was stationed before the portal. There Mara's party was signaled to halt. "Lady," one of the soldiers commanded with scant sign of deference, "the Light of Heaven permits you to enter with but one soldier, lest more bloodshed defile his palace."

Mara could only bow before an imperial edict. After an instant of swift thought, she inclined her head to Lujan. "Return to our quarters and await my summons."

Then, from the ranks of her guard, she signaled Arakasi to stand forth. The splint beneath his right bracer might decrease his advantage as a fighter, but she did not wish to be without his counsel. And after the past night, even if a Lord was rash enough to try violence in the presence of the Emperor's guard, Kevin had proved he could handle the sword in Arakasi's scabbard.

Yet as Mara also waved her body slave from her retinue,

the guard put up a restraining hand. "One soldier only, my Lady."

Mara returned a disdainful look. "Do slave robes look like armor today?" Her eyes narrowed, and with all the arrogance she could muster she added, "I will not subject an honorably wounded warrior to the duties of a common runner. When I need to send for my escort, the slave will be needed to carry my orders."

The guard hesitated, and Mara swept past before he could rally and offer argument. Kevin forced himself to follow without a glance back, lest unsubservient behavior precipitate a quick change of mind about his worthiness to be admitted.

The hall seemed sparsely populated after the previous day, and those Lords present were considerably more subdued. Mara acknowledged a few greetings as she moved to her seat, her eyes busy between times taking stock of empty places. To Arakasi she murmured, "At least five Omechan Lords are absent."

The instant she settled in her chair, a flurry of activity commenced. A dozen notes were placed before her by soldiers who simply bowed and left without waiting for reply. Mara scanned each quickly, then handed the papers to Arakasi, who put them in his tunic without a glance. "We have gained," she said in amazement.

She pointed to an area that had stayed empty throughout the previous week. Now elaborately robed nobles were arriving to take their seats, with warriors that looked untouched by combat. "The Blue Wheel Party is among us."

Arakasi nodded. "Lord Kamatsu of the Shinzawai comes to bargain with others, gaining whatever advantage Lord Keda can command. He and Lord Zanwai will do little more than keep their party from deserting wholesale in the first ten minutes."

Mara glanced at the company, seeking the familiar face of Hokanu. Only one soldier wore Shinzawai blue, and he was a stranger, wearing the high plume of a Force Commander. Obviously, the heir to the Shinzawai estate was no longer permitted to come where he would be at risk. Mara felt disappointed.

A hush fell over the room as the two highest-ranking Lords entered last. Axantucar, now Lord of the Oaxatucan, stepped down to his chair at roughly the same moment as Tasaio. Both walked with haughty bearing, as if they were the only men of consequence in the room. Neither one so much as glanced in the direction of his major opponent.

As soon as each candidate was seated, a number of Lords stood up and moved as if to confer with either Tasaio or Axantucar. Each would halt a moment, as if exchanging a quick greeting, then return to his chair.

Kevin asked, "What are they doing?"

"Voting upon the office of Warlord," answered Arakasi. "By this act each Lord confirms his allegiance to the claimant he prefers to wear the white and gold. Those who are undecided"—his hand swept the room—"watch and choose."

Kevin looked down and observed that Mara closely measured the play of the Great Game. "When do you go to Oaxatucan?"

"Not yet." Mara's brow furrowed as she studied the order of nobles who moved across the floor to either the Lord of the Oaxatucan or the Lord of the Minwanabi.

Then, for no reason that was apparent to foreign eyes, Mara abruptly rose and descended the stairs. She crossed the lower floor as if heading toward Tasaio. A hush fell over the room. All eyes watched the slender woman as she mounted the stairs toward the Minwanabi chair. Then she turned and in three short strides came alongside the seat of Hoppara of the Xacatecas. She spoke briefly to him and returned to her place.

Kevin whispered, "What was that? Could the boy take office?"

Arakasi said, "It is a ploy."

Several other Lords moved to speak to Hoppara, and soon it was clear that no other claimant would declare himself. Kevin quickly calculated in his head and said, "It's roughly equal. A quarter for Minwanabi, a quarter for Oaxatucan, a quarter for Xacatecas, and a quarter yet undecided."

For a long quiet moment no one moved. Lords sat in their finery and looked about, or spoke to advisers or servants. Then another Lord here or there would rise and move to one of the three claimants. After a few moments another pair would rise and make their preference known.

Then Kevin said, "Wait! That Lord in the feathered head-

dress spoke to Minwanabi before. Now he's speaking to Oaxatucan."

Mara nodded. "The balance shifts back and forth."

The afternoon wore slowly on. As bars of sunlight moved
across the high expanse of the dome, the High Council continued the strange custom that determined primacy among
Ruling Lords of the Empire. Twice Mara rose to speak with
Lord Xacatecas, showing that her support for the young man
was unshaken.

Then, as evening approached, Mara nodded at some unseen signal. The next moment both she and Lord Hoppara
rose. As one they moved from their different vantage points
and arrived before the chair of Axantucar. A rustle swept the
chamber. Suddenly another score of nobles left their places
and advanced to stand before the Omechan Lord.

Then Mara returned to her seat and said, "Now."

Kevin saw her eyes move to where Tasaio sat. The Lord
of the Minwanabi returned a look of such pure malevolence
that Kevin felt chills touch his skin. By now his wounds
ached, and his robes itched, and every bruise acquired the
night before made standing a trial of endurance.

As Kevin wondered how much longer the council could
drag on without resolution, the climate in the hall changed
suddenly from waiting stillness to charged expectancy.

Tasaio rose. The great chamber became silent, every Lord
motionless in his chair. In a voice that rang loudly in the
quiet, the Lord of the Minwanabi said, "It is fitting a message
be sent to the Light of Heaven that one among us is willing to
wear the white and gold, that he will stand first among us to
guarantee continuance of the Empire. Let it be known his
name is Axantucar of the Oaxatucan."

A cheer arose from the council gathering, a vast echo of
sound that filled the chamber to the highest arch in the ceiling; though Kevin noticed more than half of the Lords responded with little enthusiasm. He asked Arakasi, "Why did
Minwanabi give up?"

Mara herself returned answer. "He was defeated. It is tradition for the Lord who is closest to the victor to proclaim to
the Emperor."

Kevin smiled. "That's a bitter draught."

The Lady of the Acoma nodded slowly. "Bitter indeed."
As if she noticed the discomfort that wore away at her love's

reserves, she added, "Patience. By tradition we must wait until the Light of Heaven sends his acknowledgment of the appointment."

Kevin bore up as best he could. Despite today's call to council, and the selection of a new Warlord, the barbarian remained unconvinced that Ichindar was as much a slave to tradition as his Lady thought. Yet he chose to say nothing. Within a half hour a messenger in white and gold livery entered, with a company of the Imperial Whites. They carried a mantle of snowy feathers, the edges trimmed in shining gold. They bowed before the chair of Omechan and presented the cloak to Axantucar.

Kevin studied the new Warlord as the mantle was laid upon his shoulders. While the uncle, Almecho, had been a barrel-chested, bull-necked man, this nephew looked like a slender poet or teacher. His frame was thin to extreme and his face ascetic, almost delicate. But the triumph in his eyes revealed as rapacious a soul as Tasaio's.

"He seems pleased," said Kevin under his breath.

Arakasi spoke quietly. "He should be. He must have spent a large portion of his inheritance to have a half-dozen Lords murdered."

"You think the black-clad warriors were his?"

"Almost without doubt."

Mara said, "Why would he send soldiers against us? We would support any rival of Tasaio."

"To prevent unpredictable alliances. And to ensure blame for the general slaughter was placed at Minwanabi's door." Arakasi's mood turned expansive, perhaps from satisfaction over an enemy's defeat. "He is the victor. Minwanabi isn't. The tong almost certainly worked for Tasaio. Logically, the other soldiers were Omechan."

Order returned to the council, and after an uneventful interval of speechmaking, Mara gave Kevin the order to fetch Lujan and her warriors. "We return to our town house tonight."

The Midkemian bowed to her as a proper slave might, and walked slowly from the huge hall with its bejeweled, enigmatic Ruling Lords. Again he concluded that the Tsurani were the strangest race with the most convoluted customs a man might ever encounter.

•   •   •

Calm returned to Kentosani. For an interval Mara and her household rested, healing wounds and assimilating the changes effected in politics since Axantucar's assumption of the Warlordship. Evenings were festive in the town house as the Lady of the Acoma entertained several influential Lords whose interest now favored her house. Kevin seemed more disgruntled than usual, but between exhaustion and her social obligations, Mara had little opportunity to deal with his dark mood.

Arakasi sought out his mistress on the third morning as she reviewed communications from several Lords still within the city. Clad in a clean servant's robe, and content for the moment to let his splinted arm rest openly in a sling, he still gave her the deep bow her rank entitled. "Mistress, the Minwanabi retinue has boarded barges upon the river. Tasaio is returning to his estates."

Mara stood, her pens and papers and messages forgotten in the joy of the moment. "Then we may safely return home."

Again Arakasi bowed, this time lower than before. "Mistress, I wish to beg your forgiveness. In all that occurred, I was not prepared for the Lord of the Oaxatucan to rise so quickly to replace his uncle."

"You take yourself too harshly to task, Arakasi." A shadow crossed Mara's face, and she moved restlessly to the window. Outside, the trees were shedding blossoms over the streets. Servants still pushed vegetable carts, and messengers still ran on swift feet. The day seemed bright and ordinary, like waking after a nightmare. "Who among us could have anticipated the murder that was done that night?" Mara added. "Your work spared five Lords, myself among them. I would venture no single person did more, and the result gained the Acoma great prestige."

Arakasi bowed his head. "My mistress is gracious."

"I am grateful," Mara amended. "Come. Let us go home."

Later that afternoon, the Acoma garrison marched smartly from the town house, Mara's litter and carry boxes and a wagon bearing the wounded securely in their midst. At the docks, boats waited to take the mistress and her retinue downriver. Settled upon cushions beneath a canopy, with Kevin at her side, Mara regarded the everyday bustle of trade along the waterfront. "It is so tranquil. You would think nothing untoward had occurred in the last week."

Kevin also watched the dock workers, fishermen, and laborers, the occasional beggar and street child interrupting the organized flow of commerce. "The common folk are never caught up in the affairs of the powerful—unless they have the misfortune to find themselves in the way. Then they die. Otherwise, their lives go on, each day of work like the next."

Troubled by an undercurrent of bitterness in his tone, Mara studied the man she had come to love. The breeze ruffled his red hair, and the beard she could never quite become accustomed to. He leaned intently against the rail, the set of his shoulders stiff, the result of the scabs left by battle. The wrist beneath her hands was still bandaged, and the look in his eyes held a bleakness, as if he saw sorrow in the sunlight. She wanted to ask him his thoughts, but a shout from the shore distracted her.

The boatman cast off lines. Polemen began their chant, and the craft slipped away from Kentosani and turned downriver on the seaward pull of the Gagajin. Afternoon breezes snapped the pennons above the canopy, and Mara felt her heart lift. Tasaio had been defeated, and she was returning safely home. "Here," she said to Kevin. "Let us sit with a cool drink."

The boats passed beyond the lower boundary of the Holy City, and the banks showed the green of land under cultivation. The smell of river reeds mixed with the rich aroma of spring soil and the pungency of ngaggi trees. The towers of the temples receded, and Mara drowsed contentedly, her head against Kevin's thigh.

A cry from the shore aroused her. "Acoma!"

Her Force Commander hailed back from the prow of the first boat, and presently the servants were all pointing to a cluster of tents at the river's edge. A war camp of impressive size spread over the meadow, and from the highest pole a green banner with a shatra bird emblem blew in the wind. At Mara's signal the steersman changed course for the bank, and by the time the boat reached the shallows a thousand Acoma soldiers waited to greet their mistress. Mara marveled at their number, and her throat tightened with emotion. Scarcely ten years before, when she had assumed the mantle of Ruling Lady, there had been but thirty-seven left to wear the Acoma green. . . .

Three Strike Leaders greeted her litter and bowed as Kevin assisted her out onto firm soil. "Welcome, Lady Mara!"

The warriors cheered as one to see their mistress again. The three officers formed ranks and escorted her through the troops to the shady awning of the command tent.

There Keyoke waited, standing tall upon his crutch. He managed a formal bow and said, "Mistress, our hearts are joyous at the sight of you."

Fighting a sudden rush of tears, Mara answered, "And my heart sings for the sight of you, dear companion."

Keyoke bowed at the kindness, and moved aside so she might enter and settle in comfort on the pillows piled upon the thick carpets. Kevin sank to his knees beside her. He kneaded her back with the hand that had sustained no injury, and under his touch he felt her tension dissolve into quiet contentment.

Still at his post by the entrance, Keyoke saw the calm that settled over his mistress's face. As he had in the past for Lord Sezu, he faced the outer world, where Lujan approached with Arakasi, Strike Leader Kenji, and the few hale survivors from the night of the bloody swords. A secret smile twitched the old retainer's lips as he held up a hand in restraint.

"Force Commander," said the former holder of that office, "if I may presume. There are times when it is best to let matters wait. Return to your mistress in the morning."

Lujan bowed to Keyoke's experience and called to the others to share a round of hwaet beer.

Inside the cool tent, Kevin glanced questioningly at the old man, who nodded his head in approval, then slipped the ties on the door curtains and let them slap gently closed. Outside the door now, Keyoke faced the sunlight. His craggy features remained impassive, but his eyes held a clear light of pride for the lover of the woman he counted the daughter of his heart.

Arakasi's messenger had made very plain what the Acoma owed to Kevin's courage with a sword. Keyoke's grim face softened a fraction as he considered the stump that had been his right leg. Gods, but he was getting soft in his dotage. Never had he thought to see the day when he would be grateful for the impertinence of that redheaded barbarian slave.

Evening shadows dimmed the great hall of the Minwanabi in the hour Lord Tasaio returned. Still clad in the armor he had worn on his trip upriver, his only concession to formality the silk officer's cloak he had tossed over his shoulders, he strode through the wide main doorway. The chamber was filled. Every member of the household stood arrayed to meet him, and behind them, every second cousin and vassal that had serviced the years of warfare and conflict. Tasaio strode between their still ranks as though he were totally alone. Only when he reached the dais did he stop, turn, and acknowledge the presence of others.

Incomo stepped forward to greet him. "The hearts of the Minwanabi are filled at our Lord's return."

Tasaio returned a curt nod. He handed his battle helm to a servant, who bowed and retreated hastily. Never a man to waste words on banalities, the Lord of the Minwanabi turned a flat gaze upon his adviser. "Are the priests ready?"

Incomo bowed. "As you requested, my Lord."

New black-and-orange cushions adorned the high dais, along with a rug sewn of sarcat pelts and a table fashioned of intricately etched harulth bones. Tasaio gave the change in furnishings what seemed a passing glance; yet no detail escaped him. Satisfied that nothing left over from Desio's rule remained, he sat and gave no other sign beyond laying the bared steel blade of the Minwanabi ancestral sword across his knees.

There followed a pause, in which Incomo belatedly realized that he was expected to act without further sign from the master. Where Desio had insisted on control over even the tiniest action, Tasaio expected to be served. The Minwanabi First Adviser waved for the ceremony to commence.

A pair of priests approached the dais, one wearing the red paint and death mask of Turakamu and the other clad in the full-sleeved white robes of Juran the Just. Each intoned a blessing from the god they served. There followed no offerings, and no grand ceremony in the manner that Desio had orchestrated. The priest of Juran lit a candle, for constancy, and left it burning in a stand woven of the reeds that symbolized the frailties of mortal man before his god. The priest of the Death God did not dance or blow whistles. Neither did he ask his deity to show favor. Instead, he trod up the stairs to the dais and reminded in cold words that a promise of sacrifice remained unfulfilled.

"A vow sworn upon the blood of House Minwanabi," the priest reminded. "The family of the Acoma must die in the name of Turakamu, with Minwanabi lives as surety. Who would accept the lord's mantle must also complete this charge."

Tasaio said thinly, "I acknowledge our debt to the Red God. My hand on this sword confirms it."

The red priest traced a sigil in the air. "Turakamu smile upon your endeavor . . . or seal your death and that of your heirs should you fail." Bones clacked and rattled as the priest spun around and left the dais; while the draft of his passage guttered the candle of the Just God.

The new Lord of the Minwanabi sat silently, without expression, as first one and then another family member or retainer came forward to bow and pledge loyalty. When the last vassal had affirmed fealty, he arose and called to the Strike Leader posted by the side door. "Send in my concubines."

Two young women entered, both wearing rich clothes. One was tall, slender, and fair-haired, her wide-set eyes jade green, and delicately enhanced with paint. The other, robed in gauze lace dyed scarlet, had a dark complexion and a rounded figure. Of different types, both women owned a beauty that stopped men's eyes, and they advanced in tiny steps, in the fashion of those trained since childhood to give pleasure. Both bowed gracefully before the dais, slender legs shown to advantage by short robes, and loose-wrapped gowns revealing an ample glimpse of breast. Although such women were chosen from among the loveliest in the Empire, neither held status above the meanest servant. All who were gathered in the hall stilled in curiosity to see what their Lord wished with his courtesans.

Before Tasaio's dais, both women fell to their knees, touching foreheads to the floor.

"Look at me," commanded Tasaio.

Frightened, but in all things obedient, the two young

women did as instructed. "Your will, my Lord," they intoned in voices of practiced softness.

The new Lord of the Minwanabi regarded them with dispassionate eyes. "Incarna," he addressed the dark one. "Are your children close?"

Incarna nodded, dread draining the color from her cheeks. She had born her Lord two illegitimate children, but their father's rise in status might not be to their benefit. It was not uncommon for a man come to the mantle of Ruling Lord to kill such offspring, preventing any claim upon the family.

"Bring them," Tasaio commanded.

A shimmer that might have been tears brightened Incarna's almond eyes. Yet she jumped to her feet and hurried out of the Minwanabi great hall. Tasaio's regard shifted to the fair woman who remained on her knees before the dais. "Sanjana, you've told my First Adviser you are with child?"

Sanjana held her hands clasped, but the beadwork on her robe shimmered in the light as she trembled. "Yes, Lord," she replied, the huskiness in her voice no ploy to seem seductive.

Tasaio said nothing. His face and his manner did not change even when Incarna reappeared, half dragging a small boy behind her. He had Tasaio's auburn hair and his mother's rosy complexion, and though he did not cry, his mother's nervousness frightened him. Carried in the concubine's arms was a second child, a girl not yet old enough to walk such a distance on her own. Too young to understand, she rode with her fingers in her mouth, her pale amber eyes on the gathering of people in the hall.

From his place on the dais, Tasaio looked the children over as a man might inspect merchandise for flaws. Then, almost absently, he motioned to Force Commander Irrilandi. Pointing at Sanjana, he said, "Take this woman outside. I will see her die."

Sanjana's fist came to her mouth. Her magnificent jade-colored eyes filled with tears of terror, and her poise failed her. Unable to rise, she remained trembling on her knees until two warriors stepped in and gripped her by the arms. Her efforts to choke back shameful sobs echoed over the stillness of the gathering as the men half led, half carried her from the hall.

Alone before the dais, Incarna stood shivering, her hands clenched to her children, and her face sweating with fear. Tasaio regarded her without pity or tenderness and said, "I take this woman for my wife, and name these children—what are their names?"

Incarna blinked, then hastily managed to whisper, "Dasari and Ilani, my Lord."

"Dasari is my heir." Tasaio's voice rang out over the gathering and echoed off the vaulted ceiling. "Ilani is my first daughter."

Then stillness broke before a rustle of movement as all in the room bowed to the new Lady of the Minwanabi. Tasaio instructed Incomo, "Have servants prepare suitable quarters for the Lady of the Minwanabi and her children." To Incarna he said, "Wife, retire to your quarters and await my call. Teachers will be sent for the children tomorrow. I would have them begin instruction in their duties to their family. Dasari will someday rule this house."

The former concubine bowed, her movements still tense with terror. She took no joy from her sudden rise in station, but hurried her son and carried her daughter from the dais, past hundreds of staring strangers.

To his guests, relations, and vassals, Tasaio said, "We shall have the wedding ceremony tomorrow. You are all welcome to share the feast."

At this, Incomo's long face froze against showing alarm. A wedding required careful planning, to ensure the most favorable auspices. The timing, the food, the ritual marriage hut—all required the blessings of priests and meticulous attention to tradition. Unions of great Lords were seldom undertaken at short notice, lest details be overlooked and ill luck visit the new couple and carry through the next generation.

Yet Tasaio gave the matter short shrift. With the silvery steel of his ancestral sword set at rest on his shoulder, he said, "See to the arrangements, First Adviser."

Then, the bared blade flashing under the skylight as he turned, he motioned for Incomo to follow and strode from the hall without further speech. Tasaio moved toward the outer door, certain that the two soldiers who were stationed on either side would have it open in time for him to pass through.

As their Lord emerged from the house and stepped into the courtyard, two warriors snapped to attention, the terrified Sanjana between them. She had shaken her hair from its pins, and the length of it fell in waves down her back, rare gold enhanced by the sun. She held her eyes downcast, but at Tasaio's appearance she looked up entreatingly. The soft white skin over her breasts showed her quick breathing, but her courtesan's skills did not fail her. Even frightened, even driven by desperation, she still managed to husband the only advantage she possessed. Sanjana parted red lips and arranged her slim body so that no man who beheld her could mistake her for what she was: a magnificent ornament whose sole purpose was pleasure.

The effect was not lost upon Tasaio. His eyes brightened as he followed all of her curves and hollows and drank in the promise of lust that her provocative pose implied. He licked his lips, bent down, and kissed her fully and long. With one hand he caressed her breasts. Then he stepped back and said, "I have found you a satisfactory bedmate." As hope filled her magnificent eyes, he smiled at her. He savored the moment, and the sparkle of relief in her expression, as he added, "Kill her. Now."

Her face blanched in stark terror, but she had no chance to cry out. One warrior caught both of her wrists and yanked them high, forcing her to look at Tasaio, while the other, stiff-faced, pulled out his sword and drove the blade home in her stomach.

She jerked and gave one thin, high scream of abject agony. Then blood fountained from her mouth, pattering in drops on the courtyard path. Her legs crumpled. Held pinioned by the warrior's grip, she hung through the throes of her dying. Bright blood darkened brighter hair. Then her muscles sagged, and her head rolled forward, and the lovely long white thighs went limp.

"Take her away," Tasaio said on a wild, ragged breath. His eyes were round and his color high. Then he inhaled deeply as if to calm himself and said to Incomo, "I shall bathe. Send two slave girls to attend me, and see that they are young and beautiful, preferably untouched."

Faintly sick, and distressed that it might show, Incomo bowed. "As my Lord wishes." He began to leave.

"I am not done with my instructions," Tasaio chided. He

walked on down the garden path, his mouth curled at the corners in the faintest beginning of a smile, as he signaled Incomo to follow. "I have given some thought to the matter of the Acoma spies. The time has come to turn our knowledge into advantage. Come, I will instruct you before I retire."

Incomo forced his mind away from the memory of the dying courtesan; he must pay attention. Tasaio was not a man who took kindly to incompetence; he would give orders once, and expect them to be followed to the letter. Yet the avid gleam in the master's eye left the First Adviser deeply discomforted. He held up a hand that shook despite his best efforts. "Perhaps," he suggested tactfully, "my Lord would prefer to discuss such matters of business after the comforts of his bath?"

Tasaio stopped. He turned amber eyes to his First Adviser and studied the older man intently. His smile deepened. "You have served my family well," he said finally, his tone like unmarked velvet. "I will humor you."

Then he continued down the path, saying, "Consider yourself dismissed, until I call."

The old adviser remained, his heart pounding as if he had finished a hard run. His knees shook. He sensed with uncanny certainty that the master had perceived his weakness, then let the matter pass, as if he knew his First Adviser's imagination would torment him with abuses far worse than the sport Tasaio planned in his bath with his slave girls. Too shaken yet to feel sadness, Incomo faced facts: against his deepest hopes, Lord Tasaio had inherited the family predilection for viciousness and appetite for pain.

The Lord of the Minwanabi rested in his bathing tub while a servant poured hot water over his shoulders. He watched his First Adviser bow through lazy, half-closed eyes, but Incomo did not deceive himself. Languid though Tasaio might seem, the hands left poised on the rim of the tub were neither slack nor relaxed.

"I came as my Lord required." Incomo straightened, his nostrils flaring as he caught a pungent, sweet odor on the air, explained a moment later as Tasaio reached over and lifted a long pipe of tateesha from a side table. He set the stem between his lips and sucked deeply. The First Adviser of the Minwanabi buried his surprise. The sap of the tateen bush contained a substance that induced euphoria—the nuts were often chewed by slaves in the field to lessen the drudgery of their lives—but the silks, at bloom, contained a powerful narcotic. The smoke brought first an enhancement and then a distortion of perception; prolonged use brought the mind to a trancelike stupor. The First Adviser considered the lure of such a drug to a man who enjoyed inflicting pain on others, then thought better of such musing. It was not his place to question the practices of his master.

"Incomo," said Tasaio with sharp and incisive clarity, "I have decided that we must move forward with our plan to destroy the Acoma."

"As my Lord commands," Incomo said.

Tasaio's fingers tapped arrhythmically on the tub rim, as if he ticked off points. "Once that is accomplished, I shall then destroy that preening calley bird Axantucar." His eyes abruptly flicked open. He gazed at his First Adviser, every fiber of him angry. "If that buffoon of a cousin of mine had done his duty and destroyed Mara, I would wear the white and gold today."

Incomo thought it politic not to remind his Lord that it had been Tasaio who had devised the plan to destroy Mara, not Desio. He returned a stiff nod.

Tasaio waved away the bath servant. "Leave us." Alone with his adviser, and wrapped in rising curls of steam, he drew again on his pipe. Physically, he seemed to relax, and his eyes grew drowsy once more. "I want one of those two Acoma spies promoted."

"My Lord?"

Tasaio leaned over the edge of the tub and rested his chin upon it. "Need I repeat myself?"

"No, my Lord," Incomo murmured quickly, warned by the spark of fire under the master's lashes. "I am just not sure what you mean."

"I wish to have one of the Acoma spies close at hand." Tasaio considered a rising ribbon of smoke as if it told him secrets. He went on, "I would observe this servant. Let him believe that he can eavesdrop upon critical conversations. You and I shall be certain that nothing he overhears is inherently false; no. Never false. But we'll also remember anything we say will also be heard by Mara. The deep plans we keep to ourselves, discussed only when we are alone. The little things we say before the spy will be offered as a gambit. I want this servant observed, and followed, until this network of Acoma spies is infiltrated."

Incomo bowed. "Anything else, my Lord?"

Tasaio set the pipe to his lips and drew another lungful of the intoxicating smoke. "No. I am tired. I will sleep. Tomorrow at dawn I will hunt. Then I will dine with you and the other advisers. At midday I will marry, and throughout the afternoon we shall celebrate the wedding festival. Send to the nearby villages for entertainers." Nothing if not concise, Tasaio summed up. "Now leave."

The Minwanabi First Adviser retired from his master's presence. Upon return to his own quarters, he determined the time was appropriate to begin composition of his death prayer. A careful man addressed this task when he got on in years, that his final appeal to the gods be read by someone who survived him. To name the Lady of the Acoma for destruction seemed a perilous enough course, but to mark as a target the new Warlord, who had just come to power over the bodies of five other claimants, was suicide.

As he shed his formal robe of office, Incomo wasted no time wondering whether Tasaio's planning was a dream that would disperse with the tateesha smoke—the eyes beneath their heavy lids had been all too dangerously aware. Sighing at the discomfort of stiff knees, Incomo knelt before his writing table. Three Minwanabi Lords before Tasaio he had called master, and while they were not men he admired, they were Lords he was pledged to serve with his mind and will, and, if needs be, his life. Taking a deep breath, he took up his pen and began to write.

The festivities were modest, but those in attendance seemed to enjoy themselves. The food was ample, the wine was abundant, and the Lord of the Minwanabi sat atop his dais in the great hall of his ancestors, looking every inch the quintessential Tsurani warrior. If he was not overly solicitous to his wife, he was polite and observed all the forms. Incarna's skimpy courtesan's garb had been replaced by a robe of stunning richness, black silk embroidered with orange threads at sleeves, neck, and hem, and studded down the front with matching pearls of incalculable worth.

The two children sat quietly at their father's feet, the boy slightly higher and closer than the girl. Occasionally Tasaio would speak to Dasari, instructing him in some point of trivia or another. From the moment he named his son legitimate, Tasaio was determined to groom him for rulership. The boy's robe was a clear imitation of his father's, down to the embroidery upon the sleeve, the outline of a snarling sarcat. The little girl, Ilani, was content to sit below her father's feet, chewing upon a sweet fruit while a juggler entertained.

Behind the Lord of the Minwanabi stood a servant, one recently promoted to the personal service of the master of the estate. While only the least of four men assigned responsibility for attending to their Lord's needs, this one listened with a little more attention to the nuances of conversation.

Throughout the evening the festivities continued, until Tasaio rose and bid his guests good evening. Motioning for Incomo to accompany him, the Lord of the Minwanabi moved toward his private quarters. Incomo quietly requested the servant to follow and station himself at the door to the master's chamber, against Tasaio's needs. The servant did as he was bid with a patience that concealed the fact that he avidly consigned to memory every word that passed between the Lord and his First Adviser.

An ancient ulo tree clutched the soil with gnarled roots, and its branches threw the site of the Acoma natami into deep, cool shade. Mara bowed before the stone that was sacred to her ancestors and the embodiment of Acoma honor. She spoke a few ritual phrases and placed a tied cluster of flowers before the monument, blossoms in seven colors that represented each of the good gods. On this, the first day of summer, she gave thanks for the well-being of all under her protection. For a moment after the brief ceremony she lingered. The sacred contemplation glade held unique peace, for here none but the head gardener, an invited priest, or those born of Acoma blood might tread. Here she could truly be alone with her thoughts and emotions.

Mara regarded the beautiful reflecting pool, the small

stream, and the graceful shapes of the shrubs. A sudden disquiet came over her. At times she recalled, too clearly, the assassin who had once nearly brought her death on the soil before her own natami. The memory often visited her unawares, like a chill on a hot day. Restless now, and anxious to leave the confinement of the garden's high containment hedge, Mara arose. She left the lovely garden and stepped under the arched outer gate and, as always, found a servant waiting.

He bowed the instant she made her appearance. "Mistress," said a voice she immediately recognized. "Your Spy Master has returned with news."

Four weeks had passed since Mara's return from the council that elected the new Warlord. The Spy Master had been absent gathering information for most of that time, and her delight at discovering him back was most welcome to him.

"Rise up, Arakasi," Mara said. "I will hear your report in my study."

Inside, settled on cushions with the customary light meal on a tray by his elbow, Arakasi sat quietly, his arm resting in a sling of elaborately knotted string, of a fashion tied by sail hands.

"You've been on a boat," Mara observed. "Or else in the company of sailors."

"Neither," Arakasi said in his distinctively modulated voice. "But that was the impression I wished to lend the last person I paid for information. Sailors' gossip is seldom reliable," he added conclusively.

Curious who such a person might have been, Mara knew better than to inquire. She had no idea how Arakasi's network operated, nor who his agents were—that was part of her original agreement when the Spy Master swore service to her house. Mara always saw that Arakasi received whatever he needed to maintain his agents, but she was oath-bound not to ask for names. A spy in house service risked a slave's death by hanging, were he to be discovered, betrayed, or sold out; should Mara's house fall to an enemy, neither she nor any retainer could break trust. The network would survive to serve Ayaki, or in worst case, were the Acoma natami to be buried upside down, forever denied the sunlight, loyal subjects who served as spies could die on the blade without shame in the eyes of the gods.

Arakasi said, "Something fortunate has occurred, perhaps. One of our agents in the Minwanabi house has been promoted to the personal service of Tasaio."

Mara's eyes widened in pleasure. "That is wonderful news." Yet as Arakasi's face betrayed his lack of agreement, she said, "You are suspicious?"

"This is too timely." Blandest when he was troubled, Arakasi qualified. "We know one agent was discovered and escaped only by means that border upon the miraculous. The other two have been left untroubled—and their intelligence has been accurate for the most part—but something in this rings false."

Mara considered for a moment, then suggested, "Begin to insinuate another agent into the Minwanabi house."

Arakasi worried at a loose end of string and watched one of the knots come unraveled. "Lady, it is too soon after the discovery of our agent, and too near the accession of a new Lord. The Minwanabi will closely examine new candidates for service in any capacity, particularly since Axantucar's rise to power. At this time it is too risky to send a stranger into the Minwanabi estate."

Only a fool would not bow to the Spy Master's judgment. Mara made a tight gesture of frustration, that she had no clear line of intelligence into the one house she feared above all others. Tasaio was too dangerous to remain unwatched. "Let me think on this," she said to her Spy Master.

Arakasi bowed his head. "Your will, my Lady." His next item of news was still less welcome. "Tecuma of the Anasati is ill."

"Gravely?" Mara sat straight in concern. Despite an antagonism begun in her father's time, and continued through her late husband's death, she respected the old Lord. And Ayaki's safety depended heavily upon the unofficial alliance between the Acoma and Anasati. With a pang of self-recrimination, Mara saw that she had tempted trouble by not taking a suitable husband. One heir was too slender a thread on which to hang Acoma continuance.

Arakasi's voice snapped her out of reflection. "To all appearance, Tecuma is in no danger—but the illness lingers, and he is an old man. Much of his former vigor was lost with

the death of his eldest son, Halesko, during the betrayal upon
Midkemia. With Jiro now heir . . . I think the Lord of the
Anasati grows tired of the Game of the Council and, per-
haps, of life."

Mara sighed, feeling oppression in the deepening shadows.
The rest of Arakasi's information consisted of intriguing minor details, a few of which were going to interest Jican. But
worry undermined the interplay of wits she usually enjoyed
with her Spy Master, and she excused him without speculation at the conclusion of his report. Alone in her study, she
called for her writing desk and penned a note to wish Tecuma
a swift recovery. She picked up her chop, inked it, and
pressed it into the parchment, then had her runner summon
a messenger to deliver the note to the Anasati.

By now the sun hung low over the meadows. The heat
had lessened, and Mara walked alone in her garden awhile,
listening to the play of water over the rocks and the rustle of
birds in the trees. The round of the game that had brought
the new Warlord to power had been extremely bitter and
bloody. New strategies would have to be evolved and new
plans made, for while winners and losers alike were retiring
to their estates to reassess, the plotting would go on unabated.

Tasaio was far more dangerous than Desio, but fate had
given him a more perilous situation than his predecessor. His
defeat in Tsubar had left his resources lessened, and he had
gained an unpredictable—and potentially lethal—rival in the
new Warlord. Tasaio would be forced to move cautiously for
the time being, lest he overextend himself and find enemies
exploiting his vulnerabilities.

Many of the old guard had died, and new forces were
emerging. Despite its questionable role in the debacle at the
peace treaty with the Midkemian King, the Blue Wheel
Party—especially the Kanazawai Clan members, and most
especially the Shinzawai—had emerged surprisingly un-
scathed. They still held the regard of the Emperor and were
actually gaining influence.

Mara weighed possibilities in her mind as to the next
likely turn of politics. A squeal of laughter and a shout from
inside the house told her that Kevin and Ayaki had come
back from their outing. Game birds had returned to the
northern lakes for the hot season, and Kevin had agreed to

take the boy hunting, to try his growing skills with the bow. Mara had faint hopes for any success, given the boy's youth.

But against her best expectations, her son and his companion burst into the garden bearing a fine brace of waterfowl. Ayaki cried out, "Mother! See! I shot them!"

Kevin grinned down upon the small hunter, and Mara felt a surge of love and pride. Her barbarian had not recovered entirely from the black moods that had begun with the news of the aborted peace treaty. Despite his silence on the subject, Mara knew that Kevin's slavery rankled with him, no matter how deep his regard for herself and Ayaki.

But worries could not intrude to ruin the excitement of her son's first manly accomplishment. Mara made a display of being impressed. "You shot them?"

Kevin smiled. "Indeed he did. The boy is a natural bowman. He killed both of these . . . whatever you call these blue geese."

Ayaki wrinkled his nose. "Not geese. That's a dumb word. I told you. They are jojana." He laughed, for this naming of things had become an ongoing joke between them.

Abruptly Mara was chilled by a shadow from the past. Ayaki's father had been a demon with a bow. A hint of bitterness tinged her words as she said, "Ayaki comes to this gift honestly."

Kevin's expression clouded over, for Mara rarely spoke of Buntokapi, the Anasati son she had married as a move in the Great Game.

The Midkemian sought at once to distract her. "Have we time for a walk near the meadow? The calves are now old enough to play, and Ayaki and I made a bet that he can't outrun them."

Mara considered only a moment. "There is nothing I would wish for more—to spend some time with you both, watching the calves play."

Ayaki held his bow overhead and shouted enthusiastic approval as Mara clapped for a maid to bring her walking slippers. "Off you go," she said to her ecstatically happy son. "Take your jojana to the cook, and we shall see if two legs are faster than six."

As the boy pounded off down the path, the brace of birds flapping awkwardly around his knees, Kevin gathered Mara close and kissed her. "You look distracted."

Irked that he should find her so transparent, Mara said, "Ayaki's grandfather is ill. I'm worried."

Kevin stroked back a stray lock of her hair. "Is it serious?"

"It doesn't seem to be." Yet Mara's frown lingered.

Kevin felt an inward pang, for concern for her son's safety overlaid a quagmire of issues they would both rather leave unbroached. One day, he knew, she must marry, but that time was not now. "Put worry aside for today," he said gently. "You deserve a few hours for yourself, and your boy won't stay carefree much longer if his mother can't spare him time to play."

Mara returned a wry smile. "I'd better work up an appetite," she confessed. "Else a good deal of hard-won jojana meat will wind up feeding jigabirds as scraps."

20. *DISQUIET*

Mara watched.

Through the opened screen of her study she could see a runner dashing up the road from the distant Imperial Highway. The muscular young man wore only a breechclout and a red cloth headcovering bearing the mark of a commercial messengers' guild. Lacking the power of a major house, the guilds could nonetheless provide sanctions enough to guarantee that their couriers moved through the Empire untroubled.

As the runner reached the front of the estate house, Keyoke hobbled down on his crutch to offer greeting. "For the Lady of the Acoma!" cried the messenger.

The Adviser for War accepted the sealed parchment and in turn gave the messenger a token, a shell coin cut with the Acoma chop, to serve as proof the man had discharged his duty.

The runner bowed in respect. He did not linger to take refreshment, but turned back down the road, his pace only marginally more sedate.

Mara noted his departure with a stab of concern. Couriers from the Red Guild were seldom the bearers of good news. When Keyoke arrived in her study, she held out her hand for the message with trepidation.

The identifying mark on the parchment was the one she feared, the chop of the Anasati. Before she cut the ribbons and read, she knew the worst had happened: Tecuma was dead.

In the doorway, Keyoke looked with troubled eyes. "The old Lord has died?"

"Not unexpectedly." Mara sighed as she put down the short message. She glanced over the accounts of her flourishing silk enterprise that had worn at her patience only minutes before; now, as if they represented a haven against difficulties, she longed with all her heart to return to them. "I'm afraid we will need Nacoya's counsel."

Mara called her servant to tidy up her documents, then led her Adviser for War through the estate house to the chamber across from the nursery that the old woman had adamantly refused to give up, even when promotion to First Adviser had entitled her to better.

As Mara set her hand to the floral painted screen at the entry, a querulous voice called out, "Go away! I require nothing!"

The Lady of the Acoma glanced hopefully to her Adviser for War, who shook his head. He would rather have braved a frontal charge on a battlefield than lead the way into the old woman's quarters.

Mara sighed, shoved back the screen, and flinched at the outraged cry that emerged from the piled blankets and pillows on the mat.

"My Lady!" Nacoya said sharply, "Forgive me, I thought you were the healer's servant, bringing remedies." She sniffed, rubbed at a reddened nose, then added, "I wish no visitors to offer pity." Abed with a congestion of the chest and a fever, the old woman found her annoyance overcome by a spasm of coughing. Her white hair stood up in stray locks, and her eyes were red-rimmed in a face like a crumpled wet parchment. The hands that clutched the blankets looked devastatingly fragile. And yet, at the sight of Keyoke, Nacoya rallied to outrage. "Mistress! You've a cruel heart, to bring a man to a sick woman's bedside, and without warning." The Acoma First Adviser flushed scarlet with embarrassment, but remained too stubbornly proud to avert her face. Her stormy gaze fastened next on Keyoke. "You, old campaigner! You should be wise enough to know better! I'll not suffer myself to be stared at."

Mara knelt by her First Adviser's bedside, the sympathy Nacoya so stoutly disdained hidden deep in her heart. The old woman's age made even small illnesses more hazardous, as today's news made clear. Always before, Nacoya's frail appearance had hidden a whipcord resiliency, a fiber of staunchness that made her seem indestructible. But now she was miserable with her cold, and shrunken with years to a husk of her former vitality, her mortality became frighteningly apparent.

Mara patted one of the wrinkled hands. "Mother of my heart, I am here only because your counsel is sorely needed."

The tone of Mara's voice jolted the old woman from self-pity. Nacoya sat up and coughed. "Daughter, what is it?"

"Tecuma of the Anasati has died." Mara's fingers tightened on her First Adviser's hand. "He succumbed to the illness that kept him abed this last six months."

Nacoya sighed. Her eyes turned distant and fixed inward on what might have been a memory, or a thought only she could discern. "He refused to fight any longer, poor man. He was a worthy warrior and a generous and honorable opponent." Under the blankets, Nacoya's thin body was raked by another fit of coughing.

As she struggled to regain breath, Mara spared her the need to speak first. "Do you think it wise for me to approach Jiro?"

Nacoya's hand tightened inside her mistress's. "Daughter, as much as he hates you for choosing his brother over him, he is not obsessed as Tasaio is. With the welfare of the Anasati placed upon his shoulders, responsibility might bend him to reason."

From the doorway behind Keyoke, Kevin's voice unexpectedly interrupted. "Never underestimate the human capacity for stupid, illogical, and petty behavior."

Nacoya gave the Midkemian an irritated glare from her pillows. Annoyed as she was that Keyoke should see her disheveled and sick, the presence of a young man was that much worse. And yet she could not show anger. Despite the slave's odd behavior and disregard for Tsurani custom, despite his inconvenient but genuine love for Mara, Kevin had a nimble mind.

Reluctantly Nacoya admitted, "Your . . . slave gives good counsel, daughter. We must assume that Jiro will remain intractable until he proves otherwise. The Anasati have been our enemies too long, for all that they have been honorable. We must proceed cautiously."

Mara said, "What shall I do?"

"Send a letter of condolence," Kevin offered helpfully.

The suggestion brought blank looks from Mara and her two advisers.

"A letter of condolence," Kevin repeated, then belatedly realized there was no Tsurani equivalent. "It's the custom in my homeland to send a message telling someone you share their loss and wish them well."

"An odd custom," Keyoke allowed, "yet it has some sense of honor about it."

Nacoya's eyes brightened. She looked long and shrewdly at Kevin, then mustered a congested breath and spoke. "Such a letter would provide an opening for communications without conceding anything. Most clever."

"Well, one could look at things that way," said Kevin, bemused to find the concept of compassion mistaken by the Tsurani mind for another machination of the game.

The idea won Mara's approval. "I shall draw up a letter without delay."

Yet she made no move to rise. She held Nacoya's hand, and her fingers tightened as if reluctant to let go. For an interval she stared at the weave in the counterpane, as if avoiding the old woman's face.

Nacoya said, "There is something else?"

Mara glanced uneasily about the room.

The First Adviser's instincts as a children's nurse had never left her; faintly disparaging, she said, "It has been years since you played the part of bashful maiden, daughter. Speak your mind and be done."

Mara fought the burn of sudden tears. The subject she most urgently needed to broach stole her poise. "We must seek a . . . bright . . . servant to . . . begin . . . to . . . ."

The old nurse fixed her former charge with a withering look. "You mean I must begin training a replacement."

Mara all but protested outright. Nacoya had stood in place of the mother she had never known; to imagine a time without her seemed impossibly bleak and unreal. Although the subject had been lightly discussed, she had put off decision and action. Yet the mantle of rulership forced the cold truth that now, she must.

Only Nacoya could handle the subject with equanimity.

"I am old, daughter of my heart. I feel chill in my bones on warm days, and my duties begin to weigh on weak flesh. Do not let my dying come on me without the surety that you have sound guidance by your side."

"The Red God won't hurry to take you," said Kevin with a grin. "You're too mean yet."

"Don't blaspheme," Nacoya snapped, but her wrinkled lips twitched and she buried a smile behind a cough. Try as she might to dislike this barbarian, he was handsome enough to forgive much; and his loyalty to Mara was unquestioned.

Mara said, "Keyoke could—"

But the hard-bitten former warrior interrupted with a gentleness his soldiers never knew. "I am almost as old as Nacoya, Mara." Her name was spoken with an affection that showed no disrespect. "I served your father gladly and have given the Acoma both my sword and my leg. You have given my life a purpose far beyond my hopes as a young man. But I will not see you foster a weakness." His voice turned stern. "I refuse the honor of Nacoya's mantle. You must have a strong, clever mind, and young blood at your side to advise you in the years after we are gone."

Mara's grip on Nacoya's hand did not loosen, and her shoulders stayed stiff. Kevin drew breath to intervene, but a quiet touch from Keyoke restrained him.

The old warrior said, "When a Force Commander trains his young officers, he is a fool if he coddles them or shows softness. Lady," Keyoke appealed plainly, "the exigencies of an advisership require more than blind obedience: understanding of what is necessary for the good of the house, as well as the will to play the Great Game. I have had no time for children. Would you deprive me, or Nacoya, of the chance to train our successor? Such a one would become the joy to enrich my late years, even as the son I never had."

"Or the daughter?" Mara said playfully, though her voice shook.

Keyoke managed a slight upward turn to the corner of his mouth, as close as he ever came to smiling. "You are that already, Lady."

Mara regarded him and then Nacoya in turn. The old woman's eyes were bright from more than fever. She watched Keyoke as if the two of them had a conspiracy. Mara's confusion crystallized into suspicion that the matter had been extensively discussed without her. "Already you have some-one in mind, you old war dog."

"There is a man," Keyoke allowed. "A warrior who has a fast sword, but whose performance in the ranks is unsatisfactory because he thinks too much."

"He's an embarrassment to his officers, and he won't hold his tongue," Kevin concluded out loud. "Do I know him?"

Keyoke ignored this, steadily regarding Mara. "He has served you well, though most of his duties have been among your outer holdings. His cousin—"

"Saric," Mara interrupted, intrigued despite her unhappiness. "Lujan's cousin? The one with the quick tongue that you sent away because the two of them together—" She broke off, and smiled. "Is it Saric?"

Keyoke cleared his throat. "He has a very creative mind."

"More than that, my Lady," Nacoya added, struggling against a thick voice. "The man's a devil for cleverness. He never forgets a face, or a word spoken in his presence. In ways he puts me in mind of both Lujan and Arakasi."

Though she had met Saric only briefly, Mara remembered the young man. He had a charm about him, manners that could not be shaken, and a gift for asking embarrassing questions; both were traits to be valued in a future adviser. Thinking fondly of Lujan, and his flexibility in embracing innovation, Mara said, "It sounds as though you two have done the interviewing for me. I yield to your better wisdom."

She held up her hand, ending discussion on the matter. "Send for Saric, and begin his training as you see fit." She moved to rise, and belatedly recalled the parchment in her hands. "I must draft a letter to Jiro." She turned in appeal to Kevin. "Will you help?"

The Midkemian rolled his eyes. "I'd sooner toy with a relli," he admitted, but fell into step as his mistress left the room. Keyoke lingered a moment to wish Nacoya a speedy recovery; his courtesy was returned with imprecations. As Mara, Kevin, and the Acoma Adviser for War beat their retreat down the hallway, the sound of the old woman's coughing followed them.

Chumaka, First Adviser to Lord Jiro of the Anasati, finished the message. Rings of polished shell flashed on short fingers as he rolled up the scroll and regarded his young master with dispassionate eyes.

Seated in comfort in the great hall of the Anasati, Jiro stared into space. Fine hands drummed on the floor beside his cushion, and the sound echoed faintly through the traditional room of parchment-covered doors and beamed ceilings, age-dark and waxed to a patina reflected in the parquet floors. On the walls hung a collection of sun-faded war banners, many of them prizes of vanquished enemies, and at length the new Lord's gaze seemed to focus on these. He raised what seemed a disinterested question. "What is your opinion?"

"As strange as it is, my Lord, I judge the message sincere." Chumaka made an effort to stay concise. "Your father and Lady Mara, while not friendly, had arrived at mutual respect."

Jiro's fingers stilled. "Father had the happy capacity for seeing things in ways that suited him. He found Mara clever, and that won his admiration—above anyone, you should know that, Chumaka. Those same qualities gave you your position."

Chumaka bowed, though the master's tone implied no compliment.

Jiro fingered his embroidered sash, blandly thoughtful. "Mara seeks to disarm us. I wonder why?"

Chumaka weighed his master's intonation carefully. "If one were to view the matter in an objective fashion, Lord, one might consider this: Mara feels that there is no real cause for conflict between your house and hers. She implies there may be cause for mutually beneficial negotiations."

Despite all care, Jiro bridled. "No real cause?" His handsome features went blank to hide an unreasoning flash of anger. "The death of my brother is not cause?"

Chumaka laid the scroll on a nearby table as though he stood balanced on a silken cord. The room was airless and hot, and he could not keep from sweating. Buntokapi's death was an excuse, he knew too well, as boys, the siblings had been constantly in contention, Bunto frequently bullying and tormenting the less athletic Jiro. That Mara had overlooked Jiro and chosen Bunto for her husband had never for a day been forgiven, despite the Lady's selection having been determined by flaws, not virtues. She had taken the fool she could exploit above the better man; yet that distinction held no meaning in terms of childhood rivalry. Bunto had been a Ruling Lord first, never mind that the prize had been poisoned, and that ultimately Jiro lived to inherit the mantle of the Anasati. The wound festered because the young man nursed boyhood grudges. Though he sat in his father's seat, Jiro could not shed the resentment of an upbringing where he continually ranked second: behind the heir, Halesko, and even behind plodding Bunto.

Chumaka knew better than to argue. Unlike his father, the young master was more concerned with being right than with the subtleties of winning the Great Game. The First Adviser tempered his phrases accordingly, as finicky as a cook choosing seasonings. "Of course, my Lord, the injury still causes pain. Forgive my insensitivity, but I referred more to legal distinctions than to ties of birth. Your brother renounced his allegiance to House Anasati when he assumed the Acoma mantle. In strict interpretation, no harm was done to House Anasati—an Acoma Lord died of Mara's machinations. I was remiss not to allow for your personal grief at the loss of a brother."

Jiro swallowed frustration that his sly-witted First Adviser had outmaneuvered him. At times the man was too crafty; that his worth was incalculable for that reason did not make him any more likable. With a flash of annoyance, Jiro said, "You're cunning enough, in your own fashion, Chumaka. But I warrant you play the game as much for your own amusement as for the glory of House Anasati."

This bit a little too near the bone for Chumaka's liking, even had the remark not come to an outright accusation of disloyalty. "In all ways I strive for Anasati triumph, master." Quickly changing the topic, he asked, "Shall we send a reply to Mara, Lord?"

Jiro waved casual assent. "Yes, write something . . . suitable. But make it clear I'd as soon rape her while my soldiers burned her house as send her—no, don't put that in." Jiro slapped his thigh, disgusted with the innuendos of politics when he much preferred to articulate his true feelings on the matter.

A smile touched him as he thought of something. "No. Thank Mara for her condolences. Then make clear to her that, out of respect for my father, I'll continue to honor his commitment. I will seek no conflict with the Acoma while my nephew lives." After a poisonous pause, Jiro added, "But also make it plain that, unlike my father, I will only feel regret if Ayaki dies. If my nephew is threatened, Anasati warriors will not rush to his rescue."

Chumaka bowed. "I shall word the message in the appropriate manner, Lord."

Jiro dismissed his adviser, brusque with impatience to be back to his library. Except when it came to gratification of his passions, the new Lord preferred his collection of book scrolls to politics.

Yet the Anasati Adviser showed no trace of disappointment as he hastened back to the cubby that served as his personal quarters. There, seated behind a cramped desk, a clerk scratched figures on a slate, an opened ledger by his elbow. On a second desk that overshadowed Chumaka's sleeping mat, documents had already been separated into three piles: messages that were of no immediate concern, those that needed relatively quick attention, and those that required urgency.

One note rested alone in the last pile. Chumaka picked it up and perused the contents before he thought to sit down. He scanned the lines twice and then laughed. "Aha! At last, after all these years!" Turning to the clerk, a young man talented enough to warrant appointment as the First Adviser's personal clerk, Chumaka said, "Mara of the Acoma has been too lucky, by anyone's measure, since she came to power. Here we see one reason why."

The clerk looked myopically at his superior. "Sir?"

Chumaka settled into his favorite seat, a cushion so threadbare and faded that the cleaning slaves spoke of it as an heirloom. "Kavai, my agent in Sulan-Qu saw a clerk of a factor for the Lord of the Minwanabi passing a message to an Acoma servant. What does that tell you?"

The clerk blinked, always more comfortable with figures than conversation. "A spy?"

"Or several." Warmed to his favorite subject, Chumaka shook a demonstrative finger. "But in any event, we know that I was not the only one to insinuate an agent into the House of Minwanabi." Even now that memory was sour, for the talented courtesan sent to Jingu had ultimately become unreliable. Of course, her instability had proven a major factor in Lord Jingu's demise—a good outcome, from Chumaka's point of view. Unlike his master, who harbored ill will toward Mara, Chumaka viewed the Great Game as simply a game, more complex and less predictable than most; and right now the opponent to be wary of was the Lord of the Minwanabi. Unlike his predecessors, Tasaio not only had the power of a mighty house, but the wit and talent to use it. He was the most dangerous man in the Empire, particularly since Axantucar had bested him in the contest for the white and gold. For without the duties of Warlord to distract him, Tasaio could turn his full attention toward the game.

Picking up writing brush and parchment, Chumaka began a line in his elegant style, the characters long and fluid and precise as ones penned by a professional scribe. He mused as he worked, "We face a player of unusual talents, two actually, for our Master burns to humble Mara of the Acoma as well as Tasaio of the Minwanabi. We must be quick to seize whatever opportunity comes our way. I shall order our man in Sulan-Qu to keep a close watch upon this factor and see if we can begin to trace the route by which messages reach Lady Mara." Chumaka paused and tapped his brush against his chin. "I haven't seen this good an operation at play since Jingu obliterated House Tuscai." He ruminated further on the past. "Too bad their exceptional spy network failed to save them. . . . I presume all their agents died or became grey warriors. . . ." Softly he added, "A shame such cunning artistry had to turn to dust."

Chumaka sighed in what might have been envy, then ended his sentence with a flourish. "Anyway, our young master has decreed that we play a three-handed game—very well. We shall do so to the limit of our wits. The triumph is so much more satisfying for the difficulty."

To himself as much as Kavai, Chumaka surmised, "It was not because Tecuma was gifted, the gods know, that the Anasati became the most politically well-connected house in the Empire. If Jiro would follow his father's lead and let me do my work without interference . . ." He let the thought trail off.

The clerk said nothing. Exposed to this sort of rambling before, he was never entirely sure he understood his supervisor's odd mutterings. An apprentice was not fit to question a journeyman, much less a master such as Chumaka, even if at times the First Adviser appeared to hold his own Lord in contempt—which of course was impossible. No one with such a wrong-headed attitude could rise to such an exalted place in a great house.

Chumaka finished his missive, then said, "Now to write a response to Lady Mara, enough so that she'll not worry for the time being, but not so much that she'll count the Anasati as a friend." He took a deep breath, then softly, wistfully sighed. "Now, that would be a woman to work with, wouldn't it?"

The clerk left the question unanswered.

The formation of blue-clad warriors reached the entrance to the Acoma estate house. From a distance, Kevin watched as Shinzawai soldiers saluted, then stood at ease while their officer mounted the steps in two easy strides to stand before his hostess. He bowed with irresistible charm. "You are gracious to receive us, Lady Mara."

Kevin felt a twist of black jealousy as Mara warmly smiled in return. "Hokanu, you are always welcome."

The barbarian's sour expression did not lift as she presented her advisers and councilors to the Shinzawai retinue. A newcomer stood beside Lujan, and Mara introduced him. "This is Saric."

Saric looked nothing like his cousin, being more muscular and darker, but there was a familiar wry set to his mouth as he said, "My lord," and bowed his head slightly. In manner, he and Lujan were nearly twins.

Sweating, out of sorts, and still disgruntled by the argument he and Mara had shared upon rising that morning, Kevin lingered at loose ends while the Lady led her guest inside and Lujan ordered one of his Patrol Leaders to escort the Shinzawai warriors to quarters set aside for them.

For a week, Kevin had known Hokanu, now heir to the Rulership of his House, would be visiting. Mara had been cryptic about the reasons, but gossip around the estate said plainly that the Shinzawai son came to pay court to Mara, seeking an alliance bonded by ties of marriage.

Kevin snapped a switch off a tree branch and angrily whacked the heads off a few flowers. The motion pulled at the scars on his back and shoulder; irrationally, he longed for a practice sword and a few hours of hard physical workout. Yet despite his heroic defense in Mara's behalf, after the night of the bloody swords the members of the household behaved as though the incident had never happened. His status remained unchanged, in that he was not trusted to handle even a kitchen knife. Despite his years of association with Mara and her councilors, the Tsurani mind adhered to tradition against logic, against feeling, and against even healthy growth.

Patrick's obsession with escape held a certain commoner's wisdom, Kevin allowed. He smacked the bud off another flower, then another, and scowled at the row of razed stems that swayed unprotesting at his abuse. He had not checked up on his countrymen in far too long. His self-disgust deepened further when he realized he did not know the work roster. He would have to ask an overseer to find out which field they were assigned to.

The stick remained clenched in white fingers as Kevin left the pleasant shade of Mara's gardens and marched through open sunlight in the meadows beyond. He heard the bright trill of her laughter at his back, and then imagined the sound over again as he walked to the distant acres of the needra field he had fenced with his companions so many years before.

There Patrick and the sun-browned crew of Midkemians crouched on their knees in the heat, pulling matasha weeds, which choked out the nutritious grass the needra required for fattening.

Kevin tossed away his stick, vaulted the split-rail fence, and jogged across the pasture to where Patrick hunkered down, twisting spiny stalks around his palm, then uprooting them with a jerk from the stubborn earth. The broad-shouldered former fighter had weathered to the color of old leather under the hotter Tsurani sky. His eyes had developed a permanent squint. Without looking up, he said, "Thought you might pay us a visit."

Kevin knelt down at Patrick's side and companionably hauled up a weed. "And why is that?"

"You'll slit the skin on your fingers, doing it that way," Patrick observed. "Got to break the fibers of the stalks first, like this." He demonstrated with hands welted with brown callus, then picked up his former train of thought. "You usually tend to remember us when you've had a row with your lady friend."

"And what makes you think I've had a row?" Unamused, Kevin tugged at another weed.

"Well, for one thing, you're here, old son." The older fighter sat back a moment and wiped sweat from his temple on his bare shoulder. "For another, she's got a gentleman caller, from the talk going around."

At a shout from the other side of the field, Patrick bunched his shoulders. "Slave master's expecting us to work, old son." He shuffled forward on his knees and grasped another stalk. "Have you noticed how the plants here never stop looking wrong?"

Kevin ripped out a large matasha weed and inspected it. "Nothing like this at home." The broad leaves flared out from willowy stalks, orange-tinged at the edges, and veined in faint lavender.

Patrick jerked his thumb at the pasture. "But this grass— just like ours in Midkemia, well, most of it, anyway. Timothy, rye, alfalfa, though the runts have odd names for them." He peered at Kevin. "Do you find it strange, old son? Have you ever wondered how things could be so much alike, yet so different?"

Kevin paused and ruefully inspected a cut on the heel of his hand. "It makes my head hurt sometimes. These people—"

"Yes, there's more of a puzzle," Patrick interrupted. "Sometimes the Tsurani are cruel, and others, tender as babes. They've got natures as tangled as a goblin's."

Kevin blotted blood on his trousers and reached for another weed.

"Wreck your hands, doing that. You're not used to work," Patrick chided. Then in a lowered voice, he added, "We've been laying about for a year since you got back, Kevin. Some of the boys are thinking it's better to leave you behind."

Discomforted by runnels of sweat that soaked his shirt, Kevin sighed. "You still thinking about escape?"

Patrick looked hard at his countryman. "I'm a soldier, boy. I'm not sure I'd rather die than grub around in the dirt, but I know I'd rather fight."

Kevin tugged at his collar laces, exasperated. "Fight whom?"

"Whoever comes after us." Patrick hauled another weed. "Anybody who tries to stop us."

Kevin shrugged his shirt off over his shoulders. The hot sun burned on his back. "I've talked to a few of the boys around here who were grey warriors before swearing loyalty to Mara. Those mountains aren't so friendly. The poor sods already living up there aren't eating well."

Patrick scratched his beard. "Well, I'll admit the kit got better since you put a word in, but it's still no banquet."

Kevin grinned. "When was it, you old fraud? The best meal you ever ate was in an alehouse in Yabon."

The reference to the past brought no smile, not even a counterthrust of teasing. Patrick wrapped another tough stalk around his fist, yanked, and tossed the uprooted plant aside. The leaves seemed to wilt within minutes under the Tsurani sun, unlike the men, who might waste away for years longing for the homes and the freedom they had lost.

Kevin looked at the distant mountains, a soft blue outline against the alien green of the sky. He sighed. "I know." His cut stung unmercifully as he reached for another weed. "Some odd events happened in Kentosani last year."

Patrick spat. "There's always something odd going on."

Kevin put a hand on his friend's shoulder. "No, I mean something . . . I don't know if I can tell you. It's a feeling. When all that trouble erupted at the Imperial Games—"

"If you mean the barbarian magician who freed those slaves, that's done nothing to change our lot." Patrick moved ahead to the next patch of ground.

"That's not the point," Kevin protested, hooking his shirt and following. "Slaves were freed in a culture that doesn't have the notion of manumission. From the word upriver, those men are just living in the Holy City, doing this and that, but counted freemen."

Patrick's hands paused on a weed stem. "If a man was to slip free here and get up the Gagajin—"

"No," Kevin said, more sharply than he intended. "That's not my thought. I don't want to live as fugitives. I'd rather pursue the idea that what's been done once might be repeated."

"Are you allowed to carry a sword?" Patrick asked bitterly. "No, and there's my point. You won't see plain. You rescue the mistress, fine and good, and when the crisis is over, it's back to being a slave."

Touched on a sore spot, Kevin took out his temper on a weed, then cursed as he received another cut.

"Give it up, old son," Patrick said angrily. "The runts are tough as their plants, when it comes to giving ground. Show them change, and they pick suicide."

Kevin stood up. "But the Great Ones are outside the law. The Warlord, even the Emperor, cannot gainsay their will. Maybe now that a magician's freed slaves, a Lord can go against tradition and do the same. But no matter what else, if you get yourself hung for a runaway, you're dead—and that's not freedom by my way of thinking."

Patrick let out a bitter laugh. "That's truth. Well, I'll wait a bit. Though how long, I can't say."

Satisfied with that answer, but left disgruntled by Patrick's blunt reiteration of other thorny facts, Kevin tossed his shirt over his shoulder. He gathered the wilting weeds into a bundle and flung them onto the pile by the fence. His cut hands burned, but his feelings stung more. His fellow Midkemians gave him barely a grunt of notice as he passed on his way from the meadow. In turn, he hardly noticed them, his mind absorbed by the memory of Mara's laughter in the garden where she sat with Hokanu.

The heat of midday drove Mara and Hokanu from the garden to a little-used sitting room in the estate house, one that had stayed unchanged since her mother's time. There, in an airy chamber with pastel pillows and gauze drapes, the couple sat down to a light lunch, cooled by a slave with a fan of shatra bird feathers. Hokanu had changed from full armor to a light robe that showed off his handsome build. To the fine bones and graceful carriage, time on the practice field had added firm fitness. He wore few rings, and only a necklace of corcara shell, but the simplicity of his dress and ornament merely emphasized his natural elegance. He sipped his wine and nodded. "Exceptional. Lady Mara, you provide gracious hospitality." His dark eyes met hers, not playful or teasing as Kevin's might be, but deep with a mystery that Mara felt compelled to explore.

Unwittingly, she found herself smiling. His features were

beautiful without being either delicate or overdrawn, and the way he looked her directly in the eye touched off a deep response. Intuitively, Mara sensed she could trust this Shinzawai son. The feeling was unique, even startling, after the endless political innuendos that complicated communication with others in her rank.

Aware she had been staring and had forgotten to reply to his compliment, Mara hid a blush by sipping at her goblet. "I'm glad the wine pleases you. I will confess that I left the matter of choosing the vintage to my hadonra. He has an unfailing instinct."

"Then I am flattered that he brought out your finest," Hokanu said smoothly. As he regarded her, he seemed to see past the way her hair was arranged, and more than the cut of her robes; on an intuition akin to Arakasi's, he reached past nuance to touch her heart. "You are a Lady with an instinct for clear vision. Did you know I shared your distaste for caged birds?"

Caught by surprise, Mara laughed. "How did you know?"

Hokanu twirled his wineglass. "Your expression, when you described Lady Isashani's sitting room in the Imperial Palace. Also, Jican once mentioned a suitor had sent you a li bird. It lasted two weeks, he said, before you set it free."

Unwittingly reminded of her piercing frustration concerning Kevin's dilemma, Mara strove not to frown. "You are most observant."

"Something I said troubled you." Hokanu set aside his glass. He leaned forward on his cushion and laid a narrow hand on the table. "I'd like to know."

Mara made a gesture of frustration. "Just a concept introduced by a barbarian."

"Their society is filled with fascinating concepts," Hokanu said, his rich, dark eyes still on her. "At times they make us seem like stubborn, backward children—entrenched in our ways to the point of blindness."

"You have made a study of them?" Mara said, intrigued and openly showing as much before she thought to guard her face.

Hokanu seemed not to care, for the subject fascinated him also. "There was more to the Emperor's failed peace effort than our people understand." Then, as if regretting that mention of politics might sunder their moment of rapport, the

Shinzawai heir brushed the matter aside. "Forgive me. I did not mean to remind you of difficult times. My father understood that you had a beleaguered night in the Imperial Palace. He said it was to the honor of the Acoma that you survived." Before Mara could wave the comment away, he gave her that direct look which unnervingly stripped away her reserve. He added, "I should like very much to hear what happened from your own lips."

And Mara saw his hand move slightly on the tabletop; with the uncanny perception she seemed to share with him, she knew: he longed to take her in his arms. Tremors touched her as she imagined the firm feel of his warrior's body. He was more than attractive to her—he understood her, with none of the cultural barriers or emotional raw edges that spiced her relationship with Kevin. Where the barbarian reacted to her dark Tsurani nature, and brought her relief through humor, this man across from her would simply know, and his unstated promise to protect became a potent combination.

Again Mara realized she was staring, and that some sort of reply to his request was required if the emotional temper of their meeting was not to overturn into passion. "I remember a lot of burst birdcages," she said with a forced attempt at lightness. "Lord Hoppara joined his forces with mine, and the attackers who stormed his apartment found no victims to hack up. They spent their fury on Isashani's li birds and a good deal of purple upholstery. The next day, the lady's bird catchers ran their legs off chasing fugitives."

Disappointed to be diverted from the personal side of the issue, Hokanu's brows twitched into the faintest of frowns. His eyes had an exotic tilt, and the expression made him look haunted. "Lady Mara," he said softly, and his intonation caught her like an ice-cold chill in the heat. "I may be overbold in presenting myself in this fashion, but circumstances in the Empire have forced changes none of us could have anticipated even a few short months ago."

Mara set down her wine to hide the slight shake in her hands. She knew, oh, she knew what he was leading up to, and the feelings that warred inside her were too wild a tangle to sort out. Lamely she said, "What do you mean?"

Hokanu read her confusion as plainly as if she had shouted. He leaned forward on his cushion, for emphasis.

"My brother was lost upon the other side of the rift, and I am left to assume Rulership from my father someday."

Mara nodded, her own emotions twisted tighter by the grief she sensed inside him, left over from Kasumi's sudden loss. The boys had been raised as brothers, and Hokanu's pain ran deep.

"When I first met you . . ." Hokanu overcame his inner sorrow, and his lips curled wryly in a smile. "I will confess, Lady, I felt regret when I first saw you."

Startled into the release of sudden laughter, Mara said, "You have an odd manner of making a compliment, Hokanu."

His smile broadened, and his eyes lit in shared pleasure as he saw the flush on her face. "I should rephrase that, lovely Lady. My regret was particularly fierce because the occasion happened to be your wedding."

Mara's expression changed to bittersweet reflection. "There was a great deal of regret involved with that marriage, Hokanu." And the thrill happened again, with the unspoken knowledge that he knew, without her needing to explain.

"Mara," he said, the word as gentle as a caress. "We both owe a duty to our ancestors. I grew up knowing that my lot lay in improving the relationships of my family through marriage. I always assumed my father would match me with the daughter of some Lord or another. But now . . ."

Mara finished his thought. "Now you are heir to the Rulership of an honored house."

Hokanu's relief was palpable. "And other considerations are at play."

Mara knew a surge of hope mingled with aching disappointment, that perhaps she had misread him after all. He did care for her, and he knew how his presence affected her, and he was kindly, carefully trying to disengage his attention without hurting her feelings. "I know that political considerations might interfere with the interests of your heart," she offered back in an attempt to smooth his difficulty.

"Mara, before, when I came to call upon you, I cherished the hope that you might petition my father, asking for me as a consort." His hesitancy cleared like clouds before sunlight, and the mischief in his eyes made him radiant. "The roles of

Ruling Lady and second son forced that silence upon me. Now, as heir, I can propose a different arrangement."

Mara's smile faded. He was not going to tell her politely that he could no longer pay her court! Instead, he was leading up to a proposal. Panicked, caught where she was vulnerable, and shoved hard against the thornier issue of how to resolve her future with Kevin, she fought for presence and poise. "What have you in mind?"

Hokanu hesitated, which was very unlike him. He sensed her confusion and was puzzled as to its cause. That necessitated a change in wording, and his hand braced instinctively against the table edge, as though he expected a blow. "I ask this informally, for if you say no, I would not wish a public rejection. But if you wish, I shall have my father's First Adviser pay a formal call upon your First Adviser, to make arrangements for our meeting. . . ." He almost laughed, and his strong, direct nature reasserted itself. "I ramble. Marry me, Mara. Someday Ayaki will be Lord of the Acoma, and your second son—our son—could wear the mantle of the Shinzawai. I should like nothing better than to have you by my side as Lady, and know that two ancient houses will one day be ruled by brothers!"

Mara shut her eyes against a tide of confusion. As well as she knew Hokanu, as powerfully as she was drawn by his charm, the idea of marriage churned up her feelings like a storm. She had sensed that this moment was inevitable, and had falsely sought shelter behind a belief that Hokanu's elevation to heirship might spare her, as political considerations forced him to seek a match with better connections. No amount of rational thought had prepared her for this reality.

She felt Hokanu's eyes on her face, felt his unspoken sharing of the turbulence his words had aroused. And in that graceful way that unerringly shattered her defenses, he came to her rescue.

"I've surprised you." Apology colored his tone. "You must not feel discomforted. Let me withdraw and allow you time to think." He arose in consideration of her, every inch of him lordly. "Lady, whatever you decide, do not fear for my feelings in the matter. I love you with all honor, but I also love you for yourself. I would cherish no minute that did not bring pleasure in my company. Seek your own happiness, Lady Mara. I am man enough to find my own."

Speechless, gripping her hands together in a misery of pent-up emotion, Mara raised her eyes to find him gone. She had not heard his steps as he went. She had to look twice to make certain the sitting room was empty. She reached out with trembling fingers, caught up her wineglass, and drained it. Then she stared at the empty goblet and the untouched plates of light lunch. Kevin's face mingled with Hokanu's in her memory, until she wanted to howl her frustration at the walls.

There was no choosing between them, none, and the quandary of love and honorable political necessity ripped at her like thorns.

"Dear gods, what a tangle," she murmured, and only belatedly realized she was no longer alone. In true and gallant solicitude, Hokanu had sent her adviser to comfort and steer her through the awkwardness of the moment.

Still weak after her illness, Nacoya shook her head, indicating Mara should hold off speech. "Come," the old woman said brusquely. "Let's get you back to your private quarters and out of those formal robes. When you are more comfortable and settled, we can talk."

Mara allowed herself to be shepherded to her feet. She followed Nacoya's lead down the corridors without seeing where she was going or noticing the floor beneath her feet. "Someone has seen to Hokanu's needs?" she said in a voice that sounded limp.

"Saric has done so. Lujan will be organizing some contests at arms among the warriors." Nacoya whipped open the screen to Mara's chambers, and rallied half a score of maids and servants. "Bath water," she rapped out. "And something light and comfortable for the mistress to put on afterward."

Mara stood with her arms woodenly outstretched as her attendants unfastened the wood-peg and cord-loop fasteners of her formal robe. "This is impossible!" she exclaimed. "The time is all wrong."

Nacoya clicked her tongue. "The Shinzawai are an ancient family, with honors equal to most, but their part in the aborted attempt to force peace upon the Empire . . ."

Bemused by this switch to hardcore politics, Mara stepped out of the heavy robe. She moved mechanically into the cool bath prepared by her servants, and sat shivering in reaction as two maids sponged her back. "What's the matter with me? Why can't I just tell him no and put the issue from my mind?"

Nacoya answered obliquely. "Daughter, there is no sure way to rule the heart."

"My heart is not in this!" Mara fired back, with a sharpness that itself was a contradiction. "What is Hokanu to me but a means to an end?"

The First Adviser seated herself on a cushion and wrapped gnarled fingers around her knees. She said nothing, while Mara endured a bath she did not enjoy. She arose at the appropriate moment and stepped out of the water, and stood with a scowl while her maids toweled her dry.

Nacoya did not break silence until another maid arrived with a light lounging robe. "Mistress, the Shinzawai have been among the most honorable families in the Empire in my memory and the memory of my father. The old lord, Shatai, Kamatsu's father, was Warchief of the Kanazawai when a Keda Lord last sat upon the Warlord's throne. And no one has ever heard of either Shinzawai Lord breaking a bond. Their honor is unquestioned."

Mara knew all this. As the maids tied her robe, she regarded her former nurse with bitten-back exasperation. "But their position at the moment is questionable."

"Many resentments linger since the failed peace and the Night of the Bloody Swords," Nacoya agreed. "Many of the families left grieving insist that murder would have never have happened had the Blue Wheel and, especially, the Shinzawai not been at the heart of the Emperor's plottings."

But Mara did not need reminding that it was only because so many were injured and everyone was being cautious that no one had sought retribution upon the Shinzawai. To bind her family to them through a marriage would be to add names to her list of dangerous enemies.

No, Mara decided, as Nacoya's obvious reasoning led her from mixed emotions to clear thought. The heart of the matter was another thing altogether. Hokanu was attractive enough; her deep involvement with Kevin added painful confusion, yet she had never fooled herself into the false hope that love could replace a slave with a husband. Her turmoil stemmed from another truth: that she was loath to yield control of her life to any Ruling Lord. Buntokapi's brief tenure had left only ugly memories, but that was not all.

Mara sighed and stared through the opened screen into the garden. The day was drawing on, and long shadows striped the path between the akasi rows. The rich green land that had been her father's, and her ancestors' before his, had prospered well over the years since a young girl came into an inheritance beyond her years and experience. In the light of her successes, Mara examined a deeper truth, altogether less tangled than any conflict in her life, past or present. After a long minute she said to Nacoya, "Thank you for your counsel. You may go now."

As the old woman bowed and departed, Mara reflected. So many events in her life were the result of her being Ruling Lady. Yet the duties, the awesome responsibility, even the danger that came her way—these things were not the fearful burden they had appeared on the day she had left Lashima's temple. Since she had assumed the Acoma mantle, she had come to enjoy her power, to revel in pitting her wits against the machinations of the Great Game. These things gave her freedom to pursue new ideas. What would it be like to leave the decisions to others? she wondered. Could she be as content collecting li birds, ornamenting sitting rooms, or matchmaking as other ladies were? Women held power in their own right, sometimes with impressive result. Could she do as Isashani of the Xacatecas, and take as much satisfaction in byplay behind the scenes as she did now in the seat of unquestioned command?

Mara sighed again.

That moment a shadow fell across the screen that led from the garden. "I know what you're thinking." A familiar voice intruded from beyond.

Mara glanced up to find Kevin watching her, a wry grin on his face.

He voiced an opinion as he always did, without waiting for her invitation. "You're wondering what it would be like to take a rest and let this young warrior of the Shinzawai run things."

Startled to laughter, Mara said, "You . . . monster!"

Kevin threw himself down next to her, flung back redgold hair that was in sore need of trimming, and paused with his mouth inches away from hers. "I'm right?"

She kissed him. Hokanu's charms she could resist, but this man was a poison in her blood. "Yes, damn you."

"I'll tell you exactly what it would be like. Dull." Kevin made a sweeping gesture that wound up catching her into an embrace. He kissed her back. "You love being in command."

"I never wished for the Acoma mantle," she responded in warning sharpness.

"I know," he said easily, not rising to her challenge. "That doesn't change the fact that you love it."

Mara allowed herself a self-indulgent grimace. "Nobody asked your opinion."

She had not denied his statement. To Kevin, that was as good as an admission he was right. As she leaned back, contented, against his shoulder, he pursued his conclusion ruthlessly. "The man you court is no weakling. Once he was husband, he'd be in command, and unless I misunderstand Tsurani tradition, you'd be forever denied rulership." Grinning evilly, Kevin asked, "So, are you going to marry him?"

Mara reached up, grabbed two fistfuls of red beard, and pulled teasingly. "Fool!" Before he could howl, she released him, half-laughing. "I might." When his eyes widened, she added, "But not yet. The political timing is wrong, and there remain a few things to attend first."

"Like what?" asked Kevin in sudden, humorless concern.

Only partially aware that his banter had masked a gnawing uncertainty, Mara's face turned grim. "Like the destruction of Tasaio of the Minwanabi."

The table was festive. Paper lanterns shed arrows of light through pierced patterns, and raised rich ruby highlights in the wine the servants had left with the meal. The plates and cutlery were the finest the closets could offer, yet neither Mara nor her guest cared to finish the last of the sweet cakes and sauce. Hokanu sat at ease on his cushions, but his attitude of relaxation was feigned. "I understand, of course."

His tone was mild, unsurprised, and utterly clean of resentment. Yet Mara knew him well enough to see the small, quiet interval he had taken to muster his poise in the moment that followed her refusal, for political considerations, of his informal offer of marriage. He was not distressed—at least not with the enraged bitterness Jiro had shown when she chose his brother, nor the kicked-dog hurt Kevin exhibited in his dark moods—but he felt a genuine pain at being rejected.

Not unexpectedly, his sadness made her ache. "Please," she added, with less impassivity than she intended. "You must know my heart."

Hokanu glanced down at his hands, which were still and rested half-curled around his wine goblet. Impulsively Mara wished she could reach across the table and take his long, fine fingers into her own. But that would be awkward, if not improper. . . . She was not agreeing to become his wife. Yet she could not entirely hide her regret. "I . . . admire you more than you know. You are everything I could ask for in a father for my children. But we both rule. Our house would be an armed camp. . . . Where would we live? Upon this estate, surrounded by soldiers not loyal to you? On your father's estate, with soldiers not loyal to me? Can we ask men sworn to our family natamis to obey those of another house, Hokanu?"

The sound of his name as only she could say it raised a bittersweet smile, and her words brought a surprised lift of his brows. "Mara, I assumed you would come live with me upon my father's estate, and that we would appoint anyone you chose to act as regent for Ayaki until he came to his majority." Hokanu made a disparaging gesture aimed entirely at himself. "Lady, forgive me for thoughtless presumption. I should have anticipated that you of all women would not react in the time-honored, customary fashion." His expression turned dry with irony. "I have admired your free spirit. To make an ordinary wife of you would be like caging a li bird, I see that now."

He was beautiful, spangled in lamplight, with his eyes deep as the forest pools sacred to priests. Mara drew a deep breath to steady herself. "You assumed, Hokanu, but that was no grave fault." Before she realized she had indulged herself, she reached across the table and touched his hand. His skin was very warm, each tendon delineated clearly. "All these problems would be solved if Tasaio of the Minwanabi did not loom like a sword over my neck. If you and your family had not stood at the heart of the Emperor's plan to force peace upon the High Council. If—"

Hokanu's other hand moved and closed gently over hers. His expression shifted subtly, toward not anger, or pain, but rather, deep interest. "Go on."

"If we lived in a place"—she hesitated, unsure how to

phrase a concept largely inspired by Kevin—"where law ruled in deed as well as word, where politics did not countenance murder . . ." She paused, and realized on the moment that his silence was a reflection of her own; that the hand upon her hand had tightened with shared resentment against the ingrained flaws in their culture she herself had reluctantly come to recognize. The easy rapport disturbed her, and to set it at a distance, she focused only on words. "If we lived at a time when we knew our children could grow without knives behind every door, then, Hokanu of the Shinzawai, I would be deeply honored to become your wife. There is no man in the Empire I would rather have as the father of my next child." She looked away from him, fearful that his presence would tempt her to further breaches in protocol. "But until the council is more settled, and things as we know them are different, a union between us would bring risk to both of our houses."

Hokanu was silent. He caressed her hand as he released her, and said nothing until she turned back to him, that he might face her squarely. "You are wise beyond your years, Lady Mara. I cannot pretend I am not disappointed. I can only admire your staunchness." He tilted his head fractionally to one side. "Your rare strength makes you all the more to be cherished."

Mara found moisture in her eyes. "Hokanu, some daughter of another house will be a lucky woman."

Hokanu bowed at the compliment. "Such a daughter must be more than lucky before she could displace my feelings for you. Before I go, may I at least know that you look favorably upon friendship with the Shinzawai?"

"Assuredly," she said, giddy with relief that he had not been angry or let her rebuff displace courtesy. More than she realized, she had been afraid her refusal might turn him against her. "I would cherish that as a privilege."

"Count it a gift," Hokanu said, "One you are worthy of." He sipped the last swallow of his wine, then smoothly prepared to take his leave.

Mara forestalled him, as much to delay the unhappy moment of his leaving. "If you would allow, I would beg a favor."

He paused, balanced in the instant of rising. His dark eyes searched her, honestly, without suspicion that she might use his weakness for her to gain her own ends, but in an intense desire to fathom her motives. Mara read his look and knew, at heart, how alike they were: both of them had an instinct for the Great Game, and the will to play the stakes fully.

Hokanu said, "What would you ask, Lady Mara?"

She strove to lighten her manner, while weighing how to broach an awkward subject. "It is my understanding that a Great One calls frequently at your home."

Hokanu nodded, his face now expressionless. "This is true."

Across a pained stillness, Mara added, "I very much desire to have an informal talk with such a personage. If you could facilitate a meeting, I would count myself in your debt."

Hokanu's eyes narrowed slightly, but he did not voice his curiosity about Mara's motives. "I shall see what I can do."

Then he did rise, briskly, and gave her a formal bow in farewell, along with graceful phrases. Mara rose also, saddened that the mood of intimacy had been broken. His charm was all on the surface now, and try though she might, she could not read deeper. When he was gone, she sat in the light of the paper lanterns, turning and turning her wineglass in her hands. She could not recall his last words, but only that he had masked his emotions all too well.

The cushions across the table seemed something more than empty, and the night a bit more than dark.

In time, Nacoya came, as Mara expected she might. The old woman's instincts were unerring. After a look at her mistress, the old woman sat down at her side. "Daughter of my heart, you look troubled."

Mara leaned against the older woman, allowing herself to be hugged as if she were a girl once again. "Nacoya, I did as I must, rejecting Hokanu's suit. But I am disturbed by a sadness that has no cause. I would not have thought I could love Kevin as deeply as I do, yet feel sorrow at declining Hokanu's proposal."

Nacoya raised a hand and gently stroked Mara's cheek as she had through painful years of growing. "Daughter, the heart can hold more than one. Each of these men has his place in it."

Mara sighed, allowing herself a moment of comfort in the old woman's arms. Then she smiled ruefully. "You always warned me that love was a tangle. I never understood until now just how much of one, and how many were the thorns."

At the sound of the gong, Mara stiffened. Kevin had just begun to slide his hand down her back, but warm flesh slid away and suddenly eluded his fingers. Left entangled in bedclothes, Kevin found himself alone. Belatedly he realized that never before had he heard the tone that had roused her. Glancing up from the sleeping mat, he said, "What is it?"

His sleepy question tangled with a flurry of activity as the door to Mara's quarters slid open and two maids hurried in with combs and pins. Others followed, flinging open the wardrobe, and within an instant the mistress was inundated with formal robes, dressers, and women who started to comb out the hair left mussed from the bed.

Kevin frowned. Shaken rudely from a pleasant interlude, he realized his Lady had spoken no word to order such an untimely invasion. "What's going on?" he inquired, loudly enough that this time he was noticed.

"A Great One comes!" Mara said impatiently, then followed with instructions for her maids on which jewelry she would wear with her formal gown. "I'll want the iron necklace for this occasion, and also the jade tiara."

"At this hour?" asked Kevin, heaving himself off the mat. He picked up his grey robe and wrapped it around himself.

From the center of the activity, Mara released a sigh of exasperation. "Most days I would already be an hour out of bed."

"Well," said Kevin, clearly the guilty party. He had done his best to detain her, and at first his efforts had been reciprocated willingly. "Do forgive the inconvenience." His tone was light, but he was plainly confused by her sudden departure from his arms.

Mara let the maids fuss over her pins and her sash. "Great Ones have no time to spare for vagaries." She seemed ready to add more, but at a second stroke of the gong the softness that started to become a smile vanished. "Enough! The Great One is here!"

The maids backed away and made their bows, while their mistress stood, satisfied that her hair was bound up simply, but in neat fashion, with four pins holding the arrangement.

The rare metal jewelry and jade tiara were enough to let this Great One know she did not take his coming lightly.

As she thrust on her slippers and headed for the door, her slave reflexively began to follow. "No. You may not come."

Kevin began an immediate protest, and Mara said, "Silence! If this magician decided you had slighted him in any fashion, he could order the death of every member of this house. I would be obliged to do as he bid, no matter what the cost. A Great One's words are as law. Knowing this, I refuse to risk your unguarded tongue within earshot of him."

She permitted no more argument but hurried through the door and crossed the courtyard to another wing. There lay a small, five-sided room without furnishing or ornament beyond a shatra bird inlaid in onyx in the floor. The chamber had not been used in her lifetime, but every household had a similar room, or nook, or alcove, with a clear symbol set into the floor. Any magician in the Empire could focus his will upon the pattern of that house and call at whim. Such an arrival was traditionally announced by the gong tone, sent by magical means to the location where a Great One intended to appear. A second chime signaled arrival, and that had occurred several minutes past.

In the chamber Mara found Nacoya, Keyoke, and Saric already standing before a stern-looking man in a black robe. She bowed deeply as she reached the door. "Great One, forgive my lack of promptness in greeting you. I was but half-dressed when you arrived."

The man inclined his head as if the matter held little consequence. He was of gaunt build and medium height, and though the robe concealed details, something about his carriage seemed familiar. "Through the agency of one for whom I have some affection, it has come to my attention that you desired to speak with me."

The voice clued her: though older, this magician had the same rich intonation that Hokanu did. Mara's eyes opened slightly. This was none other than Fumita, the Shinzawai heir's blood father. Hokanu had taken her request very personally indeed; and it would seem her hunch was correct, that some tie to family yet remained between this member of the Assembly and the Shinzawai.

Yet Mara dared not speculate openly. If they chose, magicians were capable of knowing the minds of those in their presence. She could not disallow the part that magic had played in the downfall of Jingu of the Minwanabi. Politely she said, "Great One, I need the wisdom of one such as yourself, to serve the Empire."

The man nodded. "Then we shall speak."

Mara excused her advisers and led the way through a screen onto an adjacent porch furnished with low stone benches. As Fumita took a seat, Mara stole the moment to study him. His hair was deep brown, shot with the beginnings of grey. The face was clean-lined and angular, and the nose more aquiline than the son's. The dark eyes were markedly similar, except that in the Great One the depths of mystery were veiled and unfathomable.

He rested himself upon a stone bench. Mara chose a seat opposite, a narrow path separating them.

"What do you wish to discuss?" Fumita asked.

"A matter weighs upon me, Great One," Mara began. She took a deep breath and searched for a proper beginning. "Like many, I was in attendance at the Imperial Games."

If the Great One had any feelings left over from that day, he kept them masked. His piercing attentiveness unnerved her worse than Hokanu's directness. He was not unapproachable, but neither did he warm into welcome. "Yes?"

"It is said that the Great One who was . . . the center of the disruption freed the combatants who refused to fight."

"This is true." Noncommittal still, Fumita waited for Mara to continue.

He could not have made himself more plain had he spoken. She would have to plunge ahead on her own and risk the consequences. "This is my concern," Mara said. "If a Great One may free slaves, then who else may? The Emperor? The Warlord? A Ruling Lord?"

The magician said nothing for some time. During an interval that felt as strange as the isolation a fish might feel in a pond, Mara was aware of the breeze across the porch and of a servant making the rounds of the estate house. Down the path, the broom strokes of a slave sounded preternaturally loud. These things were part of her world, yet somehow seemed sealed away as the eyes of the Magician remained pinned unwaveringly upon her. When Fumita spoke at last, his tone had not altered; the words remained inflectionless and bitten off sharply. "Mara of the Acoma, your question shall be raised in the Assembly."

Without further words, and before she could proffer reply, he reached into the pocket at his belt and removed a small metal object. Mara had no chance to express curiosity, even had she dared, before he ran his thumb across the surface of the talisman. The gesture seemed like one he had made many times. A faint buzzing suddenly surrounded him. Then the magician vanished. The stone bench stood empty, and an eddy of air teased the trappings of Mara's robe.

Left open-mouthed, and distinctly at a loss, Mara shivered slightly. She frowned, as if the space where the magician had sat might answer her dissatisfaction. She had never tried dealing with a Great One, beyond that single encounter which had finalized Lord Jingu's demise. This was the first time she had tried an overture on her own initiative, and the aftermath left her unsettled. There was no fathoming the ways of the Assembly. She shivered again, and wished herself back in her blankets with Kevin.

21. *KEEPER OF THE SEAL*

The barge docked.

Seated on cushions beneath the canopy with a cup of fruit juice in her hand, Mara squinted against the morning sunlight reflected off the water. Rocked by the rhythm of the polemen as they expertly maneuvered her craft through the press of commercial boats at the wharf, the Lady recalled Nacoya's disapproval of her trip to Kentosani. Yet, looking over the traffic that jammed the dockside, and counting the merchant barges at anchor waiting to unload, Mara judged Arakasi's assessment was the correct one. At least on the streets and public squares, the city had recovered from the chaos let loose upon it at the Imperial Games six months before.

To Mara, this seemed an opportune time to return to the Holy City. Nacoya was right to suspect that Mara's motive—visiting a minor political opponent to change his alliance—was deeper, but Mara revealed her thoughts to no one.

Once her barge tied up to the wharf, she surrendered her abandoned fruit juice to a servant, called for her litter, and assembled her honor guard. She had brought only twenty-five warriors in her retinue; her stop was intended to be brief and she was not worried about assassins. Both the Assembly and the Emperor were likely to look disfavorably on public disorder; any killing by a tong in the Emperor's city would bring a much deeper investigation than any family would risk at this time. Except for a minimum of servants, and her boat crew, Mara had only Kevin and Arakasi in attendance.

The heat was already stifling. As the Acoma guards began

the chore of clearing traffic from the Lady's intended path, Kevin pushed back damp hair from his brow. "So why did you really make this trip?"

Dressed in a finer robe than she usually chose for street travel, Mara looked between the curtains of her litter, which were cracked open to admit the relief of the passing breeze. "You asked Arakasi that scarcely an hour ago."

"And he told me the same lie, that we're going to pay a social call on Lord Kuganchalt of the Ginecho. I don't believe it."

Mara extended her fan through the curtains and tapped his wrist in reproof. "Were you a free man, I would be obliged to challenge that statement. To accuse me of lying is to insult Acoma honor."

Kevin caught the fan, playfully disarmed her, and returned the item with an exaggerated flourish, in imitation of a Tsurani suitor of a lesser house paying court to a Lady of higher station. "You didn't lie exactly," he admitted and grinned as Mara smothered a laugh at his clowning behind her now opened fan. He paused a step, reminded of how dear she was to him; then he doggedly pursued the subject. "You just didn't tell what's on your mind."

The litter bearers turned a corner and swerved to avoid a stray dog being chased by street urchins. They were after the bone it had stolen, and were moving too fast and chaotically for her soldiers to change their course. As always, Kevin noticed their poor clothes and evidence of sores and sickness upon them, and felt sad. He only half heard Mara's explanation: Lord Kuganchalt was an important if minor ally of the Lord of the Ekamchi and the Lord of the Inrodaka. Those two held sway in a small faction allied firmly against her since her winning of the cho-ja Queen from a hive near Inrodaka lands. She allowed that a contact with the Ginecho would at least give her an opportunity to explain her side of the dispute, perhaps even to drive a wedge between the Ginecho and the two disaffected Lords.

"House Ginecho took heavy losses with Almecho's fall," Mara qualified. "They were heavily indebted to the Omechan, and the Warlord's two disgraces caused the debts all to come due much earlier than the old Lord of the Ginecho could have expected. He died, it is said, of the strain, though others whisper suicide. Still others claim poison was set in his dish by an enemy. Whatever the reason, his young son, Kuganchalt, has inherited his mantle, along with a heavy financial burden. I judge this an auspicious time for an overture."

Kevin's lips thinned in annoyance. She said this though she knew he had been present when Arakasi allowed that Kuganchalt's court was riddled through with cousins who were Ekamchi and Inrodaka loyalists, a few of whom probably had orders to commit murder should the inexperienced boy act in any way to the detriment of his two allies. Kevin had commented that a few might be motivated to speed the young Lord along to the halls of the Red God without any urging from Mara's two enemies. Nacoya warned Mara that entering Kuganchalt's town house would be stepping into a nest of swamp relli; Mara, she berated, was deaf to good advice when larger issues were on her mind.

As litter and bearers rounded another corner, and sunlight fell through the curtains, Kevin became aware that the Lady was looking at him. Too often he had the feeling she could read his thoughts from his face, and this was one such time. "The Ginecho would expect us to try to rearrange their alliance," she pointed out with mischievous gentleness. "Ekamchi went to such trouble to buy the loyalty of so many members of Kuganchalt's family, and Inrodaka underwrote most of the expense. They would all be terribly disappointed if the Acoma failed to put in an appearance. We will go, and give them what they want, which is belief in their own self-importance. Inrodaka and Ekamchi must always be led to believe that their enmity is of some consequence. It keeps them from allying with my other enemies.

"Gods help us if they discover the truth: that the Acoma have gained enough standing that their minor plotting has no impact; then they might brew worse mischief than they do already, just to attract attention, or do something really destructive, such as throwing their support to Tasaio."

Kevin snorted out a laugh. "You mean you're going to pat the little guy with a grudge on the head, just to keep him from getting really irate, in case he thinks you've forgotten he's got bones to pick, so he doesn't get nasty and go out and find a bigger bone to pick?"

"Inelegantly spoken," Mara said. "But yes."

Kevin swore in Midkemian.

Somewhat nettled, Mara twitched the curtains back. "That's rude. Now what do you mean?"

Her barbarian lover gave her a long look and shrugged. "In polite language, your Great Game of the Council ingests water from a infested swamp. One could say it quite often borders on the absurd."

"I was afraid you were going to say that." Mara leaned an elbow on her cushions and gazed at one of the huge stone temples that bordered both sides of the avenue.

Kevin followed her glance, by now well enough versed in the Tsurani pantheon to recognize the temple of Lashima, Goddess of Wisdom. Here, he recalled, Mara had spent months in study, in the hope of taking vows of service. The deaths of her father and brother had drastically changed that fate.

As though her own reminiscence followed his into the past, Mara said, "You know, I miss the quiet." Then she smiled. "But nothing else, really. The temple priestesses are even more bound to tradition and ritual than the great houses are. Now I cannot imagine being happy with such a life." She tipped a wicked glance at Kevin. "And certainly I would have missed out on some very enjoyable bed sport."

"Well," said Kevin, running irreverent eyes over the walls that surrounded the temple grounds, "maybe not—given luck, a length of stout rope, and a determined man." He bent over, cupped her chin, and kissed her as they walked along. "I'm a very determined man."

From the other side of the litter, Arakasi shot the couple a black look.

"You never will act the proper slave," Mara murmured. "I suppose we shall have to look over the precedent set in the arena by the Great One who was your countryman, and seek a legal way to set you free."

Kevin missed a step. "That's why we're back in Kentosani! You're going to look up the fine points of the law and see what's changed since the games?" He strode out, reestablished position at Mara's side, and grinned. "Patrick might forget himself and kiss you."

Mara made a face. "That would certainly earn him a beating! The man never bathes." Shaking her head, she added, "No, that's not my reason for being here. If we can find the time, we'll visit the Imperial Archives. But the Lord of the Ginecho comes first."

"Life would be so dull without enemies," Kevin quipped, but this time his Lady did not rise to the bait. Beyond the precinct of the temples, the avenue narrowed, and traffic became too thick to allow for conversation. Kevin fought against the press of the heavy crowds, using his greater height to prevent his Lady's litter from being jostled. He realized that his years of captivity had not been entirely unhappy ones; he might not love all aspects of Tsurani society —the misery of the poor would never cease to bother him. But given the chance to become a free man, and stay at Mara's side, he would choose this alien world as home. His horizons had widened since he had fought in the Riftwar. For him, as a younger son, return to his father's estate at Zūn would offer poor prospects, no substitute for the excitement he had found in foreign and exotic Tsuranuanni.

So caught up in his thoughts was he that when Mara's small retinue arrived at the Acoma town house, he did not raise his customary protest when the head servant there commanded him forthwith to unload the Lady's carry boxes and heft them up to her chambers.

Midday passed, and the heat lessened. Bathed and refreshed since her journey, Mara prepared for her visit to the Lord of the Ginecho. Kevin declined the chance to attend her, insisting he would be unable to keep a straight face through the proceedings. In fact, Mara knew him to be fascinated with the markets of the Holy City, and in wistful reflection she agreed that an afternoon of shopping with the head servant of the house was bound to be more interesting than exchanging stilted small talk and veiled insults with a seventeen-year-old boy whose eyes were still puffed from weeping over his father. She indulged Kevin's excuse and let him stay, and instead took Arakasi, unobtrusively clad as a servant. The Ginecho were too minor a house to warrant close observation by Arakasi's agents, and the Spy Master himself desired the opportunity to pursue gossip with the house servants.

The litter departed from the town house courtyard in the late afternoon, accompanied by twenty warriors, a suitable number to impress Lord Ginecho that his enmity was taken seriously. For quickness, the entourage held to back streets, less packed with traffic.

They passed through cool tree-lined avenues lined by the garden courtyards of wealthy guild officials and merchants. Few folk noted their passage, and the only impediment was the occasional hand-pushed cart filled with vegetables that the servants of the very rich wheeled home. The soldiers stayed alert, though Arakasi held belief that no great house in the Empire would feel confident enough to attempt an assassination in public.

Mara had always loved the side streets of the Holy City, with their long glades of flowering trees, and their neatly swept stone cobbles. She enjoyed the wooden gates, with their patterned lattices, and their posts netted over with akasi and hibis vines. Although Kentosani was a river city, like Sulan-Qu, by imperial edict no dyers, tanneries, or other crafts requiring unpleasant procedures had been permitted within the city walls. Unless one was downwind of the holding pens for the arena or the crowded markets in the central waterfront area, this was a city that smelled of flowers, spiced with the scents of temple incense as day closed and priests and priestesses of all the Tsurani deities began their night's devotions.

The Acoma bearers conveyed their burden from the side lanes and entered one of the many wide squares. Half-lost in reflection brought on by the quiet of the hour, Mara almost missed Arakasi's hesitation.

She looked over to see what had captured his attention. Across the square rose two gilded columns framed by an arch and a span of smoothed slate. This was one of many message boards reserved for the word of the Light of Heaven. Although the messages were usually scribed in chalk, and of a religious context, today a crew of Imperial Whites stood guard over the site. The event was unusual enough to draw notice. Closer inspection showed two plain-garbed craftsmen repairing the gilding on the frame, which had been damaged in last year's riots. Even the minute amounts of gold they used were too costly to risk thieves; this seemed to explain the presence of the Emperor's guards. But what drew Arakasi's closer inspection were three dark-robed figures who stood at the board in process of affixing a scroll heavy with imperial ribbons and seals. Mara frowned, puzzled.

Great Ones from the Assembly of Magicians did not usually perform the errands of clerks.

"It's a proclamation," Arakasi mused, sharing his thoughts with his mistress. "With permission, Lady, I should like to see what it contains."

Mara nodded her permission, diverted from her enjoyment of Kentosani's loveliness to considering the Light of Heaven; imperial proclamations were a rarity, and the fact that one was being posted by Great Ones augured a momentous matter. It was no longer a topic of idle speculation that the current Emperor was not acting the exaltedly remote figure his forebears had been. This Light of Heaven, Ichindar, had not only put his hand into the game, he had overturned it.

Arakasi returned, slipping neatly between two bread sellers with shoulder yokes and laden baskets. As he arrived beside his mistress's litter, he said softly, "My Lady, The Great Ones announce to the Empire that the magician Milamber has been cast out of the Assembly. The document goes on to say that those slaves in the arena who were freed by his action are lawfully released from their masters, but no precedent may be seen in this. By imperial decree, and by the will of heaven, Ichindar pronounces that no other who wears the slave's grey may change his status. For the good of the Empire, for the sake of the order of society, and by divine will, all who are slaves must remain so until death."

Mara showed no change in expression, but the delight went out of the day. Suddenly heavy-hearted, she motioned her bearers forward, then closed her curtains, as she did when she wanted privacy. Her hands laced tightly over a cushion. She did not know how she was going to tell Kevin, whose hopes had risen so dizzyingly after her careless reference that morning.

Until recently, she had not considered his slavery to be an issue of importance. As Acoma property, he was guaranteed food, and housing, and a measure of public standing by right of the honor of her house. As a freeman, he would have no position, even in the eyes of a beggar. Any Tsurani in the street might spit on him without fear of retribution. Much as Mara might love him, she had not always understood his pride, so different from Tsurani pride, for he was safer as a slave in her house than as a clanless barbarian freeman. Anyone who spent time at the docks in Jamar would see the occasional renegade Thuril or dwarf from Dustari and their misery and know this was true.

But this much she had come to grudgingly understand: if he remained a slave, in some manner, at some time, she *must* lose him. The Night of the Bloody Swords had shown her beyond doubt that he was a warrior; he deserved freedom to further his honor. Since then she had felt uncomfortable with the concept that he should finish his days as her property. Her views had changed: she understood that his Midkemian code of conduct, alien as it was, had its own intrinsic honor.

No longer could she regard him as disgraced for failing to take his life rather than be captured by an enemy, as a Tsurani warrior would have done, or for hiding his rank to avoid summary execution.

Troubled to discover that her plans to give him happiness were permanently dashed, Mara stayed withdrawn throughout her visit to the Ginecho. She performed the proper social display expected of her, but afterward she would have been hard put to recall a word of the conversation or recite a detail of young Lord Kuganchalt's appearance. If Arakasi noted that she seemed distracted as the litter wended its way homeward through Kentosani's torch-lit streets, he said nothing. He provided his hand with the skill of a man assigned such duties lifelong as she got out of the litter in her courtyard, and disappeared unobtrusively at her dismissal.

Mara called for a light supper, and for once did not ask for Kevin's company. She sat in solitude in the study overlooking the courtyard, picking at her meal and staring at the shadow patterns the flowering shrubs threw onto the screen. From the kitchen she could hear laughter, and Kevin's boisterous voice describing some escapade concerning a jigabird seller in the markets. He was in high humor, and the other servants were enjoying his performance with the enthusiasm of bystanders at a street entertainment.

But for Mara, tonight, Kevin's laughter only cut. She pushed aside her barely tasted plate with a sigh, and asked a servant to bring wine. She sipped, and let the night deepen without calling for lamps. Her mind and her memory circled endlessly, reviewing the leading questions she had asked of the Great One, Fumita. His reticence stung her even yet. Over and over, she pondered his chilly reception, and she wondered, now that it was absolutely beyond hope to change, whether the edict against freeing slaves had been prompted by her inquiries.

She could never know for certain. That was the painful part. If she had more wisely kept her own counsel, Kevin's chance of freedom might not have been destroyed.

Mara sighed and waved for removal of her supper tray. She retired early, though her mind churned, and when Kevin came she feigned sleep. His touches and his tenderness could not break through her dark thoughts, and she feared to risk bringing him into her confidence. When at last he fell into contented slumber by her side, she felt no better. All night she tossed and sorted words. Hours passed, and she still did not know what to say.

She gazed at his profile, lit softly golden by the screen-filtered light of the courtyard lanterns. The scar he had gained from the overseer at the slave market had nearly faded away over the years. All that remained was a fine crease over his cheekbone, such as a warrior might gain from a sword cut. The blue eyes with their laughing depths were closed, and in sleep his face showed abiding peace. Mara ached to touch him, and instead wound up blinking back tears. Angered by her shameful softness, she rolled over and stared at the wall, only to find herself turning back, studying his profile and biting her lip not to weep.

Dawn came, and she was exhausted. She arose before Kevin, tense and miserable in a cold sweat. She called for maids to bathe and dress her, and when her beloved roused with his sleepy questions, she covered her reticence by seeming brusque.

"I have a most important errand to do this morning." She tilted her head away, ostensibly to help the maid who was arranging her hair, but in fact to hide her puffy eyes before cosmetics could disguise the evidence of her unhappiness. "You may come or not, as you wish."

Stung by her coldness, Kevin paused in the act of stretching. He looked at her; she could feel his gaze on her back and did not have to see to be sure of his reproach. "I'll come, of course," he said slowly. Then, chagrined that his tone held an edge that reflected her own, he added, "At least, the antics of jigabird sellers will need to improve a great deal before I'll be drawn from your charms." The conciliatory tone of the comment was not lost on her; she cursed the fact he held such power over her and that even such a small remark feel could like a rebuke.

He stood up. Never quite as silent as a Tsurani warrior, but as strongly confident, he stepped over to her and slipped his arms around her shoulders. "You are my favorite little bird in the Empire," he murmured. "Beautifully soft, and your singing is the joy of my heart."

He moved away, with a sly quip that caused one of her maids an unseemly fit of giggles. If he had noticed the Lady was stiff in his arms, he attributed it to the pins that the maid was using to fasten the long, looping twists of her hair.

The elaborate coiffure should have warned him. Built to a height that indicated a Tsurani intention to impress, and fastened with dozens of fine jade and diamond pins, Mara's headdress was crowned and glorified by a feathered tiara set with corcara shell.

"We're going to the Imperial Palace?" Kevin demanded when he tore his eyes away long enough to notice that Arakasi was among the honor guard, dressed as a clerk. The Senior Strike Leader was wearing his ceremonial armor and his most imposing plumes. His spear and helm were streamered, and since the ribbons would not hold up to prolonged street wear, not to mention a fight, somebody important had to be the reason behind all the pomp.

"We're going to pay a visit to an official of the Emperor," Mara explained, her tone brittle. She let Arakasi hand her into the litter. He was better at the task than the Strike Leader, who was fine enough with a sword but clumsy when it came to managing a Lady in high-soled sandals, eight layers of overrobes, and a headdress that would have outmatched any King of the Isles' coronation crown by a factor of ten.

"You look like the confection on a wedding cake," Kevin observed. "This personage is important?"

At last he won a smile from her, though with her face painted and thyza-powdered, the expression was predictably stiff. "He thinks he is important. When one goes asking for favors, the difference becomes moot." Mindful of her finery,

Mara settled back on her cushions. "Close the curtains, please," she instructed Arakasi.

As the bearers raised the litter poles and started off, a nonplussed Kevin fell into stride. He presumed that Mara wanted privacy to discourage gawkers and to preserve her elaborate costume from dust. His cheerful mood held through a long, traffic-harried trek to the Imperial Palace, and not even the elaborate protocols of the various gate- and doorkeepers put him off. Once he had become accustomed to the grand weight of ceremony that attended all matters within the Empire, he had discovered the purpose behind such manners. No official, however minor, was ever rudely interrupted by someone from the lower ranks. Ruling Lords or Ladies were not caught unprepared by a visitor; the Tsurani attention to ceremony ensured, according to rank, that all things happened in due course, and that the proper papers, or clothing, or refreshments would all be in place the moment the caller at last crossed the threshold.

The Keeper of the Imperial Seal was well prepared when his secretary finally let Mara and her retinue into the audience chamber. The cushions had been plumped since the last petitioner had departed. A fresh tray of fruit and juices sat upon the low side table, and the official himself had his robe on, his weighty collar and signet of office adjusted and straight, and his fleshy anatomy arranged with dignity.

A middle-aged man, the Keeper of the Imperial Seal had a florid face, a mouth all but lost amid multiple chins, and hooded, darting eyes that could probably name the coin worth of every jewel in Mara's costume at a glance. He also liked sweets, as evidenced by the keljir leaves piled in his refuse basket. The gummy confection made from an extract of tree sap had rimmed his teeth and his tongue a faint red-orange, and his bow was perfunctory, owing to his bulk and his equal-sized sense of self-importance.

The chamber smelled of fat man's sweat and old wax, by which Kevin deduced that the screens were probably stuck shut. Holding a satchel of inks, pens, and parchments for Arakasi's needs, he braced himself for a boring wait as Mara began the phrases of greeting. The official used this interval to open a drawer in his lap table and unwrap a keljir as if the task were a sacred ritual. He popped the sweet in his mouth, sucked noisily, and then condescended to reply.

"I am well." His voice was deep, and too loud. He cleared his throat carefully, twice. "Lady Mara of the Acoma." He sucked, considered, then added, "I trust you are well?"

Mara inclined her head.

The official shifted his weight on his cushions, and the floor creaked ponderously. He shifted his candy with a click of teeth to the other bulging cheek. "What brings you to my office this fine morning, Lady Mara?"

Kevin heard her reply as a murmur, but could not make out single words.

The official's jaws stopped working on his treat. He cleared his throat, three times, very deliberately. His fingers drummed on his knee, leaving white spots in the flesh that the hem of his robe did not cover. Then he frowned, his eyebrows snarling together over his baby-round nose. "That's —that's a most unusual request, Lady Mara."

The Lady elaborated, and hearing her mention "Midkemia," Kevin pricked up his ears.

The Lady of the Acoma finished most clearly, "It is a whim." She shrugged in a manner that Kevin recognized as purely feminine, and calculated to disarm. "I would be pleased."

The Keeper of the Imperial Seal shifted again. His frown became uncomfortable.

Mara said something.

"I know the rift is closed!" the official blurted, startled into biting down hard on his sweet. He looked briefly as if he had cracked a tooth. "Your asking on this, a seemingly worthless concession, is odd. Most odd." He cleared his throat and said, "Most odd," again, as though he liked the sound of the words.

Kevin discovered himself leaning forward, and realized he had better not; a slave in this land must not be caught taking an interest in the affairs of his betters.

Mara spoke again: maddeningly, too low to be heard.

The official scratched his chin, obviously stymied. "Can I do that?"

"It is written so, as a point of law," Mara returned. She beckoned to Arakasi, who strode forward and bowed behind her shoulder. "My clerk will be pleased to explain."

The Keeper of the Imperial Seal crunched the last of his

candy, looking anxious. He waved, as if Arakasi were of little more consequence than a slave.

The Spy Master reached into a pocket in his smock and withdrew a document. He slipped the ribbon, unrolled the scroll with brisk industry, and read a passage copied from a book, which held that the Keeper of the Imperial Seal could use his discretion and assign those dispositions concerning trade and guild rights, and authorize limited collection of minor taxes upon goods or services that were deemed too small to bother the imperial council with.

"Well." The huge man rearranged himself and began unwrapping another keljir sweet. "The matter you ask for is certainly a petty one, of no merit for discussion by the council." He paused and turned the candy over and over between his fingers as if he expected to find insects. "But, if I may guess, no man in my position has initiated any sort of private dispensation for hundreds of generations."

"Exalted sir," Arakasi ventured. "I point out that the law has not changed." He bowed again and backstepped to stand beside Kevin, a clear hint that he expected to collect his writing utensils and commence setting up a document.

"What's she asking for?" Kevin questioned, as softly as he could.

"Shh!" Arakasi gestured for the slave to be silent, while Mara added another point in favor of her argument, and the official across from her became distinctly more flummoxed.

Kevin observed, and deduced that the Keeper of the Imperial Seal was a bureaucrat with a sanctimonious devotion to order. With the obstinacy typical of his kind in every country, he was going to refuse Mara's request, not because her demand was unreasonable, but because it was unusual and outside the method of paper work and filing he was bound by habit to follow. Arakasi seemed to sense an imminent rejection also, because his pose grew quietly more taut.

Kevin stared at the floor and feigned unconcern. But in a low whisper to Arakasi he said, "Why don't you suggest that Mara try a bribe?"

The Spy Master twitched no muscle, his sole evidence of surprise the interval before his response. "Brilliant!" he whispered back. "Is that what your people do with reluctant officials in Midkemia?"

Kevin returned a barely perceptible nod, and one corner

of his mouth turned up. "Usually it works. Besides, I'd bet Mara's jewels that's what he's waiting for."

But Arakasi had already moved forward to tap his Lady discreetly on the arm. He spoke into her ear, swiftly, before the Keeper of the Imperial Seal could finish his snack and end deliberation.

Mara was gifted with the knack for thinking on her feet. As the fat man across the lap desk from her drew a ponderous breath to frame his answer, she interrupted.

"Exalted sir, I realize such a request would require effort on your part, to ensure that you were acting within the dictates of your office. And as you are under no obligation to do so simply because I ask, I would be pleased to recompense your time and industry; say, a hundred centuries of metal and three thumb-size emeralds, if you would undertake the needed inquiry to resolve the issue properly."

The Keeper of the Imperial Seal swallowed his keljir ball whole. His eyes bulged out. "Lady, you are too generous." He did not belabor the issue; after all, her request was ludicrously useless. He had even most honorably emphasized that the rift connecting Midkemia to Kelewan was closed. But if Mara wished to be eccentric, the Emperor and the High Council certainly should not be bothered to consider such a worthless point of trade. Transparently content with his reasoning, and already greedy for his gift, the official motioned to Arakasi. "My duty requires I research such tasks, but I shall be happy to take your gifts and . . . pass them along to the temples as devotion." He smiled. "Now that I've had a moment to ponder, I am certain your interpretation is the correct one. Fetch your pens and parchments. We shall draw up the agreement directly."

Imperial documents in Tsuranuanni were never short-order items. Kevin shifted from foot to foot, while the closed chamber grew more stifling. Arakasi and the Keeper of the Imperial Seal argued endlessly and amicably over wording, while slaves came and went with braziers, pots of various colors of wax, and spools of ribbon. Afternoon had come before the document proving Mara's dispensation had been recorded under the Imperial Seal. Another interval elapsed, while the ink dried, and the captain of her honor guard sent a warrior to the town house to fetch back the centis and emeralds. While they waited, the fat man chewed keljir and discoursed on the poor quality of this season's dyed feathers. He had purchased an indigo robe, which had proceeded to rot into dust.

"The merchants think nothing of selling second-quality goods since the riots," he lamented, while his own clerk was sent for, just to knot the official ribbons that tied the parchment into a scroll. "The fabric of our clothing is going to ruin," the Keeper of the Imperial Seal ended sadly. "Some say that the order in the Empire will sour next."

"Not with the Assembly of Magicians guaranteeing order," Arakasi interjected. He moved fast enough to intercept the parchment, before the official could wave it about as emphasis to expound a further point.

Blessedly fast, after that, Kevin was handed the satchel of scribe's implements, the document safely inside. Mara arose and bowed, and as her party took their leave of the sweltering chamber, the Keeper of the Imperial Seal could be heard bellowing loudly for his servant.

"There are no more keljir candies in my jar! Where is our efficiency these days? The clothes dyers are lazy cheats, the merchants sell defective goods, and now my own servants think they can ignore my needs and not be punished! We are coming to ruin, in this Empire, and who beside me seems to care?"

Mara did not linger in Kentosani after her visit to the Keeper of the Imperial Seal, but boarded her barge for the return voyage to Sulan-Qu and home that afternoon. The weather continued hot, sultry even for Kelewan, and as often happened during travel by river, Mara kept to her quarters, by herself. She spent long hours in conference with Arakasi, or reading scrolls her factors had sent her from the markets in the Holy City. The rest of the time she stared at the water, deep in thought, and not much noticing the stream of passing traffic on the river.

Kevin amused himself joking with the polemen, or playing at dice with the off-duty warriors from the Lady's honor guard. As a slave, he could not legally keep his winnings, which was well from the standpoint of the losers, who claimed he had ungodly runs of luck. The barge docked without event in Sulan-Qu, and Mara's retinue regrouped. Her goods and carry boxes were dispatched to a warehouse, to head home with the next inbound caravan, while the Lady transferred to her litter. She had dinner in a travelers' hostelry in one of the fashionable districts of the city, then set off for home at twilight, her warriors carrying lanterns to light the way. Tired from the sun, Kevin had spent the interval in the city napping with the litter bearers, rather than seeking street gossip from the beggars, who were unfailingly surly because he was a foreigner and a slave.

Since the visit to Kentosani, events and chance circumstance had conspired to keep Kevin from private time with the Lady. He did not take this amiss. She wore the mantle of the Acoma, and her responsibilities did not always leave her accessible. Usually this suited Kevin's independent turn of mind. He had moments when he preferred solitude, or jokes in the company of men. Still, curiosity impelled him to know what Mara had transacted with the Keeper of the Imperial Seal. The parchment that granted her concession of rights had stayed rolled up in Mara's personal chest of papers. She had not left that box in Sulan-Qu with her other baggage, but had kept it in her litter at her feet the whole way home.

Ayaki's boisterous greeting prevented Kevin's finding out where the box was taken. But Mara must have ordered it locked away first thing, for by the time she finished scolding servants for allowing her son to be up so late, Kevin realized the box was gone. The bearers had already vanished in the direction of the stores shed, and Jican was nowhere to be found. Wise enough to know that information could not be wheedled out of Arakasi, Kevin waited through the hour while Mara caught Nacoya up on the news over cups of chocha and a late snack. He was waiting for her in the bedchamber when, exhausted by travel, she at last came in to retire.

He realized the moment he embraced her that something was wrong. Her lips were cool on his, and her smile was forced. He was on the point of asking what it was when she clapped for servants to bring bath water. What followed distracted him completely. After passion had cooled, he lay on the bed cushions with the screens cracked open and a copper flood of moonlight slashing a square across the floor; he noticed that the woman in his arms was still not relaxed. In retrospect, he realized their lovemaking had been hurried, not at all the slow, languorous spiral into ecstasy that Mara was inclined to prefer. Her responses to his touches had carried a buried sense of desperation that Kevin had almost failed to notice.

He reached out and gently stroked the hair away from her temple. "Is something the matter?"

Mara rolled over. Her features stayed shadowy, but Kevin could feel her gazing at his face. "I am tired from the journey," she said, but the words were studied.

Kevin caught her wrists and pulled her warmly against him. "You know I love you."

But she buried her head in his shoulder and refused the invitation to talk.

Attempting an innocuous approach, Kevin cupped her chin in his hand. "You have something of importance up your sleeve. What was that secret dispensation you bribed from the Keeper of the Imperial Seal, anyway?"

Mara answered with surprising pique. "You must not expect my confidence in all matters."

"No?" Kevin sat up, unsure of the source of her antagonism, and stung just enough not to handle it without rancor. "Do I mean that little to you?"

"You mean a great deal to me," Mara said at once. Fear made her voice cold, but in the dark he noticed only her tone. She drew away from him and sat up with her arms around her knees and her hands tightly clasped. "You mean everything."

"Then tell me what agreement you made in Kentosani." Kevin swept back a fallen lock of hair in a gesture so habitual it made her ache. "I know it concerns Midkemia."

"Arakasi did not tell you that," Mara accused, still snapping.

"No. I overheard." Kevin's admission revealed he felt no shame, which angered her.

Mara released a pent breath. "Only my Spy Master and I know the contents of that document. That is according to my wishes."

Now convinced she was hiding something, and fearful that it might be a matter detrimental to his people, Kevin tried to pressure her. "You said I meant something."

Against the square of moonlight, Mara was perfectly still. Her profile went hard, expressionless, and thoroughly, infuriatingly Tsurani. She said nothing. Unaware that she was caught up in personal conflict that had little to do with the subject, Kevin reached for her.

"Have we no trust between us, after all these years of intimacy?" His voice was persuasive enough to wound; still she could have withstood him if he had not reached out and stroked her shoulder with all of his tenderness. "Mara, if you are frightened of something, can't I know?"

She flung away from him, which was totally unexpected, and painful in a way that took his breath. "Of what would I be afraid?" Her words were harsh, and he had no means to guess that he had hit upon exactly the point that troubled her. She was afraid—of the power he had over her, and of the tangle he had made of her emotions. Coldly, self-defensively, she reacted with the one thing she knew beyond doubt would distance him. "You are a slave," she said with icy, bitten clarity. "It is not for a slave to suppose what I fear or do not fear."

Angry himself, and beyond thought, Kevin let his words take on a sharp edge. "Is that all I am to you? A slave, to be numbered among your things? Am I of no more account than a needra bull, or a scullion?" He shook his head and tried valiantly through his pain to soften his voice. "I thought, after Dustari, and a certain night in Kentosani, that I had earned some worth in your eyes." He felt a tremble invade his middle, and hardened himself against the emotion her people deplored. "I killed men for you, Lady. Unlike yours, my people do not lightly take the lives of others."

His pride caught her heart and twisted. In a moment she would be crying, and in a desperate attempt to contain her own hurt, Mara held herself in grim control. As if she faced her direst enemy, not her most beloved companion, she said, "You forget yourself. You forget that your life could have been forfeit for daring to set hand to a sword. You are a slave, like other slaves, and to remind you of your station, it would be best if you left my chamber and spent the remainder of this night with your fellows in the slave quarters."

Kevin sat, motionless with astonishment.

"Go!" Mara said, not shouting, but with all the finality of an executioner. "That is an order!"

Kevin arose, lordly in his fury. He snatched his breeches from the chest by the bed cushions but did not bother to dress. Naked, tall, and prideful, he said, "I have all but deserted my companions in sharing my love with their enemy. They might be barbarians and slaves, but they are not ones to cast aside loyalty. It will be a pleasure," he finished, and he spun and left without giving her a bow.

Mara sat, stone-stiff. She did not cry until long after he had departed. By then he was knocking on the lintel of the hut where Patrick lived, politely requesting admittance.

"Kev?" a sleepy voice responded. "That you, old son?"

Kevin stepped across the threshold, then cursed when he recalled: the slave huts had no lanterns. He crouched in the dark and sat on the clammy dirt floor.

"Damn," Patrick muttered. He sat up on the poor pallet that served him as bed, chair, and table. "It is you. Did you have to come calling in the middle of the bloody night? You know we have to be in the fields before dawn."

There was more than accusation in his fellow Midkemian's tone. Having already made one mistake concerning another's feelings that night, and sobered by that into sensitivity, Kevin chose tact. "Something wrong, old friend?"

Patrick sighed and ran a hand over his bald head. "You can bet on that. Very wrong. And I'm glad you didn't wait until tomorrow to come, really. I suppose you heard about Jake and Douglas."

Kevin drew a careful breath. "No," he said gently. "What's to hear?"

"They were hung for trying to escape!" Patrick leaned forward, distressed and bitter. "We heard about the imperial decree from a tradesman passing by. You weren't here to dissuade them. God, I tried. They pretended to listen, then sought to bolt the next night. Keyoke, the old fox, knows our ways well enough by now that he guessed somebody might attempt to run for the hills. He had warriors waiting for our boys, and both of them dead before dawn."

Kevin felt a sting as an insect sampled his calf. He slapped it away with a fury he withheld from his voice. Carefully, weighing this news from the beginning, he said, "You mentioned an imperial decree. What was it?"

"You didn't hear?" Patrick laughed incredulously, with a heavy underlying sarcasm. "You were in the Holy City, in the company of gods'-almighty nobility, and *you didn't hear?*"

"I didn't hear," Kevin snapped. "Now will you kindly tell me?"

Patrick paused, scratched at a scab on his knee, and sighed. "Damn me, but you're telling the truth, at that. That's maybe not surprising, seeing as slaves mean no more than needra bulls to the runts of this accursed land."

"Damn it, tell me, Patrick! If there's been an imperial decree concerning slaves, I want to know about it."

"Simply this," said the bald man, who over the years had nearly become a stranger. "That the slaves freed from the arena by that Midkemian magician, Milamber, were a freak. Milamber's been tossed out of the Assembly for what everyone says was not doing his duty by the Empire—he's an outlaw for good reasons, they say, and has a death price on his head. And the Emperor has set his hand and seal to a document posted in every city that no other slaves, ever, can be freed. That does tend to wreck the hope you held out to us, old son. Poor Jake and Douglas lost their stomach for waiting, and there are others as impatient that won't be hanging on here much longer." With a bitter note, he added, "They were so ruined by the word, I believe they knew they were going to be caught and didn't care." He sighed. "It's hard to think how all these years we've been hoping one way or another we'd get home. I guess the prospect of doing this slave work every day until we're dead . . ."

A silence developed as Kevin absorbed the implications of the news his countryman had related. Patrick caught up in his thinking and realized that his two dead companions had not been the reason for Kevin's sudden visit.

"You had a fight with her," he accused abruptly.

Kevin nodded ruefully, his lover's feelings less raw since he had learned of Milamber's disgrace. Mara's odd reticence since Kentosani at least had an obvious cause. Upon sober reflection, in a clammy hut full of stinging insects, he saw he had been a fool to let his fur get ruffled. She had never been a woman given to hysterics. And indeed, she must feel as frightened of losing him as he was of being parted from her. If he could not, by her orders, return to mend matters until morning, at least he could give the difficulties of his countrymen long-overdue consideration.

"I had a bit of a tough night," Kevin admitted ruefully. "But that's no reason to lose hope."

"Damn you, man, the rift is closed," Patrick interjected. "That means no return for us, and our only chance is an outlaw's life in the mountains."

"No." Bitten by another insect, Kevin slapped his breeches and politely asked for a place on the pallet.

Patrick grudgingly moved over.

"The rift is closed now, very true." The blankets were rough, and Kevin wondered which was the more evil of two irritants, his companion's bedclothes or the bugs. The mattress was sweat-damp and lumpy, no fit place for a man to spend his nights. Kevin sighed, torn inside between his love for Mara and his responsibility as the only Lord's son with a chance to find help for his countrymen. As always, he sought comfort in humor. Rather than rail over Tsurani injustice, he regaled Patrick with a jocular account of Mara's visit to the Keeper of the Imperial Seal.

He managed to coax a dry laugh from Patrick when he got to the part about the bribe. But the central issue did not pass unnoticed.

"You don't know what was in that dispensation," the bald man pointed out. "It may have nothing whatever to do with us or even slavery at all."

"Probably not," Kevin confessed, then said quickly, "But that's not the issue."

A skeptical quiet followed. The pallet shifted as Patrick sat back against the wall. "What is the issue, then, old son? I'm waiting."

"She negotiated for some concession that had to do with Midkemia," Kevin added as though the conclusion were plain. When Patrick failed to catch on, he qualified. "Obviously our Lady believes that someday the rift will be reopened."

"And that's supposed to keep the boys living in vermin and putting up with being beaten?" Patrick asked. "Damn you, Kevin, you're too much the optimist. All that silk and woman flesh have gone straight to your head. You know these runts have a history going back thousands of years. They make plans for the next fifty generations and consider them important in this lifetime."

Kevin did not gainsay this, but gestured in honest entreaty. "Patrick, talk to the men. Make them hope. I don't want to see them hung one by one by Mara's warriors, while I'm working for a way to send them home."

Patrick grumbled something unintelligible that had the ring of swear words. Dawn light filtered through the shack's single window, and the tramp of feet from the barracks signaled a changing patrol. "I got to get up, old son," Patrick said morosely. "If I'm not on time for grub, it's a long day's work with an empty belly."

On impulse, Kevin touched his companion's hand. "Trust me, old friend. For just a little bit longer. When I lose hope, I'll tell you, and I promise you this: I'm not going to die as a slave. If I give the word, I'll lead the break for the mountains and the outlaw's life."

Patrick eyed him closely in the lightening gloom. "You mean that," he admitted, surprise showing through. "But it's going to be hard, convincing the boys. They're angry about Douglas and Jake."

"Then don't let them join Douglas and Jake," Kevin said forcefully, and he rose and stepped through the door.

Well aware that Jican would be pleased to set him to work, Kevin crossed the estate grounds between the slave quarters and the main house by a roundabout route through the gardens. Dew drenched his bare feet and dampened the bottoms of his breeches. Occasionally he passed one of Keyoke's sentries. They did not trouble him; since the campaign in Dustari, and especially since the night of the assassins, word of his martial prowess had circulated in the barracks. Mara's warriors might not acknowledge him openly, but they did in their way grant him a wordless respect. They no longer questioned his loyalty.

If the guards by the door to Mara's chambers had overheard the argument in the night, they gave no sign as Kevin stepped through the akasi hedge and sauntered down the path. As if he were a ghost, they ignored him when he cracked the screen and let himself back in.

Light fell like pearl over a disarranged mass of cushions. Mara lay sprawled in their midst, her arms hugging a snarl of twisted sheets, and her hair in tangles from tossing. She might not have been gnawed on by insects, but she appeared to have had as unpleasant a night as he had. Even while she dreamed, her forehead was troubled by a frown. Her profile, her small clenched fingers, and the curve of one visible breast melted the last of Kevin's annoyance. He could not stay mad at her. Perhaps that was the worst of his faults.

He slipped out of his damp breeches. Aware that his skin was cold, and angrily red from his scratching, he reclined on the edge of the cushions and tucked a fold of blanket around his chilly feet. Then, waiting for circulation to restore him to warmth, he looked at the Lady he loved.

Her nearness took the sting out of slavery, almost made him forget who he was, the rank he had been born to, all that he had lost, and all of the problems of his countrymen. Too well he understood their peril if the thin hope he had dangled before Patrick proved to be only a hangman's noose. Then Mara flinched and cried softly in her dream, and concern for her overrode all else.

Kevin reached out with warm hands. He straightened the sheets entangled between her knees and freed one of her wrists from an imprisoning loop of black hair. Then he gathered her to him and tenderly kissed her awake.

She must have worn herself out with crying, for she roused slowly and her eyes were puffy and red. He had caught her off guard, and she relaxed enjoyably against him. Then memory returned and she stiffened with the beginnings of outrage.

"I ordered you to leave!" she said angrily.

Kevin tipped his head sideways toward the screen. "Until morning," he answered equably. "Morning's here. I came back."

She opened her mouth to say more. Gently but fast, he set his finger over her lips. "I still love you."

She moved in protest against him, stronger than she appeared; he had to be firm to keep hold of her. Aware if he kissed her she might explode, he settled for laying his lips against her ear. The hair at her temples was damp, perhaps from tears. Softly he said, "I heard from Patrick about the imperial decree concerning slavery." That she had not told him herself stung yet, but he laid it aside. "If I leave you, it won't be now."

"You're not angry with me?" she asked, and at long last the uncertainty showed through.

"I was." Kevin kissed her, felt her starting to warm

against him. "If you had spoken to me, I might not have acted like such an oaf."

"Oaf?" The word became tremulous as Kevin's hands made headway under the sheets.

"Karagabuge," Kevin translated, choosing the term for a mythical misformed race of giants that inhabited mountain caves in Tsurani children's tales, creatures who were comically maladroit and constantly creating their own downfall.

"You're that anyway, you're so tall," Mara teased. Relief had left her giddy, and the fact he had forgiven her flung her headlong into passion.

"Well then, if that's the case, a karagabuge doesn't ask permission to rape and pillage." He caught her closer, rolled her across his chest, and sighed into the spill of her hair that streamed across his face. Within a few minutes, both of them had forgotten which was the slave and which the master; for they were both inseparably one.

22. *TUMULT*

Months passed.

The rainy season returned. The fields turned green with new growth, and the trumpeting call of needra bulls heralded yet another breeding season. The day began like many another, with Mara and Jican in conference over slates of chalked figures, trying to determine the most profitable crops to plant for the fall markets. Then at midmorning they were interrupted by word that a bonded runner from the Commercial Guild of Messengers raced toward the Acoma estate house.

"Running?" Mara inquired. She continued to check her strings of notations on hwaet yields in a new property recently purchased in Ambolina.

"Yes, mistress. Running," said the guard. The affirmation did not surprise her; the warrior who brought her word was breathless still from hurrying himself to carry the news.

Mara gestured for Jican to conclude the year's assessment without her. Then, stiff in the knees from sitting, she arose and picked a path through precarious piles of slates to reach the screen that led to the corridor.

She arrived at the front door in time to see the stocky messenger round the last curve from the outer pasture road. He was not walking briskly, or trotting, but running as fast as possible on an errand of obvious urgency.

"I wonder what it can be?" she asked herself aloud.

Recently arrived at her shoulder, Saric typically answered with a question. "Trouble, mistress, or why else should a man be hurrying in mud?"

The Lady of the Acoma cast a wry smile at her adviser, who seemed not to miss his former place in the barracks as a warrior. His dry, sarcastic wit differed from his cousin Lujan's flirtatious humor. Saric's insistent tendency to know the why of things might have slowed his advancement as a soldier; yet that quality made him a natural talent in his new post. Blind obedience was not a virtue in an adviser.

Already he had proven his worth. For over six months the Empire had been quiet under the iron grip of Axantucar. Since Mara's visit to the Holy City to see the Keeper of the Seal, Imperial Whites had intervened three times in what should otherwise have been a dispute between neighboring nobles. Axantucar's justification was that the Empire needed stability, but Saric had sourly noted that somehow the new Warlord always managed to tip the scales in favor of those who had supported his rise to power. Repayment of political debts was common currency in the Game of the Council, but involving Imperial Whites in what amounted to border quibbles was excessive and showed an enthusiasm for bloodshed that rivaled the Minwanabi's.

The Acoma benefited by default, since Tasaio had been forced to assume a posture of quiet patience. As the Warlord's most powerful rival, the Minwanabi Lord needed no adviser to predict how Axantucar might react should his family find itself overextended. The man who wore the white and gold ruled as ruthlessly as his predecessor, but even more unpredictably. Even on his near-impregnable estate, Tasaio dared take nothing for granted.

The guild runner reached the steps, rousing Mara from reverie. Glistening with sweat, and clad only in a loincloth and an armband bearing his guild's insignia, he bowed. "Lady of the Acoma?"

Mara said, "I am she. Who sends a message?"

"No one, Lady." The runner straightened from his obeisance and flipped back sweat-damp hair. "For the good of the Empire, my guild sends word to all Ruling Lords and Ladies."

For the good of the Empire . . . With that phrase the runner indicated his guild had thought this matter of grave enough importance that they acted without recompense. Concerned now, Mara asked, "What has occurred?"

The messenger seemed not to mind that her request came

without any offer of refreshment. "Lady, the Empire stands imperiled. The gods have turned their anger upon us. The renegade magician, the former Great One, Milamber, has returned."

Mara sensed a stir of movement behind her and knew that Kevin had joined her. In a note of rising excitement, the Midkemian said, "Then the rift is opened once more!"

"As your slave observes, my Lady," the runner answered, looking only at Mara. "More. The Warlord sought to capture this magician, using allies in the Assembly. There is no clear account of what occurred, save that a battle was fought in the palace between the Imperial Whites and an army led by Kamatsu of the Shinzawai."

The air seemed suddenly to lose brightness. Mara clutched her robe around her shoulders, unaware that her knuckles had gone white. With a calm she did not feel, for there could be no doubt that Hokanu would have marched beside his father, she prompted, "A battle in the palace?"

"Yes, mistress." Unaware of her personal discomfort, the messenger seemed to relish his dark news. "To this end: the Warlord was pronounced traitor and has been put to dishonorable death."

Mara's eyes widened. Dishonorable death could only mean hanging. Only two powers in the Empire could order such an execution, and Axantucar had allies among the magicians. "The Emperor . . . ?"

Barely able to restrain his excitement, the messenger confirmed. "Yes, Lady, the Light of Heaven condemned the Warlord and now himself suspends the right of any Lord to sit upon the white and gold throne."

In the shocked interval that followed, Mara did little but try to order her reeling thoughts. The Emperor condemning the Warlord! The event stunned, breaking as it did all former tradition and precedence. Even in times of gravest threat, no Light of Heaven had dared to act as did Ichindar.

The messenger summed up. "Mistress, the High Council is dissolved and will not assemble without the Emperor's command!"

Mara struggled to show no surprise. "Is there more?"

The messenger crossed his arms and bowed. "Nothing in common knowledge. But no doubt official word should follow."

"Then visit the kitchen and eat," Mara invited. "I have been remiss in my courtesy, and would invite you to replenish your strength before you make your next call."

"My Lady is generous, but I must depart. By your leave?"

Mara waved the young man on his way. As he hurried down the road at a run, she bent a keen look at Saric. "Get Arakasi back here as soon as possible."

Her urgency needed no explanation. For if the runner's news was accurate, this was far and away the most momentous event ever to occur in her lifetime. Now the rules of the Great Game were forever altered, and until such day as the Light of Heaven changed his mind, he was the absolute power in the Empire. Unless, Mara thought, with a twist of irony like Kevin's own, someone decided otherwise by killing him.

It took nearly two weeks to recall Arakasi, given the circuitous methods he insisted upon. Throughout the delay, Mara fretted, while rumors ran rampant through the Empire. Contrary to expectation, there came no official tidings of the upheavals surrounding Axantucar's execution. Yet the days dawned damp and humid, and the afternoons brought fine drizzle and showers, as they did each year at this season. Plots and speculation abounded, but the Emperor indisputably remained alive and in power in Kentosani. Word held that eight of his slaves had died of various exotic poisons left in dishes of food, and that three cooks and two imperial chambermaids had been hung for connected acts of treason. Commerce went on, but uneasily, as if in the calm before a storm.

The oppressive weather made even fidgeting uncomfortable. Mara spent restless hours at her writing desk, penning notes to her various allies. Only missives sent to Jiro of the Anasati remained unanswered, which came as no surprise. Mara sighed and reached for another parchment, then checked the next name on her chalk slate. She dipped her nib, and the soft scratch of her pen wore away yet another afternoon.

Kevin tended to wilt in the heavy, moist air of the wet season. Less volatile than Mara when it came to intangible matters, he lay dozing upon a mat in the corner of her study, lulled by the soft tap of rain from the eaves, or by the scrape of Mara's pen. Into the grey-green gloom that lingered from yet another shower came a shadow.

Mara started upright, her breath stopped in her throat. Her movement roused Kevin, who scrambled up on a fighter's reflex, his big hands grasping for a sword that was not there.

Then the Midkemian relaxed with a self-deprecating chuckle. "Gods, man, you gave me a fright."

Arakasi stepped in from the rain, a heavy black robe slapping around his calves. His sandals were sodden, and slicked with bits of grass, which meant he had come in by way of the needra pastures.

Mara subsided in relief. "You took long enough to get here."

The Spy Master bowed, a silvery fringe of droplets falling off his hood and running down his aquiline nose. "Mistress, I was very far afield when your recall reached me."

Mara clapped for her maid. "Towels," she demanded. "And a dry robe, at once." She motioned for her Spy Master to sit and help himself to a cup of chocha from the tray at her side.

Arakasi poured himself a steaming drink, then bent a keen gaze on his mistress. "Lady, I ask that you not tell anyone I am back. I slipped past your guards and took pains not to be seen."

Which explained the pasture grass caught in his sandals, but not the reason behind it. When Arakasi did not elaborate on his own initiative, Mara was forced to make inquiry.

Her Spy Master twisted the fine porcelain cup in his hands in uncharacteristic agitation. He frowned, thought, and ignored the towels and dry clothing left for him by the maid. Still in his black, and still dripping, he said, "My informants . . . Something may be amiss. The possibility exists that we've been compromised."

Mara raised her eyebrows and, with unerring intuition, tracked his thought to a long-past event. "The ambush set for Keyoke?"

Arakasi nodded. "I think the late Lord Desio let our man escape at the time, to lull me into believing our other agents in the Minwanabi household were undetected. If so, then the promotion of one of my men to Tasaio's personal service . . ."

"Is suspect?" Mara finished as his words trailed off. She waved her hand in dismissal. "Deal with that problem as you wish. If you think a Minwanabi spy may have insinuated himself upon my lands, dig him out. At this moment, I wish to know what actually happened in Kentosani."

Arakasi sipped at his chocha. For an interval he seemed reluctant to leave the subject of a possible breach in his network, but as Kevin had settled back in his corner, and as Mara seemed rarely out of patience, the Spy Master turned to the requested subject. "Much occurred, but little was public." Arakasi put down his cup so softly the china made no sound. "I lost an agent in the fighting."

Mara did not know the man who had died, and never would, but he was an Acoma servant. She bowed her head in respect, as she might at the word that one of her warriors had lost his life in her service.

Arakasi shrugged with none of his usual lightness. "The man was simply at the wrong place when the fighting started. He was killed by a stray arrow, but the loss was regrettable. Candidates for posts in the Imperial Palace are carefully screened, and he will be very difficult to replace."

The Spy Master was taking the loss personally, Mara realized, and despite her wish that he would address the matter directly, his lapse was unusual enough that she waited for him to resume of his own accord.

Arakasi tucked folded hands under the cuffs of his robe and seemed to come back to himself. Briskly he said, "In any event, the magician Milamber, though banished from the ranks of the Great Ones, has returned by way of a rift."

"Where is this rift?" Kevin interjected, suddenly not half so sleepy as he appeared.

Mara frowned at him, but it was Arakasi's look of withering scorn that caused the Midkemian to fall silent. "I do not know yet," the Spy Master conceded pointedly to his mistress. "Milamber was taken captive in the city of Ontoset, by two magicians who served Axantucar. He, two companions from his homeworld, and another Great One were taken under guard to the Imperial Palace."

Mara interrupted. "The Warlord took a Great One prisoner?"

"It could be argued that the two Great Ones restrained one of their fellows," Arakasi corrected dryly. "About the Warlord little is known, though speculation abounds. At a guess, Axantucar was not content to wear the white and gold. He may have been harboring greater ambitions."

"Murder the Emperor?" Mara cut in. "There were rumors that someone tried poison."

"Half of such hearsay is true." Arakasi tapped his fingers, and water puddled from his sleeves onto the polished wood floor. "Ichindar gave that reason for the execution. And since one of Axantucar's pet Great Ones turned in his loyalties and brought testimony, who can doubt the truth of the issue?"

Mara's eyes opened at that. "A Great One denounced him?"

"More." Warming to his subject at last, Arakasi qualified. "Two Great Ones, brothers, lent their aid to this Warlord, as they had to his uncle." Mara nodded. She remembered the pair well, as they had been instrumental in proving her innocence in the tangle of conflicting accusations that had culminated in the ruin of Jingu of the Minwanabi.

Arakasi continued. "Brother turned against brother, with one Great One now dead, and the other publicly denouncing all who conspired against Ichindar. At the moment no one moves in the Great Game, for fear of retribution. But for our own part, I judge this a time for caution. If Tasaio believes himself to be the most powerful among the Lords of the Empire, he may choose to strike."

Mara held up her hand for silence while she thought. After a moment filled with the sound of rain dripping from the eaves, she said, "No. Not now. Tasaio is too clever to attempt to steal a march when so many swords are unsheathed. Who commands the garrison at the Imperial Palace?"

"Kamatsu of the Shinzawai," Arakasi replied. "He acts as the Emperor's Force Commander, though he wears the armor of a Kanazawai Warchief, not the Imperial White."

Mara's brow furrowed as she weighed political ramifications. "So, for the moment we may surmise that the Alliance for War is done, with the War Party shattered as well, since only the Minwanabi dominate that faction." She tapped her chin with a finger, then said, "We can assume Jiro of the Anasati will distance himself from both the Omechan and Tasaio, and that the Anasati and other families of Clan Ionani will turn firmly back into the fold of the Imperial Party. No, the Blue Wheel may not be the most powerful faction, but they sit at the Emperor's right hand, and at this juncture that counts for a great deal."

Arakasi added, "As for the council, two attempts by Minwanabi to call a formal session have been openly rebuked by Ichindar. The Light of Heaven reiterates his command that the High Council is dissolved until he decides to recall it."

Mara was silent a long time. "I know there is more to this than treason," she concluded at length. "Something else is at play. We have had attempts upon Warlord and Emperor before, but neither ever resulted in suspension of the High Council."

"Maybe this Emperor has more brains or more ambition than his predecessors," Kevin offered from his corner. "I'd stake my guess that he desires absolute rule."

Mara shook her head. "To take over by these methods would court revolution. If Ichindar truly desired power, to turn the council to his bidding, he would make them his dogs. The imperial court can do many things, but it cannot govern the Empire. Our system is not like yours, Kevin, with both ruling lords and their servants all subject to a king." She made a frustrated gesture that showed such concepts were alien to her still.

"The Great Freedom," Kevin recited. "The law that clearly shows the relationship of each man to his master and his servant, so that no one can suffer unjust treatment."

"A polite fiction, I am certain," Mara interjected. "In any event, that's not what I was speaking of; we do not have the system that allows for replacing a corrupt Lord with a noble one. If a Lord falls, his estate falls with him, and if enough of our number fall, the Empire itself must fail."

Kevin shoved back sleep-tousled hair. "You're saying the Empire doesn't have the infrastructure to withstand so widespread a change. Tsurani nobles are too spoiled and self-indulgent to administer their own lands unless they're also allowed to be absolute dictators. They won't do it just because the Emperor tells them."

Mara found Kevin's comments rankling. "No. What I'm saying is that if the Light of Heaven thinks, by whim, to turn a body of rulers into no more than clerks, he'll learn that ordering a thing is not the same as doing it, or seeing that others get it done."

Kevin set his back against the wall and nonchalantly inspected his fingernails, which had dirt beneath the rims. "I can't argue that with you."

Uncertain why he should choose this moment to be difficult, Mara directed her attention to Arakasi. "I think we need to go to Kentosani."

Suddenly still, a shape cut from shadow in his dark cloak, the Spy Master said, "Mistress, that may be dangerous."

"When hasn't it been?" Kevin questioned with a bite of sarcasm.

Mara waved a hand to silence him without even looking in his direction. "I must chance that the Emperor would have no argument with a meeting of Clan Hadama in the council chambers. And if some members of the Jade Eye Party are also in the city at the same time, and we choose to dine. . . ."

But the social byplays of politics held no interest for Arakasi this day. "These are matters to discuss with your hadonra and First Adviser, mistress," he interjected with the slightest trace of sharpness. "I must return to my agents and ensure that you are safe."

Caught up in her own thoughts, Mara missed his abnormal abruptness. "Do so," she said in vague reference to words she had interpreted only by surface meaning. "But I will expect you at my quarters in the Holy City in one month's time."

"Your will, mistress." Arakasi bowed with no trace of hesitation. As unobtrusively as he had entered, he slipped through the screen and vanished into the silvery afternoon drizzle. Still deep in thought, Mara allowed him time enough to leave unseen. Then she clapped for her runner and sent for her advisers.

The rain held almost everyone indoors, and within a few moments Nacoya, Keyoke, and Saric entered. Lujan arrived last, smelling of the oils used to preserve laminated armor. He had been in the barracks instructing young recruits, and his sandals added to the puddles left by Arakasi's black cloak.

Without preamble, Mara said, "Nacoya, send messages to all the Ruling Lords of the Jade Eye Party, informing them that one month from this day we shall be in residence at our town house in the Holy City. The Acoma would be pleased to host each at a lunch or dinner . . . according to rank, of course." Almost without hesitation she added, "Send word to all members of Clan Hadama that a meeting will be held in the High Council hall in six weeks' time."

Nacoya paused in the act of straightening a drooping hairpin. "Mistress, many of the Hadama Clan were allied with Axantucar. They will have little inclination to return so soon to Kentosani, despite your request."

Mara turned a hard glance toward her First Adviser. "Then make it clear: this is not a request. It is a demand."

On the point of argument, Nacoya gauged the look in her mistress's eyes. She reconsidered, nodded once, and with poor grace said, "Your will, mistress."

From his corner upon the sleeping mat in Mara's study, Kevin regarded the evening's exchange with a growing sense of disquiet. Something in Mara had changed, he intuited, though he could not put his finger on precisely what. Certain only that a distance had grown up between them, despite his best efforts at patience, he regarded the cold, remote look on the face of his Lady and decided. Whatever the resolve behind her thoughts, this time he was unsure that he wanted any part of knowing it. The game was no game, not in any sense he could understand. And by now familiar enough with the politics of Tsuranuanni, he could sense when events led to danger. Changes, he had learned, did not occur in this land except through bloodshed, and the fall of yet another Warlord promised the direst of trouble.

The rain beat on the rooftree, and darkness fell, and though the air remained every bit as humid and close as before, Kevin found he had lost all inclination to sleep.

The storm passed, and while clouds on the horizon proclaimed the approach of showers later, the day blazed brilliantly. Mara stood in the hot sun, her bearing erect and her expression unreadable. Lined up before her on the expanse of the practice field stood her entire garrison, every fighting man wearing Acoma colors. The only absent warriors were those assigned to far holdings in distant cities and the current patrol on duty along the perimeter of the estate itself.

At her right stood Nacoya, looking tiny under the weight of a formal robe. Her diminutive height was emphasized by the wand tipped with a fan of shatra tail feathers, official token of her office as First Adviser. Behind her and to the left stood Keyoke, Saric, and Lujan, also wearing formal garb. The lacquered dress armor, the jewels, and the shell inlay on the officer's staves glittered blindingly in the morning light.

Squinting against the sunlight scintillating on polished armor, Kevin regarded the scene from inside the house, his vantage point a window seat in the large hall where Mara held court. Ayaki stood with his elbows propped on the cushion by the Midkemian's knees. Behind the young master, with a pot of wax and a polishing cloth dangling forgotten from his hands, stood the elderly house slave, Mintai, who was assigned this chamber's upkeep. The old man enjoyed the free moment that such ceremony brought, this being one of the rare times he could lapse into idleness without fear of reprimand.

Mara had started off giving awards and promotions, then had gone on to accept the oath of loyalty of an even dozen young warriors called to Acoma service. Once the new recruits completed their final bows and stepped back to take places in the ranks, she addressed her army as a whole.

"Now have the Acoma grown in strength to match their honor. Kenji, Sujanra!" As the officers who were named stepped forward, Mara accepted two tall, green-dyed plumes from Keyoke. "These men are elevated to the rank of Force Leader!" she announced to her companies, and as the two men bowed before her, she affixed the badges of their new rank to their helms.

Kevin dug Ayaki in the ribs. "What's a Force Leader? I thought I knew all your ranks."

"Tasaio of the Minwanabi has four of them," the boy said unhelpfully.

The Midkemian's blue eyes fixed in turn upon the house slave, and, flattered to be consulted as an authority, Mintai flourished his polishing rag toward the expanse of Mara's army. "It is an assignment made sometimes when a force is too large for one commander. These will now be subofficers to Force Commander Lujan, and each will command a company." A puzzled look crossed his face. "This must mean she's dividing the army."

Kevin waited for Mintai to qualify, then belatedly realized when no explanation followed that the old man must be a bit simple. "What's that mean?" he prompted.

He received a Tsurani shrug. "Perhaps the mistress wishes to call more soldiers to her service."

"So we can beat Tasaio," Ayaki broke in. He made a noise in his throat that was his idea of the sound a man might make while dying, then grinned brightly.

Kevin poked the boy in the ribs again, and the sound effects dissolved into laughter. "How many men exactly are in a company?" he demanded of Mintai.

The old slave repeated his shrug. "Many. It is all to a Lord's liking. There is no fixed rule of quantity."

But Kevin's curiosity was only whetted by vagueness. "Then how many man answer to the Patrol Leader?"

"A patrol, obviously, barbarian." Mintai showed signs of wanting to return to his polishing. The outworlder might be his Lady's lover, but he was due no respect for asking silly questions.

Predictably, the barbarian missed the cues that his interest had become a bother. "Let me ask in a different way. How many men are usually in a patrol?"

Mintai pursed his lips and refused answer, but now Ayaki was eager to show off. "Usually a dozen, sometimes twenty, never less than eight."

That a child could keep such a nonsensical system straight was just another anomaly on this crazy world. Kevin scratched his head and tried to make order out of chaos. "About ten, say. Now, how many Patrol Leaders does a Strike Leader command?"

"Sometimes five, other times as many as ten to each company," Ayaki declared.

"You don't need to shout like you're on a battle field." Kevin reprimanded, and tried, despite several retaliatory pokes in his own ribs, to figure in his head. "So each Strike Leader can command as few as forty men and as many as two hundred." He blinked as he looked back into the hot sun, where the newly promoted officers arose and reassumed their places. "Then how many Strike Leaders do you need before you split your forces like this?"

Ayaki was laughing too hard to answer; Mintai tired of the window and scooped a dollop of wax onto his polishing cloth. As if the floorboards might vanish from under his feet for lack of attention, he knelt and began vigorously to rub. "I don't know. How many men does our Lady command now? I think from the extra help in the kitchen this last two years it must be close to two thousand—we have twenty or twenty-two Strike Leaders, or so I heard Kenji boasting. Now let me do my work, before my back gets whipped."

The threat was pretense; Mintai was a household fixture, and too well liked by the overseer to receive much more than a scolding. Kevin fended off Ayaki's boisterous play and calculated. Most of the garrison rotated, spending part of the month in barracks near the house, so they could be with wives and children. The rest were housed in small huts near various points along the perimeter of the estate, or were out protecting caravans or river barges bearing Acoma goods to distant markets. It would be hard to judge, precisely, but the slave's estimate could be accurate. Mara might well command as many as two thousand warriors. Kevin whistled low in appreciation. From gossip he knew how small a garrison she had inherited when she first assumed her ruler's mantle, something like thirty-five men. Now her forces were growing to rival those of the very strongest of families in the Empire.

A pity, he thought, that the location of her estate was so poorly suited for defense.

But the disquieting thought followed naturally, that perhaps the Lady did not amass her military might for protection only.

A cloud crossed the sun, harbinger of the first afternoon shower. The ceremony on the practice field was ending, square after square of green-armored warriors facing about and marching at Lujan's command. Mara and her advisers made their way toward the estate house. Suddenly anxious to meet her, Kevin suggested that Ayaki go to the kitchen and bother the cooks, who were making fresh thyza bread, by the smell riding the breeze. The perpetually hungry boy needed little persuasion, and by taking shortcuts through the courtyards, Kevin managed to be waiting for the Lady as she entered her private quarters. He preempted one of the maids and helped her out of her heavy robe. She allowed him, still and silent, and less responsive than usual to his touch.

Keeping his tone light, Kevin said, "Do we marshal for war, my Lady?"

Mara smiled without humor. "Perhaps. If my clansmen show sense, we do not, but if they prove recalcitrant, I need this show of force. It will not take long for word to travel the river that the Acoma garrison has grown to the point of needing two Force Leaders." She shed a heavy collection of jade bangles and dropped them into an open coffer. Her set of matching hairpins followed with a chiming cascade of sound as each was tossed in with the rest. "No one need know our companies are fewer than before."

The empty robe was surrendered to the maids to freshen and hang; Kevin regarded his Lady's naked back and sighed as she covered herself with a light, indoor lounging robe. "The game continues?"

"Always." Mara knotted her sash, ending any hopes of an interlude on her sleeping mat. Unaware that her lover entertained the idea of intimacy, she added, "The Emperor may have suspended the council, but the game always goes on."

Except that it was no game at all, Kevin concluded inwardly. Not when armies entered the picture. Despite his recent decision not to become entangled in politics, he could not help but wonder what course his Lady considered this time.

Shadows painted the Imperial Palace in shades of rose, orange, and deep charcoal blue as the first sun of morning breasted the horizon. The city along the riverfront and in the poorer sections was already awake and busy, but the halls of the powerful rang only with the footfalls of servants and one patrol of warriors armored in Acoma green.

On this, the day Mara had appointed for the meeting of Clan Hadama, she wished to be first into the Council Hall. The proceedings she had in mind must not go amiss, or her demands upon the clan would do nothing but gain her more enemies.

Lujan and a hand-picked escort of twenty men escorted Mara to the inner circle of the council, but at the point where they would normally be asked to stand and wait, the Lady of the Acoma continued to walk. After a brief hesitation, Lujan signaled to his warriors to maintain ranks. They followed their mistress down to the lower level of the chamber, and if they were startled that the Lady passed by her usual chair, they showed no sign.

In his pose as her body slave, Kevin raised one eyebrow, then chuckled to himself as he guessed his Lady's intention. Mara crossed the open floor on the lowest level, then mounted the raised dais reserved for the Warlord during council sessions, or for the Clan Warchief during gatherings.

By now the upper dome was golden with new sunlight. Mara sat upon the elaborate ivory-inlaid throne and composed herself. Kevin stood close behind, ready to answer her needs, and as if her action had required neither courage nor audacity, her warriors arrayed themselves in a semicircle behind her position.

Kevin regarded the ranks of vacant seats from his place on the central dais. As the hall was empty but for Acoma soldiers, he spoke freely. "Some folks are going to have their bowels in an uproar before this day is done, Lady."

But Mara had already assumed the air of superiority that accompanied the throne where she sat; she said nothing. She waited in her formal pose for close to three hours, until the arrival of the least-ranked members of Clan Hadama.

The Lord of the Jinguai was first to step into the Council Hall, his guard in yellow and red armor trimmed in black at his back. By then the sun had risen high enough that slanting shafts lapped over the central dais. Anyone who entered could not miss the Lady on the throne, in her sparkling jewels and flowing ceremonial robes. The old man gave one surprised glance and precipitately halted. He hesitated, then smiled in genuine amusement and proceeded to his place near the back of the hall.

Kevin whispered, "Well, there's one who's ready to watch the show."

Mara moved her decorative fan in a manner that meant he should keep his thoughts to himself. Her face remained impassive as alabaster beneath layers of thyza-powder makeup; all her nerves and excitement were invisibly pent inside.

Within the hour, another five Lords arrived. Most simply moved to their allotted place after one look in Mara's direction. Two others conferred briefly, exchanged subdued gestures, then went on to their chairs. Noon brought in a delegation of a half-dozen Lords, with them one who numbered among the most powerful of families in Clan Hadama.

Upon crossing the upper threshold, this Lord signaled to the rest, and as one body, the group came to the center of the hall. By now the sun shone down upon the gold and ivory throne, lighting Mara like the statue of a goddess in a temple niche. Before the Warchief's chair, the Lords paused. Rather than take seats, they clustered together, muttering among themselves.

At length one who wore deep blue moved to address the motionless woman on the throne. "My Lady of the Acoma—"

Mara interrupted him. "You have something to say to me, my Lord of the Poltapara?"

The man seemed about to bridle; like a bird in full plumage in his finery, he puffed out his chest, then measured the Lady on the dais. Her gaze did not waver, and the soldiers at her back stayed statue-still. Yet in the culture of Tsuranuanni, such brazen lack of reaction became an emphatic statement. The Lord cleared his throat. "Are you well, Lady?"

Mara smiled at his polite capitulation. "I am, indeed, my Lord. Are you well?"

The man in blue acquiesced, then nonchalantly returned to conversation with his fellows. Kevin spoke sotto voce, "One down."

"No," Mara corrected, hiding relief behind a flutter of her fan. "Six down. The Lord who greeted me ranks above the others, two of whom are his vassals. The other three are sworn allies, and since they are still speaking to one another, all will defer to his choice."

The victory was telling, for as more Lords entered, they saw that one of the more powerful families had accepted Mara's position ahead of them. Plainly unwilling to challenge her popularity, they gave her greeting and assumed their places with varying degrees of enthusiasm.

Then the formerly acknowledged Warchief, Lord Benshai of the Chekowara, swept into the hall, his colorful robes billowing like sails around his voluminous body. Deep in conversation with one of his advisers, and entrenched in his own self-importance, he was halfway down the stair to the lower floor before he noticed the figure who occupied his accustomed throne.

He stopped dead for the briefest moment, his eyes widening in his dark face. Then he gestured to his garrulous adviser to be silent and moved his bulk the remaining ten steps at surprising speed to confront the Lady of the Acoma.

Kevin restrained his comment, for Mara's tactic was now plain. Despite the fact that early arrivals were for lesser-ranked rulers, anyone on the floor below who stood looking up at the person in the seat of primacy was set at a disadvantage.

"Lady Mara—" began the Lord of the Chekowara.

Mara cut him off. "I am well, my Lord. Are you well?"

Several lesser nobles in the clan smothered smiles. Mara's answer to a question not asked lent the impression the Warchief of the clan had conceded her position as superior to his own.

The Lord Benshai spluttered and strove to recover. "That's not what—"

Mara interrupted again. "That's not what, my Lord? Forgive me, I assumed you were being mannerly."

But a man accustomed to power could not long be put off by adept verbiage. In a tone of ringing authority, Lord Benshai called, "Lady, you sit upon my dais."

The Lady of the Acoma returned her most penetrating gaze. In a voice of equal command, that none in the chamber could miss hearing, she pronounced, "I think not, my Lord!"

Lord Benshai of the Chekowara drew himself up to his full height. Ivory ornaments rattled at his wrists and neck as he bristled. "How dare you!"

"Silence!" Mara demanded, and the rest in the room obeyed.

Their compliance was not lost on Lord Benshai. He twisted his short neck and glared at the Lords who had failed in their support of him. Pride alone kept his posture from wilting. Not just to the Lord of the Chekowara, but to all in the gathering, Mara announced, "The time has come for plain speaking, klnsmen.

Now profound stillness fell over the vast hall. Terms relating to blood ties were rarely used in public, for Tsurani set great store upon relationships. Any claim of kinship, however vague, was considered both important and personal. Although all in the clan shared blood ties in the far distant past, the relationships had grown tenuous with time and were never stressed lest implications of debt or honor be implied.

As if the Lord of the Chekowara did not stand nonplussed

at the foot of the dais, Mara continued to address the Lords in the galleries. "By fate's ruling, you are members of a clan long considered steeped in honor"—as many in the hall murmured agreement, Mara's tone punched through—"but lacking power." Voices fell silent. "My father was considered among those most noble Lords in the Empire." Again several rulers in the hall concurred. "Yet when his daughter faced powerful enemies alone, not one kinsman sought to lend even token support."

No one spoke as Mara surveyed the galleries.

"I understand as well as any of you why this is so," she said. "Yet I also feel that political reasons are insufficient justification. After all," she qualified in bitter inflections, "conscience does not trouble us. Such is the Tsurani way, we tell ourselves. If a young girl is killed and a honorable family's natami is turned downward in the dirt, who can argue it is not the will of the gods?"

Mara searched each face in the room, looking for adverse reaction. In the instant before the boldest rulers could raise their voice in protest, she cried, "I say it is not the gods' will!" Her words rang across the galleries, and the near to unseemly emotion that colored them held every Lord in his chair.

"I, Mara of the Acoma. I who forced the Lord of the Anasati to give quarter, and I who destroyed Jingu of the Minwanabi under his ancestral roof! I who have molded the Acoma into the mightiest house in Clan Hadama! I say that we make our own destiny and seek out our own place upon the Wheel! Who here says not?"

A stir greeted this concept, and several Lords moved, as if made uncomfortable by what sounded like blasphemy. One ruler toward the rear called out, "Lady, you voice dangerous thoughts."

"We live in dangerous times," Mara shot back. "It is time for radical thinking."

A general if reluctant agreement followed. Low-pitched grumbles deepened to a buzz of animated discussion, cut short by the Lord of the Chekowara, who barely contained his rage at being forgotten where he stood. He shouted across the general noise, "What do you propose, beyond usurping my office, Lady Mara?"

Jewels blazing in the sunlight that fell from the dome,

Mara removed a document scroll from the depths of her sleeve. Now Kevin had to fight against his desire to express admiration at her timing. "Show them the carrot," he whispered to himself.

In the brightness of the light, the yellow-and-white ribbons that denoted a writ from the Keeper of the Imperial Seal could not be mistaken. Aware she had drawn every eye in the chamber, Mara regarded the gathering with imperious composure. "I have here, under official seal, an exclusive trading option granted to the Acoma."

"Trading option?" "With whom?" and "For what?" came various queries form the galleries.

Only Lord Benshai seemed unimpressed. He stood like a mountain and glowered. "Did you hold a writ from the hand of the Light of Heaven himself, I would not bow to you, Lady."

Lujan slapped a hand loudly on the grip of his sword, clear warning that no insult to his Lady would be tolerated. The Chekowara warriors bristled likewise, and aware of how real was the threat of bloodshed, Kevin sweated beneath his robes and longed for a knife to his hand.

Yet as though the tautness of her warriors were nothing more than posturing, Mara read the document aloud to the gathering. The chamber grew still as a tomb. "I hold the key to wealth, my Lords," she concluded. "I have exclusive rights to these goods, both import to and export from the world of Midkemia."

A hush descended. Into a profound stillness Mara said, "You realize how the wholesale importation of any of these listed items, in particular those of metal, would affect your wealth?"

The silence in the Council Hall took on a strained quality. A few Lords conferred in whispers with advisers, while the ones in the highest-ranking seats slowly turned pale. The Lord of the Chekowara sent swift signal to his warriors to relax their battle-ready posture; better than any, he realized that Mara had him beaten. Had she tried force, or called upon political allies, her position might yet be in question. But as she had strength enough to equal if not best him, and, now, the certain power to undermine the finances of every family in the clan, not a Lord present would dare to support their former Warchief. A look of baffled fury on his dark face,

Lord Benshai sought furiously for means to back down without disgrace.

Around him, his fellow rulers of the Hadama clan seemed too self-absorbed by their own predicament to relish his defeat. One in the front balcony called out, "Lady, are you offering participation?"

Mara answered guardedly. "Perhaps. I may be willing to establish trading consortiums and allow others to participate —those of you who prove yourselves my kinsmen in deed as well as word."

Many looked askance at this suggestion, and by the flurry of movement as the advisers present leaned over to whisper to their lords, the idea was not taken with enthusiasm. The Lord of the Chekowara saw his opening. In a voice well practiced at persuasion, he said, "Mara, your proposition is well and good, but we have seen nothing to suggest trading with the barbarians is feasible, even should you hold exclusive rights from the Emperor. Besides," he added with a wave a father might use to reprimand a wayward girl, "these things change, don't they?"

Mara heard Kevin murmur, "Now show them the stick."

She had to struggle not to laugh. The Lord of the Chekowara exhibited a confidence that in another moment was going to make him seem regrettably pompous. Choosing her tone carefully, Mara said, "My Lord, understand this: when I leave this hall, I shall know those who number among my friends, and those who stand apart." She directed a meaningful glance around the hall and tempered her lines with restrained patience. "I have proven myself a dozen times over since becoming Ruling Lady."

A thoughtful pause made the most of general murmurs of agreement from the galleries. Mara resumed. "Those who doubt me may stand aside and face whatever comes to them, firm in the knowledge they can rely upon their own wit and resources. Those who accept my call for clan unity and cast their lot with mine shall have the Acoma beside them to face whatever dangers may arise. For, my Lords, if anyone believes the Great Game can be ended because the Light of Heaven so commands, let that man remove himself from power and seek out a temple to pray for mercy. For that man is a fool, and only by the gods' indulgence will he and his family survive the days to come.

"I offer a better choice," she cried in the loudest voice she had employed so far. "You may continue as you have done, a small clan, empty of promise, or you may rekindle the fire that our ancestors once used to light their way. Tasaio of the Minwanabi will fall or I will fall. If I fail"—she looked directly at Lord Chekowara—"do you think Tasaio will not plunge our Empire into civil war? What family is strong enough to stop him, with the Omechan in disgrace?" She sat back and quieted her tone, so that all in the galleries had to lean forward to attend her. "But if I succeed, then one of the Five Great Families will vanish. Another family must rise to fill that seat. Most would assume the Anasati would claim the honor, or perhaps the Shinzawai. This is yet to be written. I say the prize might also fall to the Acoma. The clan of the ascendant family will rise in standing, and those who are kinsmen of that Ruling Lord will number among the mighty"—she waved the document—"and the wealthy."

The old Lord of the Jinguai had not moved from his seat throughout the entire proceedings, but now he stood. His back might be stooped with age, but his tones were firm as he called, "Mara! I name Mara of the Acoma my Warchief!"

Another Lord joined his call, followed by a chorus of others from the upper galleries. Suddenly many were shouting, and in consternation, Lord Benshai of the Chekowara realized that the majority of the clan were upon their feet hailing Mara. At last, as the commotion began to subside, the Lady of the Acoma regarded the former Warchief. "Benshai, surrender the staff."

The Lord of the Chekowara looked sour. He hesitated an almost imprudent interval, then held out the short wooden staff with ceremonial carvings that marked the rank of Warchief. As Mara accepted the token of office, he gave a shallow, stiff bow and backed to the first seat next to the dais, the position reserved for the second most powerful Lord in the clan. Others reorganized themselves accordingly down to the chair that had formerly been Mara's, while those of lesser rank remained undisturbed.

With clan order readjusted, Mara waved a hand to indicate the gathering. "All of you shall be counted loyal and faithful friends. From this moment forward, let it be known that the Hadama is again a clan in both name and deed. For, kinsmen, trying times are coming, days to make the Night of the Bloody Swords seem a mild disturbance unless we undertake plans to prevent such a pass.

"I call upon Clan Honor!" With those formal words a shock ran through the room. Lords exclaimed aloud in surprise and consternation, for by her choice of phrasing, Mara proclaimed beyond recall that whatever came next impacted upon not only the honor of the Acoma, but that of the entire clan. No Lord would dare such a move in a capricious or trivial way, for the invocation bound every family within the clan to stand with the Acoma. Should any Warchief embroil clans in conflict, the stability of the Empire could be overturned. The point did not have to be reiterated, that to threaten social continuity would invite intervention by the Great Ones. More than the wrath of the Emperor, or even the vengeance of the gods, the Tsurani feared the Assembly of Magicians, those whose words were as law.

Yet Mara allayed the worst fear, that she might use a Call to Clan Honor for her own ends. "The first duty of Clan Hadama is to serve the Empire!"

In a flurry of relief, all in the room cried out, "Yes! To serve the Empire!"

"I tell you this: all that I undertake from this day forward is not for the glory of the Acoma, but to serve the Empire. You, my brave and loyal kinsmen, have cast your lot with mine. Know by my word that no matter what may come, I act for the good of all."

Like a change in tide, the undercurrent of conversation faltered. Mara placed Clan Hadama under a dreadful burden, for with those ritual words, "good of the Empire," she committed her clan to a course that could end only in victory or in utter destruction.

Yet before the mutters could swell into cohesive protest, Mara swept on. "From this day, all party affiliations outside the clan are ended, save those with the Blue Wheel and Jade Eye." Several Lords nodded in approval, while others, whose political interests lay elsewhere, scowled their displeasure. Yet no one spoke out. "All ties with factions outside the clan must be made known to me," Mara demanded. "I shall not force any of you to act dishonorably or forget vows, but in the days to come, some of us will find that former friends become the most bitter of foes." She took a deep breath, as if waiting for a challenge.

"Look around this room, my Lords. These are your family, upon whom you may depend. The ancient ties of blood have today been renewed. Any man, no matter how highly placed, who raises a hand against even the least of my kinsmen raises his hand against me. Our clan heritage has fallen to disunity for generations. No more. For whosoever strikes at my kinsman strikes at me. My army has been divided, my Lords, and fully one half of my warriors under a newly promoted Force Leader stand ready to answer should you call." She let that sink in, then added, "And when the coming dark days have passed, it is my intention to meet again in this room, and to see no absent faces among us. For as a mother shatra bird brings food to her young and spreads her wings to shelter them, so shall I be to you, one who feeds her family and protects them."

Most of the Lords in the hall stood at this, and the ones least in rank and strength cheered in appreciation of Mara's vow. Even the most powerful who had been displaced were forced to look upon their new Warchief with respect. And if the Lord of the Chekowara's dark face held other than admiration for the woman who had replaced his primacy in the clan, he hid his sour feelings as he stood and applauded her brave words.

Only Kevin observed with a man's perception, and he did not miss the flash of bitterness in Lord Benshai's eyes. Although the Midkemian himself felt warmed that his Lady had dared to turn his influence upon her thinking into public policy, he wondered with concern whether she had yet again won many new allies at the price of creating another mortal foe.

The Keeper of the Imperial Seal paused with a keljir candy halfway raised to his mouth. Caught at a loss, he visibly sagged when he saw who called upon him. He shoved his bulk form his cushions with a suppressed grunt of effort and adjusted his robes around his girth. "My Lady of the Acoma. What a . . . surprise."

Glancing at the apologetic servant who stood behind Mara, the Keeper understood that Mara and her not inconsiderable entourage had simply swept past the usual maze of servants, depriving the Keeper of the news an important visitor was approaching.

The candy was suddenly an embarrassment. The Keeper of the Imperial Seal dropped it hastily back into the bowl, though it was unwrapped already and beginning to melt in the heat. He wiped his sticky palm on his sash, since the robe he was wearing had inconveniently short sleeves. Then he extended his palm to his visitor.

Mara took the proffered hand and let the man lead her to a seat before his writing desk. As the official stowed his bulk on his cushions, he wheezed, "Are you well?"

"I am well, my Lord Keeper," she replied with the faintest hint of deference.

"Word holds that you've risen to primacy in your clan." The Keeper of the Imperial Seal wasted no time retrieving his sweet. "Much honor to you, I think."

Mara inclined her head as if accepting a compliment.

Around a softening mouthful of candy, the official said, "To what do I owe the honor of this visit?"

"I think you know, Webara." By the shift to first-name usage, Mara indicated her demand that she be treated with all honor due her rise in station. She removed a roll of parchment from her sleeve. "I hold a warrant under Imperial Seal for trading concessions and now I require my claim to be made public."

Webara forced a friendly smile and shrugged. "Mara, you may do anything you wish." His reciprocal use of her first name showed that he claimed still to hold position in power equal to hers. "You may employ runners of the Commercial Guild of Messengers to carry word of your exclusive trading rights to the far corners of the Empire, for all it matters."

Taken aback, Mara fought not to show surprise. "I assumed that when the time was appropriate, the imperial messengers would undertake the duty of posting such notices."

"They would do so if I directed them." Webara inspected his robe over his navel and removed a flake of keljir leaf that had stuck itself to the fabric. "However, as the rifts are not under imperial control, I am not concerned with who uses them."

Mara bit back outrage. "What is this? I hold exclusive trading rights!"

Webara gave a long-suffering sigh. "Mara, let me be blunt.

You hold trading rights with the barbarian world. While it can be argued that no one else is entitled to import the commodities you have licensed, still, you hold no monopoly on the use of a rift on another's lands. Neither of the two rifts is under imperial jurisdiction."

"Who controls them?" Despite her best efforts, Mara's query came out acerbic. She blotted sweating hands, worried now, for yesterday's bold advancement had been based upon her use of her license to control certain Midkemian imports.

Like many officials whose post held hollow forms that brought pomp but poor prestige, Webara sensed at once that he had the upper hand. He sucked on his sweet and twined his fingers across his ample stomach. "The first rift is upon the lands of a man named Netoha of the Chichimechas, near the city of Ontoset." His self-satisfied manner informed more plainly than words that this man might be difficult to convince when it came to granting access for trade purposes.

"Where is the second rift?" Mara asked through a stab of annoyance.

Webara returned an unctuous smile. "The other rift is located to the north, somewhere within the City of the Magicians." He smacked his lips as the last of his candy dissolved. In sugary tones, he added the unnecessary: "It is controlled by the Assembly, of course."

The man's patronizing scorn galled as deeply as insult. Mara arose without the grace of any courtesies. Certain the Keeper of the Imperial Seal was gloating at her frustration, she swept from the chamber without a word or a single glance back.

The chuckle that followed her departure into the corridor went unheard. Plunged into furious thought, Mara frowned. Her escort of warriors fell into step behind her without the benefit of any signal. Their mistress was too preoccupied with her own mistake to attend to such details. She had made an assumption, and paid. Acting on power she did not entirely have, she had presumed that the reopened rift would be under imperial control, as the last had been; then her warrant would have given her undisputed access.

But the magicians were far too capricious and powerful a body to approach, and this Netoha might certainly prove intractable. Mara uttered one of Kevin's favorite curses under her breath. Whoever Lord Netoha was, or whomever he held as allies, she was going to set Arakasi to the task of sounding his strengths and weaknesses. She had to gain access to a rift. Her newly won position as Clan Warchief depended upon this; and if she was thwarted in her needs, her house was set on perilous ground, both militarily and financially.

If she was frustrated—Mara forced herself to keep breathing evenly, to walk as though nothing were troubling her—Tasaio must not find out, or she begged swift ruin, not only for herself, but for all of Clan Hadama as well.

Arakasi reported back within the hour of Mara's return to her town house. Agitated still over her dilemma concerning trade concessions, the Lady of the Acoma immediately summoned the Spy Master into her presence in the garden courtyard. There, surrounded by perfectly groomed flower beds and the songs of fountains that did not soothe, Mara asked point blank for information concerning the man Netoha, upon whose estate the secondary rift to the barbarian world was reputed to lie.

As if her need had been anticipated, perhaps because of her desire to free Kevin, Arakasi had an astonishing supply of ready facts. He completed his bow, his secretive features more than usually impassive. "The magic gate is not located upon Netoha's lands by chance. He was the hadonra of the renegade magician, Milamber, who resided there before his expulsion from the Assembly. My inquiries established that the man had been a servant or hadonra of the previous owner of that luckless property."

Arakasi paused at this, for Tsurani superstition held against occupying residences or employing the servants of those fallen from power; when a lord or a family lost favor with the gods, his goods, his lands, and his staff were believed to be accursed along with him. Yet Milamber had been a barbarian, no doubt ignorant of such points. And ill luck had dogged him also. Arakasi shrugged Tsurani fashion. "But while both Netoha's masters have fallen upon ill fortune, his cause seems on the rise. Through some distant relation, he was able to claim kinship with the Chichimechas, who needed capital at the time. An arrangement was made. Now Netoha of the Chichimechas is fourth in line for succession to the Ruling Lordship of a tiny house, and he's in good standing with the Hunzan Clan."

Mara resisted an urge to rise and pace the flagstone walkway. "Clan Hunzan is radical in their thinking. Nothing they do would come as a surprise."

Arakasi rounded off his report. "Little else is common knowledge, save that Netoha's wife is a former slave."

Mara raised her eyebrows, diverted from her troubles by interest.

But her Spy Master's explanation dashed any hope she might hold for Kevin's benefit. "Milamber freed all the slaves upon his estate before leaving Kelewan," Arakasi said. "As his status had yet to be called into doubt at the time, the act became as law. Even without slaves, Netoha has turned his small holdings to profit. Given his industry, he is a man who will likely continue to rise. He might someday become a powerful Lord."

Mara seized upon the one point that mattered. "Then he could be open to a commercial transaction concerning this rift?"

"Perhaps." Arakasi's mood stayed guarded. "There is something else, mistress. A great deal is not clear to me, beyond the certainty that something vastly beyond the ordinary is in play. The renegade magician's return has sparked much activity, all of it clandestine. There are disturbed patterns running through imperial circles—high officials in long conferences with scholars sworn to secrecy, and a lot of close-mouthed, nervous correspondence carried back and forth by the Light of Heaven's personal messengers, none of it written, and all of it bonded by suicide oath, according to court gossip. I shall endeavor to penetrate and discover the heart of this, but as the Assembly is involved . . ." He shrugged again, to indicate the effort might not bear fruit.

Too concerned for her own difficulties, Mara forwent curiosity over the affairs of Great Ones. She dismissed her Spy Master with uncharacteristic abruptness, then called for a scribe, her intent being to send messages to Lord Netoha and to Fumita of the Assembly, offering generous terms for use of the rift gate into Midkemia.

Once her missives were dispatched by the guild of messengers, Kentosani held little to retain her. Mara opted for a swift return home, as much to avoid inopportune contact with other members of her clan as to assuage a sudden longing to spend time with Ayaki. The boy was growing so fast! He was halfway to becoming a man, she realized; she must speak to Keyoke soon about selecting a warrior to teach him weaponcraft, with his tenth birthday scarcely a half year off.

The return barge trip down the Gagajin passed without incident, but upon arrival at the border of her own estates, Mara's worry lessened as she felt something of the familiar calm that came from the knowledge of being home. And yet, for the first time in her life, she felt gnawed from within by a sense of something missing. She pondered why as her bearers took her litter up the road to the estate house.

Yet the cause eluded her until the moment she set foot in her own front dooryard and accepted greetings from Lujan, Keyoke, and Nacoya. The house seemed suddenly insignificant. Mara felt a passing sadness that she no longer looked upon the home of her father as the grand and wonderful place it had seemed throughout her childhood. As Ruling Lady and Clan Warchief, she now saw only a spread of land that was difficult to defend, and a dwelling that was comfortably appointed, but lacking the grand presence and state guest suites needful to a ruler of her status. For a moment Mara entertained the bitter thought that her most hated enemy should thrive in a place that was both the most defensible location in the Empire and the most beautiful.

As Mara crossed the threshold, Kevin in his customary place behind her, Nacoya pursued. Nettled that the mistress had returned only perfunctory salutations, the old woman nearly abandoned composure. "What has overcome you, Mara? Are you bereft of wits?"

The reprimand stung the Lady out of her thoughts. She spun to face her adviser, her frown an open warning. "What do you mean?"

"This assumption of the Warchief's staff." Nacoya wagged her finger, much as she had in her days as a children's nurse. "Why didn't you discuss your intentions before you acted?"

Mara stood firmly, her arms folded. "The idea never occurred to me until I was halfway to Kentosani. When I left, I thought I could convince the clan to do as I asked, but upon the river I had time to think—"

"I wish you had put the time to better use!" the Acoma First Adviser cut in.

"Nacoya!" Mara's eyes flashed rage. "I will not be scolded like a girl. What do you object to?"

The First Adviser bowed precisely to the correct degree, which meant she was not cowed. In tones near to scorn she said, "I beg your pardon, Lady. But since you have compelled Clan Hadama to recognize your primacy, you have also forced public notice that you are now a power to be contended with."

Caught off guard, Mara tried to wave the matter off. "Nothing has changed, save—"

Nacoya put her old hands firmly upon Mara's shoulders and looked her mistress in the eyes. "Much has changed. Before, you were seen as a resourceful girl, who could escape traps and strengthen her house and defend herself. Even after Jingu's death, the mighty of the Empire could cast your success off as luck. But now, by making others relinquish honors, you announce to the world that you are a threat! Tasaio *must* act. And he must do so soon. The longer he waits, the more his allies and vassals will come to doubt his resolve. Before, he might remain content to wait for a clear opportunity; now he must do something. You have made him desperate."

Mara felt a sudden current of cold. With certainty she knew Nacoya was correct in her appraisal. Made nervous as fresh worries tangled with others arising from her trade difficulties, she closed her eyes a moment. "You are right." Smiling thinly in chagrin, she regained her poise and added, "I have acted precipitately and . . . well, the best that can be done is to hold council with my staff as soon as I have refreshed myself. We must . . . make plans."

Nacoya nodded grumpy approval. As Kevin escorted Mara to her quarters, the old woman fretted, not only because Mara acted without thought, but also because she looked tired, truly bone-tired. As many years as Nacoya had served, she had never known the daughter of her heart to appear so worn.

The Acoma First Adviser sighed and shook her head. The Acoma ministers could meet and talk all they liked; plans might be made and acted upon, but truly, what could be done to ensure Acoma security and prosperity that had not been tried already? Feeling her age, and the ache in every joint that suffered from arthritis, the old woman shuffled slowly down the corridor. Every day since the Lord Sezu had died and left his holdings to his daughter, Nacoya had known fear that her beloved Mara might become a casualty of the Great Game. Yet the Lady had proven herself a capable, cunning player. Why, then, should the fear be worse today, or was it just an aged woman's bones protesting a life of long service? Nacoya shivered, though the afternoon was warm. At every step she took, she seemed to feel the earth of her own grave beneath the soles of her feet.

Word returned from Ontoset. Mara read the message twice, a stormy frown on her face. Restraining a vicious urge to tear something, she hurled the parchment onto her writing desk. The move was entirely unexpected. But Netoha had refused her very generous fees for the use of the rift on his lands.

"It makes no sense!" Mara exploded aloud, and in the corner of her study, Arakasi raised one eyebrow.

Dressed as a gardener, the Spy Master contemplated the edge on the small sickle he had been using to prune kekali bushes. He still insisted on keeping his return to the estate a secret, for his suspicions concerning Tasaio's penetration of Mara's security were far from laid to rest. The mistress might not wish to talk the matter through, her mind being diverted by other things, but Arakasi had his own worries. He currently spent as much time investigating servants and slaves upon the Acoma estates as he did conducting the business his mistress required of him. Only Nacoya knew of his concerns, as the old woman was above suspicion.

Arakasi tested the edge on the laminated tool with his finger and assumed a posture that would appear to an onlooker as if the Lady berated a servant for carelessness. "Mistress, I have discovered little about this man, Netoha. His motives are not public. He must have cogent reasons for refusing your offer; obviously, he cannot do business across the rift himself, because of your trading rights. Yet I cannot tell you what his reasons may be."

Mara tugged at a tight hairpin in frustration. Her message to Fumita of the Assembly had been returned unopened, so her last recourse to gain her trade concessions was this

Netoha. Although Arakasi did not care to be pressured, she said, "Can you get someone close to the Chichimechas to discover what these reasons may be?"

"I can but attempt to, Lady." Trying hard not to look harried, Arakasi added, "It is unlikely we shall learn anything new, but I can have someone exchange gossip with the house and field servants. Netoha's workers are largely barbarians—"

Mara broke in, "Midkemians?"

Arakasi nodded. "The renegade magician, Milamber, freed all his countrymen before leaving, and this Netoha employs them as workers. I would say from reports out of Ontoset that they do well enough as farmers. In any event, these are likely to be more garrulous than our own slaves, so getting information shouldn't prove difficult. If, that is, they know anything worth hearing."

Aware of Nacoya's taut stillness at her elbow, Mara turned to the next issue at hand. "What of Minwanabi?"

Arakasi's hands stilled on the sickle. "I worry, mistress, precisely because I have nothing to report. Tasaio conducts the business of his household much as you do your own, but with nothing that I would account extraordinarily significant." The Spy Master exchanged glances with Mara's First Adviser. "This goes against expectations. Upon hearing of your rise to the primacy of the clan, Tasaio should have been moved to act at once. But instead . . ." Arakasi glanced about, then said, "One other thing: the Minwanabi have begun a primitive spy network and are attempting to insinuate agents into several locations throughout the Empire. They are not hard to spot, since Incomo, the Minwanabi First Adviser, proceeds in a heavy-handed manner. I have men watching his men and am reasonably certain we can infiltrate his ring soon. That will give us a secondary access to his household and affairs, and when this is accomplished I shall feel reassured. Yet I dare not proceed too quickly. The whole operation may be an elaborate ploy to draw us out."

And yet, Mara sensed, that would not be Tasaio's style. The subtleties in his nature tended toward cruelty, and his tactics to military violence. Involved in deep thoughts once again, she absently waved dismissal to her Spy Master. She did not notice him leaving, and had forgotten Nacoya was in the room until the old woman spoke.

"I feel a chill in my bones, daughter."

Mara started slightly. "What worries you, Nacoya?"

"Minwanabi plots. You rely too much on Arakasi's informants. They may be well placed, but they are not everywhere. They are not at Tasaio's side when he squats or when he lies atop his wife, and you must believe that this is a man who plots murder even while relieving himself or taking a woman to his bed."

Mara found nothing humorous in the images, for Nacoya spoke truth. Arakasi's agents might have ferreted out nothing overtly threatening toward her house, but the reports were disturbing nonetheless. Tasaio ruled his household with a wayward, cunning viciousness. His abuses were those that tormented the mind and heart, and yet, where a sworn enemy was concerned, Mara knew there was no blood in the Empire he would rather spill than her own, and her young son Ayaki's.

23. *SORTIE*

The year passed.

Distracted with worry over continuing trade difficulties and Tasaio's apparent lack of activity, Mara waited as the rainy season came and went. Needra calves were weaned from their mothers, and the little bulls charged around the meadow; when they were sufficiently grown, the herdsmen picked out those that were gelded and those that were to be used for breeding. Crops were planted and harvested and an uncertain peace held sway. Days slipped by without any resolution to Mara's uncertainty. A thousand responses to a thousand possible assaults were discussed and discarded, and no Minwanabi threat materialized. A thousand moves in the Game of the Council were planned, but the Emperor did not relent in his edict against the High Council.

Seated in her study in the cooler hours of early morning, and clad in a loose, short robe, Mara studied the slates and parchments Jican had left for her. Since her frustrating setback in Kentosani, Acoma fortunes were improving. Her assumption of the position of Clan Warchief had precipitated no disasters. Gradually, the herds were recovering from the outlays made necessary from the Dustari campaign; the silk trade at last was flourishing. Although Nacoya seized every opportunity to nag that her mistress was neglecting the matter of marriage, Mara refused to be moved. With Tasaio consolidating his power as Lord of the Minwanabi, even someone from a family as favorably placed these days as was Hokanu's would be foolish to agree to a union until the issue between Minwanabi and Acoma had been decided. Except for Xacatecas and, less dependably, Anasati, alliances with the Acoma had become tentative. Mara sighed and pushed back a fallen lock of hair. Not yet strong enough to initiate the first overture, she had grown practiced at waiting.

A soft tap at the screen disturbed her.

Mara gestured for the servant hovering beyond the door to enter.

He bowed. "My Lady, there is a bonded messenger awaiting you in the antechamber."

"Send him in." Mara had enjoyed two hours of quiet contemplation since dawn and, now that the inevitable interruption had occurred, she was anxious to know the news.

The courier brought before her was dusty from the road and clad in a tunic of bleached cloth, tagged on the sleeves with the badge of a guild from Pesh. Since Mara had no dealings with any family from that city, this piqued her interest.

"You may sit," she allowed as the courier completed his bow. He carried no documents; the message he brought would be oral, guaranteed by his life oath of silence. Mara waved for a servant to bring jomach juice, in case the man's throat was dry from travel.

He inclined his head when the refreshment arrived and gratefully took a long swallow. "I bring greeting to the Acoma from the Lord Xaltepo of the Hanqu." The messenger paused for another sip, politely allowing the Lady an interval to call to mind what she knew of this Lord's house, clan, and political affiliations.

Mara needed the time, since the Hanqu were a minor house that had never previously dealt with the Acoma; they were of the Nimboni, a clan so tiny that it regularly associated with other, larger clans; which other clans it was allied with at present Mara didn't recall. Arakasi would know. He might also confirm whether Xaltepo had renewed his participation in the Yellow Flower Party since the demise of the Alliance for War. The Yellow Flower Party had no ties with the Minwanabi, but had occasionally supported common interests with them before Almecho wore the white and gold, and the changes effected by his successor, Axantucar, had disrupted the old alliances. The Yellow Flower Party currently fended for itself, and Nimboni quite likely inclined to favor the Kanazawai Clan. Perhaps this was an overture in that direction.

Mara sighed over this season's unrecognizable snarl of politics. Without Arakasi's network, she would be floundering, relying upon guesswork, and not leading her clan decisively through the moil.

The messenger finished his drink and politely awaited her attention. At a wave from Mara, he resumed.

"The Lord of the Hanqu formally requests that you consider an alliance with his house. If you judge the matter to be in Acoma interests, Lord Xaltepo asks for a meeting to discuss his proposal."

A house slave unobtrusively removed the emptied juice cup. Mara used the interval to formulate a swift decision. "I am flattered by the offer from the Lord of the Hanqu, and will reply through one of my own couriers."

This was politely noncommittal, and not unusual, since a ruler near Sulan-Qu would be unfamiliar with the guild of another city. Conscious of security, Mara intended to hire from a known guild. But to dismiss this courier without thanks was to insinuate mistrust, if not to imply dishonor. The Lady sent her runner to summon Saric. By now familiar with the duties of a second adviser, he would accompany the guild messenger to a distant chamber and see him occupied with banalities until the heat passed, and the man could politely be dismissed.

Financial reports no longer gripped Mara's attention. Throughout the morning she pondered the Hanqu's unexpected overture without assuming what their motive might be. Lord Xaltepo might earnestly desire an alliance, and this must not be treated lightly. Since Mara's public rise to the office of Clan Warchief, it could be but the first of many such approaches. To ignore this would be folly.

Far more dangerous, he might be puppet for some other, better known enemy, who used him to disguise another plot against her. She waited until the courier's departure before dispatching Arakasi to make inquiries.

After supper, she called council. Weary of the stifling stillness of her study with screens and drapes drawn closed, she decided that a meeting in the garden courtyard adjacent to her quarters, under the light of lanterns, would be more comfortable. The garden had a single entrance, securely guarded.

Settled on cushions under the tree beside the fountain, Mara regretted her preoccupation with security. For an envious moment she once again recalled Tasaio's estate, a beautiful building on spacious grounds, fortified by steep hills and the naturally defensible valley with its lake and narrow tributary. Unlike other nobles situated in the low country, the Minwanabi Lord need not vigilantly keep guard over broad acres of borders. He required only sentries in watch towers on his hilltops, and patrols stationed at key points along the perimeter of his estates. Where the Acoma required five full companies of a hundred warriors each dedicated to the main estate to optimally maintain its defenses—a goal still unrealized after over a decade of carefully building her resources—the Minwanabi could do better with as few as two hundred soldiers guarding twice the land. That lower cost of security for the home estate provided Tasaio with resources for political mischief that Mara lacked, despite her rapidly expanding financial empire.

Mara regarded her circle of advisers, larger than before, with younger faces added and older ones the more aged by contrast. Nacoya became more wrinkled and hunched with each passing month. Keyoke could not sit quite so erect, yet he remained a stickler for appearances. He kept his good leg crossed over his stump, and his crutch painstakingly out of view. For all his care, Mara could never quite accustom herself to the sight of him in house robes instead of armor.

For formal meetings of her council, no servants were present; but in the role of body slave, Kevin sat beside and behind her, surreptitiously playing with her hair, which she had let down from its pins. Then there were Jican, with his hands dusty from chalk, and Saric, young, eager, and shrewd around the eyes where Lujan was deceptively carefree. Her Spy Master had not yet returned from the docks of Sulan-Qu, where he had gone to meet the contact who carried intelligence from Pesh. Since Arakasi's word would bear heaviest influence, Mara began before his arrival to lend time to hear her other advisers.

Nacoya opened. "Lady Mara, you know nothing of these upstart Hanqu. They are not an old family. They shared none of your interests politically, and I worry they may be the glove for an enemy's hand."

The First Adviser's views had grown increasingly cautious of late. The Lady of the Acoma was unsure if this resulted from Mara's rise to the Clan Warchief's office or from a fear of Tasaio that was deepening with age. Increasingly, Mara looked to Saric for a more balanced weighing of risk and gain.

Though barely out of his twenties, the soldier turned counselor was quick-witted, sly, and often sarcastic in his advice; his overt playfulness seemed at odds with a deeper barbed cynicism, but his observations were consistantly astute. "Nacoya's reasoning is sound," he opened, his eyes boldly on Mara, and his hands running over and over a lacquered bracelet on his wrist as though he tested the edge on a blade. He gave a soldier's shrug. "But I would add that we know too little about the Lord of the Hanqu. If he acts in good faith, we would offend if we refuse to hear his case. Even if we could afford to affront this little house, we do not wish the Acoma to gain a reputation for being unapproachable. We might politely reject his alliance after hearing his cause, and no offense will be given." Sarik tipped his head slightly and ended with his customary question. "But, can we afford to refuse him without inquiring what his motives may be?"

"A telling point," Mara conceded. "Keyoke?"

Her Adviser for War reached to straighten a helmet no longer there, and ended by scratching thinning hair. "I should look closely at the arrangements proposed for your conference. The Lord could have an assassin waiting, or an ambush. Where he wishes to meet with you, and under what conditions, will tell us much."

That the former Force Commander did not question the necessity for a parley was not lost on Mara.

Lujan, from his days as a grey warrior, gave a new perspective. "The Hanqu are regarded as mavericks by the powerful houses of Pesh. I was acquainted with the cousin of one of my subofficers' wives, who served Xaltepo as Patrol Leader. The Hanqu Lord was said to be a man who seldom shared his confidences, and did so only upon occasions of mutual advantage. That they are a new house has been said, but the rise of the family is due to their powerful business interests in the south."

Jican followed Lujan's lead and widened the picture. "The Hanqu have an interest in chocha-la. Being weak, at one time they were mercilessly exploited by the guilds. Lord Xaltepo's father tired of losing his profits. When he came to power, he hired in his own bean grinders, and reinvested his chocha-la profits back into that enterprise. His son has continued to broaden the business, and now they are, if not dominant, a major factor in the southern markets. He boasts a thriving trade and processes crops from other growers. It is possible he desires an arrangement that will bring the beans of our Tuscalora vassal into his drying sheds."

"In *Pesh?*" Mara straightened, interrupting Kevin's attentions. "Why should Lord Jidu risk the mold and damp of shipping his crops by sea, or the expense of an overland caravan?"

"For profit," Jican speculated in his inimitably neat fashion. "The soil and the climate are wrong for chocha-la that far down the peninsula. Even the Hanqu's inferior beans yield high revenues there. Most growers grind their crops close to home, to save the weight of shipping the husks. But the bean keeps better in its unshelled form, and the Hanqu spice grinders could get luxury prices for any chocha-la they could process in what now is idle time between seasons. And they effectively remove a potential rival from the local market. Eventually, such a relationship might provide an entrance for their goods into the heartland of the Empire."

"Then why not approach Lord Jidu?" Mara argued.

Jican spread placating hands. "Lady, you may have allowed the Lord of the Tuscalora his rights to negotiate his finances, but among the merchants and factors in the cities you are spoken of as his overlord. They cannot conceive any ruler being as openhanded in policy as you have been; therefore, word in the markets says you are in control."

"Jidu would protest," Mara objected.

Now Nacoya leaned forward. "My Lady, he does not dare. He has his man's pride; it rankles him to have been bested by a woman. Lord Jidu would rather avoid being the object of more street gossip than turn to you with complaint."

The discussion of this point continued in depth, with Kevin listening raptly. The Midkemian was silent not so much out of deference as fascination with the intricacy of Tsurani politics. Lately, if he contributed an opinion, it was less from ignorant impulse and more out of insight lent by an alien viewpoint.

Mara weighed the counsel of her advisers and tried to avoid the looming distraction of how much she was going to miss her barbarian when she finally faced her neglected responsibility and chose a suitable husband. Unsettled as the current politics became, she cherished this moment, surrounded by people who cared for her, and the soft, familiar warmth of the summer night.

Lantern light fell kindly over the faces of Keyoke and Nacoya, softening the lines of adversity; it caught in Saric's eyes in a moment of fired enthusiasm; and it hid the weariness in Jican's posture.

Not a day passed that the hadonra failed to visit the remotest field on the estate; since Dustari, he visited the city every morning, leaving before sunrise and returning before midmorning, enduring two hours of travel to gain earliest word of trade fluctuations from his factors. Few opportunities escaped his diligence, but Mara wished adversities would ease, that she need not lean so heavily on his resources. Jican had taught her much in the intricate world of finance. And her other advisers had rescued the Acoma from disasters invited by her inexperience in her first days of leadership. Silently she thanked Lashima for the guidance of good people. With her pledge to Clan Hadama binding her, and the Minwanabi blood feud against her, she dared not contemplate the loss of any one of those present.

The talk at last wound down. Mara reviewed the major points, a pensive frown on her face. "It looks as though I should send a message to Lord Xaltepo, setting a meeting that will most favor my safety. Jican, could you arrange to rent one of the guild halls in Sulan-Qu?"

But a dry voice interrupted before the hadonra could answer. "My Lady, with all due respect, a public place might not be the best of choices."

Unnoticed, quiet as shadow, Arakasi had slipped into the garden; as he bowed, Keyoke's lips stiffened. Annoyed with himself for missing the moment when the guards at the entry granted a newcomer entrance, the old warrior would never admit his hearing was growing less acute.

Arakasi bowed, his face veiled by the loose cloth of a priest's cowl. He waited in his distinctively quiet manner for

Mara's leave, then added, "I should warn at once that this request by Lord Xaltepo is known to the Minwanabi. My sources indicate that Tasaio is personally intent upon finding out where a meeting between my Lady and the Hanqu might take place. If a guild hall is rented, I fear there may be spies in the walls. And if there are presently no niches for unfriendly parties to eavesdrop, you can presume such would be constructed in time for our mistress's conference. Tasaio is that persistent when he wants a thing."

The Spy Master hesitated, as if his own words were distasteful to him. "My source was emphatic, much more so than usual. Tasaio wants knowledge of this meeting quite badly."

Mara's fingers tightened on her cuffs. "By this, I conclude that the Hanqu's interests go against those of our enemies."

"It lends weight to the notion that the Hanqu's desire for alliance is valid." But Arakasi did not seem entirely settled. "Too many unanswered questions remain. Expansion of the Hanqu's spice enterprise seems a motive, but that is speculation. Also there's a vague rumor that the Nimboni have been approached by Clan Shonshoni." The Spy Master's manner betrayed disquiet. "There are things here that are *too* clear, given how much is unseen."

"You worry?"

"Aye, Lady. Something in his . . ." He shook his head. "Perhaps I've grown wary of too much information gained easily." He shrugged. "Not having kept a close watch upon the Hanqu, it's not unreasonable that their affairs would escape my notice. I urge caution, though, in the extreme. Meet with Lord Xaltepo somewhere easily defended; here, upon your estates; or if not on home ground, then somewhere close at hand where we keep an advantage."

Mara weighed the advice. "You speak wisely, as always. Caution must be exercised. No opportunity for advantage can be wasted, however slight. I'll meet with Lord Xaltepo, not in a guild hall, but in that glen in the mountains where Lujan's band once made their camp. It is not upon Acoma soil, yet we have the advantage should any trouble arise."

Arakasi looked dusty and gaunt after his hurried trip to town; Mara dismissed him to seek refreshment, and the rest of her advisers disbanded, talking among themselves. Once outside the garden, all would be silent concerning the subject of Lord Xaltepo.

Kevin alone remained seated. He slid his arms around Mara's waist and buried his cheek in her hair. "What do you say to a special sort of council between the two of us?"

Mara turned her face to be kissed. Kevin's hair glowed russet in the lantern light, and his hands well knew where to touch; as his lips closed over hers, Mara prepared to surrender her worries for the night.

"My Lady," snapped Nacoya's acerbic voice. Unwanted as a state visitor, the First Adviser lingered in the courtyard. "Stop your foolishness and hear warning."

Mara disengaged from Kevin's embrace. Her eyes were bright, her hair slightly mussed, and her temper short. "Speak, mother of my heart. But do not presume upon my patience." Lately her First Adviser seemed to seize upon every opportunity to insinuate the folly of Kevin's presence. Though Mara understood that the old woman's persistence stemmed from care, tonight she was determined to enjoy the few moments she had left with the man she loved. However kindly meant, Nacoya's concern was not welcome.

The First Adviser did not lecture about her inopportune choice of bedmate, but crossed her wrinkled arms and stood firmly. "You rely far too much on those spies of Arakasi's."

Mara's gaze darkened. "They have never failed me."

"They have never dealt directly with Tasaio." Nacoya waved a stern finger. "Remember the silk caravans! Desio discovered one of Arakasi's agents, and ill came of that. His cousin will not be so stupid. He'll not be lulled into thinking he has no watchers in his house. But unlike Desio, Tasaio will not be led by hate on discovery his security was compromised. He would spare his traitor, even nurture the man, and await his moment to exploit."

A breeze swayed the lantern. Netted by a moving play of shadows, Mara gestured her irritation. "Do you suggest we should rent the public guild hall? Depend upon the security provided by clanless men?"

Nacoya pinched her sleeves as the errant wind flapped her robe. "I say no such thing, except to beseech you to beware. Arakasi is very good, the best of men who work in secret I have ever heard of in my years of serving this house. But his former master of the Tuscai was ruined despite his spy ring.

Remember *that*. Informants can be helpful, but they are never infallible. All tools can break, or be turned into weapons."

Mara stiffened, acutely feeling the chill as Kevin's warmth drew away. "Old mother, your warnings are heard. I thank you for your counsel."

Nacoya knew better than to persist. She bowed in deep disapproval, then turned and limped out of the garden.

"She's right, you know, the old nag," Kevin murmured fondly.

Mara spun and snapped at him. "You too! Does every evening have to be filled with warnings and fear?" She tossed her dark hair, aching inside more than she would ever put into words; though Kevin perhaps thought better of it, he indulged her whim, and gathered her close. He kissed the hardness out of her, and on the cushions, in the flicker of a breeze-tossed lantern, he made her forget the enemies who sought her life and the utter ending of her family.

Within three weeks, high summer set in; the grasses lost the last green that lingered from the rainy season. Mara stepped out of the estate house into the misty predawn gloom. Her litter awaited, surrounded by a picked guard of thirty warriors led this day by Kenji, who needed the field experience. For her journey to meet with the Lord of the Hanqu she planned to be in the mountains before the heat of midday, and, at Arakasi's suggestion, she kept her escort light for speed and secrecy. Her Adviser for War had insisted on seeing her off; since Nacoya was no longer up to rising in early morning.

Yet no adviser waited in the dooryard as Mara made her appearance, Kevin following at the proper pace behind her shoulder, but ever unmindful of propriety. "The old codger must have slept late," the barbarian said lightly. "I should take the chance to get back at him for the time he kicked me awake with his war sandals on."

"I heard that," called a voice well trained from the drill field. Keyoke emerged from the ranks of Mara's bodyguard, a craggy silhouette incongruously propped on a crutch. He paused to speak emphatic instructions to Kenji, to snap at a man for sloppy posture; then, plainly reluctant to leave the warriors, he shot a disparaging glance at Kevin and assumed his post before Mara's litter.

"My Lady." He bowed with well-practiced balance and replaced his crutch beneath his shoulder. Then he looked intently at his mistress, as if he marshalled words instead of troops. His voice dropped, so that the soldiers would not overhear. "Daughter of my heart, I feel uneasy about this trip. The fact that Lord Xaltepo sent speech in the mouth of a messenger rather than written above his family chop has suspicious overtones."

Mara frowned. "They are a small family with few ties. If I were to decline alliance, and that parchment with their personal chop should fall into Tasaio's hands, what do you think would become of them? The Minwanabi have obliterated other families for far less cause." She bit her lip. "No. I think Arakasi is right, and that Tasaio finally sees that much of what we've done has been built upon financial gain and now he must counter further Acoma expansion."

Keyoke raised his hand, as if he had begun to scratch his chin and then thought better of it. Instead he took Mara's wrist and gently settled her into the litter. "Go with the good gods' grace, my Lady."

He stepped back as Mara waved for the bearers to lift her litter. Then Kenji gave the command to march, and the small cortege started forward. As Kevin moved to fall into step beside his mistress, Keyoke caught his elbow in a grip still calloused and strong.

"Protect her," he said, an urgency in his tone that Kevin had never heard before. "Let no harm come to her, or I'll kick you with more than my battle sandals."

Kevin grinned insouciantly. "Keyoke, old friend, if harm comes to Mara, you'll have to settle for kicking my corpse, because by then I'll already be dead."

The Adviser for War nodded, allowing that this was true. He released the slave and turned quickly away while Mara's escort and bearers marched into the mist. Kevin hastened to catch up, looking often over his shoulder. Far less the foreigner than he once was, the Midkemian would have sworn that the crafty old warrior had something pressing on his mind.

•   •   •

By the time the rising sun burned the mist off the valleys, Mara and her honor guard were deep in the forest that covered the foothills of the Kyamaka Mountains. Before the day's traffic of caravans began, and out of sight of early couriers, they turned off the main road, striking down a narrow trail that threaded ever deeper into the wilds. Daylight was not strong here, and the mist lingered, lending a gloom to the wood and the drip of wet trees. Already the damp heat was oppressive. Force Leader Kenji motioned his small column of warriors to halt for a short break, and to allow a change of bearers for Mara's litter. The escort was too small to include a water boy; the slaves carried crocks from the spring by the roadside, helped by Kevin, who felt sorry for their plight. Mara was not a heavy load to carry, but this day her haste was great, and the bearers just relieved from duty were sweat-drenched and panting.

Crock in hand, Kevin knelt at the verge of a still, mossy pool fed by a spring from a fissure in the rocks. Intrigued by the alien orange moss that clothed the banks, and by the iridescent flash of fish that darted through aqua strands of weed, he only half heard Force Leader Kenji say to Mara that the scout who held back to watch the trail for followers was slow to report.

"We shall delay to see if he arrives," the officer decided. "If he does not come within a minute, I suggest we slip into the cover of the trees, until a man can be sent to investigate."

Kevin grinned to himself and bent to fill his basin. The scout in question was Juratu, a quick-witted, lively man who liked his pleasures; he had kept late hours gambling with friends the night before. If he had drunk half as much wine as barracks rumor claimed, he'd likely be found moving at less than anticipated speed, slowed by a grandfather of hangovers.

One of the soldiers said as much to Kenji, then added that this was the haunt of grey warriors, and perhaps Juratu had paused to observe their movements. Another dryly suggested he might be bartering with them for a wineskin. Kevin indulged in a chuckle; had the Lady herself not been present, such an antic would certainly be within Juratu's reputation. Thinking of grey warriors, and his few Midkemian companions who had escaped and taken refuge in these forests, Kevin peered through the trees as he rose.

The mist was lifting. Pale spears of sunlight fell through the canopy of branches. Had Kevin not been half-expectantly looking for the chance-met shape of a man, he would have missed the movement: the brief, flickering sight of a face through the leaves, there, and then hastily gone.

The nose had been narrow and hooked, and the helm was not Juratu's.

Kevin's hands tautened over the crock, and water spilled, wetting his knuckles in a flood. He dared not cry out, or even run, lest he reveal that the hidden watcher had been seen. Sweating, more than a little shaky in the knees, Kevin turned his back on the spring. In imitation of a slave's listless shuffle, he made his way step by nerve-racked step back to Mara's caravan.

The skin between his shoulderblades itched, as if at any moment he expected the terrible stab of an arrow.

The dozen steps that separated him from Kenji and Mara's litter seemed to take an eternity. Kevin forced his feet to walk sedately while his thoughts raced. The litter curtains were cracked open, with Mara on the verge of leaning out to address Kenji.

Fear shot like a bolt through Kevin's nerves. He pinched the water crock in a death grip and inwardly willed the woman to lean back out of sight in the shadow of her litter.

Being Mara, she did not. She shoved the curtains wider, looked up at her Force Leader, and opened her mouth to speak.

Feeling danger like a breaking wave at his back, Kevin acted. He tripped, hard, on a rock and flung the contents of his water crock over the Lady and her officer. He followed up this clumsiness by crashing full length into the litter.

His mistress's cry of surprise and outrage became smothered under his chest as he forced her down and back, deep into the cushions, safe behind the protection of his body as he flipped the litter on its side, turning it into a breastwork.

His action came none too soon. Even as Kevin disentangled himself from the silk curtains, enemy arrows began to fall.

They sang out of the air, smacking through dirt and armor with an evil flat sound like the blows of punitive hands. Kenji was first to fall. He went down screaming orders, while arrows hammered and hammered the underside slats of the spilled litter, raised now before Mara like a barricade.

"It's an ambush," Kevin snarled in her ear, while she beat with her fists to try to tear from his embrace. "Keep still."

An arrow whapped through a cushion and rammed a groove through the dirt. Mara saw and instantly went still. She listened, stricken, to the shouting as those warriors left alive to heed their dying officer's call to rally threw themselves in a heap on top of the litter, their bodies her living shield.

The situation was desperate. The arrows crashed down in a rain, and the flimsy underpinnings of the litter bounced and splintered with the impact. Kevin tried to see out and caught a raking slash across his shoulder. He cursed, ducked back, and in a rush peeled off his slave's robe.

Two of the warriors nearest Mara were dying, wounded as they dove to her defense. Now the cold hiss of shafts was replaced by the rattle of swordplay as ambushers charged from the forest in a wave and engaged the tatters of her guard still left standing.

"Quick," Kevin snapped. He held out his robe. "Bundle my Lady in this. Her fancy clothes makes too clear a target."

One of the bearers threw back a look of uncertainty.

"Just do it!" Kevin shouted. "Her honor is dust if she's dead."

More warriors charged from the cover of the wood. Mara's few survivors closed in a ragged ring around the litter; they were too few, a pitiful dike against an avalanche of foes. Kevin abandoned further argument, for a swordsman charged out of the melee with lowered blade to take him in the back. Kevin snatched up a fallen weapon and snapped off a length of curtain that he wrapped around his arm to serve as shield; then he spun at bay and prepared to kill until he died.

At home on the Acoma estate, Ayaki scowled blackly at Nacoya. His face turned red and his fists clenched, and she and two slaves and a nurse all prepared for a warrior-sized tantrum.

"I won't wear that!" Ayaki shouted. "It has orange, and that is the color worn by Minwanabi."

Nacoya regarded the garment at hand, a silk robe fastened with shell buttons that might, with imagination, be called orange. The real reason behind the argument was that Ayaki preferred to wear no robe at all in the heat and humidity of high summer. That he was too well born to charge about naked as a slave child through the hallways made no impression on nine-year-old priorities.

But Nacoya had years of experience at managing high-spirited Acoma children. She caught Ayaki's stiff shoulders and gave him a shake. "Young warrior, you will wear the robes you are given, and deport yourself like the Lord you will be when you are grown. If you do less, you will spend the morning scrubbing dirty plates with the scullions."

Ayaki's eyes widened. "You'd never dare! I'm not a servant or a slave!"

"Then stop acting like one and dress like a noble." Nacoya closed a puffed, arthritic hand over Ayaki's wrist and hauled him firmly across the chamber to the servant who waited with the robe. Even stiff and sore, she still had a grip like iron. Ayaki stopped struggling, shoved his bunched fist into a waiting sleeve, then stood scowling and rubbing at the red mark where the skin on his wrist had pulled.

"Now the other hand," Nacoya snapped. "No more nonsense."

Ayaki's dark look lifted and he grinned. "No more nonsense," he agreed in one of his instant shifts of mood. He submitted his other hand to the servant, and presently the offending robe was settled over his shoulders. His smile widened until he showed his missing front teeth, and he deliberately reached up and jerked off the first shell button. "The robe is all right," he announced defiantly. "But I will wear no orange!"

"Demon!" Nacoya swore under her breath. She was definitely too tired to manhandle willful little boys. She settled for smacking his cheek, which shocked him into a loud shriek of rage.

The yell was loud enough to defeat thought, and the servants winced. The guards in the corridor were distracted and did not hear the soft footfall as a black-clothed figure leaped on silent feet through the screen.

Suddenly the servant standing nearest reeled aside with a knife in his back.

He fell without a cry. Even as the assassin's shadow sliced across the sunlight, the second servant toppled with a cut throat.

Nacoya felt the thud as the corpse struck the wooden floor. Instinctively attuned to danger, she reached down and caught the Acoma heir, who still howled, and flung him headlong into the corner. He landed rolling amid bed mat and cushions still in morning disarray.

The First Adviser called for the guards, but her voice was aged and weak. Her warning went unheard. Ayaki screamed now in blind rage, intent on disentangling himself from his bedclothes. Only Nacoya saw his peril, and the servants bleeding out their lives on the nursery floor.

"Demon!" she said again, but this time to the black-clothed figure of the tong assassin. He had pulled another knife from his belt, and a cord looped the fingers of his left hand. His face was hidden behind a black gauze caul; his fists were gloved. Nothing showed but his eyes as he stalked to take his victim, the boy who was Mara's heir. Only Nacoya stood in his way. Already the knife rose for a throw to cut her down.

"No!" Nacoya flung forward as the knife left his hand. She made a dive for his left wrist and the cord held ready for Ayaki's throat. The blade flashed over the first Adviser's head and thunked in the plaster wall.

The assassin cursed and sidestepped. But Nacoya caught his garrote. Her nails tore through thin leather, raked his knuckles like claws, and twisted in a deathgrip on the cord. "You won't." She again called for guards, but her thin voice was not equal to the task.

The assassin wasted no time in wrestling. His eyes narrowed in contempt, and his right hand closed on a wooden handle and drew the next knife in line on his belt. He seemed perversely delighted as he drove the point deep between the old woman's ribs.

Nacoya's lips curled back from her teeth with the pain. She hung on.

"Die, old woman!" The assassin gave the knife a vicious twist.

Nacoya shuddered. An agonized cry escaped her, but her hands tightened harder on the cord. "He will not be killed in dishonor," she wrung out.

Behind her, Ayaki's cries died. He saw the knife in the wall above his head, and then the blood that snaked across the floorboards. One of the fallen servants still quivered in his death throes. Paralyzed with terror, an orange shell button still clenched in one fist, Ayaki bit back a whimper. The assassin, he decided, must be Tasaio. With that realization, the courage that was his father's reasserted itself in force.

"Attack!" he shouted. "Attack!" And with his head filled with visions of warriors, he scrambled from his pillows and beat upon the intruder's thigh.

The tong took no notice. He shoved the knife deeper into Nacoya. Blood ran hot over his hand, soaking his glove as he jerked his garrote from her grip. She crumpled quickly, fell over into Ayaki, and pinned the boy under her dying weight.

"The Good God's curse upon you," she croaked hoarsely at the tong. Her strength inexorably ebbed. Ayaki wriggled free.

The assassin grabbed at the boy and tripped. Nacoya had caught his ankle, but her life was fading fast. The assassin recovered instantly, stamped on her wrist, and yanked free.

Across the chamber, through failing vision, the old woman saw the guards had finally reacted. They charged through the nursery doorway, their armor shining unbearably in bright sunlight. With drawn swords they ran, bellowing battle cries, across the chamber toward the tong.

Behind her, the assassin pounced. Little Ayaki howled wrathfully. Nacoya struggled to raise her cheek from a puddle of pooling blood. She could not see but only hear the scuffle of Ayaki's bare feet drumming on the floorboards. Her vision went dark, and her dying thought was recognition: the cord was still tangled in her fingers. She had done nothing more than force the assassin to use his knives. . . . A boy who died honorably by the blade would still be dead.

"Ayaki," she murmured, and then, heartbrokenly, "Mara . . ." as darkness took her.

Kevin lunged, thrust, and cleared his sword. An enemy fell screaming at his feet. He leaped over the thrashing, gut-wounded man, and met another. Somewhere in the fray he had picked up a foe's shield, and it had saved his life. He had taken another cut in his left shoulder, and a glancing slash across the ribs. His movements were hampered by the sting. Blood flowed over his bare skin and soaked soggily into his loincloth. Every movement hurt. The enemy swordsman exchanged three strokes with him before realizing he fought a slave. He snarled an oath and dodged past. Kevin stabbed him unceremoniously from behind.

"Die for Tsurani honor," the barbarian cried savagely. "Gods, please, let the runts keep being stupid."

Let them keep underestimating his war skills, that Mara might stay alive.

But there were too many. Enemies kept sallying from the trees. As Kevin whirled to stave off another attacker, he realized the Acoma were more than just surrounded. Their circle was breached. Foes charged through and started hacking at the bodies that lay across the litter which sheltered Mara.

The Midkemian screamed like a banshee and ran a man through. He abandoned his blade in the corpse, snatched up another from the ground. In the same unbroken movement he kicked over the fallen litter. The wooden frame hammered down, driving enemy soldiers into a scattered rush back; then the litter thumped to a rest, with Mara and her shield of dying bodyguards fenced underneath.

Kevin charged over the barrier. "Back, you pig-licking dogs!" He added obscenities in Tsurani and hurtled over the wreckage.

His blood-streaked, near-naked body and berserker's howl startled the lead ranks into hesitation. He landed on an arrow, felt the sting of its four-bladed head cut his heel, and cursed again in Yabon dialect. "May Turakamu eat your heart for breakfast," he ended, and then the swords came at him.

He could not parry so many. Nor could he wonder if his use of the litter for a ram had injured Mara. He only understood he would die here and was not pleased with the prospect.

A sword sliced his shin. He stumbled, fell, rolled. The air above his head became bisected by weapons driving to impale him. They narrowly bit earth; he felt the disturbed dirt strike his shoulders. He unlimbered his shield and rolled hard over again, bringing it upward in a vicious blow to the groin of a man who moved too slowly. Kevin's body wedged at last under the canted litter. His searching fingers encountered a fallen shield. He twisted, scraping against wood, and came up with the shield in front. His palms stung as enemy blows rained down, momentarily thwarted.

"Gods, this can't last." His curses now sounded suspiciously like crying. And the swords hammered his shield, incessantly. They split toughened needra hide and wood, and left him clutching splinters. Very far off, perhaps in the wood, he heard shouting and the clatter of more fighting. "Damn them, damn them." He loosed a bitter laugh. "We're defeated, and still they want to butcher us."

The sword sliced air with a whine and bit flesh. A black-haired head tumbled in a bouncing roll among the bed-clothes.

Still the Acoma guard kept yelling, and before the assassin fell, he had slashed the body three times. The corpse collapsed in a ruck of sodden fabric, and shuddered convulsively amid the cushions.

Spattered with the blood of the tong, and crying in wild-eyed terror, Ayaki wormed out from under the corpse. A gash on his young neck bled freely, and he threw himself mindlessly against the wall in attempt to escape from stark terror.

"Fetch Keyoke," cried the warrior with the dripping sword to the other who bent over the body of Nacoya. "There may be other assassins!"

The slap of running sandals sounded outside the screen as armed warriors rushed through the courtyard garden. Drawn by the disturbance, they saw the puddled blood and corpses through the screen, and almost instantly a second Strike Leader arrived, giving fast orders for a grounds search, while detailing six men to surround the Acoma heir.

A moment later, Jican appeared, his composure vanishing as he saw the carnage on the nursery floor. He shoved his load of slates into the hands of the stupefied slave who followed him and, in atypical haste, threaded a path through a room suddenly filled with armed men. Beyond a wall of sticky cushions crouched the Acoma heir, pounding the wall with bruised fists and screaming, "Minwanabi, Minwanabi, Minwanabi!"

The warriors who gathered to help seemed unwilling to touch him.

"Ayaki, come here, it's over," Jican said firmly.

The little one appeared not to hear. Mara's hadonra reached out anyway. He ignored the child's flinch from his touch, extracted the traumatized boy from the mess, and bundled him against robes that smelled like chalk instead of slaughter.

"Let's get him out of here," he instructed the nearest warrior. "Get the healer. He's injured." Looking at the motionless forms of Nacoya and the two nurses, he said, "And somebody find out if he has a nurse left alive."

The blows on the shield redoubled. Kevin yanked one hand away from the rim, an instant before losing a finger. He was dimly aware of a heave of movement in the bodies behind his hip, as one of the mortally injured warriors he leaned on thrust a dagger handle into his palm.

"Defend our Lady," croaked a voice. "She's alive."

Kevin rejected the defeated realization that she could not remain so much longer. Naked and bleeding and half-crazed with battle fury, he accepted the blade, reached under the rim of the shield, and stabbed an enemy foot. The knife was promptly lost as the skewered enemy jerked with a scream of rage.

"Happy dancing," wished the barbarian, turned drunken with blood loss and adrenaline. He took a moment to notice that the blows on the shield had stopped.

Hands in green-lacquered gauntlets caught the rim a moment later and strongly lifted the battered wreckage away. Kevin peered up, blinking against the sun. Through vision that danced with dizziness he made out an officer's plume and the face of the Acoma Force Commander.

Relief overturned his sense of humor. "Thank the gods you're here," he said. "We found ourselves in a sticky situation."

Lujan regarded Kevin's bloodied hands and the dripping gash on his forearm. " 'Happy dancing'?" he quoted, puzzled.

"Later," Kevin muttered. "I'll explain everything later." He turned awkwardly against the pain of his bleeding side, and cursed bilingually. He felt sick, and the sun was too bright.

"Where is our Lady?" Lujan demanded, sharply now, and taut with worry.

Kevin blinked bemusedly at the overturned litter. Acoma dead lay crushed like so many impaled beetles underneath.

"Light of Heaven, not under there!" Lujan called another order that to Kevin's ears sounded like noise. Then many hands were reaching down and dragging his battered body out from under the splinters.

"Don't," Kevin protested weakly. "I want to know if Mara . . ." Words were hard; the air burned his lungs.

Still protesting, he was pushed supine on the ground, and darkness closed over his ears just before the shouts of amazed discovery from the warriors who righted the litter; they sorted the tangle of dead and injured and found a blood-stained, crumpled figure who was not conscious but had no wound beyond a purple bruise on her head.

Mara was laid on the soft, dry moss by the spring. Surrounded by a hundred soldiers, her head pillowed in Lujan's lap, she roused as a rag that dripped icy water bathed the lump on her brow. "Keyoke?" she murmured as her eyes first flickered open.

"No," her Force Commander answered gently. "Lujan, mistress. But Keyoke was the one who sent me here. He thought you might run into trouble."

Mara stirred, faintly reproving. "He's not your commander, but my Adviser for War."

Lujan stroked the hair from his mistress's face and gave her his most insolent smile. "Old habits die hard. When my old commander says jump, I jump."

Mara shifted painfully. She seemed battered and sore in a hundred places. "I should have listened." Her eyes clouded. "Kevin," she said, "Where is he?"

Lujan inclined his head toward his field healer, who crouched over a second figure lying on the moss. "He survived. In a loincloth, without armor, and with a hero's complement of wounds. Ayee, what a warrior that man is."

"Wounds!" Mara shoved up in distress, and Lujan required a surprising amount of strength to keep her quiet.

"Lady, be still. He will live, though he'll have a pretty set of scars. He might limp, and he will be a long time regaining full use of his left hand. The muscles were badly slashed."

"Brave Kevin." Mara's voice shook. "He saved me. My foolishness almost killed him."

Her Force Commander touched her again, almost tenderly. "It is a pity the man is a slave," he commiserated. "Such courage deserves only the highest honor."

The air suddenly hurt to breathe; Mara turned her face into Lujan's shoulder and shivered. Perhaps she wept, soundless in misery; if she did, the officer who comforted her would never expose her shame. Somehow he understood that her agony did not stem from her narrow escape in the glen alone. And his abiding love and devotion would never permit him to acknowledge his Lady had betrayed herself in a moment of public weakness. The surrounding soldiers quickly found tasks to occupy themselves, allowing Mara her moment of release.

The Lady of the Acoma wept for Kevin, whose bold spirit had captured hers, and whose actions had finally made her understand beyond denial that he was not, and never would be, a slave.

She would have to set him free, and that could not be done within the borders of the Empire of Tsuranuanni. To give him his due, to acknowledge him as a man, she was going to lose him forever. Following through that realization was going to be the hardest thing she had ever undertaken.

Regrouping from the ambush in the forest took the better part of the day. The bodies of the slain warriors had to be gathered up onto makeshift litters for rites and cremation at home; the enemy dead were left as food for jagunas and other carrion eaters. Lujan sent out scouts, who returned from the appointed place of rendezvous with report that the Hanqu were nowhere in evidence.

Mara took this news badly: that her proposed meeting with Lord Xaltepo was unequivocally fiction, and more probably a Minwanabi plot. She fretted, too tired to keep still even in the heat, and worried now for more than Kevin's hurts.

"Tasaio does not strike just once," she complained to Lujan, as the gloom of twilight fell around the firelit encampment of warriors. "Though our wounded will suffer for being moved, we must return home tonight."

Her Force Commander did not argue the necessity, but strode off and mustered his warriors and efficiently made arrangements to depart. Battle-weary and bandaged, the three survivors from Mara's original guard were given places of honor at the head of the march. Kevin and two litter-borne wounded were carried next, and after them, the honorably slain. Mara insisted on staying afoot. Her bearers lived, but with their trained ability to manage burdens without jostling, they were assigned to carry the injured. The Lady of the Acoma walked beside her unconscious body slave. Kevin had been given a draft for his pain that left him deeply asleep. She held his unbandaged hand and alternated between aching sorrow and fury.

She had not heeded warnings that Tasaio might have compromised Arakasi's network. She had seen only her growing power, had been lured into thinking that because she was now Clan Warchief, it was her natural due that lesser families should clamor for her favor. Nacoya had cautioned her; Keyoke had most pointedly avoided a confrontation with her, precisely that he could be free to forestall the disaster of the trap she had foolishly conceded to Tasaio.

Twenty-seven good warriors from her honor guard were dead. Lujan had lost another twelve in the course of her rescue, and Kevin might never walk again without a limp.

The price was far too high.

Mara clenched her hand, then belatedly relaxed her grip; she squeezed only Kevin, who had stood as staunchly as any of her warriors. She did not feel the stones under her feet, or notice the occasional hand on her elbow as Lujan steadied her over the gullies. She barely noticed the coming and going of the scout patrols, as they repeatedly swept the surrounding woods for enemies; she thought only upon the shame of her own false pride; and she wondered, over and over, what she would say to Arakasi.

The moon set. The darkness under the trees matched the darkness in Mara's heart as she marched numbly, dwelling long and hard on recriminations until she reached the borders of her estate.

Another patrol of soldiers awaited her there, armed and carrying torches. Mara was weary enough that it took her a moment to realize the anomaly of this added company's presence. Lujan was speaking with the Patrol Leader, and as she heard Ayaki's name, a chill washed over her, fright jolting her alert.

She pushed away from Kevin's litter and hurried to her Force Commander's side. "What has happened to my son?"

Lujan caught her shoulders firmly. "He is alive, my Lady."

That reassurance did not blunt the edge of Mara's urgency. Even in the wind-caught flicker of the torch light, the reporting Patrol Leader's face showed strain. Terrified that the disaster that had overtaken her might not have been confined to the glen, Mara demanded, "Has there been an attack upon my house?"

"My Lady, an assassin was sent." The Patrol Leader tersely bowed. Trained by Keyoke to be concise, he delivered the news like a battle report. "Ayaki suffered a minor cut, but is otherwise unharmed. Two nurses died, and Nacoya, First Adviser, was killed in the child's defense. The estate grounds have been searched, with no sign of other enemies found. The assassin apparently stole in alone. Keyoke reinforced all border patrols and sent us to bolster your escort."

But Mara heard none of the details, past knowledge that Ayaki had suffered hurt and that Nacoya, who had been a mother to her since childhood, was dead. Her knees felt weak, and her mind was shocked past thinking. She did not feel the arm that Lujan slipped under her elbow to steady her. She heard but did not comprehend the words her Force Commander said to the Patrol Leader, dispatching a runner to fetch a replacement litter.

Nacoya was dead, and Ayaki injured. She needed Kevin's arms around her, and the comfort of his love through this nightmare; but he lay bandaged in a litter, unconscious from a healing draft.

Mara stumbled forward. The night felt bitterly desolate. Trouble seemed to roost unseen in the dark, and the road through her own prayer gate seemed menacing with unnamed danger.

"I must go home," she said blankly.

"Lady, we shall take you there with all haste." Lujan snapped orders to his company, and the patrol integrated with the guard already surrounding the Lady and her wounded and dead. Then, without awaiting the runner's return with the litter, the warriors marched for the estate house.

Mara hurried in a numb haze of disbelief. Nacoya was dead; that fact seemed incomprehensible. The Lady felt she ought to be crying. Instead, she could not see past placing one stumbling foot in front of the other. She was aware of the Patrol Leader giving the details of the assassin's raid to Lujan, but inside her head she could hear only Nacoya's voice, scolding and scolding her for folly, vanity, and headstrong actions.

Ayaki had been injured.

Her heart cried out in outrage, anger, and grief, that one so little should ever be threatened by the machinations of the Great Game. She thought blasphemies: Kevin was right; deaths for political gains were a senseless, cruel waste. Her sense of family honor warred outright with her pain. How narrowly Tasaio had missed ending the Acoma line in the passage of a single day!

Keyoke's wisdom, Nacoya's courage, a slave's disregard of propriety: those had been all that stood between her house and total destruction. Almost, Minwanabi had fulfilled his blood oath to Turakamu. Chills chased over Mara's flesh. She remembered the rain of arrows that had hissed over her head, even as Kevin's weight had knocked her down, out of the way. She hurried faster, and did not protest when the litter at last arrived and Lujan caught her up in his arms and bundled her inside without pause to break his stride.

These bearer slaves were fresh. Mara signaled Lujan to appoint an honor guard and let the other soldiers escorting the wounded and dead proceed more slowly. Distraught beyond restraint, she screamed for the slaves to sprint the last quarter mile to the lighted hall of the estate house.

Keyoke met her there, grim and wearing armor from the waist up. He had donned his old helm, shorn of plumes, and his sword was strapped to his side, prepared for the worst if word came back that his mistress had been killed in the forest.

Mara stumbled out of her litter before Lujan could catch her hand. She flung herself into the arms of the old warrior, and with her cheek against his hard breastplate, she fought to hold back tears.

Keyoke stood staunch on his crutch, and his free hand stroked her hair. "Mara-anni," he said in his deep voice, using the diminutive as a father might address a beloved daughter. "Nacoya died most bravely. She will be sung into the halls of Turakamu with all of the honors of a warrior and make proud the Acoma name."

Mara repressed a deep, shuddering sob. "My son," she gasped. "How is he?"

Over her bent head, the Adviser for War and Lujan exchanged a quick look. Needing no words, the Force Commander gently took Mara's elbow and eased her weight off Keyoke.

"We shall go at once to see Ayaki," the older adviser said. He pointedly did not ask after her crumpled appearance, or the evidence of bloodstains on her robe. "Your son sleeps, attended by Jican. The cut on his neck was attended to promptly, but he lost a lot of blood. He will be well enough in time, but you should know: we could not stop his crying. He has had a terrible shock."

Mara froze, resisting all attempts to lead her away. "Kevin," she said frantically. "I want him brought to my chambers and tended there."

"Lady," Lujan said firmly. "I already presumed to give orders to that end." He caught her more firmly around the waist and propelled her into the corridor that led to her chambers. Someone thoughtful, probably Jican, had ordered every lamp lit, so no step she took was in shadow.

Again the eyes of Force Commander and Adviser for War met. Keyoke knew that Mara's party had suffered ambush; he was impatient to hear the details. Lujan nodded in wordless indication that he would relate the event, but out of Mara's hearing. She had grief enough on her heart without being made to endure a repetition of the day's unpleasantness.

They reached her private apartments. The screens were opened wide and attended by a dozen armed warriors. Inside, half-lost in a sea of cushions, a small figure lay with white bandages wrapped around his neck. Someone sat with him; Mara did not look to see whom, but pulled herself out of Lujan's hold and fell to her knees by her child. She touched him, transparently surprised by his warmth. Then, tenderly cautious of his hurts, she gathered him into her arms. She wept then, beyond all control, and her tears rinsed Ayaki's cheek.

Her officers averted their faces in staunch disregard of her shame, and the person on the cushions tactfully rose to leave.

Mara glanced through brimming eyes and identified Jican. "Stay," she said shakily. "All of you, stay. I don't want to be here alone."

For a very long time the lanterns burned, while she sat and rocked her young son.

Later in the night, after Kevin had been placed on a mat by Ayaki's side, Mara ordered the lights put out. She dismissed Keyoke, Jican, and Lujan to their long-deserved rest, and, guarded by a relief watch of warriors at every entrance to the house, she sat in silent vigil over her loved ones. She thought, and saw too clearly where selfishness had steered her near to ruin. Her arrogant assumption of the Clan Warchief's seat now seemed the act of an idiot.

She did not undress for bed, though the healer who came periodically to check on his two charges begged her to take a draft to bring rest. Her eyes stung unpleasantly from crying, and she did not wish the oblivion of sleep. Guilt weighted upon her heart, and too many thoughts upon her mind. At dawn she gathered her courage, rose stiffly from her cushions, and left her room and her loved ones. Alone, watched only by her guarding soldiers, she moved like a waif through darkened corridors to the nursery, where the body of the woman who had raised her had been laid on a bier of honor.

Nacoya's bloody robes had been changed for rich silks bordered by Acoma green. Her wrinkled old hands lay at peace by her side, sheathed in soft leather gloves to hide the cruel cuts from the assassin's cord, and the knife that had slain her rested on her breast, as badge of homage to Tura-kamu that she had died a warrior's death. Her face, nested in silver-white hair, seemed more peaceful than it ever had in sleep. Cares and arthritis and hairpins that never stayed straight could not trouble her now. Her loyal years of service were over.

Mara felt fresh tears spring under her swollen eyelids. "Mother of my heart," she murmured. She sank to the cushions beside the dead woman and gathered up one cold hand.

She fought and steadied her voice. "Nacoya, know your name shall be honored with the ancestors of the Acoma, and your ashes shall be spread inside the walls of the sacred glade, within the garden of the natami. Know the blood you spilled today was Acoma blood, and that you are as family and kin." Here Mara paused as her breath caught. She raised her face in the grey light through the screens and looked out into the mist that clothed the lands of her people.

"Mother of my heart," she resumed, shamefully unsteady, "I did not listen to you. I was selfish, and arrogant, and careless, and the gods took your life for my folly. But hear me: I can still learn. Your wisdom lives yet in my heart, and on the morrow when your ashes are delivered to the gods, I will swear this promise: I will send the barbarian Kevin away, and write a betrothal contract to Shinzawai asking for marriage with Hokanu. These things I will do before the season turns, wise one. And to my sorrow, to the end of my days, I will regret that I chose not to heed while you were alive at my side."

Mara gently laid the withered hand back at the dead woman's side. "Not enough did I tell you this, Nacoya: I loved you well, mother of my heart," she ended, "and I thank you for the life of my son."

24. BREAKTHROUGH

The drums stilled.

Silence fell over the grounds of the Acoma estate for the first time since the funeral rites three days past. The priests of Turakamu summoned for the occasion packed their clay masks and departed in single-file procession. Only the red bunting on the front door posts remained as a visible reminder of the recently departed; but to Mara the estate house would never again seem the secure haven she recalled from her childhood.

She was not alone in her disquiet. Ayaki cried himself to sleep nights; Kevin rested beside him, a strange ghostly figure in white bandages, who cheered him when he could with stories, called servants to light lanterns when the boy lay trembling in the dark, and calmed him when he woke up distraught from nightmares. Mara sat often at the boy's bedside, quiet, or speaking desultorily with Kevin. She tried to ignore the twelve warriors who stood guard at each window and door. Now she could not pass even the shadows beneath the shrubs in her gardens without looking sideways for assassins.

After an exhaustive search, Lujan's trackers had discovered the dead assassin's trail onto her estate; the killer had taken time to complete his infiltration, here spending a night in a tree, and there leaving a depression under a hedge where he had lain for hours, waiting motionless for a break between patrols or a servant to pass. Plainly Tasaio of the Minwanabi had reversed his tactics since the Night of the Bloody Swords. Where numbers and sheer force had failed before, his most recent attempt had been furtive, involving just a single man. Lujan did not have soldiers enough to beat every bush and vine and fence row daily to search for lurking intruders. The Acoma sentries had not been the least bit lax; simply, the estate lands were too wide and too open to be maintained in flawless security.

Nacoya and a patrol of brave warriors were ashes, but aching failure lingered in Mara's mind. A week passed before she steadied enough to ask for Arakasi.

The hour was late evening, and Mara sat in her study beside a nearly untouched supper tray. Her request for the Spy Master's presence had been carried by her little runner slave, who now bowed until his forehead touched the waxed floor.

"Lady," he said, still prone. "Your Spy Master is not here. Jican regrets to inform you that he left your lands within the hour after the attack upon your person and son. He told no one of his destination, nor did he give a date for his return."

Seated on her cushions under the hot lamplight, Mara stayed motionless for so long that the slave boy began to tremble.

She stared at the painted murals commissioned by her last husband, Buntokapi, the ones that depicted bloody battle scenes in rioting brilliance. From the rapt look on Mara's face, she appeared to be seeing them for the first time. It was most unlike the mistress not to notice her slave boy's discomfort, for she was fond of him, and patted him often on the head when he rendered quick service.

"Lady?" he offered timorously, when minutes passed and his knees began to ache.

Mara stirred and came back to herself. She realized the moon stood well up in the sky beyond the screen, and the wicks burned low in her oil lamps. "You may retire," she bade with a sigh.

The boy scurried from the room in grateful haste. Mara continued as she was, while servants entered and removed the untouched dishes. But she waved away the maids who expected her to retire, and stayed toying with a dry quill pen, a blank parchment sheet spread before her. Hours passed, and she did not write. Night insects sang in the garden beyond the screens, and the relief watch changed guard at midnight.

It simply was not conceivable that Arakasi was a traitor; and yet, in low words, members of her household suggested so. Mara twisted the pen, anguished. She had delayed any formal summons, hoping the man would present himself and prove beyond any question he had no part in Tasaio's attempt on her house. Keyoke had stayed closemouthed on the subject, and the usually outspoken Saric was reluctant to speak. Even Jican took care not to linger for a chat after his reports on estate finance. Mara tossed the quill pen aside and massaged her temples with her fingers.

It was most painfully plain that Arakasi could be suspect.

Were he to turn coat, her danger was multiplied. Over the years, he had been entrusted with her household's deepest secrets. There was no aspect of her affairs that he did not know intimately. And he detested the Minwanabi as she did.

Or did he?

Mara sweated in torment. If his desire for revenge had been an act, what better ploy to gain her confidence than to revile the same enemy that had ruined her father and brother?

Arakasi, who was so gifted at changing roles and guises; he was a consummate actor, easily capable of feigning passionate hatred.

Mara closed her eyes and recalled conversations between herself and Arakasi over the years. The man *couldn't* have betrayed her. Could he? She sighed, indulging herself in that simple release in the privacy of her quarters. She was certain in her heart that Arakasi couldn't be a Minwanabi agent; the hatred for Tasaio and his family was too real, but could someone else have turned the Spy Master? Someone who could, perhaps, offer Arakasi a better position from which to conduct his war against the Minwanabi? With the price for that more secure position the Acoma's betrayal?

Mara's fingers tightened until they left white marks on her flesh. If the Spy Master was the real in her nest, everything she had done was for naught. At this moment Nacoya's carping would have been welcome, a sign that errors could be rectified.

But the old woman was now ashes, dust amid the dust of a thousand Acoma ancestors whose honor Mara was entrusted to keep.

Again she tormented herself with the question: How

could she have held such a deep, instinctive rapport with a man who wished her harm? How could she?

The night held no answers.

Mara dropped tired hands in her lap and regarded her abandoned quill pen. Though the lamps blazed brightly around her, and her best guards stood vigilant at her door, she felt cornered. With a hand that shook distressingly, she reached out and took up pen and parchment. She scraped dried ink from the nib, dipped it in the waiting ink jar, and wrote in formal style in the center of the top of the page the name of Kamatsu of the Shinzawai.

An extended interval passed before she could force herself to continue. Neither could she simplify her pain by sending a servant to fetch her scribe. Her promise to Nacoya was sacred. In her own hand, she completed the ritual phrases of the proposal for marriage, asking Kamatsu's honored son, Hokanu of the Shinzawai, to reconsider after her former refusal, and take her hand as consort of the Lady of the Acoma.

Tears welled in Mara's eyes as she reached the final line, added her signature, and affixed her family chop. She folded and sealed the document quickly, clapped for a servant, and gave her instructions with her throat tight with emotion.

"Have this paper delivered at once to the marriage brokers in Sulan-Qu. They are to present it with all speed to Kamatsu of the Shinzawai."

The servant accepted the paper and bowed before his mistress. "Lady Mara, your will shall be carried out at first light."

Mara's brows gathered instantly into a frown. "I said, at once! Find a messenger and send the document with all speed!"

The servant prostrated himself on the floor. "Your will, Lady."

She waved him impatiently away. If she noted his quick and puzzled glance at the darkness beyond the screen, she did not call him back in allowance for the unreasonable hour. If she delayed the proposal to Kamatsu until morning, she knew well, she would not be able to send the document on at all. Better the messenger stand a few hours in the dark, waiting for the broker to arise, than risk another opportunity to change her mind and break her vow.

The chamber suddenly seemed too stifling, and the scent of the akasi cloying. Mara shoved her writing table aside. Filled with a desperate need to see Kevin, she stumbled to her feet and hurried down the lit corridors, past rows of vigilant guards, to the nursery wing.

At the entrance, half-blind in the sudden dark, Mara hesitated. She blinked back a fresh flood of tears and waited for her eyes to adjust; the pungent healer's herbs and poultice scents lay heavily upon the air. Finally she crossed the threshold.

Moonlight turned the closed screen copper and carved the rows of watchful warriors outside into dark silhouettes. In no way comforted by their vigilance, Mara made her way to the mat where Kevin lay, his bandages white smears in the gloom, and his torso twisted in the sheets as though his rest had been troubled. She paused, looked to Ayaki, and reassured herself that the boy was more settled, asleep with his mouth open, his hands half-curled on his pillow. The scratch on his neck was healing more quickly than Kevin's hurts, which had been treated less promptly in the field. But the assassin had left more lasting marks on the little boy's mind. Relieved he did not suffer another nightmare, Mara moved past, careful not to disturb him. She dropped to her knees by Kevin's mat and tugged to disentangle his limp weight from the constricting snarl of the bedclothes.

He stirred at her touch and opened his eyes. "Lady?"

Mara silenced his murmur with her lips.

Kevin reached up left-handed and captured her around the waist. Strong despite his injuries, he pulled her to him. "I've missed you," he whispered into her hair. His hand moved, and under his practiced manipulation, her light lounging robe fell open.

Mara buried her grief and strove to match his light humor. "My healer threatened dire consequences if I came to your bed and tempted you past restraint. He said your wounds could still open."

"Damn him for being a grandmother," Kevin said amiably. "My scabs do well enough, except when he chooses to pick at them." Sure and warm, the Midkemian stroked her breast with the back of his fingers. Then he hugged her tighter. "You're my cure, all by yourself."

Mara shivered, half from sadness, half from poignant

arousal. She banished the painful wish that the marriage contract to Hokanu could be recalled, and snuggled closer.
"Kevin," she began.

From her tone, he realized she was anguished. He gave
her no chance to speak, but leaned across and kissed her. Her
arms clasped him around the shoulders, avoiding his bandages. Kevin cradled her, instinctively offering her what his
soul knew she needed; and in familiar and natural companionship, they lapsed into lovemaking. His enthusiasm seemed
in no way diminished, except that he fell asleep very quickly
after his passion was spent.

Mara stretched out at his side, her eyes wide open in the
dark. She ran her hands over her flat belly, much aware that
her tryst in the nursery had not been planned with propriety.
She had taken no elixir of teriko weed, to prevent conception.
Nacoya would have been shrill with reprimand over the
lapse.

Nacoya would have been wise.

By the dim, filtered moonlight, Mara studied Kevin's profile, nested amid a tangle of red hair. She found she did not
wish to be wise. Marry Hokanu she must, if Kamatsu would
allow, and he would have her; but if Kevin was to be sacrificed, she did not possess the will to relinquish his love and
her happiness without any trace of a tie.

Foolish she might be, even selfish. But she wanted Kevin's
child. All she had accomplished had been for the honor of
her family name and ancestry. Her heart felt battered, eaten
up by rulership's endless griefs. This one thing she had to
have for herself.

"I love you, barbarian," she whispered soundlessly in the
dark. "I shall always love you." Her tears flowed freely, for a
very long time after that.

A week passed, and another week, and the healer permitted
Kevin short bouts out of bed. He found Mara seated in the
east garden, the one the kitchen staff used for growing herbs.
Clad in the light, loose robes she habitually used for meditation, she had set her discipline aside to sit amid dusty stems
of aromatic plants and watch the front road. Messengers
came and went, mostly on Jican's errands. Whether she stud-

ied the traffic or whether she was lost in thought did not matter.

"You're moping again," Kevin accused, setting aside the cane he used to keep his weight off the leg that had taken the sword cut.

Mara twisted a mangled bit of greenery between her hands. It had once been a slender tira branch, now wilted, stripped entirely of its spicy leaves. Peeled strips of bark emitted a heady, pungent odor on the noon-heated air. The Lady who tortured the sprig did not answer.

Kevin settled with some difficulty beside her, his wrapped leg stretched out before him. He lifted the poor stem from her hands, and sighed at the sap beneath her fingernails.

"She was a mother to me, and more," Mara said unexpectedly.

"I know." He did not need to ask if she spoke of Nacoya. His response was gentle. "You need to cry more, spill your grief out and let it go."

Mara stiffened, sharp-edged. "I've cried enough!"

Kevin tilted his head to one side and shoved his fingers through unruly hair. "Your people never cry enough," he contradicted. "Uncried tears remain inside you, like poison."

He did not intend to drive Mara away; but she rose abruptly and he could not regroup in time to follow, not with his leg bound in splints. By the time he reached his feet, found his cane, and pursued, she had disappeared through the hedges. He decided it would be tactless to give chase. Tonight, in bed, he would try once again to console her. But forgetting the tragedy that had upset her was not possible, with soldiers in armor standing guard almost everywhere one stepped. The assassin might not have killed Ayaki, but the event had left other damage. Troubled, withdrawn in unhappiness, Mara could find no peace within the walls of her own home.

Kevin shuffled out of the herb garden and decided to seek out young Ayaki. In a sheltered courtyard, out of sight of the house servants, he had been teaching the boy how to fight with a knife. It might be forbidden for a slave to handle weapons, but on the Acoma estate none would interfere. True Tsurani, they all looked away from this latest breach of protocol. Kevin's loyalty was proven, and he reasoned that the boy might stop screaming from bad dreams if he learned a few tricks in self-defense.

But today the courtyard was not deserted when Kevin arrived with a purloined kitchen knife and the Acoma heir in tow. Keyoke rested in the shade under the ulo, two wooden practice swords between his knees. He saw Kevin, and the contraband, and a rare smile creased his eyes. "If you are going to train the young warrior, someone should be on hand to see that the job is done properly."

Kevin grinned insouciantly. "The lame leading the lame?" He looked down, ruffled Ayaki's dark hair, and laughed. "What do you say, little tiger, to the idea of beating up two old men?"

Ayaki responded with an Acoma battle cry that caused the servants within earshot to dive for cover.

Mara heard the shout from the secluded corner of the kekali garden where she had chosen to make her retreat. The corners of her mouth lifted with the barest trace of amusement, and then stilled; her melancholy stayed in force. The sun beat down, sucking life and the color from the glade. The bushes seemed grey in the glare, the deep indigo flowers scorched at the edges from the heat. Mara paced the walkways, fingering her mourning robe's red tassels. Almost, she seemed to hear Nacoya's ghost behind her.

"Daughter of my heart," the old woman seemed to say, *"you are foolish and thrice to be pitied if you persist with this idea of bearing a child to Kevin. A messenger will be returning from the marriage broker's anyday with word from Kamatsu of the Shinzawai. Dare you enter into marriage with the son of an honorable house while carrying a slave's baby? To do so would shame the Acoma name past all mending."*

"Then I will tell Hokanu outright whether or not I am with child," Mara interrupted the imaginary voice.

She stepped around a gardener who raked away dead growth, and meandered aimlessly down another path. Behind her, the servant set his tool aside and followed.

"Lady," called a voice as soft as velvet.

Mara's heart missed a beat. With the blood gone cold in her veins, she slowly turned around. Fear raised a sweat on her body. She examined the servant in his sun-faded robes:

Arakasi . . . With a grace quite outside the ordinary, he approached holding a dagger. As a cry of alarm was almost on her lips, he prostrated himself on the gravel path and held out the blade, hilt first.

"Mistress," said Arakasi, "I beg your permission to take my life with my dagger."

Mara stepped involuntarily back, numbed by shock. "Some say you betrayed me," she blurted, clumsily, without thought. Her words were accusingly rough.

Almost, Arakasi seemed to flinch. "No, mistress, never that. He paused, then added in a tortured tone, "I failed you." He was gaunt. The gardener's robe hung awkwardly over his shoulders, and his hands were drawn as old parchment. His fingers did not shake.

Suddenly desperate for shade, or any sort of surcease from the sun, Mara swallowed. "I trusted you."

Arakasi moved no muscle, unmercifully exposed by the daylight; all of his deceptions seemed stripped away. He looked like an ordinary servant, worn, honest, and frail. Mara had never noticed before the attenuated bone structure of his wrists. He said, his voice as whipped as his appearance, "The five spies in the Minwanabi household are dead. By my order, they were killed, and the tong that I hired brought me their heads as surety. Eleven agents that passed their messages from Szetac Province lie dead also. Those men I killed with my own hand, mistress. You have no spies in your enemy's house, but neither does Tasaio have any avenue left to exploit. No one lives who might be forced to betray you. Again, I beg leave to make atonement for myself. Allow me to take my life by the blade."

He did not expect her to grant his request; he had been no more than a grey warrior, once, and not born to service in her house.

Mara stepped back again and sat sharply upon a stone bench. Her sudden movement attracted her sentries' attention, and several came running to investigate. The officer in charge spotted the servant at her feet and recognized him for her Spy Master. The warrior signaled, and his small patrol closed at a run. A heartbeat later, armored hands seized Arakasi's outstretched wrists. Very fast, they had him dragged upright and pinioned.

"Lady, what should we do with this man?" The Patrol Leader briskly demanded.

Mara watched, quite silent. The warriors, she noticed, handled their prisoner with care, as if he carried poison, or as though he might somehow strike back. Her gaze shifted to encompass Arakasi's still face and his hollowed, shadowed eyes. No secrets lingered there. The Spy Master seemed an empty husk, all his spirit sucked out of him. He expected an ending, a hanging, and his mien was desolate. The fire and the pride that, along with a razor-sharp intellect, had marked him apart were missing.

"Let him go," she said dully.

The soldiers obeyed without question. Arakasi lowered his arms, twitching his sleeves back into place out of habit. He stood with bowed head, and a seemingly endless patience that was painful to observe.

If he was acting, his extraordinary talent had her beaten.

The air seemed sluggish and heavy as Mara dragged in her breath. "Arakasi," she said slowly. Almost, she waited for a carping voice to raise protest; then she remembered. Nacoya was dead. She pushed on with the matter at hand. "You served as you saw fit. You and your network provided intelligence; you never guaranteed facts. You have not made decisions. I, as your ruler, decide. If there has been failure, or misjudgment, the blame must be mine alone. Therefore, you shall not be permitted to take your life with your dagger. Instead, I ask pardon for my shame, for demanding more than a loyal man should ever be expected to deliver. Will you still serve me? Will you continue to maintain your network, and bring ruin to the Lord of the Minwanabi?"

Arakasi slowly straightened. His eyes grew penetrating, disquietingly, uncomfortably direct. Through the sun's glare, and the dusty scent of the flowers, he appeared to see through flesh and read her invisible spirit. "You are not like the other rulers in this Empire," he said, the velvet restored to his voice. "If I could dare to venture an opinion, I'd say you were quite dangerously different."

Mara lowered her eyes first. "You may be right." She twisted the jade rings on her hands. "Will you still serve?"

"Always," Arakasi said at once. He released a long, audible sigh. "I have news, if you would hear it."

"Later. You may go now, and refresh yourself." When

Mara looked up, she watched her Spy Master off, the spring in his step rejuvenated as he hurried away down the path.

"How did you determine he was innocent?" asked a patrol leader, just past his youth.

Mara shrugged slightly. "I didn't. But I looked at him, and remembered his formidable competence at his job." She arose before her puzzled warriors, her eyes almost distant with thought. "Do you think, if such a man wanted me dead, that he would have bungled the task? If he were Tasaio's agent, or someone else's, the Acoma natami would be no more. This I believe. So I trust him."

Twilight threw a mantle of silver-green light over the garden when Arakasi reappeared to make his report. He had eaten and bathed, and now wore a house servant's robe, tied with a crested green sash. His sandals were laced with meticulous perfection, and his hair had been freshly trimmed. Mara noticed these details as he bowed, and other servants walked softly around her, lighting the first lamps of the evening.

He straightened, slightly hesitant. "My Lady, your faith in me is not misplaced. I say again, as I did once before, that I would see your enemies dead and their names obliterated. Since the moment I swore by your natami, I have been wholly Acoma."

Mara received this reaffirmation in considerate silence. At length she clapped for a servant and asked for a tray of fresh sliced fruit. When she and her Spy Master were alone once more, she said, "I have not questioned your loyalty."

Arakasi frowned and struck to the heart of the matter. "It is important to me as my life that you do not." He looked at her, his dark eyes for once unshadowed. "Lady, you are one of the few rulers in this Empire who thinks past ancient traditions and the only one willing to challenge them. I might have come to serve you once out of shared hatred for the Minwanabi. But now that has changed. I serve for you alone."

"Why?" Mara's own gaze flashed up, also free of any posturing.

The shadows of the lamps darkened as the sky deepened overhead. Arakasi made a gesture of impatience. "You are not afraid of change," he observed. "That one bold trait is going to take you far, perhaps even make your house last-ingly great." He paused, and a startlingly genuine smile lit his face. "I want to be there, be part of that rise to power. The power itself does not interest me. But what can be done with it—there I admit to shameful ambition. Times of great change are upon us, and this Empire has stayed settled in its ways for many centuries too long." He sighed. "I do not know what can be done to alter our fate, but in more than fifty years of life, I have met no other ruler more able to accomplish reform."

Mara released a quiet breath. For the first time since she had known the man, she realized that she had pierced through his reserve. At long last, she looked upon the real motive that drove her most enigmatic adviser. Master of deceit, Arakasi sat now stripped of deception. His face showed the longing of an excited boy, and with that, she saw also that he cared deeply for her, and would provide her with anything she might ask. At last convinced that Nacoya had been right, that there were limits beyond which no ruler should press a loyal heart to perform, she smiled. In the most banal tone she could manage, she said, "You mentioned you had news?"

Arakasi's eyes sparkled with sudden enthusiasm. He reached for a fruit slice and opened: "The magicians have been very busy with a plot of their own, it appears. The rumors are intriguing, and almost beyond imagination."

Settled back on her cushions in relief, Mara waved for him to continue.

Finishing his snack with a neat swallow, Arakasi licked his teeth. "It's very thought-provoking. The word is that ten Great Ones from the Assembly went through the rift to Midkemia, along with three thousand Kanazawai warriors. A battle was fought, and wild speculation abounds concerning why. Some say the Emperor wished vengeance upon the King of Isles for the traitorous slaughter at the peace talks." Here the Spy Master held up a hand to forestall his mistress's eager questions. "That's not the unbelievable motive. Others say—persons in reliable offices—that the Magicians made war upon the Enemy."

Mara looked blank.

"The Enemy," Arakasi repeated. "The one from the

myths before the Golden Bridge. Surely your teachers recited stories to you as a child."

Recalling those tales, recognition dawned. "But those are fables!" Mara protested. She glanced around at the lamps, as if the shadows they cast might suddenly have grown larger and darker. "Not real."

Arakasi shook his head, mystified and excited at the same time. "So we thought," he agreed. "But who can rightly guess what enemies might challenge the Great Ones, particularly since the renegade, Milamber, had his name mixed up in the events? Those myths are older than history, as ancient as the names of the brothers who began the Five Families. How can we judge what is truth in that long-distant past?"

Suddenly poignantly troubled, Mara bit her lip. "Kanazawai were involved? Then we can inquire what has passed when I hear from Lord Kamatsu." Her thoughts skipped ahead. "We could surmise that the Emperor's interference with the council might have been in cooperation with this action of the Magicians."

"So I presume." Arakasi helped himself to another slice of fruit. "But that's speculation. My sources closest to the Light of Heaven suggest negotiations may be under way for an exchange of prisoners between the Empire and the Kingdom of the Isles."

"So the rift is opened!" Mara cut in. Her voice held a strangely emotional note.

Rightly attributing that to some concern with her barbarian lover, Arakasi coughed lightly. "None of what I tell is common knowledge. But it would seem that if you applied again for a hearing in the right places, you might be able to gain the benefits of your trade concessions with Midkemia, at last."

Mara seemed only distantly interested in a subject that had once been a hot source of frustration. Arakasi tactfully used the interval to clean off the last fruit on the tray. He recalled Mara and Kevin's discussion of the rift in Kentosani; the subject had revolved around granting the barbarian his freedom. Cued by shrewd intuition, Arakasi knew the idea was emotionally painful.

"I will probe the issue for you, Lady, and try to find more facts."

Mara shot him a glance of wordless gratitude. "For

Kevin's sake," she said in a small voice. "He does not deserve to stay a slave."

As if shrugging off the torments of unseen ghosts, the Lady changed the subject. "If power continues to shift away from the council, there will be upheavals. Minwanabi will consolidate his allies and make a bid to revive the Warlord's office."

She sighed, frowned, and added, "It would be nice if all of us were alive to enjoy the gains of my exclusive trade rights." Then her eyes narrowed. "You had spies killed under Tasaio's own roof, you said. Why, then, does our enemy still breathe?"

Arakasi settled his elbows on his knees like a killwing ruffling feathers. "My arm is not long enough to reach beneath Tasaio's roof to take his head—but his servants? They are a long and different story."

In the soft summer night, under a brilliance of lanterns and stars, he told her.

The servants were discovered, finally, in a lime pit in a vegetable garden that was occasionally used for burials to enrich the soil; only the dishonored were interred there, without rites, and where the stink of decomposition would not waft beyond the domestics' quarters. The five corpses were headless, and when the runner boy who made the find reported it to one of the overseers, the older staff member understood at once that the master must be informed. Shaking in the knees, and ducking his white head in consternation, he hastened off to report to Murgali.

The Minwanabi hadonra was hunched over ledgers stacked precariously high, doing his best to stay inconspicuous. All the household had felt Tasaio's temper since his ambush had failed to kill Mara. Bristling at the interruption, he heard the house servant's news and cursed as he recognized its import. This matter of dead bodies was not something he dared to ignore.

"Go," he commanded the house servant. "Have the bodies removed from the garden and laid out in an empty bed suite."

As the old man left, Murgali arose, feeling tired. He chafed an arthritic wrist, put on his softest slippers, and, as soundlessly as he could shuffle, hastened to find Incomo. The Minwanabi First Adviser was perhaps the only person who could approach Tasaio with impunity. As the hadonra crossed through the corridor that led to the nursery, he clicked his tongue; even the children were quiet, as if aware of their father's lingering wrath.

Incomo was none too pleased with the interruption, either. Sitting, dripping, in his bath, with a slave girl one quarter his age sponging his stringy back, he sighed soulfully at the water that poured over his knees. "This is most inopportune," he murmured in the direction of his privates.

Murgali bobbed agreement. "Most. The corpses are being installed in an empty bed suite. My Lord can examine them there."

Then, as Incomo heaved himself up from his tub and submitted to a rubdown by a towel slave, the hadonra stole his moment to escape.

Left dry and naked and alone to carry the news, Incomo indulged in a rare string of oaths. He forwent his chance to fondle the slave girl who gave up her sponge to robe him, and that put him in a spiteful temper. He tied his tasseled belt in a quick, irritable knot and set off to locate his Lord and master.

The search carried him from the dining chambers, through the grand hall, past innumerable meeting rooms, into and out of Tasaio's personal study, the scriptorium, and an exercise chamber; he finally ended his search on the archery range that lay on the far side of the guards' barracks. By now Incomo was puffing, and sweaty as if he had not just stepped from his bath. He bowed and spoke very deliberately and loudly, that his Lord could not mistake his presence for that of another warrior.

Clad in the lightest silk robe and an incongruously battered war helm, Tasaio shot off seven arrows in rapid succession. They cracked with uncanny accuracy into a small shield's center, painted as a target, held upright by a trembling slave.

"Bodies," snapped the Lord of the Minwanabi. He punctuated the word with another arrow, loosed whistling between the slave's legs to smack into dry summer earth.

The slave flinched and forgot himself. He stepped back in white-faced terror.

Tasaio showed no change in expression. His next arrow took the hapless man exactly in the hollow of the throat. "I have told them, and told them, they are not to move!" The Lord snapped his fingers, and a servant rushed to relieve him of his bow and quiver. Tasaio stripped off his shooting glove, and his amber eyes turned to his First Adviser. "By 'bodies,' I presume that you have located the missing Acoma spies?"

Incomo swallowed. "Yes, Lord."

"Five, you said," Tasaio snapped back. "But we knew only three."

"Yes, Lord." Incomo followed the proper step behind as his master spun briskly and walked from the archery grounds.

Tasaio pulled at the knuckles of his left hand, cracking each of the joints. "I will inspect the bodies. Now."

"Of course, Lord." Incomo stretched to keep up with the taller warrior's stride, the sweat springing freely from his face. When they reached the estate house, it took him some minutes to determine which bed suite housed the corpses. Domestic staff made themselves scarce, with the master present, and he had to make too many inquiries to get answers.

Tasaio tossed his helm to a hovering slave, then spent the interval in coiled impatience. "You have not been efficient," he observed to Incomo, but fortunately he was in haste to inspect the corpses, and made no further comment. He strode the length of a painted corridor, shoved past a bowing guard, and whipped aside a screen.

The stench of corrupted flesh wafted with the breeze of his motion. Tasaio was unfazed. Apparently nerveless in the presence of horrors, he entered the bed suite and knelt to examine the dirt-streaked lumpish forms of what had once been five men.

Incomo lingered outside the door. Engaged in a silent struggle to master the heaving of his stomach, he watched his master finger the remains with long, inquisitive fingers. Tasaio ran his hand along an indentation in the neck of one body, barely a hair's breadth below where the head had been severed. "This man was strangled," he muttered. "This is the work of a tong assassin." He examined the last body and discovered a tiny cloth fragment embroidered with a red flower, hidden in the corpse's robe. "Hamoi!" He arose, showing his anger as he spun to address Incomo. "After my gifts of metal, *I should own that tong!*"

The Minwanabi First Adviser interpreted his master's glare as a warning. He bowed in instant obeisance. "Lord, your gifts were copious."

"This should not have happened!" Tasaio said in ice-cold rage. "Send a messenger at once. I would have the Tong Master before my dais to explain himself."

Incomo sank lower. "Your will, my Lord."

He could not move his old knees fast enough to avoid the shove of Tasaio's elbow as the master shouldered through the doorway.

"Send this carrion back to the lime pit, then send word to my wife," the Lord barked at the nearest servant in earshot. "Tell her I wish a bath to remove the stink of rot from my flesh."

Incomo reached his feet and considered the idea a sound one. He reflected soulfully on the little slave girl, and the delicious massage of her sponge, but the day's upheavals were not over.

From his tub, Tasaio summoned in an endless succession of servants for interrogation. Many admitted to having seen the tong assassin who had come to commit the murders; a Patrol Leader even confessed to allowing the assassin entry through one of the checkpoints in the hills at the border of the estate.

The man's explanation for allowing the murderer passage was inherently logical. "All soldiers know that my Lord purchased the tong's loyalty. The man came openly to the checkpoint, stating he was on my Lord's business, and showing a document."

Tasaio heard this with narrowed eyes and tight lips. He motioned to Incomo in the negative, and sadly the First Adviser instructed the house scribe to write the warrior's name on the list for immediate execution. The soldier would be dead before Tasaio was dry from his bath.

The Lady Incarna continued mechanically to sponge her husband's back, but her cheeks were wax-white, and she looked sick around the eyes. Like a puppet on strings she soaped the lean muscular shoulders of the Lord of the Minwanabi over and over, until Tasaio tired of her attentions and snapped suddenly to his feet. Incarna dropped her sponge with a splash into the bath water and snatched back with a startled cry.

"Silence, woman!" Tasaio jerked his wet head, and towel slaves flew to attend him.

The guild messenger could not have chosen a worse moment for arrival, nor could the servant who scratched at the doorway to announce the man's presence in the foyer, awaiting the master's attendance.

In no mood to hurry, but impatient with his dresser nonetheless, Tasaio snatched the lightweight but heavily embroidered robe from his body servant. He flipped it over his shoulders, held out his hand for his shell-decorated belt, then accepted the black-lacquered sheaths of his sword and dagger newly threaded on a soft needra-hide baldric. A slave laced on his sandals, and he finished his dressing with a light, padded jacket sewn with bone rings that offered the same protection as light armor without being as cumbersome.

"Send the messenger to me in my personal armory," he instructed his runner. Then he motioned for Incomo to follow and strode out, leaving his wife to oversee the slaves in the bath chamber as if her standing were no higher than an overseer's.

The Minwanabi Lord's armory was a small, windowless chamber with sanded wood walls, laid out with pegs for swords and stands for storing body armor. Tasaio's single personal indulgence since becoming Ruling Lord had been to purchase extravagant sets of arms for himself, some plain and deadly, designed for the rigors of war, others resplendent with lacquer and chasing, for dress occasions; yet a third variety was thin and strong and without fluting, designed to be secretly worn under clothing. Tasaio roved from stand to stand, stroking helms and breastplates and sword hilts, then examining his fingertips for dust. The slaves and servants who attended this chamber knew well to keep it immaculate; predecessors who had failed the Lord's inspections had not survived his displeasure.

Uncomfortable in the small, airless room, Incomo compromised his uneasiness by standing farthest from the lamp, which was hot, and drew unwanted attention to his actions, should the master's narrow scrutiny fall upon him. Still as every Minwanabi servant had lately learned to become, he waited while the Lord roved from sword to sword, and helm to helm, stopping occasionally to arrange a buckle or a boss, or to finger the edge of a blade.

Tasaio was testing a dagger when the courier bowed at the door. The Lord flicked the barest glance over the man's guild badges, just enough to note the colors of the Sulan-Qu denomination. He spoke in his deceptively gentle manner. "What message do you carry?"

The man straightened. "An overture from Mara of the Acoma," he began, and silenced instantly as Tasaio whipped around in a breathtaking blur of speed.

The messenger swallowed awkwardly against the pressure of a sword tip against his throat. He looked into the eyes of the man who held the weapon, and saw there a flat lack of expression that terrified him to his soul. "My Lord," he quavered, "I am but a guild messenger hired to bear letters."

Tasaio moved no muscle. "And do you bring me a letter?" His voice had not altered a hairsbreadth.

Incomo cautiously cleared his throat. "My Lord, the guild's runner is blameless, and his life protected by oath."

"Is he?" Tasaio fired back. "Let him speak for himself."

The messenger sucked in a difficult breath. "Mara requests a meeting," he began, and stopped at a twitch from the blade.

"You will not mention that name under this roof, within these walls." Tasaio gave another light dig with the weapon, and teased a trickle of scarlet from the skin beneath the point. "What does this thrice-accursed Lady ask a meeting for? I wish no parley. I want only her death."

The messenger blinked uncomfortably. Suspecting that he reported to a madman, and convinced he would end with a cut throat, he gathered his dignity and bravely concluded the words he had been employed by his guild to deliver.

"This Lady asks that the Lord of the Minwanabi visit her estate for the purpose of a mutual discussion."

Tasaio smiled slowly. Impressed by the little man's courage, he lowered the sword, wiped the point clean on a polishing cloth, then replaced the weapon on its pegs. As an afterthought, he tossed the rag to the messenger, along with gestured permission to tend the scratch on his throat.

The guildsman lacked the effrontery to refuse; he lifted the lightly oiled cloth to his neck and began tentatively to dab. And as though no stranger were present, Tasaio resumed his inspection. Roving between items in his collection, he spoke to his adviser as if they were the only occupants of the room.

"Ah, Incomo, I believe I have frightened her badly," he said. "My ambush and my assassin might not have accomplished my ends, but Sezu's little bitch is running scared. Luck has helped her cause, but fortune never endures. She knows she cannot last another year." The Minwanabi Lord abandoned one armor stand for the next. He fingered a plated gorget as if probing for a weakness. "Perhaps the Lady offers compromise, say, a sacrifice of the Acoma name and line, in exchange for survival for her son?"

Incomo bowed with due respect. "My Lord, that is a dangerous assumption. As well as you, the Lady knows the time for compromise is past. She initiated blood feud with your uncle Jingu; and Desio made pledge to Turakamu. For the sake of her ancestors' honor, and against the Red God's displeasure, she must know she has no position from which to bargain."

Tasaio let the plates of the gorget fall with a click like the rolling of game dice. "She is desperate," he insisted. "Let her come to me here, if she has a desire to speak."

The armor room seemed stiflingly claustrophobic. Incomo risked a small movement to mop his brow, and dared another interruption. "My Lord, I hesitate to remind: the Lord Jingu underestimated the girl, and in this very home she forced a situation that required him to take his own life."

Sandals scraped lightly on waxed wood as Tasaio leaned an elbow on a fine suit of armor. The tawny eyes he fixed on his First Adviser were wide and bright in the lamplight. "I am not a coward," he said softly. "And my uncle was a fool."

Incomo nodded hasty agreement. "But even the bravest man should do better to act with caution."

Tasaio's eyes narrowed dangerously. "Do you suggest she could threaten me?" He tipped his head and spat upon the polished floor. "Here? Just because she is presently too strong to succumb to an open attack, make no mistake. It is only a matter of time before I will step in and finish her. Indeed, I should relish the chance to see my warriors sack and burn her estate. Perhaps I should use this request for parley as an opportunity to go there and study the site for assault tactics."

The guild messenger seemed uncomfortable with the turn the conversation had taken. His task as a courier required discretion, but the discussion at hand was not one he cared to witness. Rival factions might torture him to learn just what he was overhearing; his guild was well respected, but that did not make him sacrosanct for those hours with his family when he was not wearing his official badges.

Incomo mopped his brow again, but the sweat continued to trickle down his collar. Learned in the ways of three generations of Minwanabi Lords, he offered argument by his silence.

Tasaio had examined all the armor. He could not leave the chamber without confronting his First Adviser in the doorway; and Incomo stood like a rock jammed immovably in a river current when he had a point to make.

"Very well," the Lord of the Minwanabi concluded. "I will not meet the bitch on her accursed Acoma soil." To the messenger he snapped shortly, "Here is my reply. Tell the Lady I will consider a meeting, but in the open, on my lands. Let us see whether she has the courage, or the stupidity, to accept."

The messenger bowed in relief, and bolted promptly through the opening that Incomo edged aside to create. Straight as the doorjamb against his back, and canny in years, the adviser regarded Tasaio.

"My Lord, if it is trickery you have on your mind, still, I would counsel you to take care. Mara is not just a girl, but an enemy to be feared. She has united the Hadama clan, no child's task, and even were you to have her brought naked and bound before you, surrounded by your bodyguards, still, I would have you be wary."

Tasaio stared into his adviser's spaniel eyes. "I am wary," he said quietly. "Most wary of letting this matter become the obsession that it was for cousin Desio. Mara I intend to kill. But I need no grand promises to the Red God to carry the matter out, and neither will I give her ancestors the satisfaction of losing even one night's sleep over the matter. Now move aside. I would have the armory locked, now, and a light meal brought to the terrace garden down by the shore of the lake."

• • •

The Lord of the Minwanabi lingered in the terrace garden long past the hour of sunset. Great torches burned on poles in ceramic containers; a carpet had been laid over the stones, and a wooden dais brought, and upon this, Tasaio sat twirling a wine goblet between his fingers, exactly as he had while on campaign. The lake shore looked much like a war camp, with warriors in full armor performing a mock attack on a knoll overlooking the water. The soft splashes of feeding fish were interspersed with shouted commands. At Tasaio's feet sat a boy lately apprenticed to the house scribes, a sharpened chalk clutched in fingers that were tense to hide their shaking. As the Lord commented on his soldier's performance in low, half-whispered phrases, the boy scribbled down his words with a frown of desperate concentration. He was but duplicating the efforts of the scribe set to teach him the craft, but should the Lord of the Minwanabi decide to appraise his work, he could be beaten for failing to achieve some arbitrary standard.

The warriors on the rise advanced in timed unison, and, absorbed in every nuance of the drill, Tasaio did not at first notice the house runner who lay prostrate in obeisance at the top of the terrace stair. The unfortunate man had to raise his voice to catch attention.

"What is it!" Tasaio snapped, so suddenly that the scribe dropped his slate. The chalk fell bouncing across the carpet and rolled to a stop against the runner's forehead, which was pressed into the stone of the last stair.

"My great Lord, the Hamoi Tong Master has arrived in answer to your summons."

Tasaio briefly weighed the displeasures of meeting the tong and interrupting his evening battle drill. Interrogating the tong won out. "Bring him here." Then, obviously preoccupied with a subject that vexed him, he glanced at the apprentice's slates and compared the clumsy lettering to the finely practiced script of his teacher. "Take that away, and be glad I didn't order you beaten with it." Motioning to the older scribe to remain, he glanced at the soldiers on the hill.

Bowing profusely, and trying bravely not to cry despite the disgrace of a reprimand, the apprentice collected his materials. He hurried off, almost crashing into the house servant who escorted the summoned visitor to the Lord's dais.

The Tong Master, the Obajan in the ancient tongue, was a

man of immense breadth and girth, but not one ounce of fat. Save for a long scalp lock tied high and cascading down his back, he had a shaved head tattooed in patterns of red and white. His nose was flat, his skin deep tan, and his ears multiply pierced. His jewelry consisted of bone pins and rings that jingled lightly as he walked, and his belt held loops sewn into the leather, each of which held a variegated array of instruments of death: a half-dozen daggers, a weighted strangling cord, throwing stars, knuckle guards, picks, vials of poison, and a long metal sword. While considered an outlaw by Tsurani standards, he demanded the respect due a Ruling Lord from any he encountered in person. He was accompanied by two assassins, clad in black, as much of an honor guard as Tasaio would permit. The Tong Master came to Tasaio and bowed his head slightly, asking, "Are you well, my Lord?" His voice was an ominous rumble.

Tasaio ignored him for a long, pointed moment. Then he nodded once, acknowledging he was well. But the Lord of the Minwanabi did not inquire after the Tong Master's health, a pointed insult.

Silence wore on the Tong Master. As if the metal wealth he had received from the personage on the cushions suddenly left a taste like curdled milk, the chief of the tong spoke in sour tones. "What does my Lord require?"

"This: the name of the one who hired your tong to assassinate five servants in my house."

The Tong Master unwisely raised his hand. The warriors arrayed behind Minwanabi's dais instantly shifted their positions, as if to attack, causing the huge man to freeze. But he was not a slave, nor a man of weak nature. Fixing his host with a level gaze, the Master of the Hamoi tong slowly raised his hand to scratch his chin. His tone bit as he replied, "Lord Tasaio, the order was your own.

Tasaio jumped from his cushions with a speed that had the two assassins slap hands to their own swords. The Tong Master motioned for them to resume their former positions. "I?" demanded Tasaio. "I ordered this? How dare you utter such a lie!"

The Tong Master locked stares with Tasaio, his eyes narrowed in the flickering light of the torches. "Harsh words, my Lord." He hesitated an instant, as if weighing the need to take offense at the insult to his honor. "I will show you the document, with your signature and your personal chop."

Dumfounded, and clumsy for the first time in his life, Tasaio sat back down. "My personal chop?" His manner turned icy. "Let me see."

The huge man reached into his tunic and removed a parchment.

Tasaio all but snatched the item out of red-stained hands. He sliced the ribbons with his dagger, cracked the rolled document straight, and studied the contents with a frown. He twisted the paper this way and that, and barked for a slave to hold one of the torches closer, turning his back upon the Obajan. He scratched a fingernail over the ink-marked chop. "Turakamu's breath," he murmured. Then he looked up, a light of murder in his eyes. "What servant delivered this message?"

The chief of the tong picked at an earring. "No servant, my lord. The order was left in the usual place for such communication," he said calmly.

"It is a forgery!" Tasaio hissed, his hereditary Minwanabi temper breaking free of restraint. "I did not write a word of this! Nor did one of my scribes."

The Master of the Tong's face remained impassive. "You did not?"

"I just said that!" The Minwanabi Lord spun suddenly, his hand clenched fast to his sword hilt. Only a gesture from their leader prevented the assassins from again making ready to strike.

Tasaio stalked from one end of the dais to the other and rounded like a hungry predator upon the bulky figure of the Obajan. "I paid you a fortune in metal to serve me, not to wreak havoc in my own house, or to jump at the orders of any rival with the wits to forge documents! Some fool has dared to copy the Minwanabi family chop. You will find him for me. I want his head."

"Yes, Lord Tasaio." The Master of the tong touched his forehead with his left hand, signifying agreement. "I will have the message traced, and the culprit sent to you in pieces."

"See that you do." Tasaio drew his sword and slashed air with a sharp whine of sound. "See that you do. Now get out of my sight, before I give your flesh to my torturers for live experimentation."

The Tong Master said, "Seek not to anger me, Lord Tasaio." He motioned for his assassins to step back as he moved forward to confront the Minwanabi ruler. In a low voice, he said, "The Hamoi are not vassals, a fact you would do well to remember. I am the Obajan of the Hamoi. I will do this thing because *my* family has been dishonored, even as yours, not because you order it. Fate has given us a common enemy, my Lord, but *never again threaten me.*" He glanced down and Tasaio followed his gaze. Between forefinger and thumb the man held a small dagger, masked from any other's sight.

The Lord of the Minwanabi did not flinch or move away. He simply returned his gaze to the eyes of the Obajan. He knew the man had but to twitch and the blade would kill before the Minwanabi Lord could possibly raise his sword. Something like savage humor flickered in Tasaio's eyes as the Tong Master said, "I enjoy blood. It is mother's milk to me. Remember that and we may remain allies."

Tasaio turned his back, ignoring the risk, and said, "Depart in peace, Obajan of the Hamoi." His knuckles whitened upon the hilt of his sword.

The Tong Master turned away, nimbly for a man of his size, the dagger vanishing into his tunic before any other could see it. He left at good pace, his honor guards falling in on either side as he strode from the terrace, leaving a frustrated and enraged man slashing at phantoms in the air.

25. *CONFRONTATION*

Trumpets sounded.

A dozen liveried bearers carried a platform, upon which Mara firmly held the wooden railing before her. She strove to appear assured, despite the inward conviction that she looked silly wearing the newly fashioned armor of a Hadama Warchief. Unaccustomed to the stiffness of laminated-hide greaves and bracers, and decidedly ill at ease with fittings and buckles and breastplate, she reminded herself to stand erect. Keyoke and Saric had insisted that while she could continue wearing formal robes during meetings, for her first public appearance as Clan Warchief she must dress the part.

How a man could fight and swing a sword under such a weight of constricting gear, Mara could not guess. Newly appreciative of the warriors who marched in ranks behind, she led the army of Clan Hadama, nearly ten thousand strong, toward the gates of the Holy City.

Seated at her feet as befitted her rank, Kevin tried to look like a meek body slave. But with the grassy verge on either side of the road jammed with cheering, waving commoners, he could hardly repress his excitement. Speaking with his face turned up toward his mistress, so that few could hear him over the crowd's noise, he laughed. "They seem quite taken with you, my Lady."

Mara unbent enough to return a surreptitious reply. "I certainly hope so. Women warriors are rare in the Empire's history, but the few who are remembered were legendary, almost as unique as the Servants of the Empire." She attempted to shrug off her newfound notoriety. "Any mob loves a spectacle. They'd cheer no matter who stood upon this platform."

"Maybe," Kevin allowed. "But I think they sense the Empire is in danger and see you as someone they can look to with hope."

Mara regarded the people who crowded the way to the outer gate of the Holy City. All castes and trades were represented, from sunburned field workers to cart drivers, merchants, and guild masters. All seemed earnest in their approval of the Lady of the Acoma. Many shouted her name, while others waved or tossed tokens made of folded paper for luck.

Mara still looked skeptical in the face of such admiration. Kevin added, "They know who your enemy is and they are as surely aware of Tasaio's dark nature as you are. You nobles may not speak ill of one another out of courtesy, but I assure you that commoners don't share that constraint. Given the choice, they endorse the one whose policy is likely to be the more merciful. Is it yours or the Minwanabi Lord's?"

Mara forced herself to exhibit a calmness she did not feel; Kevin's logic seemed reassuring. It might even be true. But the support of the common folk would have no bearing on the outcome of the pending struggle. Aware that the next few days would find her either triumphant or dead, Mara tried not to dwell upon consequences. There could be no other choices. The attack upon her and her son had forced the issue. She must move, or maintain a defensive strategy until the day that her warriors, her guard, or her spy network failed her again, and Tasaio's blade found her heart.

On the day her father, Sezu, had fallen victim to a Minwanabi trap, he had chosen to fight to the death rather than shame his ancestry by choosing flight, and a coward's life. Mara could do no less; she had tried to precipitate events by her demand to meet with Tasaio. If he refused her, she must confront him. And yet, with no plan in mind to spare either her house or her honor, her posture was no more than bravado. As she rode in triumph on the platform at the head of Clan Hadama's war strength, her mind held a morass of fears.

"Look at that!" exclaimed Kevin.

Jerked out of morbid introspection, Mara glanced where he pointed and felt her throat tighten. An army camped to the west of the Holy City. The hills were a patchwork of colored tents and banners, which Kevin swiftly counted. After rough calculation, he said, "I guess that encampment holds fifteen thousand warriors."

Mara's initial jolt of nerves eased as she identified the banners. "That is a part of Clan Xacala. Lord Hoppara has brought the Xacatecas in strength. Others follow him." But not only her allies were present in force. Mara nodded across the river. "Look over there."

The road followed the Gagajin, and on the far bank Kevin saw another army, its tents so thickly clustered, the land bristled with banner poles. "Gods! There must be fifty, sixty thousand warriors in those hills. It looks like half the Lords of the Empire brought every man capable of wearing armor and carrying a sword."

Mara nodded, her mouth drawn grimly taut. "The issue will be decided here. Those across the river answer to Tasaio. That is the might of Clan Shonshoni, other families in vassalage, and the Minwanabi allies. I can see the banners of the Tondora and Gineisa near the river's edge. And, of course, the Ekamchi and Inrodaka have at last sided with Tasaio." She made a sweeping gesture with her hand. "I will wager Lord Keda and Tonmargu are encamped to the north of the city, with their allies, close to forty thousand swords. And I am certain beyond sight of the city another hundred thousand warriors are within a day's march. Scores of lesser families stay out of harm's way, but close enough to pick over the corpses if we come to conflict." She lowered her voice as if fearful the wrong ears might overhear her. "With so many soldiers ready to do battle, can we avoid a civil war even if we wish?"

The crowd's cheers and its festive mood of gaiety suddenly rang hollow. Aware that his Lady was trembling beneath her armor, Kevin returned a reassuring shrug. "Few soldiers are keen to kill. Give them an excuse, and they'd just as soon get drunk with one another—or indulge in a little friendly brawling. At least, that's how it is on my world."

Yet the contrast between the animated expressions he remembered from Midkemia and the masklike bearing of even the meanest beggar on Kelewan could not be ignored. Kevin kept the thought to himself, that he had never known a bunch so willing to die as these Tsurani. As long as people kept calm and didn't start insulting one another's mothers, all these factions might be able to avoid bloodshed. But if only one loud-mouthed sod got rude . . .

The thought did not bear finishing. Even with the point left unsaid, Mara would not be blind to risk. One sword drawn for honor's sake and all the Empire would shake. Could it be avoided? After witnessing the massacres that occurred on the Night of the Bloody Swords, Kevin did not care to examine the odds.

As her vanguard neared the arching city gate, the crowds of admiring gawkers fell away. Into stillness and a suddenly emptied road, a patrol of imperial warriors stepped forth to meet the Hadama entourage. Mara ordered a halt before the gate as the Strike Leader approached, his white armor with gold accents brilliant in the morning sun. "Mara of the Acoma!" he called.

Unaccustomed to the weight of the plumed helm that shaded her brow, Mara nodded careful acknowledgment.

"For what cause do you marshal Clan Hadama and bring them to the Holy City?" demanded the Emperor's officer.

From the height of her platform, Mara stared down at the arrogant young man, supremely confident of his imperial rank. At last she said, "You shame the Light of Heaven with your lack of manners."

The officer ignored the reprimand. "Lady, I will answer for my actions when Turakamu judges where I will next mount the Wheel of Life." The young man glanced first at the armies encamped upon the riverbanks, and then with pointed reproof at the warriors following after Mara's platform. "Manners are the least of our difficulties. As the gods will, many of us could encounter our fate soon enough. I have my orders." Obviously strained that he had only twenty soldiers at his back, and many thousands stood ready to answer Mara's call, he finished in blunt command. "The Imperial Force Commander insists that I hear your reason for bringing the might of Clan Hadama to the Holy City."

Making an issue of this demand could prove just the flame to ignite the conflict, Mara realized. She decided it wise to ignore the slight. "We come for council with others of our rank and station, in the interest of the Empire's well-being."

"Then proceed to your quarters, Lady of the Acoma, and know Imperial Peace is upon you. One honor guard of Acoma soldiers may accompany you, with a like number of clan soldiers for each Lord of the Hadama who joins you. But know that the Light of Heaven has ordered the Council Hall closed until he commands otherwise. Anyone who seeks entry to the palace without imperial consent will be counted traitor to the Empire. Now, if you would proceed?"

The young officer stood aside to permit passage of the Warchief's platform and her honor guard. Before resuming her march, Mara bent to Lujan and gave swift orders. "Carry word to Lord Chekowara and the others: we meet at my town house at sundown."

Her Force Commander snapped a bow. "And the warriors, mistress?"

One last time, Mara scanned the surrounding hillsides with their blanket of tents and banners, soldiers and weapons racks. "Seek out the Minwanabi standard and encamp the men as close to his lines as possible. I wish Tasaio to know that whatever he does, an Acoma dagger is poised at his throat."

"Your will, mistress." Lujan hastened to relay her orders to the appropriate subofficers, and then to assemble her honor guard. In formal state, Mara signaled for her company to continue on through the city gates. As Lord Chekowara and the other Hadama Lords moved after, each in position according to rank, she wished she had some way to allay the dread lingering in the pit of her stomach. All would be determined here, within the next few days, and still she had no idea of how she would avert the fate Minwanabi had vowed, that she and her nine-year-old heir be delivered as sacrifice to the Red God. The armor she wore seemed to weigh on her shoulders, and the crowd's shouts suddenly seemed uncomfortably loud. Was there anywhere left, she wondered, where she could go to find peace for thought?

The journey though the city to her town house left Mara feeling taxed. Attributing her fatigue to poor spirits, she postponed her initial meetings and ordered the afternoon for rest. In retrospect, the change in schedule allowed Arakasi time to seek out his agents in the city and glean what information he could. She, her Spy Master, and Lujan dined alone, discussing various ways they might move to blunt Minwanabi's ambition.

No one had any brilliant insights.

Next morning, Clan Hadama met. Within the inner garden's freshly pruned greenery, the most prominent Ruling Lords of the clan, as well as a half-dozen allies, were seated in a large circle adjacent to the central fountain. Through the trill of falling water, the Lord of the Ontara ventured opinion. "Lady Mara, rulers who have no love for Tasaio will stand with him against the Emperor, simply because Ichindar defies tradition. Many in our own clan fear an Empire ruled by one man, even if that one is the Light of Heaven. A Warlord may dominate, the gods know, yet he is still but first among equals." Others murmured agreement.

Still feeling oddly out of sorts, Mara made an effort to concentrate. Kevin's dry observations on Tsurani politics were right on one point: these men were more in love with their own prerogatives than haters of cruelty, murder, and waste. Freshly aware that her own thinking had changed to a degree incomprehensible to all but a handful of her ruling peers, Mara regarded her clansmen and allies, and strove for tact. "Those who cling to tradition blindly, or out of fear of change, are fools. To embrace Tasaio is to hold a relli to your bosom. He will take warmth and nourishment, but in the end he will kill. Allow him to blunt the Emperor's power, and you choose a worse course than absolute imperial rule. The Minwanabi Lord is a young man. He could hold the white and gold for decades. He is clever, ruthless, and, if I may speak bluntly, captivated by the pain of others. He is a clever enough player of the game that he might make question of the succession a moot issue. Almecho and Axantucai came close to creating a family office. Is the ambition of Tasaio of the Minwanabi any less?"

Several of the Lords glanced at one another, for they had been among those inclined to back Tasaio's predicted bid for the white and gold. With the Omechan Clan crushed by Axantucar's shame, the Minwanabi were left unrivaled as first claimants to the office. Lord Xacatecas was too young, and Lord Keda too closely allied with the Blue Wheel Party to gainsay the Emperor. The only possible rival bid would be

Lord Tonmargu, if the Anasati lent full support; yet Jiro was not deemed reliable—his own agenda was not yet clear, and he had plainly indicated he would not be following in his father's footsteps. More than street gossips and rumormongers were convinced that Tasaio would be the next Warlord. The more pertinent question seemed to be whether he would gain the white and gold peacefully, or by means of bloody war.

Of all present, Lord Chekowara was the only one relaxed enough to avail himself of the cakes upon the refreshment trays. Dusting crumbs from his chin, he offered his own opinion. "Mara, in all you have done since becoming Ruling Lady, you have consistently shown a brilliant ability to extemporize. May we assume that you have some unexpected twist of the rope in store for Tasaio?"

Unsure how much this question might be rooted in bitterness over her assumption of his former office, and how much an honest plea for reassurance, Mara sought some hint of expression to give her clue. But Lord Benshai's corpulent face remained impassive. Mara dared not answer carelessly. By forcing her clan to unquestioned obedience to her will, she had also taken on responsibility for ensuring their survival. Although she still had no idea what she would do, rather than let her doubts shake the foundation of her newly forged alliance, she chose to be evasive. "Tasaio shall not command more than worms in the soil before long, my Lord."

The other Lords present exchanged glances. Since to challenge this outright statement would involve a point of honor, no one rushed to speak in contradiction. After an awkward minute, the lords of Clan Hadama began to rise and bid their Warchief good day. All knew that before the close of the week, Tasaio would march into the city to confront the Emperor and demand a restoration of the High Council's power. Just how Mara intended to prevent him was beyond anyone's guess; certainly she lacked the military might to challenge the Minwanabi Lord's in the field. Yet she had wits, and enough presence that even Benshai of the Chekowara dared not speak against her under her own roof.

The last Lord departed, and, returned from seeing the clan rulers to the door, Saric entered the courtyard garden and was surprised to find his mistress still seated by the fountain. Unofficially filling Nacoya's role as First Adviser, he inquired gently if there was anything his Lady might require.

Mara took a long moment to answer. Turning a face that seemed shockingly pale, she murmured, "Have my maid attend me, please."

The phrasing was most unlike her. Aware that in some things he could never fill Nacoya's sandals, and also by canny intuition sensing that somehow his mistress needed more understanding than he had the background to offer, Saric floundered at a loss. "Are you ill, Lady?"

Mara seemed to struggle for speech. "Simply a disagreeable stomach. It will pass."

But Saric knew naked fear. She looked suddenly very frail. Afraid she might be taken with the summer fever, or, worse, that an enemy might have found means to poison her food, the Acoma adviser took another quick step forward.

His worry was sharp enough for Mara to take notice. "I will be recovered within the hour," she reassured him and followed with a weak wave of her hand. "My maid will know how to make me comfortable."

Saric's alarm transformed to a look of piercing inquiry, which the Lady shied away from without comment. She had not lied. At last she realized her tiredness of the past few days was not simple fatigue; the difficult stomach in the morning was a familiar sign of pregnancy. With Ayaki, she could not keep breakfast down for the first nine weeks she had carried him. Abruptly recalled to the fact that Saric had been a soldier long enough to have observed the condition of the army's camp followers, she peremptorily ordered him to leave before he had time to make his suspicions a certainty. Left alone until her maid's arrival, Mara felt sadness well up inside. She permitted the tears that gathered in her eyes, aware that her feelings were amplified by the changes within her body. She would indulge herself now, when contemplating bitter choices, for the time would arrive soon when she must act with . . . what had Kevin called it? Nerves of steel! Yes, she must have only hardness in her soul. And thinking of her beloved, sitting quietly in her quarters awaiting her summons, or her return to his side, the tears flowed freely down her face.

Above anyone else, Kevin must never find out she carried a child by him. That single fact would bind him to her in a way that would be cruelty to sunder. His devotion to Ayaki had established how much regard he held for children. Though he had never spoken on the subject, Mara had read the longing in his eyes. She knew he yearned for a son or a daughter of his own, and that by his homeworld's code of honor, such things were not ever taken lightly. On Kelewan the bastard child of a slave would not be an issue. The illegitimate children of nobles often rose to high office within their own houses. But to Kevin, the matter would lie closer to his heart than his own life. No, the man she loved must never know, and that meant her days with him were numbered.

The maid arrived and, seeing her mistress in distress, came at once to her side. "Lady, what may I do?"

Mara held out her hand. "Just help me so I may rise without becoming ill." The request was voiced in a strained whisper.

As the Lady of the Acoma stood on shaky feet, she understood that pregnancy was but a small part of the reason she was ill. The tension within her was like a bowstring, drawn until it threatened to snap.

Someday, she hoped the child within her womb would be counted Hokanu's son and rise to be Lord of the Shinzawai. . . . That he—already she hoped for a boy—would be Kevin's was simply her way of discharging the debt of honor due the barbarian who had won her heart and repeatedly saved her life. His line would continue in distinction upon the soil of Kelewan, and so his shade would be revered and remembered.

But Mara knew she must first survive the next three days. Even as powerful a Lord as Kamatsu would not bind his heir to a house with an enemy as threatening as Tasaio. White now from more than stomach cramps, Mara leaned heavily on her maid's supporting arm. She must formulate a plan to snatch the victory that seemed assured from the grasp of the Minwanabi. She simply must; the alternative was utter obliteration for her son, and for Kevin's unborn child.

Sunset threw red light through the wide screens of the chamber. Tasaio of the Minwanabi perched like a monarch upon a pile of cushions in the largest, most opulent suite of his residence in the Holy City. Unlike most other Ruling Lords, who owned town houses, the Minwanabi possessed a sizable mansion on a hilltop above the city, overlooking the heart of the imperial precinct. Gazing through slitted eyes at the changing of the white-armored guards at the Emperor's inner gate, the Lord hardly glanced at the message handed to him by his First Adviser.

With utmost patience, Incomo prompted, "Master, Mara is but a short distance from the city gate, with her honor guard. She is also accompanied by an imperial messenger bearing a staff of office, and an Imperial Peace is upon the city. At your word, she will travel to the appointed meeting place."

"Her choice of timing will not save her." Tasaio ran his thumb along his jaw as he followed the movement of the guards in their sparkling white armor. "That silly boy who calls himself Emperor can delude himself for a few more days, but no call of Imperial Peace will prevent me from destroying an enemy." After an interval, Tasaio added, "However, it might be useful to wait to strike until we have a time and place of our choosing. And it might be entertaining to hear what the Acoma bitch desires, simply to learn what I may do to frustrate her."

Incomo grew tense with apprehension. "Master, I would be remiss in my duty if I did not advise against this meeting. The woman is more dangerous than any other ruler in the Empire, as she has demonstrated on numerous occasions."

Drawn at last from contemplation, Tasaio silenced his First Adviser with a glare. "I have an army with me, Incomo."

"But do you stand to gain?" the First Adviser asked urgently, more than mindful that his Lord's uncle had died under his own roof with his army about him, as a result of Mara's plotting. "If the Lady of the Acoma desires talk, anything she will say must be to aid her own cause against you. I see nothing to benefit the Minwanabi in this, my Lord."

Tasaio drummed his fingers upon the cushion at his knee. "Send this message to the bitch. I will honor the truce and speak with her." Seeing Incomo's features cloud over, he narrowed yellow eyes. "I see no point in all this needless worry. Mara and her brat might have escaped death by a narrow margin, but when I win the white and gold, she shall be the first of my enemies to be removed." Graceful, fast, and intent upon his beliefs, he stood. "I may be magnanimous. Those silly fools in Clan Hadama will perhaps be allowed to live, but only if they become my vassals after they see me end the Acoma name forever." With a rare smile, he added, "You worry too much, Incomo. I can always say no to whatever offer Mara makes."

Incomo remained silent. He had the terrible feeling that if Tasaio rejected Mara's offer, that would be exactly what she wished. The First Adviser bowed, turned, and went to send the message.

The wind was called butana in the ancient language of the Szetaci people of the Empire. The translation meant "wind from demons," and it blew for days, even weeks at a time. The gusts were dry, whipping out of the distant mountains in fitful, howling bursts. In the hot season, such winds could desiccate a piece of uncovered meat or fruit in hours. In the cool season, the air carried a chill, and at night the temperature dropped, sending people indoors to huddle around fires and under layers of robes. When the butana blew, the common folk said dogs went mad and demons walked the land in the guise of men. Husbands were known to run screaming into the night, never to be seen again, and wives became melancholy to the point of suicide. Legends abounded of supernatural beings who appeared when the butana whined across the land. The Grey Man, an ancient myth, was said to walk the Empire on nights like this. Should a lone traveler meet him, he must answer a riddle, and be rewarded if his solution was found pleasing, or suffer loss of his head if the Grey Man proved dissatisfied. Such were the stories of the butana, the bitter dry wind that blew this night.

Under brilliant stars, atop a hill outside the city walls, two small armies waited, facing one another. Torches guttered and banners flapped in the gusts, casting a flickering transience of light and shadow over faces taut with apprehension. Plumed officers waited before the ranks in motionless formation. And at the head of each army stood a ruler, on one side a woman clothed in shimmering green silk and emeralds and upon the other a lean, predatory figure in jet armor with black and orange bosses.

Positioned equidistant between them, an imperial herald

waited, his robe of office gleaming like bone under a wan quarter moon. In a voice loud enough to carry over the wind, he addressed the two forces in attendance. "Let it be known that the Imperial Peace is upon this city and the surrounding countryside! Let no man draw his sword in anger or retribution. So commands the Light of Heaven!" Turning toward the band who surrounded Tasaio, the herald intoned, "This Lady, of noble rank and line, claims that she comes to treat with you for the Good of the Empire. My Lord, do you acknowledge?"

Tasaio inclined his head, and the messenger deemed that sufficient. Turning to where Mara waited across a narrow expanse of grass, the herald raised his voice above the wind's rising whine. "My Lady, this Lord answers your call to parley and acknowledges your intent to speak for the Good of the Empire."

Mara returned a bow, making a point of correct courtesy to contrast with her enemy's lapse.

The herald received his due without reassurance. His stance between two enemies sworn to blood feud was precarious, and he knew it; family honor might be trustworthy when two such ancient lines were involved, but a single hothead among the ranks of common warriors could precipitate a massacre. He needed all of his training to speak steadily to those within earshot. "What is the highest duty?"

Every man, woman, and warrior present answered with the phrase: "To serve the Empire."

By crossing his arms, the imperial herald signaled for the principal parties to approach. That moment the butana drove down in a whipping gust, its sound like the moan of a dirge. Trying not to take the incident as omen, the herald completed his office. "My Lady, my Lord, I shall await at a distance, so that you may discourse untroubled."

He withdrew at a rate that was barely within the limits of propriety, leaving Mara and Tasaio faced off with but two paces between them.

Unwilling to succumb to the indignity of shouting over the wind, Mara left the opening words to Tasaio. Predictably, he did not begin with politeness or salutations. His thin lips curled slightly at the corners, and in the uncertain flicker of the torches, his eyes seemed to shine like a sarcat's. "Mara, this is a situation I had not anticipated." He waved his hand, indicating the odd surroundings, the poised warriors, and the snapping banners that were all in the tableau that seemed alive. "I could draw my sword and end this now."

Defiantly matching his malice, she answered, "And disgrace your house's name? I think not, Tasaio." Her tone turned dry. "That would be too much"—she fixed him with dark eyes—"even for a Minwanabi."

Tasaio laughed, the sound unexpectedly bright over the dissonant undertone of the butana. "You will be made to understand a truth. A man with enough stature may do as he pleases with impunity, Mara." He studied her from under veiling eyelids and said, "We waste time. Why are you here?"

"For the Good of the Empire," Mara reiterated. "You bring your army and the bulk of Clan Shonshoni to Kentosani. I believe you come to make war upon the Emperor."

Tasaio's manner showed interest, but under his veneer of civility, Mara sensed an almost physical wave of hatred. She resisted an instinct to step back and barely managed to keep her composure. As with dogs who circled before a fight, she sensed that the first one to turn away would be the one to invite attack.

"You bring the bulk of Clan Hadama behind you," the Minwanabi Lord replied in deceptively lazy inflections. "Yet I do not accuse you of preparing treasonous assault upon the Light of Heaven."

Mara spelled out the obvious. "I am in no position to claim the white and gold."

As if conceding a compliment, Tasaio inclined his head. Yet his feline, watching eyes tracked her every movement, seeking opening.

The Lady of the Acoma gathered courage and added a barb. "Cease your preening, Tasaio. Your position of ascendance has nothing to do with merit. The other claimants are in disarray because of their dealings with Axantucar."

"A fine point," snapped Tasaio. Then he smiled. "In the end, for whatever reason, I win."

"No." Mara allowed a slight pause. "A stalemate could go on indefinitely. That would serve the Light of Heaven, since delay would allow him to bring the Empire under his own control. The Imperial Government may be asleep, but it is not dead. Over time, more and more Lords would accede to the jurisdiction of the imperial court and governors, and less power would reside with the High Council. Should Ichindar order the smaller Lords, one at a time, to send support to his Imperial Whites, consolidating his authority, soon the roads and the river between your estates and the trade cities would be commanded by his army. Already the Kanazawai serve alongside the Whites. Who next? The Xacala? How long before you become a Lord only within the boundaries of your own lands?"

A light touched Tasaio's eyes, hard-edged as the burn of the stars in a sky stripped of haze by the butana. "You speak of possibilities, Mara, and remote ones at that."

Yet his manner had become subtly guarded. Pressing her narrow advantage, Mara sought to unbalance him. "Not that remote, Tasaio, and well you know it." Before he could speak, she said, "There is another possibility: what if Lords Keda and Xacatecas threw their support to Tonmargu at the outset?"

Tasaio's attention focused instantly upon Mara. Beyond that he concealed his surprise. He was aware Lord Hoppara was her ally, but mention of the Lord of the Keda was unexpected.

As Tasaio continued his flat stare in silence, Mara said, "I have a proposal. The other three claimants to the white and gold could form alliance only to frustrate you. Even joined, they cannot win their own choice. Given that, I control enough votes in the council to swing the outcome."

Tasaio's patience seemed suddenly worn. "Then do so, Mara. Give the white and gold to Frasai of the Tonmargu and go home."

Mara felt the wind like a tingle of chill against her skin. She played a dangerous game for perilous stakes, and knew it. Yet she saw no other option. Too much innocent blood would be spilled if events were permitted to run their worst course. Choosing her phrases with care, she said, "The difficulty is that while I would rather die than see you gain the white and gold, you are the only man who could hold the throne. Lord Tonmargu is not the sort of man to face down the Light of Heaven inside his own palace. So, we are left with two choices: a Warlord who is the Emperor's puppet . . . or you."

Wary, and not so vain as to swallow all he heard without suspicion, Tasaio considered. "If a figurehead Warlord is a fate worse than death, but you wish my instant obliteration, what solution do you propose?"

"I can do for you what I could also offer Frasai of the Tonmargu: should I bid, enough Lords will support you to put you firmly upon the Warlord's throne."

The wind held sway through another interval of silence. Tasaio stood motionless, his plumes whipping in the brisk air. His face became too still, a mask, and his hands rested like carved stone on the hilt of his sword, while burning amber eyes never moved from Mara's face. After considering her words, he said, "Suppose for a moment you are correct. Tell me why I should care, given the fact, Lady, that I can seize the Warlord's mantle without your help."

The reply came as gall from Mara's lips. "At what price? Would you bring the Empire to ruin to take the prize? You will win, I have no doubt, for while few would openly back your claim out of love for House Minwanabi, many will oppose Ichindar's break with tradition—and to protect their own prerogatives. So, in the end, after a ruinous war you will sit on the white and gold throne, marry your son to one of the departed Ichindar's many daughters, and have him become the ninety-second Light of Heaven. Then you'll have no trouble having the new Emperor ratify your election. But you will rule a shattered people." Mara strove to maintain poise; merely imagining the costs of such a bid for power caused revulsion in every fiber of her being. After a necessary interval to keep herself from shaking, she added, "Such a conflict will certainly leave you critically weakened. Are your reserves deep enough to cope with those likely to prey upon your borders after such mighty conquest? The lesser houses would swarm over you like ravenous insects."

Tasaio broke eye contact with Mara for the first time. Loftily remote, and in his secret depths convinced he had gained the key to Mara's gravest weakness, he turned and surveyed his forces. Under his scrutiny, they seemed flawless, arrayed in rows across the hillside, and ready for his instant orders. In their impeccably clean armor and correct bearing, they were a sight to bring pride to any commander. The glorious Minwanabi banner of alternating squares of black and orange snapped smartly in the wind. What else Tasaio saw in the night that sheltered his army only he knew. At length his gaze swung insolently back to Mara. "Do continue on the assumption that your supposition is true, Lady. What do you propose in exchange for my not seizing what I perceive is already mine?"

Mara stifled a fury that had nothing to do with enmity or blood feud, but held root in her personal desire to nurture life. "I treat with you for the Good of the Empire, Tasaio. I am not without resources." She motioned, and an unarmed servant approached from her lines. The Lord of the Minwanabi could not know that the man in the simple robe was actually Arakasi in disguise; in flawless imitation of servility, the Spy Master carried a wrapped bundle, unrolled the parchment covering, and tossed a human head that reeked of preservative across the grass to Tasaio's feet.

Barely shy of shouting, Mara said, "You should recognize the face. Behold the remains of the man you attempted to use to compromise my spy network."

Tasaio returned a startling rictus of hate. "You!" His word came out as a snarl. "You were the one who ordered murder in my house! Only *I* may command death upon Minwanabi lands!" A mad light entered his eyes, icily without compunction. Touched by an involuntary shiver, Mara sensed threat in the air. The wind ruffled her robes, tugged at her elaborately piled hair, and chilled the sweat on her skin. No words were spoken, but Mara knew in her soul that only the thinnest thread of reason remained to remind Tasaio of his pledge of truce. At this moment, she knew, her enemy wished for nothing more than his hands around Mara's throat, perhaps as he took her in brutal rape.

Then, with equally frightening abruptness, Tasaio's expression shifted to a satisfied smile. "So you admit to killing your own agent?"

Mara willed herself to outer calmness. Inwardly she was frightened by his shattering shift of mien, and aware that she was dealing with a man who could only be judged insane. She inclined her head. "More than one, Tasaio."

Tasaio's teeth flashed white as his smile turned cruel. Through a long and uneasy interval, the only sounds upon the hillside were the crack and flap of battle standards and the hiss of the wind through the grass. Then Tasaio said, "So you forged my family chop? And paid the Hamoi tong to murder your own agents in my house? Lady, you have unexpected turns of originality."

He did not threaten or posture, which Mara found disturbing. That his heart held murder, and worse, could never for an instant be doubted. And yet she pressed him. "You must consider the frustration in coming years of not being able to bring strangers into your service, Tasaio. You know as I stand here, my agents shall be among them. Perhaps you should have all merchants and visitors banned from your estates, and even refuse the wagons of traders lest you admit an Acoma spy."

Tasaio's patience suddenly vanished. He shouted, "Do you really think such pathetic threats worry me, Mara? Upon your death, all your servants become slaves and grey warriors. What dread will I know when you are food for worms?"

With a droop to her shoulders that was not feigned, Mara drew a tired breath. "I bring you a proposal."

Tasaio took a half-step forward. Uncannily composed, and beautiful as a predator, he did not twitch a muscle at the sound as a hundred Acoma soldiers slapped hands upon their sword hilts. Reckless in his disdain, the Lord of the Minwanabi said, "I have no interest in listening, Mara. My predecessor swore blood oath to Turakamu that this feud would end in Acoma obliteration. While I lack Desio's passions and count the pledge regrettable, still I am bound to it. I must see the Acoma line ended. The alternative need not be discussed. There can be no cessation to our conflict."

Mara sensed Arakasi's alarm, but she could see no other way beyond this impasse. "Would you consider . . . a suspension?"

Caught by surprise, Tasaio blinked. "What do you mean?"

"Quarter. No end to our enmity—that will never abate until one family or the other is dust—but a postponement of conflict, until the Empire is once again on a firm footing for peace?"

"The Good of the Empire," Tasaio murmured. His humor was cutting. Intrigued despite his sarcasm, he added, "Say on."

"I propose a meeting with the Ruling Lords of the Empire, but in the Imperial Palace. There we confront the Light of Heaven with our need to resolve this confrontation and prevent a crisis that will plunge our land into ruin. Or would you wish to govern an Empire where the eastern frontier is dominated by Thuril captains and their marauding highlanders? A northern border overrun each spring by Thün raiders seeking Tsurani heads as trophies? A return of pirates to the Outpost Isles?"

"You do paint a bleak picture," Tasaio allowed. "If I agree to this meeting, you'll deliver the votes needed to grant me the Warlord's throne without bloodshed?"

"Should you agree to meet with the Emperor, peacefully, I will pledge to make every effort, to the last of my resources, to ensure no one ascends to the Warlord's throne before you." Mara drew a shaky breath. "Upon this you have my most holy oath, sworn upon my family's name and honor, from now to the last generation of the Acoma line."

Tasaio raised his eyebrows at this most sacred of vows. A skeptical twinge of malice colored his tone. "If any of your descendents are worth swearing by, how long a truce would you wish?"

Although offered the most mortal of insults, Mara steeled herself against irrational anger. More than her family's name was at stake here, and more than the affairs of nobles—servants, children, craftsmen, and thousands of nameless slaves would suffer if the Empire's rulers were to indulge in a senseless war. Changed from the woman of limited perspective that she had once been, Mara did what she could not have conceived of prior to being influenced by Kevin's foreign ideas: more, she swallowed her family's honor. Rather than merely a phrase, *to serve the Empire* was now her only guiding motive. Swallowing mortification, she said, "Hold off your final assault until I have returned home and seen to the affairs of my house. After that, let our struggle resume without stint until the bitterest end."

Her tone of capitulation drew a bright laugh from Tasaio. Unable to resist toying with the vulnerability she had exposed, he said, "Already you presume to guess my answer, Lady. You overestimate my love of the Empire. My honor is my own, not my nation's." He looked her avidly up and down to see if she showed discomfort.

But Mara was familiar with his malice. She revealed not the slightest hint of discomfort to gratify his lust for torment.

After apparent thought, Tasaio amended, "However, a quick solution to my accession to the white and gold would spare me a certain degree of bother." He smiled, and Mara saw how well this madman could mask his depravity behind military propriety and courtly manners. "I will agree. Let the High Council meet before the Light of Heaven and have an end to his dictatorial rule. You shall marshal your allies, and when the moment comes, you will have them support my claim. Then, when such things as fate requires are finished, you shall have my safe conduct back to your estates until you have put your affairs in order. Be sure that I will march against you, Mara, but until then you may count the hours you live as payment for your service to the Empire."

Drained, and feeling desolate beyond words, Mara sealed her pledge with a bow. She dared not wonder how her father or brother would have reacted, were they alive to know of her commitment. All she could hope was that war might be averted, lives might be spared, and the unborn child within her womb might be permitted enough time to achieve birth. Whether she and Ayaki died for the pact she sealed this moment, perhaps the cho-ja Queen would consent to keep one newborn infant alive in secret. . . .

"When shall we meet?" Tasaio said in a voice that betrayed satisfaction.

"The day after tomorrow," said Mara. "Send word to the Emperor, and the other council members, and leave me free to muster the support I have promised."

"It shall be interesting to see whether the Lady can meet her obligation. If she forswear, she will not leave the city alive," Tasaio ended. He returned the shallowest of bows, barely more than an inclination of his head. Then he spun with the quickness of a sarcat and walked back to his own lines.

Beaten down by a sense of hopelessness greater than any she had known in life, Mara returned to Lujan's protection.

From the sidelines, the imperial herald proclaimed, "This conference is ended! Depart in peace and honor, and know the gods are pleased that no blood was shed this night."

As Mara's officers called orders for the Acoma army to disperse, the Minwanabi First Adviser drew breath to address his master; but Tasaio held up his hand. "She is defeated, Incomo." He watched Mara's retreating figure, a knowing smile on his lips. "I have seen that look in the eyes of warriors waiting for death upon the battlefield." He gave a half-shrug. "Oh, they fight well, and do honor to their ancestors, but they know they are fated to die. Mara *knows* I have won."

"Master," pleaded Incomo, "I would be less than your dutiful servant if I did not point out that there may be unexpected turns in your assessment. There are other issues at stake beyond who may claim the white and gold. Ichindar has fathered no son. At this moment, many of the Imperials might whisper that the time draws nigh to install another member of the royal line upon the throne. Jiro of the Anasati could be their choice; Kamatsu of the Shinzawai can trace ties to royalty, and his son is well regarded. What if you were to discover this offer is but—"

Tasaio sharply cut off speculation. "Mara knows *I have won.* It is over." Oddly piqued, as if he had relished a challenge that would not materialize, the Lord of the Minwanabi signaled his Force Commander to wheel his columns of soldiers and march back to their camp.

Left alone with the mournful song of the butana, Incomo lingered behind. He could not imagine how Mara might contrive to shift the course of events yet to come. But he knew this conflict was far from over. At best, Mara had bought herself the gift of a few months more in which to plot; at worst, she would have some trap in mind, and the Minwanabi would be swallowed by it. Chilled by a heavy gust, Incomo caught his flapping robes about him and hurried to overtake his master. As he picked his path downhill in the darkness, he mulled over the most prudent course: to send inquiries to his agents for the latest information they might uncover about Mara's intentions, or to complete his unfinished last testament and death poem. Caught by a deepening sense of finality, Incomo decided to do both.

The night's progression of events did not end with the meeting on the hilltop. Mara arrived back at her town house feeling tired to her bones. She shed her outer robe and pushed back strands of hair torn loose by the incessant wind, and only then came out of her daze long enough to understand what Saric was telling her.

An imperial messenger had called in her absence.

"What did he say?" Mara asked dully, and by the concern on Saric's face, she realized she had asked him to repeat himself.

Tactful, Saric explained; and the particulars of Ichindar's latest proclamation struck Mara like a blow to the heart.

Her mind went numb after the first words: that the Emperor of Tsuranuanni was buying up all Midkemian slaves belonging to subjects of the Empire. The words "fair price" and "Imperial Treasury" seemed sounds made by cold winds, an evil extension of the nightmares brought by the butana. Reeling as if the underpinnings of her life had all been torn asunder, Mara did not feel Saric's hands help her from the hallway into the sitting room. The cushion that supported her did not seem real, and the tears that sprang into her eyes seemed those of somebody else.

Her body, her mind, her heart—all seemed open wounds of anguish.

"Why?" she asked dully. "Why?"

Saric had not released her hand, mostly because she clung still to the warmth of his touch. He offered what comfort he could, though he guessed the futility of such efforts. In the gentlest of tones, he tried to soften the insupportable. "It is said that the Light of Heaven will sell Kevin's countrymen back to the Midkemian King. The original rift has been re-opened outside the City of the Plains. All slaves who were prisoners of the war will be shipped downriver and sent through the rift."

Flinching outright at the mention of her beloved's name, Mara could not prevent brimming eyes from spilling over. "The Emperor makes free men of slaves?"

Calmly, Saric qualified. "Out of respect for our gods, one could say that act would be the province of Lyam, King of Isles."

Mara regarded the whitened fingers twined with those of her adviser. Her resolve to keep nerves of steel had availed nothing! She felt defeated down to her core. The threat posed by the Minwanabi had at last overtaken her scant resources, and now she was to lose Kevin. The fact she had already resolved to send him away into freedom made no difference. The immediacy of the moment devastated.

"When does the Light of Heaven require the slaves to be

surrendered?" she asked, surprised that her tongue could shape words.

Saric answered with profound sympathy. "By noon tomorrow, my Lady."

There had been no warning for this, none. Mara choked back a sob. Shamed by her show of emotion, and hearing the shade of Nacoya scolding her for ignoble sentiment, she grasped for one single thought upon which to bolster her courage; for bravery alone would see her through the ruins of her only happiness, and the hopes she had dared to cherish concerning the continuance of the Acoma name.

Only one hint of good came to mind amidst the bleakness: Kevin would be spared the disaster that must follow her support of Tasaio for the Warlordship. If the barbarian's recitations of Kingdom Law and the Great Freedom were truths, then his King Lyam would free him. He would live out his days honorably in Zūn, and escape the madness and carnage to come.

Mara tried to convince herself that her beloved was better off gone, but logic did not appease the lacerating pain in her heart. She found the hand not gripping Saric's cradled over the small spark of life engendered deep in her womb. Like a spill of light through a doorway, revelation came. She realized that all she had done this night had been for Kevin's unborn child. She and Ayaki were Tsurani-born, dedicated to centuries-old tradition that held to honor before life, and they would unhesitatingly chose death before disgrace. But the spirit that quickened in her womb was half-Midkemian; somehow she had acknowledged its future right to live and prosper with the values the father would have accorded such things. Recognition dawned, with no small portion of fear, as Mara of the Acoma understood she had again stepped beyond the bounds of her culture. She had accorded the common folk of the Empire consideration before her family name; once she would have believed such a concept would have shamed her father and her ancestry, even earned the wrath of Tsuranuanni's many gods.

Now she could conceive of no other viable choice.

Torn between tears and the sense of relief that soon, very soon, the years of tribulation would be ended, Mara came back to herself. She loosened her fingers from Saric's and blotted awkwardly at her eyes. "I will need the services of my maid," she managed tremulously. "Kevin must not see that I have been upset."

Saric made to rise and bow, but a small shake of Mara's head detained him. "Send word back to Keyoke that all of our outworld slaves are to be sent forthwith to the City of the Plains. Then choose our strongest warriors to escort Kevin to whatever staging area the Emperor has set aside for the Midkemians. Say nothing of this to anyone save Lujan, lest word of this development be carelessly mentioned by the servants." Here Mara paused to wrestle past a catch in her throat. "For my lover has a contrary and stubborn nature. Although he longs for his freedom, he may have a mind to argue over the manner in which it is bestowed upon him."

Here the Lady was unable to continue, but Saric understood. Kevin had never submitted to orders, except through choice, or brute force. He had proved himself a formidable fighter, and where Mara was concerned, no man might predict how he would react to being parted from her. For his own safety's sake and the lives of the warriors who must deliver him into the care of the Emperor, he must not hear of the fate that awaited him beforehand.

Saddened, for he had come to like the Midkemian's odd humor, and his decidedly strange views of life, Saric bowed to his mistress's wisdom. But as he hurried off to send in her maids, he reflected that he had never seen a more bleak expression in the eyes of any woman he had known.

The night passed in terrible, restless torment for Mara. While the butana wailed across the rooftree, she made frantic love to Kevin, the last time ending in tears in his arms. He stroked her with a tenderness that threatened to break her heart. Hurt by her silence, her unwillingness to speak her fears, he nevertheless ignored his own pain in a profound effort to comfort her.

Mara clung to him in a mounting tide of hysteria. Her world seemed unhinged and she could not conceive of a life without the solid presence of the man who had caused her to reexamine every aspect of her beliefs, and forced her to see the deficiencies of her culture. Kevin had become more than lover, more than a man she could confide in: he was the taproot of the tree of her resolve. She had to rely upon his strength to change the Empire and make it honorable in a new and moral way. Without him, the power, the goals, and the shining vision she held for a future now shadowed by her recent vow to Tasaio seemed things devoid of joy. Mara lay in the warmth of Kevin's embrace and listened to the soft, steady beat of his heart blended with the hollow dirge of the winds that rattled the screens.

Somehow, against his volatile barbarian nature, Kevin sensed that her turmoil would not support questions. His sensitivity wounded her, robbed her of a perverse excuse to fly into anger and send him away. Mara endured the tender caress of his hands, cut by the knowledge that this was the last night she could touch him. At last, exhausted, she fell into restless dreams. He lay awake, her head cradled in the hollow of his shoulder.

Through all the years he had known her, he had never seen her so distraught. Open in revealing his own passions, it never occurred to him that her love for him might be the hidden cause of her anguish.

Dawn came, unwanted as an executioner's arrival. Mara found a grain of courage amid the wreckage of her nerves and ordered Kevin away, before the onset of her morning sickness. She spent a miserable interval torn between tears that would not flow from swollen eyes, and dry heaves. Her maids worked tirelessly to restore her to a semblance of proper appearance. By the time she was fit to be seen in public, noon had already drawn nigh. Mara emerged from her quarters to find the escort quietly arranged by Saric already waiting by the door. Unaware of the Emperor's proclamation, Kevin waited in his usual place by her litter, his red hair familiarly tousled, and a concerned expression on his face. At the sight of his blue eyes on her, Mara all but broke down.

Then the stern fiber of her warrior forbears sustained her. Drawing upon all her temple-taught training, she shut off her clamor of emotions and forced herself to step forward, one foot after another, until finally she reached her litter. Of desperate necessity, she chose Saric to assist her to her seat. Then, in a voice unrecognizable as her own, she said, "We must leave."

She named no destination; this detail Saric had already attended to, and Lujan knew what lay ahead. But the anomaly roused Kevin to suspicion. "Where are we bound for this day?" he asked on a fixed note of sharpness.

Mara dared not try speech. Aware that her eyes were flooding, she quickly snapped her curtains closed, and it was Lujan who waved her bearers to rise, and her honor guard of soldiers to march out of the town house courtyard, as Saric held his gaze upon the Midkemian with something resembling regret.

"Will somebody please tell me why everyone acts as though we were going to a funeral?" Kevin demanded plaintively. He received only Tsurani blankness for reply and resorted to a spectacular attempt at banter.

His extravagance at any other time would have sorely tried the deportment of her warriors, but today the most devastating of his repartee fell upon deaf ears. No one so much as hinted at a smile, far less indulged in a laugh.

"Gods, but everyone's as lively as a corpse." Mournful that some of his best jokes had been wasted, Kevin lapsed into silence as the escort crossed the bustle of Kentosani and took a turn toward the less fashionable district by the south-facing riverside.

Ahead lay a palisade constructed of wide, thick planks. Kevin stopped dead in the roadway, and only their fighters' reflexes prevented the warriors behind from slamming into him. "I've seen the likes of this place before," he accused in a tone that snapped with reckless insolence. "Why are we going to the slave markets, Mara?"

The Acoma warriors did not wait for any signal; Kevin's reactions were far too unpredictable for such nicety. Firmly, swiftly, and in force, they closed around the Midkemian and caught him back by the wrists.

Pinioned, and startled into rage, Kevin twisted, half an instant too late. The warriors grunted at the effort, but managed to keep their grip.

Traffic in the street was stopped by the commotion, and heads turned to stare.

"Gods!" Kevin exploded in a tone of blistering betrayal. *"You're selling me!"*

The cry all but shattered Mara's heart. She whipped aside

the curtains of her litter and looked up into blue eyes that burned with fathomless rage. Words failed her.

"Why?" cried Kevin, with such terrible lack of inflection she felt clubbed. "Why should you do this to me?"

It was Lujan who answered, and roughly, for his own voice threatened to show feeling unseemly for a warrior, far less an officer of his status. "She does not part with you willingly, Kevin, but by the Emperor's order!"

"Damn the Light of Heaven," Kevin exploded. "Damn your sod of an Emperor to the deepest pit of the Seventh Hell!"

Gawkers poked their faces out of windows, and more passersby stopped to stare. Several farm matrons made a sign against blasphemy, and a sour-faced merchant on the verge expressed thought of sending for a priest. Unwilling to be tried by the temples for the mouthing of a miscreant barbarian, a warrior less well acquainted with Kevin reached out a hand to cover his mouth.

The barbarian exploded into violence. He wrenched a fist free, knocking two of Mara's guards aside before any others could move. The men were under orders to refrain from drawing blades, but as Lujan joined the heaving knot of struggle that centered around the Midkemian, he prayed no one would forget. Kevin battled as if possessed, and with his great height, no one watching from the sidelines could miss that he transgressed sane limits. He was irate enough to forget protocols, and should he succeed in his attempt to snatch a sword from one of the warrior's scabbards, the Emperor himself could not keep him from dying.

Lujan glimpsed the fear on Mara's face. Then he dared a fury more focused than any harulth's, and dove headlong into the press.

The wrestler's move he employed prevailed and he struck Kevin squarely off balance. Lujan bore him over backwards onto the cobbles of the street, while another soldier added his weight to the Force Commander.

Most men would have been stunned by the fall. The Midkemian seemed unfazed. Driven by a rage that dulled physical pain, and goaded by emotions that no line of reason might stay, he tore into Lujan with a ferocity well capable of killing. Narrowly avoiding a knee in the groin, the Acoma Force Commander grappled a whirlwind of moving flesh.

Somehow he managed to rap out orders to his men. "Close in! Use your shields and bodies to hide this fracas from public view."

A fist grazed his cheek. Feeling the burn of torn skin, Lujan indulged in a rare curse. "Damn it, man, will you stop, or must I be forced to hurt you?"

Kevin snarled an obscenity. ". . . if you had a mother!" he finished.

Aware that the slave he sought to subdue had not hesitated to pitch himself weaponless against armed ranks of enemy warriors, Lujan reacted by reflex. Desperate, and moved by care and admiration for Kevin, he employed the honorless, brutal tactics learned in the mountains as a grey warrior. Another criminal might have recognized the moves; any proper Tsurani warrior would have been shamed to employ a fist to an opponent's groin. Felled by a blow that held nothing of fairness, and blanched dead white with the pain, Kevin rolled into a moaning knot of limbs on the filthy paving of the street.

"Sorry, old son," Lujan murmured, his inflection and choice of phrase borrowed intact from Kevin. "You will finish your life in freedom and honor, whether you wish to or not."

Then, feeling battered inside as well as out, Force Commander Lujan raised himself to his feet. "Bind and gag him," he said with whiplash curtness to his men. "We dare risk no further incident."

Then, aching for the mistress who watched all from the shadow of her litter, he forced his face back into a semblance of Tsurani impassivity and ordered the party forward on its errand.

At the gate of the compound, the master of Kentosani's slave guild stepped out of his hut to inquire after the needs of the Lady of the Acoma.

Mara choked words past numbed lips. "This slave . . . is to be returned to his homeland, by order of the Light of Heaven."

A limp weight in the grip of her guardsmen, Kevin turned blue eyes toward her. The light in their depths beseeched, but the child in her womb kept her strong. "I am sorry," she murmured, heedless that the master of the slave guild stared at her in dumbfounded curiosity. Unable to voice the words, she moved her lips to mouth the phrase "my love." The rest of what she wished to say stuck impossibly in her throat.

The slave broker nodded. "He's very strong, though a bit past prime. I would think a fair price—"

Mara held up her hand, silencing the man. "No. Send him home."

If the slave master found this behavior odd, he said nothing. He was having enough difficulty understanding why the Emperor would chose to buy slaves simply to send them away to some alien palace. The edict had created enough confusion, and if this Lady chose to be generous, he would not object. "My Lady," he said, bowing deeply.

At last, unable to bear the wild, haunted pain she saw in her loved one's face, Mara whispered, "Live a long and noble life, son of Zūn."

She managed to achieve the impossible and summon the courage to order her warriors onward to take Kevin away to the compound set aside for the Emperor's purchases. The Slave Master directed the way, and dimly Mara heard one of her warriors speak words to the effect that Kevin was to be treated with respect and care, once his bonds were removed. . . .

The stockade doors swung closed, forever cutting off her view. Lujan remained by her side, his face a stone mask beneath the shadow of his helm. Most atypically, he did not realize that his officer's plumes had been bent and knocked awry during the foray in the street.

Mara sank back on her cushions, wrung dry of tears, and too debilitated to lift even a finger to close her curtains. The shadow thrown over her by the great wooden gates seemed utterly frigid. She could not banish the memory of Kevin's eyes, in the moment she had ordered their parting. Always, to her grave, it would haunt her, that she had sent him away bound and helpless. Dully she wondered how long Tasaio would spare her, after the coming truce came to its inevitable end. How many nights would she lie awake aching with the now unanswerable question: Would Kevin have left her reasonably, or willingly, if she had owned the nerve to consult him beforehand?

"Lady?" Lujan's soft voice intruded into a wilderness of pain. "The time has come to go home."

The warriors had returned, unnoticed.

Mara returned a limp wave. How, she wondered, with a pain sharp as a knife thrust, was any place in the Empire ever again going to feel like home?

The day and the night that followed seemed desolate and without ending. Alternately ravaged by grief and cruel nightmares, Mara tossed on her sleeping mat. Waking, sleeping, and in dreams, she seemed to see Kevin standing at her bedside, a look of naked accusation in his eyes. By now the barge that carried him would be well on the way downriver. By the time she and Tasaio and the Lords of the High Council resolved their differences with the Emperor, the man she loved above all others would be far beyond reach, on the soil of a distant, other world.

Stung awake time and again as she reached out and encountered the empty place where he had lain, or jolted bolt upright in terror by the vision of Tasaio of the Minwanabi holding a sacrificial sword over the gutted body of her son, Mara prayed. She begged Lashima for insight that would grant her the miracle she needed to thwart the enemy who cared for power more than peace, and who would see the natami of her ancestors buried face down, forever beyond reach of the sunlight. Hagridden, and feeling ill, she at last abandoned her pretense of rest. She paced the floor of her chambers until dawn, and then called a meeting of her advisers.

The butana continued to blow. Its whipping, tireless gusts pried at the shutters and screens as Mara, her Force Commander, and her acting First Adviser sat down in conference in her sitting room.

Huskily, as though her throat had been scraped with sand, the Lady of the Acoma opened. "I have one day to prepare for the confrontation between the Emperor and Minwanabi."

Painfully bright in his confidence, Saric said, "What have you planned, mistress?"

Mara closed swollen eyes, worn through to her soul. "I have no plan. Unless you and your cousin have considered something I have not, we march into this moment of destiny with nothing more than our naked wits. I have promised Minwanabi that no one shall ascend to the Warlord's throne before him."

"Then," said Saric, in a tone of patent reason, "the only choice must be that no one sits upon the Warlord's throne."

For a prolonged moment, only the wail of the butana held sway. A maid entered with a tray of chocha and sweet rolls and quietly left. No one seemed interested in refreshment.

Mara regarded the faces that all turned toward her with maddening expectancy. "Well, how shall we contrive to make a miracle?" she said in thinnest exasperation.

Showing a bruise and a scabbed cheek from his fisticuffs with Kevin, her Force Commander said without humor, "Mistress, it is for such things that all look to you."

Mara stared bleakly back. "This time I have run out of inspiration, Lujan."

Her Force Commander shrugged with total impassivity. "Then we shall die honorably killing Minwanabi dogs."

A surge of protest moved within Mara. "Kevin is—" Her voice caught and a rush of emotion caused a sting of tears beneath her eyelids. Forcing her grief and pain behind rigid control, she ran a damp hand over her face. "Kevin was right. We are a murderous race, and we waste ourselves in killing one another."

The butana howled, shaking the screen, and sending chill drafts across the room. Mara repressed a shiver and did not at first notice Saric's request to speak. When she saw, and signaled her acquiescence, he questioned her condemnation with a buried hint of impatience. "Mistress, the answer is plain? It does not matter if Minwanabi is not defeated, so long as the Emperor wins, yes?"

Mara's eyes opened wide. "Explain this."

Saric searched for words to express the concept which hovered upon the edge of his mind. "If the Light of Heaven can bolster his position, can find enough support in the High Council for his absolute rule—"

Mara shot upright, causing her loosely pinned hair to tumble in waves down her back. Ignoring the maid who rushed to remedy the untidiness, the Lady of the Acoma knotted her brows in a frown. "Then he could order Minwanabi . . ." She fought against the reflexive instinct to oppose any break in tradition and embrace the alien concept of absolute rule. "Leave me," she said with sudden sharpness to her circle of advisers. "I have much to think about."

As Saric arose with the others, Mara retained him with a

command. "Send word to the Light of Heaven, Saric. Beg him for an audience. Swear upon whatever honor our name holds that the safety of the Empire depends upon this meeting."

The young adviser repressed curiosity. "When, mistress?"

Over the incessant noise of the butana, Mara called, "As soon as he is able, but no later than one hour before noon today." Her voice ceased sounding whipped, as her mind weighed options, discarding those that were based on unfounded hope, rather than sound possibility; for inspiration had arrived at a moment nearly too late. "If Tasaio's ambition is to be thwarted, I will need every minute of time."

26. *RESOLUTION*

The Emperor listened.

In his grand audience hall, a chamber large enough to house twenty companies of warriors, Ichindar, ninety-first in an unbroken line, sat atop his ceremonial throne. The imposing chair was ancient wood, overlaid with gold and topaz, with massive rubies, emeralds, and onyx stones faced into the sides and back. It rested on a raised pyramidal dais, with a course of steps upon each side. The floor at the base was inset with a vast sunwheel pattern in warm tones of agate, white opal, and more topaz. Upon each side of the huge pyramid, twenty Imperial Whites stood guard upon the stairs. The floor directly before Mara held chairs for high priests and advisers, but only three were present: a scribe who took notes for distribution to those temple representatives who were absent, the Chief Priest of Juran, and the High Father Superior of Lashima. Mara had been grateful for the prelate of Lashima's presence, hoping it was a favorable omen, for that man had officiated at her interrupted ordination, on the day Keyoke had arrived to take a seventeen-year-old child home as Ruling Lady of the Acoma.

Stripped of even her honor guard, for warriors were forbidden in formal audience with the Emperor, she voiced the last part of her proposed plan. An imperial scribe sitting to Mara's right hurriedly transcribed her words for the archives, as her phrases echoed into the cavernous chamber. With the hall's vast domed skylights, gold-and-crystal-framed windows, and polished marble floors, the sound of her voice made her feel physically diminished.

At the close of her last phrase, she bowed deeply and stood as protocol dictated, her hands crossed in salute at her breast, behind the low railing beyond which no petitioner might approach. Trembling despite her best efforts, she awaited the Light of Heaven's reaction. As the minutes passed, and the silence became prolonged, she dared not even raise her eyes for fear she might find disapproval on the youthful countenance atop the dais.

"Much of what you propose rests upon speculation, Lady." The Emperor said on a note of unquestioned authority.

Her eyes still locked upon the elaborately patterned floor, Mara said, "Majesty, it is our only hope."

"What you suggest . . . is unprecedented."

That Ichindar considered tradition ahead of his own personal safety suggested much. This slender, solemn-faced young ruler was not greedy for absolute power; neither was he too timid to embrace bold concepts in the light of pending crisis. Admiring the maturity and courage apparent in one so physically slight, Mara said, "Much of what you have done, Majesty, is also unprecedented."

Ichindar inclined his head, the long, golden plumes of his headdress swaying as he nodded a stately acquiescence. Enveloped in elaborate layers of robes, he sat with painful formality, his face already marked by the ruler's burdens. Green eyes in dark hollows and cheeks gaunt from sleepless nights marred what should have been a carefree visage. Beneath the jewels and pomp, Mara perceived a spirit beaten down with worry. Young he might be, but the Light of Heaven was aware that he stood upon ground more perilous than quicksand. He held no delusions. His strength stemmed from the incalculable reverence the Tsurani people held for his office, but although deep-seated, such sentiment was far from limitless. Although uncommon among Ichindar's ninety predecessors, regicide was not unheard of. An Emperor's death was considered proof unto itself that the gods had already withdrawn their blessing from the Empire. Circumstances must already be disastrous for any but the most ambitious of Lords to attempt such a deed. Yet Mara knew Tasaio harbored just such ambition. And there were those, this day, who considered abolishment of the Warlord's office a dire enough offense against tradition to justify such an act.

Aware of the perils she invited by encouraging a course that departed further from the familiar, Mara raised her eyes to the enthroned figure on the dais. "Majesty, I offer only hope. I can stem Minwanabi's ambition alone, but only at great cost. Tasaio would have to be granted the Warlord's title. A bloodless succession to the white and gold might send these armies outside Kentosani home in peace. I submit to you this is an easy choice. Take it, and you may retire from the Great Game, return to the High Council its license to act, and retire to your divine contemplations. But all personal feuds and differences aside, I submit that this course would only buy time. A Minwanabi on the Warlord's throne would lead to a future of strife.

"I believe the chance exists, here and now, for permanent change—an end, perhaps, to the needless bloodshed that riddles our concept of politics. I believe that honor need not be rooted in killing for supremacy. Our moment to instill a more compassionate governance may never come again in our lifetimes. Humbly, I implore you: think what that could mean."

The Emperor's green eyes regarded her piercingly, even from his place high upon his dais. When he did not offer opinion, the priest of Juran the Just arose from his seat; a flick of one thin hand from the enthroned figure allowed him permission to speak.

"Mara of the Acoma, does it occur to you that your words might not be pleasing to heaven? Yours is an old and esteemed name, and yet you appear to have laid aside your family honor. You pledge one thing to Tasaio of the Minwanabi, but even now you seek to forswear a most sacred vow."

Mara knew a terrible, invasive shadow of fear. The perils of inciting accusation of heresy were not far from her mind, so she directed her reply solely to the Light of Heaven. "If I have laid aside the blessing of my ancestors, I say this is my own affair. I have transgressed no laws, nor offended heaven. In all that I have done, through all that I implore you to consider, I act for the Good of the Empire." She shifted her regard to the priest as she added, "Even if I should dishonor my family's name, this I would willingly do to serve the Empire."

A stillness greeted this statement, and then a stir of murmurs from the handful of advisers and priests. The representative from Juran's temple sat down with a look distinctly shaken.

The Light of Heaven turned wide, intelligent eyes upon the lady who stood in erect defiance at the foot of his throne. After an interval of unhurried thought, he gestured to his priests. "Let none present impute disgrace to the Lady. She does no shame to her house and name, but honors the Empire with her courage and service. For who else among our thousands of ruling Lords has dared to approach us with this truth?"

He paused, reached up with his own finely drawn hands, and removed his ceremonial headdress. A servant rushed in from the sidelines, knelt, and relieved him of its burden. With the high, feathered crown gone from his head, Ichindar seemed to shed his formality. He ran a hand through tousled brown hair and turned reflective. "When I first embarked upon my course within the Great Game, it was because I saw my uncle, Almecho, manipulate the Empire for the sole purpose of keeping himself in power as Warlord. The results brought suffering to many. His ambition was a threat to the nation . . . and myself," he added ruefully. "In working with Lord Kamatsu and others to end the bloodshed, I came to question the manner in which we live our lives, and I believe I understand something of the necessity that moves you."

Ichindar stood. He waved away the guards who would close at his shoulders, and descended the steps from his dais. "Let me share something with you, Mara of the Acoma, something only a handful of men know." The Emperor's manner was sure, but behind the mask of a ruler born, Mara saw a boy who was still vulnerably young and as human as she under the enveloping weight of his state finery. He crossed the floor in measured steps. The priests watched, the one from Juran's temple rapt as a carrion bird, and the High Father Superior of Lashima's order faintly smiling as the Light of Heaven reached across the rail and took her hand from its position of salute.

Since such unexpected familiarity appeared to disconcert Lady Mara, he looked directly into her eyes. "Originally, I tried to force peace upon the nations, for I saw great danger to us as a people if conquest were our only goal. But after Milamber returned, my reasons changed. You may have heard rumors of a great conflict upon the world of Midkemia. I confide to you now that the foe confronted there was the being our legends name the Enemy."

Mindful of a past discussion with Arakasi, Mara was unsurprised to hear this confirmed. She had reread the ancient tales of some unknown horror called the Enemy, which had destroyed her ancestor's homeworld, sending them across a mystic Golden Bridge into refuge on Kelewan. Although most of her peers had no cause to believe the old tales were anything other than myth, her quiet, earnest manner held no hint of scorn or disbelief. This was not lost on the Emperor.

Warming still more, Ichindar said, "The menace from before the dawn of our history existed, and was more terrible in fact than in story. The Assembly of Magicians stood with me in my desire that should such an evil conquer our former enemies in the Kingdom and turn their wrath upon us, we as a nation must stand united to face them. For this I suspended the High Council, that the machinations of the Great Game not be allowed to weaken us against such awesome threat. At my command, ten Great Ones and three thousand soldiers of the Kanazawai clan, led by Hokanu of the Shinzawai—"

"Hokanu has been upon the other world?" Mara blurted. Then realizing her rudeness before the Emperor, she added, "I beg my Sovereign's forgiveness."

Ichindar smiled. "You hold the young man in some regard, I see. Yes, Hokanu spent some weeks at war on Midkemia, and more time with his brother, Kasumi." The Emperor smiled. "We do not understand our former enemies in the Kingdom. Kasumi's bravery in serving his new master in the conflict won him appointment to a lordship among the nobles of the Kingdom. I am unfamiliar with their titles, but the one granted Kasumi is no mean thing, I'm told."

The Great Freedom that Kevin had recalled with such fondness was true, then! Mara blinked back sudden tears, this certain proof setting final seal upon her changed beliefs. Forever after, she could not live comfortably with her own people's rigid concept of caste. Men and women were only human beings—gods did not appoint them slaves, or nobles, or craftsmen with irrevocable finality. That in her culture a son might be born and live in exemplary honor, and yet never be awarded the rank deserving of his deeds, was injustice and waste of the first order.

"It is to our shame," she murmured unthinkingly loud, "that a captive might gain freedom and begin a noble house that might someday rise to greatness among his former enemies—those *we* call barbarians—and yet many equally worthy sons taken prisoner into our Empire could become no more than slaves. I fear we are the barbarians, and not the Midkemians."

Taken aback by this concept, which previously had only been aired with Kamatsu of the Shinzawai, the Emperor of Tsuranuanni regarded the woman across the rail. "So I thought, also. Perhaps you will appreciate the fine point, that all slaves returned across the rift will be free men on their home soil. Their King Lyam swore such to me, and though the first peacemaking was a disastrous mishap, I now know him for an honorable ruler."

Torn by memories of Kevin, Mara could only nod.

"I am loath to relinquish control of the Empire back to the High Council," Ichindar resumed, returned to the subject that had brought her. He lowered his voice so the priests and the scribe would not hear. "I also have come to understand that the chance arises to begin afresh." He released Mara's hand with a half-smile of chagrin that oddly reminded her of Hoppara. Then, gesturing for his servant to return his formal headdress to his brow, he swept back up the stair to his lofty throne.

Once again seated in state, he framed his official answer. "Whatever will occur on the morrow, the Empire will be forever changed. The magicians have held council on this issue, but they are reluctant to intervene further in politics, since the risk of the Enemy is past. Many of my allies against that threat have withdrawn"—he indicated the empty chairs upon the pyramid steps—"some as a result of my condemnation of Axantucar." Ichindar studied Mara a long and final time. "I think your plan has merit, but the risks you court are equal to, if not greater than, others you wish to avoid." The point did not have to be stated that more than Lords might fall if Mara's proposal went awry. The Empire itself might be plunged into bloody ruin. "I shall send word in the morning of my decision," Ichindar allowed. "Tasaio has already requested a meeting, with all Ruling Lords in attendance—it's just this side of a demand I appear before the High Council to answer charges, I think."

Now seeming only a boy wearing a costly weight of jewels, sparkling metals, and silk, Ichindar sighed. "I expect I have no choice. I shall confront Tasaio." He ended the audience with a tired smile. "Whatever befalls, Lady Mara, you have my regard. Await my word tomorrow, and may the gods protect you and the name of your ancestors."

Mara bowed low, feeling admiration for this young man, trained since childhood to revere tradition, and yet gifted with imagination and intelligence enough to see beyond false glory to the higher good of his people. Aware that he was special, and that his office might never be blessed with another of such unbiased perceptions, Mara left the great hall.

In the imperial anteroom her own party awaited, including Saric and Lujan, and Arakasi as attending servant, along with a picked honor guard of warriors. As one of Ichindar's ministers escorted the Acoma contingent out of the imperial quarters, Mara remained deep in thought. Outside, as she was helped by Arakasi into her litter, she said, "Home, quickly. We have much to do and dangerously little time."

Mara held council throughout the night. Lords of many parties and clans made their way to her town house to seek her wisdom. Two hours before dawn, the Lady gathered an escort and departed in her litter to appear before the one ruler who had failed to call. To the sleepy guard who answered Lujan's knock upon that man's town house gate, she demanded, "Tell Lord Iliando that Mara of the Acoma waits without for his welcome."

The disgruntled Lord of the Bontura arrived a short time later, his hair still in spikes from his pillow, and his robe mismatched with his slippers. Through an expression still surly from being wakened, he spoke the words to welcome Lady Mara into his home. When she was comfortably installed in his sitting room, and servants were called from their beds to attend to the courtesy of refreshments and chocha, he spoke bluntly. "Mara, why do you arrive unbidden at this hour of the night?"

Mara signaled for Lujan and her honor guard to withdraw. "I come to ask your help."

Iliando held up a hand. "You have my sympathy in your time of difficulty, but as for opposing Tasaio—"

Mara snapped erect. "What?" Had the Lord of the Bontura spies among the Minwanabi retinue, or had one of Incomo's staff been too free with his tongue? None but her inner circle should have known the contents of her discussion with her enemy on the hill.

"Come, girl, your meeting with Tasaio atop the hill with two armies at your backs could hardly be kept secret, could it?" Mara's expression showed that she had hoped it could. "I will save you time. I have already given my support to Jiro of the Anasati," the Lord of the Bontura confessed.

A slave arrived with the chocha tray and unobtrusively began to fill cups. While the older Lord blew on his cup to cool the scalding drink, Mara's eyes narrowed. "Jiro? What is he seeking in this?"

"You'll have to ask him." The Lord of the Bontura unwisely tried a sip, burned his tongue, and set down his cup in distaste. "Mind the chocha," he warned unnecessarily. Out of patience, but tactful enough to keep still, Mara waited for the elderly Lord to qualify his statement.

"Jiro has sent word to all members of Clan Ionani, making plain his belief that he considers his house in better standing than that of Lord Tonmargu."

"So he bids to be Warchief," Mara surmised. Suddenly she needed the chocha as an excuse to busy her hands. Nerves, and tension, and the uneasy adjustments her body was making to pregnancy were all exacting a toll.

"If Frasai of the Tonmargu fears to confront Jiro, we'll have a major shift in the ranks of the great families. It may be overdue," the Lord of the Bontura surmised. He did not need to belabor the fact that Frasai detested conflicts.

Stunned, Mara absorbed the implications of this unexpected twist. Sadly, she realized that Nacoya and Kevin had been right: after long years of brooding, Jiro was still angered that she had chosen his brother over him as her husband. Jiro apparently had discerned the only course left open to her, and had taken steps to ensure that she would fail—for if she lacked the support of Clan Ionani in a coalition to block the Minwanabi majority, her years of garnering influence and debts of vote all amounted to nothing. The Anasati heir could refuse to support Minwanabi and Acoma both, deadlocking the High Council. Her prediction to Tasaio about encroaching imperial rule by slow default would come true.

But Mara would gain little satisfaction, for a sworn enemy would then turn his full attention to the obliteration of her house in the instant that impasse became obvious. Clearly, the Lady of the Acoma would not live long enough to see her prophecy come true. Her hands instinctively touched her middle, as though to shelter the seed of Kevin's child. Boy or girl, the babe might never know birth.

And if Jiro was patient and clever enough to survive as the conflict raged on, he could emerge as the logical compromise candidate for the office of Warlord. Deep in thought as she sorted implications, Mara lost herself in the tangled turns of the Great Game.

"Lady, are you ill?"

Lord Iliando's question snapped her from contemplation. "No, I am only . . . tired." She waved away her host's concern and said, "You are in my debt."

The man inclined his head, acknowledging this was true. Regret colored his tone. "I may not compromise my honor, Mara. You hold but my single vote in council, and only under circumstances that cause me no family or clan dishonor. Those were our conditions."

"I would demand no such breach of integrity," Mara assured him. "Instead, I request that you marshal Clan Ionani's support. If you can convince your kinsmen to support the Ionani Warchief against House Minwanabi, you will have satisfied your debt to me as well as your clan's honor."

Iliando shrugged. "Even those who will back Tasaio in the end will go through the motions of supporting Lord Tonmargu's bid through one round of voting, Mara. It is expected."

"Don't confuse my request with a pro forma show of respect for Frasai," Mara interjected. Beyond the screen, the first grey pallor of dawn had begun to drive back the night. She was rapidly running out of time, and that realization vastly shortened her patience. "I require as many vows as possible against the chance that conflict might arise between Tasaio and your Warchief. In that event, I depend upon the assurance that Clan Ionani will stand resolute until I clearly show you it is no longer useful. *Particularly* since Jiro of the

Anasati may replace Lord Tonmargu as Warchief by this time tomorrow."

Lord Iliando sighed deeply. "You ask a difficult bargain. I will see what I can do, starting with Lord Ukudabi. He is influential, and his cousin, Lord Jadi, was ruined by Tasaio's uncle, so his house bears no love for the Minwanabi."

"Good." Mara set aside her half-emptied chocha cup and arose. "I will see the Lord of the Tonmargu myself." As her host saw her through to his outer door, she concluded, "This is more than a matter of feud between myself and Tasaio, my Lord Iliando. The Empire has been plunged into change, and it is up to you and me and others like us to decide whether the result is for good or ill. Remember this: no matter what else you may think, I serve the Empire."

Once she was outside, Mara's need for haste took over. She gave rapid instructions to Lujan, climbed into her litter, and endured a jostling ride as her bearers trotted through the city. The streets at that hour were deserted but for vegetable sellers driving laden needra wagons, and priests chanting daybreak devotions. Too fraught with nerves to feel sleepy, Mara closed stinging eyes until she arrived at her destination, an unobtrusive but beautifully appointed villa in the old city, with guards in blue armor at the gates.

Even as her bearers bent to set down her litter, Mara pulled aside the curtain and called, "Mara of the Acoma!"

The officer on duty approached and offered a salute. "My Lady, what service?"

"Announce to your Lord that I wish to see him, at once!"

The plumed officer returned a bow of impeccable politeness and strode inside the gates. Despite the early hour, Kamatsu of the Shinzawai was not in bed. Already finished with breakfast, he sent word that Mara was to be escorted inside, to the comfortable study off his garden.

In a secluded chamber surrounded by flowers and greenery, Mara found the Lord of the Shinzawai in conference with another figure in the black robe of a magician.

Caught off guard, Mara hesitated, then bowed low. "Great One. I crave pardon for my intrusion."

The cowled figure turned. Mara recognized Fumita as enigmatic dark eyes swept across her. "You do not interrupt, Mara of the Acoma. You merely find two old men reminiscing."

His statement was kindly meant, but even the casual scrutiny of a member of the Assembly was disquieting in Mara's state of barely contained agitation. "I would return later," she apologized. "But time is limited, and I have need to speak with Lord Kamatsu."

The Warchief of Clan Kanazawai waved the Lady toward a sumptuous pile of cushions. "Have you eaten, Lady Mara? If not, my servants might being you refreshment."

Mara accepted the seat gratefully, but the thought of any food caused her stomach to feel queasy. "A little tesh will be sufficient for my needs." As one of the Shinzawai servants departed unobtrusively for the kitchen, she glanced around the room. "Where is Hokanu?"

The elder Lord of the Shinzawai smiled in a warmth of indulgence. "He will be distressed to learn that he missed your visit, Lady Mara. But as acting Force Commander of the house, and Subcommander to Lord Keda, he is needed in the hills with the army." Sadness touched his expression as he added, "Like every clan in the Empire, the Kanazawai make ready for war."

Then, presuming she called to learn what had become of her contract of marriage proposal, Kamatsu sighed. As if a weight bore down upon his shoulders, he gestured to his visitor in appeal. "Mara, in other, calmer times, nothing would please me better than to bind my house to one as honored as the Acoma." His honesty was genuine as he qualified. "Nor could I wish for a daughter-in-law more resourceful than you. But although my first son was not lost, as we first supposed, he will not be returning to rule after me. He has been granted his own title to lands by the King of Isles. As his father, I honor his choice to remain in the land of Midkemia. Hokanu remains as my heir."

Aware that the older man paused to search for words, Mara tried to relieve him of his discomfort. "It was not for the marriage contract that I came here. Please, do not feel obligated to deliver your answer to me in times when other difficulties surround us."

Kamatsu returned a warming smile. "Your thoughtfulness is appreciated, Lady Mara. I have always understood Hokanu's reasons for favoring you. In fact, if the choice were simply personal, he would have had me send acceptance on the day your writ arrived. The delay in answering your request was mine alone, since the future of our land is precarious. I'm not certain any of us will be in position to enjoy weddings after tomorrow."

So he also had heard about Tasaio's call to confront the Emperor. Forgetful of the presence of the Great One who sat motionless as shadow in the corner, Mara regarded the man who was among the most honored rulers in the Empire. His age lay lightly upon him. The silver hair at his temples made him look distinguished rather than old, and his eyes were kindly with laugh lines. Where Hokanu's intelligence held an intensity like fire, the father had weathered with years to a quiet, confident wisdom. Intuitively, Mara sensed that this was a ruler to whom she could speak her true mind.

"Hear me out," she said earnestly. "For what I say is intended for the Good of the Empire." With that formal beginning she outlined a plan she had been contriving to set into play since sundown the day before.

Before the entrance to what had been the High Council section of the palace, Tasaio and his black-and-orange-clad honor guard were halted by a contingent of a dozen Imperial Whites. In full ceremonial regalia, and commanded by a Strike Leader whose golden plumes spread like a fan over his polished helm, they stood in neat ranks across the entrance, barring the way.

Before Tasaio could speak, the Imperial Strike Leader held up his hand. "My Lord of the Minwanabi, you are commanded to present yourself to the Light of Heaven, who awaits your presence within the chamber formerly employed by the High Council." The officer motioned, and his warriors stepped smartly aside, allowing Tasaio clear passage.

Resplendent in his finest suit of armor, and carrying his heirloom family sword in the scabbard at his black-lacquered belt, Tasaio ordered his retinue forward. As they traversed the lofty halls of the council complex, he gave his First Adviser a dry, satisfied smile. "Ichindar knows enough to keep the illusion of command, even if the reality of his authority is in question."

Incomo gave no reply. Hot in his ceremonial clothing and too breathless from brisk walking for even a pretense of dignity, he barely maintained the correct distance behind his master as he attempted to ascertain what might go wrong during the coming confrontation. As they reached the entry to the council hall, Incomo was caught by surprise as Tasaio stopped suddenly on the threshold of the main portal; the elderly adviser barely avoided a collision. Yanked from his preoccupation over possible disasters, Incomo peered over his master's shoulder to see what caused the delay.

The chamber was filled with Ruling Lords, not unexpectedly, since the lowest ranks took their seats first, and as the current most powerful family in the Empire, Tasaio was privileged to assume his place last. That this was no ordinary council stood confirmed by the fact that even the highest tiers of galleries were packed. The least significant Lords in the Empire had seen fit to attend this gathering, surest indicator of a time of crisis. Incomo squinted nearsighted eyes to better make out the central dais. In the dazzle of sunlight from the dome, he made out a figure in shining white overrobes and armor of precious polished gold. Ichindar, ninety-one times Emperor, stood at the top of the central dais. Through the flash of jewels and metal, Incomo took a moment to notice what had changed.

When he did, the reason behind Tasaio's precipitous stop became plain: the ivory and gold throne that had seated generations of previous Warlords was no longer in place upon the dais.

"Curse the name of her ancestors," Tasaio hissed under his breath. After the absence of the gold and white throne, he had spotted Mara, clad in shimmering green silk, and standing below the dais at the feet of the Light of Heaven.

"My lord Tasaio," addressed Ichindar in the awkward interval while Tasaio was still not recovered from surprise. The Lord of the Minwanabi had plainly intended to enter the chamber and, before the entire High Council and the Emperor himself, presume to mount the dais and take the Warlord's seat. Mara had arranged to have the chair removed to rob him of such theatrics. As all eyes turned, catching the Minwanabi Lord in his moment of furious embarrassment, the Light of Heaven continued. "You sought my attendance at a meeting with the Lords of the Empire. *I have come."*

Tasaio recovered his poise with a reflex as swift as a sword stroke. As if he had intended to speak all along from his position in the central doorway, he looked loftily over the hall. "Your Majesty, my Lords." He glanced at Mara. "Lady." Entering the chamber to a hushed audience, he slowly descended the stairs. "We come to demand an end to this interruption of the traditional course of governance in the Empire." Without pause to make a bow he said, "Majesty, I say it is time for the High Council to reconvene for the appointment of a new Warlord."

Quiet for only a moment as Tasaio reached the wide concourse above the lowest floor, the glittering figure on the dais inclined his head. "I agree."

Taken aback a second time in moments, Tasaio stopped. He realized that to descend the stairs farther would put him below the Emperor, so he remained where he was, looking at Ichindar at eye level. Yet he hesitated. Of all the answers he had anticipated, this was the last he expected to hear. "You agree, Majesty?"

Ichindar raised his jeweled rod of office. "Before this day is ended, we must arrive at a clear consensus. The High Council must ratify my decisions of the last year, or the old order must be reestablished." He glanced down at Mara. "I am in debt to the Lady of the Acoma for lending me understanding. I now perceive that a single dictate is not the way to gain support for the changes necessary to ensure our future. If our Empire is to survive, the time has arrived *for us all* to rethink our needs. Other worlds and cultures are now open to us through the rift gates. In our first experience we have learned to our sorrow that the old ways of conquest and war are poor coin to treat with the peoples of other realms.

"Not only have our former enemies shown themselves to be honorable men," continued the Emperor, "they have generously kept us apprised of their struggles against the ancient horror known in our history as the Enemy." A buzz of talk greeted this, yet Ichindar raised his voice above it. "To deal with the Midkemians, and others who may come after them, we need to change our ways."

Tasaio cried out in heartfelt appeal to the council Lords. "To deal with foreign powers, we must be strong! We suffered shame because Almecho lacked the courage to forge a million swords into one weapon yielded by a single, strong hand!" Looking in scorn upon the young Emperor in his many layers of finery, then down at the diminutive Lady at his feet, the Lord of the Minwanabi gestured in outright scorn. "It is time."

Mara returned his hard look without flinching. Before all, she said, "I gave my vow that I would see no other upon the throne of white and gold before you, Tasaio. Behold, the ivory and gold seat has been removed. By this you will see that I keep my sworn word of honor. No one shall sit upon that throne before you, Tasaio."

A murmur swept the packed galleries, and Tasaio's lips twisted with rage. Yet before he could manage rejoinder, a voice near the front ranks called out. "I will let my choice be known."

All eyes turned to observe as Jiro of the Anasati arose from his seat and crossed to a point midway between the Emperor on the dais and the figure in orange armor on the stair. After a moment of dramatic confrontation, he moved to stand beside the Lord of the Minwanabi. From there he directed a triumphant sneer at Mara. "Lady, this settles an old debt between us. Perhaps my brother's shade will find rest in the knowledge his murderer has been punished."

Mara suddenly felt every hour of missed sleep and the ache of every dashed hope. The error she had made was now past all chance of remedy. Again she had underestimated Jiro's thirst for revenge and placed too much stock in his ambition. Still, like her father, she faced defeat with a fighting spirit. "You think to support Tasaio now," she called with a derision that carried to the uppermost tier of the galleries. "Is it your intent to catch him weakened after he spends himself destroying me?"

The conjecture was preposterous, given the current Minwanabi ascendance. Jiro simply smiled and looked at Tasaio. "I stand with the new Warlord, for order must be restored to the Empire."

The words touched off a wave of motion as a score of Lords joined Jiro's bid to reestablish the old ways. They rose in a rustle of robes to array themselves behind Tasaio, until the stairway where he stood became packed, and then overflowed into the adjacent ranks of seats. Some Lords were trapped in the press, and no small number lost the spirit to fight against the prevailing surge, to win free of the crowd. Their numbers added to those of the truly dedicated, forming a formidable wedge of support behind the Minwanabi Lord.

Yet Mara persisted, against reason. "My Lord Xacatecas?"

Hoppara of the Xacatecas stood and crossed to stand with her beneath the Emperor. A score of loyal Clan Xacala nobles joined him, their features grimly determined.

Lord Iliando of the Bontura came to Mara's side. Then members of Clan Kanazawai entered in a flood, ringing the central dais.

Still, these gains were rendered impotent at a stroke, as most of Clan Ionani moved to stand with Tasaio. The few members of the Omechan who had attended divided evenly.

When all the Lords in attendance had taken sides, the majority backed Tasaio. Lounging at ease against a railing, his expression suavely assured, he turned languid eyes to his enemy. "Well, Mara? Is this the best you can do?"

Less showy, but every bit as commanding in presence, Mara squared her shoulders. "Lord Jidu of the Tuscalora, you have sworn allegiance to me."

The recalcitrant vassal, who had thought to hide himself to the rear of the Minwanabi's faction, shamefacedly removed himself from the stair. Compelled to apologize profusely as he squeezed his corpulent body through the press, he arrived in Mara's camp red-faced and sweating with embarrassment.

Mara paid his discomfort no heed. "Lord Randala," she cried. "You have sworn me a vote in council. I now call in that debt."

A major Lord in Clan Xacala, and a potential rival to the young Lord of the Xacatecas for the office of Warchief, the sandy-haired ruler of the Xosai removed himself from Tasaio's side of the hall. Two other Xacala Lords abandoned other allies and followed. After them came another man from the upper galleries, armored in scarlet and brown. "Let all know that Tasaio of the Minwanabi used the honorable name of the Hanqu in an attempt to ruin the Acoma. I take offense at such presumption, and cast my lot with the Lady."

Accorded unexpected satisfaction from the disastrous past ambush in the glen, Mara advanced onto the lowest stair of the dais. To all present she announced, "Never again will a noble of the Empire wear the office of Warlord." As a stir threatened to drown out her words, she looked pointedly at five others who stood with her family's blood enemy. "My

Lords, all of you have committed one vote of my choosing. I call in the debt at this time."

Reluctantly, the rulers in question vacated their chosen position. As they and a trickle of their vassals and allies swelled the crowd gathered behind Mara, others reacted to the shift of power in the room. More and more supporters left Tasaio's ranks and added to the throng around Mara.

Tasaio's features twitched with irritation. In tight tones he said, "You have your stalemate, Mara, and I concede the cleverness that allows you to keep your vow to the letter, without embracing its gist. You've gained a few days, at most, so why not end this pretense?"

"I do not play the Great Game this day for personal gain or glory," Mara interrupted. "For the Good of the Empire, I call on my Lord of the Tonmargu."

From the rear of the hall, the second most powerful claimant to the Warlord's office entered amid an honor guard of twenty. Erect despite his advanced age, he made careful progress down the stairs past Tasaio and came to stand beside Mara. If his body seemed wasted with years, his voice was still powerfully resonant. "By the honored blood of my ancestors, hear my pledge. I act for the Good of the Empire." So saying, he mounted the dais and bowed before the dazzling figure of the Emperor. "Majesty," he intoned, "in the best interests of all of my people, I surrender my authority to your care." He raised the staff that was his badge of office as Warchief of Clan Ionani and handed it up to Ichindar.

Jiro started forward in a rage. "You can't do this!"

Lord Frasai of the Tonmargu turned his silvered head in the direction of the young man who had inherited the mantle that had formerly been Tecuma's. Sadly he said, "Son of my kinsman, you are mistaken. Ichindar is of our own blood. Dare you claim that any stands above him in our clan?"

Red faced with fury, Jiro looked ready to argue. But a swelling roll of sound drowned his voice as excited talk broke out. Amid the commotion, two more entered the hall, Lord Kamatsu of the Shinzawai, wearing the armor of his ancestors and carrying the staff of Kanazawai, and beside him, Lord Keda, his predecessor, and another from a line with recognized claim to the Warlord's office.

Kamatsu reached Ichindar's dais and bowed. "We speak as one, and act for the Good of the Empire." With grand dignity for all his lack of ceremony, he surrendered his staff of office as Warchief of the Kanazawai into the hands of the gold-armored figure on the dais.

Over a cresting murmur of surprise, Tasaio shouted, "This is a violation of *tradition*, Kamatsu!"

The Lord of the Shinzawai called this accusation down in rebuke. "My family is as noble as any in the Empire. We can trace our line back to the twenty-fourth Emperor and are related by blood to the Light of Heaven. Tradition says that anyone of clan lineage may hold the office of Warchief." He ended on a note of ringing challenge. "Dare you deny the blood claim of Ichindar?"

Mara said, "Tasaio, you may be a brilliant commander in war, but your grasp of history is deficient. Has it never occurred to you why only five families have traditionally been allowed to claim the office of Warlord, first noble of the Empire after the Light of Heaven?"

At a loss, Tasaio returned a Tsurani shrug.

"Those first five houses, including your own, are the most directly related to the Empire's founders!" Mara regarded her sworn enemy with contempt. "If you had asked, any Master of Lore or the Keeper of the Imperial Archives could tell you. The original High Council was begun by five brothers, all of them siblings of the first Emperor!" With a sweep of her hand, Mara concluded, "We *all* stem from the same origins, Tasaio. Trace back far enough, and one way or another, all the major families in the great clans are related."

Lord Xacatecas spoke from Mara's side. "I act for the Good of the Empire!" He joined his two predecessors on the dais stair and handed up his staff of Xacala Warchief to the Emperor.

Gold armor flashed as Ichindar held up his hands, and all present took note that he held, not three staves, but four. Into the rising uproar the Light of Heaven called out, "I received the staff of the Omechan Clan this morning, Tasaio. Take note and beware: in my province are four claims to the throne of white and gold."

Jiro of the Anasati turned a look of naked anger upon Mara before he bowed to necessity. "Tasaio, fate has decreed this. I am sorry." So saying, the second most bitter enemy of the Acoma abandoned his position at the Lord of the Minwanabi's side. His desertion precipitated the withdrawal of the remaining Ionani nobles, leaving Tasaio alone with a handful of vassals and cowed followers.

One of these abruptly turned away. As he stepped down the stair toward the gathering around the dais, Tasaio gave way to rage. "Bruli of the Kehotara! You disgrace the memory of your father! He gave a generation of honorable service to the Minwanabi, and in your cowardice his steadfastness is shamed!"

Handsome as few men could be in cumbersome formal trappings, Bruli spun lightly on his heel. "Shamed, you say! That is insult from one whose family once sought to use me as an instrument to destroy the Lady Mara. Neither you nor Desio condescended to treat me, your vaunted vassal, as generously as this Lady at the time she defeated me." Bruli spat in contempt toward the stair where Tasaio stood. "I am done with the Minwanabi."

"I will see the lands of your ancestors sown with salt, and your natami shattered!" screamed Tasaio in a surfeit of rage.

The threat left Lord Bruli unfazed. He moved off without a look back until he reached the floor before Mara. There, in public view, he bowed. "Some may say you have deserted family honor this day, Lady Mara." Then he smiled. "I think not. Despite our past differences, I believe in my heart that you truly do serve the Empire, Lady. May peace hold between us from this day forward."

Mara smiled in return. "Before the High Council, I acknowledge friendship between the Kehotara and the Acoma."

Tasaio's eyes blazed with frustration. "You may have played into Ichindar's hands, Mara, but this is not the end. I've given my word that you may return safely to your home, but the moment my scouts bring news that you've set foot upon Acoma soil, then shall I unleash the might of the Minwanabi upon you. More," He spun in command upon those still behind him and cried, "I call upon Clan Honor! The Acoma have disgraced the Empire and Clan Shonshoni! Let war come to Clan Hadama!"

Ichindar said, "I forbid this!"

Tasaio's smile twisted with overweening malice. "I have fifty thousand soldiers ready to march at my command." Although the baring of blades was deplored within the great hall, he flouted custom and drew his sword for emphasis. The rare metal blade caught the light like fire, while an uproar swept across the hall. Over the clamor, in his commander's shout, Tasaio cried, "If you seek to make an end to this, Ichindar, let us do so on the field of war! Will your supporters stand with you then?" demanded Tasaio, his face flushed in challenge.

Mara felt a chill pierce her being. Before her stood a madman who would see his civilization reduced to ashes rather than suffer a rival to claim victory. Numbed by the sight of her worst nightmare made real, and stabbed through by recognition that her hope had been ground down by the caprice of the gods, she closed her eyes to hide her anguish. Because of her pride, and her ill-founded attempt to wrest the course of the future into a new mold, more than the Acoma would fall. With her she dragged down the best among the mighty, and in that most terrible recognition came the personal grief that Ayaki would die before manhood, and Kevin's unborn child might never know the chance to draw breath.

Mara felt withered by responsibility, for in cold truth, this impasse had happened because of her. Her acts had brought her nation to civil war.

Numbly she heard Ichindar murmur words of apologetic consternation. Too devastated to speak, she turned to bow to his better grace. Seeing the young man standing without sign of fear, Mara forced herself to speak. "The Acoma are yours to command, my Emperor." At once many Lords pledged support, or made a display of putting distance between themselves and their neighbors; bloody chaos was too close at hand not to make it clear where one stood. Those who wished no part in the coming clash sought to escape being swept along.

That instant, a voice from the edge of the chamber rang out in absolute command. "There shall be no conflict!"

The uproar died. Mara snapped her eyes open to find silence as the nobles surrounding her looked upward in disbelief. Dozens of black-robed figures descended into the hall in a ring through every entrance and side door. Eerily silent, and contested by none, the Great Ones of the Assembly advanced down the steps to the lowest floor of the High Council.

The whim of the magicians was as law, even above the

might of armies. Mindful of the havoc unleashed by just one man trained to the black in the arena, no Lord present was fool enough to stand against the will of the Assembly. Tasaio stood frozen in abject fury, fully aware that he had lost. The last color drained from his features as he resheathed his sword in disgrace.

Fifty magicians closed in a ring around the Lords who surrounded the Emperor. Their spokesman gave a formal nod to the Lady of the Acoma. With a faint start, Mara recognized Fumita. In a giddy rush of fear, she recalled that he had been present throughout her entire discussion with Kamatsu. At his side were two others she did not know, a short, very stout magician and a thin one with angular features. Confronted by their stern, impassive gazes, unknowably steeped in power, Mara knew an instant of terror. Surely they came to take her, to punish her unpardonable boldness.

For if Tasaio was greedy with ambition, she was as much at fault, for her presumptuous attempt to shatter tradition. Yet the Great One did not speak to berate her. Taking a stance between her and the sworn enemy of her family, Fumita addressed the gathering at large. "We speak for the Assembly. Our council has met and determined that Mara of the Acoma has acted for the Good of the Empire. She has jeopardized herself in selfless honor to prevent strife, and her life in this moment is sacrosanct."

The stout magician took up where Fumita ended. "We are divided on many issues, but one thing must be made clear. We shall not permit a civil war."

The thin magician spoke last. "Tasaio of the Minwanabi: you are forbidden to conduct any conflict with Mara of the Acoma, from this day forward. This is the will of the Assembly."

Tasaio's eyes widened as if he had been slapped. His hand tightened again on his sword hilt, and a disturbed light glittered in his eyes. In a hoarse whisper he said, "Great One, my family has sworn blood oath to Turakamu!"

"Forbidden!" repeated the slender magician.

White to the lips, Tasaio bowed. "Your will, Great One." He unbuckled his sword, an heirloom of steel with an elaborately carved bone handle. Reluctance stiffened every line of his bearing as he descended the stair and surrendered the weapon to Mara. "To the victor." His hands shook from closely contained rage.

Mara accepted the trophy with hands that openly trembled. "It was a close thing."

Tasaio loosed a bitter laugh. "I think not. You have been touched by the gods, Mara." He glanced around the room. "Had you never been born, or had your family not died to make your inheritance possible, I have no doubt that change might have come. But this!" He gestured in white rage at the assemblage of Lords, Magicians, and Emperor. "Nothing so momentously conclusive would ever have come to pass. I think I prefer facing the Red God to seeing the Great Game of our ancestors reduced to a paltry charade, and our Lords cast away pride and honor for subservience to the Light of Heaven." His hard topaz eyes roved one last time over the council he had dreamed he might rule. "Gods pity you all, and the Empire you surrender into disgrace."

"Be silent!" Fumita snapped. "Shimone of the Assembly will conduct you back to your estates, my Lord Minwanabi."

"Wait, I beg you!" Mara cried out. "Desio vowed to the Red God, on the blood of the Minwanabi line. By the terms of his oath, none who claim kinship with Tasaio may survive if the Acoma are not sacrificed."

Hard as stone, Fumita faced the Lady of the Acoma. "Foolish is the Lord who presumes that the gods take such a particular interest in his enemies. Desio transgressed prudent limits to make such a pledge. The gods do not suffer recanting such vows. His kin must suffer the consequences."

But Mara felt as if Kevin stood at her shoulder, and his irrepressibly foreign beliefs left a clamor in her mind that not even the Great Ones might still. "What of Tasaio's innocent wife and two children?" she appealed. "Should their lives be wasted for honor?"

Desperate to see her point through, she spun and faced her enemy, only pity in her eyes. "Release your children from fealty to the Minwanabi natami and I will adopt them into House Acoma. I beg you, spare them their lives."

Tasaio looked at her, aware that her concern sprang very near to the heart. Only to deny her, expressly to hurt, he cruelly shook his head. "Let their blood be on your conscience, Mara." So saying, he tugged the Warchief's staff of Clan Shonshoni from his belt. "My Lord of the Sejaio," he called to a thick-necked man on the sidelines, "this is now your trust."

As the staff of office was removed from his hand, he gave one last glance around the halls of power. Then, with a flat look of mockery at Mara and the Emperor, he turned with all his grace and arrogance to the slender magician beside Fumita. "I am ready, Great One."

The magician took a metal device out of his robe, and a faint buzzing sounded through the hall. As he placed his hand upon Tasaio's shoulder, both of them vanished without warning, the only sign of their passing a faint inrush of air into the space that they had occupied.

The Lord of the Sajaio regarded the Warchief's staff he now held, and reluctantly came to stand before the Emperor. "Majesty! I do not know if I act for the Good of the Empire or not." He glanced at the other Lords who clustered unanimously around Mara and Fumita. "But it is said that in the Great Game the gods favor the winners. I surrender to you the office of Warchief of the Shonshoni."

Ichindar accepted the last of the five staves of office. Clearly, in words of newly unquestioned authority, he pronounced, "The office of Warlord is no more!" Without further ceremony he snapped each staff in two halves and cast the fragments on the floor. Then, over the echoes as the broken rods tumbled down the stair of the dais, he called upon Kamatsu of the Shinzawai.

Hokanu's father returned a bow of deep courtesy. "Majesty?"

"The Empire has need of you," decreed the Light of Heaven. "I appoint you to a new office, Imperial Chancellor."

Again Kamatsu bowed. "To serve the Empire, Majesty, I will gladly accept."

To the assembly of nobles, Ichindar proclaimed, "Kamatsu of the Shinzawai is my voice and my ear. He shall hear your requests, your needs, and your suggestions as we undertake to reshape our nations." When the new Imperial Chancellor was dismissed, the Light of Heaven called another name.

"Frasai of the Tonmargu!"

The old soldier made his way forward. "Majesty!"

"We shall have need of one to oversee military matters. If Kamatsu is my eyes and ears, will you act as my good arm?"

"To serve the Empire!" Lord Frasai returned in his basso voice.

Clearly, Ichindar outlined new duties. "Frasai of the Tonmargu shall bear the title of Imperial Overlord. He shall conduct the business of the Empire as did the Warlord in days past, but only at my bidding." Then Ichindar inclined his gleaming helm toward a figure nearest to Mara. "Further, I instruct Hoppara of the Xacatecas to act as his second-in-command."

The youthful Lord grinned at Mara. "To serve the Empire!" he cried exuberantly.

Mara gave him Tasaio's sword. "Send this to the desert men, to honor your father's vow."

Hoppara of the Xacatecas received the ancient sword from her hands and bowed respectfully.

And then the Light of Heaven turned his visage to the Lady who stood patiently in robes of shimmering green silk. "Mara of the Acoma!"

The woman who had given him a throne, and the burdens of absolute power, looked up, her eyes unreadably deep and her emotions locked behind impeccable Tsurani bearing.

"You have prevented chaos from overtaking the nations," Ichindar stated to those at large. And then his tone turned personal. "What reward can we offer?"

Mara found herself blushing. "Majesty, in truth, I wished for nothing beyond the chance to conduct the affairs of my family in peace and prosperity. I fear I have sacrificed too much of my honor to deserve any reward."

"And yet you set aside those very needs, and honor, to serve the greater good," Ichindar pointed out. "You have reminded us of forgotten truths and true greatness." He paused to sweep the air with one golden-armored hand. "You have recalled to our times a concept neglected for centuries. By your sacrifice, by setting aside family for the good of the nation at large, you have defined the highest of all honors. Is there no reward we might grant?"

Mara considered barely a moment. "Majesty, I would ask for title to the estate and lands that belonged to the Lord of the Minwanabi."

A harsh, uneasy mutter ran the breadth of the hall. Tsurani tradition dictated that a fallen house was accursed by the gods, to be avoided by commoner and noble alike. Many fine estates were gone to ruin and weeds as a result of the deep-seated conviction that a Lord's luck was tied to the soil.

The Emperor made a gesture of uncertainty. "Why such an ill-omened gift, Lady?"

"Majesty," she said gravely, "we gather today to embrace change. To my mind, it is the greater offense against heaven to allow a dwelling of such magnificence to be abandoned to waste and decay. I hold no fear of ill luck. Allow me, and I shall send to the Red God's temple and seek clear notice that Desio's blood vow stands fulfilled. Then may the priests of Chochocan bless the property, every foot if need be, and on the day when the restless spirits of the Minwanabi are banished in peace, I will make my home there."

Struggling to hide tears of relief, Mara continued. "Too many good men and women have died, Majesty. Others are slaves, their talents denied, their potential ignored." Poignantly struck by the memory of Kevin, she fought her voice level and continued. "I work for a future of change, and for that, I ask to be first to break a profitless tradition."

To her startling request, Ichindar nodded acquiescence. And into a stillness grown profound, as each Lord present examined his land and his people in a new light, Mara called out in appeal. "This waste must end. Now. To all who have stood against me in the past, I make this vow. Come to me with peace in your heart, and I will put an end to old conflicts." She glanced at Jiro of the Anasati, but he returned no flicker of feeling. His face under his red and yellow helm remained unreadably remote.

On the dais, the Emperor watched the exchange, and the wonder in the expressions of many of the nobles who were gathered. He sensed something of Mara's emotions, and yet he understood but a fraction of what motivated this deep and complex woman. Profoundly moved by her vision of a forgiving victory, he said, "Lady Mara, lands are insufficient compensation for the gift of enlightened thought you have brought into this council. You have wealth and power, influence and prestige. At this moment none stands above you in influence and greatness in this hall." He smiled in sudden wry humor. "I would offer to make you my tenth wife if I thought you would accept."

At Mara's blush of confusion, a wave of gentle laughter filled the hall. Over the general mirth, the Emperor raised his final command of the day. "You have chosen to serve others ahead of your own self-interest. Therefore you shall be recognized, throughout life and all of history. In past ages, when the Empire was yet young, when a citizen came forward to undertake extraordinary service at risk of life and honor, my forebears bestowed on them a title, that all in the land might recognize them with highest acclaim. Mara of the Acoma, I give to you the ancient title Servant of the Empire."

Stunned speechless, Mara clung to the tatters of her bearing. Servant of the Empire! No man or woman in living memory had received such a lofty accolade. Only a score of times in two thousand years had the title been awarded. Those twenty names were recited for luck, and memorized by children as they learned the history of their people. The rank also brought formal adoption into the imperial household. Reeling mentally at her unanticipated rise in status, Mara realized that she and Ayaki could choose to retire to the palace and live upon imperial largesse for the remainder of her days.

"You overwhelm me, Majesty," she managed at last.

And she bowed to his presence like the humblest of his servants.

Then Lord Hoppara of the Xacatecas let out a battle cry and the High Council hall erupted in cheers. Mara stood at the center of a circle of admirers, giddy with the recognition that she had won, and more: she had ensured that her family was forever safe from the machinations of House Minwanabi.

27. *BEGINNINGS*

Hokanu stood motionless.

Then, in the wash of golden light that fell through the western window, the son of the Shinzawai rested his hands upon the sill. His back to Mara, and his gaze directed outward into the colors of a brilliant sunset, he remained in silent contemplation.

Seated upon the cushions in Kamatsu's private meeting room, Mara agonized that she could not see to read his face and gauge his reaction to her presence. Her distress was further heightened by anticipation of the difficult words she had yet to utter. She caught herself in Kevin's habit of picking at the fabric's fine fringes, and forced back sadness and longing as she stopped. She must live out her days as Lady of the Acoma, even as her beloved must as a free son of Zūn.

"Lady," Hokanu said softly, "things between us have changed, since we spoke last." A tinge of awe touched his tone, and his hands tightened against the beautifully inlaid wood of the window frame. "I am heir to the Shinzawai Lordship, true, but you . . . are Servant of the Empire. What life could there be between us, with such a vast gap between our ranks?"

With an effort, Mara shook off her memories of a roguish barbarian slave. "We would live as man and woman, as equals, Hokanu. Our families and our names would continue through our progeny, and both our ancestral estates would be managed by factors."

Bemused, Hokanu finished for her. "We would live in the mansion that once belonged to Minwanabi?"

Hearing a catch in his voice, Mara said, "Do you fear bad luck?"

Hokanu gave a short laugh. "You are all the luck I or any man would ever need, Lady." Absently he murmured, "Servant of the Empire . . ." Then, in swift recovery of the topic at hand, he added, "I have always admired the home of the Minwanabi. With you at my side, I would most certainly find happiness there."

Sensing he had reached the point of speaking formal words of acceptance of the marriage proposal his father Kamatsu had given him permission to decide, Mara spoke fast to forestall him.

"Hokanu, before you say more, there is one thing I must tell you."

Her serious tone caused him to turn from the window. She wished he had not. His directness made the task ahead more difficult. Fine dark eyes caught her in earnest appraisal, and at their clear depths, and the honest admiration in them, Mara felt a twist to the heart. Her words became painful to complete. "You should know: I am one month with child to another man, a slave I held in highest regard. He is returned forever to his homeland across the rift, and I will not see him again. Only if I marry, I add the insistence that his child be counted as legitimate."

Hokanu's handsome face showed not a flicker of expression. "Kevin," he mused aloud. "I know of your barbarian lover."

Mara waited, tautly braced for an outburst of male jealousy. Her hands tightened on the cushions until fringes threatened to tear.

Her worry and nerves did not pass unnoticed. Hokanu crossed the room and gently pried her grip from the cloth. His touch was light, and trembling ever so slightly with emotions he politely did not show. "Lady, I would expect that you did not enter into this pregnancy lightly, knowing you as I do. Therefore, I can only presume that Kevin was an honorable man."

Her surprise brought a light of joy to his eyes. Suddenly smiling at her, he asked, "Did you forget I had spent time on Midkemia? My brother Kasumi made sure I was well educated in their 'barbaric' concept of fairness." His tone made it clear he used the term in jest. "I am not a complete stranger to the fiber of the Midkemian people, Lady Mara." Then his smile twisted. "I was the one who chose to bring the 'barbarian' Great One Pug to my father, sensing in him something rare." When the name didn't bring a reaction from Mara, he added, "The one who came to be known as Milamber of the Assembly." Mara couldn't contain a giddy rush as she saw the ironic humor. As she laughed lightly, he said, "In my own meager way I played some small part in the tremendous events we have known."

The Lady of the Acoma looked up into Hokanu's face, and there read a rare understanding. She might not bring the fire of passion to any union with House Shinzawai, but this was a man whom she could honor, one with whom she could share her new vision of the future. Together, they might shape a greater Empire. He crossed to stand before her, then began to kneel.

"You could care for two boys not your own?" she asked as he knelt before her.

Hokanu regarded her tenderly. "More, I could love them." He smiled at her profound astonishment. "Mara, did you forget? I am the foster son of Kamatsu. Though we do not share the blood tie of father to son, he taught me the value of a strong and loving family. Ayaki's merits are apparent. Kevin's child we will shape as his father would have desired."

Overwhelmed suddenly by emotion, Mara ducked her head to hide tears. As Hokanu's arms closed in comfort around her, she gave way to a flood of relief. She had hoped for nothing beyond having her child by Kevin accepted; the gift of Hokanu's complete support was more than her wildest expectations, certainly more than her wayward, headstrong decision had deserved. Almost, she could hear Nacoya's voice carping that the man who held her was special, and deserving of regard. Softly she said, "The gods have chosen wisely, Hokanu, for no man born of this world could better understand and respect my needs."

"I accept your proposal of marriage, Lady, Servant of the Empire," Hokanu murmured formally into her hair. Then he kissed her, in a manner different from Kevin's. Mara tried, but her body could not warm to the sudden change immediately. His touch was not unpleasant, simply . . . different.

In his uncanny manner, Hokanu seemed to sense that she

needed time to become used to him. He drew back, still holding her strongly, and a light of humor touched his eyes. "How in the name of the good gods can you know that the child you are carrying is a boy?"

Mara's last apprehension dissolved in a rush of pleased laughter. "Because," she said, for once a woman rather than a ruler, "I would have it so."

"Then, my strong-willed future wife," announced Hokanu, drawing her to her feet, "it must be so. We had best go out and inform my foster father that he will need to spare time from the Emperor's duties to be attending a wedding."

Mara signaled and the company halted. The priest of Turakamu turned his red-masked face in her direction in unspoken, formal inquiry. He stood in full dress attire, which meant more paint than clothing. His nude flesh was stained red, and a feather and bone cape over his shoulders mantled his necklace of baby skulls. Yet he came in regalia only, without any acolytes in attendance to conduct ceremony, his purpose to oversee the relocation of the prayer gate off Minwanabi property.

Mara arose from her litter to treat with him.

"My Lady," he greeted formally. "Your generous offerings to the temple have been looked upon with favor."

Mara indicated a bonfire some distance up the road, where several large timbers lay burning. "What is that?"

"Desio's ill-omened gate that was never finished. The temple has decreed: by their fall from power, the Minwanabi have demonstrated beyond doubt that their cause found no favor with the Red God. Therefore the gate is neither consecrated nor blessed and may be destroyed without fear of divine retribution."

He indicated a pair of large needra wagons drawn off to one side, awaiting the dismantled timbers of a second gate. "This structure will be sent to the site you provided. That soil will be reconsecrated." From behind the grim skull mask the priest sounded almost conversational. "It was something of an odd request, this relocation of a prayer gate, Mara, but upon discussion, no blasphemy or sacrilege was seen. Given the association of this gate and the vow that was made, it was understandable why you might wish to have it removed once you hold this land." The priest gave a Tsurani shrug. "Now that the High Council is an advisory body only, the temples may again take a more active role in the well-being of the Empire. Your part counted for much, and the servants of the gods are grateful."

He motioned aside to a worker who approached the west post with a shovel. "Gently!" he called out in warning. "The remains of the sacrifices must not be disturbed. Be sure there is ample soil around their graves!"

The overseer to the workers acknowledged the priest's instruction. Satisfied the matter was in hand, the servant of Turakamu reminisced in friendly fashion with Mara. "We who serve the Red God are often misunderstood, Lady. Death is part of life, and all come to Turakamu's hall eventually. We are not in a hurry to gather their spirits. Remember that in the future should you ever have need of our counsel."

Mara nodded her respect. "I shall, Priest." Then she turned to Lujan and said, "I will walk for a while."

She led the march down the gentle rise to the landing where boats waited by the docks to cross the lake. On the far shore in the sunshine lay the vast house that soon would honor the Acoma and their visitors and emissaries. "Lujan," she murmured, as her eyes followed the magnificent vista of lake, and mountains, and the distant inlet from the river, "did you ever think we might lose?"

Lujan laughed and Mara felt a rush of affection for this man, most like her rakish barbarian with his pleasantly teasing nature. "Mistress, I would be a liar if I said I had not contemplated defeat on more than one occasion." More seriously he added, "But never for a moment did I doubt you."

Mara impulsively took his hand. "For that I humbly thank you, my friend."

Together, Lady and Force Commander made their way to the docks where boatmen waited to take them across the beautiful lake. Lujan, Saric, and Keyoke assumed seats in the vessel with Mara, while her two Force Leaders directed the other Acoma soldiers into craft to follow after. Soon the water was crowded with the flotilla of her army. Mara glanced back to where Keyoke sat, holding a bundle in his lap as if it were fragile and precious. Under a mantle of green cloth beaded with jewels rested the Acoma natami. Mara's Adviser for War had drilled endlessly with an old wooden coffer to perfect the handling of both burden and crutch. He counted this trust as the highest honor ever awarded him, even over accolades won in battle.

The boats floated swiftly across the water. Wishing poignantly that Kevin could have been at her side, Mara was surprised out of her reverie to see a magician waiting for her upon the docks outside the great house. Behind him stood priests of Chochocan, who had been overseeing the blessing of the new Acoma estate, in preparation for Mara's coming union with Hokanu of the Shinzawai.

The first guests would arrive within the week. Mara had been relieved, for by her estimation, Kevin's child would be born slightly less than eight months after the wedding, close enough to raise only eyebrows, and not giving incontrovertible evidence that the father was other than her pledged husband.

The lead boat reached the landing. Helped to the dock by Lujan, Mara bowed to the magician. "Great One, you do us honor."

The stouter of the two Black Robes who had accompanied Fumita in the Council Hall, the member of the Assembly introduced himself. "I am Hochopepa, Lady."

Mara felt a stab of concern. "Is there a problem, Great One?"

The Great One waved a pudgy hand. "No. I remain only to inform you that my colleague conducted Tasaio here, then witnessed the ceremony as the former Minwanabi Lord made ready to honorably end the feud and take his own life."

Mara was joined by her advisers as the Great One added sadly, "Please, come with me."

The Acoma party followed him down spacious paths on the opposite side of the great house. There more than ten thousand people waited in silent ranks. Before them stood a large bier fronted with red bunting. Mara raised her eyes to the four shrouded figures that lay in their final rest.

Tears flooded her eyes as she saw that two were children. Servants had tried to make them look presentable, but their fresh wounds could not be hidden. Tasaio had cut their young throats. Sickened by the thought that the boy might have been her own Ayaki, Mara felt Lujan reach out and steady her arm.

"I would have spared them," she murmured numbly.

The Great One regarded her with sorrow. "The Minwanabi line is ended, Lady Mara. The Assembly officially stood as witness. Now that my charge is complete, I will excuse myself. Live a long life, and a happy one, great Lady."

Hochopepa reached into his pocket, where he kept his talisman of transport. A buzzing sounded upon the air, and he was gone.

Mara was left at a loss before the host of former Minwanabi retainers who still survived. The first six rows of people had all donned grey robes of slavery. Behind were ranks of soldiers, with weapons and helms stacked at their feet, and heads bowed in defeat.

An ancient man, garbed as a slave but aristocratic in bearing, stepped forward and prostrated himself before Mara. "My Lady," he intoned respectfully.

"Speak," the Lady bade him.

"I am Incomo, former First Adviser to Lord Minwanabi. I present myself to assist you in whatever dispensation you decree for all of us who served that unlucky house."

"Their fates are not mine to dispense," Mara whispered, still shaken by the bodies of the dead children.

Incomo looked up, emptiness in his dark eyes. "Lady, my former Lord commanded all blood relatives to their ancestral home. He ordered and saw each kinsman kill his own wives and children, then fall upon his sword, in turn. But he waited until an hour ago, when he heard you had set foot upon Minwanabi soil, before he took the lives of his own family. Only when they were dead did he fall upon his sword." Trembling in abject fear, Incomo performed his last duty to his master. "Lord Tasaio bade me tell you that he would rather see his children in death's hall at his side than live in an Acoma house."

Mara felt a stab of horror. "That murderous animal! His own children!" Blind rage shook through her, then dwindled to grief as she again regarded the small forms of the little boy and girl upon the bier. "Grant them full honors," she said softly. "A great name ends this day."

Incomo bowed. "I am your slave, mistress, for I have failed my master. But I beg you, have mercy, for I am old and ill suited for labor. Grant me the boon of honorable death."

Mara almost snarled in her outrage as she said, "No!" Her eyes bored into the startled man as she cried, "Stand up!"

Stunned by her unseemly emotion, Incomo was taken aback.

Mara could not bear the sight of his subservient attitude an instant longer. Taking his arm in a surprisingly strong grip, she pulled the elderly adviser to his feet. "You were never sold into slavery by Tasaio, were you?" Incomo couldn't speak, he was so taken off guard. "You were never ordered into slavery by an imperial court, were you?"

"No, Lady, but—"

"Who calls you a slave?" Her disgust was palpable as she half dragged the old man to where her own adviser stood. To Saric, wearing an adviser's formal robes, she said, "Your training under Nacoya was sorrowfully cut short. Take this man as your honored assistant, and heed him well. His name is Incomo, and as all of Tasaio's former enemies know, he gives competent counsel."

The old man gaped at his new mistress, who smiled at him in a surprisingly friendly way. She looked from his astonishment to a wry, nearly laughing Saric and said, "If you have ambitions to become my First Adviser, you will listen to whatever this wise old man may tell you."

Mara turned away and the former Minwanabi adviser said, "Master, what is this?"

Saric chuckled. "You'll discover that our mistress has her own way of doing things, Incomo. You'll also find you've been given a new life."

"But freeing a slave?"

At this Mara spun back in a fury. "You were never pronounced a slave! In my house you never will be. It is tradition that made freemen slaves when their masters fell, *not the law!* Now serve me well, and cease this discussion."

As she moved on, Saric raised eyebrows in his personal brand of bemusement. "She is a Servant of the Empire. Who will say no to her if she changes another tradition?"

Incomo could only stand mute and nod. The concept of working under a mistress who was blessedly not afflicted with temperament, or an insane lust for cruelty, seemed a vision of perfection from the gods. Uncertain whether he was dreaming, he shook his head in wonder. The old man raised his hand and was shocked to find tears flowing. Forcing himself back to an honorably impassive mien, he heard Saric whisper, "When you've reconciled yourself to death, a new life is something of a shock, yes?"

Incomo could only nod, speechless, as Mara returned her attention to the priests of Chochocan. The clerics finished their rites over the bodies of the Minwanabi Lord, his wife, and his children. As they lit their candle to start the death fire, Mara looked one last time at the hard, clean profile of the man who had nearly come to ruin her, and whose hand had brought the deaths of her father and brother. "Our debt is settled," she said to herself, then raised voice in formal call. "Soldiers of the Minwanabi! Give honors to your master!"

As one, the waiting warriors retrieved their helms and arms from the ground. They stood at attention, saluting their former master as his earthly form and extravagantly fine armor were engulfed in curtains of fire.

As the smoke rose toward heaven, Irrilandi stood forward and was permitted, in a voice almost tremulous with gratitude, to recite the long list of Tasaio's honors in the field. Mara and the Acoma retinue stood and listened with impeccable politeness, and out of respect for her feelings the fallen Minwanabi Force Commander omitted the names of Mara's father and brother when he mentioned the battle that ended their life. When his recitation came to an end, Mara turned to face those arrayed before her. Raising her voice to be heard over the roaring fire, she cried, "Who among you were advisers, hadonra, servants, and factors, you are needed. Serve me from this day forward as the freemen you are." Several of those in grey robes rose uncertainly, then moved to stand to one side. "You who are slaves, serve me also in the hope that one day this Empire will find the wisdom to grant the freedom that should never by right have been forbidden you." These others followed, hesitantly.

Then Mara shouted to the soldiers, "Brave warriors, I am Mara of the Acoma. Tradition holds that you now lead a masterless existence as grey warriors, and that all who were your officers must die." The front rank of men who had once worn plumes received her words impassively. They had expected no less, and their affairs were settled in preparation for the end.

Yet Mara did not order them to fall upon their swords. "I

find such a practice a crime and a dishonor for men who were but loyal to their lawful Lord. It was not your choice to be led by men of evil nature. That fate decrees a death without battle honors is a foolishness I have no intention of perpetuating!"

Softly, to the Force Commander at her side, Mara murmured, "Lujan, did you find him? Is he here?"

Lujan inclined his head to speak in her ear. "I think he stands on the right in the first rank. It's been years, so I can't be sure. But I'll find out." Stepping away from his mistress, he called out in his field commander's voice, "Jadanyo, who was once fifth son of the Wedewayo!"

The soldier who had been identified bowed in obedience and came forward. He had not seen Lujan since boyhood and had thought him dead in the destruction of the Tuscai, so his eyes widened. "Lujan, old friend! Can it be you?"

Lujan waved introduction to Mara. "Mistress, this man is Jadanyo, by blood my second cousin. He is an honorable soldier and worthy of service."

The Lady inclined her head toward the former Minwanabi warrior. "Jadanyo, you have been called to serve the Acoma. Are you willing?"

The man stumbled over his words in dismay. "What is this?"

Lujan gave back a devilish grin. In a laughing voice he said, "Say yes, you idiot, or do I have to wrestle you into submission as I did when we were children?"

Jadanyo hesitated, eyes wide. Then, in a joyful shout, he cried, "Yes! Lady, I am willing to serve a new mistress."

Mara saluted him formally, then signaled Keyoke forward.

In the tone that once commanded armies, her battered Adviser for War cried out, "Irrilandi, who was my friend as a child, present yourself!"

The Minwanabi Force Commander took a moment to recognize a former friend and rival, resplendent as he was in the glittering finery of an adviser. With a glance in wonderment at the crutch, and the face whose chiseled lines still held vitality and pride, he moved from his place before the front ranks of his dishonored soldiers. By every tradition he expected to die this day, along with all his subofficers. Too old a campaigner to set any store in miracles, he heard without belief as Keyoke said, "Mistress, this man is Irrilandi, who is brother to one who married my cousin's wife's sister. He is therefore my cousin and worthy of service to the Acoma."

Looking at Tasaio's former Force Commander, and moved by the iron courage that masked a turmoil of confusion, Mara said kindly, "Irrilandi, I will not kill good men because they faithfully discharged their duties. You are called to serve the Acoma. Are you willing?"

The old officer searched the Lady's eyes for a long moment, speechless. Then restraint, suspicion, and disbelief gave way to boyish abandon. Swept by irrepressible elation, he said, "With all my heart, my most generous mistress, with all my heart."

Mara gave him her first command. "Marshal all of your soldiers and compare bloodlines with those in my retinue. Most will have ties to soldiers serving the Acoma, or at least they will have, by the time the last of you have sworn service. All here are worthy; therefore, let the forms be observed that all may be lawfully committed to duty. If there are any among you, officers or common warriors, who feel they could not give loyalty to my house, you have my leave to permit them to fall upon their swords or depart in peace, as they choose." A handful of soldiers stepped from ranks, and departed, but fully nine men in ten remained. Mara said, "Now, Irrilandi, will you come before the Acoma natami and vow your obedience, that the task ahead may begin?"

The older officer bowed deeply in gratitude, and as he rose with a shining smile, the ranks of leaderless soldiers erupted into uncontrollable cheers and shouts. The name "Acoma! Acoma!" rang on the morning air, until Mara was nearly deafened by the clamor. The cheering continued unabated for long minutes while the rising smoke from the Minwanabi pyre rose on the clear air, forgotten.

Over the waves of noise, Mara told Saric and Incomo, "Sort this out and ready these men to swear before the glade. I am going now to place the natami in its new home."

A priest of Chochocan, the Good God, and Keyoke accompanied Mara to the contemplation glade. Waiting outside with a shovel in hand was the gardener who was the traditional keeper of the grounds. He expected the Minwanabi natami to be buried face down forever, in the timeworn custom of a house fallen to conquerors. The moment came at last, and Keyoke surrendered the burden of the Acoma natami to Mara. Her escort halted outside the entrance, while the priest and gardener accompanied her inside.

The glade was much larger than the one upon the Acoma estates and was tended in impeccable fashion, with fragrant flowers and fruit trees, and a series of pools interconnected by the trilling splash of waterfalls. Mara gazed in wonder upon a beauty that stopped her breath. Half-dazed, she said to the gardener, "What is your name?"

All but trembling in apprehension, the dutiful servant replied, "Nira, great mistress."

Softly she said, "You do honor to your office, gardener. Great honor."

The sun-browned man brightened at the compliment. He bowed and set his forehead to the earth he had tended so lovingly. "I thank the great Lady."

Mara bade him rise. She walked on down shaded paths to the place where the ancient rock bearing the Minwanabi crest rested. For a long moment she regarded the talisman, so much like her own; except for the weatherworn sigil, it might have been twin to the one she carried. Poignantly reminded that all the great houses of the Empire shared a common beginning, she renewed her dedication to make that a common future as well. At last she said, "With reverence, remove the natami."

Nira knelt to do her bidding as she turned and faced the priest. "I will not bury the Minwanabi natami." She needed no symbolic act to rejoice in the recognition that the struggle she had fought most of her life had at last come to an end. She had risked much, and lost a great deal that was dear to her, and the thought of even ritual obliteration of a family's memory made her feel sour inside. Too easily, all too easily, the defeated house might have been her own.

In deep recognition of her own strengths and failures, and the legacy they might leave to her son and future children, she nodded to the Minwanabi family talisman. "Once heroic men bore that name. It is not fitting they should be forgotten because their offspring fell from greatness. The Acoma natami shall rest here, where I and my children may sit in peace with the shades of our ancestors. But another place on a hilltop overlooking the estate will be set aside for the Minwanabi stone. I would have the spirits of those great men see their ancestral lands are well cared for and nurtured. Then they, too, will rest easy."

To the gardener she said, "Nira, you are free to choose this site. Plant a hedge and a garden of flowers and let no feet tread there but yours, and those of your appointed successors. Let the ancestors who participated in the founding and continuance of this nation know sunlight and rain, that the memory of a great house shall endure."

The man bowed low and expertly dug around the base of the ancient rock. While the priest of Chochocan intoned a blessing, his work-calloused hands raised the talisman and shifted it aside. Mara gave over her own family stone into the hands of the priest of the Good God. He raised the Acoma natami toward the sky and recited his most powerful incantation for Chochocan's everlasting favor. Then he returned the Acoma natami to Mara, who in turn passed it to the gardener. "Here is the heart of my line. Tend it as you would your living child, and you will be known as a man who has done honor to two great houses."

"Mistress," Nira said, bowing his head over his new charge in respect. Like every other servant on the estates, he had expected slavery, but instead he discovered he was being given a new life.

The priest consecrated the ground around the natami as Nira tamped soil around the base. At the completion of the ritual, Chochochan's servant sounded a tiny metal chime and departed, the gardener following on his heels.

Mara remained alone with the stone that bound her ancestors' spirits to renewal on the Wheel of Life. Careless of her fine silks, she knelt in the earth and ran her fingers across the surface, the faint lines of the shatra bird crest worn with age.

"Father," she said quietly, "this is to be our new home. I hope the site pleases you." Then she added words for the dead brother whose absence even yet left a wound in her heart. "Lanokota, rest you well and know peace." Then she thought of all those who had died in her service, those close and loved and others barely known. "Brave Papewayo, who gave your life to save mine, I hope you return to the Wheel of Life as a son of this house. And Nacoya, mother of my heart, know the woman you raised as a daughter sings your praises."

She thought of her beloved Kevin, who now was back

among his own family, and prayed that he would find a happy life without her. Tears flowed freely down her cheeks, for both losses and victories, joys and sorrows. The Game of the Council as she had known it was forever changed, and by her hand. Yet as she knew her people, she understood that their nature would accept this new order slowly; politics would shift and she would be required to work hard to preserve the peace. The wealth she would gain from her Midkemian trading concessions would help underwrite such efforts, but the difficulties ahead in establishing Ichindar's power would require as much nurturing as any plan she had completed to defeat enemies.

Mara arose, both sobered and exhilarated by the weight of new responsibilities. Inspired by the beautiful gardens, and by old trees lovingly tended, she arrived at the gate that marked the entrance to her family's sacred glade. There she encountered her inner cadre of advisers, and thousands of Minwanabi soldiers upon their knees with Lujan before them. "Mistress," he called gladly, "to a man, these remaining warriors embrace Acoma service."

Mara waved him a salute. Even as she had restored hope and honor to a band of houseless outlaws as a girl green to the ways of power, she said, "Swear them to honorable service, Force Commander Lujan."

Proud in his plumes, the Acoma Force Commander led them in the short vow that he had undertaken those same years before, when he had been among the first soldiers in the Empire to receive the grace of a second chance at honorable life.

As he finished and marshaled the warriors newly dedicated to the Acoma natami, Mara's eyes lifted to the distant shores of the lake. A flash of movement there snagged her attention, and her spirit soared with emotion. Setting a hand upon Keyoke's shoulder, she said, "Look!"

Her weathered Adviser for War turned his gaze where she indicated. "My eyes are not young, mistress. What do you see?"

"Shatra birds," came Mara's awed reply. "By the grace of divine favor they come to nest in the marshes on our shores."

From his place beside the youthful Saric, Incomo said, "The gods seem pleased with your generous heart, mistress."

"We can only hope, Incomo."

To her circle of advisers she said, "Come. Let us make our new home ready. My husband-to-be shall arrive soon, in the company of my son and heir." Mara led old ministers and new toward the house she had so long admired, now to be home to her family, and a roof to join two great houses dedicated to the betterment of the Empire.

Mara of the Acoma passed the ranks of her newly sworn soldiers, men who but days before had been her confirmed enemies, zealous in their duty to bring ruinous ending to her house. That she could work miracles was now firmly believed by most who watched her, for not only had she defeated three Lords of the most powerful house in the Empire, she had forgiven their servants and embraced them as if they had never done her harm. Such generosity and wisdom would shelter them and make them prosperous.

And she bore the most ancient and honorable title ever bestowed: Servant of the Empire.

ABOUT THE AUTHORS

RAYMOND E. FEIST is the *New York Times* bestselling author of *Magician: Apprentice, Magician: Master, Silverthorn, A Darkness at Sethanon, Faerie Tale, Prince of the Blood,* and *The King's Buccaneer.* He has also coauthored three Riftwar-related novels with Janny Wurts: *Daughter of the Empire, Servant of the Empire,* and *Mistress of the Empire.* He lives in San Diego with his wife.

JANNY WURTS is the author of the Cycle of Fire trilogy (*Stormwarden, Keeper of the Keys,* and *Shadowfane*), *Sorcerer's Legacy,* and three collaborations with Mr. Feist: *Daughter of the Empire, Servant of the Empire,* and *Mistress of the Empire.* She is also a cover illustrator. She lives in Florida with her husband.